CW01270708

Witney Library Welch Way Witney Oxon OX28 6JH Tel: 01993 703659	AB	7/09·	BA
11. JUL 08.	23. OCT 08		
04. SEP 08	02. SEP 09.		
	27. MAR 09		
14. APR 09	19.		
ABINGDON LIBRARY The Charter, Abingdon Tel. 01235 520374	21. AUG 10		
7/09	19. OCT		
07. AUG 09			
09. JAN 10			

To renew this book, phone 0845 1202811 or visit
our website at www.libcat.oxfordshire.gov.uk

www.oxfordshire.gov.uk

WARLORD

S.M. STIRLING
DAVID DRAKE

WARLORD

This is a work of fiction. All the characters and events portrayed in this book are fictional, and any resemblance to real people or incidents is purely coincidental.

Copyright © 2003 by S.M. Stirling and David Drake

All rights reserved, including the right to reproduce this book or portions thereof in any form.

A Baen Books Original

Baen Publishing Enterprises
P.O. Box 1403
Riverdale, NY 10471
www.baen.com

ISBN: 0-7434-3587-7

Cover art by David Mattingly

First printing, February 2003

Library of Congress Cataloging-in-Publication Data

Stirling, S.M.
    Warlord / by S.M. Stirling & David Drake.
    p. cm.
    "The General series was originally published as five separate novels: The Forge, The Hammer, The Anvil, The Steel, and The Sword. Warlord contains half of the Raj Whitehall saga, which will be concluded in the second omnibus volume, Conqueror."
    ISBN 0-7434-3587-7
    1. Life on other planets—Fiction. 2. Space warfare—Fiction. 3. Generals—Fiction. I. Drake, David. II. Title.

PS3569.T543 W37 2003
813'.54—dc21
                                        2002034190

Distributed by Simon & Schuster
1230 Avenue of the Americas
New York, NY 10020

Production by Windhaven Press, Auburn, NH
Printed in the United States of America

10 9 8 7 6 5 4 3 2 1

Contents

The Forge
-1-

The Hammer
-311-

I
The Forge

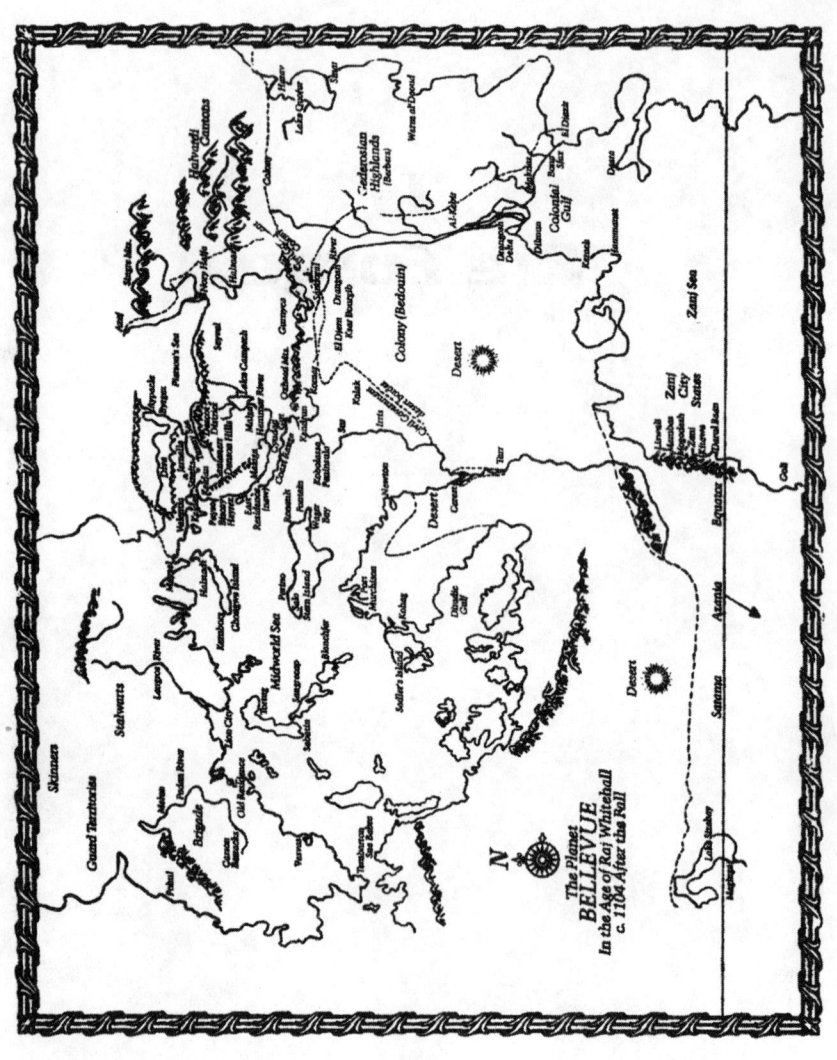

CHAPTER ONE

The rat screamed.

Raj Whitehall spun on one heel, the beam of his carbide lamp stabbing out scarcely faster than the pistol in his right hand.

"Shit," he muttered, as the light fell on the corner of the underground chamber. The rodent was dead now, dangling from the jaws of a cat-sized spersauroid, a slinky thing with a huge head and slender body carried high on four spidery legs. It blinked at them with eyelids that closed to a vertical slit, and then was gone with a rustle of scales against rubble. Raj grimaced. One of the few pleasant things about living in East Residence was that Terran life had mostly replaced the local. But not in the catacombs, it seemed.

Thom Poplanich laughed. "Careful, Raj," he said. "Those bullets will bounce, you know."

Raj grinned back a trifle sheepishly as he holstered the weapon. A genuine five-shot revolver, it was as much a badge of nobleman's rank as was the saber he carried slung over one shoulder. Both were as familiar as his clothes: Whitehall had been born in Descott County, hard country two weeks' journey north of the capital, where men went armed from puberty. The platinum stars and hunting scenes inlaid in the steel of the revolver were a badge as well, of membership in the Governor's Guard.

"Spirit of Man of the Stars," Raj said, and touched the silver wafer etched in holy circuits that hung around his neck. "This place makes my skin crawl." Everyone knew the catacombs under New Residence were ancient and huge . . . but those were just words until you *saw* it. This complex could house the whole population of the capital, with room to spare—and New Residence was the largest city on Earth.

"Not a spot for a picnic," Poplanich agreed.

The abandoned elevator shaft he had found below his apartments ended in this floor of rubble; from the hollow sounds and the way it shifted, there must have been levels below. Rust-streaks marked the lines of ancient machinery. Now there was only the cool gray surface of fused stone, and one half-open door . . . no, wait.

"Look at this," Poplanich said. He walked quickly over the broken rock and flicked his lantern's beam downward, moving with a studied grace. "*That* hasn't been here since the Fall."

It was a tallow candle stub, resting in a congealed puddle of its own grease. There was a smokemark above it, but dust lay thick over all.

"But it's been there long enough," Raj commented, trying the door. It was frozen in its half-open position, but there was just room for his barrel chest. "Hand me the paintstick, will you, Thom?"

They would need to be very careful not to lose their way, down here in the catacombs. He touched his wafer again. Everything around them was a product of men who had lived before the Fall, when the Spirit of Man of the Stars had infused their souls. You could see it in the way the rock was carved, seamless and even, in the strange bits and pieces of shattered machinery, the very materials unfamiliar. There might even be . . .

"If we come across any computers, we'll have to tell the priests," he said.

Thom laughed. "They don't need *genuine* relics any more," he said with easy cynicism. "Haven't you heard what the last synod ruled about the Miraculous Multiplication?"

Raj flushed; they were both just turned twenty-five, but there were times when Thom Poplanich made him feel very much the raw youth, a rustic squire in from the provinces. Even in tweed and leather hunting clothes, the other man had a slim self-assured elegance that spoke of ten generations of urban aristocracy. Raj touched his amulet again. It was comforting to know that this was the genuine article, recovered two centuries ago and blessed by Saint Wu herself. Even if the Church had ruled that belief made the relic holy, rather than the reverse.

He forced himself into the door and pushed with knees and hands, back braced against the wall. For a long moment nothing moved, until he took a deep breath and threw the strength of shoulders and back into it, timing the contraction to the exhalation of his breath the way the family armsman had taught. A seam parted along the side of his tight uniform jacket, and the thick slab slid open with a protesting screech of tearing metal. Raj dropped to the floor in a crouch, panting slightly.

"Showoff," Thom said as he sidled past. There was surprise and slight envy in his tone; his friend grinned.

"A strong back comes in useful for other things than pulling a plow," he said, raising his own lantern. "Let's keep turning to the right."

Raj genuflected again, touching brows and heart to the ancient, dust-shrouded computer terminal.

"Look, there's not much point in going on," he said. This was the fifth level down from their starting-point. Emptiness, offices and storage space, eerily uncorroded metal and the smell of damp stone. And enough computer equipment to stock every church in the Civil Government and the barbarian lands as well.

Poplanich ran a hand over the swivel chair before the terminal. Dust puffed up behind his hand, silver-yellow in the light of the lantern.

"Feel this," he said, fascinated. "It *looks* like leather, but *new* leather. This area's been abandoned since the Fall, it should have rotted away to shreds." He swung the chair back and forth. "A greased axle won't turn that smoothly, and this doesn't even *squeak*."

Raj shrugged. "They had powers before the Fall. The Spirit withdrew them when they proved unworthy."

Thom nodded absently; that was from the Creed. "I still think this was a naval installation," he said, picking up a plastic sign from one desk. It was made of two strips joined at one long edge; one side was blank, and the other bore black letters in the Old Namerique tongue. *Wez cainna bie fyr'd: slavs godda bie sold.* His lips moved silently, construing it first into modern Namerique, and then into his native Sponglish. He frowned absently. *Well, of course,* he thought.

"I don't know," Raj replied, heading cautiously out into the corridor again. "The Book of the Fall—hey, there's a stairwell leading down here, hand me the paintstick again—says the military joined the Rebellion." They had both sat through enough droning sermons on *that*.

Thom's teeth flashed in a grin. "Just as my own interpretation—and please keep this from the Invigiles Against Heresy, will you?—I'd say that the Brigade and the Squadron and the others were pretty low-echelon units, out in the wilds when the Fall came. They didn't cause the breakup of the Holy Federation, they just seized power where they could when we were cut off from the Stars."

Raj felt a slight discomfort; that was not outside the canons of interpretation, but it was dangerously free-thinking. "Come on," he said. "Two more levels, then we go back."

"That's a light," Thom said in a hiss as they turned the corner. His foot brushed aside a crumbling human femur; they had seen enough skeletons on this level to grow blasé. A brittle pile of brown-gray bone, hardly marked by the teeth of the rats, bits of rope and stiff leather and rusted metal scattered about it.

Raj squinted, then turned off his lamp. His friend followed suit, and they waited for their eyes to adjust. He could feel the darkness fading in around him, and with it the enormous weight of the catacombs. His mouth felt dry. *That is a light*, he thought. A soft white light that was unlike anything he had ever seen; not like sunlight, stars, fire, or even the harsh actinic arclights that you sometimes saw in the Governor's Palace or the mansions of the very rich. This was the light of the Ancients; the light of the Spirit of Man of the Stars.

"Live equipment," he whispered, genuflecting again. *Blasphemy. Fallen Man's eyes are blind to the Light of the Spirit. I am not worthy.* With an effort of will he relaxed the rock-tense muscles of his neck and shoulders.

"Thom, we shouldn't *be* here. This is something for a Patriarchal Council, or the Governor." There was a slight tremor in his hands as he drew his pistol, swinging the cylinder out and checking the load. The unnatural gleam shone off the polished brass of the cartridges. He was conscious of the uselessness of the gesture; what good would a revolver be against the powers of the unFallen? Of course, it was no more useless than anything *else* he might do . . .

"Priests . . ." Thom visibly reconsidered. "Priests aren't notably more virtuous than you or I, Raj," he said reasonably. His eyes stayed fixed on the unwinking glimmer, shining slightly with an expression of primal hunger. "Of course, if you're . . . uncertain . . . you can wait here while I check. I wouldn't think less of you for it."

Raj flushed. *I'm too old to be pushed into something stupid by a dare*, he thought angrily, even as he felt his mouth open.

"I'll use the pry bar," he said. "Get it out, would you?"

Thom rummaged in his rucksack, while Raj advanced to examine the door. The feeling in his stomach reminded him of waiting behind the barricade during the street fighting last fall, when the sound of the rioters had come booming around the corner, thunder of feet and massed chanting of voices: *Conquer! Conquer!* Just like then; he had seen the eyes of the rankers flick toward him, as they stood at parade rest. He had strolled up to the chest-high barrier of carts and furniture and paving stones as if he were walking out the front gate of his father's manor, going to inspect the dogs. *Sergeant major, first company to the breastwork; prepare for volley fire, if you please.* His voice hadn't been the shaky squeak he'd expected, either.

You could get through anything, once you'd decided you had to. Look at it as a job to be done, and then do it, because *somebody* had to and it cursed well wasn't going to happen if you waited for the next man. Not to mention that his role in putting down the riots had gotten him a Captaincy and the still more important position of Guard to the Vice-Governor.

Closer, and the light was a narrow strip along one side of the door rather than a wedge; he pressed an eye to the crack, but it was reflecting around a tongue-and-groove socket that was almost closed. The air blew from inside to him, dry and metallic and tasting of . . . *old bones*? he thought.

"Maybe I can get it open," he said experimentally, trying for a grip with his hands. The crack was too narrow, but his friend slapped the octagonal steel of the pry bar into his hand as he reached around behind for it. The metal was as thick as he could comfortably grip and about a meter long; one end flattened out into a wedge, and the other into a hook. The wedge slipped in easily enough, a hand's width, and he braced one foot against the jamb of the door.

"Wait a second," Thom murmured. He pointed to a rectangular plaque beside the blank gray rectangle of the portal. "I've seen an old manuscript that describes doors like these, Annaman's *Records of the Settlement*. The inscription said *'touche thi squaire, und recessed it shall by.'* "

"But will it work now?" Raj said, a little sharply. A Descott squire had better things to do with his youth than pour over ancient manuscripts and parse verbs in Old Namerique, to be sure. But it was still a little irritating, when some city noble trotted out a classical quotation. *At least Thom's usually have something to do with reality*, he thought.

For answer, Thom pointed at the light that picked out the highlights of their faces, and then slapped his hand on the control. There was a *chink* sound deep inside the wall, and the door shifted slightly. So slightly that he would not have been conscious of it, except for the tremor of metal against his palms.

"Well, let me try muscle if scholarship won't budge it," Raj continued, forcing cheerfulness into his tone. "And *hssssssaaaa!*"

There was a moment of quivering tension, and then the door began to move; in a squealing jerk for the first centimeter or so, then more rapidly. Halfway open it stuck again with a soundless authority that told him something solid had fallen across the trackway. Raj leaned head and shoulders through, squinting and blinking against a fall of dust and the dim light.

"I can see where the light's coming from," he said.

Thom crowded up beside him, craning for a look. Beyond the door was a corridor five meters across, running right into darkness; on their left was a square of brighter light, another door. And the floor was two meters down from where they stood, the sagging remains of a metal stairway offering more hindrance than help.

"If you lay and held onto my wrists, I could drop to the bottom, Thom said.

"And how in the Outer Dark would you get back *up*?" Raj said dryly. "Here, let me have your belt."

The smaller man handed over the narrow dress belt of his jacket; it was rogosauroid hide traded down from the Skinner country north of Pierson's Sea, and strong enough to hold four times their combined weight; Raj's was much the same, except that it was broader and less elaborately tooled. He looked thoughtfully at the door, tapping the heel of his palm experimentally on the edge. It seemed to have stuck fast. On the other hand . . . The pry bar was just a little shorter than the width the door had opened; he laid it in the opening and stamped on it until it seated firmly, the wedge-end driven under the bottom between runway and door.

"This'll hold the belts," he said, buckling one to the other. "I'd better go first."

Raj took the leather in one hand and his pistol in the other, bracing his boots on the wall and rappelling down in three bounds. Dust spurted up under his feet and bone crunched, spurting more dust. He swore and spat, unpleasantly conscious of how long it had been since he had a drink. Then he swore again, softly, as Thom dropped down beside him and the nature of the floor he was standing on became plain.

"Bones," he whispered. Thom unshuttered his lantern and swung the beam around, brighter than the white glow from the doorway and better for picking out detail.

"*Lots* of bones," his friend agreed, sounding more subdued than usual.

Not quite enough that you could not find clear space for your feet, but nearly, and the crumbled dust between them spoke of others still older.

"And look," Thom continued. "What the hell's *that?*" *That* was a rust-crusted weapon; Raj picked it up, and pursed his lips in a soundless whistle.

"It's a koorg-rifle," he said. "The Civil Government Armory stopped issuing them two hundred years ago."

Raj might not have been to the schools of rhetoric, but there was *nothing* wrong with his grasp of military history. "Double-barreled muzzle loader with octagonal barrels."

His friend's light picked out other items of equipment; off by the other wall there was what looked like one of the ceremonial weapons the mannequins of the Audience Hall Guard carried. Raj looked closer: it was not, it was a real *laser*, the ancient Holy Federation weapon. The metal men in the Hall of Audience carried non-functional replicas, but this was the real thing. The soldier's eyes narrowed as he followed the line of the muzzle; there was a deep pit to the upper right of the door, melted into the stonework, with a long dribbling icicle of lava below it. Nothing on the metal of door or frame, although the melt would have crossed it.

"Thom," Raj said briskly. "This has gone too far; this is seriously strange. We should fall back and report. *Now*."

Reluctantly, the other man nodded. And—

CRANG. The door above their heads slammed shut so quickly that the huge musical note of the pry bar breaking was almost lost in the thunder-slam of its closing. A fragment of the steel bar cannoned across the corridor and ricocheted back, falling at Raj's feet. He bent to touch it, and stopped when his skin felt a glow from the torsion-heat of breakage. Thom was standing and examining the linked belts; the buckle that had fastened them to the bar was missing, and the tough reptile hide cut as neatly as if it had been sliced with a razor. Raj felt a giant hand seize his chest, squeezing, tasted bile at the back of his throat.

"Well," he said, and heard it come out as a croak. "Well, it *is* still active."

Thom nodded jerkily. "Notice something about the skeletons?" he said.

Raj looked around. "Pretty dead."

"Yes, and no marks on the bones. Looks like they fell in place, *and nothing disturbed them*."

Raj Whitehall nodded. The surviving skeletons were eerily complete, like an anatomy model; no toothmarks, nothing disturbed by scavengers.

"I don't think there's much point in going that way," he answered, waving to the darkness on their right. The beam of his lamp showed nothing but the walls of the corridor, fading to a geometric point with distance. "That heads due east, near as I can tell." Out from under the city and towards the hills. "If there's anything beyond that . . . light . . . we might find another shaft leading up."

Thom nodded, wiping a sleeve across his mouth. "Maybe. I wish we'd brought some water."

Raj grinned. "I wish you hadn't said that," he said. "I really do."

"Mirrors," Thom said. For the first time in Raj's memory, there was real awe in his friend's voice. "I've never *seen* mirrors like this.

"I've never seen a *light* like that, either," Raj said.

The room was circular, floored and roofed with mirrors, and with a single seamless sheet of mirror for the walls. The center of the circle was a pillar of light; white, glareless, heatless, odorless, shining on the endless repeated figures of the two men. Raj felt himself stagger in place, lost and splintered in fractions of himself. It was a moment before he noticed the last, the intolerable strangeness.

"Thom," he said urgently. *"Why don't the mirrors reflect the light?"* There it was before their eyes, a column as physically real as their own hands, a light that was all that kept this place from being as dark as a coffin. Yet in the mirrors there was no trace of it, only the two men and their equipment.

Thom blinked for an instant; then his eyes widened and he turned to run. *Did* run, one single step before freezing in place as if turned to stone. Even his expression froze, and Raj could see that his pupils shared the paralysis. The doorway that had been Thom's goal had . . . not closed, simply vanished; only the direction of the living statue that had been his friend enabled Raj to tell it from any other part of the smooth mirror curve. The light-pillar in the center of the room blazed higher.

Raj fired, with his second finger on the trigger and the index pointing along the barrel, the way the armsman had taught him: at close range, you just pointed and pulled. The five shots rang out almost as one, the orange muzzle flashes and smoke dazzling his eyes. Almost as loud was the *bang-whinnnng of* the soft lead bullets ricocheting and spattering off the diamond hard surfaces of the room; they left no mark at all. Something struck Raj in the foot with sledgehammer force, a bullet tearing off the heel of one boot. A long tear appeared in the floppy tweed of Thom's breeches . . . Then nothing, nothing except an acrid cloud of dirty-white powder smoke that made Raj cough reflexively.

Raj's muscles seized halfway through the motion of reloading. A voice spoke: not in his ears, but in his mind. Spoke with an inhuman detachment that had a flavor of hard-edged crispness:

yes. yes, you will do very well.

CHAPTER TWO

The floor had vanished, and the pillar of light. There was nothing beneath him, although he could feel the pressure of weight under his feet. The off-white haze of powder smoke cleared rapidly, as if the air was being circulated without a detectable breeze. Thom hung suspended also, still in the first motion of flight, as if this was the Outer Dark where those who rejected the Spirit of Man fell frozen forever.

He heard his throat trying to whimper, and that brought him back to himself. He was a Whitehall of Hillchapel, and a soldier, and a man grown. The worst this whatever-it-was could do was kill him, and a paving stone in the riots could have done that. Or a scropied in his boot on a hunting trip, or a Colonist bullet or a Brigade bayonet. His soul only the Spirit could damn or save.

yes. excellent.

"Who the Dark are you?" Raj said, trying for the tone his father had used on machinery-salesmen back at Hillchapel. Hillchapel, sweet wild scent of the silverpine blowing down from the heights, the sound of a blacksmith's hammer on iron—

I am Sector Command and Control Unit AZ12-b14-c000 Mk. XIV.

Awe struck the human; he tried to genuflect, found himself still immobile. "Are you . . . a *computer*?" he asked incredulously.

yes. although not in the sense you use the term.

"What do you mean?"

i am not a supernatural being.

"What are you, then?"

i am a sentient artificial entity of photonic subsystems tasked with the politico-military supervision of this sector for Federation Command.

That's what a supernatural being is, dammit. Raj frowned; that was straight out of the Creed, and even the phrasing was the archaic dialect the priests used. *First it says it isn't a supernatural being, then it says it's working for the Holy Federation*, he thought in bewilderment. *An angel.*

"What do you want of me?" he continued bluntly. Although the skeletons outside had given him a few grisly notions along those lines.

observe. think.

Thom and the mirrored sphere vanished. This time Raj did cry out, but it was as much wonder as fear; he was hanging suspended in air, flying as men had done before the Fall. It took a moment for him to recognize precisely where; the bird's-eye-view was utterly unfamiliar, and the scene below was not that which he knew. It was the shape of the land itself that finally shocked recognition out of him, known from a hundred maps. The New Residence, the city of the Governors and the capital of the Civil Government. The near-perfect circle of the bay, cut by a single three-kilometer channel; the buildings were laid out on the Silver Antler hills, just in from the passage to the sea. Off south he could see the delta of the Hemmar River, misty in the morning light . . .

But it was not *his* city, not the city that Governor Vernier ruled in this Year of the Fall 1103. Instead of tight-packed streets within great defensive walls, there were towers and low domed structures scattered through forest and park, as if the whole town was a nobleman's pleasaunce. The streets were merely cleared lanes, with vehicles floating along not touching the thick green turf beneath them; and the city was *huge*, stretching off into the distance beyond what he could see. Metallic eggs moved across the map-like landscape beneath him in slow-seeming traceries. A ship was making passage in through the channel, a slim thing without sails or oars or fuming smokestack—the perspective snapped home, and he knew it was a thousand meters long or more.

The view swooped down to show people in odd, rich clothing strolling amid unearthly splendors. In a fenced garden with a strange double-helix sign above the gate children played with fabulous beasts, griffins and centaurs, miniature bears and tiny dogs no higher than a man's waist; even the ordinary riding dogs were odd, the usual breeds seeming shrunk to no more than five hundred pounds, smaller even than a lady's palfrey.

"Holy Spirit of Man of the Stars," Raj whispered. Tears of joy formed at the corners of his eyes and leaked downward. "I am not worthy!" *A vision of time before the Fall!* he exulted inwardly. *Why* me? *I'm just a soldier, not a priest. I . . . I try to live by the Spirit . . .* Sins he had neglected to Enter at the Terminal floated up, making him wince.

no. Was there a trace of exasperation in the passionless non-voice? **this simulation is of a period roughly twenty years after the events you refer to as the Fall, after the last faster-than-light transit from bellevue. observe.**

Something flashed by him in mid-air, something moving too quickly to see as more than a streak. Fire blossomed below; his heart cried out in shock as the lacy towers crumpled, and he could feel the small hairs along his spine struggling to stand erect as the ball of flame expanded out toward him like a soap bubble of orange and crimson. Thunder rolled impossibly loud and long.

Wait a minute, he thought. *I don't feel anything different. The air even smells the same as it did before the vision. Why don't I feel the wind?*

this is a simulation. consider it a very good map. you may alter your point of view by concentrating.

There was a feeling like a click behind his eyes, and the scene swooped dizzily. Raj tumbled for a moment before regaining control; it was as if he was a disembodied pair of eyes and ears with the power of flight. Cautiously, he swooped downward. The beautiful ancient buildings lay tumbled, or burning, or shattered in zones of overlapping circles out from the center of the fading ball of flame. He moved until the radius of complete destruction was behind him, watching like a god as little swooping vehicles came to collect the wounded; hideously burned figures writhed or lay still, and the ground-cars that had zipped along the roadways of turf were tumbled like toys, some driven through the fronts of houses.

There must have been a wind like a hurricano, he thought; the scene matched the description of the terrible storms of the far southern Zanj Sea. *Fire like the heart of a star, then a killing wind*. Raj had received the rudiments of a classical education, despite the pragmatism of his country-gentry family. There was only one thing that fit that description: fusion bomb, the agency of the Fall.

Then other flying cars touched down. He grunted in shock as he recognized the blazon on their sides—a double lightning flash, with the numerals 591 between—the insignia of the 591st Provisional Brigade. The barbarians who held the Old Residence, the original seat of planetary government, on the other side of the Midworld Sea. *But those aren't barbarians*, he thought dazedly, as the hatches opened and troops stormed forth. He could recognize their arms and armor, too. The clockwork and compressed-air automatons that lined the walls of the Hall of Audience were formed in that shape, and bore such arms. Lines of fire stitched back and forth as other troops in similar gear but bearing the insignia of the Federation Guards charged to meet them.

enough. The voice interrupted him as he watched the Brigade troops smash the last resistance and move on to sack a huge structure whose foundation outlines matched those of the Governor's Palace he knew. His viewpoint moved without his willing it, and locked on the face of a man lying with half his chest burned away despite his powered battle-armor; the mouth worked behind the visor, but nothing came out of it but clotted blood.

next.

There was a silent snap, and he was back in his original position. The city was intact again, unscarred by the fusion bomb, but as he looked more closely he could see that the outskirts had been abandoned, overgrown with green Terran vegetation and the reddish brown-green of native plants. Fewer of the flying eggs zipped by . . . This time the attack was from the sea, in giant square vessels that floated on flexible skirts in billowing clouds of mist. Impossibly fast, the ships drove up from the sea to the land; laser fire stabbed out from them, and flashes that ended in explosions where oddly slender cannon pointed. Then ramps dropped, and armored soldiers poured out into the streets. The resistance was even less this time, and the attackers less disciplined; they began to loot and rape almost immediately. He recognized their insignia as well; 3rd Cruiser Squadron, the overlords of the Southern territories. Angry puzzlement grew at the back of his mind; even the Brigade considered the Squadron to be savages, and they had trouble maintaining flintlock shotguns, much less unFallen technology.

Again the swoop, and a lock on a man with visor raised who directed resistance from behind a barricade of wrecked vehicles. A flash, and there were only body-parts mixed inextricably with metal and synthetics.

next.

Again Raj found himself back at his starting point. The city was almost completely overgrown except for a core around the Palace, and that was being disassembled for building material. A checkerboard of farm fields and dirt roads stretched around; walls of rubble on dirt mounds protected the core, and a beaten pathway stretched down to improvised docks where sailboats lay. The broadest road stretched south and east; he estimated distances with an officer's trained eye, triangulating off hills he recognized. Yes, that was the course of the Great River Way, the main highway out of East Residence. Far smaller, and without the superb stone-block paving . . . and there was an army marching up it, fighting its way through the overgrown ruins. He swooped lower.

Colonists, this time: dark men, many in billowing robes, bearded, with the green crescent flag of Islam at their head, alongside the scarlet peacock of the Settlers, the family that claimed to have led the first humans from Terra to Bellevue. Few of the beam weapons this time, and they were being sparingly used. Raj frowned, directing his attention from one unit to the next. *Odd,* he thought. The Colonists were mortal enemies of the Civil Government—had been the first to rebel after the Fall, in fact—but they were civilized, in their fashion. This looked like a mob, and a badly equipped one. No cavalry at all, not a single riding dog even for the officers; ox-drawn guns, but so primitive! Muzzle loaders all, that looked to have been cobbled up out of some sort of tubing, and the footmen carried everything from spears to matchlocks. Their opponents wore the blue and crimson of the Civil Government, but were no better armed and far less numerous.

Raj relaxed slightly, felt his stomach muscles unclench: he could understand *this* fight, at least. Much like a gigantic brawl, with numbers overwhelming position. The lock on a single commander was expected, this time: a tall elderly man with a hook where his left arm should have been, wearing a primitive version of the Governor's diadem and wielding an energy-weapon in his right hand. It failed, and a wave of Colonists swarmed over him, hacking and stabbing. A minute later and a spear surged up out of the ruck with the man's head on the end.

next.

The ruins were mostly gone, the odd exotic materials of the unFallen weathered into the soil—*unable to bear the corruption of the Fallen world*, his childhood catechism reminded him—and the central core of the Palace was as he knew it, but shining in new blue limestone, without the patina of centuries. He could see a few of the familiar street patterns, and a bulky stone barn-like structure with the Star on its roof, right where the Temple stood in Raj's own time. A naval battle was raging out on the harbor; galleys only, many open-decked like giant rowboats, not a steamer in sight. There were dozens of flags beside the Civil Government's; Brigade, Squadron, a wild variety of tribal blazons, even the clenched fist with single upright finger of the Skinners, and *they* were wild nomads on the steppes of the far north. Cannon roared, vomiting a fog of smoke that lay like a dirty carpet on the bright blue of the harbor; ships burned; wreckage floated, some of it still living and moving, until the tentacled mouths of downdraggers sucked them under.

Raj's vision locked on the poopdeck of the largest galley. A man lay there, head cradled in the arms of a subordinate, wearing the insignia of a Civil Government Fleet Admiral. Not much was left of his legs beneath the tourniquets, but he was still trying to give orders when he yawned and slumped into unconsciousness.

next.

East Residence was half-built, and men were laying the foundations of the Temple. Or had been; now they were trying to hold walls that were closer to the Palace than the ones Raj knew, but well-made and of stone. Trying and failing. The banners of the Colony waved over a gate; it swung open and troops poured through on dogback, but the animals were small, no more than six hundred pounds. *Like a dream*, Raj thought; half-familiar but distorted. The Colonists charged against a line of Civil Government infantry armed with muzzle-loading rifles, percussion models. They had time for a single volley, and then the dogs were snarling and rearing at the line of bayonets.

A counter-attack about— Raj began; then he saw the column of Civil Government riders pouring down the street behind their infantry. The Governor's banner was at the fore, a Mercator-projection world map, and another that looked something like the sandlion flag of the Descott hills; beneath it was a man whose face had the cast of Raj's home district, square, hook-nosed, brown-skinned, and black of hair and beard. The column crashed into the enemy in a saber-swinging melee. The swooping focus centered on the Descott man's face just as a Colonist trooper fired a pistol loaded with buckshot into it.

next.

The disorientation was worse again, as the city grew more familiar. The Inner Walls were complete, as were the Temple, and all of the Palace except the Long Galleries and their gardens. Noblemen's estates stood outside the Inner Walls, with no trace of the workshops and slum tenements that should cover that ground; the harbor was full of sails, with a few tall, thin smokestacks of uncouth design. The walls were under siege, though: a formal affair, zigzag trenches and revetments, with heavy guns pounding the crumbling ramparts and little return fire. Columns of smoke rose from the East Residence streets; mobs moved through them, and the soldiers struggling toward the perimeter seemed to be having more trouble with their own people than the enemy. Outside the wall were the camps of the attackers; a huge, neatly laid out rectangle around a giant pavilion that bore the Settler's flag, surrounded by field-works; a series of clumps and unit-lines for the Brigade, a sprawl of tents and brush shelters for the Squadron. And odds and sods from everywhere; Skinners on lean hounds with their two-meter rifles—but muzzle-loaders, not the ones he was used to. The dogs were full-size this time, many of breeds he could identify, eight hundred to a thousand pounds.

Few of the attackers were in their camps. Columns and groups and swarms flowed forward into the communication trenches; his training told him the final assault was near. The viewpoint swooped; not to a battle, but into the Audience Hall of the Palace. The decoration was different, but the basic layout the same; the ancient sea ivory and gold of the Chair newer, the jewel inlay more lustrous. The man on it was ignoring the chaos below, the shouts and pleas for orders. Instead he touched the Governor's diadem about his brow, then raised the slender muzzle of a single-shot breech-loader pistol, a type that had been declared obsolete in Raj's grandfather's day. He put the barrel in his mouth and . . .

"Wait!" The shot crashed out; the man's body slumped sideways, showing the cratered exit wound and a fan of gray spatter and pink boneshards across the gold and iridescence of the Chair's back. Memory returned, of a portrait in the Gallery of the Governors. "Wait, that's Muralski IV, he died of the Trembling Plague campaigning on Stern Island, two hundred and twenty years ago, there *wasn't* a siege of East Residence in his reign!"

next.

Raj opened his mouth to protest, closed it again. There was no battle, and the city was as he knew it; a sprawling chaos of avenues and alleys, streets and plazas, running down from the garden-greened heights of the Palace to the tarry bustle of the docks, all within the double circuit of the walls. He swooped his invisible eyes down to ground level. A lumbering traction engine drew a heavy load from a foundry; a litter went by, and then a squad of Palace Guards, jingling and arrogant on their curriecombed Collies. He withdrew to bird-height again, and looked more closely, felt a prickle up his spine; not *quite* as he knew it now. The East Railway was still under construction. As it had been on his first visit to the city, a six-year-old in from the provinces, with his brigadier father to show him the sights.

A mental push, and he was beside the embankment. Just as he remembered, from that never-to-be-forgotten day, the dirt and gravel, the crossties, the long timber rails with their top-strap of rolled iron; engineers in tailcoats, craftsmen, slave gangs swinging picks and hoes and shovels.

The scene slid away, and he was in a room he knew. The Governor's council chamber, the smaller informal one used for the real work, high up over the Long Galleries. And . . .

"Father," he whispered.

Young again, in his thirties, wearing a Corps General's epaulets, which was five ranks higher than Huego Whitehall had ever risen. Standing braced to attention before the old Governor, Govenor Morris Poplanich. Thom's childless uncle, who had died a decade ago. There was a campaign map on the table; Raj focused, saw the wooden counters arranged to show a massive thrust of Colony troops over the passes of the Oxhead Mountains, down into the Hemmar Valley that was the heartland of the Civil Government.

"No!" Raj shouted.

"And I don't know if you're a traitor or just criminally incompetent, Whitehall," the Governor was saying. "And it doesn't matter. I'm removing you from command."

"But, sir, I know *that if you do* . . . !" Huego Whitehall began. He stopped with a resigned shrug, and made no objection when the Guards seized his arms and began stripping him of insignia and sidearms.

"No," Raj whispered. Time blurred: East Residence burned, and Colonist soldiers dragged his father from a prison cell, through corridors thick with smoke and littered with the bodies of Civil Government troops. Huego wrenched free as they emerged, onto a vantage point that showed a panorama of East Residence in flames. He leaped to the balustrade of the terrace, but the guards bore Colony lever-action repeaters; they managed to shoot him at least three times before he went over the edge.

"Lies!" Raj shouted. "All lies!"

calm yourself. consider.

Raj fought his breathing under control, felt the sheen of sweat dry on his skin in the unmoving dead air. "Those . . . battles. They're what *might* have occurred if . . . If what?"

if one earlier than you had been allowed to leave this place, with my help.

He felt the grip on his body relax, and found he could move torso and arms and head. It was inexpressible relief to rub a palm across his face.

"Your help doesn't seem to be worth much," he said bluntly.

consider a general with faultless intelligence staff, who *always* knows the most probable results of his actions, The mental voice of . . . Center, he supposed . . . continued, **yet the universe is a structure of probabilities, if the probability of success is sufficiently low, even my assistance is not enough. sociopolitical and economic factors often count for more than winning a battle. outside this complex i can only advise and observe through my agent, not compel. my calculations indicate the time is ripe at last, for your mission.**

"What mission?" Raj asked.

to unite bellevue, as a preliminary to the rebuilding of the Tanaki Spatial Displacement Net. Even in the soundless voice, he could hear the capitals on the Holy Name of Faster Than Light Travel.

"To unite *Earth*?" Raj said incredulously, touching his amulet.

bellevue, Center corrected pedantically. **earth will come later.**

The young man's lips shaped a soundless whistle. The Whitehalls of Hillchapel had served the Governor in arms for half a thousand years, riding at the head of troops recruited from their home county's tough hill-farmers; the Descott district bred soldiers, not tax-broken peons like the lowlands. He remembered vague boyish dreams of glory, dreams that had grown more specific as he passed into manhood. Beating back a Colony grab at the disputed territories in the southeast, perhaps; there was a border war with the rag-heads every generation or so. Or smashing a raiding column of Brigade troops, over northwest across the Kelden Straits, where the Civil Government kept a foothold in the Middle Territories.

But to reunite the *world*!

"That's a job for a hero-saint," he protested.

I am Sector Command and Control Unit AZ12-b14-c000 Mk. XIV. Without sound, the words roared like the thunder of massed cannon. **I say you are the One.**

Raj genuflected. You did not argue with an angel. "I know my duty," he said, straightening.

that is one of your qualifications, Center observed.

A thought struck the young man. "You don't mean I have to be Governor, do you?" he asked, worry in his voice. "Governor Vernier has my oath. And Vice-Governor Barholm, too; I swore allegiance as his Guard."

vernier will die within the year, Center said, **his nephew barholm will take the chair.** That was no news; Barholm was the real power now, not his ailing kinsman. And Raj was Barholm's man. **you will act as governor barholm's shield and sword, and in any case you will be abroad on campaign for many years: your talents are military and administrative, not political.**

Raj nodded in instant agreement; he could keep his feet in the snakepit intrigues of the Palace, but knew he lacked the gift to excel. Perhaps only the interest, but that was enough. Politics was like fencing, one mistake, one momentary lapse of attention, and you were dead. He thought of having to deal with the Chancellor, Robert Tsetzas, and shuddered; that would be like having a spitting fangmouth grafted on your hand. There was a joke, whispered rather than told, that a fangmouth actually had bitten the Chancellor one afternoon, at a levee: Tzetzas hadn't even missed a nibble on his truffle, while the poison-lizard had died in convulsions . . .

"I took an oath," he said, "to uphold the Civil Government against all enemies, to restore it to its rightful place as the Holy Federation's agency on this world. I guess this covers it."

excellent.

A cone of light focused on Raj's forehead; he slitted his eyes, but honor forbade him to flinch. There was a moment of intense pain, that vanished in a lingering sensation of cold between his eyes and behind the skin. Thoughts moved just below the surface of consciousness, fragments of memories of events that he had never experienced. They died away, leaving a residue of dizziness, a ringing in the ears that was wholly non-physical; he felt as if his body was slightly too small to contain him.

the sensations will fade, Center said, **you will now be in constant communication with me at all times, remember that your actions must be** *yours*: **my help is informative only.**

Raj nodded, still dazed by the echoes within his head, wanting nothing so much as a long sleep, and . . .

"I'll have to tell Suzette; she'll . . ."

observe.

There was a blinking before his eyes, and suddenly he was in his rooms, near the Vice-Governor's section of the Palace. Suzette was across from him, and he could see bewilderment giving way to horror on the smooth aquiline features. She nodded, smiled, left: then the priests came, the Healers of the Troubled speaking soothingly and maneuvering him toward the coat with the crossed arms.

The chamber snapped back. "Shit," he said disgustedly, then blushed at the sacrilege of swearing *here*. "I thought she'd believe me."

not without proof which i will not furnish, Center replied, **knowledge of my existence would render further calculation impossible.**

Raj shrugged. "All right, let Thom go."

no.

The man remembered the bones outside the door; it suddenly occurred to him what it would be like, waiting in the dark unable to control so much as the expression of your face. Unable to blink, feeling your eyes drying out, waiting for thirst or madness to take you.

"Oh, yes you will, angel or no," Raj said flatly. His hand fell to the butt of the useless pistol, not so much a threat as a statement of intent. "A Whitehall doesn't abandon a friend, not for any reward."

poplanich is too close to the old dynasty. Which Vernier had overthrown; old Morris Poplanich had died without male issue . . . of natural causes, or so most thought. Vernier Clerett had been CIC, Residence Area Troops, which had usually counted more than heredity in succession disputes, throughout the Civil Government's history, **now thom poplanich is of age, and is popular, widely respected**

among the older families. Which the Cleretts were *not*; Vernier had been no wealthier or better born than Raj Whitehall himself, an upstart to the ancient kindreds. Just another uncouth Descotter, who wore his spurs indoors, **when barholm clerett assumes the chair, poplanich dies, observe.**

Images. The gongs of the Temple ringing out in mourning, black headbands in the streets. Barholm ascending the steps to the Chair, cheeks flushed, a hard triumph glittering beneath the mask of grief. Troopers of the 2nd Gendarmerie dragging Thom Poplanich out the gate of his family's townhouse; the young man wrenching his arms free and smoothing his coat, walking with quiet dignity toward the black two-dog wagon. Raj watching in the ranks of Barholm's Guard as Thom was strapped to the iron column in Remembrance Square, with the heralds reading out his crimes—"treason against the Civil Government and the Spirit of Man of the Stars"—while the bare-chested executioner in his black hood stood by the scissor-switch to the thumping generator. Barholm stood; the crowd jeered and pushed behind a threatening line of dragoons. The thunder-growl of five hundred wardogs was the louder, until the switch went home and Thom screamed, screamed and sizzled and smelled like roasting pork.

Raj felt sweat on his palms, trickling down his flanks, but there was no controlling these visions. More: Raj with officers he recognized, talking quietly in the rear room of a tavern. Older men there; Berzetayz of the Governor's Council, leader of the Hemmar River clique, the big landowners. Alois Wijolska the iron-smelting magnate. Gunfire in the Palace; men falling before the two-meter cast-bronze doors of the inner chamber, and his own dog rearing to crash it open with its forepaws. Barholm startled out of bed, standing back naked against the tapestries with his hands before his face. His wife Anne, equally naked and cursing defiance as she raised a pistol. Volley fire from behind him.

Fragments. A view that it took him a second to recognize as being from the Chair, and the High Priest raising the Diadem over his own head. Suzette dying—*Suzette!*—her lips blue with poison. Chancellor Tzetzas going to the pillar himself; the crowd cheering this time, and the

Chancellor spitting at the executioner's feet as Governor Raj Whitehall raised his arm. Raj leading troops, but the enemies were Civil Government forces, others in the outfits of noblemen's household retainers. Other battles, a kaleidoscope.

One final scene. Raj Whitehall stumbling at the stirrup-iron of a man he recognized all too well, from Intelligence reports, his hands tied to the leather. Tewfik, amir of the Army of the South, one-eyed eldest son of the Settler; not his heir, no man not whole in body could be, but certainly his commander in the field, and not because of his blood, either. This field was the East Residence, burning, with bodies lying in the rough heaps as the death-squads had left them. Another row fell before a Colonist firing squad as he watched, and a white-bearded *imam* preached from an open Koran behind them as a new batch marched up. Others, women and children mostly, stumbled by chained neck-and-neck under the whips of mounted guards. Wagons of white salt rumbled up the street.

"We will sow it with salt," Tewfik said, looking down at the bloodied face of his captive. "But do not worry. The hot irons will ensure you see no more."

"No," Raj said. He could taste the iron-and-copper of his own fear, smell it. Suzette had died hard, blind animal pain in her eyes, nothing human left. "No. I still won't let you kill Thom. A man who doesn't stand by his friends is no man." *And if I give in on this, I'm a dove. I'll serve the Spirit of Man, but damned if I'll be a dove even to a god.*

again, excellent. Amusement at his indignation. **a successful general must know loyalty, before he can evoke it. poplanich will come to no harm: i can hold his body in complete stasis, and provide more than sufficient mental stimulation.** Was that some sort of joke?

you may return and visit occasionally, when this will not excite suspicion.

He hesitated.

remember that if he leaves here now, he dies, and not him alone.

"Raj." Whitehall's head shot up. Thom's voice; the smaller man turned to face his friend. "Raj, I'm all right . . . it's showing me the most amazing . . . the most amazing things. . . ."

He froze again, but this time the expression was one of wondering delight, not fear. Raj took a tentative step forward, and found that he could. His fingers reached out and touched his friend's skin; it was already cooling, slightly rubbery under his palm. There was a slight shimmer in front of Thom's eyes, like a trick of vision seen out of the corner of the eyes, and Raj could see his pupils expanding and contracting, as if they were moving across a landscape of light and shadow.

"Goodbye," he said; and saluted, for some reason he could not have explained even to himself.

The corridor of bones was as he had left it, save that the door two meters above its surface was open. No other help was offered; evidently Center expected him to make his own way in the world.

Raj Whitehall nodded once, and stopped to reload the revolver before he jumped to plant fingers on the edge. It was lucky not many knew Thom and he had gone exploring together; he had not even told Suzette, she had been dropping more and more hints about how dangerous Poplanich was to know.

Not that dangerous, Raj thought, grinning humorlessly into the dark as he chinned himself and threw a knee over the doorsill. *Not nearly as dangerous as knowing* me *seems to be.*

CHAPTER THREE

"Captain the Honorable Messer Raj Ammenda Halgern da Luis Whitehall, Whitehall of Hillchapel, Hereditary Supervisor of Smythe Parish, Descott County, Guard to the Exalted Vice-Governor, presents himself for duty!"

Raj winced as the herald's bellow rang deafeningly in his left ear; she was using a megaphone that was no less functional for being built of thin polished silver with decorations in niello and diamond chip. The jostling crowds of petitioners fell silent for a moment, craning their necks towards the main doors and pressing against the line of Gendarmerie troopers in dress uniforms. The rifles they held were richly inlaid but loaded and in perfect working order; the whole hall where the Gubernatorial Levee was held was like that, he supposed.

All of two hundred meters long and fifty high; the ceiling was a mosaic, a wheeling galaxy of stars against indigo night, with the head and shoulders of the Spirit of Man looming above it. Much like the one in the Temple, and like that it always gave you a slight creeping sensation between the shoulderblades, as if the huge dark eyes were following you and looking into your soul. The floor was tessellated marble, and the walls point-topped windows filled with stained glass, mostly Scriptural scenes—computers, spaceships lifting off—or gruesome martyrdoms, or the triumphs of the Governors. A blare of trumpets, and the mechanical men spaced at intervals along the walls came to attention from parade rest, slapping the replica lasers with their left hands as they brought them to the salute. There was a hiss and whir from the compressed-air machinery of the automatons, and the arc lights along the angle of ceiling and wall popped and flared, shedding an actinic blue light and the occasional spark. The crowd moaned, bowing in unison before the awesome technology of the ancients.

Raj increased his pace slightly, the gold-alloy spurs on his high boots jingling. He was in full dress fig for this, and as always it made him feel like a dancer in a revue down on Carcossa Street; skin-tight crimson pants with gold piping down the seams, codpiece, jewelled saber-belt and tooled pistol holster, a tache so long and elaborate that he had to hold the scabbard of his sword in his left hand to keep it from dragging on the floor. The blue jacket hugged his shoulders so tightly he could feel the tickle of the epaulets, and the split tails nearly reached his ankles.

The horseshoe shaped end of the Hall was focused on the Chair, standing alone and untenanted at the top of a semicircular flight of white marble stairs. Vice-Governor Barholm was sitting in his usual chair of state on one of the lower steps; to either side were the Chiefs of Department at their inlaid desks. The ceremonial view-screens in each were symbols as well, the actual paperwork would be handled by the crowds of flunkies and aides who hovered at their rear.

Raj went down on one knee, bowing deeply: all that was necessary, considering Barholm's official status and his own. The Vice-Governor's long robe was so heavy with embroidery and jewelwork that it was probably as uncomfortable as Raj's uniform, even on a cool spring day like this. His face showed as little of that as did the other nine Guards who stood behind the bureaucrats. Or the bureaucrats themselves; this was part of the ritual of power, after all.

"Rise, Whitehall of Hillchapel," Barholm said. He was more typical of the Descott Hills than Raj himself, lacking the younger man's rangy height; stocky, with a torso like a brick, a heavy-muscled man who moved with a tensile quickness despite a sedentary life. But his accent was pure East Residence, smooth as a hired rhetor's.

Raj came to his feet, saluted smartly with his free hand and buckled on the plumed helmet; at least on his head it didn't tickle his nose the way it did under one arm. He settled to parade rest beside Hemlt Stanson, the Guardsman next in seniority. Their station was directly behind the Vice-Governor, and they rested their palms on the butts of their pistols. Not that they expected trouble, a very expert crew of chamberlains inspected everyone before they were allowed this far into the Palace. For that matter, there were two dozen *very* expert riflemen with 'scope-sighted weapons behind various pieces of ornamental grillwork. The status of Guard did not appear on any muster roll, but it could count for a good deal more than formal military rank. The Guards were all well-born, well-connected; fighting men who could be relied on for anything that needed doing.

a need shared by both vice-governor barholm and myself, Center observed, **someday inquire as to the meaning of the term "bucellari."**

Raj managed not to jump, and subvocalized: *be careful, you might distract me.* Consciously, he schooled his mind to acceptance; numinous awe was all very well for church, but he had work to do in this world, that was why the angel had chosen him. *Act as if everything was normal*, he told himself. *Act well enough, and you'll grow to believe it in your gut as well as your head.*

Silence, while the ushers shepherded forward the first batch. Three of them, two men and a woman in expensive but unfashionably up-country clothes, without the hired cicerone who could have shown them how to *really* penetrate court ritual. They began to go down in the full prostration, to be halted by the hissed outrage of the usher; that was for the Governor alone. Raj blinked, catching slight alterations in Barholm's expression—*funny, I was never this good at that before*—and decided that the yokels had done themselves no harm and the usher herself no good. It had been a long time since anyone got to the Chair without wanting it bad enough to wet-dream about it waking and sleeping; that was one of the Civil Government's problems. It would probably be better if somebody like Thom Poplanich could inherit the job for once.

Of course, Thom was a gentleman and a scholar; he wouldn't last a week.

"Messer Bendict Cromar Buthelesi, representing sundry

gentlefolk!" the herald announced. Unusually blunt; somebody must have under-bribed.

"Your Exalted Vice-Governorship," the leader of the delegation began; Raj placed the accent, Gaur County, about halfway up the Hemmar River. "We represent the Gaur County Locks Association, and the Seven Hills coal proprietors." The voice was gathering a little assurance as it spoke, though his hands fumbled with the sealed package of documents. "As Your Exaltedness knows, the locks are being reconstructed to be passable for steam riverboats." Those had become numerous, over the last fifty years or so.

Most of the bureaucrats affected an elaborate boredom; an educated man learned of the doings of the unFallen, not the grubby, oily expedients which passed for technology in this degenerate age. Two were fully alert; Chancellor Tzetzas and Barholm. Who, being a Descott man and practical to a fault, was keenly interested in anything that increased the tax revenues of the State.

"Yes, yes," Barholm said, waving a hand to urge the man past the background data. "I've seen the plans."

The petitioner continued doggedly, obviously plowing through a rehearsed speech. Too wired tense to do anything else, even when a new factor entered the equation.

"Your Exaltedness . . . ah." Barholm's glare finally forced the speaker to summarize. "That is, His Supremacy the Governor Vernier, Vice-regent of The Spirit of Man of the Stars, we're orthodox in Gaur County, my lord . . . that is, the State advanced part of the cost of the renovations . . . but the materials have been so late, my lord! While the locks are out of operation, we . . . there's no cash flow, my lord, and the expenses . . . and, well, the coal has to go by animal haulage to below the falls. Your Exaltedness, we beg for relief, either on our interest payments or our taxes."

Barholm frowned, his fingers drumming on one arm of the chair while he beckoned an advisor. Tzetzas' face stayed as calm as a mosaic Avatar, but his fingers riffled through a small box of index cards.

I wonder what's behind all this, Raj thought idly. Porifro Rifera's *Tactics and Strategy* had a whole chapter on the importance of transport in extended operations, and the Gaur Falls were the major break on the river between East

Residence and the head of navigation in the Oxhead Mountain foothills. *Wonder how it'll turn out.*
observe:

A rectangle blanked in the air in front of him, then split: the left side flashed
action by the Vice-Governor.
The falls, and the canal around them. Barges unloaded casks of cement, gangs of laborers, bundles of new-forged pickaxes and barrels of blasting powder. A side-wheel steamer tug pulled a train of barges into a basin whose sides shone with new-cut ashlar blocks; the barges were loaded with bales of hides, cauldrons of pitch, grain, dried fruit, others had holds piled high with gleaming coal. The town behind bustled.
reference to the Chancellor.
The same scene, but he could tell it was nearly a year later. The steamer tug bore the weighing-scale blazon of Tzetzas' family on the side of its stack; as did the carts bringing down coal from the mines. A coffle was being driven onto a barge by armed guards in the Chancellor's livery; the people on the chain had the black brands of debt-bondsmen on their cheeks. Raj recognized the petitioners, in rough burlap prison tunics rather than the quietly affluent clothing they wore today; behind them were their families, others that were probably their retainers. There was a scuffle as the guards unhitched a girl of fourteen from behind Bendict, began pushing her forward under the overhang of the barge as they stripped the tunic up over her head. She screamed and struggled, and so did Bendict until a truncheon struck the side of his head with a sound like a rock on melon.

"Well, delay is certainly a serious . . ." Barholm was beginning. Tzetzas's messenger threaded his way to the Vice-Governor's chair, leaned to murmur in his ear. Barholm's face changed, going smooth and hard. " . . . serious matter," he continued, in a harsher tone. "I expect better of those the State sees fit to aid than excuses! Direct your petition to Chancellor Tzetzas, and perhaps something can be done."

Beside him Stanson whispered *sotto voce;* with the acoustics in here, you could do that pretty safely.

"*Yeah, talk to Tzetzas and you're* done, *the way the monkey did the miller's wife.*"

Raj made a noncommittal grunt; there were some people it was *never* safe to talk about.

"But my lord!" the petitioner wailed, dropping the package of documents. "He—the Honorable Chancellor—he owns the firms that have been delaying delivery of the construction materials!"

"Are you making allegations about my Chancellor? Perhaps you question my judgment, my uncle His Supremacy's judgment?"

"No, Your Exaltedness," the man whispered.

Barholm smiled like a wardog in a butcher's shop. "Well, move along then. As you mentioned, Chancellor Tzetzas has extensive interests in enterprises dedicated to the upbuilding of the State and the furtherance of the designs of Spirit of Man. Perhaps you could arrange a loan."

observe.

. . . and a banker in a skullcap was handing over deeds in a small office richly paneled in Zanj ebony, eyes cold with distaste as Tzetzas riffled through them. The gaslights glittered on the elaborate seals.

"*And with these as security, I'm sure the further loan to His Exaltedness will go through at, oh, half of prime.*" *Silence, then:* "*Unless, Joshua, you feel that you should join your compatriots in buying the forced war bond? Granted that it pays no interest at all, but given the Church's position on nonbelievers . . .* "

Stanson nudged his foot, less likely to be seen. "What's that funny shimmer in front of your eyes?" he said.

Shut up, Raj said mentally. Whispering: "Quiet."

The other Guardsman shrugged slightly; Raj knew Stanson thought—what was the phrase he'd used—that Raj Whitehall had a serious pickle up the ass, and was too freshly down from the Descott hills. *And I think he's a fop who feels his birth puts him above discipline.* Not that it would be wise to say it; Stanson had killed four men in duels, and Raj had better things to do with his time than learn how to be a duelist-gunman. Now, with a saber it might be interesting . . .

The next petitioners were complaining about the tax formers in their district; everyone expected them to squeeze—that was where their profit came from, the difference between what they bid for the district to the government and what they could collect from the populace—but these were supposedly stripping productive assets, not just money and goods.

observe.

A peasant stood in the furrows, watching gape-jawed as the tax-farmer's men walked away with the oxen, and the plow itself for good measure. A typical low country peon in a rough linen tunic of unbleached fabric, his beard reaching to his chest and half his teeth gone. Middle-aged even at the thirty he looked to be, with a burlap sack wrapped around his head against the gray slanting rain and more rags about his feet. The animals bawled in panic, their great brown eyes rolling. It must be a more than usually prosperous farm, to afford a team so sturdy. At the sound the peasant seemed to shake himself, take a few lumbering paces forward.

"'are!" he said. "'are, wait nu, Oi've t' barley t'git in, y'kenna tek—"

The leader of the tax collectors was mounted on a fine black Alsatian, fifteen hands at the shoulder, whose bridle did *not* include the usual steel-cage muzzle. He was armed as well, pistol and shotgun, but he made no move toward the weapons; the dog half-turned, baring finger-long teeth and rumbling like thunder in the deep chest. The peon stopped, well out of snapping range, and stood with his fists clenched in impotent rage. The mounted man rode closer, the dog's feet sinking deep in the wet plowed earth; then he leaned over and slashed the peasant across the face with his crop.

"Well, then tell your master to pay his taxes, you clod! The oxen first, and your brats next year. Twenty pieces of silver, or two hundred bushels of corn, or a bale of first-grade tobacco; that's the assessment on this plot."

Raj's lips tightened.
action by the Vice-Governor.

The tax collector, face covered with tears and mucus as soldiers cut him down from the flogging triangle. Wagons unloading china and silverware at a small manor house, with the squire's lady bustling about giving sharp-voiced directions:
"Watch tha clod feet, ninny! Like enough half is stolen nor broke already!"
Movement: the peasant looking up, an incredulous gap-toothed grin on his face as he dropped the rope over his shoulder and ran toward the gravel-surfaced road where gendarmes lead his plow team. He had been pulling the plow, his wife beside him, shapeless in her rags with a face as wrinkled as a winter apple, and a half-grown boy holding the handles.
action by the Chancellor.

Nothing but the peasant's face, bent beside his wife's as they strained against the ropes. Their breathing sounded deep and labored, and their feet made wet sucking sounds as they came free of the mud, carrying twenty-pound lumps at each step.

Barholm made a slight gesture, the usher said, "Take your petition to the Honorable Chancellor, good sirs."
The next two petitions were for leave to exercise eminent domain; one for an ox-powered railway to bring marble to the coast, down on the Kolobassa peninsula, another to build a reservoir and canal system on the edge of the southern desert, in the foothills of the Oxheads. Both approved, and sent to the Minister of Writs and Sessions. *Real action,* Raj thought dryly. *Well, even Tzetzas can't steal* everything.
"Your Exaltedness."
A crisp military bow from this man; in conservative landowner's Court dress, his plain blue robe showing the tips of riding boots polished but worn. There were places worn shiny on his belt, as well, where a holster and sabertache would hook. A thin eagle face, black eyes above high

cheeks and a nose hooked enough for a Colonist or a Descotter. The usher brayed:

"Messer Mustaf Agrood Naxim, Hereditary Watch-keeper of Deep Fountain, County of Sna Barbra."

Raj pricked up a soldier's ears. That was on the upper Drangosh River, far to the southeast, not a hundred kilometers from Sandoral. On the border of territory controlled by the Colony, and yes, the man had the look of a borderer.

"My lord," Naxim said briskly. "The blessings of the Spirit of Man of the Stars be upon you." The border folk were notoriously orthodox. "Your wisdom—and that of His Supremacy, of course—is our shield. Yet Your Exaltedness cannot be everywhere, and it is my duty to tell you that your servants have been shamefully neglectful on the frontiers of my county. Within the last year, two villages on my lands alone . . ."

"Bandits are your responsibility, man," Barholm said impatiently.

Naxim lowered his eyes and continued. "My lord, these are no bandits, they are regular troops of the Colony and household retainers of Colonial noblemen, acting under orders. They brought artillery on the last raid! My lord, they burn and kill and carry off free folk as slaves. They trample the irrigation canals and cut down orchards to let in the desert! Those farmers are Your Exaltedness's barrier against the Muslim, and . . ."

"And you are authorized to fortify your manors and raise a militia for exactly that purpose," Barholm said. "The Civil Government remits taxes to the extent of . . . how much?"

The Minister of Finance turned to confer with his aids. Tzetzas' voice came smooth as water over tile in a courtyard garden. "To the extent . . . this is for the County of Sna Barbra alone, Your Exaltedness . . . of fifty thousand silver credits annually. That is the land tax; adding in the loss of the hearth tax, poll tax, salt monopoly, excise tax, water rates, billeting and tax-in-kind for garrisons, assumption tax . . . as much again, my lord."

"Well." Barholm sat back, steepling his fingers.

Naxim's eyes closed, and his lips moved in prayer for a

moment. "Your Exaltedness, Sna Barbra—and the other border counties—finance from their own resources ten battalions, mounted and armed, the beacon system..."

"And yet you come whining to Us for help at the least trouble."

"My lord, we can deal with bandits, bedouin, even the amirs of the over-frontier, even the *ghazi* fanatics who come from all over the Colony to plague us... but we cannot deal with the regular armies of the Settler!"

"Take your petition to the Chancellor," Barholm continued coldly. "If further detachments of regular troops must be sent to the southeast, then the tax remittances must be reconsidered or altered. There are many calls on Our resources." Naxim bowed silently—

observe.

Naxim sat a lean-muzzled riding dog with a sand-colored coat, on a ridge overlooking a broad dry valley. Behind him were nearly a thousand troops; not regulars, but well-equipped and looking as tough as any Raj had seen, riding the same long-legged mongrels as the nobleman. Many wore turbans, with veils drawn across their faces, most were in long billowing robes, but a Star medallion gleamed on every chest, and there was a Hierarch Starpriest riding at Naxim's side. The snowpeaks of the Oxhead Mountains towered behind, floating on the horizon.

"Lord Naxim," the priest was saying, pointing down the rocky slopes. "You cannot let the infidel pass!" There was a growl from the men behind him, a clank and rustle of equipment, whines from the mounts.

An army was passing below, an army in scarlet and green, with the crescent banner of Islam before it. Ordered ranks of dog-dragoons under their regimental flags, infantry in solid blocks around the ox wagons of the supply column. Couriers dashed about on light agile Dobermans, and a galloper-battery of one-powder quick firing guns clattered along, drawn by Ridgebacks.

"I cannot stop them," Naxim said, slowly beating one gloved hand on his thigh. "They come twenty thousand strong."

"You could harry them, ambush their foragers..."

"As we have done before," Naxim growled. He spat on the sandy ground. "When we had support from the regulars. Where are they now? Drunk in barracks and pissing out our taxes! Should we leave our homes to be burnt and flee to the hills, when it will accomplish nothing?"

A rumble of assent came from the armed men. The priest bent his head and wept, clutching his medallion.

"The Ambassadors of the Free Canton of the Halvardi!"

Barholm crooked a finger; Raj leaned forward, whispering. "Lord, they're the eastern mountain tribe, the one that controls the best passes through to the Skinners in the northern steppes. And for the Skinners to come south, southwest into the Peninsula, southeast into the Colony."

The Vice-Governor nodded, and smiled affably at the dozen or so barbarians grouped before him. It was obvious even at a dozen meters that they greased their hair with butter, and never washed it; the hair was mostly blond, and both sexes wore it in long braids that fell to their waists on either side. They were dressed in jackets and pants of cowhide, adorned with horns and feathers and beads, draped about with enough edged weapons to arm a company, although they had been persuaded to leave the crossbows and halberds outside the Hall. Two brought a litter heaped with gifts forward; round yellow cheeses, wood carvings, small cedar kegs of beer, and some spectacularly beautiful fercat pelts, pure white and a meter long.

A shaman capered before them, waving a cross and ceremonial wooden house with a small jeweled bird within; he chanted, an eerie nasal *kuku-kuku* that sent not a few hands reaching for their amulets. The Supreme Hierarch Starpriest glared from the midst of a group of her ecclesiastical bureaucrats, but tradition and treaty kept foreigners not settled in the Civil Government outside the Church's jurisdiction. A hired diplomat paced beside the horn-helmed figure of the Halvardi chieftain, and he *was* a citizen, conspicuously holding a Star medallion to show he had not been tainted by his employers.

The Halvardi chief bowed slightly, raised both hands and began to chant: the hired diplomat translated line for line from *Zvetchietz*, the mountain tongue. To Raj it had a monotonous sameness, a *hburni-burni-hrji* sound endlessly repeated.

hburni-burni-hrji

"—Lizsauroid-Slayer Fren-kel, chief of the Houses of the Halvardi—"

hburni-burni-hrji

"—greets the Great Chief of the Rich Houses—"

An aside: "Such is their rude way of acknowledging Your Exaltedness" *hburni-burni-hrji*

"—thanks him for the continued ah—" he glanced aside at the Halvardi, who evidently knew the Sponglish of civilization, or at least enough to keep a translation honest "—tribute for barring the passes against Skinner raiding parties—"

hburni-burni-hrji

"—and also for the additional bribes to allow the Skinners through to burn and pillage the Colonist territories around Lake Quofur—"

hburni-burni-hrji

"—which they have done. However—"

hburni-burni-hrji

"—Jamal, the Settler of the Colony—"

All the Halvardi spat at the name, and the watching ushers winced.

"—has sworn to send an army into the mountains—"

hburni-burni-hrji

"—kill or castrate every Halvardi of fighting age—"

hburni-burni-hrji

"—and seize the passes for Islam. Worse, he is sending—"

hburni-burni-hrji

"—his one-eyed general Tewfik to do it."

hburni-burni-hrji

"In which case—"

hburni-burni-hrji

"—*you* had better do something yourself."

Barholm frowned. "You," he said, addressing the diplomat. "Are you empowered to negotiate?"

"Yes, Your Exaltedness, provided that the chief and his council agree and finalize it," he said. A grimace. "The shaman has to cut open a sheep, too." He made a gesture that anyone around Court knew, thumb and two fingers rubbed together: *bribe him.*

"Take them over to the Minister of War," Barholm said decisively. "This is serious." He signed to the usher.

"*This audience is at an end!*" the megaphone bellowed. "*All hail, his Exaltedness, Vice-Governor Barholm!*"

"Be seated, gentlemen. My dear," Barholm added to his wife Anne.

The conference room dated to the reign of Negrin III, three centuries before; the walls were pale stone, delicately painted with scenes of reeds and flying dactlysaroids and birds, daringly unreligious unless you counted the single obligatory star up in one corner. The conference table was a relic of preFall days, a long oval of plastic that no force known to modern man could scratch or scar. Raj seated himself at the end furthest from the Vice-Governor, nodding to Anne with a smile. She responded with one of her own, cool and enigmatic. Anne, Lady Clerett, was a tall woman, an inch or so taller than her husband, and from her figure she had kept up the dancer's training. In her thirties, but with an ageless look; long dark-red hair that fell to her waist, braided with silver, conservatively dressed in wide pleated trousers and tunic of maroon silk that set off the green of her eyes.

You could see how she had captivated a younger Barholm; it took a closer acquaintance to understand how she had maintained that hold, gone from kept courtesan to official mistress to Church-wedded wife, despite all the cries of scandal and political liability. Raj remembered her on the Plaza Balcony, during the riots, standing calmly and looking down at the sea of upturned faces; he had stood beside her, in an agony of indecision over whether he should force her within. Then she had raised her glass to the crowd and laughed, while torches and bricks fell short and the occasional bullet spanged off the ornamental stonework.

She'd smiled at him then, too, as she turned and walked back into the dubious safety of the Palace. Smiled, and said: "I always *did* perform best with an enthusiastic audience." Laughing at the shock on his face . . . She was a very good friend of Raj's wife, Suzette, who was *still* the only lady of rank who would receive her. Raj suspected that social blockade would be broken with a ruthlessness even greater than that of the society matrons, when Barholm ascended his uncle's Chair. There were weapons sharper than a snub, and Anne would have no hesitation whatsoever in using them.

"Lady Anne," he murmured. This was a semi-formal occasion; greetings went from most junior to the second-senior present. Then to the others, the men with formal power: "General Klostermann." Commander of Eastern Forces, the second-most important field command. Commander of Residence Area Forces was the most important, of course. Which was why the Vice-Governor kept it firmly in his own hands. "Chancellor Tzetzas." Lidded eyes and perfect courtesy. "Captain Stanson." A brisk nod. "And Delegate Hortanz." The hired diplomat of the Halvardi.

Servants ghosted in, set out trays of wine, kave, nibblements on trays, left with the silent self-effacement of the Palace staff. A military aide brought the big relief-map and spread it out on the table; such were a priceless asset of the Civil Government's military, rivaled only in the Colony and unknown elsewhere.

"Well, there it is," General Klostermann said sourly, when Barholm had nodded the meeting open for business. He was a middle-aged man, weathered by the savage winters and summer heat of his command. There were deep crinkles beside the slanted hazel eyes that looked out the gallery windows, down into a courtyard of fountains and flowerbeds. "Tewfik's closer to the Halvardi than I am, and they've got the farmlands around Lake Quofur to draw on. He can reinforce and we can't, and that's the truth. If we'd kept the roads up better . . ."

Tzetzas frowned. "General," he said quietly, "the Civil Government's resources are limited, though one would wish otherwise. One inquires if the distinguished general would prefer to have roads and no pay for his troops?"

"That's late often enough," Klostermann said. "My lord." Turning to Barholm, "Your Exaltedness, perhaps we could send the Halvardi a subsidy; arms, maybe, or some engineering officers to fortify the passes?"

Barholm leaned back and sipped moodily at his kave. He looked down at the cup, blinked. "No, we don't *want* to make the Halvardi stronger, we want to *keep* them dependent on us. Klostermann, surely we could send *something* in the way of troops?"

"Ah, your Exaltedness . . . well, perhaps a couple of companies of Daud's Dragoons?"

Tzetzas laughed. "One is confident they would feel at home, being mostly barbarians themselves."

The general visibly forced himself not to scowl at the Chancellor, who was not a safe man to antagonize. "They may be irregulars, but they can ride and shoot."

"Not fast enough to stop the sort of force Tewfik will bring," Stanson said, prodding at the map.

"Ah, if *something* could be sent, relations with the Halvardi could be improved considerably," Delegate Hortanz said. He made a refined gesture. "In which case, the, ahh, subsidy for this year could be forgone . . . perhaps distributed to worthier causes?" His eyes crossed Chancellor Tzetzas', a byplay lost on none of the others.

Raj looked down at the map. It showed the eastern portions of the Midworld Sea and the western provinces of the Colony, the lands of civilization. The Civil Government held the thumb-shaped peninsula on the northeastern shore, and areas to the north and south; they shaded out into vaguely tributary provinces inhabited mostly by tribal peoples. The mapmaker had been remarkably optimistic; the Skinners, for example, were listed as "vassal tribes."

Outer Dark, they have enough trouble getting on with each other, he thought. *To business.* The southern edge of the peninsula ended in the Oxhead Mountains, running inland from the sea to the deserts and the headwaters of the Drangosh; the fortress-city of Sandoral stood at the head of navigation. Southward and eastward were the deserts. Colonial lands, centering on the rich irrigated districts of Drangosh delta and the city of Al-Kebir. Rich and anciently civilized, the first parts of Bellevue to be settled.

observe.

Center's holograms overlaid the map with other projections: force ratios, roads and their conditions, march-times.

tewfik will also find it difficult to shift forces to the northeast, Center continued. A line traced up from Al-Kebir, then east into the rocky highlands of Gederosia and north through difficult country to the great oasis around Lake Quofur. **it will strain their grain and dogmash supplies, and the heavy ordnance is in their capital, tewfik's own army of the south is still near hammamet, resting and refitting from the zanj wars.**

"Ahh, my lord?" Raj said. Barholm looked up quickly. "My lord, it occurs to me that we're reacting to what the Colony threatens. We should be making *them* react to *us*."

Raj was uneasily conscious of Tzetzas' level gaze, of the throttled impatience of Klostermann, like a hard knot in his stomach. *To the Outer Dark with Klostermann,* he thought. *He hasn't won so much as a skirmish in twenty years.* Few Governors wanted *too* able a general in command of so many experienced and mobile troops.

"Tell us something that the manuals don't," the general said.

"Well, to secure the Halvardi passes, Tewfik would have to bring up most of their field army from the lower Drangosh, and then call out the *amirs* and their *ghazis* along the way through Gederosia." That was tough highland country, much like Descott, and contributed soldiers rather than taxes to the Settler. "Then they'd link up with the garrison forces around Lake Quofur and move west... and if they *did* take the passes, it'd put them in a position to move on Novy Haifa." His finger tapped the map at the extreme northeast corner of the peninsula, where the coastline turned north to form the eastern shore of Pierson's Sea.

Tzetzas winced slightly; Raj remembered that the Chancellor's family had tobacco plantations in the area, and interests in the grain and hide trade up into the steppe country. Barholm nodded.

"Well, how do we stop them?"

"We make *them* afraid of an invasion by us," Raj said, keeping his features immobile and cursing the sheen of sweat on his forehead.

For a moment Raj could not tell whose objections were making the most noise; Barholm pounded a fist on the table for silence, and glared at the young Guardsman in the quiet that followed. "Are you serious, Whitehall?" he asked. "I took you into the guard because you could think, not because I wanted a hillman fireater."

Raj swallowed. "Perfectly serious, my lord. I didn't say we should invade the Colony: I said we should make *them* think that we're going to."

He looked down at the map again, blinking. It was still a little unsettling, seeing the physical reality of the parchment overlain with the shining colored lights of Center's projection, moving unit-counters to Raj's command and finger-tip.

"First, we tie down the Colonist forces in the northeast."

"How?" Klostermann said sharply.

Raj looked up, and smiled with an expression copied from the Chancellor's cool malice. "Bribe the Skinners," he said flatly. Barholm grunted in interest and leaned forward, his eyes locked on the map. "And the Halvardi, to let them through. It's going on for harvest in the Quofur country, good pickings . . . ten thousand gold FedCreds ought to do it, to the *Shefdetowt* of the Bekwa and Traryvier tribes. That'll bring a couple of thousand warriors down from the steppe at least; or we could give part of it in powder, shot, and cartridges, even better."

"I hate to let those savages through into civilized country," Klostermann said. Raj found himself joining all the others present in staring at the older man; his eyes met the Vice-Governor's, and Raj knew they shared a thought. *He's been out in the* bundu *too long.*

"Five thousand gold," Tzetzas said decisively. "Half in cash, half in munitions." A quirk of the lips, half-hidden behind a hand. "One must remember these savages are not accustomed to East Residence prices."

You'd think it came out of his own *pocket*, Raj thought. Then: *Well, it does, in a manner of speaking.*

"Then we make demonstration raids all along the southern border," Raj continued. His finger traced an arc from Ty-Och in the west to Sandoral in the east.

"That'll be like sticking your dicks into a hornet's nest!" Klostermann half-shouted. Then, turning to Anne, "Begging your Ladyship's pardon."

"Granted," she said dryly, raising a sealion ivory cigarette holder to her lips and puffing.

"You'll set the whole bloody border aflame!" the general continued.

Raj remembered the petitioners. "It's *already* bloody aflame, you idiot! On *our* side!" His hand swept along the dotted line on the map. "If we let them think we're softening them up for an attack, they'll have to concentrate their forces. Which means they'll have to draw into places with enough food surplus to support large bodies of men and dogs; pull in their horns and group at the riverbank fortress-cities."

"Enough." They all looked up: the Vice-Governor had settled back in his chair, resting his chin on one fist. His orders rapped out, clear and decisive; it was no accident that Barholm Clerett had held the reins of power in East Residence for more than a decade. "We'll send the five thousand to the Skinners: Tzetzas, coordinate with the Ministry of Barbarians and see to it." A hot black glare. "And I want it *done*, Tzetzas, understood? None of your little games now. This isn't the time for them."

The Chancellor bowed with hand on heart. Barholm continued. "General Klostermann, you'll mobilize your forces, down to the infantry rabble, and deploy strong blocking forces in the passes over the Oxheads, leaving enough to cover the Halvardi if necessary—and to keep those devils of Skinners in line, remind them which direction they're supposed to go."

"Whitehall, Stanson," he went on. "You'll each take one battalion of Residence Area cavalry—pick as you please—with appropriate guns and supporting elements, and proceed east to the fortress-city of Komar. You'll take command there and use it as base for the demonstration raids. Kill and burn, chop up any Colonist units you can, make them think we've gone out of our minds. Oh, and don't leave a mosque standing, I've got that Outer Dark cursed ecclesiastical synod to oversee and I'd better show some zeal. Tzetzas, further orders to the Ministry of War, to General Heartwell in Sandoral. Probing attacks down the river and into the farm country to the southeast; maximum devastation, and I want to see some worthwhile loot, prisoners from the Settler's Regulars, and captured guns."

He stood. "Is that clear, gentlemen?"

Hard, Raj thought, as they all rose and bowed. *Barholm's a hard man . . . but brittle.* Cool decisiveness now; it was difficult to remember the Vice-Governor's hours of trembling panic during the riots. He shrugged mentally; there were plenty of men who could handle physical danger, the immediate and unexpected challenge, but who froze when they had to make the big decisions. Barholm's weaknesses were tolerable ones in a Governor, as long as he had a staff to handle the pressures he could not. *And Lady Clerett; Anne has backbone enough for two.*

"Dismissed. Not you, Whitehall."

The Vice-Governor's manner changed completely as soon as the door closed behind the last of the men. "Good work, Raj," he said, coming around the table and slapping the younger man on the shoulder. "Damned good work. We're not ready for a real war yet, Tzetzas is still filling the treasury, but by the *Spirit* this'll put the fear of civilization into that ragheaded wog bastard Jamal."

He handed Raj a glass, raised his own. "To victory!"

"To victory," Anne murmured. Raj became conscious of her with a slight start as she rose and came to stand beside her husband, laying an arm around his waist. It was amazing how self-effacing she could be at need; part of her theatrical training, he supposed.

"And," Barholm said, "good work taking care of the Poplanich matter. Smooth, getting him going on those trips with you before you dropped the axe. Very smooth." Anne was nodding and smiling in a way which nearly blanked out the undertow of attraction nearly every male felt in her presence. *Spirit of Man, if I woke up with that on my shoulder I'd gnaw my arm off to get free without waking her*, Raj thought in horrified fascination.

Aloud, he managed, "Ahh, I'm sure I don't know what you mean, sir."

Barholm laughed aloud, jovial and proud. "And they say we Descott men are bluff and simple!" He gave Raj an elaborate wink. "To be sure, the dirty little traitor—" for a moment his face twisted, then settled back into man-to-man good nature "—just happened never to come back. To be sure. Well, I won't keep you from your duties, Raj. A young man who'll go far, eh, m'dear?"

As Raj bowed salute Anne gave him a slow nod and another smile.

deadlier than the male, Center observed.

The young man felt the skin between his shoulder-blades ripple slightly as he turned to go.

CHAPTER FOUR

"Apologies, master," the servant said.

Raj grunted, pulling himself out of a bright hologram of Tewfik's Colonists digging in around a border hamlet. The two slaves maneuvered themselves through the doorway, a huge wicker hamper of household goods slung between them on poles.

He blinked in surprise, then slid past them into the antechamber of his apartment. As a Captain, and more importantly a Guard, Raj and his wife qualified for a six-room suite in the South Wing, one side of a two-story block around a small garden quadrangle. It had seemed grand enough when he arrived, a single officer fresh from the backcountry. Hillchapel manor house was much larger, but it was as much fort as dwelling place and severely plain within. Nothing like these cool gray marble floors covered in Colony-made rugs, mosaic walls, tall clear-glass windows looking out on the fountain and lilac and potted lavender bushes of the courtyard.

The air was cool from shade and thick stone; there was a smell of dust in it, overlaying the usual odors of beeswax and incense and flowers. Most of the furniture had been pushed back against the walls and draped in canvas sheets, but everything else seemed to be going into hampers, and *where* had all that bedding and knicknacks and clothes and general folderol come from? Raj suppressed an uneasy consciousness that much of it had been Suzette's. She had agreed with matter-of-fact practicality that the jewelry she had received as gifts *from* others before their marriage should be sold—he had been surprised at how much it came to, and how shrewdly she invested the proceeds. He had no need to live on his pay or draw much on the estate, unless he wished. Many of the finer artwork and ornaments had come with her as well. The Wenqui line was as ancient in the City, as old as the Poplanich *gens*, and a few of the antiques were her family's heirlooms. Those that had not been sold in the long losing struggle against bankruptcy that had left her orphaned and not-quite-penniless at fourteen.

"Tingra, Mustfis, be *careful* with that!" Suzette's voice rang sharp from one of the inner rooms. Then: "Darling!" as she saw him and ran over to give him a kiss of greeting.

Raj felt something loosen in his chest at the sight of her; it was always that way, had always been since the first day he met her at Uncle Alois' garden-party. He had to bend to meet her face as she put her hands on either side of his; she was a small woman, barely up to his shoulder. Slim-built, with the greyhound grace of long breeding and a tensile alertness that did not make her look in the least jumpy. Feather-soft black hair was cropped close to her head, convenient for the long blond Court wigs she often wore; her eyes were a hazel-green, wide and startling in the dusky olive of her oval face, tilted by the fold at the corners.

"Congratulations, darling," she said, a trifle breathless after the kiss. The servants bustled on around them, ignored as such always were. *Except that Suzette said you should always remember they had ears, that was one reason she insisted on paying them all a cash allowance, they heard things and repeated them to her.* "Your first independent field command!"

"Well, Stanson's along," Raj said, unfastening the collar of his dress uniform. "Turbo, get my field blues," he added to the valet.

"They're laid out in the bedroom, master," the servant said, bowing over clasped hands.

"Stanson," Suzette said, waving a dismissive hand as they walked together into the inner chamber. "Anne said Barholm gave you seniority. The Vice-Governor knows who's competent. And who can be trusted."

Raj snorted, but looked around before he added: "Then why's Tzetzas still Chancellor?"

Suzette frowned slightly. "He's a very able man," she said seriously.

"Crooked as a dog's hind leg."

His field kit was laid out on the broad surface of the canopied bed; blue wool-linen jacket and red pantaloons, both rather baggy and unadorned except for the Captain's bars and strips of chain mail sewn to the shoulders of the coat. Saber, a plain good curve of Kolobassi steel with a brass basket hilt, revolver, pouch with fifty rounds, binoculars, map case and slide rule, boots, steel bowl helmet with a chain mail neck-guard. And beside it all Suzette's riding clothes, and *her* personal kit; a Colonial repeating carbine and a derringer.

Raj scowled. "Now wait a minute, Suzette-Lady-Whitehall," he began, stripping off the confining dress tunic and throwing aside the silk shirt beneath. "Where in the Outer Dark do you think *you're* going? Unless you want to take another ride up to Hillchapel and stay with Uncle Alois." Raj's father's brother was managing the family estates in Descott County while the younger Whitehall fulfilled the family tradition of service.

"I'm going with you, of course," Suzette said.

He turned, and found her wearing nothing but that slight enigmatic smile. "I ride as well as you, after all," she said, letting one eye drop in a slow wink. Her fingers touched lightly on the tight, sweat-damp skin of his shoulders and traced downward over the hard rippled muscle of his chest and stomach, toying with the belt buckle. Her fingers felt cool and delicate; there was a faint scent of hyacinths in her hair.

"And every second trooper," she continued, unbuttoning the trousers, "is going to have his poopsie or pretty-boy along, not to mention servants. Should you have to go alone?" She knelt to remove the skintight fabric. "You know," she whispered, looking up at him and moistening her lips, "unkind people used to say that when I wore riding clothes I looked like a pretty-boy. Did you?"

"Spirit of the Stars!" Raj shouted, leaping out of bed with a glance at the clock over the fireplace. "It's been better than an hour, the couriers will all be here."

The apartments rated a hot water shower; he washed and dressed with feverish haste, trying and failing to scowl. Suzette curved her lips and set her chin on her hands, lying on her stomach and swinging her feet up behind her; it made her look absurdly young.

"It won't hurt them to mill about for a while," she said lazily; she rinsed off quickly and threw herself back on the bed, towelling and pulling pieces of clothing towards herself. Dressing without standing; the process was distracting enough that Raj misbuttoned his tunic; their eyes met, and they laughed in unison.

"Get yourself covered, for the Spirit's sake," he said, redoing the garment. "Or none of us will ever get any work done."

"Which units are you and Stanson taking?" she asked, winding the cumberbund of her riding clothes around her waist. That hid the holster of the little two-barreled derringer; Raj hid a grimace of distaste at the sight of it. A gambler's weapon.

"Well, Stanson's taking the 2nd Gendarmerie Battalion," Raj said with a snort. He stopped to examine himself for a moment in the long mirror, part of the luxury of the bedroom. Buckling on the helmet and feeling the leather-lined neck guard rustle across his shoulders was like stepping across a barrier, away from this quiet room with its subdued elegance. The figure tapping his gauntlets into his palm did not belong in palaces.

Suzette raised a brow, as she stamped a foot into a tooled-leather riding boot with high heels. "It's a very fashionable unit," she said. "Overstrength by fifty men, and beautifully equipped."

"Poodles," Raj said briefly.

His wife sat back and rested her elbows on her knees. "Alsatians," she said. "They're mounted on Alsatians."

Raj quirked a smile. "How did I ever manage to pick someone with your combination of qualities?" he said.

"Oh, you didn't," Suzette said calmly. "I picked you, and mean to keep you . . . but about the 2nd?" There was genuine interest behind the question; she had started reading his military texts as soon as they returned from the honeymoon and he took up his duties.

"Palace poodles," he continued. "The 2nd aren't just Residence Area troops, they practically never *leave* East Residence."

"Father used to take me out to the Gendarmerie Picnics, when I was a little girl," Suzette said reflectively. "When they were on maneuvers up in the Bay Hills."

He looked around for a second, saw brief reflective melancholy on her face. *Odd*, he thought. *How seldom Suzie's talked about her childhood.* Suzette, Lady Whitehall, nee Wenqui, was twenty-six, a year older than her husband, and looked younger, but it was usually difficult to imagine her as a *child*.

Aloud: "That's a hunting park. And most of the 2nd are either city toughs, or scions doing some military service where it won't take them too far from the races, the theater, or their favorite cathouses. They've got beautiful gear because the scions compete with each other to rig their units out pretty for parades. About the only real soldiers in it are some long-service NCO's, and most of them are past it; the scions sponsor them in to polish the drill, and it's a retirement post for good men."

"They're useless?" Suzette asked.

"No, not useless. Reliable enough putting down strikes and riots."

For a moment the room vanished, and he was walking down a flight of outdoor stairs in the naval harbor, a vision of memory more vivid than Center's. The rank of Gendarmerie troopers was walking ahead of him, in their white "field" uniforms. *Reload!* over the screams of the mob—the people—below. Metallic clicks, tinging as the spent brass and paper cartridges bounced on marble and the fresh rounds clacked home. *By platoons, volley fire—fire!* And the *CRASH* of two hundred rifles, the rippling and thrashing along the line of the crowd where the heavy 11mm bullets struck. The bodies on the steps were dead, mostly; the blood flowed in little rivulets that made the bottoms of his boots stick to the stone with little *tak-tak* sounds.

"—and they'll die bravely enough. I'm going to take a Descott Hills unit with Field Force experience; the—"

observe.

✦ ✦ ✦

Faces this time, a comparison left-right between the Company officers of the 12th Residence Battalion, the unit he had meant to take, and another. Faces thin and square, fox-mean and bovine, with a murmured commentary from Center on each.

"Darling! Are you all right?"

Raj staggered slightly, took his hand down from his forehead. "Why, certainly, sweetheart. Why?"

"You looked so . . . so *strange* for a moment," his wife said, raw anxiety in her voice.

"*Aya, dummerlin,*" he said, shocked back into dialect for a moment. "It's all right, I was just . . . ah, lost in thought. I'd decided to take the 12th, but I've changed my mind. It'll be the 5th Descott Guards, instead."

Suzette stepped back, the immediate concern fading from her face. "But . . . darling, they're understrength."

Raj nodded. "But they've got a better set of Company commanders, and that will be crucial. It's a raiding mission, they'll have to split up into smaller groups and perform on their own, without always having me there to hold their hands."

Suzette's fingers tapped her chin. "You *do* know, Raj, that they're understrength because those officers are pocketing the pay and rations of the men who aren't there?"

Raj nodded. "Well, of course," he said, grinning. "I have been in East Residence for four years, my sweet. That *proves* they're sharper than the 12th, doesn't it?"

"But they're still short two hundred men," Suzette said thoughtfully. "Perhaps an order to draft replacements?"

Raj shrugged ruefully. *Center, this had better work*, he thought, then corrected himself for doubting . . . the Spirit of Man of the Stars? An angel, at least. "I'd look pretty silly, asking the Vice-Governor for that," he said. "After asking for the 5th in the first place."

"*You* might," Suzette said. "Men care about things like that. I'll talk to Anne, and I don't think she'll feel silly at all, when she talks to the Reassignments officer. I will *not—*" her voice took on an icy clarity "—have you endangered needlessly, Raj."

He inclined his helmeted head. "It's good of you to have made a friend of her, back when Barholm wasn't the heir," he said seriously. "And smart, too."

Suzette looked at him with a slight flare of her patrician nostrils. "The only difference between Anne and me," she said coldly, "is that I was older and had more money and choices when I was thrown out on my own. And a few contacts. *She* was sold to be an 'entertainer' at ten. I'll see you at dinner."

"Whew," Raj muttered, following more slowly. "Nobody can say married life is dull." A glance back at the rumpled bed. "Or uninteresting."

The first task would be a general inspection, *without* warning. As Raj stepped out into the anteroom he slipped out his watch and clicked open the heavy brushed-brass casing. *1100 hours,* he thought.

The couriers were waiting, some leaning against the walls, a few chatting-up the more presentable of the maids—two were even helping with the lifting, true dedication—and one was even *reading;* Raj noted his face and name.

"At ease," he said as they braced to attention. A Palace courier was equivalent to a corporal in a line regiment; the post was a plum and eagerly sought. "First, to the officers of the 5th Descott Guards, platoon level and above; with the warrant officers, the Battalion Master Sergeant, the vet and the quartermaster. Battalion meeting at—" another glance at his watch. "—1550 hours, in the wardroom. Have the Surveyor General's office send down the designated maps, please."

He turned to the next brace of couriers. "You boys are going to have to earn your pay: this does *not* go out on the heliograph." Mirrors, signal-towers, telescopes, and lanterns provided the fastest means of long-distance communication, but they were unfortunately wide open to counter-intelligence. "Take the following, to depots 7 through 38, East Residence, all station commanders. 'Greetings. By order of the Civil Government, all supplies and refreshments necessary to the passage of the 2nd Gendarmerie and 5th Descott Guards, minimum 900 effectives—" an exaggeration, but better safe than sorry "—with the usual dependents, to be available from this date until further notice."

The couriers scribbled. They were all young men, fit and dressed in tight fringed leathers, armed with shotguns; they would ride fast down the post relays, changing dogs every fifty kilometers. The next five finished their messages, sealed them with prestamped wax and saluted before dashing off towards the stables. Raj followed them out the door, his remaining couriers trailing. The orders continued, metronome-steady.

"To the Master of Ordnance," he said. "Indent for three 75mm fieldguns, with full limbers and teams to report not later than—"

observe.

This time he could manage to walk, talk, despite what Center was showing him.

—Colonist banners waving above a walled village; he recognized the green-and-silver of the Lions of Medinha, Tewfik's personal guard regiment. The lean brown dogs were staked on picket lines, lying and panting resignedly in the bright sun; their masters and the camp followers were digging in, shoveling the earth out of rifle pits. The hologram swooped in, showing muscular, brown-skinned troopers stripped to their baggy pantaloons, sweating as they threw basketloads of sandy dirt out of the entrenchments. Quick-firers were being manhandled into revetments; a detachment of mounted scouts trotted out into the fields in column of twos, the butts of their carbines resting on their thighs. He focused on the leader's hairy brown hawk face, the beard trimmed to a rakish point under a spired helmet with a spike and canvas neck flap. The man turned and said something to the troop sergeant riding to his rear; the NCO laughed, making the brass hoop earring in one ear dance.

A blur, and he saw the command council of the regiment on a hilltop, the same red jellaba robes but more gorgeously embroidered. Military engineers were working over a mapboard, with slide rules and compasses and steel straightedges; the commander peered through a tripod-mounted telescope, and a detachment was putting up a heliograph tower.

—and in a riverport town on the Drangosh a train of barges was unloading, muscle-powered cranes squealing as they swung crates with the Settler's phoenix stencil on their sides to the dock. Wardogs were being led down a ramp, and black-tanned porters in loincloths and headdress were trotting down another gangway with 50-kilo sacks of soya dogmash meal on their backs, filling ox-drawn wagons that moved out with a squeal of ungreased axles.

There were lighter-skinned folk on the docks as well, more naked than the porters but wearing chain hobbles on their ankles, bound neck-and-neck with long ropes. They crouched, waiting to be loaded on the barges for the return trip downriver when the munitions were ashore. The porters sometimes paused to kick them as they passed, or loft a gobbet of spit in their direction, and a group of boychildren lurked at a distance, throwing clumps of garbage or occasionally darting forward to poke with a stick. Many of the chained slaves were slumped in an apathy so deep they did not even dodge the lumps of ordure. Flies buzzed, and Raj could imagine the stink so well that it was almost a physical presence, on the slow-moving river.

Clumps of townsfolk, all men in long robes, examined the fresh-caught slaves from the Civil Government. One wore a robe of dazzling white linen edged with silver, and a cord-bound ha'ik headdress. He was bargaining more seriously with a uniformed officer in charge of the prisoners; at last they slapped palms in a bargain-sealing gesture.

"By Allah," the civilian said, smoothing his gray-streaked beard with one hand, "I would have bought more if they were in better condition. Not worth my while to pay for transport if all they're fit for is the mines or the sugar plantations."

They were speaking Arabic, but somehow Raj understood far better than his nodding acquaintance with that language would allow.

"Look at that moon-faced beauty!" the slaver continued. He pointed with a long ebony staff at a plump girl who sat staring before her, ignoring the hardtack in her hand and the woman beside her who urged her to eat. "I could have gotten, two, three hundred for her in Al-Kebir, except for those infected bites all over her breasts. And she's mad besides; now, no more than fifty for a sailor's brothel."

The officer shrugged, glanced up at the cloudless sky and

pulled a fold of his helmet's cloth neck-guard across his face. "By the Prophet, you can't keep troops too much in line when the loot's so scanty," he said, clapping his hands and pointing out one slave, then another. The guards untied them and hustled them forward; the slave trader's assistants formed them into a new coffle with bonds of woven coconut-fiber rope. All were males, prepubescent.

"But look at these," the soldier continued. "All healthy, sound of mind and limb; you'll get good prices for these, even if the fashion is for black harem guards."

"*Kaphars* have a certain value as well," the trader nodded. "But we lose half when we geld them; sometimes more, and then where is my profit?"

There was a crash behind them. Both men wheeled to look; the ropes had slipped unloading a heavy gun from one of the barges, a muzzle-loading siege gun with a barrel shaped like a soda bottle, built up with extra bands around the breech. It hung for a moment, teetering, then crashed onto the dock as the crew pulled frantically at ropes. There was a hollow thudding shudder through the brick arches beneath their feet. The soldier strode off, waving his riding-crop in the air and screaming imprecations.

"Peace be with you!" he shouted over one shoulder to the merchant, before returning to cursing the dockworkers.

"And upon you, peace!" the slave trader called back, patting one of the boys on the head. The child smiled up at him uncertainly. "But not too *much* peace," he continued happily.

Confident, Raj thought grimly. *It's been a long time since the Civil Government won a major battle with the Colony.*

Forty-three years two months seventeen days, Center prompted helpfully.

Thank you, Raj replied. *Thank you very much.* He looked up; they were nearly at the stables, the familiar rank odors of boiling mash and dog shit muted by the cool stone smell.

"We'll just have to make sure the record doesn't run to forty-four," he said aloud.

CHAPTER FIVE

"Get that thing off the road, get it the *fuck* off the road, do it *now*, er I blow yor fuckin' *head* off!"

Raj Whitehall heard the high-pitched scream of the 2nd's Battalion Master Sergeant and sighed. It had taken fifteen minutes for the huge procession formed by the two battalions to lurch to a halt, another fifteen to become frustrated enough to go forward and see for himself, and ten more to ride and edge his way forward to within hearing distance of the front.

Half a day, he thought. *We can't get half a day out of East Residence and this sort of thing happens.* He looked up at the reddish-orange disk of the sun; the glance at the position of Miniluna was a reflex from his youth, when the only watch on the estate was an heirloom his grandfather had brought back from the Army. Only one of the moons was up right now. *And three hours just getting out of the gates.*

Raj pressed his heels to Horace's sides. The wardog swerved out of the slow-moving column, ignoring the occasional sniff or yelp from the other mounts. And teams; half of the 2nd were in light overland carriages, big enough to carry four. *Only a quarter of the 5th Descott's officers in coaches*, he thought sardonically. *Hooray, we're hardy sons of bitches, we Descotters. Spirit of Man of the Stars, give me strength!*

that is not my function.

"Literalist," he muttered. Even a pious man could not talk with an angel daily and not become familiar.

no. ironist.

The column seemed to go on forever, filling most of the eight-meter width of the road. This close to the capital the surface was of poured concrete, over a bed of stabilized earth and gravel; the shoulders were three meters wide, of crushed rock, and right now occupied by scores of indignant travelers. Most were peasants, with handcarts or single-ox two wheel wagons of fresh produce; a substantial minority were pilgrims, afoot and dressed in burlap robes, with staffs in their hand carved with mystic circuit diagrams and topped with the Star. The peasants waited with stolid patience, the pilgrims the same, or with a serenity that Raj found slightly disquieting. A few of those pushed *off* the road were wealthy enough to have carriages or riding dogs of their own.

One merchant on a high-bred borzoi tried to edge along beside the stalled, irritated troopers. The two soldiers nearest merely turned their heads in blank disinterest. Their mounts turned their heads as well, twisting them down and half-sideways in a snakelike gesture. Their ruffs stood up, but the dripping bare teeth were only incidentally and functionally a threat display. The borzoi's muzzle was encased in a steel basket as law required for civilian animals, while the wardogs wore only light halters that deliberately left their jaws unencumbered. Not that that made much difference, since each of the massive beasts was half again the borzoi's weight and a killer by breeding and training besides.

It backed away, crouching and whining and urinating in a thin stream on the dusty rock of the road verge. The dogs waited, visibly hoping it would come within reach. They ignored Raj and Horace; most wardogs recognized a sort of vague pack-sentiment to anything smelling of the Army, although putting a scratch unit together always led to weeks of trouble as they settled the pecking order. And to even worse trouble when that pecking order did not correspond with the human ranking of their riders.

Raj had expected Stanson to be at the head of the column; the other Guard had insisted that the 2nd have precedence on the road, after all. Instead there was still only the advance piquette of the Gendarmerie, and the Master Sergeant he had heard cursing half a kilometer back. The color-party were sitting their dogs uncomfortably; the standard-bearer was slumping a little, letting the long pole with the bronze Star and the citation ribbons of the five companies making up the 2nd Gendarmerie slant out from the cup in his right stirrup. The dogs were looking hackles-up at the thing in the roadway before them.

It *was* impressive; a steam traction engine, like a locomotive with a brace of wheels on a pivot at the funnel end of a long riveted iron boiler, and two huge spoked iron driving wheels at the rear; there was a tasseled canopy over the driver's seat, and behind it four huge six-wheeler wagons. They were loaded with hand-thick sheets of nairstone, fossilized quasi-coral cut from the occasional reefs of harder stone that rose from the alluvial floor of the Hemmar Valley. Rare and quite precious, used to pick out ornamental details on important buildings; the surface was basically a lustrous silver, streaked with swirling patterns of reddish ochre and blue.

There were a half-dozen armed guards with the train, even this close to the East Residence; they sat their dogs in a clump, surprisingly truculent, several with rifles across their knees. There was a stoker perched sullenly beside the driver's bench of the traction engine, a dark stocky huge-muscled man with a steel collar around his neck. And the driver himself, as broad as his slave assistant and much taller, in stained overalls, his woolen hat respectfully in his hands.

"Well, good sir, I *can't—*" he broke off as Raj rode up, taking in the three-star insignia of a Captain on the brow of his helmet. "Oh, thank the Spirit! Good my lord—"

"Sor—" the 2nd Gendarmerie NCO began.

"Quiet." Silence fell, even the crowds on the shoulders of the road ceasing their chattering. "Sergeant, could you tell me what the darklord is going *on*, here?"

"Ahh, well, sor." The NCO was elderly for this line of work, fifty if he was a day and bald as an egg. The narrow mustache on his upper lip still had streaks of yellow in it as well as gray, and his eyes were blue; Raj put that together with the accent and decided he was probably from Chongwe Island County, over on the western border. Skin tanned to the consistency of old leather, and a voice to match. "We've gots a bit of a transport problem, like. The other civvie stuff, it's moved aside, but this bastard here won't." The sergeant brightened, and dropped a hand to his saber. "Kill hem, sor?"

The guards stirred, and the dogs of the two parties exchanged tail-down snarls. The civilian opened his mouth to protest, looked up at the sergeant and suddenly realized there was real hope behind the request. He wrung the cap between his hands again, then burst out:

"Noble lord! Star Spirit and Holy Federation witness, I *can't* run this off the road, not *here,* m'lord. This thing weighs twenty *tonnes,* m'lord, not counting the cargo, the ground won't hold it, not unless I was an Avatar of the Spirit 'n could walk on water."

"Well, that's your problem," Raj said flatly, looking around.

They were headed south on a road that ran south-southeast, two kilometers from the river, with the Coast Range mountains floating on the western horizon, snowpeaks merging with low cloud. The ground rose up-valley, so the ramparts of the East Residence wall were still visible to the north, earthworks and ramparts and outlying forts larger than most cities, all a dim line on the horizon. The fields to either side were tabletop flat, long-reclaimed marshland; the road itself was raised two meters above ground level on an embankment. They had left the rice paddies of the delta behind, but the turned earth showed black and spongy between rows of young maize, and irrigation canals laced the landscape until it disappeared in the haze along the horizon. The wheat was just starting to head out, streaks of gold among the green, orchards in full leaf; sharecropper shacks were scattered across the fields, occasionally clumping into a hamlet with the spire and Star of a chapel at its center. Now and then a manor, although most landowners hereabouts would live in the city for all but a few months of the year.

"Right, sergeant, get a squad up here. We'll push—" "My lord, I'm under contract to the Church!" Raj touched his amulet. *Oh.* Now that he looked, the guards had Star emblems pinned to their shoulders, and they were the real electrum the Church issued to its secular servants, not brass. The 2nd's Master Sergeant sighed in vexation and let his sword slip back into the scabbard, the handspan of bright metal dropping into the lapwing-oil greased leather and wood with a slight *shhhhp* sound. This *did* put a different complexion on things. Sinful to offend the church, and stupid as well; the Governor was the Spirit's Viceregent on Earth, but . . . Raj cursed under his breath and unfastened his helmet; the mild damp breeze was a little chill on the sweat-dampened curls of his dark hair. It was from the south, smelling of turned earth and growing things, a wet fecund smell.

"It's for the New Temple, m'lord," the driver said eagerly. "The Vice-Governor hisself's in charge; a great work to the glory of the Spirit, it'll be!"

and to the glory of barholm.

The Spirit operates through human instruments, Raj thought tartly. It was widely known that the Vice-Governor had employed Abel Yunner, a heretic Earth-Spiritist from the Old Residence, as architect. "His soul may go to the Outer Dark, but his designs will honor the Spirit of Man of the Stars," Barholm had said.

exactly. human instruments such as yourself.

Raj felt himself flush with embarrassment, then wrenched his attention back to the practical problem at hand. The thought of himself as an Avatar, one in whom the Spirit in-dwelt, was profoundly disturbing . . . and seemed to be literally true.

"What's in that first wagon?" he said, pointing.

"Why, coal, your lordship."

Raj looked at the side of the road, the meter-deep ditch, the long slope down to the edge of the cornfield. Less than fifty meters beyond that to a row of poplars along a canal. "How much do those wagons with the nairstone weigh?"

"'bout two tonnes each, m'lord."

"Hmmm." He closed his eyes, estimating distances. There was a long length of cable coiled at the rear of the traction engine, first-quality woven-wire stuff.

"All *right*," he said. "Now, here's what we'll do. Sergeant, get . . ." he looked back down the column. "Oh, three twelve-ox teams from the baggage. Driver, uncouple the engine and pull the coal-wagon over there." He pointed to the right side of the road. "We'll tip it over—"

"M'lord!" Almost a bleat.

"—to form a ramp. Then we'll run that cable out to those

poplars, rig that nice block-and-tackle I see you've got to one of them ... better make that two, use a Y brace ... and run the wagons one by one down the embankment."

"They'll bog, m'lord, right to the axles."

"Not if we use the cable to haul them out of the way. Then we run the traction engine down"—the driver's eyes bulged—"and all the Church's property is nice and safe, as soon as they want to come out here with equipment to dig it out."

"M'lord, the Reverend Sysup will skin me, and the damage to the fields, m'lord—"

"Sergeant, squad-present, if you please," Raj said.

The NCO's expression changed from one of blank disinterest to anticipation.

"Squad, saddle-fire, *present!*" he barked.

The color-party were troopers of the 2nd without enough money or influence to travel by carriage, street toughs from the capital; they looked sullenly out of place even this far into the countryside, and their white field uniforms were already soiled. There was absolutely nothing wrong with their basic drill, however. Their hands snapped down to the scabbards before their right knees in one movement, gripped the butts of government issue East Residence Armory rifles in the next, then flipped them up and out. The rein-hands slapped on the forestocks in unison, and the thumbs of the right hands caught in the trigger-guard levers. There was an oiled metallic *snick* as the bolts swung forward and down, leaving a grooved ramp on top to guide the shell into the breech.

Slap and the hands struck the bandoliers. A clicking rustle as they undid the clasps and brought their hands out with a paper-and-brass cartridge: *click* as thumbs pushed the heavy 11mm rounds into the breech: *snick* as the levers drove them home and cocked the firing pins.

"Aim!"

The muzzles came up unwaveringly on the driver. He paled and began to shake. Some of the guards looked irresolute for a moment, then toed their dogs to the side.

"Certainly m'lord, at once!" the driver said. The confrontation dissolved into bustle.

"Where's Captain Stanson?" Raj asked, as he and the Master Sergeant rode aside to oversee.

The older man smoothed down his mustache. "In his carriage, sor," he said. "With his girl, like."

"Girl?" Raj said casually. The troopers were interpreting their instructions liberally, conscripting a few score of the sturdier locals stalled on the side of the road to unhook and push the coal wagon; well, whatever got the job done.

"Yes, sor, the boys was just fashion last yea—" The NCO spoke absently, attention focused on the group clearing the road, then brought himself up with a cough. "Well, I wouldn't be knowing, sor."

"Whitehall." A bored voice, down at his stirrup. Raj looked down; Stanson stood there, smoking a cigarette in the ivory holder the Vice-Governor and his Lady had popularized. His tunic was unbuttoned, and there was a wineglass in his hand. The bottle was behind him, in the hands of a spectacularly endowed redhead; from the way she stood with one hip cocked in her slit-skirted gown, it was obvious that the red hair was as natural as her other assets. Rare coloring, even rarer than blond. "What is going on here, my man?"

Raj showed his teeth in something approaching a smile. "Well, we've had a little problem, but it's cleared up now."

The squad leader handling the coal wagon had two dozen peasants and pilgrims lined up on the road side of the wagon, where it stood tilted with two wheels on the edge of the ditch.

"Right, you horrible lot," he shrieked, booting one of them in the buttocks with a flat smacking sound. *"Push!"* The heavy vehicle went over with a roar of loose coal. One by one the other wagons were manhandled to the edge of the road, dragged across the coal and down the low slope. The Gendarmerie troopers surged back, cursing and beating at the coal dust on their white uniforms.

"We wouldn't have *had* this problem if we'd gone up the river in barges. *And* we'd have gotten where we're going sooner. What's the problem, Whitehall?"

Well, you, for starters, Raj thought. Aloud: "The men need toughening up," *though dick-all they'll get in a sprung carriage with a whore*, "and sitting on their butts in a barge isn't the way to get it," he said mildly.

Stanson began to speak, then waited for a long mournful

blast on the traction engine's whistle as it trundled over the verge, across the ditch on the bridge of coal, and into the cornfield. It began to sink into the soft uncompacted earth immediately. When the noise level sank low enough to permit conversation, he continued:

"Are you implying my men aren't ready to fight?" Stanson asked, dangerously quiet.

Raj opened his mouth: *Fight their way out of a tavern brawl, perhaps—*

observe.

—Raj saw himself, *that's the worst of all, seeing myself*, standing across from Stanson. It was early in the morning, from the slant of the sun: tomorrow, perhaps, Miniluna was still three-quarter and a waxing crescent of Maxiluna showed just above the horizon. They stood in a meadow, ten meters apart; Raj was under the shadow of an apple tree, with a few last blossoms still in the branches. Dewdrops sparkled from the tops of the tall grass blades, and birds were singing, a skin-winged dactosauroid the size of his palm flitted by to clamp miniature toothy jaws on an insect . . .

"Ready, gentlemen," an officer said. In 5th Guards blue; he raised a handkerchief. Raj saw/felt himself turn sideways, presenting a minimal target, working his fingers on the pistol's grip. Stanson did likewise, his face as calm as a carved saint in the temple. The images slowed as the handkerchief fluttered towards the ground, and Raj knew *exactly* how he was/would feel, the paper-dry mouth, glassy clarity of vision, it *touched* and both pistols came up, *crack* almost at the same time—

—and Raj was/would crumple, staggering. Open his mouth, and a gobbet of blood came out, spinning, Raj could see the wound on his own body. Below the armpit, through the tops of both lungs, massive exit-hole on the left side, *my, nasty, he was using hollowpoints*. Suzette rushing to hold the dead Raj's head in her arms, pale as the dying man, ignoring the blood that slicked the whole front of her jacket. Stanson stood over them, mouthing something. Suzette smiled, she smiled and rose and put one hand on his shoulder, and he was smiling when the derringer came out in her right and fired twice, pointblank range.

Blackness, and the voice of Center: **Observe. the alternative, but the last projection is common to both.**

—Raj saw himself beneath the apple tree, but this time they had sabers in their hands. Stamp-stamp-stamp of feet on the dew-wet grass, little hurried recoveries when a boot sole slipped, harsh panting breath, and the atonal music of steel on steel. His viewpoint swooped, until he was looking out at the eye level of the possible future Raj. Stanson's mouth was open in a snarl of effort; there was no fear in his eyes, only a merciless concentration on the task at hand. Stamp-cut-thrust; Raj saw the opening, Stanson was tiring, not in the hard condition of his opponent. Their swords formed an X, and then it was slide turn twist *thrust*, and he was shocked not to feel the resistance he knew, the soft heavy feeling and the jerks as the point went through membranes and muscle-sheaths. The blade before his eyes withdrew with the wrenching twist his wrist would execute without volition, and the other man fell.

"Expected . . . *huhn* . . . to be killed . . . jealous husband," Stanson managed to say, through tight-clenched teeth. Then he screamed, thrashing for a moment, and died.

observe. consequences.

Vice-Governor Barholm signed the paper. It was an execution notice, with the name of Raj Ammenda Halgern da Cruz Whitehall inscribed in the black ink and blocky letters traditional in such matters. "Well," he said in disgust. "That's the last of *that* idea on how to deal with the border situation."

General Klostermann smirked, picking up the decree and waving it to dry the ink. "Thank you, Your Exaltedness," he said. "These young hotheads would have done even more harm on the border . . ."

—and Tewfik was riding his dog into the waves of the sea, an army drawn up behind him. Raj recognized the location, it was the Kolden Straits, a hundred kilometers *northwest* of the East Residence, almost into the Middle Territories. The dog took a lap at the foam that broke on its chest, the salt taste producing a whine and slight jerk backwards. Tewfik's heels pressed the beast forward; his right hand held the banner of the Settler and his faith, and he plunged it into the waters and the sand beneath.

"Allah, I take you to witness!" he shouted, rising in the stirrups. "There is no ford here! If there was, I would cross!" Cheers rolled like thunder down the long ranks of the army on the hills behind.

"Well?" Stanson asked, his impatience growing. The girl tried to refill his glass; he turned on her suddenly, putting a palm on her face and pushing. "Get *away*, you stupid blowsy cow!" he barked; she fell on her backside and began to cry quietly, looking no older than the seventeen she probably was. "Well?" he continued, looking back to his nominal superior. "Daydreaming again, Whitehall?"

"I meant," Raj answered carefully, "no insult whatsoever to you or your troops, of course. Now, if you'll excuse me?"

He neckreined Horace around and clapped his heels to the hound's ribs.

Dusk had fallen by the time the column crawled into the way-station's yard and pasture, overflowing the weedy five-hectare plot and the stone-walled yard. The last arch of the sun was disappearing behind the distant peaks of the Coast Range to the west; a final ray blinked red-bright from the signaller's platform at the top of the six-story heliograph tower. Raj sat his saddle grimly, ignoring Horace's occasional efforts to sit down; hounds were like that . . . not undisciplined, exactly, just self-willed. The last of the 2nd had pulled their mounts or carriages into their assigned areas long ago; the 5th Descott were still milling around the area, as the NCO's Raj had assigned directed the carriages into a square apart from the other wheeled transport. Most were light four-dog models, with steel-rimmed wheels on leaf-springs and room for four inside, with baggage racks above, but there were a good half-dozen of the heavier six-dog vehicles. Almost all had collapsible leather roofs, and one—he noted it was Captain Staenbridge's, commander of the most understrength of the five companies—actually had movable windows, with eisenglass curtains and a fringe.

"Trumpeter," he said quietly. "Sound *'Officers to the Standard,'* if you please." Raj waited impassively, until the second series of notes. "*General Assembly*, now."

There was a fresh burst of shouting and confusion, the

thunder-deep barking of wardogs sensing their master's frustration and rage. The officers of the 5th Descott had all realized that their men were their capital assets, too valuable to allow to go slack, and the ranks formed fairly quickly. The officers cursed and dogwhipped their way through to fall into a ragged line before Raj where he waited with the signallers and Battalion standard; the companies fell in to the shouted commands of their NCO's, in no particular order with respect to each other but in columns of platoons within their own units.

"Gentlemen," Raj said, once the officers were together. "First order of business: Evening service." To the trumpeter: "Sound, *dismount* and *stand to reins*."

There was a long rustle as the other ranks swung down on the left side of their mounts and gathered the reins in, just under the lower jaw of their dogs. The mounts were mixed-breeds, mostly the spotted reddish Hills farmbred strain; sturdy strong-legged beasts of about fourteen hands with blunt muzzles and floppy ears and black whip-tails, but there was a scattering of everything from Border Collie to Newfoundland. They stood as motionless as the men; the 5th recruited from the yeomen class, men born to saddle and gun and the hunt. Most farmsteads in Descott sent a son to the Army, in lieu of taxes, and they sent him mounted and paid the price of his gear and uniform as well. Experienced recruits, blooded fighting Military Government raiders or bandits. *Or blooded* as *bandits,* Raj reminded himself sardonically. Stock theft was an old Descott tradition, and not considered disgraceful unless you were caught.

The unit chaplain stood forward, walking into the gap between the command staff and the assembled Battalion. He was an under-Hierarch, the sort of man they might all have known as Parish priest at home in the Descott hills, dressed in a simple kirted white robe with a silver Star around his neck. A saber scar down one cheek hinted that he had had some other calling before he took the ear-to-ear tonsure of the Church.

"Hear us, O Spirit of Man of the Stars," he intoned.

"*Hear us,*" the group returned. It was a deep sound, a little blurred with three hundred male voices slightly out of synchronization.

The priest lifted both hands to the first of the stars appearing in the east. The assembled soldiers assumed the attitude of prayer, one hand over the left ear and the other raised with the fingers bunched.

"Code not our sins; let them be erased and not ROMed in Thy disks."

"Forgive us, O Star Spirit!"

"The Spirit of Man is of the Stars and all the Universe: this we believe."

"Witness our belief, O Star Spirit!"

"As we believe and act in righteousness, so shall we be boosted into the Orbit of fulfillment."

"Raise us up, O Star Spirit!"

"Deliver us from the Crash; from the Meltdown; from the Hard Rads; spare us."

"Spare us, O Star Spirit!"

"We receive diligently the Input from Thy Holy Terminal, now and forever."

"Forever, O Star Spirit!"

"As we believe, so let Thy Holy Federation be restored in our time, O Spirit of Man of the Stars; and if the burden of a faithless generation's sin be too great, may our souls be received into the Net. Endfile."

"Endfile!" The troops relaxed.

"My children," the priest continued, "the Honorable Captain Whitehall has graciously allowed compulsory unit purgation of sins, as of 20:00 hours tomorrow." There were a few subdued groans; that meant penances, usually fasting. "The Spirit be with you." A mumbled chorus of *and in thy soul* followed.

"Master Sergeant da Cruz," Raj said, his face more impassive than the priest's had been in the midst of the liturgy.

"Ser!" A Descott man of the old breed, this one, brick-built and hook-nosed and dark. He moved easily; one of the fast heavy men, rare and dangerous. About thirty-five, a decade older than the Captain. A finger missing from his left hand, and shrapnel scars all down the right side of his face. It drew his lips up into a slight perpetual sneer, but there was a hint of a smile in it now.

"Carry on as ordered, Master Sergeant."

"Battalion, attention t' orders," he bellowed, turning to face the men. Their ranks were a series of rectangular clumps in the gathering darkness; firelight from the windows of the rest station and the campfires of the 2nd picked out a detail here and there. Oily gleam from the chainmail neck guard of a helmet, light from a buckle or the bronze buttons of their blue coats, eyes, the teeth of the wardogs. "Battalion will encamp." A grin, made ghastly by the pulling effect of the scar. "Full kit inspection at 0600 tomorrow. Workin' party, report to me as instructed. Dismissed!"

"Inspection?" one of the Company commanders remarked, as they dismounted and handed their reins to their batmen. He stripped off his gloves and smoothed the kidskin; there was a shimmerstone stud in one ear as well. *Kaltin Gruder*, Raj thought, prompted by some internal filing system. *Just in from Descott two years ago. Bit of a dandy. Devil with the ladies.* And a distant relative of sorts, although you could say that of most of the County's gentry. At least there were no blood feuds between their families.

"Isn't that rather rushing things?" Kaltin continued, with a winning smile.

"Sir," Raj added.

"Sir," the younger man said, flushing slightly.

"That's exactly the point, gentlemen," Raj continued. "We made . . . what, twenty-one kilometers today, on a poured-stone road?" Looks of protest. "Yes, I know, the baggage train slows us. But we have to be *prepared* to move; and in the meanwhile, I don't intend to waste the time these lumbering oxcarts and our, ah, *lavishly equipped* comrades of the 2nd confer."

That brought a general chuckle; the 5th might have been in garrison for some time, but the 2nd had never been *out* of the immediate vicinity of East Residence, not in living memory.

"Speaking of which, I'd like to thank you gentlemen for the loan of your carriages."

Dead silence, a tension. Heads turned; a platoon-sized group of enlisted men were working on the vehicles, under the profane direction of da Cruz. Detachable hoods were stripped, thrown to vanish in the darkness, black leather against the ground. The fine springs jounced as the troopers climbed in and began handing down the luggage within, none too gently; shrieks of complaint turned to outrage as various servants, women and other hangers-on were elbowed aside. Another working party came up, bent under loads from the baggage carts. Ammunition boxes mainly, with medical supplies, bandages, and portable heliograph equipment.

"It'll greatly increase our tactical mobility once we reach our objective," Raj continued equably. "With the fine teams you so generously brought, those ought to be able to keep up as well as the guns do, nearly as much cross-country capacity as the troops. We won't have to return to base nearly as often."

Mouths dropped. Raj continued more gently: "You may note that my wife's carriage is on the end of the row, there." It was a spidery-fragile shell, deceptively slender; the body creaked as the metal-edged hardwood boxes of rifle ammunition were dropped in. The sound was muffled on the quilt-padded linen upholstery. "As I said, a very patriotic and pious gesture; especially as it might be misunderstood." His voice lost the undertone of banter, went flat and hard. "Since bringing nonregulation vehicles into the field is strictly forbidden under the Civil Government Army Code."

There was a crash of breaking glass. A uniformed aide walked over, blinking back tears; a boy of fifteen or so, with a fresh and livid bruise discoloring one cheek. Well-born by his manner, with an almost pretty face that showed promise of strong-boned regularity later.

"Gerrin!" he said, grasping Captain Staenbridge by the hand. "Gerrin, that brute of a trooper *struck* me, and they broke the windows!" He looked around, met Raj's eyes and those of the other officers, and straightened. "Sir," he continued, releasing the company commander's hand.

Staenbridge turned on Raj. "Sir, are you going to permit indiscipline of this sort?"

Raj met his eyes, held them until he saw a sign of wavering. "Messer Senior Lieutenant Staenbridge," he said dryly, "your . . . young friend is an aide by courtesy"—*and because he's a Meffred cousin and of good family*, Raj remembered—"and not in the chain of command." He looked pointedly at the youth's pistol, inlaid with mother-of-pearl, and the light saber at his other hip. Both were exceedingly nonregulation;

Civil Government law was quite strict on possession of arms, here in the heartland territories. "I suggest that if he looks to you for example"—the traditional way of putting it—"you should set one. Any further questions?"

"No, *sir*."

"Now, we're having inspection at 0600, as you heard. We're also having a field problem at 0730, which I expect to last all day. Since we're out of the city and have room . . . so, if you please, report to my tent by 0500, and we'll plan it." Suddenly he smiled. "These lowlanders have so much good land, they surely won't begrudge us enough to ride over . . . No questions? Dismissed."

"Did we *really* have to give up the carriage, darling?" Suzette asked.

Raj was lying on his stomach on the cot; his wife was astride his back, her strong slender fingers kneading at the muscles of his neck and shoulders. The muted sounds of a night camp came through the dark canvas; a sentry's challenge and response, and raucous singing from somewhere over in the 2nd's area. There was a strong smell of sweat, dog, canvass, leather and oil, blending oddly but pleasantly with the healthy female sweat and jasmine perfume from Suzette's body.

"Spirit," Raj said, laying his head face-down in the thin bedroll. "Don't *you* start."

She laughed softly, starting to rub his back from the waist up. "Something's got you tense; were the 5th that bad?"

"No," he sighed. "Crash and Meltdown, that's good . . . No, they're fighting men, or were, or they're boys who think war is glorious, which with training is even more useful, sometimes. It's that bastard Stanson."

Her hands paused for an instant, then continued. "Watch him; he's dangerous." The lazy affection had gone from her voice, without affecting the mellow tone. "And you got on reasonably well, back at Court."

"That was before I had to see him try to command a battalion in the field," Raj said. "He's not stupid, better at Court affairs than I am . . . but at this he doesn't know how and won't learn."

"Don't let him make you fight him," she said sharply.

"I've seen him kill; he loves it. And he loses his temper, completely loses it, doesn't think about consequences until it's too late."

"I won't," Raj said bitterly. "I *can't* fight him; it would . . . ruin everything."

"You're tensing up again . . . that's right, relax . . . He's very well connected, too."

"A relation of the Welman County Stansons, isn't he?"

"Yes. And the Minister of Finance . . . who's a nonentity personally, but not somebody who can be ignored."

"Some sort of connection of the Chancellor's, too."

"Married to his wife's aunt's third cousin," Suzette said absently; she was better than the *Book of the Starborn* for noble genealogies. A pause, and her hands continued.

"Why *did* Barholm put him in joint command?" Raj asked, after a while.

"Well, at a guess, he wants to see how you both shape," Suzette continued, in the same abstracted tone. "This is the turning point in both your careers . . . and it was a bone to throw to the Minister of Finance. The man's so stupid he doesn't know he's a puppet, but he's got an uncanny memory for favors and slights." More briskly. "You'll just have to manage Stanson. He's not stupid, there's a nasty streak there, but he's mentally lazy and a man like that can be manipulated."

Raj groaned. "As if I didn't have *enough* to do!"

"Now you've tensed up again. Don't worry, something will work out . . . turn over."

He did; their faces were almost touching, as she slid down along his body. "I love you," she said; her face was shadowed, backlit and haloed by the dim light of the coal-oil lantern slung from the tent pole. Her voice was softly fierce, and the kiss that followed was bruising. Breathless, she laughed throatily. "And now, I *will* make you relax."

"Sweet, we have to sleep."

"Ah." The grin was urchin. "What was it you told me once about . . . field expedients? I know what you need."

Later, drifting off, he half-heard a whisper: "And I'll see that you get it, too."

CHAPTER SIX

"Rust! Rust! Rust!"

The five troopers jogging by with rock-filled packs held their rifles at arm's length as they chanted in unison; the sergeant behind them was keeping his mount to a slow lope, whistling merrily and occasionally giving a crack of his dogwhip. The punishment detail looked in bitter envy at those whose shortcomings had been in their personal gear or harness rather than their weapons; *those* lucky bastards were only forced to carry the big tin bowls of soyamash from the cookfires out to the dog lines. Servant's work, generally, but a much milder penalty than running until your lungs burned and your legs turned to rubber and your feet blistered in the riding boots and your arms felt like they were going to drop off . . . and *then* you did a normal day's work.

After cleaning your gear, of course. Now that the 5th Descott Guards had been two weeks on the move, the number of men caught out by the snap inspections was falling fast.

The rest of the Battalion stood easy by their mounts, grinning at the miscreants or calling an occasional comment. It was no skin off *their* asses if the new CO was hard-nosed, and they were heading out where mistakes didn't mean a noncom reaming you out, they meant getting seriously fucked. And everyone who was depending on you as well. The dogs, more pragmatic even than their masters, concentrated on the big five-kilo loads of boiled soya flour. There were enough whining complaints at the quality to keep the troopers busy soothing and rubbing ears and scratching ruffs; in East Residence it was easy and cheap to buy bones and offal to add to the ration. A cavalry trooper was supposed to find his own food and his mount's out of his pay, which on the move meant basics only.

"Right, gentlemen," Raj said. The other officers were there, and one or two noncoms he had had his eye on for possible detached duty. A Battalion in garrison was an administrative unit, and had no regular staff . . . and a commander needed men he could rely on, no less than a Vice-Governor. "We're leading off today, but I don't think that will be a problem."

They all looked over to the 2nd's camp, which was barely stirring. A fair number of the troopers were up, many working on their uniforms. The Gendarmerie were beautifully equipped; their jackets and tunics of the best fine-combed bleached wool, boots and harness of supple iridescent sauroid leather from the northern steppes. The neck guards of their helmets were sauroid leather as well, nearly as strong as chain mail and much lighter, and they were reinforced with studs of brass or silver. The officers competed in their men's turnout, of course, so many of the helmets were silvered; one platoon had theirs gilded, and the privilege of wearing plumes was generally granted. The quality of their arms was unsurpassed in all the Civil Government; glass-beaded match rifles with stocks inlaid in flamewood and Torsauroid tooth, drawn-brass cartridges, Kolobassi watered steel sabers and bayonets.

Their dogs were all pedigreed Alsatians from the Governor's private stud; very impressive on the Field of War drill ground, quartering and leaping in unison and passing in line as they did dressage practice five mornings a week. Half the children in the city perched on roofs and trees to watch.

There was an explosion of yips and snarls from their lines; two of the dogs were fighting over their mash bowls, rearing and lunging on their checkreins, snaking heads down for a leg-grip and then rising to wrestle with their forelegs while their teeth clashed. A servant ran up with a bucket of water and pitched it at the combatants; they broke apart, but one snapped at the attendant, managed to grab him by the thigh. A trooper sprang in and began hammering at the dog's head with the butt of his whip; by the time it released the moaning groom, his leg was dangling by a thread. None of them thought that the tourniquet his friends applied would do much good.

Highbreds are like that, sometimes, Raj thought judiciously. *Testy*. It was the inbreeding. Not all of them, of course: most were like any Alsatians—lazy, happy, puppy-friendly doofus-dogs, very trainable and as likely to lick an enemy as bite him. It was a pity that crosses between the basic breeds produced only sterile mules. Legend said the ancients had fixed them with their unFallen powers.

"No, I don't think they'll be bumping our butts on the road," Kaltin Gruder said. He was not wearing his shimmerstone earring this morning, but his uniform was noticeably more spruce than the others. He finished the hard roll he was gnawing and dusted his hands. "All that brightwork takes a mort of polishing."

"Unlikely," Raj agreed. The 5th's personal servants and camp followers were striking tents and bundling gear, quickly if messily; even hookers who wanted to stay on in the Battalion's rear echelon had realized they could not earn all their keep on their backs under the New Order of Captain Whitehall.

"Well, gentlemen, today we'll do basic fire and movement, by platoon and company, and a Battalion movement from line of march into column as per a meeting engagement in the afternoon."

"Sir?" Gerrin Staenbridge spoke, giving his curly black hair a final vigorous scratch before donning his helmet. "Were you planning on grading?"

"Of course," Raj said. Performance was improving rapidly but unevenly, and you had to know your weak points.

"I think a little sporting proposition would improve the mens' spirits. Hambone and stick, as it were."

"Hmmm." Raj flashed the other man a smile; he was doing better and better, now that he was waking up. Perhaps he would be a Captain himself now, with more ambition or better connections.

"Well, let's say . . . double ration of wine and no sentry

go to the winning platoon. And—" he turned to the clump of NCO's. "Master Sergeant, from now on we'll be pitching camp in hollow-square formation, baggage in the center. Establish a crapground for the dogs, as well." The wind was bringing them unmistakable evidence that such had not been done here. "Losing platoon polices it before we pull out." He slapped one fist into the other, tightening his gloves. "To the day's work, gentlemen."

"Battalion—"

The 5th Descott was trotting in column of twos down the little farmlane. There was an orchard to their left; to the right, an open flat pasture stretching a hundred and fifty meters. It had been mown for hay recently, and the smell was heady-sweet in the afternoon sun. The field was bordered by a rise, a terrace of the alluvial plain marking an old shoreline of the Hemmar in some age long before men came to Bellevue. It was in heavy forest, oak and wild cherry and pine and native thongtree, tall reddish-ochre things with smooth bark and a cluster of thin whippy branches on top, big sword-shaped leaves set like feathers along the edges of each.

"—to the right, fire mission, *wheel-halt*."

"Company—" the unit commanders relayed it; the men kept their pace. There was an imperceptible slowing in the manifold thudding of dogs' pads on the dusty dark-brown earth of the lane. Cavalry mounts were bred for intelligence, and most knew the drillbook nearly as well as their riders. The trumpeter called it out as well, brassy and cheerful in the slanting sunlight. Two weeks travel from the Capital had tightened drill considerably.

"Platoon—"

"*Right face, wheel-halt!*"

The dogs stopped, sinking their haunches toward the ground and bracing their column-thick forelegs, then whipped around to the right in half their own body lengths. Or tried to; some of the troopers had been a little late or early with the crucial rein signals. There were collisions, the heavy *thud* sounds of thousand-pound wardogs meeting unexpectedly. Raj had his watch out, the second hand sweeping inexorably as the men jumped from the saddle with barely time enough for the mounts to stop. Many tumbled, shouts of pain and clatter of falling rifles; a shot cracked out, and Master Sergeant da Cruz's lips tightened. Raj did not envy the luckless trooper who had been riding with a round up the spout and, worse, the safety off.

"Ragged, ragged," the noncom cursed as the units formed in a staggered line along nearly a thousand meters of roadway; like two lines of dashes, the rear covering the empty spots in the front. The dogs dropped to their bellies, lying flat while their riders aimed over their backs. "Three minutes, that's *ragged*, try that with Colonials and we're fucking *dead*. Ser." The Master Sergeant had less of the nasal twang of Descott in his voice than most of the other ranks; a surprisingly well educated man, if you could get him to talk.

"Well, we're here to give them some polish, aren't we?" Raj said mildly. The exercise was supposed to be a response to a charge from the treeline. The crucial thing was to make the zone of beaten ground as wide as possible, to break the momentum of shock action before the enemy could get home with cold steel. Such a charge was more likely with the western barbarians of the Military Governments, who had what amounted to a religious reverence for edged weapons, but Colonial dragoons would jump you fast enough if they could.

The platoons were sounding off as they came ready; Staenbridge was noting the times on his noteboard. Raj waited until the last hailed in, before he pressed the stem of his watch.

"Call it five minutes," he said. "Down by half from where we were first day out, but not good enough . . . volley fire on the treeline; by platoons, four rounds." He raised his field glasses to his eyes and focused on the edge of the trees, where bushes grew thick between the trunks.

"Battalion, treeline target—" the Master Sergeant's voice carried easily, raised two octaves to pierce the ambient noise and propelled by his deep highlander's chest. The trumpeter duplicated it between phrases, and the noncoms down the battalion front were like multiple echoes.

"Volley fire, four rounds. *Load.*"

A giant rattling click, that lasted far too long. Raj turned his head aside for a moment. The field gun with the 5th was setting up on the crown of the road behind the troops, a few meters to the left of where the command group sat their mounts about the banner. A 75mm rifle, standard issue, with a six-dog team and caisson, a breechloader with chest-high wheels. The crew were in uniforms of a darker blue; they were Area Command troops, detached for this duty. They moved smartly, swinging the long barrel of the cast-steel piece toward the putative target, letting the steel pole trail thump to the dirt. The gunner squatted over the trail and sighted through the opened breech and down the barrel, standard for point-blank work. The shell clanked home just as the riflemen were ready.

"Volley fire—*fire!*"

There should have been a rolling *crash* down the line, a separate BAM from each platoon. Instead there was a staccato stuttering *kkt-kkkt-kkkt*, overlapping bangs. He watched the treeline carefully; the bushes were thrashing as if caught in a high wind, but far too many branches were pattering down from as high as four meters up. Raj's teeth showed beneath the binoculars. Some people were not adjusting their sights properly. Some people were going to be sorry and sore.

PUMPF. The field gun cut loose, adding its long plume of dirty-white smoke to the clouds puffing up along the firing line. The shell burst neatly at the edge of the forest, and a medium-sized pine quivered, swayed and fell outward with slowly gathering momentum.

"Reload." The process was quicker this time. "Volley fire, *fire.*"

The platoons opened up again and this time the sound was more like the *BAM-BAM-BAM* that it should have been.

Reload . . . *fire.* Reload . . . *fire.* The fourth volley was almost acceptably crisp, except that a lone shot rang out several seconds after the rest.

The Master Sergeant made a sound that would have done credit to an angry wardog. *"Get me that man's name,"* da Cruz shouted into the ringing silence. There were muffled coughs as the slight breeze carried the cloud of powder smoke back across the road; for a few moments it was dense enough to hide the prone men and dogs from the mounted officers.

"We'll have to do better than this," Raj said neutrally.

"Fire in the hole!" called the gunner; his team had rolled the gun back into batter after its recoil. Raj glanced over to him: "Give me an airburst just short of the treeline," he said; that was a real test of skill.

The gunner swung the crank that opened the breech and removed the round; taking a small wrenchlike tool from his belt, he fastened it to the point of the shell and twisted three careful turns. The fuse was dual-purpose. It would explode on contact, or when a perforated brass tube of powder burned past an outlet into the body of the bursting charge. The tool rolled the tube up or down to vary the length of time that took . . . but the speed of combustion was not entirely uniform.

The gunner rammed the shell home and cranked the breach closed, stepped aside and jerked the lanyard. The gun recoiled, rolling almost across the road to the ditch; there was an instant of ripping canvas sound, and a burst of black and off-white ten meters short of the trees. An irregular circle of alfalfa beneath the airburst flattened, ripped by the shredded iron of the shell casing. Raj nodded; some of the troopers winced. Air-burst shrapnel was something you could *not* guard against, it killed with the impersonal arbitrariness of lightning.

"Hey!" someone shouted. "Sicklefeet!"

Surprised, Raj brought his glasses up again. Yes, sicklefeet, a pack of about twenty breaking out of the trees and halting for a moment, bobbing and tense on their long legs. They were native carnosauroids, about twice the size of a large man, bipeds whose snaky two-meter bodies were balanced by an equal length of tapering tail. They held themselves almost horizontal to the ground, the slender forearms with the grasping claws tucked into their chests. The heads were slender as well, with forward looking vertical-slit eyes, and mouths that split three quarters of the length of the skull to reveal back-curving teeth.

Those were for tearing flesh; the killing tools were on the feet, half-meter rear claws that folded up along the shank of the birdlike leg. When muscle and tendon swung them down they were ready to slice and tear; in the wild steppe country a pack of sicklefeet could bring down a giant grazing sauroid, leaping twice their own height to kick slash wounds man-height and arm-deep. The carnivores milled, opening their mouths to hiss-roar at each other, sounding like a locomotive about to explode. Their mouths were shocking pink, holding only teeth and a tongue fixed all along its underside to the floor of the mouth; it was a mechanism for ramming large chunks of meat down the throat, since the creatures could not chew. The mouth was a striking contrast to the mottled reddish-green and dull blue of their pebbled hides, a color that faded to dull cream on their bellies.

"Sicklefeet, all right," Raj said, spitting on the road. The things were still quite common in Descott County, which was mostly rocky pasture or open mountain forest with scattered pockets of arable land; men had killed off the big grazers that were their natural prey, but sicklefeet were thoroughly opportunistic feeders, and had found human livestock a perfectly acceptable substitute. Or humans; Raj remembered watching one bounding up a near vertical cliff with a crofter's toddler clamped in its jaws and still screaming. They were one reason no male and few women in their native hills went beyond hailing distance of their hearths without a gun.

"Gerrin." Senior Lieutenant Staenbridge looked up. "Which platoon scored best, today?"

"First of the Second," he said. That was Kaltin Grader's Company; his younger brother Evrard was the lieutenant.

"Kaltin, my compliments to Lieutenant Gruder, and his men are to take those things out. See to it."

"I'm surprised there are any of the filth in close-settled country like this," Gerrin said.

"So am I," Raj said. "But this pack is leaving soon."

The beasts were milling around, moving in darting-swift bounds; some of them were pointing their bodies at the road and flaring the single broad nostril on the ends of their snouts. One of those was a male, and it lifted the crimson skin ruff around its neck and bugled a challenge. No pack back in the County would do that; they had learned to be afraid of men, although they had a disconcertingly sharp notion of how far a rifle could shoot.

Crack. The pack male leaped straight up, an astonishing

fifteen-meter jump, landed spinning and snapping at its flank. *Crack-crack-crack,* thirty rifles on independent fire, in the hands of men whose livelihoods had depended on guarot. The heavy hollow point bullets hammered at the sauroids, punching fist-sized exit holes that gouted blood a darkish brick color. The pack scattered like glass exploding away from a sledge hammer, but none escaped; sicklefeet were open-country creatures, and their instinct was to run rather than shelter in the bush behind them.

Raj looked up at the sun, westering; the Battalion had made more time on the side roads in the course of its training exercises than the transport column would have all day. They would cut back north and west to intersect it.

"Skin them," he said. Sicklefeet heart and liver were quite tasty, and the tail made acceptable stew. The dogs would be glad of the rest. "Then mount up, and we'll head back."

"Sir—"

Raj looked around; it was young Lieutenant Gruder, looking much like a model of his older brother Kaltin in nine-tenths scale, without the self-assurance.

"Just a second, Lieutenant," Raj said, and turned back to the local landowner who had ridden up to the head of the column just as they were about to pull out. "Excuse me, Messer . . ."

"Minh, Messer Captain," the noble replied. A wave to indicate the estate. "Stevin Trahn Minh, Guardian of Twinford."

"Raj Ammenda Halgern da Luis Whitehall," Raj said, using the older long form common at home.

Trahn's mount was a cream-colored wolfhound, worth half a year of Raj's pay; there was an equivalent amount in the jeweled clasp that held a spray of peacock feathers to the side of his beret, and the buckle on his gun belt. His clothes were almost offensively fashionable, long-sleeved tunic and white-silk roll-necked shirt, baggy trousers, tooled boots. The half-dozen guests behind him were similar, and there was a positive train of attendants.

"I must protest, Messer," Minh was continuing, "over this high-handed violation of the game laws."

"Game laws?" Raj rocked back in his saddle, surprise

striking like a physical blow. He had been expecting a complaint of damage to the timber, and a demand for compensation. No problem with that, write out a chit and let this big frog learn what size puddle the Ministry of Finance was. Game laws, though?

"Messer, I grant that the forces of the Civil Government have the right to conduct exercises on my land, but this wanton slaughter of my carnosauroids is inexcusable! The Law clearly states that sport hunting on any Messer's land is his and his alone; these sauroids have been preserved at enormous expense and trouble for the sport of my guests." He waved a hand over his shoulder to indicate the bright-clothed assembly. "Those were the last pack between here and the coast range."

"*Slaughter*?" Raj asked. "Of *sicklefeet*? Messer, you mean you were keeping those vermin around *deliberately*?" Raj looked at him, a tall slender man with a narrow face and eyes so black that the pupil merged with the iris; thirty, and in good hard condition, the way you'd expect an enthusiastic hunter to be. "In Descott County, there's a *bounty* on them."

"Ah. Descott." There was a freight of meaning in the single syllable, in the hard-edged accent of the Home Counties. "Well, *Messer* Captain,"—he stressed the honorific as if Raj was a member of the gentry class only by courtesy "—this is *Harzon* County, don't you know."

A slight tension at his back, as the other officers heard the implied insult to their birth County. *Is this man insane?* Raj wondered, forcing back the pounding at his temples. No, he decided, watching the eyes that held no trace of fear or doubt; it was the face of someone who could not *imagine* contradiction or opposition on his own territory. No doubt this Trahn could drop the purchase price of Hillchapel across a gaming table and laugh at the loss, but it required an arrogance of truly interesting proportions to act this way with three hundred killers at Raj's back. A Descott squire could be stiff-necked enough behind the ramparts of his manor . . . but the biggest landowner in the hills wouldn't have *this* sort of gall.

Of course, they still practiced the vendetta back home, and not just between social equals, either; a sniper behind a rock could vanish into the canyon lands, and who could say it wasn't bandits? *There are times I'm glad I come from the backwoods*, Raj decided. Lieutenant Gruder's voice broke in again.

"Sir, you should see this." There was something strange in the tone. "We found it when we paunched the last sicklefoot."

Raj turned in the saddle; Horace kept up his curious sniffing at the muzzle of Minh's wolfhound. The other dog was uncertain how to handle it, unwilling to reciprocate and too well-trained to back.

A trooper was riding beside the younger Gruder, his face as green as his commander's. He had a scrap of bloody sauroid hide in his hands, with a lump of something half-digested on it. It took a minute's stare to realize it was a leg; of a child about six, from the size, still wearing the remains of a hide shoe. Home-made, a peasant's moccasin, but with blue beaded flowers on the toe. Raj swallowed, looked from the trooper to Minh.

"Well?" he said.

"I *told* you, Messer, it was expensive to keep the beasts in the neighborhood." A shrug. "They got two other brats, and chopped up a team of perfectly good plow oxen, and the Spirit of Man of the Stars alone knows how many sheep. Crafty devils, and good sport."

Raj heeled his mount forward, to within hands-reach of the landowner. Horace shouldered into the wolfhound, which tried to push back and rebounded from the bigger dog's weight; the hound's lips were drawn back just enough to show his teeth, and he raised his head to look down on Minh's slender mount. Raj reached out, grabbed the wrist of the hand that had begun to swing the dogwhip towards him.

"Now that, *Messer*," the officer said, "was unwise. It might be construed as an assault on a serving officer, highly illegal." The muscles of his forearm tightened; Minh tried to jerk free, found himself in a grip as unyielding as a vise. He looked down, and his eyes widened slightly as he took in the thickness of Raj's wrists; the Descotter was a big man, but they would have been impressive on someone half again his size. The fingers clamped inward, and Raj felt bones bend towards their breaking points.

What? he said inwardly. *No disastrous consequences?*

none that i can calculate, Center replied dispassionately, **act as you think advisable.** Minh was snarling himself, white about the lips and sweat beading on his forehead.

"I . . . apologize!" he said tightly. Raj squeezed again, then slacked at the sickening rush of pleasure he felt, as fear invaded the other's eyes for what was probably the first time in decades.

"Accepted, Messer," Raj grated, working his hand. It had been years since he last slipped his tether like that, and he did not like to think about what the consequences had been then. A thought struck him. "Your estate, Messer; it includes a town?" That was a legal term rather than a descriptive one, but it usually meant something bigger than a village.

"Yes," Minh said, with the glazed look of one who cannot *believe* what is happening to him. "At the ford over the Toluravir." That was a left bank tributary of the Hemmar, and they had to cross in any event, heading south for the passes over the Oxheads and into the border Counties.

"Expect two Battalions and complement, for billeting, sundown tomorrow," he said crisply. Minh's face fell slightly; the soldiers would pay for their supplies, but they would do so in Government script . . . re-claimable in East Residence, two weeks travel away. A banker would take the paper, at a 10% discount. And it would empty storehouses that would otherwise have turned a healthy profit. "Now, if you'll give us the road, Messer?"

The first thing that Raj noticed as he rode down the expedition's column of march was Suzette stepping down from Captain Stanson's carriage. She waved gaily to him, before turning and extending her hand. Stanson bent over it as she laid fingers on his palm, touching it to his lips; standard courtesy, from an officer to a Messa, a lady of the Messer class. Horace gave a short complaining whuffle-whine as Raj reined in with a brutal jerk at the bridle. Suzette's dog Harbie was tied to the rear hitch of the passenger vehicle on a leading rein.

"Oh, Raj!" his wife said, with a glow. "Messer Stanson so *kindly* invited me to ride with him and Merta."

"Good evening, Captain Stanson," Raj said shortly. The co-commander of the expedition was leaning back against the curved rear seat of his carriage; the top was down, on this fine spring day. The redheaded girl—*Merta*, Raj remembered, she had been a seamstress or something of that sort in East Residence—huddled against the other side of the vehicle.

"Thank you for your hospitality, Messer," he continued: a social pleasantry, for which social rather than military rank was appropriate. Stanson looked cool and elegant in his spotless white uniform with the gold trim, slender and tough and pretty as a fangmouth. Raj was acutely conscious of his own state, all the bright-work on his uniform browned with varnish as he had ordered for the 5th, soaked with sweat and sweat-caked dirt besides, smelling of powder and dog. He held out his hand, noticing the rims of black under the nails.

"Oh, no problem," Stanson said, leaning over from the carriage and shaking it. "We had such a *marvelous* time discussing the old days. We met each other back when, you know."

"Yes," Raj grated. "I know."

Back when Suzette had been a desperate hanger-on to the fringes of polite society, nobody to bring her out for the first season but an aunt as shabby-genteel as herself. While this young spark had been doing the rounds of the parties and spending his father's rents, and Raj . . . Raj had been dividing his time between the armsman and his tutors and lonely hunts in the high hills, dreaming of winning a commission, glory, something beyond the endless sameness.

"Messer Stanson has very kindly invited us to dinner," Suzette said, a bare hint of wasp-warning in her voice.

"Yes, we can discuss the new draft," Stanson said.

"New draft?" Raj said. *God, I'm tired*, he thought.

"Yes, the Master of Soldiers, East Residence Area, saw fit to send us along about two hundred odds and sods in the way of reinforcements. Countersigned by the Vice-Governor's office." He produced the personnel order; Suzette's eyes dropped slightly. *Anne*, Raj knew. "We'll have to decided how to split them up."

"Oh, *Helmt*," Suzette said pettishly, using his first name.

"I thought you were going to tell me how you arranged for old Ebnzar's barge to sink at the water picnic!" She slapped at his hand lightly with her gloves. "You *know* you've got more men than you can use; besides, they look so fine, all on those beautiful Alsatians, wouldn't it be a pity to spoil it?"

Stanson smiled genially and patted her hand where it lay on the door of the carriage. "Of course, my dear Suzette, by all means." He raised his eyes to Raj. "You *will* be able to join us, fellow soldier?"

"Sorry," Raj said with an abrupt jerk of his head. "I'll have to call an officer's meeting, handle the details." With patently forced courtesy: "But by all means, Suzette, don't let me detain you; the meeting should last until 1100 or so. And if we could return the courtesy in a day or two?"

"Done," Stanson said, ignoring the patent insincerity. "Day after tomorrow it is." He turned to Suzette. "And tonight, do wear that fetching tweed riding outfit; quite dashing, my dear."

"Ser—" da Cruz began.

"I know, I know," Raj said shortly; he had changed and sponge-bathed in an echoing silence as Suzette dressed for her dinner party.

Now he looked about him; it was two hours past sundown, with Miniluna nearly full. Light enough to see the neat tent lines of the 5th, laid out as they were every night, and the mathematical arrangement of their campfires. An axe was falling on wood, somewhere, and some of the men were singing at their evening meal. A mounted squad trotted by, on their way out to night-patrol veddette duty; the duty corporal saluted smartly as he passed, and Raj returned it.

"It's the new draft. We're getting them all."

Master Sergeant da Cruz looked as if he had bitten into an orange and found it half-sour. "They isn't no prizes, ser," he said. "Only 'bout one in two's a Descott man, and a mort of 'em, they looks loik their sergeants was happier for their space 'n their company. And first and fifth companies is so unnerstrength, we put enough in to bring them up they'll be one-third replacements."

Raj nodded. All the companies in the 5th Descott Guards

had originally been recruited from the personal retainers of some County nobleman or other; yeoman-tenants and *vakaro* herdsmen putting on uniform to follow their squire in the Governor's service, as they might have against bandits or raiders or in a feud at home. Over the years brother had followed brother and son father, and throwing strangers into those close-knit unities was asking for trouble. For that matter, moving men around from the other companies to ensure a better mix of old hand and newcomer would be almost as bad.

"I'll discuss it with the company commanders," Raj said. *Duty is release from care*, he thought to himself, quoting scripture. "But sound out the men, find a few due for promotion who'd be willing to move into the first and fifth companies as corporals, platoon sergeants, that sort of thing." The officers who had been shorting their companies preferred to keep dead noncoms on the strength, since their pay was higher. "Then we can keep those two from being overrun with newbies, at least."

Da Cruz nodded. "Ser." A pause. "There's also a matter of a discipline offense. Seein's yer gave the foraging order, I suggested to Senior Lieut'nat Staenbridge as you'd like to deal with it, beggin' yer pardon for the liberty, ser."

"All right, let's see to it."

The Senior Lieutenants' tents were pitched at the head of their company streets; two-room tents, a bedchamber at the rear just large enough for a cot and an office/sitting chamber collapsible at the front, filled by a collapsible table and a couple of chairs. Staenbridge and his aide were sitting at the table beneath the open flap doing paperwork when Raj arrived; they rose smartly and saluted, fist touching brow and shooting straight up in allegiance to the Stars. A hangdog looking trooper was standing before them, with evidence piled around his feet, and a few other figures were lurking at the edge of the circle of light cast by the lantern on the tentpole. And a full squad lined up with their rifles at port.

Raj returned the salute. "Evening, Gerrin," he said, putting things on an informal basis as for as the officers were concerned.

"Raj," the other man replied. His smile was slight but

genuine; they had settled into a truce of wary mutual respect without much liking. *In fact, I have a sneaking suspicion I'd be much like him if I was stuck at company command level for a while with no prospect of anything else,* Raj thought. One thing they *did* have in common was a like of getting the job done; Staenbridge had just gotten discouraged enough to forget what the job *was*. With a genuine military task at hand, things were going much better.

"Ensign Foley," Raj continued. Regularizing the boy's rank had seemed the most sensible thing to do. And hell, there were worse ways of learning the trade than as a military apprentice, and his birth was perfectly acceptable. The youth nodded and brought out some papers.

"You have a problem, Gerrin?" Raj continued.

"No," the other man answered. "One of my troopers has a problem. Sergeant?"

"Trooper Antin M'lewis, front and center!" da Cruz barked.

The soldier was rather thin for a Descott man, with a reddish tinge to his bowl-cut black hair, limping a bit on one leg that also sported a rip in its red trouser leg. Piled behind him were two pig carcasses, neatly gutted and with the edible organs inside the body cavity in burlap bags. Another burlap sack beside sagged open, showing onions, dried apples and figs, a loaf of dark-crusted bread and a clay jug. "Yer other sods, too!" Two nondescript soldier's servants; every eight-man squad was officially allowed one in the field, but the ratio was generally exceeded.

"He's in third of the first," Gerrin said. "Salman"—Nkita Salman, the Lieutenant of the first company's third platoon—"is out on veddette duty, so I'm the one that called you." He raised his voice slightly. "Complainants, step forward." A farmer, old enough to be stooped, in his Starday-go-to-church linen shirt and kerchief, with wooden clogs on his feet.

"Yis, m'lud," he said, going down on one knee, then bobbing erect at Gerrin's nod. "Koleman's m'name, lud. Farms on shares for Messer Trahn Minh, I does, n' pays m'crop to his collector at Broken Hill; twenty year've brought m'harvest an' Star Spirit witness never mor'n a stroke a' the rod to warm me back—"

"Yes, yes, goodman," Gerrin said. "Get on with it."

"Yis, m'lud. Out seein' t' the tobaccy wormin', me 'n muh sons an' son-in-law. 'M granson Tuk comes runnin', says there b'trouble at the house. Go there. Find thissere gun-boy—" he jerked a thumb at Trooper M'lewis "leapin' 'n hoppin' around the front door, like. Those other two, the slavies—" the servants, being freedmen, stirred angrily but subsided at the noncom's glare "—drivin' off in a one-dog cart. With m'pigs. Gun-boy jups up an' rides off on his dog. Yis. Askin' muh wife an" daughter what happenin'. Says t'gun-boy rides up, chases 'em into t'house, sets he slavies to slaughterin' t'pigs. That done, talks m'daughter—garmless frikkin' fork—into open door, says he payin'. Grabs her tits. She kicks 'n hollers, muh wife come out, slap a ladlefull 'a hot bran on his leg. Bar t'door agin while he yellin'."

The farmer ducked his head again. "We's law-abidin' folk, m'lud. Pays our taxes and tithes and rent regular, goes to Church ev'r second Starday. Enters our sins at Terminal. Gun-boy there ain't no Messer t' take muh pigs 'r grab muh daughter's tits. Askin' yuh justice, m'lud."

Gerrin blinked, kept his face straight with an effort that Raj, at least, could see. "It seems," he said, "that the women were direct witnesses. Why aren't they here?"

The peasant's jaw dropped. "Ah, t'forks, m'lud? As well bring a chicken to a law-speakin' as a fork."

Raj raised his brows. In Descott, the women would have blown a single-armed intruder in half with a shotgun, and put up his head for the men of the family to find when they got home, and mocked them with it at every rural frolic and meeting for a year and a tenday . . . Well, there was only one Descott County, more the pity; some of the other backwoods areas were almost as tough, though.

Gerrin turned to him; it was as much a test as a courtesy.

Raj crossed his arms and spoke: "Master Sergeant, this man's service record?"

"Ten year enlistment, seven served," da Cruz said; his voice took on more of an officer-class tone as he recited. "Marksman, first class; watch-stander." A good shot and literate, both accomplishments which meant extra pay. "Gold-of-valor durin' the Stern Isle skirmishes." The trooper's face had relaxed somewhat. "Twice promoted corporal, twice demoted. Strikin' a superior while drunk; theft from a fellow soldier." It fell again, and he looked at Raj out of the corner of his eyes.

Something in the expression and the man's name struck a cord in Raj's memory. "Home parish, soldier?" Softly: "It's a run-the-gauntlet offense to lie at a hearing, soldier."

The man swallowed. "Bufford parish, ser," he said flatly.

Da Cruz smiled openly, and Gerrin put a hand before his face to muffle his snort. "Messer Cap'n, ser!" the trooper burst out. "That's not justice, there's a mort of honest men in Bufford parish!"

"And they stay there, we don't see 'em," da Cruz said.

"No volunteer comments, Master Sergeant," Raj said, remembering the old saying: *an ordinary Descotter bandit will steal your sheep and rape your daughter. A Bufford parish man will sell your daughter because the price is better, and be content with raping the sheep instead.*

"What's your side of the story, soldier?"

"'Tis all lies and damned lies," M'lewis said passionately; his face shone with conviction. "Bought the food with good siller, ser, I did. Then the woman, she grabbed m' cock and dragged me towards the bushes, and cried rape when her men came home!"

"Let's see your leg, then," Raj said. Motionless for a moment, the soldier gave the peasant a glance that made him flinch, pure feral menace. Then he bent to roll up a pantleg.

"The *right* leg, M'lewis: the one yer limpin' on, man. Don't waste the Captain's time."

There was a splotched purple burn on the wiry flesh of the soldier's leg.

"Well, that settles it." Raj nodded toward the pile of meat. "Do you know the punishment for unauthorized plundering on Civil Government soil, Trooper M'lewis?"

"Ahh . . ." A hopeful smile, with crooked tobacco-browned teeth. "Stoppage of rum, ser?"

"Flogging."

"Messer Captain ser, I'm a freeborn man and a Descott!"

Raj nodded. "For which I'm commuting the offense to one month's pay, and one month's punishment drill, and one month's . . . stoppage of rum." He met the man's eyes: as well lecture a feradog on its obligation to protect the sheep. "And be glad," he continued slowly, "that I don't add attempted rape and absent-without-leave in the face of the enemy. Your record says you've the makings of a good soldier, M'lewis. Don't make me hang you."

"Ser."

Raj looked over at the two servants. "Have them given twenty-four with the lash and a bucket of salt water," he said. They began to wail, struggling as the squad clubbed them down and manhandled them off to execute sentence. Raj raised an eyebrow at Gerrin, who nodded.

"We've got to get this under control," Raj said. "It's not just wrong, it's bad for discipline . . . Master Sergeant, announce it at muster tomorrow: from now on, no private purchases except what sutlers bring in to camp. The Quartermaster is to collect whatever's needed and buy in bulk; only men designated by the Quartermaster to leave camp for purchase of forage."

"Ser!" da Cruz saluted, stamped a heel and marched off.

"Ah, Captain." It was Ensign Foley, looking up from the muster roll he was annotating.

"Lad?"

"The 2nd . . . well, the men won't like it, that they're restricted and the 2nd aren't. I think they're, ahh, grumbling." He flushed, looking down at the pen in his hands.

"Good thinking, lad . . . Ensign," Raj said. Gerrin put a prideful arm around the youth's shoulders. "But we'll have to live with it; if you let men be jackals, don't expect them to fight. Looting and rape are their privileges on foreign soil, not among our own people. Otherwise we're bandits. . . ." Raj grinned tiredly. "And I'm perfectly well aware they call me Brass-Ass behind my back. When a soldier stops grumbling, worry: if he's a Descott man and he stops grumbling, watch your back. . . . By the way, speaking of the 2nd, I'm having Stanson over tomorrow for dinner, and I'd appreciate it if you could attend. In fact—" he coughed, embarrassed "—I'd appreciate it if I could borrow your cook, Gerrin."

"Delighted."

CHAPTER SEVEN

"Not bad at all," Stanson said, leaning back in his camp chair and sipping at the wine. "I'm surprised we don't see more of this vintage in the capital."

"It doesn't travel well," Staenbridge said. "Be glad while we've got it; over the passes the wine is thick as syrup, you have to cut it with water, *and* they put pine sap in it."

Silence fell again. It had *not* been a convivial evening, here under the outstretched flap of the 5th's command tent. For one thing Stanson had brought his mistress Merta with him. No problem, if it had been an all-men affair, but there was a married gentlewoman present, which made it something of an insult. Or simply slovenly, even for a war-camp. They had begun with pan-fried trout, easy enough now that they were getting out of the lowlands; then a main course of roasted lamb stuffed with spicy sausages on a bed of saffron rice, salads and quick-fried vegetables on the side. Staenbridge's cook had even managed to whip up a chocolate compote, which was next to a miracle under field conditions.

Raj grinned behind the mask of his face. *Expected to condescend to a pack of monkeys from the wilds, eh?* he thought. Staenbridge had turned out to be, of all things, a gourmet and oenophile; Kaltin Gruder and his brother talked fashions and racing dogs with the best; young Foley had an encyclopedic grasp of classical drama . . . And none of them was particularly impressed by their guest's reputation as a duelist; in East Residence he might pass for a killing gentleman, but the other men around this table had been brought up to the traditions of the blood-feud. In the end, Stanson had spent most of the time talking to Suzette, who had dropped into the intricate jargon of the Palace without missing a stride. A private language of their own, filled with in-jokes and malice.

Raj held out his cup again for the server, then drank. Staenbridge winced and sipped.

"Captain?"

The duty squad's corporal came in, drew to attention, and saluted. "Captain, we'z got summat strange here. Woman out here, says sommat of bandits, says you know 'er man. Speak strange-like, she does, cannat tell snout from arse of it, beggin' yer pardon, ser, Lady." Which was not to be wondered at; the noncom's own Descotter brogue was thick as tar, and the local peasant dialect was radically different.

Raj stood, glad that whatever-it-was had come up before the drinking seriously started, because if he had ever been in a mood to get fighting-drunk, this was the time. Then a woman stumbled in between two troopers. Grey-haired, as her fallen headscarf showed, wrinkled face fallen in on a near toothless mouth, body like a shapeless bag of potatoes under a good wool skirt with some stitching on the hem and a dirt-grey linen blouse. Probably about forty . . .

"Justyc, mlud," she gabbled; between the dialect and her toothlessness and the sweating exhaustion that left her panting, he caught about one word in three. "Hep uz." Hands work-gnarled and covered in cracked callus reached out as she knelt.

"Stop," he said. "Nod yes or no. Your man came here yesterday?" *Yes.* "Bandits have attacked your farm, and you think they're still there?" *Yes.* "Can you guide us." *Yes.* "Were the men who attacked your holding in uniforms?" He splayed fingers towards his own blue tunic. *If it's that Bufford parish bastard M'lewis I'll hang him from a tall tree—* The woman looked doubtfully at him, more doubtfully still at Stanson in his whites, then shook her head.

"All right," Raj said. He straightened, fastening his jacket and picking the webbing belt with his saber and pistol from the back of his chair. "I'll take—"

"Me for one," Gerrin Staenbridge said. Foley stood as well, then Kaltin and Evrard Gruder, and several of the others he had invited.

Stanson laughed, turning so that he did not notice how for once that evening Suzette did not echo him. "Well, this is just like one of the old songs," he said. "The hero and his loyal companions off to slay the monster and rescue . . ." his gaze fell to the sobbing peasant woman, with an expression more suitable for a man scraping something off his boot as he went indoors " . . . the beautiful lady." He made a moue. "Actually, I'd think it was more a matter for the parish constables, but I'd be glad to come along?" He pushed back his chair and half-stood.

"No, enjoy your dessert," Raj said, watching dispassionately as the man sank back into his chair and reached for his wineglass.

"And *do* save us some of the compote," Gerrin said with a toothy grin, scooping up a finger load and eating it. "It's so hard to get fresh ingredients out here, don't you know?"

Stanson covered a yawn with the back of his hand. "Certainly," he said, and reached for a dried fig from the bowl, across Merta's bosom. He ignored her, glancing over at Suzette. "There'll still be one lovely lady here; we shall sing songs and gossip until dawn, awaiting your return."

Raj's last sight of the tent was Merta looking pure hatred at them both.

The air outside had turned cooler and drier; they were a hundred meters up from the flood plain of the Hemmar, and the increased altitude was more than compensating for the lower latitude as they headed south. The moons shone on the Oxheads to the south, making their peaks gleam like silver or salt, up in the high knot where they united with the Coast Range. The passes would be chilly, high tumbled rock, and then they would be down into the baking plains of the border Counties, foothills smoothing down into sparse pasture and then out into the *erg* of the deep desert, where nothing grew except around the salt lakes or the rivers of the east. Down where the riders of the Colony were waiting for them.

Someone led a dog in out of the darkness; it was da Cruz, the lamplight slick on the keloid lumpiness of his facial scars.

"Thought yer mought be needin' me, ser," he said.

"A positive plague of volunteering, eh, *loyal companions*?" Kaltin Gruder said softly, with a chuckle under it.

Raj slapped his gauntlets into his hand. "Five minutes, gentlemen," he said. "Evrard," he continued, and the younger Gruder straightened, "turn out your platoon . . . twenty-seven rifles, isn't it?"

"Twenty-five, sir: two men down with the flux."

"By all means. The rest of you, sabers and sidearms, please." He paused. "Oh, Foley." The young man drew himself up, bristling-ready to defend his right to come along. "Get yourself something with a little more stopping power, eh?" He nodded toward the 8mm pistol at the boy's belt.

"I've got *just* the thing," Foley replied.

They all paused for a moment, and then turned as Raj drew on his gloves. "Gentlemen?" A check. "Thank you."

The dogs' feet padded through the night at a loping trot beneath the stars and the moons, thudding and crunching softly on the crushed rock surface; the chink and rattle of equipment was louder, but still not enough to break the peace of the night. Dew was beginning to settle, bringing out the spicy scents of the crops and trees, the spoiled-honey scent of native vegetation. The peasant woman perched on his saddlebow stank, too, a hard dry scent like an ox that has been working in the sun, no more unpleasant than any soldier who had been in the field for a week or two; it was the things that crawled across from her clothing and bit that were a nuisance. Her shoulders were still shaking with an occasional hiccupping sob, and he patted her back absently.

"Hier," she said, pointing.

The main military highway turned eastwards, and a local track continued south of east, bordered by eucalyptus that filled the night with their sharp medicinal smell. The track was graded dirt, just wagon-wide, but well-kept, arrowing off into the rustling darkness. Raj flung up a hand.

"Yo!" da Cruz's voice was pitched low, and the column came to a halt.

"How far?"

He listened to the woman's breathy gabble for a moment, cursing inwardly. She had apparently never heard of kilometers, and judged all distances by the time they took to walk; the campground the soldiers had been using was as far as she had ever travelled, and everything beyond was "foreign parts," the land of legends and monsters.

"Ah, ser," a voice said.

Raj handed the peasant woman down and turned in the saddle. It was Trooper Antin M'lewis, holding himself straight in the saddle and looking blankly ahead.

"What the fuck are you doing here, soldier?" Raj asked.

"Gettin' my rum ration unstopped, ser," the man answered; his face was pure regulation, but . . . "Thought the Messer Captain might needs me, seein' as I knows this ground."

You have to give him credit for effrontery, Raj thought. "Tell me," he added, and gave a gesture of reassurance to the woman, who had recognized M'lewis and shrunk back.

"Draws a dirt map, ser?"

Raj gestured to da Cruz, and a whispered order to dismount brought men and dogs crouching; it was not a dark night, and they did not want to be noticed before they struck. M'lewis flattened a stretch of soil and sketched with his ringer.

"Ser, 'tis no more than half a klick up thisshere laneways," he said, with quick efficiency. "Farmstead scattered out, loik they does hereabouts." In Descott, an isolated dwelling was built around a courtyard and walled. "Barn by the road; house back mebbe ten meters, sheds n' whatnot, chickenhouse, a well, kitchen-garden. Road turns just before, go quiet 'n yer doesn't get seen 'till yer right up their arse."

"Good, very good," Raj said. "Hmmm, we need someone to scout it."

"I's yer man, ser," M'lewis said cheerfully. They stood, and their eyes met for a long moment. The trooper's grin died away for an instant.

"Good man," Raj said. "See to it, then. We'll be—" he nodded to his right "—about five hundred meters that way."

M'lewis nodded. To Raj's surprise, he did not go for the rifle in its scabbard by his saddle; instead, he stripped off jacket and boots, hung them on his saddlebow with his saber-belt. He was wearing a black cotton shirt, not the off-grey most men bought; the kerchief he took out and tied around his head was the same color. For weapons he tucked a long curved skinning knife in its sheath through the narrow waist belt of his trousers, over the small of his back, and took something out of the pocket of his jacket. Raj stepped closer and looked; it was a wire cord with wooden toggles on both ends, and M'lewis tucked it through his belt with care, the handles secured but easy to reach. Then he bent, rubbed dirt over his face.

"Loik old times t'home, 'tis, ser," he said, and was gone into the night.

"Evrard," Raj said.

"Sir?"

"Leave four dogholders; we'll go up the lane, quietly please, and wait. Clip the stickers, a round chambered. Quietly is the word, gentlemen," he repeated to the others around him, drawing his pistol and snapping the cylinder out for a final check. Just habit, but habits saved your life or killed you, in this line of work.

"Forward, Companions," Gerrin whispered, and the others chuckled softly; they seemed quite taken with the archaic title.

The noncoms relayed the orders, and the men stepped out of the saddles of their crouching dogs, with firm murmurs of *stay* to keep them in place. A series of rapid *click-chick* sounds as the forearm-long blades of the bayonets snapped home under the muzzles, spring-clips holding them to barrel and cleaning rod, and the oiled-metal sound of loading. Raj heard the platoon sergeant go down the squads, giving the men a quick check and delivering softly fervent promises:

"En I *will* cut a new asshole in any yer bastids pops it, unnerstan?"

The trees left a narrow slit of moonlight down the crown of the dirt road; the men of the 5th advanced up the sides by sections, alternating right and left. There was surprisingly little noise, but then these *were* hunters, after all; part of a boy's training back home was to be sent out with a rifle and one round, with a beating and no supper if he came back without game. Raj could smell the sweet-yeasty scent of barley in the milk ear stage behind the low adobe wall of the field on his left; water gurgled in an irrigation ditch, and pale silver light flickered through the leaves. Then they were coming up to the curve; a vineyard on their right, and broad-leafed tobacco on the left. *Good cover*, he thought, motioning backward with his hand. The column halted and sank down, men resting on one knee.

"I think I can see light, about four hundred meters ahead on the left," Foley whispered. Gerrin laid a finger over his lips. Raj strained his eyes. Nothing, but then Foley had the eyes of youth. *Damn, stop being a teenager, start dying*, he thought, then a figure rolled over the fence wall at their left and landed on noiseless bare feet.

"Ser," it said, as a dozen bayonets poised. It was M'lewis; Raj motioned his Companions close. "Warn't no problem, ser. It ain't no bandits, neither. It's them pretty boys from the 2nd."

"Numbers and positions, M'lewis," Raj said.

"Four of them carriages out in the yard, dogs tethered an' eatin' on the stock they's killed. Men and boys— I figger five, six, family and mebbe a slave—tied up in one the sheds. Six mebbe seven from the 2nd, officers an' gentleman-rankers, with they whores and slaves, they party pretty loud. No sentries." M'lewis seemed faintly sorry at that, and touched the garrote at his belt.

"How do we handle it, Raj?" Gerrin asked. As if to punctuate his remark the faint echo of a scream drifted down the road from the farmstead.

Raj opened his mouth. *Now, how do I say "kill them all" suitably?* he thought. Then—

observe.

—troopers of the 2nd falling screaming before their guns and Raj and the companions broke into a farmhouse kitchen. Reaching for their weapons, jerking, dying, slammed back by the lead. Servants and mistresses screaming and bleating pleas for mercy, holding their hands over their faces as troopers of the 5th drove the bayonets home again and again. Blood flowing sticky into the dirt floor, splashing on walls and ceiling in trails of red—

—and Stanson's face behind the pistol on the duelling ground. It was a different place this time, the other/Raj was standing on bare ground beside a road. Spectators, Trahn Minh looking on with satisfaction on his thin arrogant face;

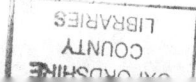

Suzette white-lipped with anxiety. Stanson sneering, bringing the pistol up in a smooth arc as the handkerchief touched ground—

—Stanson falling as Raj's saber gashed his throat—

—Tewfik riding his dog into the surf, and the ululating cheers of the Colonist army behind him, the great green banner snapping in the wind.

"—we do this by the regulations," Raj said. "No firing on," the next words seemed to choke him slightly, "fellow soldiers of the Civil Government except in self-defense or on my order." With deadly precision: *"Is that understood?"*

"What about the camp followers?" Kaltin asked.

"Fair meat, but don't start anything unless they try to fight or run . . . best we keep the platoon outside for a blocking force, unless it drops in the pot. Evrard, send your platoon sergeant around back with M'lewis and half your men. The rest will come with us and secure the farmyard and the vehicles. We'll deal with the scum inside ourselves. Follow my lead. Understood?" A chorus of nods. "Let's go, people."

Raj poised his foot above the doorlatch. The rhythmic screams from the farmhouse had stopped a minute ago; now they started up again, weaker and more shrill, muffled as if they came from a room behind this one. The peasant house was a single-story square, whitewash peeling from adobe walls and tiles missing from the roof; probably this single large kitchen-cum-everything in the front, a bedroom behind, and a half-loft above. The old farmer lay outside, his hands clutching a wooden pitchfork and his eyes staring upward. The face had been recognizable, even after a careless saber slash left half of it dangling down in a slab of meat and gristle, baring the pink bone and an eternal smile. Eight-legged native quasi-insects walked across his tongue to reach the eyeballs.

The air smelled of poverty and dog shit and blood and cooking; raucous noises of celebration and snatches of song came through the plank door, almost louder than the screams. Smoke ghosted white from a squat mudbrick chimney in the center of the roof.

"One," Raj said. There was a small metallic sound behind him; Foley had brought a sidearm with stopping power, all right. A double-barreled shotgun, cut-down to riot gun size, about 18-gauge.

"Two." Gerrin was at his side, pistol in one hand and saber in the other, quivering eager. Behind him Kaltin dusted one sleeve absently, and Evrard's lips moved silently in prayer; Master Sergeant da Cruz's mutilated face looked closer to peace than Raj had ever seen it.

"Three." Raj felt the world pause and go crystal clear, attention narrowing down to a diamond-bright focus. There was a taste of metal in his mouth, somewhere in his head the knowledge that he might be dead in a few seconds. Namelessly dead in this squalid little yard where nothing had ever happened but the endless repetitions of misery . . . And there was a job to do.

The sole of his boot crashed against the cheap pine-wood of the door next to the latch, and it came away in a shower of splinters. The door banged open. Raj fired a round into the ceiling as he stepped forward, moving aside to let the others file in.

It took a moment for the activity in the room to cease. It was L-shaped, lapping around the bedroom on two sides, with a single wickerwork door between them. There was another door at the end of L's short arm, out to the rear yard and the well. The long arm was filled with a table, crowded with the remains of a feast, roast piglets, a goose . . . more chickens were turning on spits in the fire, and a small ceramic crock of a clear yellowish liquid was surrounded by a scatter of cups. Raj glanced at it and was no longer surprised at the slow stunned looks of many of the feasters; that was the local homebrew, distilled from grape skins left over after the wine was pressed, and it had a kick like a sicklefoot.

There were four people he judged to be part of the farm family: all women, from one who looked to be a blousy-but-attractive forty and was probably a decade younger at least, to a just-pubescent girl; he could tell that easily, because like the others she wore only dirt and bruises. The older three women had been cooking and serving, while the youngest was on her knees before a seated 2nd Gendarmerie officer, her head bobbing up and down as she fellated him. His left hand stroked her hair; he smiled dreamily, and rested the point of a fighting knife on the skin between her neck and collarbone. Four others in stained white uniforms were sprawled around the table; and three times as many servants, mistresses and general hangers-on, frozen at the sound of the shot in every activity from drunken sleep through vomiting and shouted song to vigorous fornication.

The oldest of the peasant women screamed sharply as the door flew open. The girl stopped at her task as she felt the knifepoint lift from her arteries; looked up and scuttled on all fours over to a wall-side bench and hid beneath it, curled into a ball with her eyes closed. Silence fell as the Companions stepped through behind Raj, weapons ready; silence except for the last shriek from the bedroom. *That* door banged open, too, and a man in the 2nd's uniform stepped through.

"What the Outer Dark—" he began, then focused owlishly on the gun-muzzles staring at him across the room. His trousers were unbuttoned, and there was blood on the slack genitals and clotted in the wool. Raj could see him forcing alertness, eyes narrowing and hand dropping to his pistol as a man in servant's livery stepped through the door behind him. The servant's trousers were stained as well, although it was harder to tell against the burgundy fabric. He was pushing a nude boy of about ten ahead of him, gripping his neck.

"I'll put the tightass snottie back with the others, Messer—" he began. Faster than his master, or simply less drunk, he pushed the boy away sprawling and crouched. *That would be the boy Tuk*, Raj thought, surprised at the clarity of his mind, watching the child haul himself across the packed dirt with a red sheet glistening in the firelight across the backs of his thighs. Center's scenarios played themselves through his mind; he did not need the angel-computer to prompt them now. Tewfik riding his dog into the sea . . .

"Messers," Raj began, his voice high and clear. It was very important to enunciate clearly. "Thank you for your timely aid, in, in apprehending these bandits."

More silence, broken only by the whimpering of the raped

children. Then a babble of voices, hooting laughter from some of the servants and mistresses, shouts of anger from the soldiers of the 2nd.

"Spirit curse you, what bandits?" the man with the fighting knife still in his hand said, blinking; the other hand fumbled his garments closed, a human male's first instinct in a conflict situation. Adrenaline was sobering him a little, but not much. "Thersh . . . there's nobody here but our servants, man!" He peered. "Why, it's the Descotter sheep-diddler, the one who spends all day wallowing in the dirt while his wife—"

Raj fired into the ceiling again; it was roughly-barked pine logs with lathes laid over, and dust filtered down from the bullet hole. He suppressed a sneeze.

"It shows great initiative of you to hold them helpless here, after the atrocities they've committed on Civil Government subjects," he went on, overriding the man's voice. Ignoring him, in fact; instinct told him that only the one in the door to the bedroom was much problem. *That* one hadn't bothered to button his fly, and his weight had gone forward on the balls of his feet. A glance went between the officer and his servant.

Raj smiled, an expression much like those of the sicklefeet his men had killed the previous day. "Because now we are going to take the bandits out and kill them, each and every one."

Movement: the servant by the bedroom door snatched up a cleaver from the board that served as a mantle and lunged. Movement: Foley's shotgun roared. The target was less than five meters away, far too close for the double-buckshot load to spread much. It *did* chew the man's stomach into a pink mass, through which red-grey loops of intestine showed; he flew backward into the fireplace, toppling the spit with the chickens. The smell of burning pork added itself to the fug of the room, and scorched wool as his clothes caught fire. The young companion turned like a gun turret, the stock of his weapon clamped against his ribs. The stubby barrels stared at the officer of the 2nd, who had managed to clear his pistol and bring it up to half-port in the fraction of a second it had taken to kill his servant.

"Drop it," Foley said; his voice cracked in the middle of the words, but the cut-off shotgun did not waver, one barrel smoking and the other black readiness. "This one's for you, *Messer*."

Several of the 2nd's hangers-on were whimpering now. "Since your valiant part in this is over," Raj continued, "perhaps it would be better, fellow-soldiers, if you all undid your gun belts . . . yes, just carry them in your hands. Out now, please. You bandits, too, and if you don't think fifteen minutes more of life matters, try something."

One of the liveried men did; he plunged erect and out the rear door of the kitchen with an athlete's agility. The door banged closed behind him, and there was a short wet *thunk* sound that many of the men present could identify; a bayonet driving home. A choked grunt, and then a long bubbling scream; more of the thunking, and the door swung open for an instant. The severed head bounced on the table, spattering gravy, and rolled to a stop against the crock of white lightning.

The 2nd's officers were still babbling protests as they filed out, but none of them were resisting. Raj smiled at them again, nodding and making a depreciating gesture.

"No, no, no thanks," he said cheerfully. "Just doing our duty. Now," he continued, when everyone was outside, "separate those women."

While the men were being roughly bound, troopers' bayonets prodded the mistresses to one side; they were in varying states of undress, but all of them wore their jewelry. The primary store of liquid assets, in their trade, and not likely to be let out of the wearer's reach. Some of them were quite spectacular, if genuine. Much of the gold was, certainly.

"Strip them, and take the jewels." He took a blanket from one of the carriages and spread it. "Pile the gauds here. *All* of them, trooper M'lewis." Raj waited until the women were huddled together, staring at him in wide-eyed fright. "Go," he said softly, when they were still. "And if you're ever within the perimeter of my camp again, I hereby announce you're not under my protection."

They were professionals, too, in their way; they looked around at the troopers' wolf-grins, turned in a body and began trudging down the dirt lane, heading south toward the town at the ford.

Raj noticed that the old woman who had run to bring him was back, panting and wheezing up past the barn. She stopped at the sight of the farmer lying with his pitchfork in hand, then squatted beside him, rocking herself and moaning. One hand reached out to touch the corpse's face, then drew back. The moaning continued, low and eerie; the next-oldest of the farmstead's women was standing on the porch. She had clothed herself, but looked uncertainly around at the armed men.

"Goodwife," Raj continued: there were a number of things to be done, before this *cursed* night was over.

"Yes, Messer?" she said, her voice surprisingly strong as she went to her knees. Well, you had to be strong, to survive the sort of life these people led. "Thank you, Messer, but . . ." there was a tremor to her voice as she looked about " . . . they ate everything we needed for the season, Messer, and—"

"You see this?" He toed the pile of ornaments and dresses. "It's yours." Her mouth dropped open; there was enough there to *buy* a farm the size of the one her family sharecropped, and stock it besides. "I'd advise you to hide it under the hearth and sell it carefully and in small amounts." Because a peasant who came into money was like one of the legendary cooked pigs who ran about with knife and fork in its back, squealing "eat me." "Don't let your men out of the shed for an hour or so." No point in having enraged civilians complicating matters.

"Master Sergeant," he continued.

"Ser?"

"M'lewis is a watch-stander?"

"Ser. Readin', writin' and numbers, summat."

"Have him transferred to Battalion staff as a courier." The scrawny trooper whooped as he rebuttoned his uniform tunic; there was a suspicious hang to one sleeve, but Raj decided to ignore it for the moment. "M'lewis, there should be woodworking tools on a steading like this; bring anything in the way of mallets and hammers, and stakes, wooden treenails, anything like that. Run." As he sped off: "Now bring the prisoners down this way. You, too, Messers," he added to the soldiers of the 2nd Gendarmerie "You should watch the results of your *valiant* work."

The outer wall of the barn was only five meters from the laneway; it was a little more than head-high, built of large adobe bricks mortared with mud, and no whitewash had ever been wasted on it. *Quite sturdy enough*, Raj decided.

"Line them up against it." Rough hands pushed the men to stand against the hardened mud; some of them were weeping, and a few fell to their knees to beg. Raj looked up into the crystal purity of the night.

"Ahh, firin' squad, ser?" da Cruz asked.

"By no means, Master Sergeant: by no means." There was a wait; Raj remembered to turn and clap Foley on the shoulder. "Quick work, Ensign," he said.

The boy had been looking nausea-pale; he straightened. "Thank you, sir," he said, looking down at the shotgun and fumbling it open. It took several seconds for him to unload it. "It's . . . a good weapon, Gerrin— Senior Lieutenant Staenbridge got it for me."

"Use it well," Raj said; the youth snicked it closed and went to stand beside Staenbridge, accepting an arm around his shoulders with a grateful sigh. M'lewis came panting up with his arms full.

"Messer Captain, gots a bit," he said. Quite a bit; three large wooden hammers, the sort used to drive vine-props, and several dozen stakes of turned hardwood the length of a man's forearm.

"Excellent, M'lewis," Raj said, bringing his eyes down to the line of men against the wall . . . eleven of them. Fifteen to fifty, East Residence born, you could see the mark of the streets on them. Eyes bewildered, eyes defiant, cringing.

"Master Sergeant," he continued, listening to his own voice as he might have a strange sauroid calling in the forest. "This laneway leads to the ford over the Torunavir, doesn't it? Passable for the Battalion?"

"Yes, ser. Bit more direct than the highway. Take a little longer, mebbe."

"Excellent," Raj said again. "Have the men draw straws for a crucifixion detail, if you please. And a detachment to see nobody touches the bodies until tomorrow morning."

Raj heard the Gruder brothers hiss in surprise behind him. The servants stared uncomprehending until the soldiers spread-eagled the first of them against the wall and brought up the stakes. They began screaming, then.

Raj walked into his tent; the table had been cleared and the flap lowered. Suzette sat in a folding chair under the single lamp, a snifter of brandy in one hand and a cigarette in the other, with a book open in her lap. Unspeaking, he walked to the sideboy and poured himself a stiff shot of Hillchapel plum brandy, tossing the clear liquid to the back of his throat. He followed it with another, motions as controlled as a machine, then threw the glass out of the tent, listening as it crashed and tinkled in the darkness outside.

"Raj?" Suzette said, closing the book and laying it aside. Some detached portion of his mind noticed the gold-leaf title on the spine: *Gentry, Nobility and Estates of the Southern Counties*.

He walked to her side, moving like one of the compressed-air automatons in the Hall of Audience, sank to his knees and laid his head on her lap.

"Suzette—" he croaked.

"Shhh," she said, stroking his hair.

"What I . . . had to . . ."

"Shhh, my brave one. It'll be all right. Shhh, sleep now."

Ten of the servants were still alive, spiked to the wall like butterflies in a specimen box, when the banner of the 5th Descott went by, twelve hours later.

CHAPTER EIGHT

Crash.
The volley rang out in crisp unison, and the boulder designated as target went pockmarked as seventy or eighty rifle bullets from First Company struck as one. Raj lowered his binoculars with a grim smile, scanning across the rolling plain. Second Company were hauling in out of a gallop five hundred meters ahead of their comrades and sliding to the ground, running for cover.
Crash. Their volley had the same mechanical perfection, and the clump of daggerbrush that was their aiming point disintegrated in a cloud of dust and fragments. The First was already remounted and pounding forward in line abreast, leapfrogging to a new firing line. Raj nodded to the signaller beside him; the man was using a portable heliograph, an affair of mirrors and lenses on a collapsible tripod. He began to click the slatted cover in coded patterns, setting pulses of reflected sunlight to the lip of a gully nearly a thousand meters away. The Captain raised his glasses once more; the erosion slash looked like a thousand others on the rolling plain, deserted, rimmed in saltbush.
Then it flashed and smoked, as Third Company popped their heads above the rim and opened up. *Couldn't see them myself, and I knew they were there*, Raj thought. Fourth and Fifth surged over the rim a moment later, mounted and sabers out. Without pausing to dress ranks or needing to they joined into a blunt wedge and charged, screeching exultantly. Shells burst ahead of them as the two 75s below

Raj's hilltop command post bucked and roared. Grey smoke drifted in clumps across the scrubby plain smelling of brimstone, but the sounds of firing seemed to disappear into that endless waste.

"Not bad at all, Master Sergeant," Raj said.

"Mebbe, ser. Mought wish the new men'd been with ussn longer, gots doubt about how steady they is."

"Well, there's only one way to find out, isn't there?" he replied. "Sound *Regroup and Reform*, trumpeter." He stood in the stirrups and stretched; Horace took that as a sign to lie down, and Raj pulled firmly on the reins.

"Up, you son-of-a-bitch," he said affably. The dog sighed and looked over its shoulder at him, mournful eyes and drooping floppy ears, tongue the size of a washtowel out and jiggling as he panted.

Horace was a premier product of the Hillchapel stud, but his sleek black coat put him at a disadvantage under the merciless southern sun. The peaks of the Oxheads were to their left and north, now; the last week since they crossed the passes had been a steady eastward trudge through the foothills, where great wedge-shaped spurs ran out into the steppe. Easier to put the road further out, from an engineering standpoint, but there was very little point in having a road without water and fodder for the men and beasts that travelled it.

"Water and fodder," Raj remarked aloud as the Battalion formed up behind the colors.

"Messer Captain?" the guide sent out from the County Legate in Komar said, smiling.

He smiles a lot, Raj thought, looking at the rather dashing face, white teeth gleaming in the dark-tanned face against black point-trimmed mustache and beard. The guide wore an odd little cap with a fore-and-aft peak, wound 'round with a snowy white cloth whose end dangled down his neck and could be drawn across the face in a sandstorm. Muzzaf Kerpatik was a sleekly prosperous person, in his long light-brown jellaba and curl-toed boots, a Star medallion around his neck in silver and diamond chips, two amulets dangling from his belt, mother-of-pearl inlays on the scabbard of his dagger and the butt of his pepperpot revolver.

"Not much water or fodder around here," Raj amplified.

The 5th was drawn up in column of march; the command party took its place at the head. He held up a hand and chopped it forward.

"Battalion . . ."

"Company . . ."

"Platoon . . ."

"Dressing by the left . . . walk-march . . . *trot.*" With a jingle of harness and a mass panting of dogs, the Battalion broke into motion, a single great blue-and-dun snake a thousand meters long coiling across the plain like some steel-tipped centipede of war.

Muzzaf nodded, stroking his beard; he was a travelled man, a man of affairs, who had been east to Sandoral, west to Kendrun, and to the capital several times. He looked about, seeing with a northerner's eyes. The southern slopes of the mountains were themselves dry, unlike the dense broadleaf forest of the other slope; open scrub, grass, a few glades of cedar or bottletree higher up. Down here was pasture, verdant enough in the winter rains, but drying out now, the carpets of wildflowers long gone. Already the sheep were being herded up the valleys and into the high meadows, vast bleating herds surrounded by mounted guardians. Several were in view from here; the land was not really flat, it rolled like the frozen waves of the sea, and from a ridgeline like this you could see a score of kilometers.

"Yet there is good trade in wool done here, Messer," he said; his Colony-bred whippet kept pace with the great black wardog easily enough.

Raj looked at the man the legate had sent, frowning slightly as his body adjusted with a lifetime's practice to the up-and-down sway of a dog's travelling pace. This Muzzaf Kerpatik was neither soldier nor bureaucrat, landowner or peasant, nor a shopkeeper or an artisan or laborer . . . "You're a merchant, Citizen Kerpatik?" he said politely.

"Ah, not exactly, Messer Captain," the man said, gesturing widely as all these southerners seemed to do. "That is, I have trading interests, yes. And in manufacturies; then again, shares in mines and the alum pits, and in a property of rents in the city."

Raj made a rapid mental adjustment: "rent" was familiar, at least. "My apologies, Messer," he said.

"Simply 'Citizen' will do. My father was a man of middling rank, and my mother a concubine from the Colony; hence my inheritance was small, and I had my own way to make in the world." Another of those flashing smiles. "I am as we would say here in Komar County, a—"

The word that followed was unfamiliar to Raj: something like "person-of-doing." "That's a dialect term?"

"No, no, common in many cities these days, though I think first in Kendrun. One who risks moneysavings in affairs of profit."

Extraordinary, Raj thought. *Getting rich without inheriting or stealing it*. Odd, and rather unsettling; and if he had so much wealth in cash and goods, why didn't he buy land, the only wealth that was really real?

The Komarite hesitated. "Your pardon, Messer Captain . . . you think, then, that your force will be sufficient to defend Komar County against the Spirit-Deniers?"

Raj looked at him in puzzlement. "Defense is the local garrison's concern," he said. "We're here for offensive action."

Muzzaf paused again, moistening his lips as if considering speech, then shrugged. "As you say, Messer." Oddly intent: "Yet if there is any way I may aid you, however humble . . . Komar is my home, and it has been good to me. A man should pay his debts."

Raj nodded abstractedly. Behind him he could hear the Master Sergeant talking, agreeing, by the sound of it. Then a Company noncom bellowed:

"Sound off, 5th Descotters!"

The Captain grinned; they all knew that one, and it was a good sign after a hard day's work in this heat. Five hundred strong young male voices roared it out:

Oh, we Descoteers have hairy ears—
We goes without our britches
And pops our cocks with jagged rocks,
We're hardy sons of bitches!

Raj laughed aloud, drawing a deep breath of the hot dry air. *I like this country*, he thought. They were angling east of south, now, and the dust column of the 2nd and the transport was visible in the far distance; they rounded a mountain spur, and the valley on the other side was inhabited. The villages were high up along the sides, wherever there was a spring. *Like home*, he thought, *but different*. Patches of cultivation around the houses, growing olives and figs to supplement the grain, mostly, rather than the apples and plums and cherries of his homeland. The architecture had a functional similarity, walls and defensive towers, but these lacked the grimly foursquare build of the County's black-basalt farmhouses and keeps. Descott County's prime exports were plum brandy, fighting men, dog trainers and skilled masons; here they seemed to be content with fieldstone cemented by mud, like giant dactosauroid nests.

We fuck the whores right through their drawers
We do not care for trifles—
We hangs our balls upon the walls
And shoots at 'em with rifles.

I like the people, too, he decided, as they passed a shallow depression in the plain; it had collected enough water to grow a catch-crop of barley, five hectares or so. Women were throwing the stooked grain onto two-wheel oxcarts. They wore vests over their striped robes, sewn with coins and brass bangles and bits of shell, and wide hats to shelter their faces from the sun. He had noticed no woman covered her face in the border country, although many men veiled for comfort; it was for the same reason the borderers made a point of eating pork and drinking wine, and spitting at the name of Mohammed, he supposed. The wars in this strip of land had been long and bitter.

Much joy we reap by diddlin' sheep
In divers nooks and ditches
Nor give we a damn if they be rams
We're hardy sons of bitches!

Not much chance of giving offense, Raj thought. The Descott dialect of the common Sponglish tongue was archaic to outside ears, and the local country folk talked a singsong version larded with Arabic loanwords. The column slowed as the women ran to the edge of the field, holding up leather bottles of water or pieces of dried fruit, giving an ululating cheer to the passing soldiers. Raj swung his hand out, and the order passed down:

"March . . . *walk!*"

The women trotted along beside the dogs, holding up their gifts and refusing offers of payment; the soldiers passed the jugs among themselves, blasphemously happy when they found the water had been cut one-quarter with the strong local wine. A trooper swept a girl up before him one-armed, trying to steal a kiss; she returned it with enthusiasm, then reared back and punched him neatly in the face, hard enough to bloody his nose. He shouted with pain and clapped his hands to it as the girl dropped nimbly down and ran to rejoin her friends; his comrades howled laughter, nearly falling from their saddles.

So did the male kinsfolk of the women who were riding guard for the harvesters. They were men much like those who had been trickling in to volunteer by ones and twos for the past hundred kilometers, drawn by a hatred older than the hills and the smell of loot. *Glad they're taking it in good humor*, Raj decided, saluting as the riders waved. Slight, lean men, whipcord next to the bull muscle of his Descotters; about the same shade of skin, where they were not burned black, which made them rather darker than most in the Civil Government, and they dressed for rough use, in sand-colored doghair robes and headcloths. Some carried buckets of light javelins, a few lances; more had short horn-backed bows or long-barreled flintlock rifles, and nobody seemed to feel dressed without half a dozen knives up to a foot long.

Raj looked upslope to the rock-built villages, and imagined fighting his way into the foothills. Long guns and hairy hawk-faces behind every rock, screaming rushes out of the side gulleys, ambush, rockslide, guerrillas . . . and these people were fanatics, they didn't just hate the Muslim enemy. Apart from Muzzaf he had heard scarcely a person south of the Oxheads who didn't invoke the Star Spirit every second sentence, and every hamlet had a church, usually large, no matter how squalid a flyblown slum the town was.

Raj's hand chopped forward once more, and the 5th rocked into the steady wolf-lope again. The riders who had been guarding the women spurred alongside for a moment, shouting and waving their weapons in the air:

"Aur! Aur! *Despert Staahl!*" Awake the Iron, the local warcry.

"Star Spirit of Man with you, brothers! Kill many! Kill!"

"I'm surprised the Colony finds it pays to raid," he said, as they peeled off back to their charges.

"Hmmm, you might be surprised what a Bedouin will do for a sheep, Messer," Muzzaf said. "Also, there are mines of precious metals and silver in the mountains . . . and," he added with a smile that seemed less assumed than most of his expressions, "you have not yet seen the Vale of Komar."

"Tomorrow," Raj said, glancing up at the moons. *There's something odd about this Muzzaf*, he thought. He gave an impression of always being about to sell you a rug, and that was normal enough, yes. But there was also . . . *as if he can't decide whether to be glad to see us or to run for the hills*, Raj mused.

"Oh, Raj," Suzette whispered. "It's . . . *beautiful*."

They were sitting their dogs on the crest of the ridge, while the long creaking stream of baggage flowed down the slanting cutbacks of the road into the valley. It was . . . *green*, Raj decided. *Spirit of Man of the Stars, I hadn't realized how much you could* miss *green*. In form much like any other foothill outwash cone, but bigger. Canals threaded it, and where they passed there was life. Plots of dark-green sugar cane, waving in ripples like the sea; grain stubble already showing verdant with the next crop; orchards of bushy glossy oranges and lemons . . . And in the center of the valley, rising on a hill, the city: glowing with a white that blazed in the noonday sun, like a heap of cubes of pure sugar, like a set of blocks carved out of snow, the White City of Komar.

"Well," he said to Suzette, "let's go down." *I really shouldn't be snatching time like this*, he reminded himself. Then, savagely: *At least she's not in the carriage with bloody Stanson*. That was a *little* unfair, the 2nd had been in the saddle and doing some field drill these past four or five days . . .

" . . . and here," Muzzaf droned on, "you see the canal extension: wonderful are the works of the Spirit! The new concrete dam, another ten thousand hectares under cultivation, financed by the city and our most benevolent and well-loved Vice-Governor, may the Spirit . . ."

Raj tuned him out for a moment. The civil administration seemed to be moderately efficient, here: not much traffic to be pushed aside, at least. The road was arrow straight, up to East Residence standards. The long-settled part of the Vale was to their right, small holdings intricately cultivated. Tall date palms, with fruit trees beneath; beneath *that* were grain or vegetables, cotton or sugar or grass, with even the goats tethered and hand-fed. The farmers' dwellings were white cubes, sometimes surrounded by flowers; he could see that almost every one had a craft/workshop of some sort attached, men and women weaving cloth or baskets, tanning leather, embroidering, hammering at brass-ware or tinware, turning pots. Everyone waved, and many ran out to cheer. Dainties were handed up; split pomegranates, huge golden-skinned sweet oranges, joints of sugar cane and clay cups of fruit juices.

A girl ran along at his stirrup for a moment, holding up her laden hands. Raj bent to take the grass plate she offered, and the strong brown fingers threw a flower wreath around his neck.

"Dammit," he muttered, watching the grins on the faces of his command group. The plate held fresh dates; dried dates were a one-a-year luxury for gentlefolk back home, expensive even in New Residence. "Dates," he muttered. "We've been eating the bloody things for two weeks, and *I* get dates." Gerrin Staenbridge was peeling an orange, feeding segments to a laughing Foley. M'lewis had a banana, bit into it and made a grimace; da Cruz showed him how to peel it, looking as near to smiling as Raj had ever seen him.

The left side of the road was less festive; the new lands had been laid out in large fields of sugar cane and cotton and indigo, slave-worked. Mounted guards watched field gangs, many in chain hobbles, Colonists by the look of them. He peered closer: one or two were actually *black*, with the wooly hair and flattened features he had heard of. Zanj, or even Azanians, from southwest of the Colonial Gulf. *They don't look glad to see us at all*, Raj thought sardonically.

Muzzaf spoke, responding to his last words. "Yes, Messer; if you have eaten dates in the North, you have eaten our dates . . . See, many of the sugar-mills are run by steam; marvelous is Progress and the works of the Spirit of Man of the Stars. This year, our first steam-powered cotton mill! And there—" he pointed to the northeast of the city, visible now through the thick vegetation "—our railroad!"

Raj looked up with genuine interest, dropping his mental calculation of billeting ratios. Railroads were important, the only means of moving bulk goods cheaply overland, although the need for that was limited. Most people were peasants, after all, and lived from what they grew or made; cities fed from their immediate hinterlands. But a railroad could be very convenient from a military point of view, it was a pity they were so few.

"North from tahe city to the mines," Muzzaf was saying. "Our Vice-Governor, the Exalted Barholm Clerett, upon whom the Spirit of Man shall surely shed Its light, loaned us half the cost. No less than sixty kilometers, finished this year!"

He nodded, impressed; that made it the third-longest in the Civil Government, and the only one south of the Oxheads. Muzzaf bowed low in the saddle.

"It has been an honor to assist you, noble Messer," he said. "But . . ."

They turned the corner into the cleared space any city kept before its walls, here used for low-growing crops, tomatoes and beans and garden truck. Komar's defenses were formidable, even if you could see the buildings on their hill behind—a twenty-meter ditch, and steep turf earthworks before the stone curtain-wall. A hexagonal shape overall, quite modern, with outlying bastions, not one of those high flimsy affairs that rifled guns could batter down in an afternoon. All familiar, there were layout plans and perspective drawings of the fortifications of every city in the Civil Government stored in East Residence, and Raj had gone over them thoroughly. The main gates were open between their fortress-bastions, and a procession was filing out. Litters with the County Legate, officers in dress uniforms, choirs of children in white tunics. A Grand Hierarch ArchSysup of the Church, with acolytes in goldcloth jumpsuits swinging incense censors, bearing a circular computer-core set in gold and silver and lapis lazuli . . .

"Shit," Raj muttered.

"URRA! URRA!"

The line of men and dogs moved with glacial slowness through the narrow twisting streets. Sprays of flowers flew toward the troopers from the crowds that blackened the rooftops and crowded up against the walls, leaned from wrought iron balconies and windows . . . *And pushed in where they bloody don't belong,* Raj thought savagely; they were handing bottles up to the soldiers, as well, and not fruit juice this time, either. Crowd noise was deafening, though not quite loud enough to drown out the sound of an NCO screaming:

"*Next sumbitch takes a bottle I will personal gouge out his eyes and* skullfuck *'im to death!*"

There were priests on every corner, spraying holy water and scented smoke with abandon; voices were calling the blessings of the spirit on the Governor, on the Vice-Governor . . . *and I'll be dipped in shit if somebody wasn't calling a blessing on* Tzetzas, *there's a first*. Somebody else ran out with a pork-roast and tried to feed it to one of the dogs, nearly losing an arm in the process. Renunciate Nuns would be handing out blowjobs, at this rate.

Da Cruz came up on his left. "*What do they think this is, a bunch of groomsmen on their way to a wedding?*" Raj screamed.

"*Wait 'till the 2nd settles in, they'll think* we're *an outing from a girl's school!*" the noncom shrieked back.

They passed what looked like a fancy cathouse, with the whores leaning out of *their* balcony, squeezing their breasts together and shaking them at the troops, with a sign unrolled below: "One Free Trip to Paradise For All Members of the 5th Descott and 2nd Gendarmerie."

Even the Master Sergeant grinned at that. "*It's a first.*" Then he paused. "*Ser, we need to talk.*"

"Companion's briefing after we dismiss," Raj returned. "*Two hours past sunset.*"

" . . . and *anyone*," Raj was saying, from the steps of the Tribunate building; it fronted the only square in the city big enough to address the Battalion, "who abuses billeting privileges will be up on charges. And if I get any complaints from husbands, brothers or fathers, the malefactor will be looking for work as a harem guard south of here." A rolling cheer at that; he looked down on the sea of grinning faces and felt a twist at the base of his stomach. *How many of them will be alive in a month?* he thought. The weight of responsibility descended on his shoulders, heavier than the world.

"All right, boys," he continued, forcing a smile. "Everyone loves us here. Just remember why." He pointed south. "*They* don't love us, and they're not going to be throwing flowers, either." There was a murmur, not displeased but slightly sobered. *Good.* "Enjoy yourselves, but remember we're heading out on Starday next. A day to play, a day to recover and a day to go Enter your sins—" he pointed to the city temple, towering in traceries of glass and stone on the opposite side of the plaza "—in the Terminal booths and wash your grimy souls. Then we earn our pay. Spirit of Man of the Stars pervade you. Up the 5th! Descott Forever!"

"DESCOTT FOREVER!"

"Trumpeter, sound *Dismissed to Quarters.*"

Suzette, Lady Whitehall paused on the steps of the tribunate; the plaza was dimly lit by the glow from the windows above her, and the municipal lanterns set high in brackets on the public buildings roundabout. The chanting of a MainFrame service came from the Temple, and the paving stones were being swept and shoveled by City convict gangs, swept free of bougainvillea and roses, dogshit and fruit rinds and shattered bottles. Lights were coming on all over the city, and she could hear the tinkle of water in fountains, and the plangent sounds of *gittars,* and singing; Komar was still celebrating what it nervously hoped would be deliverance.

Captain Stanson cantered his Alsatian up to the steps, sweeping off his silvered helmet and bowing; there were hyacinths woven in his hair.

"Ah, my dear," he said, kissing her hand. "A lovely evening for the loveliest of ladies. I've found the most enchanting little place, and reserved a table for two."

"I'm sure you and Merta will enjoy it," she replied, with an ironic lift of her eyebrow, gently tugging on her hand.

Stanson's face fell. "But, I mean, I had planned . . ."

"Table for two, bed for three? Very sorry, my dear, but that's *your* particular fantasy." She pulled harder on her hand, slipping the other under her sash to the hard lump of her derringer. It remained there, when he released her fingers. "The Prancing Bitch is offering a free first-time, they'd probably give you a very good discount on that."

"You lying slut!" Amazement struggled with rage. "You . . . you promised— You lying whore!"

"Tsk, tsk, my poor Helmt, all your life at Court and you believed a *promise*? And the word you're looking for, under the circumstances, is 'tease,' not 'whore.'" Suzette watched a baffled curiosity overcome anger, for a moment: *that surprises me*, she thought distantly.

"Why?" he said.

"Well, you see, Helmt, I don't need you any more, that's all."

He jerked the dog's head around and heeled it savagely; with a whining bark, it sprang across the pavement, nearly running down the sweepers. Suzette made a moue and tapped a finger against her lips.

"A mistake, perhaps," she murmured. "But occasional fits of truthfulness are so enjoyable."

"Everyone's here," Gerrin said, as Suzette slipped through the door and seated herself at the foot of the table.

Raj glanced around the table. The Companions had grown to nine, not counting him or his wife: Gerrin Staenbridge and Foley, of course, and the Gruder brothers. Another Lieutenant from Kaltin Gruder's Company, Mekkle Thiddo by name, Raj and he were cousins of a sort and near-neighbors back home; two gentlemen-rankers from Thiddo's platoon, Holdor Tennan and Fitzin Sherrek, younger sons of bonnet-squires who were clients of the Whitehall family.

"M'lewis isn't, ser," da Cruz said. Several of the others winced. Descotters were less class-conscious than most, nobody objected to da Cruz's membership; he came of respectable yeoman stock. The scruffy trooper was something else again, even *gentry* from the Bufford parish district of the County were not well-regarded.

"Probably out picking pockets," Kaltin muttered.

"I hope so," his brother Evrard said: both of them were sensible enough to listen to their noncoms, but a platoon leader was closer to the enlisted men's grapevine. "If he's just drunk . . . well, sober he could talk a Renunciate Nun flat. Drunk he wouldn't know a sow from his sister, and either would do willing or no."

"He's on an errand for me," Raj said, seating himself at the log ebony table. There was a wall fountain behind him, a blaze of colored tile against the stark white marble of the walls—and a useful plashing that made it unlikely anyone listening at a peephole would get much of a quiet conversation. "Now, Companions, we've got a situation here."

"Arserapin' right," da Cruz said. An informal etiquette had already established itself for these meetings, rather different from the one they used when wearing their official hats. "What keyed me, was the way the *townsfolk* were poppin' off t' welcomes us. Especial the Messers, they was sweatin' happy to see us, but commonfolk, too. The *whores* is givin' it away. Only reason fer that I kin see, they're certain-sure the ragheads was comin' over the wall, real soon now, least we didn't stop "em."

"My thoughts exactly," Raj said. *Sweet Spirit, I could use a bath and a neckrub and twenty hours' sleep in a bed.*

Gerrin Staenbridge frowned. "This town's as close to impregnable as any its size can be," he said in a slightly pedantic tone; siegecraft was a hobby of his. "It's only fallen, what, twice—"

"Three times, once in a civil war," Foley interjected.

"*Thank* you, Barton," Gerrin said. "To continue, there's over fifty fixed pieces on the walls—muzzle loaders, but good ones—and a garrison of, what, three battalions of regular infantry." There were a few snorts at that. The foot soldiers of the Civil Government were conscripted from the peons of the central Counties around East Residence, and even the barbarian mercenaries who made up a third of the army ranked higher. "I know, I know, but they *are* trained soldiers with Armory guns. If all they have to do is sit in bunkers and fire out the slits at the ragheads as they run up, well, really now."

At least they didn't send them down here with flintlocks, Raj thought, tapping at his pad with a graphite stick. Not uncommon, in the interior Counties; the trade guns made for export to the savages were much cheaper. A knock sounded; Evrard sprang up to open it with his hand on his pistol, and Antin M'lewis stepped through. He slid into a seat down the table, grinning through his bad teeth and looking somehow furtive even now. *It's amazing. When he's trying to cheat somebody, butter wouldn't melt in his mouth. It's when he relaxes you put your hand on your valuables.*

Kaltin took up the argument. "And even if the garrison isn't worth much, there's forty thousand people within the walls; you saw the way it's built." A maze of laneways, twisting and turning between blank stone walls. "This is a rich city, too, with a secure water supply. Holy Avatars of the Spirit—"

Raj forced himself not to wince; technically, that term included *him*, now. *I am not worthy!* something cried within himself. He forced it down, like the tiredness and the sore butt that came of too long in the saddle.

"—you'd need twenty thousand men and a siege train to take this place."

"M'lewis?" Raj said. "What did you find?"

"Best dam' party I ever missed on m'own, Messers," he said. "Couldn't pay fer booze 'r cooze if yer wanted to.... Beggin' yer pardon, Lady. Anyways, I finds out what yer wanted."

Raj nodded. "I got suspicious when I saw a beggar saluting us from an alleyway," he said dryly. "More remarkable than girls with flowers, if less sightly."

"Bought 'im a drink, ser. Well, passed on one I's given, loik. Private in the 23rd Foot; they's here, with t'81st Rifles an' the Kelden County Foot."

"Wait a minute," Kaltin said. "Those aren't the units that were supposed to be here!"

"Ay-up. Moved in last month, ser. Ain't gots they land grants settled yet, either. Sellin' they uniforms, beggin', workin' at that'ere cotton mill, which is worse to my way a—

Another knock at the door. The Companions exchanged glances, and Kaltin and his brother bracketed the entranceway. Foley reached over his shoulder for the shotgun in its leather scabbard and drew it, clicking the breach open for a second and snapping it shut, then laying the weapon in his lap under the table.

Raj was lighting a cigarette as Muzzaf Kirpatik walked through the opened door and threw himself on his knees. That startled the Gruder brothers, but not so much that they did not seat the muzzles of their revolvers in his ears and half-carry him forward to their commander's end of the table. Hands plucked his weapons away as they moved, frisking him thoroughly. The pepperpot revolver, two derringers, a long knife from one boot, a stiletto punch-dagger down the collar of his robe . . . *Indeed, a man of affairs*, Raj thought.

"Forgive me, lord," the local said brokenly; the singsong southern accent was more noticeable, and he tried to bend his head to the marble tiles of the floor.

Raj blew smoke. "It might be easier if I knew for what," he said.

"I have betrayed you—I have betrayed the Spirit of Man of the Stars, may I be damned to . . . well, forgiven—I have betrayed the Civil Government."

Kaltin Gruder thumbed back the hammer of his revolver. "Spying for the ragheads?" he said, in a voice as metallic as that sound.

"No, no! The Tribune arranged with . . ." a visible internal struggle " . . . with authorities in East Residence, I think the Chancellor . . ."

"*Tzetzas*," the Companions chorused.

"Watch your language," Suzette observed.

" . . . to transfer the garrison. It is the land grants, you see, until title is cleared the rents are still collected but the soldiers get nothing, nothing!"

Raj nodded sickly. There was never enough money in the central government Fisc to pay the foot soldiers directly, not and keep the more important cavalry units supplied . . . not to mention the mercenaries from outside the Civil Government, who wanted good hard cash in sound coin, no bank drafts please. Revenue melted on the way from the Counties to the capital, and on the way back out for disbursements; instead, the infantrymen were each assigned a farm. Worked by tenants, so that they had time to drill, although many ended up spending more time helping in the fields than marching. If the unit was transferred, the soldiers were supposed to be settled into equivalent holdings immediately. Even when it worked the way it was supposed to morale dropped hideously every time an infantry regiment moved.

Kaltin was nodding thoughtfully. "You know, one of the infantry Captains was wearing a uniform coat tailored from Azanian *torofib*." That was a fiber spun to line its nests by a burrowing pseudoinsect that lived in the savannahs inland from the Zanj coast. "The real thing. He didn't buy *that* on an infantry officer's pay. I couldn't afford it, myself." And the Gruder estates pastured ten thousand head of pedigreed Angoras.

"But . . ." Evrard burst out, "that's . . . that's *despicable!*" The others looked at him pityingly; he had been out from Descott less than a year.

Gerrin shrugged. "That's Tzetzas," he amplified.

Muzzaf nodded, tears streaking his face. "The Legate suggested it, but he's the Chancellor's appointee. That was before Tewfik moved, nobody thought there would be more than raids on the outlying settlements."

"What was your share?"

"I . . . acted as agent, to collect the rents. Five percent to me; out of . . . three thousand silver FedCreds. A quarter to the officers, and the rest to the Legate, I don't know how he split that with the Chancellor." Brokenly: "My lord, I did not know . . . it seemed that all the others were doing it, and they said Komar would still be safe. The Spirit of Man and of the Stars and the Civil Government have been good to me, my lord: now I see you are Their true servant. I have served a corrupt man in corruption—let me serve you in honesty!"

"*Merida*," Raj said quietly. *Shit.* "So much for our secure base. How many actual troops are there in this town?"

He looked at Muzzaf: a man of mixed blood, probably bitterly determined to make his loyalty unquestioned, as many such were. Who could blame him, for following the lead the Legate and Chancellor gave? An able man as well, invaluable if his remorse was lasting and not a mere fit . . .

"Ahh, there is the Legate's personal guard, mercenaries from Asaura County." A few snorts; that was in the mountains north and east of the plateau-and-canyon country of

Descott, part of the Civil Government only by courtesy. The County Legate of Descott was chosen by the area's gentry, in practice if not theory; the County Legate of Asaura was appointed in East Residence and stayed there, if he had any sense. Even Descotters considered Asaurans backward, but they were much in demand as elite infantry.

"Well, good enough fighters, except that when they're drunk, which is usually, they cut every throat in sight and rape the corpses," Mekkle Thiddo said. "How many of them?"

"About a hundred. Then, there is the town militia, but they are for manning the guns, only. And one of the infantry Captains, he has been maintaining two hundred of his men at his own expense, I think that the others forced him to go along with the billeting scheme by threats. And perhaps as many again, among the retainers of the Messers in town, but they are not organized."

"Not nearly enough to hold the walls," Raj said. Heads turned toward him, eyes full of unspoken questions. And **observe.**

—he was looking through his own viewpoint, seeing the hands on the table before him move as they would when he shrugged.

"Well," he said/might say, "there's nothing we can do about it but pray; the Legate's in charge here. We'll just have to be sure we don't *need* a secure base, let the *enemy* worry about that—"

POM-POM-POM—the quickfirer shells slashed into the mass of screaming humans and animals that jammed the gates of Komar. It was dark, lit only by the moons and the fires that were turning the buildings of the White City crimson and black. White-hot metal slashed dogs and oxen and men into things that fell twitching, to be trampled underfoot; others were pushed off the edge of the bridge, into a moat whose bottom bristled with angle-iron stakes.

Raj was halfway through the gates himself, blood from a scalp wound coating one side of his face in a glistening sheet. "Rally!" he shouted, beating at fugitives with the flat of his saber, forms in the blue of the 5th and the white jackets of the 2nd Gendarmerie, or the dun robes of peasants. The noise overrode everything he could say; everything but the triumphant roar of the Colonist troops as they scrambled down into the moat on ropes and raised the scaling ladders against the inner side. A cannon fired from the ramparts, another, loads of grapeshot cutting paths of moaning, twitching meat through the bright-clad ranks. But they were too few, and only the odd rifle cast its muzzle flame beside them.

"*Ul-ul-ul-Allahuu Akbar!*" The shrieks were like files on stone, thousandfold, as the soldiers of Islam poured over the walls in a flood, a flood whose surf shone in the firelight with eyes and teeth and the edges of their scimitars.

A jump; morning, that would have been bright if the smoke had not lain so heavy. A pile of bodies was growing in the center of the plaza before the Tribune's palace; Colonist infantry were pitching new loads onto the growing heap. One was Barton Foley, his eyes wide and a gaping cut from ear to ear that nearly reached the backbone. The foot soldier at his shoulders giggled, calling attention to it:

"Hai, this one has had the *hallal*, brothers!" he said, giggling. The ritual throat cutting which the Shari'ah, the Road to a Watering Place, prescribed for animals slaughtered for meat. "Would any feast on this tender dainty?"

A mounted officer leaned over and lashed a nine-thonged whip on the soldier's back, bringing a yelp of pain.

"Silence, you blasphemous son of ten Berber pigs and a syphilitic whore!" he shouted. There was a huge crash from the temple across the plaza, as the great silver starburst was thrown down and shattered its way through the roof to a chorus of jeers. The officer looked up with a chill satisfaction, then down at survivors of the 5th lined up against the palace; two of them supported a half-fainting Raj, with bandages swathed around his head.

"You *kaphar* dogs have seen," the officer said, waving his lash over the burning city, "that there is no strength in *shirk*, idolatry. Indeed there is no God but God. Which of you will renounce your idols and embrace the Faith?" Glares and silence. "As God wills. These are strong men, they will work well in the mines—wait," he continued, as the soldiers began to prod them away. "That one." He pointed at Suzette. "She will be comely, once she puts some flesh on her bones. Cover her face from the sight of men and take her to my quarters."

observe:

—he was looking through his own viewpoint, seeing the hands on the table before him move as they would when he shrugged.

"Well, we'll just have to try and pry the supplies for the infantry loose," he said.

A blur, and he was watching a pouting bureaucrat stamp his seal on a document.

"You could have done this *last* week," Raj said, snatching it up.

The civil servant was about to speak when the door swung open, and an orderly leaned in with a casual salute.

"Beggin' yer parden, ser, an' the officer of the day requests yer presence. Raghead columns approachin'."

Enough, Raj thought: Center's holograms faded. "We've got to do something, and do it *fast*," he said, tight-lipped. "What was the name of that infantry officer, the one who's paying his men out of pocket?"

"Messer Captain Jorg Menyez," Muzzaf said, drying his eyes with the back of his hand, then pulling a handkerchief from one sleeve to blow his nose.

"I know the family," Raj said. Landowners up in Kelden County, by the straits of the same name, the narrow waters between the Midworld and Pierson's Seas. Quite well-to-do, you saw their wine sold by name in East Residence, and they had . . . oh, yes, marble quarries, too. "What's he doing in an infantry outfit in the bundu? Never mind; Mekkle, if you'd be so good, look him up and have him come by my quarters tomorrow at, hmmm, 1400 hours, that should give us enough time." He planted his fists on the table and rose. "Now, here's how we're going to implement a little matter of administrative reform. At reveille, Gerrin will—"

"This is utterly irregular!"

The Vice-Assistant Legate of Komar was a local man, but dressed in the height of East Residence fashion. The corridor

Raj and Staenbridge and Foley had tramped down was lined with open rooms, clerks sitting cross-legged at low desks and chattering as they read and annoted reports and letters; they had fallen nervously silent as the Descotters tramped through, boots ringing on the pebble-surfaced concrete. This office was rather different, walled in hand-painted tiles; the outer wall was stone fretwork laced with a flowering jasmine vine, dew-spangled with the cooling water that flowed down from jets above the ceiling. A secretary huddled wide-eyed on a bronze-legged couch in one corner of the room, almost as ornamental as the vine in her tight red dress. The bureaucrat's desk was at chair-height, northern style, a slab of porphyry almost empty save for neatly arranged pens and a lithograph of the Governor, Vice-Governor, and Chancellor in court robes.

"If you read carefully," Raj said, plucking the parchment sheet out of the man's hands, "it authorizes me to levy contributions and assert the authority of the Civil Government by any means necessary." In gold, vermilion, and silver ink, complete with six ribboned seals, starting with the Vice-Governor's and running down through the Chancellor to the Minister of War and the Master of Soldiers, Residence Area. "And it enjoins all civil authorities to cooperate."

"But—that is for operations over the border!" The Civil Government recognized no other state on Earth—

bellevue, Center interjected in Raj's inner ear.

—on Earth as sovereign; all other territories were in rebellion.

"Oh?" Raj said, unrolling the document and giving it a quick scan. "Not that I can see; not a mention of borders in here; it just specifies 'Komar and area.' This is Komar; so I'll thank you to sign that order for immediate transfer of title on the land grants, if you please. Plus arrears of rent, to be met out of the County treasury."

"Out of the question," the bureaucrat began, then faded into silence as Raj turned his back and braced a steel-toed boot against the door, wedging it shut.

Foley reached over his shoulder and drew the shotgun. He swallowed, visibly nervous, but even a man as unacquainted with first-hand violence as the plump Vice-Assistant did not doubt his willingness to use it. If anything, the slight tremor in the twin muzzles made it more terrifying still.

Staenbridge came up behind the civil servant and pushed him back into the chair with a thump. "You're right-handed, aren't you, Citizen?" he asked politely.

"Yyyyes," the Vice-Assistant stuttered.

"Good, wouldn't want to leave you unable to sign," the Descotter continued cheerfully, and grabbed his left wrist. There was no struggle—or rather the bureaucrat struggled; Staenbridge laid the hand on the smooth stone of the desk without noticeable delay. Whistling between his teeth he drew his pistol with his right hand, flipped it around to grip by the barrel, and brought it down in a blurring arc that ended on the pudgy clenched fist.

The sound of impact was like a bundle of sticks breaking, combined with the thump of bread dough on a kneading board. The Vice-Assistant screamed in antiphonal chorus with his secretary, then slumped out of his chair, sprawling. The Companion's grip on his wrist pinned the limb to the surface of the desk as effectively as an iron staple would have, however, so he could not slump all the way to the floor. His face had gone grey-brown and saliva dribbled from the corner of his mouth to match the tear streaks around his eyes. Then he spasmed and whinnied as Staenbridge shifted a thumb and ground it into the soft mush of shattered small bones at the center of his hand.

The Companion bent low, tapping the other man's nose sharply with the pistol butt to attract his attention. "Now, *do* sign the papers, there's a good little capon," he said. "Or shall I continue?" The thumb brushed across the wound once more, lightly.

"It's out of the question," the Director of Municipal Supply said, glaring at the Gruder brothers; their blocky shoulders filled the space in front of his desk. "Two thousand infantry tunics and trousers, shoes, belts, cartridge cases . . . out of the question! I have their rifles in store, for reissue *when* the land grants are cleared and they resume regular duties, but this—!" he riffled at the request form. "Ridiculous!"

"The land grants are bein' taken care of right now," Evrard said patiently. Someone who knew him well would have realized how dangerous the trace of brogue was. "And this is Komar? Got cotton mills, dyeworks, tailors, tanners, cobblers? Export cloth and boots? Just append an authorization for rush contracts, down there at the bottom."

"Get out of my— Here, you man, what do you think you're doing?" he said, looking sharply around the blocky forms of the Gruder brothers.

Antin M'lewis looked up and grinned, snaggled brown teeth and cold brown eyes. "Stealin'," he said, wrapping the silver paperknife in a dirty handkerchief and tucking it into one of the patch pockets of his jacket. "Gives us summat in common, loik, eh?" The office walls were lined with shelves for knickknacks; he picked up a glass bubble with a miniature house inside, laughing like a child as he shook it to produce a tiny snowstorm inside, then dropped it in beside the knife.

The Director's eyes bulged, and his face turned purple, but the bellow died in his throat as Evrard's saber came out with a smooth *sshhunng* sound. The tip settled under his nose, touching just enough to dimple the skin of his upper lip.

"Evrard," Kaltin said. He touched a statue of a dancing girl, only six inches high but vibrant with life; it was of honey-toned spicewood, and he rubbed his fingertips on it before holding them under his brother's nose. "Excellent taste, don't you think?"

"Mmmm. Smells almost as nice as a real girl," Evrard said.

"But these," Kaltin continued, indicating a set of blown-glass animal figurines, "are definitely common." He began picking them up and dropping them over his shoulder, one tinkling crash after another.

"Damn you all to the Outer Dark, crash your cores and burn, demons eat your *eyes*," the Director hissed. There were beads of sweat on his forehead and upper lip. "You can't intimidate me this way!"

"Oh? How disappointing," Evrard said, wiping the tip of his sword on his sleeve and sheathing it. "M'lewis, what do you think we should do, then?"

"Dunno, ser," the trooper said, frowning. He brightened. "Throw 'im out the window, ser?"

They pounced, lifting the writhing, yelling form between them. "One—" The windows were glazed, with the outer wooden shutters latched against the sun "Two—

"*Heave!*"

The scream was cut off by a brittle crash and the crunch of breaking wood. The Director bounced back into the room; there were half a dozen superficial cuts on his face, and he spat out a tooth as he tried to climb to his hands and knees. The Descotters came around the desk and the Gruders seized him by ankles and belt; then they used his head and shoulders as a battering ram, to clear what was left of the windows and shutters out of the way. His bloodied hands scrabbled frantically at the frame, careless of the spikes of glass, before the inexorable pressure left him dangling head-down, supported only by their one-handed grips on his ankles. The struggles ceased then, as he realized that kicking free would send him fifteen feet straight down onto the cobbles.

M'lewis came up and pulled off one of his shoes. "Wouldn't fit nohow," he said regretfully, standing on one leg while he measured it against his own sole. The shoe went out the window, followed by the other and the red-and-blue checked socks; M'lewis reached behind his back and drew the skinning knife, held the hilt in his teeth while he rolled up his sleeves. "Tum-te-*tum*," he hummed, testing the edge by shaving a patch of hair from his corded forearm. "Well now, sers, m'father always said, you want a man to accommodate yer, skin 'im from the feets *up*. Er down, as we has heres."

"*Keep him away from me!*" the Director squealed, kicking again as the trooper drew a line of thin red down the bottom of one of his feet. "*I'll sign!*"

"I knew you would," Kaltin said.

"As per orders," Mekkle Thiddo said, dropping the documents on the table in front of Raj; the Companions were meeting in the same room as they had the day before. They rustled against the stack of papers already there, as the Companion sucked on a skinned knuckle and then went to rinse the hand in the fountain.

"Three months' rations for the full complement. No killing, but mine's going to be eatin' real careful."

Raj nodded briskly. *And the men these penpushers depend on for their lives won't be begging in the streets*, he thought with bleak satisfaction. "Is that infantry Captain here yet?" he asked. *And what sort of a Menyez is he, to end up commanding an infantry Battalion?*

Captain Jorg Menyez was a tall man, with much the same broad-shouldered, narrow-hipped build as the cavalryman he faced; Raj remembered suddenly that his maternal grandmother had been from the Kelden Straits country. There was little resemblance otherwise; Menyez was in his thirties, a pale-eyed, straight-nosed man with russet brown hair, sun-faded and thinning on top. The pale eyes were red-rimmed now, watering behind the wire-rimmed spectacles; he sneezed into his handkerchief and cleared his throat repeatedly as he scanned the documents. His lips thinned as he looked up:

"Thank you," he said. "For the men's sake. I tried, but—" A shrug, that turned into a grab for the handkerchief. "*Chooo*! What will Colonel Dyaz say?"

"Colonel . . . Messer Dyaz has taken indefinite leave of absence for reasons of health, Messer Acting Colonel," Raj said, in the same gun metal flat tone.

Menyez sat silent except for his wheezing. "Well." Another pause. "It must be . . . satisfying, to have such power."

"No it isn't!" Raj roared suddenly. "It isn't satisfying *at all* to have to act like a mountain bandit to get people to do their fucking *jobs*. It isn't satisfying that the agents of the Civil Government won't perform without a fucking *pistol* up their nose! But it's better than having this city undefended." He nodded to the documents in Menyez's hands. "Now you've got the tools, at least."

Menyez straightened, saluting crisply, respect in his voice along with the unwilling gratitude of a man who has been given a long-denied due. "Well, I'd better get out there and *do* my job, then." He strode briskly from the room.

"I just realized something," Gerrin Staenbridge said suddenly. "Why he's in the infantry." The others glanced over at him. "The poor luckless bastard's *allergic to dogs*."

Suzette chewed the end of her pen; the others had left quickly, overdue for the work of preparing their own departure. She stretched, alone with the sound of falling water and the lingering odors of gun oil and leather, dogs and male sweat that went with soldiers. She thought, dipped the steel nib of the pen in the inkwell of her portable writing desk-cum-briefcase, and continued the letter:

> ... *and I'm sure your husband will be as interested as mine in how Tzetzas' appointee prepared the defenses of Komar, where the Cleretts have so many investments.*

Was that a little heavy-handed? No. *Unfair*, yes; nobody had *expected* Komar to become a theater of war anytime soon. If he had, the Legate would not have allowed the defenses of his own home to become *quite* so run down, though it was amazing what men would do with the prospect of short-term gains before their faces.

Tzetzas had gambled and lost, that was all. Luck was good, or bad: bad, for example, when the child-prostitute one brutalized at age twelve became the mistress and then the wife of an up-and-coming Gubernatorial relative named Barholm Clerett . . . Coming up from the underclass meant spending long years when assaulting bureaucrats was an unattainable dream. Anne would thoroughly enjoy the description of Raj's tactics, more than the men who had carried them out and *far* more than the man who had ordered them.

You are too sweet for this Fallen world, my angel, Suzette thought with a sigh. Best not to over-elaborate, let Anne think up her own political tactics. Her pen scritched:

Your loving friend—

And *only* friend, I'm afraid, she thought,

—Suzette, Lady Whitehall.

She picked up the bell and rang once. The door opened and a small nondescript man in border County herdsman's robes padded in, bowing low.

"Here, Abdullah," Suzette said, handing over the sealed message. "To Lady Clerett, and none other. Into her own hands, not those of a servant."

"Your command, my Lady," the man said; he bowed again, touching the letter to forehead, lips, and heart. "It shall be one week, or ten days if Allah is unkind."

"And watch that!" Suzette added sharply. "Here, that could get you stoned."

The full lips quirked. "Do not worry, my Lady Whitehall," he said quietly. "Those Sunni dogs over the line would be even quicker with the rocks; I have passed for a borderer before." Druze were scarce, these days, and their weird subset of Islam had always allowed a politic lie in the face of persecution. More gravely, "For you, who saved my family from slavery, my life is always ready to stand forfeit." A grin. "And you pay well, besides!"

"Peace be with you, Abdullah. Go."

"I go, Lady. And upon you, peace."

CHAPTER NINE

The first orange rays of the sun were streaking the plain behind Raj's back, throwing shadow over the oasis of El Djem and the fortified hamlet at its center. Left and right the line of the escarpment stretched into black shadow, streaked with touches of blue and ochre as the rock began to catch the light; the high steppe was behind them, the low desert of *erg* in front. Sand leaked over the caprock of the basin; the water came from the edge below, where the limestone of the hills rested on granite and the water table was shallow enough for wells and wind-pumps or artesian springs. The air was still, a little chilly from the desert night, with a slight green smell from the fields.

Raj raised his binoculars. El Djem was built on a mound of earth two meters high, surrounded by a wall of date palm trunks twice as tall again, bound with ancient iron-hard rawhide and plastered with mud. The minarets of a mosque stood stark and white against the paling stars, one cutting across the yellow circle of Maxiluna. More to the point, so did a heliograph tower built into the stockade... and the success of this raid depended on how much damage the two battalions could do before substantial Colonist forces came up.

Three figures ghosted in; M'lewis, Muzzaf, and one of the fifty or so border irregulars who had joined the 5th. *And none stuck with the 2nd*, Raj thought with satisfaction. Thank the Spirit of Man of the Stars that Stanson and his crowd were a hundred kilometers east at Ksar Bougib; the two forces were to work towards each other. It was bad enough being responsible for his *own* fuckups.

"Went loik a charm, ser," M'lewis said. "Blastin' powder in place."

He nodded thanks to Muzzaf, who had procured that and a number of other useful items for the 5th. And whose trader's knowledge of this side of the border had been invaluable. Komar was unhealthy for him, right now, but it was his own inner demons that had brought him on the raid, rather than travelling west to his kin in Kendrun along with his family and movable wealth. The trooper and the Komarite left as quietly as they had arrived.

The borderman irregular remained for a moment and laughed softly, looking down on the oasis with much the same expression as a housewife standing in her chickenyard and picking out a roasting pullet. "These fellahin are sheep, lord," he said. "Not like the Bedouin. We cannot raid so far as this on our own, it is a great pity." His smile grew broader. "We heard their muzzein squealing, 'Prayer is better than sleep.' Soon they will squeal a different song."

"There hasn't been a Civil Government raid here in over twenty years," Muzzaf said, returning with two dogs. "And *that* was a failure." He would be riding with the irregulars. They got on surprisingly well with the man from Komar city, and they had been very useful as well. Although their high motivation had its drawbacks, this was a grudge fight for them.

"Positions, then," Raj said. He touched his amulet, eyes closed for a moment and lips moving silently in prayer. *Oh Spirit of Man of the Stars, you know how busy I must be this day. Do not forget me, even if I forget you.* Then he moved crouching to the long black shape of Horace, kneeled into the prone dog's saddle. The barrel-sized muzzle swung back toward him, and a tongue like a wet towel stropped across his leg. "Ready, boy," he whispered. Birds sang in the fruit trees of the oasis, and dactosauroids hissed.

The gates of El Djem swung open; there were sheds and barns aplenty among the palm-groves and fields, but no houses. However slack the hamlet had grown, it had been founded as a defensive outpost and some traditions remained. The laborers crowded through in clumps and straggling trickles, bearded men in long nightshirt-like garments, hoes and spades and pruning hooks over their shoulders. Raj tensed his knees, and Horace rose smoothly from his crouch. All around him there was a rustle and click as three hundred others did likewise; the other two companies were downslope a hundred meters, to provide a base-of-fire. There was a sound like a hundred iron gearwheels turning in a watermill, the sound of massed wardogs growling.

"And—" Raj muttered to himself. Timing was everything, the difference between a cheap victory and a bloody rat fight through the packed maze, against men who lived in it and were defending their own homes and families.

Whunk. The explosion of the twenty-kilo charge of blasting powder was massive but the noise was muffled, because the men who had set it had buried it a meter deep in the base of the wall. From here, Raj could see the huge spurt of dust and stones; the top of the heliograph tower quivered, swayed, lurched, then toppled outward with an initial slowness that was almost stately. A thrashing stick figure arched out from the signalling platform, to strike the ground and bounce just before the last chunks of mud and wood settled in a haze of powdered adobe. There was a solid knot of men in the gate, now, and a fan spreading out into the field beyond. About a thousand, probably most of the adult males in El Djem; they had stopped, chattering among themselves and craning to see what had happened around the circular stockade from the gate. They were theoretically soldiers, a land grant militia, possibly even fairly effective in a fixed defensive position if given time to mobilize and arm.

Which time he had no slightest intention of granting.

From the slope below Raj's position the two hundred troopers of Second and Third Companies rose and began to pour volleys into the crowd; eight hundred meters range, and Armory rifles were efficient mankillers at that distance. They were deployed in two lines, one kneeling and one standing erect, firing by half-platoons; the sound was like an almost continuous series of single gunshots, but magnified twelvefold. BAM and the long barrels of the rear rank swung down in unison, as the troopers reloaded. The front-rank weapons rose, precise as a ballet, or the shuttle of a loom. BAM. There was light enough now to tell a white thread from a black, the traditional test, but still sufficiently dim that the orange-red muzzle flashes of the rifles were long stabs of fire, hot combs teeth-on to the target. *BAM-BAM-BAM-BAM.*

Raj drew his pistol as the first volley slapped and echoed across the basin, flipped it into his left hand and drew the saber. A long slither and rasp sounded behind him as three companies of cavalry did likewise.

"Trumpeter, sound charge!"

"*UP AND AT 'EM!*"

The carnage in the gateway would have been sickening, if time or inclination had allowed such luxuries. The packed dirt of the lane between the two log-and-mud blockhouses was carpeted with bodies and turning to slimy mud with blood and body fluids. The noise that bounced back and forth between the straight confines of the gateway was stunning, the howling of men and dogs, screaming of the wounded and dying as they were pulped into a paste of dirt and flesh. Past the blockhouses the lane made a half-turn and there were more of the Colonists still on their feet; dazed, mostly, their bodies spattered with the blood of the men who had been a few paces ahead of them. Raj saw their faces go slack with new fear for an instant, before the sabers of the 5th and the teeth of its dogs were upon them.

A dozen or so of the survivors had retained enough presence of mind to try and shut the gates; futile, most of the troopers had split off from First Company and were scaling the palisade from the saddle around its whole circumference . . . but it was an improvement on standing and waiting to be killed, he supposed. Horace and three other mounts reared their forepaws against the iron-sheathed wood, and Raj felt a jar that ran all the way up his spine to whipcrack his neck and make his teeth meet with a clack. The effect on the twin leaves of the gates was to turn them into giant flyswatters that hammered back against the buildings on either side with a thud that shook the ground beneath his feet. They rebounded enough to let the remains of the men behind them drop.

"*Keep moving!*" Raj shouted, using the opportunity to pull Horace up.

The words were lost in the overwhelming roar of battle-maddened dogs in the narrow way, but the gesture with the sword might do some good. Speed and impact were the weapons here; they had to overwhelm all resistance before the locals could organize . . .

The flood of First Company poured by, riding knee to knee, then slowed to a trickle. Shots were crackling further into the alley-maze of the town; it was all mud brick, with narrow windows and jutting rafter-logs, some of the tenements four stories high. Raj could see figures in 5th Descott blue swarming on the firing platform of the palisade, some kneeling to sweep snipers off the roofs, others swarming down the ladders into El Djem. A quick glance out the gate showed the reserve rounding up the few hundred laborers who had managed to scatter into the oasis, advancing on foot at the run, and—

Horace's jumping wheel might have unseated his rider, if a lifetime's reflex had not adjusted Raj's muscle before his conscious mind was aware of the dog's movement. Two men had been close enough to the hinge of the gate to avoid being crushed, and they ignored the false promise of the open gate to attack Raj. He fired four times, and the one with the pitchfork spun and fell with a bullet in his thigh. That had been a bad choice, because the other had a pruning hook, a half-meter of steel like a giant straight-razor on a head-high pole. Also he was younger, and looked determined . . .

The dog whipped his head back at the man's first swing; the Colonist reversed the polearm and thrust at Raj's face. He caught it on the blade of his saber and let it run down the steel to ring against the basket hiltguard, used that to immobilize it for a second. The shaft of the pruning hook even provided an aiming point as he trained the pistol at the Colonist's center of mass. A bullet went past Raj's ear with a flat *whak*, and the whole side of his face crawled as if the skin was trying to suck itself in. *No time for it.* The young man froze, white showing all around his eyes as the Descotter's finger tightened on the trigger.

Snak. The hammer fell on a defective round, but Horace's teeth closed on the burrwood shaft, splintering it like a straw caught in a doorjamb. The villager had time for one scream as the horrible fangs closed again, on his face. Well-trained, the dog dropped the corpse and spun again in a circle smaller than his own length, ears almost straight as his nose pointed toward the sound of a rifle action working. The man on the roof above was wearing a robe and *ha' aik*, and armed with a light repeating-carbine; he was only ten meters away, taking careful aim from one knee. Raj seemed to be imprisoned in honey, moving in dreamlike slowness. A hot-chill flash ran across his skin, as the body's refusal to believe in death met the mind's knowledge that there was no way to dodge a bullet in the time available. All the universe vanished, outside the enormous circle of the muzzle.

The lariat that settled around the sniper's shoulders was almost as much a surprise to Raj as it was to the sniper; his brain had screened out peripheral vision. The trooper galloping his dog down the lane to the gate already had the rope snubbed to the pommel of his saddle; ten meters before he reached the Captain the braided leather cord went bar-tight and the Colonist shot off the roof as if launched by a catapult. He landed in the street with a dull thud that cut his shout of rage off knife-sharp, and dragged fast enough that he rolled to the feet of the two dogs when the trooper reined in.

"Nice work, Companion," Raj said, conscious of breathing once again; an impressive display, even though the lariat was a standard working tool back in Descott County.

"I was a *vakaro* for a while, sir," Corporal Holdor Tennan said. "With an outfit rounding up wild cattle . . . Senior Lieutenant Staenbridge's compliments, and they've secured the mosque."

There were shouts outside the gate, and Kaltin Gruder jogged through at the head of a column of dismounted troopers with fixed bayonets. Raj held up a hand as he began to speak, turned to the other Companion: "My congratulations, and he's to hold in position, stationing marksmen on the minarets and the roof of the Caid's mansion. Kaltin," he continued, turning to the man standing at his stirrup. The troopers were fanning out down the street, scanning windows and rooftops. "Ready?"

A brisk nod; even after a week's march through the desert

the elder Gruder had kept a clean tunic for the attack. He had even *shaved*, which was devotion, if you liked.

"All the ones who got out are secured, Raj," he said. "Put 'em in a livestock pen, trussed up. Two-twenty, about. No casualties."

"Well. You and Thiddo fan out—" He made an encompassing gesture "—and start doing a house-to-house; First and Fifth already have blocking forces at the intersections and fire teams on the palisade. Quick and dirty; spike anyone who gives you trouble. Separate the men out, move the commoners out to that pen. Women, children, and anyone who looks important into the center of town, we'll use the mosque to contain them. And keep the troops in hand."

"Won't be able to much longer, Raj," he warned.

The soldiers looked alert enough, their fingers on their triggers and eyes moving restlessly, but many of them were grinning. With the primal exultation of having come through an action alive, and with anticipation of the rarest pleasure of a soldier's life, the sack of an undamaged town. Two pounced on the groaning sniper and began frisking him for weapons, tying his hands behind his back; he shrieked as they wrenched at a dislocated shoulder, but it seemed to bring him back to consciousness. The trooper popped it back into place with rough efficiency.

"Off wit' yer, Mohammed," he said, pushing the prisoner toward the gate. "Any messages to yer wife? I'll be seein' 'er before you does!" Barking laughter. "Milio, put 'im in the pen."

Kaltin indicated the byplay with a jerk of his head. "Not much longer at all."

"Well, we'll just have to do it quickly, then, won't we?"

"—and that concludes this phase of the operation, except for finding the Caid. Where is the Caid?" Raj asked in frustration, lighting a cigarette. It had been the sort of action soldiers dreamed of in barracks, a rich town taken with negligible loss, but somehow his teeth were on edge.

The command group was meeting in the loggia of the mansion that had been owned by the Caid, the headman, of El Djem; a narrow, irregular cobbled triangle fronted it, with the mosque on one side and high-walled houses on the other. The Caid's was slightly different, with a sheltered verandah where he could address public meetings, give impromptu judgment, and right now the shade was welcome as the temperature built to its brain-frying noonday maximum. A rather informal type of governance, but this had not been a large town, no more than five thousand or so. It would have been convenient to have the chief administrator on hand for interrogation, but not essential.

"Probably hiding in a basement," Muzzaf said. The Komarite looked as tired as any of them, but more relaxed than he had been since they left the White City. "In any case, the Battalion has done well this day."

Raj nodded. Ten dead, which was derisory for a five-company action . . . except to the ten, of course, for whom it was infinitely significant.

"Double share for the fallen?" he said; everyone else nodded. The loot of a town taken by storm was the property of the troops, less the government's ten percent. Officers and noncoms shared half according to a complicated formula, and the rest went in equal shares to the ordinary soldiers, in Descott-recruited units. Double shares for casualties was more of a custom than a tradition; it would be delivered to the kin with the urn of ashes and the deceased's rifle, sword, and dog.

Across the way a group of troopers appeared on the flat roof of a building, manhandling a huge clay jar between them. They gave a shout of laughter as it arched out to shatter on the cobbles, spraying a flood of olive oil. The first sweep for obvious loot was over, and the proceeds under guard in the warehouses; the real value had been there to start with, anyway. Now came the "gleaning," when anything a man found was his own to take, or destroy. *Odd the pleasure they get from smashing things*, Raj thought. *Like extravagance for its own sake, all the pleasure of being a spendthrift with none of the drawbacks.* Grimly: *They've earned it, or will, before this is over.* Or the other dues of the victors; clumps of troopers waited by the steps of the mosque, grinning and pushing each other in rough dogplay as they waited. A sergeant stirred bits of paper around in his helmet, picked out one and read: "First Company, second platoon, third squad!" One of the clumps pushed their way forward. The mosque door opened, and a half-dozen young women were pushed out into the sunlight, blinking and cringing. A raw whoop lifted from the crowd, and the Colonist women flinched as if from a blow. One fainted as the squad rushed up the stairs to claim their prize, raising an ironic jeer from the spectators, and most of the others began to scream or whimper as the troopers lifted them in fireman's hoists or simply cuffed them along toward the unit's billet. Jovial shouts followed:

"Good luck, yer bullcocked bastards!"

"Show 'em why Descott girls is bowlegged!"

"Hey, Sandor! This mean yer gonna sell the ewe?"

That nearly started a fight, until friendly hands dragged the heckler away and Trooper Sandor had to make a dash to recover his prize, who made a break for the alleys through the laughing ranks of the Descotters. None of them paid any attention to Sandor's blasphemous calls to trip her; bets were called back and forth, and paid up as he closed a hand on her hair on the second circuit of the little plaza. He kept his hold on the long black tresses and bent her arm up behind her back in an efficient come-along hold, scowling at the mock-tender inquiries of his comrades who wondered aloud if he had the wind to do anything else but catch her.

"All right, yer dickheads," the sergeant on the steps said, making another draw. "Next—Second Company, third platoon, second squad! Come and get it!"

"No, yer gets it and *then* comes!" someone said. "Plunder, *then* burn."

Muzzaf had been searching in the folds of his robe while the Companions idly watched the byplay.

"Ahh, yes," he said. "I have done a preliminary calculation . . . one thousand five hundred silver FedCreds. Per share."

Shocked silence fell.

"Sweet Avatars of the all-knowing Spirit," Gerrin said, at last. He turned and fisted Barton lightly on the shoulder. "War Academy for you in a year or two, my lad! We'll make a two-semester wonder of you."

Da Cruz moistened his lips, remembering a retirement due in five years.

"Squire Dorton said he'd rent Cazanegri Farm to a man

who could stock it decent, it don't pay 'im to run it with a bailiff," he said meditatively.

"Don't price the unborn calf," Raj said, and they all spat and made the horn-sign. He eyed Muzzaf narrowly. "How do you figure that?"

The man from Komar smiled, almost his old salesman's grin, and produced a piece of paper. "These are the price estimates for the frankincense I found; this is a collection point for it . . . and I know a factor for the Church, in Kendrun, who will pay 93% of the East Residence price. The specie, the dinars, you can do better than turning them in to the Fisc for recoining—they use their own scales. There are merchants in Sandoral who will give you 3% above metal content, for the convenience in the Colonial trade. Slaves will be a glut in Komar, but—" he laid a finger alongside his nose "—your humble servant knows several mine and quarry firms that would be *delighted* to buy direct."

He continued down the list, and the soldiers looked at each other, uneasy. To yeoman and squire alike, it was a reversal of the natural order of things for mercantile skills to work to their benefit. Descott County's largest town was smaller than El Djem, and the merchants and factors there were mostly outsiders. Yet the Komarite had been one of the first over El Djem's wall . . .

"Commission for you?" Evrard said bluntly.

Muzzaf looked down, fiddling with the paper. "No," he said quietly. "I pay my debts." A shadow of his old grin: "In Messer Whitehall's service, I may do that, and profit well, and face far less boredom than I did before."

"Well," Raj said gently, and touched him on the shoulder. "I think we can spare you a full share, at least; we'll put your name on the rolls as a scout."

Muzzaf swallowed and looked away; it was a sign of acceptance, more than the money. He was still a wealthy man, with what he had been able to salvage from Komar and send west to the coastal city of Kendrun with his wife; her kindred would care for it.

Raj continued briskly, "Remind the men that we're moving out tomorrow, hangovers or no." Luckily a Muslim town wouldn't have much in the way of liquor. "We'll leave one platoon here, for base-of-communications work, and move east along the escarpment in column with two-squad units out to take the outlying farms. Master Sergeant, organize demolition squads from the duty Company, and start the prisoners on felling the orchards and destroying all pumps, wells, and irrigation canals."

Da Cruz nodded; there could be no defenses where men could not live, and they could not live far from the source of their food, not without navigable water to carry it. This raid would weaken the Colony's northwestern border for a generation or more; even then, restoring it would impose enormous expense.

"Ser," he said. "I'll have the date-palms felled an' piled about the orchards, day'r two and they'll burn enthusiasticloik. Rubble an' bodies down the wells. Blast to cover the springs . . ."

"See to it. The servants and transport should be in by this afternoon. As soon as the ammunition is unloaded, get the prisoners coffled—" there were slavers travelling with the column, they followed war like scavenger birds behind a carnosauroid, and they would have the equipment "—fill every spare wagon and anything local with the loot, and we'll send it all back immediately. They can shuttle between here and Fort Blair while we're in the field; as we move east, everything can be sent back here and staged north in relays. The Colony semaphore net will get the news to the Drangosh Valley soon enough, and I want to keep us mobile as possible."

"Consider it done, ser."

"Oh, and turn captured dogs and weapons over to the servants," Raj said. "They won't be any use for fighting, but they can plunder and burn well enough, which is our job right now."

"Immediately, ser."

"We'll start pulling back as soon as we meet the 2nd, cleaning up the southern rim as we go." The basin that held El Djem was a flattened oval lying east-west; the bulk of the habitations were on the north edge, where artesian springs were most abundant. A lesser scattering rimmed the southern edge; the water that seeped to the surface in the low center of the *playa* was too salty for food crops, but it supported rich spicebush plantations. "When the last load's assembled here—or sooner, depending—we pull back to Fort Blair and then Komar, mission accomplished. Understood?"

Gerrin was lounging against a pillar. "Good, provided the enemy cooperates."

"Mought wish they wouldn't, ser," da Cruz said. "New draft, I'd admire to see how they shape under some weight."

M'lewis spoke up unexpectedly, from where he sat crouched on his haunches trimming a hangnail with his skinning knife. "Mebbe so," he said. The others looked at him, and he responded with a shifty, snaggle-toothed smile. "Summat of the newlies, they thinkin' Messer Captain's a luck-piece, turn bullets to water. Foin while it lasts, make 'em take chances, though, mebbe turn arse when the red wine's served for really."

"Not much we can do about that," Raj said, pushing back the shimmering vision of a firing-line dissolving as men ran, abandoning their comrades . . . no, abandoning strangers they had not learned to depend on, officers they did not know enough to trust. Raj knew his own motivations, knew that he would carry out his mission *whatever* the consequences, but he would not have been an effective leader if he did not realize that most soldiers were governed by different imperatives.

Somewhere in the building behind them wood crashed. Voices shouted, in a yelping exultant falsetto, "*Aur! Aur!*"

"Spirit of Man of the Stars," Kaltin muttered. "It's those *damned* irregulars again. Bloody weasels in a henhouse."

Raj sighed wearily, rubbing a hand over his face and unbuckling his helmet. Tepid sweat trickled greasily from the cork and sponge lining. "They've been willing to listen to reason, somewhat," he said.

"Summat, ser," M'lewis added, "after the boys told 'em what they thought of spoilin' loot." The officers nodded; their Descotters could be a trifle rough—they were soldiers, after all, not schoolgirls on an outing—but they were good lads at heart. "Got a good nose for hidey-holes, true told, once they blood's cooled a bit. Few of the *kaypadros* were goin' around with them, gleanin'-loik."

More crashing, the rhythmic sound of metal on wood. Then another chorus of screams, women's voices among them this time; a single shot, and a brief clash of steel.

Shouts, the shrill yelping of the borderers and deep-chested Descotter bellows.

"Well, I think that's the Caid in his little hideaway," Evrard said, looking around and through the unshuttered floor-to-ceiling windows. "But damned—"

Raj looked back; the irregulars were kicking an elderly man along, one dressed in an expensive-looking robe. His beard was dyed green, sign of one who had made the pilgrimage to the Holy City of Sinar; where the first ships from Old Earth had landed, bearing a fragment of the Ka'bah from the ruins of burning Mecca. They swung open-handed blows at him, spitting in his face; one ripped out a handful of the beard. The Caid cried out, a prayer in Arabic.

"—if there's going to be much left."

The borderers were shouting as well:

"This for our priest you flayed in his church—

"Scream, dog! Scream as my brother did when the Bedouin burned him alive!"

Raj slapped a hand against the fluted limestone of the pillar beside him. "Well, they didn't *have* to volunteer," he said. The irregulars were invaluable at raid-and-ambush work, and they were certainly fighting men . . . but they were not any *sort* of soldiers, and the ones who'd come this far into hostile country were likely to have exceptional motivation.

Ripping cloth, and more breathless cries of pain and fear. A jeering borderman's voice, "These are your bitches, dog? Hai, an old dog like you doesn't need them!"

He glanced in through the windows again. The Caid was down on hands and knees, and one of the irregulars was sitting on his back as if on a riding dog, slashing behind him with the Caid's own ceremonial nine-thonged whip of authority. The jagged pieces of steel on the ends of the thongs were fully functional as well as symbolic, however. *Spirit of Man, what a way to make a living,* Raj thought with weary disgust.

"This dog won't answer to the lash," the "rider" joked.

"A cull-dog!" somebody else laughed, darting in with the sleeve of his robe rolled back and a knife in his hands. "Cull-dogs must be *castrated.*"

The commanders did not precisely look away, but there was no particular need to watch what was effectively out of their control. Thus they missed the first flicker of movement through the doors, and nobody heard the slap of bare feet on the sandstone floor because the Caid's dying scream was loud enough to stun their ears for a second. It did not last long; a man whose testicles have been completely severed bleeds out into unconsciousness quite quickly. Barton Foley was startled enough to jump backward with a yell as the girl ran into him, head down. He shouted, his voice cracking; the girl gave a breathless shriek, staring about wildly as weapons were returned to scabbards and holsters. Her hands stayed gripped in the harness of Ensign Foley's shoulder-strapped baldric. A torn-open vest was her only clothing apart from the thick hair that fell past her waist; she looked to be about sixteen, plumply pretty in the Arab fashion.

Boots rang on the stone behind her, not the soft-soled gear the irregulars wore. The first trooper out onto the veranda had a bayonet in his hand and his rifle slung muzzle-down across his back; four deep fingernail gouges ran across his face, and from the wide fixed stare he was fully aware that he had just missed having one eye scooped out to dangle on his cheek.

"The bitch," he said, in a strangely distant voice, panting. "The bitchcunt, we had 'er down, she clawed me, I'm gonna cut 'er four *ways*, the *bitch*."

The girl ignored Foley's tentative attempts to push her away. When the trooper started forward she swung herself behind the young Descotter, gripping his harness again and holding him like a shield in front of her with hysterical strength, jumping up with hair billowing to shout Arabic curses and spit at the trooper over his shoulder. Frustrated, the soldier checked his rush just as his weight was going onto the balls of his feet and tried to angle around the younger man, snatching with his free hand.

Gerrin Staenbridge moved sideways, putting his palm over the girl's mouth. She tried to bite; the big hand clamped, and he barked two words in Arabic that left her standing silent except for the quick gasping of her breath. The trooper with the bayonet hardly seemed to notice.

"Get out a my *ways*, pretty boy," he snarled.

Foley freed his shoulders with a jerk, straightened and set hands on hips, looking down his thin hooked nose.

"What was that, trooper?" he drawled, in a tone reminiscent of Captain Staenbridge's on inspection days.

The man blinked, looked around. A little of the glazed look faded from his eyes, and he straightened. The point of the bayonet turned down towards the ground, and his left hand fumbled automatically at the undone buttons of his jacket.

"Ah, beggin' yer pardon, ser," he said, making a sloppy salute. "That cunt, she's mine. We got 'er." Three more troopers had followed the first: one was limping, and another sucking at the ball of his thumb where sharp teeth had taken out a thimble-sized lump of flesh. "Jest step aside, ser, and we'll take care of it."

Foley cast a glance back at the fear-wide eyes of the girl and then helplessly at Staenbridge. The older man stepped closer and laid a hand on his shoulder.

"I don't think so, soldier," he said smoothly. "There's plenty more over in the mosque, and less menace to your eyes."

The trooper's fingers tightened on the bayonet, and he began shaking again with frustration and the terror of near-blinding transmuted into rage.

"Ser, it's *gleanin's*, it's our *right*." That was dangerous, when a Descott man started to talk of his rights. "An' beggin' yer pardon, ser, but what the fuck do yer two want wit' 'er?"

Staenbridge relaxed, pulled a pack of cigarettes from his jacket and offered one to the soldier with a smile, not ignoring the gap in rank but treating the matter as between one fighting man and another. The trooper took it awkwardly in one hand, then had to sheath his bayonet to light it.

"Look, soldier . . . Trooper Hylio Henyarson, isn't it? Mamorres parish?" The man had blue eyes, rare anywhere and almost unheard of in Descott County. He nodded, and the Senior Lieutenant continued: "Do you like wine?"

"*Ci, ferrementi, seyor*," the trooper said, bewildered: "Yes, of course, ser."

"Beer?"

"Summat."

"*Slyowtz?*" An enthusiastic nod; the plum brandy was by way of a Descotter national drink.

"Honey mead?"

"*Nao*, it leaves a funny taste at 't back a me throat, ser."

"But you drink it now and then?"

"Well, of course, ser—" The trooper stopped with his mouth open, frowning in dissatisfaction and visibly searching for an answer, as the officer indicated the girl with a silent *well, then*. While he thought, Gerrin bent and pulled two bottles from the personal gear piled on the edge of the verandah; they were half-liter, of thick green glass with lithographed labels bearing the outline of a spray of plum blossom, sealed with wired corks and wax.

"Tell you what, soldier . . . I'll *trade* you for her."

"Holy Avatars of the Spirit," one of the troopers behind Hylio whispered, licking his lips.

Holdor Tennan straightened up from his seat on the verandah railing and put companionable arms around the shoulders of two of the others. "Hey, dog-brothers," he said, "I happen to know Sergeant Salton over there at the mosque is keeping some of the best back for last, and for a couple of hits of that liquor, with a little persuasion . . ."

Hylio looked back at his friends, whose eyes were fixed on the bottles; *Slyowtz* and a woman each were obviously looking a lot more appealing than sloppy seconds after him and a grudge-producing pissing match with a company commander. They might have backed him anyway, on principle, but the bottles were a face-saving gesture for Hylio and a generous one at that, showing a commander careful of his men's honor.

"Ah, crash and coredump 'er," he said. "They're all pink insides, anyhow. Watch the nails, ser."

"But . . . but *Gerrin*," Foley said. "What *will* we do with her?" The girl had backed up against a pillar, one hand holding her vest closed and the other spread over her crotch.

Staenbridge smiled fondly at him, but spoke to the girl first, in slow careful Arabic, hands moving to indicate where the troopers had stood, and then the mosque. She swallowed and nodded, glancing back and forth between him and Foley, then accepted a cloak from the older man's hands.

"Continue your education, Barton dear," he said, laying an affectionate arm around the youth's shoulders. "After all, you'll need to marry and carry on your family name, someday, so you need to know something of women: I get along quite well with my wife, one week every six months when I'm back in the County. First lesson, don't hurt them; honey catches more flies than vinegar, and there's no rush."

He nodded pleasantly to the other Companions. "See you later, gentlemen. Come, Fatima." Foley's ears were red to the tips as they walked away toward their billet.

"You know," Raj said to the others, "that was a very pretty piece of officer's work."

Discipline was essential, but so were aggression and self-confidence; that was why the elite of the Civil Government's army was recruited from places like Descott County, or from the *barbaricum* beyond the frontiers, rather than the spirit-broken peons of the central provinces. Men trained to kill, and proud enough to advance into fire rather than admit fear, were never easy to control.

"Frankly, I'm a bit surprised," Evrard said.

"You didn't know Gerrin when we were stationed on the western border, Evvie," Kaltin replied.

Da Cruz spat meditatively out into the plaza. "Messer Staenbridge knows his business," the senior noncom said. "But he needs sommone t'point him in the general direction, loik. Or he lets things slide a little at a time, and goes mean with it." He dusted off the thighs of his uniform, saluted. "You knows how to work with *him*. ser."

"Think I'll do a tour of the vedettes," Kaltin said. "Keep their minds off how all their buddies are drinking and fucking while they roast in the sun."

Antin M'lewis watched the others depart, all but the Captain; *he* stayed, standing with his arms crossed and watching out over the captured hamlet as if he were seeing visions. *Don't cross 'im*, the man from Bufford parish reminded himself. There was something spooky about the young commander, but he knew how to reward good service . . . and to punish. Just as well to hitch your cart to a rising star; it would never be dull, he decided, and possibly very profitable indeed. Not safe, of course, but then neither would staying home have been, shovelling muck and branding cattle and likely as not ending with iron in his belly for something truly stupid: a cuckold mocked at a feast, a moved boundary stone, straying stock.

He reached into a pouch and fingered the dice, looking meditatively at the mosque. Headquarters noncom billet there . . . and him a new-minted corporal. The dice flicked up into the air. M'lewis decided he could wait for the women; not that he didn't like a piece as well as the next, but he was no three-ball man, and in his experience they didn't grow shut again. It had been a source of amazement to him for years how mellow, how suggestible, how trusting men were right after they'd had their ashes hauled. Probably they'd just *love* a friendly game.

His hand caught the carved bone at the top of its curve, with a motion like a trout rising to a fly. Tomorrow they'd be back in the hot sun . . .

CHAPTER TEN

The burning manor house was still smoldering, throwing a pall of acrid-tasting haze across the 5th's encampment. There was a crash as rafters collapsed in the squat four-story tower at the west end, turning it into a giant chimney casting red-shot black billows in the darkening sky of late evening. The long rows of spicebush trees reaching down to the salt marsh were burning, too, smelling like hot cinnamon and cloves; higher up troopers and soldier-servants were ringbarking mastic and terebinth trees, uprooting frankincense bushes and piling them together for burning.

"Pity they burned it before our boys got in," Suzette said. The household were dining at a looted table under a fringed marquee; Captain Stanson sat at the other end, frigidly polite. "The last two had some beautiful things."

Suzette's chamberlain stalked over from the cookfires, haughty in a plundered silver cloth robe and a staff of office. Behind him two servants walked with the care of men carrying a burden not quite heavy enough to be uncomfortable, a huge silver dish of roasted sauroids on a bed of the inevitable boiled rice and dates. The quasireptiles were of a local species that lived in salt marsh, feeding on grubs and rushes; their flesh was white and salty but otherwise remarkably similar to chicken.

"Not surprising," Raj said, ripping off a six-inch drumstick.

Off to one side came the musical *ting* of hammers on iron; the labor force of the estate were being neck-shackled, in collars on either side of a long chain. Each bent at the small portable anvil as the slaver's smith deftly inserted a soft-iron pin through the clasp of the collar and peened it over with three expert blows. Most of them had been slaves before in any case, this was a commercial enterprise and not a farm. The few surviving free guards and craftsmen were on a separate chain, and the dozen or so Civil Government-born captives were off celebrating their newfound liberty by doing camp chores.

"Ser," M'lewis said, coming up and saluting. "Them ragheads has arrived."

"By all means, send them in," Raj said. Campfires were blossoming, and there was a bleating of sheep being led to the slaughter. *The dogs are going to resent going back on a mash diet*, Raj thought idly.

you have not entrenched, Center's voice, prompted, inside his ear. He continued chewing stolidly on his drumstick while a ghost-image of men wearily digging trenches and firing-pits overlaid the landscape.

No, he thought. *This is a raiding party, not an invasion. There's a whole company out on vedette duty, and the men are camping with the dogs loose-saddled and their boots on. Good scouts and quick reaction are the best protection we can have, and we can't get our job done if we waste three or four hours every day.*

No flat-toned words spoke in his mind, surprising him. Instead Stanson spoke. "You're bringing all your people in every night?" he said in a tone of tolerant disapproval, nodding to a two-squad column trotting home, silhouetted against the sunset and the red glow of the burning buildings. The men were hung about with loot like luggage racks, and there was a train of pack goats behind them. Servants on Colonial whippets brought up the rear, laughing and waving the repeater carbines in their hands.

"They're out in groups of ten to twenty all day," Raj said. "Patrolling, as well as scorching the earth, it's a good compromise. Seems to be working quite well, in any event. We'll have to pack it in, soon, since the message got through Ksar Bourgib."

Stanson returned his attention to his plate. Ksar Bourgib had fallen after a day of hard fighting; the 2nd had lost heavily, and the town had burned before it could be plundered. Worst of all, the heliograph had gotten a message out to the east before it was destroyed. The 2nd's commander had ridden into the rendezvous with no more than his artillery, a platoon or so of walking wounded and a huge straggling trail of plunder on captured transport; the rest of his troops were out in penny packets, no more than a pair sometimes, from here all the way back to El Djem.

"Effendi." It was the Colonist delegation under a flag of truce, led by an old man in a green turban and beard, an imam of some sort. Their first tentative bow was to the gorgeously-robed chamberlain, who made scandalized gestures until they realized the dusty officer in the three-day stubble and plain uniform was the Civil Government commander. A long, sonorous, throaty roll of Arabic followed.

"Fanciful greetings and plea for mercy from all of these wogboys," Muzzaf said, pushing aside his plate and unbuckling a brass-clasped ledger book. Suzette handed a key to a servant, and the man dragged a steel trunk from under the table, opening a heavy padlock and throwing back the hasp.

"Tell him the terms are agreeable," Raj said. "And any appropriate circumlocutions." *Every ounce of gold or silver is so many tools or days' wages or livestock*, he thought. Better to lay waste to the remaining farms, but draining the capital resources of the local landowners was a good second-best.

The eyes of the imam were cool and free of fear, despite the armed men who ringed him. Small sacks of coin were produced, weighed, checked off against names in the ledger; stumbling captives were prodded forward, many weeping with joy as their relatives in the delegation embraced them.

The Komarite's Arabic was fluent; Raj remembered him saying his mother had been a slave-concubine from the Colony. "It is a providence of the Spirit that the Muslims forbid usury," Muzzaf chuckled, transferring the coins to the box and handing the key back to Suzette.

Raj nodded; the Colony was as civilized as the Civil Government, possibly richer, but its banking system was rather primitive by comparison, and largely in the hands of Jews and Christos. A comparable group of gentry back home would have kept most of their cash in paper, letters of credit and such. Nor was it surprising how much they were willing to pay to get the attackers out of their neighborhood; several of these salt-marsh manors had been looted *before* his men arrived, by the slaves who worked them, and the only things left there for relatives to retrieve would be the makings of a closed-casket funeral.

"We do not grudge the money, Messer Captain," the imam said suddenly, in good Sponglish with the accent of the southern border. Raj looked up sharply. "Such is pleasing to the Merciful, the Beneficent." A slight smile. "And who knows, perhaps someday you will need the gold to ransom yourself. Peace be with you, *kaphar*."

The delegation had brought spare dogs for the men they ransomed; the whole party trotted off with the white flag flapping in its midst. The sun was nothing more than a glow, less bright than the dying fire consuming the buildings. Sparks drifted skyward, embers against the stars. Raj met Suzette's eyes across the table; they crinkled slightly with that secret smile.

Crack. Raj glanced up. It could have been heated stone, splitting in the ruins as the cool night air descended . . . His body did not believe that, and it was rising and cinching tight his gunbelt. *Crack-crack-crack*, northward, shots from behind the low bulk of the slave barracks and the line of eucalyptus trees near it, spiteful winking red eyes of muzzle flashes. Shouts and screams followed, the long slave-chains yammering and thrashing and the huge chaotic sprawl of the 2nd's baggage camp erupting into chaos. The 5th's troopers were diving for rifles, some mounted already but uncertain of the direction of the attack. Firing was crackling from the baggage camp, probably the 2nd's people and *certainly* the servants. A round went through the marquee above him, and it had to be an Armory 11mm from the sound, not the light pistol-calibre bullet from a Colonist carbine.

"Spirit of *Man*, get your people to fucking cease fire, Stanson!" Raj barked. "Trumpeter, sound *stand to!*" Just what they needed, a blindsided firefight in the cursed *dark*, there couldn't be many of the enemy if they'd gotten through the vedettes but friendly fire could kill dozens in a few seconds—

and the Companions, his core command group, were mostly out with raiding groups, it was going to be near impossible to get things organized—

"*Ul-ul-ull-ull Allahu Akbar!*"

Much closer, well within their perimeter, the rapid crackle of Colony repeaters and the sudden clash of metal, something flammable went over on a campfire with a gout of white light. He could see them now, a solid wedge driving straight for his marquee, shooting and slashing at anything in their way.

"M'lewis—" he began, his voice steady and pitched to carry despite the crawling in his stomach: Suzette was here. "Turn out the guard, they're headed this way—"

Too late; they were *here*. Suzette's chamberlain had come running to see what the trouble was; six of the attackers crowded their dogs around him, lean whippets and greyhounds dancing and snarling as the robed soldiers leaned far over to slash. The man screamed in fear, flailing about him with his staff to win a few seconds more life. The others drove for the group about Raj.

Shove. He knocked the heavy table over with his hip, making a chest-high barricade for the noncombatants. Stanson was on his feet, and whatever his other faults there was nothing wrong with his reflexes or marksmanship. There were two revolvers in holsters strapped to his thighs; he had them both out, firing alternately in a ripple of blasts like a trip hammer, using the muzzle flash of each shot to aim the next, emptying saddles. Out of the corner of his eye he could see M'lewis unsling his rifle and take careful aim. A shot, and a dog went down in a yelping, thrashing tangle that rolled right over its rider. He worked the lever, and then gave a snarl of frustration as it jammed half-open, the fragile wrapped-brass cartridge disintegrating under the pull of the extractor.

Raj leveled his own pistol, carefully centering the foresight and V on one of the men aiming a cut at M'lewis' head. The recoil was a surprise as it always was when you did it right, and the man pitched backward, his sword making a spinning circle of light as it flew off into the darkness. The little Companion had dropped his rifle and drawn the skinning knife; he rolled under the next attacker's blade and under the belly of the dog. The animal gave a deafening yelp-howl and collapsed as its intestines spilled out of a two-foot slash, and then Raj had troubles enough of his own.

Flickering light, wet white teeth and steel coming for his life; the Colonists had shot their weapons empty on the way. The muzzle of his pistol was almost inside the long wedge gape of one greyhound's muzzle when he fired; the hollow point bullet tore out the back of its palate, through the spine and into the belly of the rider. Another shot, a miss. Another, and a dog was down but the soldier on its back rose and came forward on foot. Raj dodged backward, into the protecting guy ropes of the marquee, leading them away from the overturned table where his wife and Muzzaf fought back-to-back. Stanson was down, and his mistress Merta had thrown herself protectively over his body in a gesture that showed plenty of courage if little sense.

Raj swung himself around a pole and slashed at the muzzle of a whippet. The tip of the blade connected, and the dog bolted into the interior of the marquee; its master's head hit the ridgepole with a *bong* of wood on steel helmet and he dropped boneless from the saddle. A bound backward put Raj in the clear, and another rider was coming at him. He waited, weight on the balls of his feet and his own teeth showing, then dove forward when the Arab heeled his dog. The butt of the pistol thumped down on the sensitive nose of the Basiji, with the weight arm and shoulder behind it. The dog yelped and jerked back its head involuntarily, and then he was in past its teeth for a moment, by the Colonist's stirrup. Bright and long, the scimitar swept down in an expert overarm cut.

Raj caught it on his own sword, and it slid the length of the steel in a ringing descent, until they locked hilt to hilt. That brought them almost face to face, the Descotter staring into the set eyes of a man who had accepted his own death in order to accomplish a purpose. His left hand rammed the muzzle of the dragoon pistol into the green sash that girdled the enemy soldier's crimson robe. The Arab's eyes flew wide as the bullet hammered into his gut, filled with rage more than pain, and then he slumped away. Raj skipped back again, to get out of range of the dog, but the lean brown animal stopped stock-still, nosed its master's body frantically and then sat, throwing back its head in a mournful howl of grief.

The dismounted Colonist was coming in with his scimitar, a dagger in his left hand. Holding both as if he knew how to use them, and moving fast and smooth. Raj switched into a fencer's stance, right foot and arm advanced; the twin blades poised, and—

—a bullet snapped the Arab's head forward and to the side like the impact of a sledgehammer. His features ballooned, the right side of the skull erupting as the half-ounce pellet of soft lead blasted out an exit wound the size of paired fists over his left eyebrow. Bone fragments and something with the consistency of warm jelly

"Sssir! Are you all right?" Lieutenant Mekkle Thiddo ran up, with half his platoon behind him.

Raj opened his mouth and took the first step toward the overturned table, wiping at the brains on his face and spitting to clear the nauseating soft-boiled-egg feeling from the corner of his mouth.

observe.

Not now, *for the Spirit's sake*! he thought furiously. **precisely for the Spirit's sake, in your terminology. observe.**

A column of Colonial scouts waited silently in a gully sheltered by feathery tamarind trees; the forested bank was higher and more steep than the other, and the red-robed soldiers crouched with their dogs at its base. Looking up from their position, Raj's disembodied viewpoint could see the branches and scrub outlined blackly against the moons. There was still the tired-orange light of sunset in the air, but the base of the cliff was in deep shadow.

A thudding and rustling that carried well through the dense clay against which the Colonists huddled, the sound of dogs trotting. One stopped directly above, and there was a crackling as the rider's arms forced an opening in the branches. Words drifted down. They were in Sponglish with the accent of Descott, but Raj's mind seemed to hear them as a foreign tongue; he had to concentrate to render their meaning. The first voice was fainter, further back.

"Yah alia vi' este?" *Do you see anything there?*

"Danad, seyor." *Nothing, sir.*

"Benyo. Waymos, allaya." *Good; let's go, everyone.*

Long silence, while the sun set and the double shadows cast by the moons moved. A crouching figure in a knee-length robe of dull dried-blood red came up the gully from the south, scuttling along in the shadows. One of the waiting soldiers stepped out to meet him and Raj felt a slight shock of recognition. It was the man whose hound had mourned him.

The man Raj had killed.

"Peace be with you, soldier," the man—the commander—said. "What news?" The Arabic was as comprehensible as his mother tongue, more so right now.

"And upon you, peace, lord," the scout replied. "We are inside their outer line of patrols, and this gully will keep us out of view to the edge of their camp. Many small parties of them ride about, some of them jackals in robes from the border villages west of Komar; in the dark we could be mistaken for such. Half their camp is in confusion, the white-coats section; the manor of Youssef Ben Khedda still burns, and the blue-coats camp about it."

"Their commander?"

"He sits at meat with his fellows and their unveiled whores, lord; they speak with the learned Imam Faysal al-'Aziz, who comes to ransom captives. The platoon which guards him went to escort the Imam into their camp, and I think will ride to see that they leave by the agreed route as well."

The Colonist commander grinned and spat. "Ahh, this is good. Gather about me, warriors of Islam." The others crowded close to hear the low voice. "Brothers, there is no God but God, and nothing is accomplished save by the will of God. If we slay the commander of the unbelievers, this will be a thing of great good; his is the better-ordered band among the invaders and without him perhaps they will be easy meat for the amir. The danger will be great. Who will come with me?"

None of the men hesitated more than a second. The Colonist officer nodded, pride on his face. "Remember that he who falls in battle against the unbelievers is granted forgiveness of sins and attains Paradise." He pulled a notepad from his sash, and a graphite writing stick from the cloth winding about his spired helmet, sketching a map and writing quickly.

"Here," he said, handing them to the scout. "To the commander of the forward column, and with a recommendation that it be shown immediately to the amir himself. Follow us only half the distance; if we kill the unbeliever, I will throw a flare bomb." He touched a wooden casing at his belt. "Report our failure or success, as God wills." The scout's face worked as he prepared a protest. "Those are your orders, Husni az-Zaim, and are so written in that message."

—and time blurred, and they were surging up out of the shallow gully and into the camp, their swift agile dogs leaping tent-ropes and dodging into the dark before the soldiers could react to their passage. Carbines spat at pockets of resistance, and then the swords were out when there was no time to reload. Raj saw the marquee looming, a table overturning; a tall man in blue falling with one arm nearly severed at the shoulder . . .

"Sir, *are you all right*?"

"Better than I'd have been if that bullet'd gone a handspan to the left," Raj barked, as his surroundings faded back to normal; he wiped a sleeve over his face again, to remove the last of the brains. "Because in that case I'd be bloody dead, wouldn't I?"

Thiddo made an incoherent apology; Raj waved it aside as he wiped and sheathed his sword and snapped out the cylinder of his revolver. Anguished embarrassment was making Thiddo's speech impediment worse; that was unjust, the fight had lasted about forty seconds before relief arrived, not bad time. He took a deep breath, forcing himself to calm as his fingers handled the tubes of brass and cardboard and lead.

"And somebody shut up that damned dog!" he continued; the Basiji was still howling. Thiddo made a hand signal and several of his men faced left, firing a volley with their muzzles almost touching the animal's side. The nine hundred pounds of it fell with a thud that made the ground shake slightly under their feet; it whimpered, twitched, laid its pointed muzzle across its master's legs, and died. Relative silence fell; there were still shots from the baggage park, shouts, the sound of men and dogs moaning or whimpering in pain, but conversation became possible.

"Sir. Report." Thiddo's voice had a strained sound, as if he were making it obey by an effort of will. "Perimeter is on alert. No further enemy forces within the perimeter. Contact established with First Company on vedette; nothing to report. My men are reestablishing order among the camp followers, sir. Orders, sir?"

"Carry on, for the moment," he snapped aloud. *Why now? Why didn't you show me that five minutes ago, curse you?*

you felt it was unnecessary to entrench, despite my warning. Raj felt himself shaking, the world narrowing to a pinpoint concentration of rage. *I could have been bloody killed, and so much for unifying Bellevue!*

i have waited a thousand years, the voice said, in the same chill tones, **it is necessary to educate you. if the process kills you as well, there will be another, if not in this cycle, then the next.**

Suzette picked up the derringer she had thrown at her feet and walked to meet Raj; that turned into a sprint, and a quick fierce hug. He returned it, as the trigger guard of the carbine she was still holding in her right hand dug into his back. The place where Center's visions had shown his own death was not two meters from where he stood, and he stared at it for a moment over his wife's shoulder, dizzy with the memory of himself falling/might have fallen, arm hanging by a thread . . .

"Shit!"

That was Stanson, prone on the ground as a priest-doctor probed at his buttock; the trouser had been cut away, exposing a bullet hole in the great muscle. Next to him Merta sat, having a long shallow saber cut on her back bandaged by another. The priest grunted, twisted the probe expertly and withdrew it, holding up the piece of flattened metal that glinted dully in the lantern light.

"Got it," he announced. "Hmm, pretty small—even for a raghead carbine, more like a small caliber . . . hmmm, better see if there's more." The 2nd's commander, grey-faced and sweating, bit down on a cuff while the probe went back in. Shaking his head, the priest strapped an iodine-soaked dressing over the wound.

"Minor wound, Messer. Couple of weeks and you'll be good as new."

"Shit," Stanson muttered again. He craned his neck up and met Raj's eyes, managing a shaky smile. "I'll never live it down, Whitehall; one minute I'm pistoling them, the next I'm down, shot in the arse, by the Spirit. Didn't see any of them behind me, must have been a ricochet . . ." His gaze met Suzette's. "And then one of them was cutting at me, I think he pulled the first one because it hit Merta. And Lady Whitehall shot him out of the saddle before he could strike again. We owe you a debt, I think."

Suzette smiled, one of her charming Court expressions. "No debts between friends, Helmt," she said coolly. "You must have gotten four or five of them before you were hit . . . and better the buttocks than the spine or kidney."

Stanson shuddered. "Spirit of man, yes, only fifty millimeters difference."

Muzzaf hobbled over, clutching his stomach. "Just winded," he wheezed. "Kicked." From the way he clutched his ribs one or two might be cracked, but you could move with an injury like that. His voice took on more strength. "Those men were in the uniform of regular cavalry," he said.

Raj nodded grimly. "Here's where those irregulars earn their keep," he said. "Muzzaf, find Bani Crodor," the closest they had to a leader. "And get me da Cruz; at first light, we—"

"Lord," Crodor croaked, then hawked and took a quick swig from his canteen. "We found them."

That was obvious; the irregulars had limped in with an escort from Raj's outlying vedettes, as the huge column of soldiers and plunder finally creaked into motion. There were dogs with empty saddles among them, and others missing altogether; one saddle had a black fletched arrow standing up like a quill, and several of the bordermen were clutching wounds, gunshot and sword. Their dogs had even found climbing the last small hillock where the officers of the 5th and 2nd waited a burden.

Crodor continued. "Ten, perhaps eleven kilometers from here, lord, and coming fast. Their scout screen is Bedouin, with some of the local landowner's retainers perhaps, but we pushed through"—risking death at the hands of vastly superior forces, or capture which would be worse "—and we saw regular cavalry of the Settler, riding in columns of twos. No artillery or wagons that we could see, lord."

Stanson cut in. "How many?" he said, shifting in the saddle. The doctors had packed the wound with sterile gauze at his insistence, and he was mobile enough. It was fiendishly painful, though, and obviously not improving his disposition.

Crodor pulled at his beard. "I cannot say, Messer," he replied. "No less than five hundreds. But there was much dust further back; another five hundred again, it may be. Perhaps more."

retreat quickly, Center's voice advised: **your mission is essentially completed, destroy the remaining baggage and pull back to komar.**

"Hmmm," Raj said aloud. "This collection of junk," he indicated the transport, "is going to slow us down. We're not here to fight the Colonial army . . . if we dumped it . . ."

"*What?*" Stanson asked. From their expressions, some of his officers would have liked to say more; one or two let their hands fall to their pistol butts. "That's our *loot* down there, man!" The 2nd had preferred to keep theirs all under their eyes, rather than taking the trouble to send it off as it came in. Three-quarters of the booty here was theirs.

Raj glanced at his own Companions and officers; the reluctance on their faces matched his. Retreating was one thing, running away another. "Recommendations, gentlemen?"

Gerrin Staenbridge nodded south. "They travel fast. Even with nothing but the artillery, we wouldn't be able to break contact unless they let us." The Colonists were lighter men on slender dogs. "But even if they can match our numbers, we can give them a bloody nose as long as they have to come to us." Colonial weapons had a better rate of fire than the ones used by the Civil Government's forces, but less stopping power and considerably less range.

"Thank you, Senior Lieutenant," Raj said formally. "As long as we can avoid a meeting engagement or a melee, I don't think enemy forces of this size are much of a threat, yes. What we can do—if you concur, Captain Stanson—is to send on all the more mobile transport to El Djem; we burned the buildings, but the stockade's intact and there's water. We'll fall back more slowly, they won't dare try to send a substantial force around us under these circumstances. From El Djem we can either stand them off if they're so foolish as to attack the stockade, or simply repeat the process on a larger scale back to Komar. Agreed?"

Stanson nodded, and his followers relaxed; some of them still looked a little contemptuous of Raj and the 5th, for even suggesting a retreat.

"Why can't we take the offensive?" one asked.

Because it would be stupid, Raj thought. The man was a lieutenant; Evrard Gruder answered him, as the equivalent in the 5th.

"Because it would be . . . futile," he said. "We can't catch them unless they let us, and they could lead us off into the alkali desert and then harry us to death. It's happened to Civil Government forces down here before."

"One company for escort?" Master Sergeant da Cruz said; the officers had approved a course of action, and it was time for implementation.

"By all means. Thiddo?"

The commander of Third Company nodded; his force had the most walking wounded, and they would get less strain and a little extra rest.

"Then I suggest we move, gentlemen," Raj said, looking south. The dust cloud of troops on the march was just barely visible over the glaring white earth, standing against the faded blue of the sky.

"Range?" Raj asked.

Barton Foley raised his binoculars. They were only five kilometers from El Djem, now; apart from the attack last night on the dug-in camp there had been only minor skirmishing.

"Five-two-zero-zero, meters, sir," he said.

Raj grunted, looking to left and right. The Civil Government force was retreating toward its base in extended order by Company column; nine widely spaced groups, with the four guns trotting along slightly behind the men. The terrain was nearly flat, long gentle swells, covered in coarse dark soil and fist-sized black rocks. *At least we're off that damned alkali flat*, he thought, licking cracked lips. But it was still hot enough that shimmers and mirage made estimating distance almost impossible, and some of the dogs were whimpering and limping as they put paw to earth. Tongues dangled, panting; some of the men were sacrificing their own water ration to rub the necks of their mounts occasionally, or laying their spare tunics over them as sun blankets. For the rest they rode slumped in the saddle, eyes staring dully ahead and great patches of sweat showing dark on the crystallized salt-deposits that marked their jackets.

Those in the main body could at least be glad they were not on the wings, where clouds of dust showed continuous feint and skirmish. The flank guards were rotated every two hours or so, and it was still brutally draining.

"You're right," Raj replied. Then: "I think they're getting closer again." He raised his own glasses. Brown dogs and red jellabas sprang out at him; the enemy had been coming on in column of march, since they were less apprehensive of a sudden attack. Tewfik's seal-of-Solomon banner in the lead. Raj felt his lips crack and bleed as he snarled at the sight; far too many of Center's scenarios had turned on Tewfik's skills. Was that burly figure under the banner him? It was a little too far to see faces with any clarity, especially with this heat haze, too far even to pick out an eyepatch; Tewfik's was said to have the Seal of Solomon picked out on it in diamonds, and his men believed it carried a curse to his enemies.

The advancing columns seemed to split, multiplying. He blinked, wiped his red-rimmed eyes on a sleeve harsh with salt and dust, looked again. *Deploying*, he realized with a chill. Peeling off to either side without pausing, converting the march formation into a two-rank line suitable for . . .

"Attack," he muttered. "They're going to try us before we get to El Djem."

"Foley," he snapped. "Message: to Senior Lieutenant Dinnalsyn." The artillery commander. "My compliments, and I believe the enemy is going to attempt to press home an attack; they won't stop for a few shells, this time. He is to deploy into line on current position"—they were on the uprise of one of the swells, looking across a broad shallow valley at the Colonists—"and open fire for effect at three-point-five k meters, and I'd advise him to have the gunners prepare some point-blank fused shrapnel."

"M'lewis," he continued, "same warning to Captain Stanson, would he please inform his subordinates that under *no circumstances* are any units to leave position without orders."

"Trumpeter," he went on, as the two kicked their dogs into a fast lope. "Sound—

"*Attention to orders.*"

The battalions continued their steady advance, but there was a ripple like grass under wind—for a moment the sweet scent of the high-plateau rangelands of Descott filled his memory—as they sat in the saddle, and the dogs lifted their heads and raised drooping ears.

"Prepare to countermarch, by Companies—"

Foley's mount had already pulled up by the guns, and Raj could see the tiny stick figure salute and give the message. The field pieces stopped where they were, crews leaping down from teams and caissons; the dogs were unhitched and trotted to the rear, ready to snatch the 75's out of danger but also out of the way. Ammunition limbers were unhitched from the pole trails of the guns; the muzzles jerked up as the trails hit the ground, and the limbers were opened. A Y-shaped rangefinder went up in the center of the battery; breeches swung open, men worked the elevating screws, shells were fused and slammed home.

"*Countermarch!*"

The Company columns were four men wide; now every one split, like a reed pushed against a knifeblade, a column of twos curling back in reverse direction to left and right from each. The rear men continued in the same direction as before, until they came to the turning point and wheeled. Less than a minute, and the whole force was moving back on its own tracks; he looked over to the right, to the 2nd Gendarmerie, and found they had done the maneuver more smoothly even than the 5th, if that was possible. *Parade-ground soldiers*, he thought.

"Halt—dismount—"

They braked to a stop and pulled the rifles out of the scabbards, another long ripple, like reeds in a swamp this time as the muzzles showed slanted across the dogs, the men swinging down.

"*Prepare to Receive Cavalry!*"

The dogs crouched, laying their bellies to the ground but ready to spring, presenting the least possible target. The men rushed forward the regulation ten paces, front rank going prone, rear kneeling; the bayonets rattled onto their catches, levers worked, the flaps of cartridge cases were clipped back. Raj raised his binoculars again as he clapped heels to Horace's flanks, down to the firing line; thirty-six hundred meters, he estimated, and they had halted in line abreast. Four deep but more widely spaced than Civil Government troops would be; battalion strength, right enough. A quiver, and their scimitars came out, sloped back and resting on their shoulders.

Raj rode out in front of his men, alone but for the standard-bearer and the trumpeter, watching their faces as he cantered down to the middle of the line. Tight-gripped tension, perhaps even a little too much eagerness, after the boredom and anxiety-filled discomfort of the three-day retreat. Looking at the long glitter of enemy steel on the ridge behind his back . . . and thinking of the officer who was the squire back home, of men on either side who would witness and report their honor or their shame. He rose in the stirrups and drew his sword: best keep it short and sweet, but the men expected something to be said. He pitched his voice to carry, knowing that the ends of the line would be getting it by word-of-mouth relay.

"Well, lads," he shouted. "Here we are—we've *burned* their crops, *looted* their towns, *had* their women—and now they want to fight!" He waited four heartbeats. "Just like the ragheads to put it all arse-end first, isn't it?"

A roar of laughter, cut short by a downward motion of his saber. "That's Devil Tewfik himself coming, Descotters; a bad one and a mad one. Thinks he's going to nail our heads and our balls to his barn door, he does." Another cry, a jeer this time. "Just remember your drill, lads, and wait for the order, and we'll send them home screaming for their mothers. Show them who you are, what you're made of, and where you come from. Up the 5th! Descott forever!"

They started another cheer as he rode back to his position at the right end of the line:

"Raj!"

"Raj!"

"Well, gentlemen," he said to the officers gathered there, and nodded to the enemy on the ridgeline opposite. "I don't think they'll wait much longer." For that matter, they had waited too long as it was, giving the Civil Government force time to get settled. "Commence volley fire at 750 meters, if you please." He brought out his amulet, kissed it. "Spirit with you."

"Holy Federation uphold you," they replied. Everyone leaned inward, slapping their fists together in a pyramid of arms, then dispersed to their units.

Raj sat under the banner of the 5th Descott Guards, bullet-tattered and hung with ribbons, and allowed the ice knot of terror under his breastbone to unfold.

Something is wrong here, very fucking *wrong.* Ahead the strange shrill-sounding trumpets of the Colony sounded, and the line of enemy cavalry began to move. Two thousand paws thumped the ground, crunched through the loose rock that clattered and slid audibly. *This is the obvious move, and it's obviously going to fail.* Which was *not* Tewfik's reputation, not at all.

"Either he's stupid, or he's counting on me doing something stupid, or we are all about to be royally buttfucked," he muttered to himself.

"Ser?" the standard-bearer said; he was a veteran of fifty, and a little hard of hearing from too much exposure to the noise level of combat.

"Nothing," he said. The enemy knew the range of a 75 to a hair, and they had positioned to build their charge to full speed before they came under the iron flail. Another glitter and blink as the scimitar blades came down; full gallop now, another line of light as the points of the helmet spikes caught the sun, surging up and down with the motion of the dogs. Their dressing was faultless, which was *not* easy on terrain as rough as this. *Those are good troops*, he thought. *And disciplined.* There were Civil Government units—he probably had a battalion of them on his right—which would flat-out refuse an order to charge against rifles and artillery like this.

POOUMP. The first gun fired, ten meters behind the riflemen. A ripping-canvas sound, then a puff of dirty blackish-grey smoke a little ahead of the enemy line.

"Fire for effect, rapid fire, down ten each!"

POOUMP. POOUMP. POOUMP. The guns fired from right to left, slapping the back of his neck with pillows of hot air. More shellbursts across the enemy line, looking like misses but men and dogs were down, scythed down by a soldier's worst nightmare, artillery striking from above without anything they could do about it except endure and hope. Their ranks closed again with a veteran ripple, closing like thick liquid around the bubbles hammered by the guns, leaving figures writhing or still or scattered in pieces across the barren plain, they were half the distance closer already, and *Spirit* but it was good to have guns at your back—

Raj's eyes widened. "Foley!" he shouted. "To Stanson, *quickly*, beware of a feigned retreat." The boy kicked into a gallop. To his right: "Hold your positions under all circumstances, pass it down!" Better to be thought a nervous maiden than a dead fool . . .

Much closer now. He raised the binoculars again; no, no eyepatch . . . yelling faces, glaring eyes, beards. His mouth was dry, but he ignored the canteen at his saddlebow, stroked a hand down Horace's neck; the hound had its ears up, and it was scenting, big *woofing* intakes of breath with a pause to lick its nose between each. Thick grimy-cotton smoke from the guns drifted slowly over him, the odor of Hell. Barton Foley pulled up beside him in a spurt of gravel.

"Sir—" He paused; there were spots of color high on his cheeks under the ruddy-brown Descotter skin. "Captain Stanson directs me—"

"What did he say?" Fifteen hundred meters, the guns were firing twice a minute, another eight rounds—

"Sir, he said that you should teach your grandmother to suck eggs, and that I—he offered insult, sir."

"He was hatched himself, lad."

"May I—"

"Off to Gerrin, Ensign, and good luck."

Eleven hundred meters. A long stuttering crash from his right, a few more saddles emptied, but didn't they realize they were just pumping out smoke to obscure their aim when it counted, Spirit *curse* them for fools? A dense cloud was growing in front of the 2nd Gendarmerie's ranks, fairly soon they would be shooting from estimates and glimpses and demons knew they'd be lucky to hit their *feet* doing that. Thank the Spirit for small mercies, at least the wind was from the northwest and it was not carrying the smoke across the 5th's front. Nine hundred meters. Eight hundred.

"Ready!" repeated down the line, and the front rank's muzzles came up. He thought he could see a slight waver through the ranks of the enemy.

"Pick your targets!"

"By platoons—volley fire—*fire*!"

BAM-BAM-BAM-BAM-BAM-BAM-BAM-BAM, eight times repeated as the front-rank platoons fired. Hands opening the levers, flashing back to the bandoliers. Rear rank presenting with a uniform jerk.

"Fire!"

BAM-BAM-BAM-BAM-BAM-BAM-BAM-BAM. Chaos downrange, dogs falling in heaps, he saw two collide in midair as they tried to leap that barricade of flesh and fall, and thousand-pound bodies would be thrashing, maddened by pain, riders crushed . . .

"Fire!"

BAM-BAM-BAM-BAM-BAM-BAM-BAM-BAM. Slowing, nobody on earth could take this . . . clumps of men pushing ahead, if they kept coming the last of them would die before the bayonets.

"Tewfik!" Raj heard himself screaming, barely audible over the hammering crash of volley fire and artillery. "Tewfik, you mad evil wog bastard, you're *murdering* them, you're murdering good soldiers, call them back, call them *back*."

Then they *were* turning back, their own trumpets blowing retreat. Moving fast, too, crouched over in the saddle to lower their target profiles. Leaving a quarter of their numbers scattered down from the ridgeline; another hundred meters of charge and that would have doubled, tripled. The artillery lifted sights to harry them, and—

A trumpet sounded "charge."

Raj grunted as if a fist had struck him in the belly. The 2nd's trumpeter was blowing the simple four-note call again and again, and the men in the white uniforms were obeying. Cheering wildly, some even throwing aside their rifles as they leaped astride their dogs and drew sabers.

"Trumpeter, sound *stand fast*," he shouted. The young man gave him a shocked glance. "*Stand fast*, and *now*, soldier," he shouted, dragging Horace's head around to face his own ranks. The 5th were on their feet now, too, cheering as madly as the 2nd, waving their rifles in the air and screaming County hunting calls as the enemy fled without order, lashing their dogs as if they intended to keep galloping all the way to the equator and the Zanj Sea.

Raj saw what he had dreaded, men leaving ranks and dashing back for their mounts. A few of those and it would be all of them, beyond holding, blood up to avenge the desert chase and be in at the kill. He drew his pistol and clamped his heels into Horace's ribs; the hound dashed out and to the left, before the 5th's ranks.

"I'll shoot the first man to break ranks!" he shouted, knowing his voice would not carry through the tumult. The trumpeter blew tirelessly at his side, though; the 2nd's was two hundred meters downslope and moving fast, the sound fading. And the muzzle of his pistol was a message in itself; he managed to get in front of the first to leave the firing line. Barely old enough to shave, he saw; one of the draft that had caught up to them on the road, a Descotter but from the northern fringe of the County. Filled with sixteen years' conviction of immortality, and nothing but a few skirmishes in this campaign.

"Back!" he screamed, pushing the weapon into the boy's face. Behind him the officers and noncoms were running down the line, cursing, calling orders, knocking men down with fists and boots and rifle butts. Raj thumbed back the hammer. "I'll shoot you dead, boy."

The young man's eyes lost the berserker-blankness, and his saber wavered and fell. "Back into ranks," Raj snapped.

"Yisser," the young soldier gasped.

"Sound *attention to orders*," Raj said. It took three repetitions to get quiet; it helped that the artillery had fallen silent with no clear target except the backs of the 2nd Gendarmerie.

"Officers to me," Raj called; they were already trotting out. He looked over his shoulder; there was a fringe of saber-swinging melee at the edge of the 2nd's charge as it passed the midway point of the swale and started up the slope, the fastest of the Gendarmerie catching up with the Colonists on winded or injured dogs, but the bulk of Tewfik's battalion was drawing ahead, opening a perceptible gap. And they were nearing extreme artillery range from this position.

"All right," he said. "Shift front, space the Companies out to cover what the 2nd had, I want 15 meter gaps between each." To give the survivors of this charge somewhere to ride through and rally, if they *could* be rallied this side of Komar. *Thank the Spirit Suzette's safe in El Djem*, he thought briefly. "And I want the dogs moved up to arm's reach behind the firing line," he continued grimly. They glanced at each other; a last-ditch chance to escape, if the line broke. "Let's do it, gentlemen, let's *go*."

The line rippled and split at the seams between companies, the men trotting with rifles at the trail and their dogs' reins in hand. Noncoms were calling dressing as they shifted, checking the setting of the men's sights as they settled into the new positions; he saw men taking the time to pry out jams, or throwing down their rifles and picking up discarded weapons from the 2nd. *Presence of mind*, he thought, as he loped Horace back to the gunners. The more you fired, the hotter the chamber and the more likely the cartridge was to tear and jam rather than extract smoothly. Many of the veterans were waiting with the lever down and the bolt back.

"Shift position, Lieutenant Dinnalsyn," he said crisply, and pointed to the new line. It was like a string of four dashes across a page; his finger pointed to the middle two companies. "Two guns each behind those, if you please, and no wasted time."

"Yes, sir!" He snapped out the orders, then turned to Raj. "Ah . . . what's happening?"

"Either I'm making myself a laughingstock, or we're about to find out why Tewfik got his reputation," Raj said; he pointed with the blade of his saber to the opposite ridge.

The 2nd had managed to form a ragged four-rank formation, and were slowing a little before they plunged over the top and down the reverse slope. "If I'm right, and I pray to the *Spirit* I'm not, Tewfik's coming over that hillock in about eight minutes, dogs and guns and their little cats, too. Open up as soon as they're in range and fire as fast as you bloody can, that's all I can say."

"Hold steady, lads!" Raj called, as he cantered down the line. "The creamsuit johnnies will be coming back faster than they left, and the ragheads close behind. Stand to it, and we can still pull it off; run, and we're all buggered, it's that simple."

One man shouted out to him: "We're ready to die game, ser!"

"That's for losers, we're going to *win*," Raj replied. There was no cheering or laughter this time, only a grim boulder-stolid readiness. *Luck*, he prayed. *Just a little luck, that's all I need. No more disasters, no more surprises*. Probably Tewfik had been surprised when the whole Civil Government force hadn't taken his bait; it had wavered within a cunt hair of happening that way, too. Raj looked at the scattered clumps of Colonist dead with new respect; the enemy commander had calmly sacrificed them to make the bait convincing, nothing less would have worked. He remembered the swath of devastation his men had cut through the El Djem basin. It was unlikely in the extreme that the Colonists would be inclined to mercy.

"We'll just have to win, is all," he murmured, staring at the ridge. Perhaps he was wrong after all—

The sound of massed carbines was lighter than that of Armory rifles, but just as deadly at close range. His mind's eye could paint the picture, the 2nd going over the crestline at a full gallop, the ranks of crimson-uniformed Colonists rising as one. Volleys pouring in, and the carbines held seven rounds in a tube magazine under the barrel . . . He whispered prayers and curses under his breath, but a trained ear was estimating. A *lot* of carbines, many more than the eight hundred or so rifles the 5th and 2nd had deployed a few minutes before. And a *pom-pom-pom* sound, Colony artillery. Light quick-firing guns spraying half-kilogram miniature shells from a clip of five. Not as accurate as the 75's, and a lot less weight of shell, but they fired as fast as a carbine.... A cloud of smoke was rising from the low swale over the ridge, twin to the one that was drifting and dispersing ahead of him.

"Oh, shit, oh, shit," he murmured to himself. *I didn't really believe it was happening*, he thought. *Not really.* A minute before he had been afraid of being wrong, of ending his career with a reputation for cowardice, the man who sat and shook while Stanson's 2nd charged to glory. Now he tasted vomit at the back of his throat, and knew that fear can put a red curtain before the eyes as surely as rage.

What, no advice? he asked Center.

you are the sword of the spirit of man, the dispassionate voice answered. His spine crawled with a different fear, to hear that said of *him*. **there can be no weakness,**

The first stragglers of the 2nd shot over the ridge, like melon seeds squeezed between fingers, the ones with the fastest dogs in the rear ranks. Individuals, few of them even carrying their swords and none bothering to look behind; then clots and masses. A few of the last paused to shoot from the saddle behind them, before putting heels to their dogs. Wounded men and animals dropped or staggered out of the chase all the way down the field where the first Colonist attack had come; now you could see the difference between real panic and feigned, and it was obvious.

Spirit of Man, Raj thought in awe. *They* knew *it was a feint to draw us out, and they rode straight into the guns anyway.*

He sat Horace with his saber-arm down, the steel clicking against the stirrup iron. The fugitives from the ruin of the 2nd's charge were bunching, instinct driving most of them to aim for the gaps in the ordered line of rifles and bright bayonets. Those that didn't were going to be right in the line of fire, which would affect the actions of the 5th only to the extent of wasting some of their ammunition. Raj's attention was focused utterly on the ridge, but he could hear voices coming as if from a distance through an echo chamber: it was surprisingly quiet here, for a few instants.

"... remember, dog down, man down. Aim low." Da Cruz.

" . . . an' if yer don't have time t'adjust sights, just aim down another body length." M'lewis, talking to the young trumpeter, who had his rifle out and resting across his saddlebow while the brass horn bumped his chest.

" . . . that's right, lads, keep those pretty backsides to me and the sharp ends at the ragheads; I can restrain myself and they can't." Gerrin Staenbridge, sounding coolly amused.

" . . . first man who turns gits my bay'net in 'is gut." Some nameless noncom, with a warning as old as battles. The first task of command is to make men face death; pride, love, fear, any emotion is grist for the mill.

And Tewfik's army came over the hill. Army was the proper term; they filled it from side to side, four deep, two thousand strong. Moving fast, sliding down the hill like a solid block of crimson and green and bright metal, and *how* had Tewfik gotten that many men here so fast? Unless somebody had laid a railroad from al-Kebir out into the desert and they would have heard about that, if it was one thing the Civil Government didn't lack it was spies . . . *I may be an idiot, but at least I've the comfort of knowing I wasn't killed by an idiot*, he thought.

Aloud: "Steady, men, steady. Don't think of it as being outnumbered, think of it as having a real big target selection." Even now that drew some laughter, although a few were near-hysterical giggles. He raised his glasses. "Gerrin."

"Sir?"

"That's Tewfik personally, under the main banner, the one with the big gold crescent on top? I'd really feel better about all this if he sort of didn't make it, you know?" It would be one real service to the Spirit of Man and the Civil Government.

"Noted, sir," he drawled, and passed the instructions to his subordinates; they told off marksmen, it was out of the question to direct the whole of the Company's fire on one man. And quite likely it wouldn't work, battle was odd that way.

"Three-two-zero-zero," the man at the artillery rangefinder sang out.

A dog-drawn gun followed the cavalry over the hill, a Colonial one-pounder pompom; then two more, and another, lashing their dogs on like madmen.

"Prepare for counter-battery shoot!" the battery commander said. Raj gritted his teeth; it was necessary, his firing line could not stand being raked by streams of those deadly little shells, not now . . . but that meant the rifles would have to do most of the work.

The earth shook, and the screeching of the Colonists was like needles driven into the ears. A 75 crashed behind him, and the smell of fresh gunsmoke made him realize how raw his throat was. The others opened up, no point in trying for the pompoms until they halted, but the cavalry were a moving target too big to miss. Gaps tore in the line, but the Colonists closed ranks with insolent courage. Fifteen hundred meters. Men in white coats were streaming through the spaces between the companies of the 5th; a few were so ridden by fear of the thing behind them that they tried to gallop directly *through* the serried ranks of the Descotters. Shots crashed out and bayonets flicked forward like giant knitting needles, and hardly anyone but those involved even noticed.

Nine hundred. Eight hundred. "Fire!"

BAM-BAM-BAM-BAM-BAM-BAM-BAM-BAM. Bodies down all along the front, and the dragon glimmer of the swords was mercifully dulled by the smoke.

"Fire!"

BAM-BAM-BAM-BAM-BAM-BAM-BAM-BAM. Gaps in the Colonist line, pileups of corpses adding to the obstructions from the first charge.

BAM-BAM-BAM-BAM-BAM-BAM-BAM-BAM. The pompoms were slowing, the teams swinging around to bring the slender two-meter barrels to bear on the line of the 5th. The shellbursts lifted instantly from the cavalry, and the dirty-cotton puffs blossomed in the air around the Colonial guns; not very dramatic, but one gun team dissolved into bloodied snarling chaos, turning on its drivers as metal slashed the dogs. The first *crack* of high-velocity shot went overhead, aiming for the guns.

BAM-BAM-BAM-BAM-BAM-BAM-BAM-BAM.

More men down, and some of the Colonists were wavering, slowing, a few in the rear ranks reining in their dogs, probably without conscious intent.

BAM-BAM-BAM-BAM-BAM-BAM-BAM-BAM. Three hundred

meters, and hardly a round was missing; some of Tewfik's men were hit half a dozen times between saddle and ground. Then the great banners of black and green surged forward, the amir throwing himself into the space between the forces to draw his men through the beaten ground by sheer force of will.

BAM-BAM-BAM-BAM-BAM-BAM-BAM-BAM.

"By the Spirit, we're going to do it!" Raj shouted exultantly; they *were* slowing, half the party around Tewfik was down, the flag fell and the commander himself scooped it off the ground, waving it through the air in a swirling flourish.

A hand pulled Raj around. *"Ser!"* the standard bearer shrieked into his ear, pointing with his charge.

The slope behind the 5th was scattered with the remnants of the 2nd; some even looked as if they were rallying . . . but *another* disorganized, blue-clad mass was pounding down the trail *from* El Djem, and by this time Raj felt expert enough to know panic flight when he saw it.

"Oh, shit," he said with infinite weariness. *Suzette, Suzette . . .* Tewfik had stolen a march; Tewfik's maps had waterholes where the Civil Government's showed only impassable desert. And El Djem had been virtually undefended, garrisoned with wounded and noncombatants. A small knot of men in blue was well ahead of the rest, with another figure in their midst. Smaller, on a light boned brown-and-black dog with floppy ears.

BAM-BAM-BAM-BAM-BAM-BAM-BAM-BAM. Some of the rearmost Colonists had pulled around and were fleeing, actually running. A clip of pompom shells struck just short of First Company's line. Men fell, silent or screaming; their comrades ignored them, and a 75 shell landed just under the ammunition limber of the pompom a second later. The explosion was noticeable even through the other sounds of combat.

And Suzette was bounding up the slope toward him on her palfrey-hound Harbie.

"Where's Thiddo and the Third Company?" Raj shouted, burying relief. Hell, *he* was probably going to die within the next hundred seconds or so.

"Thiddo's dead, this is all," Suzette shouted back, wild-eyed and clutching her carbine. There were less than a platoon around her, and most looked barely fit to stay in the saddle, much less fight. One had a flap of cheek hanging down, exposing a red-and-white grin. "Tewfik's men were waiting for us, these cut their way out with me, they're about an hour behind us!"

BAM-BAM-BAM-BAM-BAM-BAM-BAM-BAM. One last full volley, and the Colonist charge shuddered almost to a halt; almost, and the first of the fugitives struck the 5th's rear, destroying the safety they so desperately sought. The firing line shattered like a glass jar dropped on concrete.

"Sound *Fall back and Rally*," Raj ordered, sweeping Suzette behind him with one arm. Tewfik's cavalry were pouring through the gaps, but the very mass of the fugitives from El Djem hindered them, as a runner would be who suddenly plunged into knee-deep water. The ones who had gotten this far were all mounted; their dogs fought, catching the madness of their riders, and each victim took a moment to saber down, if nothing else.

Seconds would determine whether anyone survived at all. "Rally around the guns," Raj was shouting. "Form square!" He saw men turn to run, men of the new drafts. One such made it only two paces before the soldier beside him drove his bayonet through his back . . . and was himself cut down by a Colonist scimitar only a moment later, a great fan-shaped spray of blood bursting out of his mouth.

A group came back in a block, turned, knelt, fired a ragged volley.

"Rally! Rally to the guns!" Raj heard them take it up; more were struggling in from the two companies in the center, men with the ability to see their only chance of survival even now. The slopes around them were scattered with individuals and small groups from the outer two companies, riding for their lives in a spatter like mercury on glass. The whole position on the ridgeline was a mass of struggling men and dogs, jammed in by the pressure from both sides; a ragged circle was beginning to form about the four 75's and the banner of the 5th, men on the outside, a milling sea of dogs who refused to abandon their masters on the inner.

"Load, load cannister," the artillery lieutenant barked.

"Out of the way there! Out of the way!" The gun squads manhandled their weapon until its muzzle poked through the thin line of 5th troopers, pointing at a mass of Colonists... mostly Colonists. "Fire!"

PAMM. A different sound; a cannister load was a giant shotgun shell, no bursting charge, just hundreds of lead balls. They hummed through the air like a swarm of giant wasps, and a gap opened through the press as if a knife had sliced paper. Another *PAMM* from the opposite side of the circle; the formation was growing like a crystal in a saturated solution. Individuals were seed crystals, a leather-lunged noncom, an officer, simply someone who didn't want to take the sword in the back. Gerrin Staenbridge came in on a back; on Barton Foley's, although he outweighed the youth by half as much again, although the wound in his side would have made most decide they were carrying a corpse.

"You there," the Ensign shouted. "Get this Messer over a dog!" The troopers obeyed; Foley paused only long enough to shove a hank of rag under Staenbridge's tunic as a pressure bandage and tie his belt to the saddlehorn. "Follow me!" he called, pulling his shotgun from the over-shoulder scabbard. "Those men need help." He pointed to a smaller knot of troopers of the 5th, stalled in a circle of Colonists. The men looked at each other, at the youngster, leveled their rifles and charged.

"Back one step and volley," Raj said. *Have to keep the guns or they'll cut us to pieces with the pompoms. Longer we hold out, more will get away. Keep as many dogs as we can.* "Back one step and volley. Make it count, make it count, *aim* damn you." The crash of rifles was ragged, but there were more of them this time. Scimitars clashed on bayonets at the edge of the circle, and it lurched northward one long pace. The gun crews ran their cumbersome weapons forward again; their recoil made them almost as dangerous as the enemies outside, but they plowed furrows through the packed Colonists and left only sausage meat behind; meat that whimpered and twitched.

"Back one step and volley!"

Other voices around the circle took it up, and the formation was beginning to look something like a square as leaders took over, pushing men into line. Suzette and two walking wounded troopers were heaving others too damaged to fight over spare dogs and dodging through the snarling chaos at the center of the formation to snap bridles onto leading lines. A half-dozen figures in the dull-crimson jellabas went down all at once; Foley led his augmented group back into the circle after delivering a point-blank load into the backs of the Arabs between them and their comrades. Raj could see the Colonist officers calling their men back, literally flogging them out of range with their nine-thonged whips. They clumped and rode to the banners of their units, into the dead ground where the cannister could not reach. Comparative silence fell; everyone who could walk or crawl had joined the little group around the standard.

"Keep moving," Raj shouted; it sounded as much a hoarse croak. "Hold your fire!" Tewfik wasted no time; a young Colonist with a white flag rode up on a beautiful snow-white wolfhound. It *had* been snow-white; now it was speckled with red, and the herald's drawn sword was red to the elbow.

"You can do nothing," he said, in excellent court Sponglish. "My lord the amir, commander of the Forces of the South, Ghazi of the Faith, offers terms of surrender to brave men. You are outnumbered, surrounded, have no water, no supplies, no place to go—"

Raj waited for the men to answer; they did, without delay:
"Go fuck yerself, raghead!"

A flourished bayonet. "Come an' sit yer wog arse on this, pimp!"

"Up the 5th—Descott ferever!"

"Spirit of Man! Spirit of Man!"

From most, a wordless growl that was matched by the riderless dogs in the center. "Keep moving!" Raj said again; he risked a quick drink from the canteen, capped it again. None of the Colonist forces had dispersed, and the two remaining pompoms were out of the line of fire; the Civil Government fugitives in sight were noticeably fewer. A flurry of orders from Tewfik's command post, just out of effective rifle range, and a block of about four hundred formed up and trotted north, giving his group a wide berth.

Raj felt his lips skin back from his teeth. "Tell Tewfik that if he thinks he can overrun us, he's welcome to try," he said. "How many men did he lose today? Twice what we did? Three times? How much burnt-out frontier does he have to hold? And every minute he watches us, more of our comrades escape. Let him come; don't be shy, we'll see to his other eye for him."

The herald bowed and reined about; the wolfhound seemed to float over the baked gravel like a mirage of snow.

"I love you," Suzette said quietly, pulling up beside him.

"I love you, too," Raj replied. "I just wish we'd had longer to do it in." He looked north, to Komar, a week's travel away and as impossibly far as Terra the lost and sacred.

"Let's go, dog-brothers," he said. "Every second man, mount. Keep it ready to about face. At a walk, *march*."

CHAPTER ELEVEN

"Ser."

"*Hunnha!*" Raj sprang erect, throwing aside a blanket he didn't remember pulling over himself.

"Ser, we're here." M'lewis' voice had a lisp to it now, with most of his front teeth missing. A thick cup of kave steamed in his hands. Raj took it, trying to stop the tremors in his own.

"I was back in the desert," he said, more to himself than anyone else. Most of the other fifteen figures scattered around the lounge of the steamboat *Orbital Paradise* were as unconscious as he had been a moment ago. All were as filthy-shaggy, uniforms caked and stained until the original color was undetectable. "On the retreat, the third night, when they tried to overrun us again, and the gun blew up, you know. I was back there."

"We're *here*, ser," M'lewis repeated patiently.

Raj took three careful deep breaths, and a sip of the kave; it had plum brandy in it, and the combination hit the acid tension in his stomach hard enough to make him gasp. The others were beginning to stir, as the city noise penetrated the shuttered windows; Suzette slept on, looking absurdly young curled on the cushions beneath a window. Then the steam whistle cut loose above their heads, and every single one of them rolled upright with a weapon in their hands, crouched and ready. The steamboat's captain had not objected to their commandeering the upper salon, not more than once, at least.

And *none* of them was going to be able to sleep without their rifles by their sides, not for a long time.

"Arrg," Foley said. "I feel worse than I did when we got *on* this tub."

True enough, Raj thought dully. When you were riding fast you didn't have time to think. The whistle roared again; they were well past the cut where the docking canal took off from the Hemmar and passed through the thick watergates of East Residence. The *Orbital Paradise* was a hundred feet long and half as wide, a shallow-draft hull just big enough to carry the engines that wheezed and chuffed beneath them, with a superstructure like a rectangular wedding cake topped by the twin smokestacks. The paddle wheel at the rear churned into reverse as they slid into the dock, nudging into the rope buffers.

The quays were as crowded as usual, all except this one. A troop of heavy cavalry waited, down where the crewmen were manhandling the gangplank across to the pavement and looping thigh-thick ropes to the bollards; men in the uniform of Vernier's Own. Twenty men on powerful Newfoundlands, in black uniforms and gauntlets, burnished black steel breastplates, helmets topped with black jersauroid plumes. All of them were leading extra dogs, ready-saddled.

The lieutenant of the escort saluted and began a speech of some sort as Raj and his Companions clattered down the gangplank; he stopped in mid-word as they walked past him without pausing.

"My, ain't they purty," M'lewis lisped, as the Descotters swung into the saddle with graceless ease.

"Barholm wanted me soonest," Raj said. "Probably for the frying post. Let's not keep the executioner waiting, shall we?"

"Out! Useless sluts, halfwits, out, *out!*" barked Anne, Lady Clerett. She was dressed in pale cream with black trim, the colors of mourning, and she swept forward toward her friend with arms outstretched. "No, wait, you, fetch refreshments, prepare the baths, fetch clothing for Lady Whitehall. Well, don't stand there gaping, go!" The slavegirls fled in a twitter of voices and fabric.

"Oh, Anne," Suzette mumbled, letting herself slump forward. Her carbine thumped to the floor and the Hammamet carpet as she rested her head on the other woman's shoulder and let the strong maternal hug support her weariness. But business could not wait more than moments.

"I'm filthy, I've got fleas, your dress," she said, as Anne guided her to a chair. A flash of acute embarrassment at her state went over her; the room was not large, but it was roofed in pale yellow glass and walled with *torofib* silk printed in delicate patterns of reeds and lotus and jewel-scaled marsh sauroids. Cool air sighed up through cast-bronze grills in the floor, driven by steam-powered fans in the vaults far below. Nobody could say that Anne used her position with new-rich showiness; she had set herself to learn an aristocrat's version of good taste with the same fierce determination she used on any other task she undertook. A good deal of it had been tutoring by her friend Suzette, Missa Wenqui as she had been then . . .

"Here, sweet," Anne said, hard triumph in her voice, as she pushed a silver frame across the inistaria table between them. "You've got just time to read this, then a bite and a shower and my masseur and a full dress-up."

Suzette blinked crusted, red-rimmed eyes down at the frame. It was the letter she had sent from Komar, but annotated in vermilion ink, a man's blocky writing. By the end of the missive the pen had been pressed hard enough to tear the paper.

"My husband was so interested," Anne said. "And Chancellor Tzetzas was . . . horrified at what his subordinates had done in his name." A lazy cat-smile. "So horrified that he signed over every inch of land and scrap of personal property in the County of Komar to the Vice-Governor." Her fingernails pressed the inlays of the table. "He's too useful . . . Barholm thinks he's too useful . . . to dispose of now. And Suzie—" the long-fingered hands closed on hers "—your man certainly came out of this better than anyone else. Better than that fool Stanson, who seems to have done nothing more than get half his behind shot off. Which should make him twice as stupid."

"I missed," Suzette mumbled, fatigue-poisons blurring her eyes.

"What was that?" Anne looked up sharply.

"I said, he won't be missed," she replied more clearly.

A thought made her blink at Anne's mourning clothes. "Someone's died?" she asked.

"Someone's going to, my dear. Someone's going to."

Raj felt himself toppling forward off the bench and jerked himself upright again. He was attracting a few glances, here in the Star Chamber, but less than might be expected; theological controversy was the city's pride and sport, and there was plenty of it here. The great round chamber was filled to capacity with Hierarchs, Sysups, Analysts, Grammers, Church dignitaries of every type and variety from all over the Civil Government; there were even representatives of the Central and Western Territories Sysuprics, in old-fashioned vestments and talking with Spajol accents. Many of them looked a little uneasy, since the Spirit of Man of This Earth was the state cult in the areas ruled by the Military Governments, and the Orthodox from those lands were not used to operating so openly.

Barholm sat behind him, on a throne that had risen soundlessly to head-height on a hydraulic column; he was in full vestments as Supreme Pontiff, strictly speaking the Governor's prerogative, resting his chin on one fist. The light through the Star-shaped skylight in the domed ceiling cast a hard glitter on the jewels and metallic thread in his robes, the gold and ebony of the chair.

"And it says clearly in the Canonical Handbook," the speaker at the podium in the center of the room was droning, "that the greater set subsumes the lesser, the metaphysical implications of this being, firstly, that all subroutines are necessary but not sufficient to the operation of the code, and secondly, that an operational subroutine may therefore be treated as a virtual entity in, though not obviously for or by, itself. Thus if—as I hold Orthodox doctrine to state—the Spirit of Man of the Stars is the Spirit governing *all* stars, and since the Star of This Earth is unquestionably a Star, and since This Earth is unquestionably in orbit around that Star and therefore under the celestial influence and governance of that Star, then the Spirit of Man of This Earth—" there was an audible gasp at the mention of the deity of the western heretics who ruled in the *barbaricum* and lost territories "—is actually no more than a facet of the Spirit of Man of the Stars!"

"*Heresy*!" Shouts of outrage from the sloping tiers of seats. The speaker was a Regional Sysup from Ayzof, a town on the northeastern shore of Pierson's Sea; she was in full cannonicals, silver jumpsuit and overrobe, and headdress with wire-rimmed glasses and Starburst over her head. "*Heresy*!" A claque of Renunciate Nun abbesses in the upper tiers tried to start a chant: *Dig up her bones! Dig up her bones*!

"Silence!" Barholm thundered. "This is a meeting of the rulers of Holy Federation Church, not a street riot!" Monastic guards trotted around the pathway behind the upper seats and pushed or clubbed the white-suited abbesses back into their seats. It was a minute before the buzz of conversation died down; Barholm's own aides on the bench beside Raj were engaged in a heated if whispered debate, arguing the use of the archaic plural in the Cannonical Handbook's terminology for "Star."

"—and therefore," the Regional Sysup was continuing doggedly, reading from the notes on the lectern before her, "the This Earth Spiritists are, though they know it not, neither heretics nor pagans such as Christos or Jews or Muslims, but rather children of Holy Federation Church *in schism from ecclesiastical authority only*, and therefore ripe for reunion." She touched her amulet, a commo unit of venerable age, the cracks in its synthetic housing inlaid with precious metals. "Endfile."

"Endfile," the assembled clergy murmured.

"The Chair logson the Honorable Sysup-Representative of the Priest of the Residential parish," Barholm intoned. The man who took the podium next was tall and lanky, with a nasal Western accent to his archaic book-learned Sponglish; the representative of the Priest of the *old* Residence, second only to the Governor in the formal hierarchy of the Church, but under the political control of the Earth Spiritist barbarians of the Brigade.

"Waaal," he drawled. "Thissehere argument is interestin', but I cain't rightly say it means much. Because whether or not *we* think the Brigaders is heretics, they surely does think *we is* heretics, and won't nohow reenter communion with

Holy Federation Church. Unless you planning to whup them." Barholm tensed, then relaxed fractionally. "Endfile."

"Endfile," the crowd murmured, sounding disappointed at the pithy brevity.

Raj remembered an ancient chronicle he had read, of a previous synod: a Sysup from the provinces had said, *In East Residence, if you ask a baker for bread he will tell you that the Spirit proceeds from the Stars; if you inquire of the bath attendant whether the water is hot, she will reply that the Spirit proceeds from the Man of the Stars.*

since you are in communion with me, and i am representative of the federation, does this not make you the avatar of the spirit?

Raj clutched at his amulet, imagining himself rising and speaking to the assembled hierarchs. He shuddered, feeling a nausea-panic almost as great as the one he had felt when Tewfik's squadrons charged home into the Valley of Death. *Bad enough to be the Sword of the Spirit, and a piss-poor job I've been doing of that—*

A page pressed through the crowd and handed a message up to the Vice-Governor; Barholm held up his hand for silence.

"Your pardon, Users of the Spirit of Man of the Stars," he said flatly. "Urgent secular business calls me away. The Sysup-Patriarch of East Residence will preside in my place."

"Captain Whitehall!" he continued, in a loud carrying voice.

"Your Exaltedness!" Raj said, crisply enough, but the dust and stubble made him feel as out of place here as a cootch-dancer in a Renunciate's cell. And the dried blood that spattered him had had more than enough time and heat to become very noticeable.

"You have your men with you?"

"Ah, that is, yes, Your Exaltedness; in the antechamber." Where they had refused all orders to stand down, and had their guns ready. For what, Raj did not like to think; by rights, they should *want* Barholm to have him sent to the frying pole.

"Here." The Vice-Governor's chair slid down with noiseless smoothness. He reached out and picked up a page of notes from an ArchSysup on the tier behind him, scribbled on the back of it and handed the paper to Raj. A simple *Pass Captain Whitehall and escort to any section of the Palace. Barholm Clerett, Vice-Governor.*

"And take this." He pulled at a ring on his finger; Raj felt a prickle of awe as it dropped into his hand. A diamond the size of his thumbnail, somehow shaped into the likeness of a Starburst, with white fire glowing within. The Vice-Governor's signet, a smaller twin to the one in the Governor's diadem, a relic from before the Fall and as holy as any computer. "Nobody will dispute your passage with this, I think."

Raj nodded stiffly and went to one knee as Barholm continued, "Report to the Governor's personal quarters, with dispatch, Captain Whitehall."

"The, ah, your quarters, Exaltedness?"

"No. My uncle's." Barholm's eyes met Raj's, as dispassionately flat as his tone. "He's about to officially designate me as his heir."

"But you *can't* go in there," the chamberlain said, wringing his hands.

"Orders of the Vice-Governor," Raj said. There was a ghostlike quality to the whole affair; it reminded him of the endless ride along the north flanks of the Oxheads. After a few days memory and sleep and waking had blurred, until he was unsure of when and where he was, of whether what he saw was reality or dream or the endless holographic scenarios that Center painted on the canvas of his eyes.

"Governor Vernier is *sick*," the man continued, as if Raj had not spoken. He ignored the signet ring as well, although the men of Vernier's Own had passed the armed scarecrows who were Raj's Companions at the sight of it. And *they* were recruited mostly from the Clerett home estates, in Descott. Barholm's estates, of course, when the childless Vernier died . . . The chamberlain wore a steel collar, and his position showed how his master trusted him. That and the jewels on his hands and belt.

"They won't stop *badgering* him." The slave major-domo's voice rose another octave. "None of them cares about him, *none* of them, I won't *have* any more people in there, not if I have to *die* to keep them out!"

Kaltin Gruder and Foley stepped past Raj, putting their faces close to the servant's. Kaltin's face showed only eyes and mouth, through the bandages that turned his head into a white ball; the eyes were dead, as they had been ever since a pompom shell exploded on his brother's chest, just before the Colonists broke off their pursuit. The bandages were spotted with blood from the wounds beneath, and the smell of disinfectant showed that his face would be considerably less handsome when they were unwound. Foley's face had all its youthful almost-prettiness, but there was no youth at all in his eyes, and no more expression than in the shotgun muzzles he rested on the chamberlain's throat.

"Well, dying's your alternative to opening that door," Foley said with supreme disinterest. "Take your pick."

Dying, thought Raj unemotionally. He could remember a time when it might have been moving, watching the old man struggle for breath in the great canopied bed; now, it was a technical judgment, listening to the rattle of breath, seeing the blue tinge to fingertips and lips. The priest-doctors were consulting, their heads inclined together; a rubber tube and needle dripped something into his arm, and a pan of repulsive-looking vegetable matter boiled on a portable stove, giving the room a strange musky-herbal odor. The lamps were turned low, letting the afternoon sun paint the blue-silk hangings of the room with red; the eyes in the mosaics on the upper walls and coffered ceiling seemed to follow movement, reproachful.

Barholm stepped up to the bed on its raised dais, a writing board in his hand. "Uncle," he said firmly. *"Uncle."* He touched the older man on the shoulder, and the various members of the household scattered around the room muttered in scandalized tones.

Vernier cried out, in pain, or perhaps in grief when he opened his eyes and saw it was his nephew, not whoever he had been mumbling to. One of the doctors looked up and took a step towards the Vice-Governor, determination on his face. M'lewis intercepted him, grabbed his hand in a complicated grip that half-twisted it with a thumb pressed against the back just below the knuckles.

"Ahh, yer Reverence," he said quietly, steering the

indignant cleric away as easily as a child might have been led. "It's these teeth o' mine. Pains me sommat awful, they does, since that fukkin' wog bastid of a raghead, beggin' yer Reverence's pardon, knocked 'em out. Now, if yer Reverence—"

"Rica was here!" Vernier's voice was shrill and breathy, leaving time for a panting breath between phrases. Rica, Lady Clerett, had been dead for nearly twenty years. "Why did you make Rica go away, Barhhie?" Tears slid down cheeks that had fallen in over the strong Descotter bones. "You're always pushing at me! Can't you leave an old man alone?"

The Companions and the survivors of the 5th who had accompanied Raj stood in a circle around the bed, legs braced and arms crossed in parade rest. None of them had a weapon in his hands, but none of the people around the walls seemed inclined to try pushing past them, either. The door opened; Raj looked up to see Suzette enter. He blinked, not quite recognizing the dusty figure he had seen that morning. She was in court dress; tight jewelled bodice, beret with plumes above each ear, flounced lace skirt split at the front and pinned back to show embroidered tights and slippers in flashing glimpses as she paced forward to where Anne stood at the foot of the bed. A golden formal wig covered her close-cropped black curls, falling past her shoulders, shining and straight.

She flashed Raj a tight smile and then stood beside her friend, looking down on the wasted form of His Supremacy, Viceregent of the Spirit of Man of the Stars, Supreme Autocrat, Legitimate Governor, Beloved of the Legislative Council, of the Clerett Dynasty the First. There was a detached compassion on her face as the trembling fingers plucked at the priceless ancient synthetics of the sheets. Anne's face held the same smile it had since she entered with her husband, lips slightly parted, and an expression in her eyes more suitable for something perching in a tree and watching a dying sheep.

"Uncle!" Barholm said again. "You must sign, *now*, it is your duty to the State."

Da Cruz moved to Raj's side, spoke *sotto voce*.

"I don't loik this at all, ser. Governor Vernier, he was a great man, in 'is time. And the Council should be called,

I knows the law. And if he weren't no more than a cottager, 'twouldn't be right to do this, not on 'is deathbed."

observe. probability sequence, if barholm not appointed.

Barholm stood in the Council chamber, shouting red-faced. Other members were glaring at each other, waving fistfuls of paper or shaking fists; it was odd, seeing men mostly elderly and formally dressed in long robe and cap quarreling like drunks in a dockside tavern. All except for Chancellor Tzetzas, holding the codereader of office as he sat smiling in the President's seat; the Chancellor presided, until the deadlock was broken. And—

—a city was burning. Raj recognized it from the perspective drawings; it was Cardahon, a County seat in the central plateau districts. Fortified with the old-style curtain wall, because it was five hundred kilometers from the eastern border; bright yellow grainfields and dusty pasture rolled away around it, where they had not been scorched by the invading army. Siege guns bellowed from the earthworks they had thrown up, big bottle-shaped muzzle loaders, and suddenly a whole section of wall tottered, crumbled downward in a cloud of dust and fell outward into a ramp that filled the moat and formed a perfect roadway into the heart of the town. Columns of robed Colony troops poured out of their approach trenches and deployed, advancing in perfect order under light fire from the stunned garrison.

They surged up the slope crying glory to their God and to Jamal, the Settler.

observe.

Barholm stood in the Council chamber, arms crossed and face impassive, as the magnates and nobility of the Civil Government shouted and argued. Chancellor Tzetzas reclined in the President's chair, a slight uneasiness on his face as he cast sidelong glances at the Vice-Governor.

"Messers!" Barholm called. "Messers, we have wrangled long enough, while the Spirit-Deniers harry the frontiers of the Civil Government and sedition builds within. The Spirit calls—"

"Shut up, Barholm Clerett!" one of the lords shouted. "You're not Governor yet, and you never will be, if I have anything to say about it."

Barholm smiled, picking up a bell and ringing it once. "I'm afraid you won't, Messer Wagger," he said, with a tight-held glee in his voice.

The main doors burst open, and Raj walked in with a column of troopers of the 5th behind him. They tramped steadily into the center isle of the long oval chamber, steel heel-plates ringing in unison on the marble flags. A sharp command, and the two files wheeled back-to-back and brought up their rifles, muzzles and bayonets silencing the storm of protests.

"Go!" Barholm shouted. "You have sat here far too long for any good you might be doing; in the name of the Spirit, *go*!" And—

—Raj was giving a staff briefing, in a lantern-lit tent. For a moment he did not recognize himself; lined face, grey-shot hair, and the insignia of high rank. The officers around him were strangers, more than half of them Brigade or Squadron mercenaries by their looks. Which was impossible, foreigners were *never* promoted to ranks some of those men held . . . The older Raj was tapping a map.

"Well, gentlemen," he said; there was an infinite weariness to the tone. "The last internal challenge to the Civil Government has been put down. Our next campaigning season will be a demonstration on the border, to show that the guerrillas in Descott County have our support, even if we cannot take the field openly."

The viewpoint switched to the map; far away, Raj could feel his body's gut tighten, his crotch shrink painfully. Nothing remained of the Civil Government, save a patch of white along the lower Hemmar River and around the capital . . .

"Just don't feel rightly about it, ser," da Cruz finished. "Ser? Yer all right?"

Raj wiped sweat from his forehead. "Tired and bruised, that's all," he said, equally quietly. There was an art to pitching your voice *not* to carry, as needful to a soldier as the bellow that could cut through the clamor of combat. "I don't like it either, Master Sergeant. But believe me, it's for the best," he continued.

Da Cruz nodded slowly at the certainty in the younger

man's voice. "I'm yer man, ser," he said. "If you say 'tis right, 'tis right."

Vernier's liver-spotted hand signed, a shaky scrawl of vermilion ink across the bottom of the formal parchment. Raj could see that Barholm was forcing restraint on himself as he gently guided the Governor's signet ring to the wax of the seal.

"It is done!" Barholm said, turning for a moment. "I call on you all to witness—" his eyes raked the faces along the wall, many of them prominent men, Councillors and Ministers "—that it is done in legitimate form. His Supremacy has abdicated, and *I*—" the eyes blazed "—*am Governor.*"

Anne came to his side, bent over Vernier's shivering body. It jerked and cried out as she pulled the signet over the swollen joint.

The faint stars of the city skies were appearing by the time Barholm finished the speech; most of the hangers-on had left, and Raj and his Companions were alone with the priest-doctors and the dying Vernier. Raj could have followed the details of Barholm's address, if he had been interested enough. As it was, fragments of platitude drifted back through the tall windows: "prosperity" . . . "Will of the Spirit" . . . "subdue the barbarians". . . . A scattering of cheers. *Probably Palace servants*, Raj thought, then they built to a thunderous roar, that shook the building even more than the sirens had when they wailed to summon the people.

They knew Vernier was sick; they want a strong hand on the reins, in these times. Barholm strode back through the windows, brisk and calm save for the glitter in his eyes, rubbing his hands together.

"That's done," he said. "Now for some work, and then I have to attend that cursed banquet for the Brigade ambassadors; we're not in formal mourning yet, and then we'll have to set the date for the coronation, there *has* to be a quiet month coming up, the ceremonies are interminable. Now," he continued, speaking to Raj: the soldier felt an indefinable flow of energy, as if some of the exultant triumph flowing through his master had been transferred to him. "There's the matter of your next assignment."

Raj's face twisted into the semblance of a smile. "If you

think the Civil Government has a use for me, Your Supremacy," he said.

"Sir will do, in private, Raj," Barholm said. He grinned and slapped the taller man on the shoulder. "I've read your report, man!" he continued. "*And* had the story from the other participants. Of *course* there'll be work for you, you're the best Dark-damned field commander I have that's trustworthy."

Raj's jaw dropped. "*Me?*" he almost squeaked. Even then, he found time to wonder: the report had been fifty close-written pages, with operational orders and figures attached. *And it arrived only 12 hours ago; he's been hosting a major synod, getting this abdication scam . . . ah, maneuver put together, Spirit alone knows what else—where did he find time for it?*

"Actually, I'm sending you out to the frontiers again," Barholm continued. Another man came through the doors; the Minister of Ceremonies.

"Your Supremacy," the man said, going to his knees and putting his forehead to the floor.

"Consider it done," Barholm said; both giving permission to rise and instructing the man not to perform the prostration on non-ceremonial occasions, standard practice for high-ranking officials.

"Your Supremacy, let me be the first to congratulate you on the blessing of the Spirit; on us as well as Your Supremacy, that we might have right guidance."

"Yes, yes," Barholm said with an impatient wave of the hand. Behind him the rasping wheeze continued.

"Your Supremacy, it has occurred to me—forgive your servant's presumption—that the investment ceremonies would be of *unprecedented* splendor, if they were attended by so many distinguished Users of the Church, as are present for the Synod." Delicately: "Not to mention the implications, considering the presence of the Sysup-Representative of the Priest of the Parish."

"Good man! Excellent! Draw up a modified ceremony, emphasizing the Governor's position as supreme head of *all* the Church, and have it on my desk tomorrow morning."

Barholm's head turned back to Raj, and he took up the thread of their conversation without missing a beat.

"We're . . . *I'm* going to relieve Heartwell in Sandoral. Your next posting . . . Brigadier Whitehall. Stop imitating a fish."

Raj closed his mouth with a snap. "But, sir—Your Supremacy, I *lost*."

"Heartwell didn't even bloody *try;* he went down the river ten kilometers, saw a boogeyman—because there wasn't a raghead within ten days' march—and didn't stop running until he had the gates of Sandoral locked again, and for all I know the door of the closet he was hiding in, as well." Barholm's voice was vibrant with scorn and conviction. "You took El Djem, sent back some really impressive loot, and were then defeated by a superior army—one which outnumbered you four to one by your account, and ten to one by every other."

I was defeated by a better general, Raj thought coldly. *Well, then, I will just have to improve.*

"Led by Tewfik himself," Barholm continued. The Minister of Finance was making polite coughing noises: the Governor held up a hand in Raj's direction.

"Yes, I know . . . Dokkermen, do I have to go over this with you again? We both know you're a fool, why do you insist on demonstrating it? Get one of your subordinates to explain 'limited liability' to you; in the meantime, take it from me, we'll make back the loans on railway extension many times over." The Minister of War tried to push past. "Yes, I'll get to that in a moment."

He turned back to Raj. "—and managed to get some of your men out, at least, as well. Tewfik, incidentally, will *not* be invading the Halvardi next spring. You were right about that, and your demonstration attacks succeeded brilliantly in their primary purpose." A grin that showed the skull beneath the square pug face. "There's only one drawback."

"Your—sir?"

"The Minister of Barbarians' agents have been as—" to the Minister of War, "I said, *wait.* Where . . . ah, yes. Jamal, the Settler himself, is going to invade *us* instead, with the whole Colonial field force; the Army of the North, and Tewfik's veterans from Hammamet as well." He nodded at Raj's expression. "Yes, right up the Drangosh Valley, it's the only practicable route . . . Tewfik will be in effective command, of course." He clapped Raj on the shoulder. "Don't worry, you've got eight months, and I'm giving you carte blanche."

observe.

"Ahh, I did wish to see the face of this so-valiant opponent," the one-eyed man was saying. The one eye was brown, and the face was remarkable enough to make you forget the eyepatch with the Seal of Solomon. "Take him away, then. We will see if he dies as well as he fought."

The crimson-robed guards dragged Raj away, his chains galling sores that wept puss.

CHAPTER TWELVE

"Well, fuck me," the trooper on the observation platform of the heliograph tower said, lifting the helmet from his head and drawing a sleeve across his face.

"Not whiles there's goats in t'world, Saynchez," the duty corporal said from below. "Keep yer eyes open, I wants to know when the El-Tee's gettin' back."

Fuck yer, too, Hallersen M'kintok, Trooper Billi Saynchez thought silently, settling the infinite weight of hot metal and leather-backed chain mail on his head again and pacing the two steps that took him to the other side of the heliograph tower. *Them stripes has gone right to yer arse and pizened yer brain.* Only early spring, and the days were already as hot as high summer back home . . . and what miserable grass there was had already burnt brown, sometimes in a crust across pits of salt mud.

Hell of a place, he thought. To the west, nothing but desert that grew flatter and more desolate the further you went. To the east the scarred bluffs above the Drangosh, and then the dense carob and legbiter bush that grew in the narrow floodplain. Across the river was the higher east bank, raghead country, and they'd love to slip across one night and bring back a Descott County boy's balls . . . the water had looked inviting the first week here; in the second it was a taunting, teasing reminder of coolness. Nothing but the tower, and the thatched shelters for the dogs, mostly empty now that the bulk of Third Company was out on patrol. Barges on the water now and then, sometimes a steamboat churning upriver towards Sandoral.

"Jine the glorious 7th Descott Rangers an' get travel, adventure, plunder, an' girls," he muttered softly to himself, leaning the rifle against the mud-and-twig wall of the platform.

The only cooze he'd seen out of this was old man M'aylez's daughter, who liked a uniform. And he'd been so drunk on his enlistment bonus all he remembered was waking up in her bed with her father whaling away at them with his dogwhip, he'd had to run barearse naked half a klick through the snow before he lost him; the other recruits had spread it through the battalion and they were *still* riding him about it. Then a snow-season march over the central plateau and the Oxheads; Sandoral would have been all right, plenty fancy enough for a country boy, if there hadn't been fifteen thousand other soldiers trying to get into the same bars and knocking-shops, with prices so high the only hookers he could afford were bag-on-the-head ugly and poxed to boot.

And field drill six days a week. And those arsemouth bastards in the 5th throwing their siller around an lettin' us all know how they'd run through a dozen harem girls each last year. Got their butts kicked good and hard after that, didn't they?

"Talkin' t'yerself agin, Snow-Balls?" Not the corporal; one of the other six drowsy soldiers taking advantage of the crowded shade below. "Talk to me: tell me why yer ain't a beautiful hoor."

He yanked open the wicker trapdoor. "Loik yer mother?" he snarled.

The corporal came to his feet. "*Next arsemouth farts out gets t'water the dogs all next week!*" he shouted. "Yer mouth cain get yer killed, place like this." Outpost duty saw more than its share of fights. "An' Saynchez, *yer supposed t' be a lookout, so keep lookin'.*"

Beer, Saynchez thought, hunching sullenly against the parapet. *I could be at Moggorsford tavern right now, puttin' back a beer.*

With that barmaid swinging her hips at him.... Or he could have done another year as a *vakaro* for Squire Hobbez, sitting his dog under the edge of the pines, rifle across his knees, watching the beefalo and sheep grazing their way across the meadows, grass rippling in the wind off the volcanoes . . . He adjusted his sword belt again, trying vainly for a spot that did not chafe the raw spots on his hips, feeling the salt-stiff cloth of his jacket grating at the skin under his armpits and at his neck.

Something thin and hard whirled around his neck. His hands flashed back toward the man who must be behind him, but there was a knee in his back and the world was fading black.

Raj wiped his face with the red-and-black checked neckerchief; there had been a warehouse full of them in El Djem, and they had become a point of pride with the veterans of the 5th. He glanced at the trooper at the right of the squad braced to attention beneath the temporary heliograph tower, the one with the circular bruise around his neck.

"Stand easy," he said. The men relaxed, except for the corporal, who stood braced with a blank expression that undoubtedly hid a mind frantically willing its own vital functions to cease, as it had been since the 5th's troopers had stuck their rifles through the tower slits with a cheery *bang, yer dead, girls*. "*I* said, *stand easy*, Corporal M'kintok. No records, no pack drill.

"And Warrant Officer M'lewis, perhaps you were just a *little* too rough on Saynchez there? You can cough, trooper."

"Beggin' yer pardon, Messer Brigadier ser, but 'e didn't even have 'is rifle slung. Powerful difficult 'tis to get the wire round the neck of a man what has his rifle next to it." A smile that shone with gold teeth. "Don't think the ragheads would'a stopped when I did, nohow, ser."

True enough. "All right, lads, just a lesson . . . now, you're Descotters, not peons, so you should be able to think. Why do you think I've got you out here in the first place, putting up these towers and spending your days in the desert? Besides my reputation as Brigadier Brass Ass, that is?"

A long moment's silence. The corporal spoke, "Keep a close eye on the ragheads, ser?" Hesitation, then, "And to keep us from spendin' too much time fukkin' off in town, ser?"

"Right on both counts, soldier. Look, we're not here for the scenery. Or the beer." A relieved chuckle from the squad; the quality of the local brew was a favorite grumble for troops from north of the Oxheads. "We're here because a bloody great wog army is coming, in a little while or so. Corporal, you were a quarryman back home, weren't you?"

"Yis, ser."

It was a safe enough bet, with those shoulders. "Ever see a man killed for not looking where he was going?"

"Summat often, ser. Rope allays breaks if yer turns arse on it."

"It's the same in this trade, lads: sweat saves blood. Habits keep you alive or get you killed, so when you're bored, think of today." The slight smile left his face, and he saw them stiffen. "Now, if we have to launch out"—the common euphemism for dying—"to get the mission the Governor assigned done, then we do. But I will *not* let any of you get your asses killed unnecessarily, not if I have to work you all to death to prevent it!"

Raj touched his foot to Horace's leg, and the dog crouched. He stepped across the saddle, feet finding stirrups as the hound came erect. "Dismissed to duties," he said, as the men of the 5th fell in behind him. "Oh, and your Company is being rotated back next week. A detached Company of the Novy Haifa Dragoons is coming in, and they need a tour of the beauty-spots."

Jorg Menyez sneezed.

"Sorry," Raj said, and maneuvered Horace around to the other, downwind side of the Kelden County officer. Menyez was mounted on one of the long-legged riding steers some of the nomads north of Pierson's Sea used, bridled with a ring through its nose; the great forward-sloping horns were tipped with steel, and it rolled its eye at the hound.

"Muuuuuuh," it said warningly.

"Werf?" Horace's head went down towards its ankles; Raj freed a foot from the stirrup and thumped the dog on the side of the jaw with it.

"Not bad at all," Raj said, as they finished their tour of the field fortifications Menyez's men had been working on for most of the morning.

Two battalions digging, and two making a route-march through the scrubby wadi-and-gully country to the west, to simulate an attack. The trenches were neatly aligned at the bottom of a low ridge, fronted with cloth sacks full of the dirt. *Good idea*, Raj thought. *Bloody good idea.* Menyez had thought of it, back in the fall when the mud had been too soft to keep its shape as the men shoveled. They'd bought the cloth wholesale in Sandoral and put the camp followers and peasant women for fifty kilometers around to sewing them. Reusable, with a slip knot to fasten them, and the foot soldiers could hump them around by the hundreds when they were empty. More up on the crest of the hill, semicircular waist-high positions where the field guns could be pushed up to fire and then recoil out of sight for reloading.

"All right, let's get on to the next bit," Raj said. They trotted in across the field of fire, past rows of straw figures on stakes, woven to roughly human shape and given sticks for rifles. There were clay jugs full of water in the stomach of each. Up to the low parapet of the trenchline, with the helmets of the troops below, waiting to step up onto the firing platform. As the two officers walked their mounts across a board bridgeway that spanned the trench, a soldier somewhere down the line called out:

"*General salute for the King of Spades!*"

"Silence in the ranks!" an officer or noncom shouted; Menyez saluted.

The men had thrown up a low observation platform behind the trenches; Raj and Menyez took their positions there, beside the infantry commander's personal guard and standard, and the lounging figures of a 5th Descott squad around Raj's banner.

"Proceed," Menyez called.

Drums and bugles sounded, and orders relayed down the long trench. The men stepped up onto the firing platform; their heads were still below the top level of sandbags, but regularly-spaced gaps had been left below that, and the rifles slanted through. Raj looked over his shoulder; the barrels of the 75's were sliding out.

POUMP. POUMP. POUMP. Shells whirred by overhead, their ten-kilo bursting charges raising poplar tree-shaped plumes of dirt three thousand meters downrange. *POUMP. POUMP. POUMP.* In a prepared position like this you could build sloping ramps behind the guns. They recoiled up the slope, gravity killing momentum, then slid down nearly into battery again, ready to be reloaded and pushed the final meter or two; it saved a good deal of time. *POUMP. POUMP. POUMP.* Barked orders, and a quivering of the rifle muzzles as the soldiers pushed at the stepped wedges under the rear sights of their weapons, setting them for maximum range.

"Prepare for volley fire," Menyez said. Repetitions like echoes, down to the platoon sergeants. *POUMP. POUMP. POUMP.* This series on the outermost row of straw figures; fragments and pieces of wooden pole spun up into the air.

"Fire."

The slamming ripple of massed rifles ran along the line, and the staggered rows of targets began to disintegrate; leg-thick poles sagged and fell, and water jugs sent out spectacular fountains of clear liquid to glitter in the late-morning sun.

"Aim low, aim low!" Shouts along the firing line, as shots kicked up dust-spurts beyond the target. There were not too many of them, far fewer than there had been six months ago. Raj listened carefully; the volleys came fast and crisp, none of the telltale stutter between. Thick grayish gunsmoke pooled before the muzzles. Officers with binoculars were standing behind each unit's section of trench, ready to run out and assess the results; drummer boys and corpsmen and stretcher-bearers were stepping up with dippers of water from the buckets they carried, not for the men but to dash over the barrels and breeches of the weapons. It hissed and sizzled as it struck the hot metal; more maintenance work afterward, but it cut down on extraction jams and the even more disastrous occasional cook-off, rounds exploding as the thumb pushed them into contact with an overheated chamber.

"Cease firing!" A long bugle call. "Battalions will pass in review, by the left!"

"Shaping nicely," Raj said to Menyez. "They don't tire as fast, they're starting to *hit* what they shoot at, and they're starting to act as if they believed they were soldiers, too."

"It helps that they know they're not getting fucked over by the people in charge," Menyez replied, cold anger mixed with satisfaction in his tone.

Half the infantry battalion commanders had been transferred or retired since they arrived to join the Army of the Upper Drangosh, and a good third of the Company Senior Lieutenants. For everything from age and incapacity, through persistent absenteeism—several had not seen their putative commands in years—to selling their ammunition allotments.

"You tell people long enough that they're shit," the brown-haired man continued, "that they're not fit for anything but to suck mud in front of the paws of anyone who rides by on dogback, and they believe it and act like it." His pale eyes watched as the thousand men of the two battalions mustered in a row of columns of fours. "They're still nowhere near as steady as I'd like, except for the Ausarians. And my Kelden County Foot."

"Tewfik's going to outnumber us badly, and if I can I'm going to make him come to us," Raj answered. *I'd better; if I can't manage to force the enemy to assume the tactical offensive when they are invading us, then I'd better just get circumcised and be done with it.* "I think they'll hold, in field entrenchments."

There was a roll of martial music, as the fife-and-drum unit behind each battalion standard struck up; they had rifles slung over their shoulders, but Raj had seen to it that every outfit produced a band. The officers had bought the instruments out of their own pockets; a "suggestion" from Raj relayed through Menyez and backed by his writ of extraordinary authority from Barholm. Some of the infantry outfits hadn't even *had* standards; he had made the men contribute to those themselves, then had the ArchSysup of the Southeastern Diocese bless them in as impressive a ceremony as the cleric and he could come up with together. That sort of thing was almost as important as prompt pay and sound boots and seeing that the sutlers kept their cheating within bounds . . .

"Pass in review!"

Tramp of marching feet, the whole line moving like a uniform centipede with a blue body and red legs; sunlight glittered on flags and bayonets and polished brightwork.

"Eyes . . . *right*." He and Menyez saluted; behind him the standard of the 5th dipped in answer to the flourish of the infantry banners as each passed. The men's arms swung briskly, their shouldered rifles in perfect alignment; officers and noncoms whirled their swords in flourishes. Perfectly useful skills . . .

"Purty," one of the cavalry troopers behind him muttered.

. . . not least because they reminded the foot soldiers that they were something other than men who had the bad luck to be visible when the press gang came around, and too poor to bribe their way out. His Descotters and the other cavalry units were mostly here because they'd *wanted* to be, or their families had . . . or at worst, because a father had come after them with compulsory weddings in his eyes and a loaded gun in his hands. They didn't need as much prompting to think of themselves as fighting men rather than victims.

Of course, it was debatable whose perception was more accurate.

The column had passed down to the end of the trenchline, wheeled and marched back. This time as the midpoint passed the mount, different orders rang out:

"Halt. Ay-bout *face*," A wheel and stamp, and they were facing him and Menyez. "Ground . . . *arms*." The rifle butts thumped the ground, held rigidly between left arm and flank; the tips of the bayonets were shoulder-high. "Stand at . . . *ease*." Each right foot moved out to shoulder-width from the left, while the rifles swung in to rest slanted across the body and held at the muzzle in the folded hands; it was an easy posture to maintain, where the rigid attention would produce a crop of men fainting, under a sun like this. Many of the men before him were from the northwestern provinces, as naturally pale-skinned as the officer beside him.

Menyez's leather-lunged Master Sergeant bellowed, "All units, attention to orders! Stand by for address by the Honorable Messer Brigadier Raj Whitehall, Commander of the Army of the Upper Drangosh."

Raj leaned forward, pommel under his palms. "Right, fellow soldiers," he said, his voice pitched to carry. There was no other sound besides the soughing of the wind through the banner behind him, and a distant hissing from a flock of dactosauroids flying toward the river.

"Today you've shown that you can march, dig, and shoot," he continued. "All good preparation for your real work, which is to kill the enemy." An almost imperceptible rustle of uneasiness; that enemy would outnumber them badly—Sandoral traded across the river into the Colony, rumor abounded, and it had exaggerated what was coming up from Al-Kebir even beyond the unpleasant probable truth.

"Before they get a chance to kill you." No harm in reminding them of the unfair but inescapable fact that in the event of defeat cavalry had some chance of getting away, and infantry none at all. "Just remember this: men aren't any more bulletproof than those scarecrows you just blew the hell out of. Put a bullet through a man, and he falls down and dies. Messer or cropper, raghead or believer, the bullet doesn't care. And if he's on a dog—" Raj slapped Horace's neck, which twitched "—it just makes him a bigger target. Spirit of Man of the Stars firm your aim, for the restoration of the Holy Federation!"

"Endfile," the soldiers murmured in unison.

"Carry on."

Menyez nodded. "Carry on, Top," he said to the senior noncom.

"Attention to orders! 17th Kelden County Foot, Fifth Company, second platoon, is hereby judged best unit of today's exercise, and will be issued a 24-hour pass to Sandoral, effective from 12:00 hours tomorrow! 21st Olgez County Rifles, First Company, first platoon, is low-ranked and will do double fatigues for the next week. Dismissed to duties!"

"Ah, Raj," Menyez coughed; it sounded embarrassed, a social gesture rather than the product of his affliction. "Your lady was kind enough to invite Aylice and myself to the entertainment tonight. Shall we arrange a carriage together?"

Semul Falhasker was staging a revival of Minalor's *Foreshadows of the Fall*, classical mime-drama. No expense had been spared: a full orchestra and troupe from the East Residence, with fireworks and illumination on the Drangosh to follow. Little enough, for the richest merchant in Sandoral.

"No, thank you," Raj said, looking aside. "I'll be, ah, that is, too busy. I'll be dropping by for the banquet and review afterwards." On torchlit barges out on the river; *that* was being staged by Wenner Reed. *Captain* Wenner Reed, if you please; Falhasker's bitter rival, second-richest merchant in

Sandoral, and commander of the city militia. That made it a matter of military courtesy to attend . . . "Enjoy yourselves by all means."

He straightened. "No rest for the weary; I've got to go drop by on the Skinners, before they forget why they're here and decide to burn down the city on a whim."

Menyez nodded, compassion flickering in his eyes for a moment.

"And I don't envy you the Skinners," he continued, changing the subject with a slight shudder. Nobody liked the barbarian mercenaries from the far northeast; compared to them, the western tribes of the Military Governments, the Brigade and Squadron and even the Stalwarts, were models of civilized sophistication.

"Well," Raj said, "they do have one great qualification."

"Their marksmanship?"

"No," he said, reining around. "The fact that they're the only people around here, Tewfik possibly excepted, who are really *looking forward* to the fighting."

"Ser," M'lewis and da Cruz said, almost simultaneously. They eyed each other, and the Master Sergeant continued first. It was his responsibility to inform the commander of possible threats, after all.

"Skinner, left about one thousand, in t'ditch, ser," he said. "Lookin' real unobtrusive like, but he's aimin' at us."

Raj rolled his head as if stretching his neck muscles. Was that a glimmer of sun on iron? Impossible to tell, and the wind was in their faces, no warning from the dogs.

"Right an' behinds us, in t'tree, ser," M'lewis said. Da Cruz was startled enough to whip his head around, swearing.

"Eyes front," Raj said. Better to ride right in and let the barbarians think all their scouts had been spotted and ignored.

There were probably more of the Skinners watching behind their heavy two-meter sauroid-killer rifles. Not because anyone had assigned them to it, simply because that was what those particular warriors had chosen to do. The camp up ahead contained half his Skinners, it would be an offense against the patron Avatars of the Army to call them a battalion of soldiers . . . and this was better organized than his *other* war band of them; he kept them well north and south of the city respectively, they came of different clans and had a habit of casual sniping whenever he brought them in range of each other. The chiefs assured him that would stop when a real enemy came in sight.

The Skinners had been assigned an evacuated village on the fringe of the cultivated lands as their camp; it was almost all destroyed now, the huts burned down, the orchard trees hacked for firewood or used for target practice or simply destroyed in idle vandalism. Some of them had rigged sun shelters of sauroid hides—they were hunters, mostly, at home on the northern plains—and more simply dropped and slept wherever impulse took them. The stink was enough to make the troopers behind him gasp and breathe through their mouths; enough to make him, too, if dignity had not prevented.

There were flyblown half-eaten sheep carcasses lying in the muddy patches between shelters, some writhing with maggots; flies clustered blackly on the mouths and eyes of men lying sleeping against their saddles. Dogshit and human dung littered the ground; as they watched, a Skinner undid his breechclout and squatted. Another staggered out of a roofless hut with a jug clutched in one hand, swayed, pirouetted, vomited, and fell facedown in the result, twitching and mumbling. Hounds of every color raised their massive flop-eared heads as the party from the 5th trotted by, scratched at fleas or simply slept.

Raj suspected that his own relative popularity with the Skinners was based on Horace; few other peoples rode hounds, with their incorrigible tendency to do exactly as they pleased with very little regard for consequences . . . which, come to think of it, was very much like the Skinners themselves.

"Spirit on crutches, this place looks like an invitation to an attack," one of the troopers in the color party muttered to another.

"That's what *they* thought," da Cruz replied with grim amusement; he had been here with Raj before.

They were coming up on a relatively intact hut, one that had not been burned down, at least, and whose tile roof was mostly still there. Also there were at least fifty heads, identifiable as Colonists by the spired helms, lined up in the eaves trough of the house or dangling from the branches of a dead orange tree beside the door; some had fallen, and been casually kicked into corners. The trooper took a look and went eyes-front, making an audible swallowing sound.

There was a hound lying on its back beside the door, rumbling a deep snore and occasionally twitching one of its splayed-out paws as it hunted in its sleep. The Skinner chief was kneeling on the threshold, behind a woman with her dress thrown up over her head; he took one hand off her hips and waved as Raj and his men reined in, without interrupting the rhythm of his thrusts. They jingled the long cartridges in the belts slung across his chest; for the rest, he wore the fringed leggings and beaded moccasins of his people's dress; the breechclout was thrown aside for the moment. Two-inch sauroid fangs were sewn onto his vest and tangled in the scalplock of hair that fell from the crown of his head to his waist; for the rest the head was as bald as an egg and brown as the rest of his body.

"Eh, my fren', *amitu*!" he called, in an atrocious mixture of Sponglish and *Kanjuk*. The woman squeaked as he finished in a flurry of grunts and withdrew. "You sojer-man who *mal cumme nus*, bad like us! You wan' *cushez cet fil*, eh? She pretty good." Massive, at least, which was how comeliness was measured among the northeastern nomads.

"Not right now, thank you," Raj replied politely.

"Eh, good, you drink wit' me." He gave the woman a ringing slap on her presented buttocks and stood, scratching his crotch energetically. "Fetch drink, woman."

She rose and scurried into the hut, returning with a clay jug. The Skinner drank noisily, liquid running down his chest, and handed the jug to Raj. Gritting his teeth and conscious of the beady eyes watching him, he took a healthy swig, spat a mouthful out.

"Dog piss," he said politely, and drank again; thank the *Spirit* he'd had the foresight to stuff himself with bread soaked in olive oil before coming out here. The liquor was basically *arak*, a sort of gin distilled from dates; the additions were those traders dealing with the steppe had found popular, chili peppers, sprigs of wormwood and a little turpentine.

"Want eat?" the chief said, pulling a stick of dried meat from a bag hanging from the eaves.

"No," Raj said: that was no breach of etiquette among Skinners, they could gorge and then go for days without a bite, as indifferent to hunger as they were to any other physical discomfort.

"So," the barbarian said, the formalities having been satisfied. "What you want, sojer-man? *Mez gars*, my men, they no kill any more farmers?"

Not since we took to shipping the liquor up here by the wagonload, Raj thought. That was a solution of limited use, though: he wanted them alive when Tewfik got here. On the whole, he wished that the Minister of Barbarians had been a little less efficient in moving the Skinners across the Civil Government and down to the frontier; it would have been more convenient had they arrived later. Most troops benefited from extra training, but if you kept Skinners in one place too long all they did was rot. On the other hand, there was no knowing *exactly* when the Colonists would make their move, now that the campaigning season was open.

"There are to be fireworks tonight," he said. The chief frowned, scratching himself again and tying on the breechclout. Raj amplified: "A great feast; meat, drink, music, women." Sandoral's dockside knocking-shops had agreed to furnish volunteers, heavily subsidized from Army funds. At that, Skinners rarely actually hurt cooperating females; they considered it beneath a warrior's dignity. "Lights—lights in the sky."

The barbarian's eyes lit with comprehension. "Ah, medicine dance!" He crossed himself vigorously. "Kill cattle for Juscrist an' de *whetigo. Fais thibodo*! We make great medicine feast before fight, take lots of heads, good fighting!"

He ran into the hut, returned with his rifle and shooting-stick. The weapon was taller than he, beautifully cared-for and gleaming with cleanliness. He opened the breech with a *snick* of oiled metal and slid in a cartridge from the belt across his chest; resting the barrel on the cross-stick of the rest he fired downrange without seeming to aim. A bronze cauldron leaped into the air, and the ringing metal pealed across the camp. Seconds later over a hundred warriors were on their feet, many mounted, all with their long rifles in hand.

"Feast!" the chieftain bellowed, shaking his weapon in the air. "*Nus fais'z thibodo*, then we fight!"

Now, how do I tell them they've got to get on a barge? Raj wondered. *Ah, I'll tell them it's part of our battle-magic.*

"Cursed if I'd have been able to handle this without you filling in on the paperwork, Gerrin," Raj said, throwing down the muster roll. *Thirty demondark cursed battalions*! he thought. All up to strength, now: fifteen thousand men, from the drummer boys to officers with twice his years and experience, every one of them convinced he could do it better. *Possibly rightly*. It was almost time to head down to the river for the celebrations, but . . . *I like it better here in Gerrin's billet*.

"Well, I haven't been bloody good for much else, have I?" the other man said. "I'm going to be ready by the time that arsecutter Tewfik shows up, if it kills me."

Thunder rolled outside the window; man-made thunder, now that the thin rains of winter were giving way to the clarity of spring; volley firing from the ranges outside Sandoral. It was still pleasant to have a blaze going in the fireplace of an evening, although noon was already giving more than a hint of the savage furnace heat summer would bring to the Drangosh Valley; the thin desert air lost warmth quickly, once the sun was down. The smell of coal smoke mixed pleasantly with kave and wet boots steaming, and the underlying tang of massage oil and tobacco; there was still a smell of the day's stew from the bowls soaking in the kitchen bucket.

"You kill yourself, not be much good fighting," Fatima said sharply, in accented but passable Sponglish, as she kneaded the scented oil into the mass of scars along Gerrin's flanks. "Lie still!" She walked away toward the kitchen.

"Insolent wench," Barton said from the corner chair, without looking up from his noteboard.

"Your own fault, you manumit me," she called, coming back in with a bowl of heated towels and laying them over Gerrin's ribs.

"And *you* teach me read, always spoil a woman," she

continued sardonically. Some of the thick muscle was coming back on his shoulders, but the bones still showed more clearly than they had nine months earlier, when the 5th Descott marched into the basin of El Djem. An infant's wail came from up the stairs. "Master calls," she said, unbuttoning her blouse as she climbed.

"You going to adopt it?" Raj said.

Gerrin nodded, reaching out from his stomach-down position to snake a sheaf of papers out of a pile. "Jellica and I aren't going to produce any, not after six years of regular attempts," he said amiably. "Doesn't matter who the father is—" he glanced over fondly at Foley, who wrinkled his nose at him "—and it'll be rather a relief to stop trying. I only did because I couldn't stand the thought of my brothers-in-law inheriting the estate; my sisters are dear girls, but lack my taste in men." Foley threw a half-eaten dried fig without looking up, bouncing it off the older man's skull. "How are the infantry shaping?"

"Better than I expected," Raj said. "That's the Kelden Brigade out there now; Jorg has a real gift for it." Getting Menyez on the strength had been a stroke of luck.

"Nice enough sort, if you avoid all mention of dogs," Foley continued. The door banged open. "Speaking of dogs," he continued, "what do you call people who track mud in the door?"

"Soldiers," Kaltin Gruder said, but he stopped to use the bone scraper. "Ground's firming up nicely, though. What's that?" he continued, looking over Gerrin's shoulder at the document in his hands. "Nice fancy seals." He turned and called up the stairs, "Can't a man get a drink, around here?"

Fatima climbed halfway down the stairs and sat on a tread, cradling the infant to her breast. "*This* man get drink first, Messer Gruder," she said. "Wine on hearth."

"It's yet another missive from our distinguished Chancellor, moaning and whining about the infantry drawing cash," Gerrin said, skimming it expertly into the fireplace. The heavy linen paper curled and browned on the bed of coals before bursting into flames.

"Well, what does he expect?" Gruder said, taking down a cup from the mantel and dipping the mulled wine out of the pot. "Field armies *always* draw their wages in cash;

there isn't enough Fisc land inside a hundred kilometers of Sandoral to assign farms to ten thousand men." Only a third of the infantry in the new-minted Army of the Upper Drangosh were part of the normal regional garrison. "And the Fisc is *collecting* the rents on the landgrants of the men stationed here."

Raj laughed, with a hard edge to it; he picked up a coal from the fire with the tongs, lighting a cigarette. The red glow highlit new lines scoring down from beside the heavy beak of his nose.

"He'd rather we let them sit in their billets all winter, worrying more about the barley than drill, and bring them here by forced marches just before the campaigning season started so they could be good and miserable as well as exhausted and slack when we needed them. It'd be cheaper."

"Spirit, does the man *want* Tewfik on his doorstep?" Kaltin asked, spinning a chair around and sinking down with a grateful sigh, his arms resting on the chairback.

"No, he's just an East Residence pen pusher who's never been more than two days' travel from the city," Raj said, leaning an elbow on the mantle. "But don't underestimate him; he's no fool, and he's not lazy . . . notice how he's been becoming steadily less polite, all winter? Getting back into favor at court, I'd say."

"I'd like to get him out here on the border . . . Spirit of Man, what am I saying, keep Tzetzas as far away from me as possible, Oh Holy Avatars!" He sipped at his cup. The scars from the shrapnel that had killed his brother were mostly healed, standing out like thin white lines against neck and cheeks, one scoring a slight v in his lower lip. "Ahh, that's good, Fatima; what did you put in it?"

"Sugar, little cinnamon, half a lime, and pinch of, how you say, *nougar*. Want I should show your girls?" The other scars had begun to heal a little as well, but it was noticeable that Kaltin avoided the highborn women who had once been his main recreation.

The Arab girl switched the baby to the other breast; Raj stared into the fire, and Kaltin watched a trifle wistfully. "Tell me something, Fatima," he said. "How did you know you were pregnant, when Tewfik kicked our butts out of El Djem?" She had shown up half-dead when they were nearly at the border, another of the steady trickle of fugitives that came in all during the nightmare retreat.

"Not know then," she said, stroking the boy's cheek as he suckled.

Kaltin blinked at her. "Then why on earth *did* you follow us?" he asked, bewildered.

"Oh, plenty reason," she said. "I fifth daughter of concubine with no sons, mother die have me. I servant, not even valuable like slave; always talk back, get beaten. No dowry, so have to marry poor man, or be small-small—" she looked over at Foley.

"Insignificant," he told her.

"In-sig-nif-icant concubine like mother." For a moment an old anger brooded in her eyes, the slights and petty cruelties of the harem. "Then, El Djem fall, I have no house and not virgin any more. No Muslim man want me; have to be whore on streets if I stay in Colony. Better here, I know these two good masters, not cruel men: take risk of dying, but better that than life so hard." She grinned. "I right, too. Now I freedwoman, my son heir to rich *shayik*. Better to be woman here anyway, not kept in all the time, go—" she broke into Arabic.

"Mad from boredom," Gerrin said.

"Yes. And besides," she said, her grin growing wider. "Concubine for these two, how you say, light work."

Foley raised another fig.

"The baby!" Fatima said sharply.

"No fair," he said, as Raj and Kaltin doubled over with laughter. "Besides, I didn't notice you complaining before Gerrin got better."

"Fair is for men," she sniffed, and cocked an eyebrow at Kaltin, whose three concubines were friends of hers; the officer's billets were all on the outer streets near the city wall. "Men all like baby, bigger here—" she pointed to her eyes "—than here," and patted her stomach. "All want, two, three, more women, walk like rooster and then don't know why . . ." More throaty gutturals. Gerrin gave a shout of laughter: " . . . the women always buy cucumbers but there are never any in the salad," he translated.

Raj threw the tail-end of his cigarette in the fire and straightened, scooping his sword belt from the table. "No rest for the wicked," he said. "Sorry to drag you away from domesticity, Barton," he continued.

"Hint, hint," the young man replied, standing likewise. A good deal of the puppy fat had left his face, the hard planes of his cheekbones beginning to match his eyes. Both men threw heavy military cloaks around their shoulders. Foley paused to touch his friend's hair. "You be careful," he said. "You've been spending more time in the saddle than you should; we've got a *little* time, and you nearly *died*, you know."

Raj watched with hooded eyes as he paused by the stairs to kiss the baby.

"Poor bastard," Kaltin muttered, bringing his chair over to Gerrin's side and handing him a mug of the mulled wine. Fatima had taken the baby upstairs to change him, and they could hear the faint crooning of an Arabic lullaby.

"Our esteemed leader?" Gerrin said, raising his brows and sipping. "Spirit, women may not be essential but they do add to the comforts of life . . . yes, for once, fellow Companion, I think we agree. He's a driven man: they may write books about him, someday, but I'll be glad to be one of the footnotes."

Kaltin stared at him in confusion. "I meant that bitch of a woman he's married to," he said, keeping his voice low.

Gerrin sipped again. "I wouldn't call her that, not in any pejorative sense," he said thoughtfully. The lamp had died down, and the coals flickered ruddily over the heavy bones of the Descotters' faces; they had a distant-cousin likeness. "A complex person, very. And not easy to know."

"It's easy enough to know what she's doing to him," Kaltin said bitterly. "A man in a thousand, one warriors are ready to die for, and she . . . first she went sniffing around Half-Arse Stanson, now it's these bloody *merchants*, of all things."

"More a matter of them sniffing around her," Gerrin said equably. "Tongues lolling, when they aren't snarling and snapping at each other."

"Parties, barge cruises, hunts, operas—" Kaltin rolled his eyes. "She's *always* on the arm of one or the other, out till all hours. Who the darkgulf doesn't know it? Men who should respect him are laughing at him behind his back."

"Not soldiers," Gerrin replied. "Unless you count Wenner Reed."

"That militia of his is a *joke*. And don't try to change the subject."

"I'm not. You may have noticed it's considerably less of a joke since he stopped interfering with us working on them. And a little dactosauroid hissed in my ear that that was Suzette's doing."

Gruder stared at him in horror: "You're not saying that Raj *pimps* to . . . to . . ."

"Oh, shut up, Kaltin," Gerrin said wearily. "Of course not. How old are you, anyway?"

"Twenty-three, and one year younger than you, O graybeard."

"There's years, and there's experience: at sixteen, Barton's got some advantage on you, I think. Fatima is years ahead, and she's not turned seventeen yet . . . Anyway, Suzette hasn't repudiated him, fostered spurious issue, or created an open scandal. He can petition a Church court for divorce, or call out any man he feels is encroaching."

"But he loves her, Spirit dammit! The man's suffering, you can see it—he drives himself beyond his strength."

"Raj was born to be a hero, which is to suffer," Gerrin said ruthlessly. "If not one way, then another: his conscience will do that to him, if nothing else, as long as he's a soldier. Working for Barholm, at that . . . As for love and Suzette, like most women she's more practical than you, m'boy, whatever she's doing or isn't. Don't confuse who she opens her knees to and who she opens her *heart* to."

Fatima stuck her head down through the stairwell, upside-down; the long hair hung a meter and a half below the urchin smile. "Take me to see fireworks," she wheedled, "and I open anything you want."

Gerrin snorted. "You're not taking that child down to the zoo on the docks, my girl."

She sighed, looking younger for a moment. "True," she said mournfully.

"We'll watch them from the rooftop," he relented. "You can bring the cradle up there."

"If you'll make another pot of that mulled wine, I'll bring

Damaris and Aynett and Zuafir over, we can all watch them together," Kaltin volunteered.

"I go get blankets."

"*Ahhhhhhh*," the crowd around Raj sighed, as the silver sphere exploded over the domes. The sound rippled across the river, from pleasure boats and barges and rafts; the water threw the light of the fireworks and their torches and lanterns back in spatters of liquid diamond.

From here, Sandoral was an enchantment, like a vision of a city before the Fall. Raj knew the reality, a city mostly of filthy alleyways and mud brick hovels, like any other . . . but from the barges lashed together offstream you saw the Legate's Palace floodlit by its arc lights, white marble domes and colonnades shining. They had been built a century ago, when Sandoral was rebuilt after a Colonial sack . . . Elsewhere in the city lamps and torches were shining points of light at windows and flat roofs, as the people clustered to watch their betters at play, kind shadow picking out the russet-colored stucco.

Raj scooped another glass off a tray, then almost choked on it; Muzzaf's face looked back with perfect aplomb from under a servant's kerchief. They turned their backs to each other, and Raj muttered, "Anything?"

"Messer Falhasker has a number of people of Colonial stock on his staff," the Komarite said. "I've had no trouble in passing myself off as a Star convert of that stock." Posing as a Muslim was a little too risky. "Yes, he deals extensively in the Colony, and has continued to do so." Technically illegal, but Sandoral was a town that lived by long-distance trade; with the locks at Giaour Falls, down past the border, you could navigate the Drangosh all the way to the Colonial Gulf. Short of actual fighting or putting people up against the wall, there was no way to stop it.

It was actually more to the benefit of the Civil Government's forces, at the moment. Fifteen thousand mouths—not to mention their hangers on—was a massive burden for a city only six times that in peacetime. Much of the Army of the Upper Drangosh was being fed from Colonial fields, and even clothed in uniforms made of cloth woven and dyed in Hammamet and Dasra and Al-Kebir itself. So there was no *excuse* to put people up against the wall; he was here to fight, not enforce border regulations made by people in East Residence. No excuse.

Not yet.

"Beyond this, nothing. I managed to glimpse his books, and his rate-of-return on ventures into the Colony is suspiciously high, but that might simply be good management, not favors for espionage."

You could not shoot a man just because his worst rival, and the town gossip mongers "knew" he was passing information to the enemy. Or because he wanted your wife. So much intelligence data passed through Sandoral that it was virtually useless, half the spies were not sure themselves who they really worked for; he had had *confirmed* reports from half a dozen sources that Tewfik was on the march . . . sent against the nomads of Sogdia . . . down with malaria . . . plotting to seize the Settler's throne . . . only a week from the border . . . Quite probably *one* of the reports was right, but how could he tell *which*? That was the whole point of spraying out disinformation, it clouded the waters until the truth was invisible even if it leaked.

"But of Messer Reed's household, I have learned something. There is a new servant there, who calls himself Abdullah ibn 'Azziz"—the Colony equivalent of "Saynchez," it was so common—"who is suspiciously functionless. He seems to have moved here from the west recently. I will try to find out more."

The fireworks display ended with a spectacular blaze of red, blue, green, and silver starbursts, almost an exact duplicate of the Holy Federation Flag. Above him on the quarter deck, Raj could hear Suzette's voice:

"Oh, Wenner, they're *glorious!*"

"Come, come, my dear, after the Governor's Court in East Residence, I'm sure you find it boring and provincial, like all our little amusements . . . pretending we're big frogs in our little pond. How all the ladies resent the way you make them seem dowdy and out-of-date!"

"No," she said seriously. "That's not true; it's Sandoral—and the people I've met here—who make the capital and the court seem . . . artificial, and unreal . . . the frontier has such . . . vitality."

Raj let the Gederosian crystal goblet drop, and marched forward to where Barton Foley was backed into a corner by three local society beauties. He seemed to be deriving considerable amusement as he egged them into competition with comments very much in Gerrin's style.

"I'm leaving, Barton," he said abruptly.

The social smile dropped off Foley's face, as if wiped away with a cloth. "Where to, sir?" he asked.

"There, first," Raj said, nodding downstream. The Skinner's barge erupted in shrieks and roars and a volley from the massive 15mm rifles fired skyward that made fireworks of its own; in the dark the muzzle flashes were longer than the weapons themselves. "To get very thoroughly drunk. And tomorrow, you and I and the 5th/1st/1st"—Foley's platoon, first in the first Company of the 5th Descott Guards—"are going looking for Tewfik. Enough of this sitting on our butts sniffing the wind."

CHAPTER THIRTEEN

"Yer shouldn't be doin' this, ser. 'Tis not yer place." Da Cruz's scar-stiffened face was rigid with disapproval. "Er at leastways, yer should be takin' me wit' yer."

"Well, I *am* doing it, Master Sergeant," Raj said, slapping his gloves into his palm. "And Captain Staenbridge will need you, if anything unfortunate should happen."

Like the Colonials cutting us all into dogmeat, he thought. The chill seemed to settle in his belly. *They're right: I'm supposed to be commanding thirty battalions, not leading forty men on a forlorn hope scouting mission.* He put the inner voice aside; arguably it was worse for the men to see the commander vacillate than to make a possibly-stupid decision, Spirit knew everyone fucked up now and then . . . and things were going well in Sandoral . . . and the *Spirit* knew it was the one place on Earth . . . Bellevue he didn't want to be, right now.

North along the chain of heliograph stations a light began to blink, a slotted cover like a lever-operated Venetian blind slapping open and closed over a mirror-backed carbide lamp. It showed hard and clear against the pale stars of midnight. High overhead Maxiluna was a thin sliver of orange-tinted silver, and the smaller, brighter Miniluna had set an hour ago. It was cold enough to make the uniform jacket and the thousand-pound bulk of Horace at his back welcome. The tower above flicked once to the north to acknowledge the message, then began to relay it south; it was a long one. Pure nonsense, as a matter of fact, meant only to deceive; if there was movement and light at *all* the temporary chain of towers, no single one would be noticeable to a chance watcher on the other shore. And they would be used to night patrols setting out . . .

"He's perfectly right," Barton Foley said, walking back along the line of men and dogs. "Barge in place, Brigadier who shouldn't be here, sir. Clear path down to the water."

"Not you, too," Raj muttered, and turned to the Lieutenant of the 7th Descott Rangers in charge of the station. "Message by rider, word of mouth only, Lieutenant: starting tomorrow night, be ready for anything we send from the other side. Otherwise, *keep your movements routine.* Understood?"

"Sir," the lieutenant said earnestly.

"Just a minute, Raj," Gerrin said. "I really think you should reconsider. . . . If you think a senior officer is necessary, I'd be glad to go"

"No." Forcing relaxation: "After all, you've got an infant son to consider, don't you, Captain Staenbridge?"

He could see the other man's mouth close. "By the Spirit, you're right . . . damnable habit of yours, Raj."

"Er, excuse me, Brigadier," the lieutenant said. "I've got a rather odd request. Squad of my men—a Corporal M'kintok—just volunteered to accompany you."

Raj snorted softly. "Who's next, Tzetzas? My thanks to your squad, Lieutenant Meagertin, and tell them they're going to ruin the County's reputation. Now, if nobody else has precious time to waste . . ."

Salutes, embraces, fists slapped together. A voice inside his skull, **this risk is strictly unnecessary.**

Shut up. **observe.**

I said, shut up: you're the voice of god, but I'm a man, *Spirit take it, and this is something I'm going to do!* There was a pause that took no time in the observable world. Then: **stochastic effects may randomize even the most rigorous Calculation,** the voice of Center said; it was the first time he had heard Center lapse into religious jargon. Consciousness returned to the world of men.

" . . . let's *go.*"

Raj held Horace's bridle as the men led their beasts onto the barge. It was a normal bulk-cargo vessel, brownish-grey native *pigaro* wood, hard and impervious and full of tiny bubbles of air. The shallow hold was roofed with arches of willow-withe, and a cover of dark canvas on top of that, also standard for cargoes vulnerable to sun or rain. Just enough room for the dogs, if they walked half-crouched and lay down in neat rows; thirty-two men and mounts of Foley's platoon, the two men and four dogs of the portable heliograph unit, M'lewis, Holdor Tennan, and himself. The vessel sank deeper against the inlet mud as fifty thousand pounds of dog and man and gear filed aboard; the steersman at the rear sweep began to look worried.

"Come on, boy," Raj said, stepping towards the plank. Last on, first off on the other side.

Horace balked, flopping himself down with a jingle of accoutrements.

"This is no time for that, you sumbitch!" Raj hissed, painfully conscious of eyes watching him, the men from the heliograph tower and others from within the barge. He hauled, with no result; kicked the dog in the ribs with the flat of his boot, and produced nothing but a hollow drum-sound, hideously loud. Dogwhips were useless on Horace; there was only one thing to do.

"Suit yourself," he said, and walked up the gangplank. Behind him the dog watched, whined when Raj jumped down into the hold of the barge, then picked up its reins in its teeth and followed, testing the footing with each step.

"Phew," Foley muttered, as the last of the men disembarked on the east bank. It had grown fairly rank inside the barge, while they drifted down toward the east bank and past the spot where the Civil Government border curved away from the west. They were in the Colony, now, and far from help.

"*Avocati*," Raj whispered back. The common dog-fodder along the river, a noxious, flabby sucker-mouthed bottom-feeding scavenger fish with no backbone; the main drawback was that it made the dogs' breath even worse than usual.

He looked up the bank; the floodplain held the same mix of carob and native thorny brush as the other shore, but the ravine-scored silt of the bluff was much higher, twenty meters, notched and slashed by winter flooding. The air smelled of river, dog, and wet mud; Raj took a deep breath and exhaled, grinning up at the dark menace of the hill. *I feel young again*, he realized with a start; which was very odd, because he had yet to reach his twenty-sixth year. Even in his teens he hadn't shared his peers' pleasure in taking useless risks, in riding vicious dogs or hanging around girls with dangerous male kin; they had called him a sober-sides for it, and for occasionally turning down a hunting trip or a cockfight to crack a book.

It's because this is a comprehensible job, he thought. No huge amorphous army, where he *had* to leave a dozen crucial things a day in the hands of men he had never fought beside; no not-quite-omniscient computer angel to show him unassailable reasons for doing things he despised; no snakepit spy-hive of a city . . . just a cavalry patrol into hostile country, go in, get the information and get out. Succeed or die.

Foley came back along the line of kneeling men and crouching dogs; there was a slight frown on his half-youthful face, the look of someone focusing on a complicated piece of work. *Learn to do it right and they'll just stick you with something more difficult, lad*, Raj thought mordantly.

"M'lewis has a way up, sir," he said. "Passable without much cutting." Native scrub was like resilient metal wire that bit; they had saw-edged clearing bars, but the noise and delay were to be avoided if at all possible.

"Let's do it then," Raj said.

"Avatars of the Spirit," Raj swore, as he poked his head cautiously over the rise.

It was morning of the second day, south from their landing point; he had been about to pack it in, the patches of cultivated land along the bank of the river were growing more and more frequent, reaching inland further and further. Another fifty kilometers, and the bluffs would fall away to the wide alluvial plains, densely cultivated all the way east to the Rushing River and the highlands of Gederosia.

"That's the biggest fukkin' raghead army I ever *wants* to see," M'lewis said beside him on the ridge.

The skin around his lips was off-white . . . well, it *was* stunning. The date groves and norias of the riverside were lost in a sea of tents, orderly clumps and rows, dog-lines running for kilometers, artillery parks with everything from the common pompoms to heavy muzzle loading howitzers. Supplies were being unloaded from riverboats, pyramids of sacks and crates and bundles; men marched through the streets of the tent city, the spikes of their helmets glinting; parties of cavalry dashed across the plain round about. In the center of the camp was a huge white and scarlet tent like a miniature mountain range. Banners hung in the still morning air above it, or fluttered briefly; the sound of the camp was like surf, spiced and peaked with the sharp music of drums and the shrill of fifes.

A muezzin had called the morning prayer; campfires were blossoming higher, carrying the sharp spices of Colonist cooking.

"There must be a hunnerd thousand men there," M'lewis whispered again.

Raj smiled; the Warrant Officer was as good a man of his hands as you could hope to find, a superb dogsman with an instinctive feel for the lay of the land and a crack shot, but the scale of this was outside his experience.

"Barton?" Raj asked.

The young lieutenant was quartering the camp with his own binoculars; his face was pale under natural olive and heavy tan, but his voice was steady:

"I make it . . . twenty thousand, or a little more," he said, writing and sketching on a pad by his head.

"Much better," Raj said. He took the drawing and laid it before M'lewis. "See, each of the standard tent holds a Colonist squad; six men, smaller than ours. So many men to a gun; banners are graded, like in our regular army. Sample a section, figure out how many equivalents, and you've got a reliable estimate, the same way you'd number a sheep herd quickly." A pause. "You're counting too many camp followers, I think, Barton: they're building that bridge with peasants they've rounded up, mostly."

"Bridge, sir?" Barton asked.

"Mmmh. See there?"

Down by the water's edge the Colonial forces had dug and pushed a huge ramp of earth and timbers down into the current of the Drangosh. Two enormous cables of flax lay coiled and ready at the head of it, rope as thick as the chest-height of the men who handled it; behind the coils further lengths were anchored in timber and stone. Working parties upstream anchoring other cables that were small only by comparison. Across the river a similar ramp was being built; Foley turned his glasses on one, then the other.

"Little men in loincloths, and bigger men in pantaloons working stripped to the waist," he said.

"Combat engineers, troops and labor-levies," Raj said. "I've read of this in some of the older chronicles. You warp the cables across on both sides, then slide . . . barges, purpose-made pontoons, even rafts . . . underneath and secure them. Brushwood and planking, then a layer of earth, and you've got a good solid bridge. It won't last forever, or even through a spring flood, but you can march an army over it like it was a firm made road for a couple of months. Much better than boats, faster, more secure . . . Get the banners, Barton: full sketches, so we'll know who's here."

The great tent bore the green flag with the crescent and star. The Settler's banner, not just the national one, Jamal was here. But not Tewfik's black-and-crimson Seal of Solomon. A group of turtle shapes, down near where the supply boats were landing, armored cars.

"Yer a great comfort t'me, ser, but twenty thousand ragheads is summat too many, I'd say."

Foley nodded. "And that's a very impressive piece of engineering," he added, handing his modified notes over to Raj. "But all things considered, sir, I'd rather be in Sandoral."

"We'll see what can be done about that," Raj said, rolling over onto his back and pulling out his watch. "Hmmm. First priority is to get the message back to the Army. They'll have that bridge up in a day or two, and it's not that far up the west bank . . . M'lewis," he continued, turning the notes over and scribbling a message.

"Take this back to the heliograph." They had set it up on the reverse slope of a hill three kilometers back, the furthest it could go and still reach the southernmost outpost of the temporary chain on the west bank. "Tell them not to bother to encode it, just send it in clear and repeat until they get acknowledgement. And hurry."

He nodded wordlessly and set off down the reverse slope,

plunging over the lip of a gully in a controlled fall. Raj and the younger man followed a little more sedately, leopard-crawling backward down the slope to keep their heads below the line, then trotting in a crouch with their sabers held in their left hands.

"It shouldn't take us nearly as long to get back, now that we know the terrain in detail," Raj said. "I added an instruction to have the ferry prepared, so—"

He halted; Foley wasn't listening. His head rotated to the right with the delicate precision of an aiming screw, and Raj had learned to respect the younger man's eyesight. The lieutenant brought his glasses up again, turning the focus wheel with his thumb.

"Shit."

Raj followed suit, blinking against the low sun-glare to the east. A dust cloud, and a line of tiny doll figures on dogback, out in the flatter land away from the riverbank and its tumbled hills. Heading straight for the conical hill where the heliograph was waiting; not that they had seen the Civil Government detachment, from the leisurely way they were proceeding, but it was the best terrain feature for kilometers around, even so, a natural place to put in a watching post. Following straight in M'lewis' tracks would be futile. The little Bufford parish soldier rode lighter and with greater skill than most of Foley's platoon, good men though they were, and where one man could go undetected thirty-odd could not.

"There's a draw, through there," Foley said with tight calm, pointing. If the heliograph team and the Colonist patrol were the bases of a triangle and the platoon the point, his arm bisected it. "We can get between them and the heliograph, I think."

An ambush, but it would be very unlikely that a firefight would go unheard or unnoticed, this close to a major camp. It would give them time, provided that there were no survivors; the Colonists would have to find their men in the maze of rough country, and a stern chase was a long one.

"Let's do it, then," Raj said.

The heliograph tower was the highest place in Sandoral, a slender pillar of concrete rising from the complex of government buildings at its center, the Legate's Palace. It contained nothing but a windowless spiral staircase and a two-story bulb at the end of that spindle; the outside was sheathed in marble, because this *was* the palace, after all. The inside was severely plain, a lower room with bunks and table and chamberpot, an upper with the signalling equipment. That was a contrast to the drabness, a great gimbal-mounted telescope and the intricate levers of brass and iron that controlled the mirrors and slides and big lighthouse-style lantern on the roof. Right now there was a smaller telescope as well, pointing south at the temporary chain set up down to the border.

Highest place and the dullest, thought the watch-stander resentfully. Learning the code and equipment was like learning to read, a great way to get promoted . . . *and stuck up here*, he thought. He looked out of the corner of his eye at the woman who sat quietly smoking in a corner, looking cool and aristocratic in white linen riding clothes. With the commander's wife hovering over them they wouldn't be able to rack out or start up the usual friendly dice game, from which he'd made a fair bit of wine-and-girl money. *Nice piece, though, if you like 'em skinny*, he thought idly.

She smiled and spoke, with a crisp Messer-class East Residence accent. "I'm not here to pull an inspection, boys. Just do your jobs as usual and ignore me."

A head rose through the circular railed stairwell. "Hey, Corporal Stainez? Gotta raghead down here, says he works for Wenner Reed an' gots a message fer Lady Whitehall?"

Stainez sighed and nodded. "Send t' wogboy up," he said.

Abdullah al'Azziz bowed low before Suzette; it amused him to do so openly, when it was so deeply secret who he served, almost as much as it amused him to use his given name. It had been a *long* time since most of those about him knew him as "Slave of God."

"My master, the Honorable Messer Wenner Reed, Commander of Reserve Forces for the City District of the County of Sandoral, sends greeting, Lady Whitehall, and wonders if there is some delay that prevents you from joining him on the excursion to his country house that was planned for this day."

"I am ill," she said. "My apologies to your master, perhaps another day." The Arab bowed again, catching the signs of furiously throttled worry and impatience.

"I will return to my . . . duties, Messa, and convey your regrets—"

"Holy Spiritshit!" The soldier glancing through the telescope to the south blurted. "Priority message!"

The corporal pushed the man aside and sat in his chair. "Kearstin, Hainez, get yer arses up here! Mefford, take it down."

The soldier grabbed up a writing board and began scribbling in shorthand:

"Relay . . . *stop* Contact with main Colonist field force thirty kilometers south last west-bank relay station *stop* pontoon bridge under construction suitable for rapid crossing whole force nearing completion *stop* estimate Colonial force eight thousand cavalry ten thousand foot one hundred light fifty medium field guns siege train engineers and support units in proportion—*oh, holy shit no don't take that down, ye dickhead*—to above *stop* Jamal leading force in person *stop* no indication presence Tewfik and southern field army *stop* estimate main Colonist force arrive vicinity Sandoral five days plusminus two *stop* relay to East Residence *stop* order full mobilization highest alert *stop* will attempt to reach eastbank ferry point eight hours soonest *stop* Gerrin have fullest confidence in your judgment Foley doing well *stop* be home soon Suzie darling *stop*."

"Shall . . . shall I sound the general alert, corporal?"

The men at the main unit were already wrenching at their controls, and the big machine on the roof was clacking out its pulses of reflected sunlight to the north. The information would be in the Governor's hands before nightfall, across more than a thousand kilometers.

"Dickhead! Why'd ye think the commander has 5th men up here and not the regular crew? Them cityfolk pussies wouldn't stop runnin' till they hit the Oxheads, er they'd burn down the whole city while they run around screamin'. The Alert list is in the duty book, start makin' copies." He spun on one heel. "You, raghead—"

"I'll be responsible for this man, corporal. And we'll get out of your way right now, don't worry."

Corporal Stainez closed his mouth. *I'd worry a lot less if his wog arse was in irons*, he thought. "Messa," he continued aloud.

"Messa Whitehall," the artillery commander said. "Ah, Messa Whitehall, with all respect, you're not, ah—"

"In the line of command, I know, Captain . . . Grammek Dinnalsyn?" He nodded; a group of gunners looked up from dragging a rope and cleaning wad through the barrel of a 75. "Nevertheless . . ." She held out a piece of paper. "I *am* taking full responsibility for giving you movement orders; you'll note that this is stamped with my personal seal."

Dinnalsyn met her slanted green eyes and swallowed. *Merciful Avatars of the Spirit*, he thought. *Why me?* There was *something* going on, you could tell that even from the palisaded camp outside the wall. A half-dozen carriages had left on the north road, light racing-shells crammed with city men in drab clothes that looked utterly out of place. And a suspicious number of peasants from the farms west and north were coming in, with food and what looked like household goods on their oxcarts and pushcarts and backs.

"Messa," he said. Then turned and bellowed, "Lieutenant Harritch! Turn out; I want batteries one through four hitched with full teams and ready to roll in twenty minutes."

Ten guns, twelve if 3/3 and 4/1 hadn't been pulled with a stripped breech-screw thread and a cracked trail respectively.

"Load, sir?"

The captain opened his mouth to order standard shell, then closed it for a second. "Twenty standard, ten cannister," he said; thirty shells was a full load for the two-wheeled caissons on which the trail of a field gun rested while it was in motion. He didn't like the ass-dangling-in-the-breeze feeling of galloping the guns off down the road without support.

Just in case anything unpleasant happened at close range, having the cannister rounds along would make him feel a whole lot better. And anyone who tried to fuck with his guns would feel a *lot* worse.

❖ ❖ ❖

There were twenty men in the Colonist patrol, men subtly different from those Raj had seen before. Their jellabas were in a mottled pattern, a few of the beards red or brown-blond, and the faces beneath were fairer-skinned compared to the general run of Colonist, or Descotters for that matter. *Berbers*, Raj decided. *Kabyle berbers from the Gederosian highlands, the Jebal al-B'heed.* Irrelevant, except that they looked uncomfortably alert, and most had their carbines out across their knees. The first man was about to leave the slough just as the last entered it, winding south and west to reach a dry watercourse running due west to the hill that was their objective. The lower slope the Civil Government platoon had chosen was scrub-covered, and the steeper one behind unclimbable.

Now, Raj thought. As if to echo his thought, Foley's clear voice shouted.

"Fire!"

Not a volley but almost as close-spaced, as the troopers rose from beneath the cloaks and scrub that concealed them. A few shots missed; more of the enemy were struck multiply. Their commander shouted a single sentence, and then the survivors were down behind their dogs in a short-range firefight with the Descotters. All except for two, who wheeled their mounts and broke into a gallop back down along their path of march; the Colonist officer had told them to retreat, while he and the others bought time with their lives. It was the response Raj would have given, and the reason he was here at the east end of the line.

The reason he slid down, blocking the only exit. The two Colonist soldiers were coming at a flat-out run, their dogs tucking hindlegs through forelegs and leaping off into each jump. Raj extended his pistol and fired carefully five times, bringing the muzzle down each time recoil kicked it back. The first punched the rear Colonist in the shoulder; he dropped his sword, and the next two took his mount in chest and neck. It went over with a howling yelp and a thud that shook the ground and ended in a crack of neckbone. That left the other uncomfortably close, and if Colonist dogs ran a man weight or so lighter than the Civil Government's cavalry breeds it could still brush him aside like a twig.

Two more shots. One creased the dog's neck, making it

check its stride and snap to one side with a doorslam *chomp* of jaws. The next took it squarely at the junction of neck and shoulder; it slowed for three more strides and folded from the front, rolling in a cloud of dust. The Colonist had his feet out of the stirrups before then, tucking and rolling forward with the massive inertia of the gallop. Astonishingly, he managed to come out of it after a dozen yards, conscious and on his feet. Even more so was the fact that he had managed to keep his sword.

"*Die, kaphar!*" he shrieked, coming in with a blurring overarm cut, too fast for a stop-thrust.

Raj met it with a high parry, and saw the Berber's green eyes flare wide at the shock of the strength in the Descotter's wrist. *These are fighting men*, he thought. *I wish all mine were as good.* His left hand punched forward with the fingers locked into a blade, sinking into the vulnerable spot below the breastbone where even a fit man's belly is unarmored with muscle. Something gave and tore before the blow; Raj unlocked the hilts of the swords and punched the other man in the face with the basket guard of his own. Bone crumpled and snapped, and the Colonist lurched back three steps and fell splay-armed.

"Sorry, I've got business first," he muttered, panting with the sudden adrenaline-wash of combat, noticing the bruises and scrapes of the quick plunge down the hillside. And the stinging in fingers; he shook his wrist. "Never hit a man with your bare hand if you can help it."

Silence fell, broken only by the whimper of wounded dogs; then a crackle of shots as the platoon finished them off. A pity to make so much noise, but nobody in their right mind would go within bayonet reach of a hurt carnivore that size if they could avoid it. Smoke hovered, blowing away in clots, as Foley's voice snapped orders.

"Get their water," he said. "Dump everything you've got on your saddles but weapons and water. Water the dogs now and feed them the last of the fodder. *Move.*" Even now the men would probably lift the enemy's coin pouches and pockets, but there was no sense in wasting time trying to stop it. They scrambled back up to their dogs, festooned with the sewn goatskins the enemy used for canteens.

The platoon sergeant came over to Foley; it was Fitzin

Sherrek, one of the gentleman-rankers Raj had taken into the Companions. *Have to get him a commission as soon as I can*, Raj thought.

"Sir," he said to Foley. "We've got a casualty."

The three men scrambled down to the bush-shielded firing position. Raj could see at a glance that this was one man—boy, rather, he was probably no more than seventeen—who was never going any closer to home than this Spirit-forsaken gully. One of the new crop of boys out from the County to bring the 5th back up to strength, awed and envious of the veterans of El Djem and the Valley of Death, eager to prove themselves. The entry hole was through the lower stomach just to the right of the navel; not much blood yet, but nobody survived a wound like that. Although it might take days to kill.

"Ser," he gasped, as Foley knelt by his head, then made a keening sound as two of his friends tried to move him. "Ser," he said again. The young Lieutenant gripped his hand; the trooper was grinning, a rictus as much as a smile, face grey with the effort and with pain, as the shock wore off.

A man lives by his pride, and dies by it, Raj thought: an old Descotter motto. Worth the effort, he supposed, if it gave you something else to do than think of fifty years you'd missed out on.

"Know . . . I'm gone," the dying boy said to the living. "I'st . . . no priest . . ."

"Don't worry," Foley said, loudly and clearly; the injured trooper's eyes had not started to wander yet, but best to make sure. He reached inside his tunic and laid his own amulet in the other's free hand; it was a piece of circuit board, overlaid with gold and crystal. "Any who fall defending Holy Federation achieve unity with Paradise."

"Thanks . . . ser," the weakening voice said. "Wayezgate Farm . . . Messer Jorgtin's estate . . . m'Da rents it. Tell 'im . . . I died game." The teeth spread wider. "Mam said I'shd wait another . . . year. Right jist loik allays." A second's panting. "Ye can't stay, ser. Finish it quick, would yer?"

The trooper brought the amulet to his lips and closed his eyes, praying in a breathy mumble. Suicide was a mortal sin, but if his comrades left him here he would likely live long enough for scavengers to find, or the enemy.

"I'll tell them," Foley said, gripping tightly on the hand lying in his. "On my honor." The hammer of his pistol clicked back.

"I *can't* take the ferry across now, Messa," the man said, wringing his hands. "That's Colony territory over there, and with war coming, the owners would *crucify* me. Anyone could walk up and seize it."

Presumably he was speaking metaphorically, since only the stokers in the hold of the steam ferry were slaves and liable for private punishment of that extent. Suzette shaded her eyes with a palm and looked across the two kilometer width of the Drangosh, over to the cluster of shacks and the dirt ramp on the other side. Water threw back the noon sun with a hard blinking glitter that hurt her eyes, but she could see there was very little activity there, the few Colonists resident had pulled out weeks ago. The river marked the border, but the east bank here was too high to irrigate and held little population; most trade went down with the water, and the road was a minor one.

She turned to the ferry. It was nothing very complicated, a big flat barge with plank drawbridges on either side. The machinery was on the port, a two-cylinder steam rocking-valve engine driving a shaft that ran across the hull under the deck and worked two paddle wheels, one on either side.

"I," she said, stepping closer to the sweating man in a mechanic's leather tunic and cotton-duck trousers, "am Messa Suzette Emmenalle Forstin Hogor Wenqui Whitehall, Lady of Hillchapel. My husband is Honorable the Brigadier Messer Raj Ammenda Halgern da Luis Whitehall, Whitehall of Hillchapel, Hereditary Supervisor of Smythe parish, and commander of this territory under martial law."

Her voice was very calm, almost friendly. "Goodman, your employers can have you dismissed and beaten. My husband can *actually* have you crucified, *and will if this boat is not ready to move very shortly.*" She reached out with an index finger, tapping the air in front of his nose in time to her words. "Do-you-understand-me?"

He bobbed wordlessly and turned, screaming at his subordinates to make steam, *quickly.*

"Hmmm, Lady Whitehall, it really would be easy for the

ragheads to grab the ferry," the artillery officer said. "Wouldn't it be better to wait on this side?"

"No," she replied. "Time is important here. I have an idea."

"Turn in here," Raj said.

A map glowed between him and reality, an overview of the route back north up the east bank. The quickest way was picked out in green, and every time they came to a fork in the tangled, knotted chain of erosion furrows the light strobed about it. Their position was a bead, a cool blue bead that slipped northward, ahead of the green clump of their pursuers.

The column wheeled left into the entrance way of the gully, and M'lewis pulled up beside him. The Warrant Officer had draped a spare shirt across his dog's neck and soaked it in water from his canteen; it was growing brutally hot here, although not as bad as it would be up on the higher ground.

"Ser?" he said, puzzled and apprehensive. The sound of paws was muffled in the soft sand at the bottom of the gulleys; the walls were crumbly silt, a natural adobe laced with rocks.

"Yes?" Raj replied, blinking. It was necessary to rely on Center for this, but it still gave him a queasy feeling at the base of his stomach.

"Ser, how in t'dark are ye keepin' track of these wadis? We came south on the ridgelines over there—" he jerked his helmet to the right, eastward "—an' Spirit, it was slower but if we take a wrong turning..."

The dust trail of the Colonist battalion was behind them, but not far; half a kilometer to the east, where the ground was not quite so broken.

"... they'll get ahead of us." He reached a hand under the rim of his helmet and scratched vigorously. "I thoughts I had a good eye fer t'ground, but this! Cain't be no map, this ground must get fucked up fresh-loike every spring."

"I watched them from the ridge coming south," Raj said. *Actually, I'm the Avatar of the Spirit of Man and an angel in East Residence is painting a magical map in front of my eyes*, he thought, and suppressed a giggle. There were times when he began to doubt his own memories, when it seemed so much more probable that he had gone mad there in the cellars last year—

"In t'*dark*, ser? From half a klick?" M'lewis protested.

"Haven't hit a dead end yet, have we, Companion?" Raj said, with a hard grin. The Warrant Officer's eyes were wide with awe and a little uneasy as he backed his dog and loped off after the others.

Raj pressed a knee to Horace's flank to follow. *Wait a minute*, he thought, a knot of unease in his own stomach. *If Center can predict the future—*

probabilities—*and show me things from long ago and far away, why couldn't it show me this route coming* south *in the first place? Why couldn't I get a* scenario *of the Colonists building that bridge without sending a patrol and risking lives?* The echo of a pistol shot bounced through his memory, and the expression in Foley's eyes as he reholstered it on the third try.

observe.

—a glowing blue shield hung against a backdrop of a black more absolute than any Raj had ever seen, strewn with hard motes of colored light. White streaks moved across the blue, and the edges of the shield were blurred, as if there was a fringe of vapor around it. The sight was so alien that it was not until a flicker of hard light outlined the continents that he understood what he was seeing: Earth—

bellevue.

from orbit.

Paradise, he thought, conscious of his hand moving toward his amulet, with the dreamlike slowness that physical things took on when he communed with Center.

my data-sources, the angel continued, **my eyes and ears.** Specks of light moved across the shield . . . the *planet* . . . and his viewpoint sped towards one. An unfamiliar shape of panels and mysterious equipment, luminous with holiness. Then he was seeing *inside* it, and then *through* it, sight keener than any cruising dactosauroid's or birds, arrowing down to the line of the Hemmar River and East Residence. It was the lacy, spread-out city of the first visions Center had given him, the city before the Fall. Once more fusion fire bloomed across it, but this time his disembodied self snapped back, into the Celestial sphere. The drifting "eye" of Center exploded soundlessly, pieces tumbling away in eerie unnatural motion, as if unslowed by wind or weight. Fingers of light reached out from the planet, and other satellites exploded as well.

You *were blinded by the Fall?* Raj thought, and shivered. That was close to heresy; sublunary humanity had been reduced, but perfection reined beyond the orbits of the moons.

to a certain extent, i have my database, and may extrapolate therefrom, and i have everything you observe or have observed, and the contents of the minds of all who touch my . . . place of being, beneath east residence.

Then I was actually telling M'lewis the truth, Raj thought, amused for a moment despite himself. *Wait, though*, he mused, frowning. *I couldn't have seen all these interconnections, it'd take a team weeks to map the gullies.*

with your waking mind you perceive only a fraction of your sensory input, and forget much of this, observe.

—night, and the patrol was jogging south. Raj could recognize the time from the position of the stars and moons; a little before dawn, thirty or so hours ago. Again it was as if he were standing a little behind his own eyes, this time as he glanced west over Horace's neck, into the tangled country nearer the river. A casual look, but it froze in place as if it were a painting or an ordnance expert's perspective drawing. Networks of lines snaked over it to mark contours, and the painting turned three-dimensional and rotated to form a map.

Raj shook himself, and looked over his right shoulder again. The bright daylight seemed robbed of heat for a moment, cold and distant as a vision, until the smell of dust and sweat returned.

"Will we beat them to the ferry?" he said.

by a very little. A pause, **very probably.**

"Dust cloud coming, Captain!" the gunnery observer perched on the engine housing said. "Two. Coming fast."

The officer grunted, and moved to the two shrouded lumps that stood on either side of the ramp. The little Colonist hamlet was deserted, not so much as a chicken had moved all day while they sat there on enemy territory with the great wooden tongue of the ramp down on the dirt. . . .

"Messa Whitehall," he said. "You should get back to the engine house, under cover." *Your pretty butt should be back on the other shore, and if you get launched I might as well put my pistol in my mouth.*

"No, thank you, Captain," she said expressionlessly, puffing on a cigarette that had gone out some time ago.

"The ferry's there!" one of the troopers shouted. "We made it!"

They were still two hundred meters ahead of the first Colonists, riding bent over to present as small a target as possible; carbines cracked and spat, but you would have to be *dead* lucky to hit a moving target from a galloping dog. Anyone you hit would be simply dead, of course, but the roadway prevented the pursuers from spreading out into the broad firing-line that would have brought their numbers to bear. Of course, once the platoon were bunched on the slow-moving ferry, nothing would prevent the better than three hundred pursuers from deploying and shooting their quarry to ribbons long before they moved out of range.

Not to mention the pompom that was bouncing along behind the Colonial cavalry; one reason the Settler's armies preferred the light quick-firers was that they really could keep up with cavalry. The quarter-kilo shells would be more than enough to deal with the ferry even without the carbines of the riders.

All of which was evident to the more experienced of the squad, as well. "Shut yer gob, dickhead!" the enthusiastic trooper's corporal shouted.

"Rifles out and take what cover you can as soon as we get on board," Foley was shouting, as he dropped back along the column of galloping dogs. "Try and take out the pompom crew."

He dropped into place beside Raj, twisting in his saddle to look at the nearest of the shouting bearded faces behind him.

"Well, I always wanted to be a social hit, and be chased after," he said. Their dogs had fallen into step. "But this is a bit much . . . one thing I forgot to tell you."

"What?" Raj said, drawing his pistol. *Not yet, that's even more ridiculous than trying a carbine.* Similar bullets, but the longer barrel gave a higher velocity.

"We wanted you to stand Starparent to the baby," Foley said.

"I'm flattered," Raj replied.

The buildings were blurring by, adobe and pole frames. The ferry bulked larger and larger, but the four-meter gap of the loading ramp was a small enough target for thirty-odd men on dogback, even without the vaguely rectangular sheeted bulks on either side. Raj grinned to himself as he thought of galloping toward it *without* pursuit; it would be terrifying. Collisions, dogs falling, men being trampled or thrown against wood and machinery with bone-snapping force. It was wonderful, how circumstances redefined the term "danger."

The chase had lasted all day, lasted until some portion of Raj's mind was ready to believe it would never end. The hollow thunder of the leading mount's paws on timber jarred him into realization, and he threw his weight back in the saddle. Horace slowed, just enough to avoid the massive pile up at the far end of the ferry; the big flat-bottomed craft was rocking and bobbing as tonne-weights of bone and muscle skidded and twisted on the planks of the hull. Dogs slammed and ricocheted of one another, twisting and scrambling to stay erect on the tilting surface, yelping shrilly in protest. A human screamed almost as loud, leg jammed against the railing at the end with axe force, but most had had enough sense to pull their feet out of the collision zone. The whistle shrieked from the enginehouse, and the paddle wheels thrashed at the water, whipping it into froth as they tried to drag the ferry out into the current.

Raj twisted in the saddle again, feeling his belly muscles tauten as they waited for the bullets. The Colonists were not even slowing; the lead element must be planning to leap whatever gap grew between gangway and ramp. There was no time to act, only to watch as Suzette—*Suzette*—stood on the walkway and chopped her hand downward in signal.

There were figures in blue jackets beneath the tarpaulins on either side of the rampway. A half-dozen at each, enough to snatch the canvas away and toss it backward. They were city men, like most gunners; it was one of the few branches of the military with a significant number of recruits from urban areas. Most of them had spent time in the bleachers of the bullrings, and they shouted the ancient cry as the cloth revealed the twin fieldpieces.

"Holay!"

PAMM. PAMM. Tongues of flame, pale in the sunlight; jets of smoke, dispersing. Twin cannister rounds, and at sixty meters the shot cones were just reaching maximum effectiveness. Every dog and man in the first four rows went down as if the ground had been jerked out from under them. Hundreds more were following at a flat gallop, closely spaced, none willing to miss the kill after the frustration of the chase. Some managed to twist themselves out of the column, riders and mounts skidding and turning with desperate skill. Some leapt the barricade of thrashing shredded meat, their dogs soaring in arcs that landed with their feet sinking into the mud of the riverbank. Many more added to that barricade, tumbling dogs and riders thrown a dozen yards or more to bounce and splinter their bones on the hard-packed dirt.

A sound over head like ripping canvas; for a moment Raj thought it was just that, as hysterical dogs behind him shredded the sailcloth that had landed on them. A black tree of mud and water blasted out of the shore, close enough to throw spray and gobbets of mud on the ferry's bow. Then another shell landed with deadly precision ten meters further inland, and another, *wham-wham-wham*, a row of towering black-grey dirt geysers. The steam winch grated, and the ramp swung erect to hide the shore; the shells pumped by steadily overhead as the ferry gained speed.

He looked up to meet Suzette's eyes; they crinkled at him in that slight quirk-lipped smile, so different from the learned charm of her public gestures. Gravely courteous, he took her outstretched hand and bowed over it as he raised it to his lips.

"Three cheers fer Messer Whitehall an' the Messa!"

The men began to whoop, helmets going up on the muzzles of rifles, gunners pounding their handspikes on the deckplanks; even the civilian crew of the ferry shouted and threw up their knit caps.

"Shut up! Silence in ranks!" Raj kept his wife's hand in his; the slender fingers drew caressingly across the heavy calluses of rein and saber hilt. "We got away from Tewfik again; and that's no cause for celebration. I'm sick of getting away from *him;* I want *him* to have to get away from me!" He grinned. "Cheer my wife as much as you like!"

CHAPTER FOURTEEN

"Gentlemen," Raj said. "That's the situation. Your Reverence."

With that he bowed to the Sysup-Suffragen of Sandoral, whose presence was obligatory. It was notable that the County Legate was absent; the head of the County's clergy and Wenner Reed were the only nonregulars present. Aside from the two Skinner chieftains halfway down the table; one of *them* had his vest before him, hunting lice and popping them into his mouth, and the other was digging at the inlays in the ancient satiny wood with the point of his knife. The battalion commanders were present, none of whom could be slighted—some of the cavalry units felt offended that their infantry counterparts were there at all—and the Companions. And Suzette, of course; after what had happened at the ferry this afternoon, no one had quite had the gall to object.

Raj watched the faces for a moment. Expecting an invasion all winter, preparing for one, was not quite the same thing as knowing the Settler's army would arrive in three days. Even now in this high cool room it seemed remote, unreal beside the glow of sunset and the blinking yellow of Sandoral's lanterns as they showed in the windows of the streets below.

Three days if they were lucky.

"My children," the Sysup said, touching the Star medallion on her chest, "I am not a soldier. The temples of the city have been cleared, and my healer-priests are ready. With the assistance of the army's noncombatants, ably organized by the Messa Whitehall." A nod of the lined, fine-featured head. "For the rest, we will pray."

"Messer Reed?" A soft-looking man, if you only noticed the body and face and not the eyes.

"Sandoral was founded as a fortress-city," Reed said. "So long as Sandoral holds, the frontier holds, and we deny the Upper Drangosh to the enemy as a route of attack. Our defenses are the strongest in the Civil Government, outside the capital itself; let Jamal and Tewfik sit in front of them, until they starve and their army rots away from disease."

There were murmurs of approval; the local authorities here had been spending continuously since the last sack, three long generations ago. Sandoral had more than walls; concrete pillboxes studded the approaches, miles of ditch filled with razor-edged angle iron, massive covered redoubts filled with obsolescent but very functional muzzle-loading guns. The Skinners looked around them, bewildered: one stood and began reciting his deeds and those of his ancestors, starting with the last man he had killed. It took a moment to restore order, and Raj felt the eyes on him like the wavefront of an explosion, crushing and twisting.

observe:

—and the Oxheads were close on the northern horizon. A long earth barrage stood across the valley mouth, with a lake backed behind it; on the hill beside, Jamal's banner stood. This day it fluttered merrily, crackling like thunder beneath a clear blue sky scattered with puffball clouds, the beards and robes of the men who stood beneath cuffing and fluttering as well. They seemed in high good humor; to the south stretched a vast flat plain, laced with the silver glimmer of irrigation canals, patchworked with crops and orchards. Pillars of smoke were spotted across it, bending before the northerly breeze; singular and emphatic where villages and manors burned, smaller trickles from the woodwork of water-lifting wheels, more diffuse where orchards and ripe grain smoldered.

Jamal clapped his hands together with a shout; he was a stout man in later middle age, dressed in a burnouse and ha'aik of classical simplicity, black and white Azanian silk, wearing no weapon but the jeweled dagger whose curved sheath was thrust through his belt. He was almost ostentatiously plain, compared to the peacock splendor of the amirs and generals ranked behind him, the glowing colors of the carpets on which they stood; plumes nodded from turbans clasped with rubies and opalescene, and servants held aloft parasols whose canopies were intricately worked with Koranic verses in pearl and lapis.

"So many fires!" the Settler laughed. "We have been careless, my sons. It is only courteous we should do what we can to put them out."

Two younger men in gorgeously embroidered robes nodded and laughed with their father; Ali, slight and nervous-faced with a twitch at the corner of one eye, Akbar fingering his goatee with a plump hand. One-eyed Tewfik stood a little apart in the blood-red uniform of his troops, his face held like a clenched fist, but it was he who signalled to the uniformed engineers. An imam knelt and prayed toward Sinar, and the engineer whirled a crank. Spouts of rock and dirt punched out from the middle of the dam's face, in the center curve where it bent against the huge weight of water pressing down from the mountains. Thunder rumbled back from the stony walls, the ground shook. Then the first spouts of water arched out, beautiful and deadly as their spray cast rainbows across the gorge.

The dam crumbled like a child's sand castle beneath their power.

—and a cart trundled noisily over the cobbles of darkened Sandoral, pulled by men in head-to-foot robes; nothing showed but a slit above their eyes, and they stopped to rest often, although there were only a few bodies in the vehicle behind. "Bring out your dead!" one called, whirling a wooden noisemaker. "Bring out your dead!"

Artillery flickered and rumbled, the flashes visible over the roofs of the buildings, because no other light showed; nothing but the orange smudge of a building that had burned down to its foundations. The men pulling the cart ignored it; so did the folk who shuffled from an opened door, carrying a small bundle between them.

"Bring out your dead!"

—and a man lay in a roadside ditch. It was spring, and

flowering vines grew across the stumps of trees; thin grass sprouted on bare clay in the fields beyond. The man had been very thin when he died; whoever had hacked the meat from his arms and legs had had to haggle chips into the bone to get a worthwhile amount. From the look of it, after a while they had lost patience and started chewing.

Raj blinked, the faces returning to focus before him. Smiles from a few of the Companions, sneers or doubtful mutual glances from some of the other battalion commanders, who had heard of his fits of introspection. He shuddered slightly; Spirit knew, a vision of a battlefield was bad enough . . .

"No, gentlemen," he said, uncovering the map on the easel at the head of the room. "Observe." He tapped Sandoral city. "There are nearly a million people in this County—" probably an underestimate, nobody liked the census takers from the Ministry of Finance "—of which no more than seventy thousand live in Sandoral City itself. It isn't the trade or manufactures that constitute the value of this city, it's the fact that it keeps the Upper Drangosh in Civil Government hands."

His pointer swept downstream. "When Tewfik comes up with the Army of the South, the Colonists will have more than enough manpower to invest Sandoral closely, then burn and kill their way north around us—while the only Civil Government field army in the east sits and eats its boots; a few months, and the dogs will have gone into the stew pots." Not so much to feed the inhabitants, as because each ate more than a dozen humans. "And there goes our strategic mobility.

"The plain truth of the matter is that the Colonists are closer to the centers of their power—" he tapped the stick down on Al-Kebir "—than we are." Moving it two thousand kilometers to the east, to the Hemmar Valley and the coastlands of the Peninsula.

"This land north of Sandoral is the only densely populated and productive area available to support a defense line. If we let them into it, the Colonists can wait for Sandoral City to wither on the vine, no matter how long it takes. And I doubt we'll be able to hold them south of the Oxheads or west of Komar. It would take centuries to rebuild what they destroyed, even if we could." He took a deep breath, closing his eyes for a moment, and then opened them with a brilliant smile that almost fooled himself.

"I am instructed to defend this frontier. The only way to do that is to remove the threat posed by the Colonist field army operating on the Upper Drangosh; which means, to meet it outside the walls and crush it utterly."

Uproar, shouting; cheers from the younger Companions, a slow nod from Jorg Menyez. Suzette met his gaze, her eyes gleaming slightly with unshed tears. Cries of horror from most of the rest. Raj held up his hand for silence, but many of those present were driven by visions of their own; running with the yelping war cries of the Colonist cavalry behind them, he suspected. Death, mutilation, slavery.

"Quiet!" he called.

"*ATTENTION TO ORDERS.*" Da Cruz's bull bellow silenced them more effectively than a gunshot might have. "Commander said quiet, Messers," he added mildly. "Ser."

"Thank you, Master Sergeant. Yes, Messer Reed."

Reed hunched forward. "But you *said* that their armies outnumber you badly—how badly, you don't know. This is suicide!"

"Not if we pick the ground carefully, and see that the enemy come to us."

The militia commander's eyes narrowed: not fear, Raj decided, but the look a man gives an enemy. "How?" he said.

Raj smiled again, rising on the balls of his feet and bending the pointer between his hands. *By praying for a fucking miracle*, he thought. Aloud, "Messers, I don't intend to fight an open-field battle of maneuver . . . not against an enemy one-third again my strength and more mobile to boot. Instead—" he flipped back the map, showing another of the city and its immediate environs. "I intend to entrench to the west of the city. Even if they have thirty thousand men, Tewfik and Jamal *cannot* invest a perimeter that includes the field army and the city both. Nor can they leave an intact mobile force of fifteen thousand in their rear, and the city with its steamboats blocks the passage of supplies by river. If I move to the west of the city, *they must destroy the Army of the Upper Drangosh or force it back within the walls before they can proceed.*"

A hand raised by one of the battalion commanders: Beltin, the 12th Rogor Slashers. "Commander, if we stretch our line so that they can't outflank it, they can punch through. And if we thicken our firing line, they can outflank us; even if we dig in, we don't have the men."

Raj nodded. "Time, space, and force, gentlemen. You know what the terrain right along the river is like; impossible, and worse as you get north. Furthermore, north of the frontier forts—" which mounted huge cast-steel rifles, capable of smashing anything that floated "—we control the river; *that* is why they're building a bridge sixty kilometers downstream.

"They'll have to *march* every meter of the way, tending away from the riverbank. Twenty, thirty thousand men, *possibly forty thousand, but let's not scare anyone*, as many animals, every one of which has to eat, and still more importantly, drink, my friends. More than once a day. How many thousand liters carried up from the bridgehead? *This*—" the stick was unsatisfactory; he snapped the tough oak across and stabbed with his finger on a dry riverbed running east just southwest of the city "—is where we'll entrench. Impassable terrain to our left; bad-to-rough to our right, and supplies only five kilometers behind us in the city—and a line of retreat, worst comes to worst. If they move to the west, they make their supply situation impossible and expose their flank to us. If they wait, fine—we're on the defensive.

"Of course," he added, "we'll have to thicken the defenses any way we can. We'll strip the city of all movable artillery—" Reed shot to his feet, genuine horror on his face. Raj looked at him for a moment, lips pulled back from teeth. *Please. Give me an excuse. I won't have even you taken out and shot out of hand for personal reasons*, please *give me an excuse*. The Companions' heads turned toward Reed like gun turrets tracking. The civilian swallowed and slumped back into his chair.

"—for the field fortifications. The militia gunners will accompany me; the remainder of the militia will hold the walls. All refugees in the city—" they had been trickling in for weeks "—all able-bodied persons not members of the militia or the medical teams, and all transport animals and equipment are hereby conscripted as labor battalions." He took out his watch. "I expect to begin in about two hours. Any further questions?"

"Sir." Menyez again, frowning down at his notes. "Sir, we'll need overhead protection for the entrenchments." An airburst could turn an open trench into an abattoir, and guns and dogs were even more vulnerable. "Timber, sir."

"There's plenty on the slopes of the Oxheads," Raj said, and laughed aloud at the expressions. "And they've been shipping it down the Drangosh and putting it into buildings for a *long* time, gentlemen; we'll just take it out." Reed looked ill; he was about to lose a considerable proportion of his income, even in victory.

Silence fell, and Raj leaned forward and rested his weight on his palms.

"Messers," he said, deliberately pitching his voice low, watching them strain forward to listen. "You're all fighting men; worse, many of you are cavalry—" a brief flicker of humor "—so you've been raised on stories of victories. Elegant victories, somebody takes somebody in the flank, a commander's nerve breaks, a dashing charge disrupts the enemy's line."

His head turned, singling out one man after another. "Those battles are like two-headed dogs; they happen, but you can't count on them. They usually turn on one side being grossly inferior, in numbers or weapons or morale, training or leadership."

One fist rapped the wood lightly. "We're not fighting barbarians. We're fighting a big, tough army, well-equipped and trained. Men not afraid to die, under commanders who've learned in a hard school. I'll use every trick, every surprise I can—but tricks and surprises will not win this battle.

"There is," he paused, and frowned as he sought for words, "a certain brutal simplicity to most engagements between well-matched forces. We're going to fight that sort of battle, and our only real advantages are interior lines and position. The enemy will march right up to us, and we're going to plant our feet in the dirt and systematically beat him to death. Kill, and keep killing until their hearts break and they run. And *then*, we will have fulfilled our mission and made this province safe."

A long quiet, even the Skinners sensing the solemnity of the mood. Raj's voice was soft, "Messers, the Spirit of Man of the Stars is with us: I know this, *know* it as if shown a vision. But the Spirit acts through fallen, imperfect men. Through us. So let us do what men may, and suffer what we must like men." Louder, "Meeting dismissed!"

The long roar of falling adobe woke the infant slung across Fatima's breast. She soothed it absently, looking back down the street of officer's billets; hers had been the last to go. Soldiers and conscript civilians surged forward even before the dust settled; mud brick has great strength in compression, almost as much as stone, but it will dissolve back into the earth it was made from under lateral stress. Townsmen shouted, dragging at lumps of clay with mattocks and shovels and picks; the Descotters tossed their lariats to be snubbed to the ends of beams, took turns around the pommels of their saddles and dragged the long baulks of pine timber back into the street, their dogs hunching and tucking their tails between their legs as they backed. Torches lit the faces of men who strained and grunted as they heaved in unison, flinging the rafters onto wagons.

It was the fourth hour past midnight; odd, she thought, for the streets to be lit like day, at an hour meant for sleep. It had often been her favorite time, catnapping between the times she fed the baby, lying quietly and listening to the breathing of the men . . . odd also to be always with men, after so many years in the world of the women's quarters. She brushed a tear from the corner of her eye with her shawl.

"Why are you sad, Fatima?" Damaris Tinnisyn said, heaving a bundle up to the bed of the wagon; Kaltin Gruder's household had been next to Staenbridge's, and they were sharing the chores of moving their gear to the temple.

She stopped to look wistfully at the baby's face for a second, and the other two concubines gathered about to coo and gurgle as well. They were all a few years older than the Arab girl, pretty but harder-faced.

"He's *really* going to adopt him?" Zuafir said.

Fatima nodded. "Papers already made," she said, with satisfaction; there was a certain . . . *solidity* to legal documents; notarized copies nestled in the money belt about her waist that Barton and Gerrin had insisted on, along with her manumission papers. "Raj . . . Messer Whitehall and his Lady stand Starparents."

The other's envy was friendly, without the edge of hostility it might have had if she had used her good fortune to try and domineer. Governor Barholm's wife had started from far lower than they, an outright prostitute rather than an acknowledged mistress: but that was a fairy-story, a tale like Djinn from a lamp or wagons that flew and talking picture-boxes; gentlemen did not marry the girls they picked up on campaign. Fatima's good fortune meant an honorable place for life, and a nobleman's status for her son. The sort of stroke of luck they dreamed of while they scrimped and saved, for a dowry that would make a working-man overlook certain things, or enough capital to open a shop.

"Then why *are* you sad?" Aynett said. The wagon creaked off, and they followed: they would all be working together in the aid station, you picked up a practical knowledge of wounds and their treatment if you followed the drum. The 5th took care of its own, but expected more in return than an ability to lie on your back.

"I happy there," Fatima said softly. "Nobody beat me, scorn me, tell me I stupid useless imp of Shaitan; house my own." Her head came up. "Pray Alia—Spirit of Stars our men return safe and victorious."

"And back two!" Jorg Menyez said, looking through the lens of the surveyor's level. The open valley where the Civil Government troops would make their stand glistened bone-white and black and orange beneath the moons.

The team of soldiers down the line of string pounded in another stake. Menyez straightened, putting his hands to his back; it was cool as the desert nights always were, and the stars had a hard brilliance. Only a winter night had that sort of clarity up in Kelden County; summer nights were softly luminous, smelling of clover and dew-damped ground. That was a rich land, rolling hills and orchards and thick oakwoods, not like this country south of the Oxheads; here the bones of the earth showed through, and the only fertility was what men had made. The desert waited, with sand to fill their canals and scorching winds, waiting for their labor and vigilance to stop.

"And we put half our efforts into killing each other," he murmured.

"Jorg?" Raj said, looking up from his mapboard. Officers clustered around it, making quick notes on their own pads, occasionally jogging off to fix a view in their minds.

"I was thinking we should have a permanent engineering corps, the way the Colonists do," he answered, a little ashamed of the unsoldierly thoughts.

"Hmmm, there are arguments both ways," the commander answered. "More flexible, our way, giving everyone the basics. Although I'm lucky you made such a study of it; too many of my cavalry commanders might as well be Squadron or Brigade nobles, not interested in anything unless they can drink it, hunt it, ride it, or fuck it. Right, here's the schematic and perspective."

The valley ran from the northwest to the southeast, out of tumbled choppy loess hills, and into the scree and badlands that ran down to the river. Water flowed here only two months of the year, but it left a broad streak of sand winding down the middle of the depression; there was a one-in-ten slope behind toward the higher ground of the city, and a long smooth rise southwest to the low ridge a kilometer away.

"From above, like this." Raj's finger traced a broad V with its point toward the enemy; the arms were of slightly unequal length. "Two-point-eight clicks on the left, two-point-two on the right; that's the easier approach and I want it defiladed from the center. Right here—" his finger tapped the point of the V "—is where the command post will be, the redoubt, and where the 5th will stand. Also half the artillery, the heavy pieces from the city. Space the rest of the stuff from the walls, and all the 75's and field-howitzers, in 4-gun batteries down the wings at equal intervals, *except*—" he tapped the extreme right, the western anchor of the line "—I want this to have six of the howitzers, sighted in on the ravines off our flank, just in case they get cute. Also, I'm putting the bordermen in there." Two hundred had shown up a week ago.

"Damned," he added "if I know why, but since I led the

5th to its notable corncobbing at El Djem, those mad bastards from the Komar hills seem to like me.

"Now, apart from the 5th, I want the cavalry battalions in a second line about fifty, sixty meters back from the first—just far enough to have a clear field of fire over the front line. Cover for the dogs just behind *them*. And behind all that, pile the spoil and then dig in a road, nothing elaborate, right across the arms of the V. Communications trenches between all positions."

"That's an awful lot of digging, Whitehall," Menyez said.

"You've got fifteen thousand soldiers and thirty thousand civilians on their way," Raj replied. They all turned and looked upslope behind them, to the lights and ant-murmur of the road out from Sandoral. Torches lit the ridgeline, and a load of squared timbers was dumped to avalanche down towards them.

"Furthermore," Raj continued, "I want a staggered line of holes, about two hundred meters up the opposite slope—" he pointed "—thirty of them. Slanting upslope in the direction of our gallant wog adversaries, just enough to hold a hundred-liter urn, you know, the type they use for oil and wine around here?"

"You don't want much, do you?" Menyez laughed.

"I want victory," Raj said flatly.

The older man looked away. "Tell me," he said suddenly. "What would you do if *you* were Jamal, or Tewfik?"

"Stay at home under a jasmine vine, sipping kave while harem girls dropped peeled grapes in my mouth," Raj replied promptly. There was a chuckle from the group of officers about them. "If I had to attack now? About what they're doing; there really isn't an alternative, as long as we have Sandoral and a reasonably-sized army and they don't control the river, which they can't since we have superior riverboats. They've got better engineers, we've got better mechanics . . . I'm glad it's Jamal in charge, though."

"Why?" Gerrin asked, glancing up from a whispered consultation with Kaltin Gruder.

"Tewfik's a saber general; feint, feint, off with your head. Jamal . . . I've studied his campaigns in the east, and down against the Zanj. He uses the hammer-hammer method; walk up to someone and start whipping on them with your hammer. If it breaks, you send back to stores for a bigger hammer."

"Let's just hope he doesn't have one big enough."

"This time, at least," Raj said thoughtfully.

"What are you doing!"

A voice called out into the street from the window above. Antin M'lewis squinted up into a carbide lantern; the house was large, with only the one exterior window above the big brass-strapped door, the sound of tinkling water coming from within where fountains played in courtyards.

"This Messer Bougiv Assed's house?" he asked, conscious of the two squads at his back, and the light wagon that had once been an officer's coach.

"Yes, it is! And the Messer will not be amused at this intrusion."

"Fuck 'im," M'lewis said casually. "This is t'place, dog-brothers."

Troopers dismounted, one rattling the gate. "'Tis locked, Warrant," he said.

"Ye, slavey," M'lewis called up to the window. "C'mon down an' open it."

"Out of the question!" indignation hardened above fear.

"Ar. Well, yer bastids heard the sumbitch," M'lewis continued.

"Right yer are, Warrant," the trooper said, holding the rifle muzzle a handspan from the lock. "'Ware bouncer."

The others led their dogs to the wall. The rifle blasted, with a chung!-*ping* of parting steel and a diminishing whine as pieces of soft lead and tempered metal bounced off stone. M'lewis dismounted and cradled his weapon in his arm, kicking the tall doors in as the broken lock rattled.

"Allays wanted to do that," he said, flashing a gold-toothed grin. "Kick in a Messer's door, that is."

"Tired a' pickin' t'locks?" one of the others asked. They formed up and tramped in his wake, gawking around at the carved-stone and fabric splendors.

"Hoo, Spirit!" M'lewis whistled. There were lords of ten thousand acres in Descott County who had nothing half so fine. Of course, back home the gentry counted wealth in livestock, dogs, fighting men, weapons and stout walls; all difficult to steal . . . from Descotters. "Nao, I don't pick locks. T'wives and daughters lets down ropes fer me; pow'rful tirin', befer I gits around to stealin'."

A stout middle-aged man in expensive nightclothes came stamping down the stairs; the guards following him with lanterns and pistols slowed to a stop as they saw the dozen helmeted soldiers staring about the foyer of the mansion.

"I am Messer Assed," he said in a tone of furious control. "Who do you think you are, soldier, breaking in here! Your officer will have you flogged, *flogged*."

"I doubts it," M'lewis said tranquilly. The broad friendliness of his smile did not alter, even as he flipped the rifle up and poked it into the aristocrat's stomach. "Allays wanted t'do this, too . . . Now, I thinks I's the man wit' t'gun, an' my officer *sent* me here. Fer one—" he looked down at the pad tucked into his belt. "El-ect-ri-cal gen-er-ator. Befer," he added genially, "we starts knockin' down yer outbuildin's fer the timber." A wink. "But don't'cher worry yer heart, Messer, I gots a government receipt, right here."

"Careful with that, yer arseface," da Cruz said.

The jar that was being manhandled off the wagon was taller than a man and nearly as wide as it was tall; even with six troopers on the stout handles the thick terracotta walls of the storage vessel made it an awkward burden. It had been full of olive oil until recently, and the smell was as disagreeable as the slipperiness.

"Ye got it?" he asked, looking down into the hole. It had been dug at a steep slant down into the silt, kept from collapsing with wicker basketwork propped on sticks. The man head-down in it was a gunner, you could tell that by the dark-blue trousers with the red piping up the seams, and by his arrogant contempt for anyone not initiated into the mysteries of his art.

"Mmm-*hmm*," the artilleryman said, "that's got her." He raised a voice muffled by the dirt. "Murchyzen, get off your useless butt and send the wire down."

There was an arm-deep trench running downhill from the pit; at the head of it a piece of wooden pipe showed, running up from the base of the hole below. Another gunner had been squatting, smoking his pipe and watching the civilians and cavalry troopers working with the enjoyment any soldier felt when someone else was pulling the detail. Now he rose and carefully lifted a length of cable; it was braided copper, the outside coated with a sap gum that was shiny and flexible, although a bit tacky in this heat. The end for a meter back had been stripped of insulation and unbraided into a fan of bright metallic strands, each one wrapped around a half-dozen big percussion caps, the type used to fire muzzle loading artillery. The gunner shook it slightly, making a clinking sound something like a sistrum.

"Ya dicking around again, Murchyzen?" the man in the pit asked with dangerous patience.

Da Cruz looked at the detonators with loathing; he had worked as a quarryman in his youth. Until his father was blown into assorted gobbets by a misfired charge; they had found his boots with the feet and sections of calf still in them. But the commander had asked him to see that the fougasses were done properly, and by the *Spirit* they would be.

"Here it comes," the gunner said, wrapping a cloth around the detonators and feeding the cable down the wooden pipe; for all his casual familiarity, he did it with a craftsman's deft gentleness. The Master Sergeant craned his head to watch the gunner in the fougasse pit working. Once the cloth-wrapped tip of the cable showed through the man spread the wires out across the canvas below him like the roots of a tree, pinning them in place with pieces of bent twig. Finished, he grunted satisfaction and called over his shoulder:

"Now the powder." Ten one-kilo cotton sacks, coarse-grained propellant charges. Whistling tunelessly, the gunner ripped each with a diagonal slash of his knife-bayonet, then turned them over and tapped them gently into place with the pommel. When he had finished he stroked the lumpy surface and wriggled out backward, squatting on his hams and blinking in the bright sunlight.

"Yer needs that many detonators?" da Cruz said, handing him a canteen.

The artillery sergeant was a wiry man, about forty; from Chongwe Island, by the accent and the blond hair that stood out against a skin tanned almost as dark as a Descotter's.

He rinsed his mouth out and spat, then poured half the contents over his head, to join the sweat-runnels through the dirt on his bare chest.

"Na," he said. "Two or three ought to do her. But I figure, what they hell, we *got* 'em, why not use them?"

Blue eyes met black, and da Cruz nodded in complete agreement. One thing you learned in this business was that it rarely paid to get too subtle, and it *never* hurt to kick a little harder than you needed to, just in case.

"Let's slip it," da Cruz said, once the gunner sergeant had had a chance to catch his breath; even if you hated explosives, it was always a pleasure to watch a good professional at work. The civilians attached to the detail were unloading the barrels and smaller jugs that would be poured into the large one to make the load of the flame-fougasse; liquid bitumen, tar, naphtha, sulphur, and the thick green vile-smelling oil rendered down from the greasy flesh of the avocat fish.

"One of my fav'rite occupations, slipping it in," the sergeant said. The troopers were manhandling the huge jar over to the hole. "Ah, friends?" They looked up. "You know, there's an earth lip around the powder, so even if you dropped that it shouldn't hit hard enough to set off the detonators, but all the same I'd appreciate it if you put her down, you know, a might soft."

"Amazing!"

Raj looked up from the lip of the bunker; a man was picking his way towards them across the tumbled earth of the trench line. A tall man, as tall as Raj, dressed in expensive cotton-drill khaki and a wrapped headdress; fifty, with sun and wind stamped into his flesh and salt-and-pepper beard. A pistol was strapped high up on his right hip, and Suzette had her arm tucked through the crook of his left. *She* was wearing elaborate Court riding-dress, complete with a wig of blond braids.

"Messer Falhasker," Raj said in a neutral tone. Although it was dubious whether he deserved the title; self-made wealth rather than inherited, and mostly in trade at that. "Good day, Messer. My thanks for your assistance." Which had been valuable; the merchant had organized his riverboat crews to help with the construction, donated every scrap of sailcloth in his warehouses for sandbags and even had them sewn up by the hundreds of women textile workers who spun and wove the fine cotton he traded up from the Drangosh Delta.

The Delta was the heartland of the Colony, and the land from which Falhasker's mother had come; she was the daughter of a prominent merchant house of Al-Kebir . . . a politically prominent family; the Colonists did not share the Civil Government's prejudice against traders.

"We're all in this together," the merchant said; Suzette gave his arm a slight squeeze. He nodded to the scene around them. "And in only two nights and a day!" he continued. "I only wish I could get them to work half as hard for *me*. And I pay them, too."

Forty thousand pairs of hands had been at work for thirty hours; the five-kilometer stretch of dry valley looked like a garden plot infested with geometric-minded gophers. The basic outlines of the trenches had been dug, the main line for the infantry to hold and the fortlets behind them where the cavalry would support their fire and be ready to block a penetration or launch pursuit. Evenly spaced semicircles marked the gun platforms, and zigzag communications trenches linked them all. The redoubt at the center was a huge pit right now, nearly two stories deep; the fighting deck would have a cellar beneath it. Even as the long timbers went in to support the floor hands were stacking powder and shot on the bottom level.

Temporary ramps had been left, and two hundred soldiers and civilians were backing a cannon down it, heaving against a spiderweb of ropes. The gun was one of the city's defensive weapons, a three-meter tube of black cast iron on wheels taller than a man, throwing thirty-kilo shot. It trundled the last few yards and set-tied onto the overlapping timbers of the redoubt's floor with a rumbling thunder; there was a ratcheting pig-snarl behind it, as one of the armored cars backed and turned, ready to follow the gun. Raj looked at the turtle shape without affection: there were a dozen of the armored vehicles in Sandoral, shells of wrought-iron boilerplate driven by the only internal-combustion engines in the Civil Government. There was room for a dozen riflemen within, and the armor would turn small-arms fire and shell fragments. It would *not* turn any sort of artillery projectile, and the things were monsters to maintain, broke down at the slightest excuse, suspensions so fragile they had to be hauled to the scene of battle on ox-drawn timber skids . . . and potentially decisive, at the crucial moment.

Unfortunately the Colony had them, too.

Falhasker cleared his throat, and Raj started slightly. "Oh, yes. Well, they're working for their lives, you know," he said mildly.

"Falhasker's called Reed out," Suzette said, when the merchant had walked a little aside to examine the armored car.

"Oh?" Raj said, looking up at the ridge opposite instead of the woman at his side. *We should have a skirmish line there*, he thought: a lot of things in life were easier to do if you focused on your work. With a goal, everything was easy. *A skirmish line would probably mean they'd encamp on the crest. Useful.* You did whatever you had to do, to get where you were going.

"Reed called him a damned raghead spy in public."

"Quite possibly true," Raj said. *Kaltin? Yes, I'll want a Companion for that. The 7th, they could handle it.*

"Falhasker said Reed was a damned fool."

"Certainly true." They stood silent.

"Suzette," Raj said after a moment. "You know, it might be . . . advisable to let Falhasker know that we were only able to scare up five generators for the fougasses. So only five on the far right flank are hooked up, the others are quaker cannon."

Actually, each generator powered a board that would fire six of the flame weapons.

A light touch on his elbow. "I'll tell him," she said softly. "He's very interested in technical things."

Anything you had to do. Anything at all.

CHAPTER FIFTEEN

"Here?" Kaltin said, reining in his dog.

"Here," Raj confirmed.

They were a kilometer southwest of the defense line; he turned back briefly, watching the torches flaring along it as the finishing touches were hurriedly completed; some of those were to make the fortifications look rawer and cruder than they were, although the Spirit knew it was rough enough, inexpert hands working in desperate haste. It was chill on the ridge, and the noise was feint, as if echoing from another world. The civilians were back in Sandoral, all except the volunteers in the first-aid stations dug in behind the communications road; after three days of their noise and confusion the position seemed almost empty with only the troops.

"Hmmm," Kaltin said, staring down the opposite slope. "You know," he continued, pointing, "I think that draw there runs all the way to the river."

Raj turned and looked. It was a steep declivity in the plain to their left and east, zigzagging away and down toward the Drangosh.

"I don't think there's much use the enemy can put it to," Raj said. "Pretty thick in there." Tanglewire weed, throttlebush, wild rose, all infested with poisonmouth and stingworms.

"I don't think the enemy could put it to any use at all," Kaltin continued, striking one fist lightly into a palm. "It's *definitely* pretty thick. Particularly along the edges. You could hide a whole battalion in there."

They all turned and looked at the Companion. "And they'd be right behind where the wogs will put their artillery," he continued; his face was shadowed by the brim of his helmet, but the teeth showed. In Maxiluna's light, they had a slightly reddish cast. Colonist shellfire had killed his brother Evrard, on the retreat from El Djem. "Payback time."

Raj nodded slowly. *Worth risking three hundred men*, he thought coldly; the 7th Descott Rangers were understrength. Counters on a board, not young men from his homeplace . . . *And Kaltin wants to be here*, he reminded himself, as they discussed the technicalities, signals and timing.

"All right" A nod. "You'd better start getting them in place, then." That would have to be done to the east, through the ravines. Gruder reined his dog around. "And Kaltin?"

"Yes?"

"Revenge tastes better as dessert than appetizer. I need you afterwards."

Trumpets were calling *Parade, fall in* down at the fortifications. *Oh, Spirit*, he thought. *The speech.*

" . . . so think of what you're fighting for," Raj continued; the words seemed to lose themselves over the sea of upturned faces. Their immediate superiors would repeat the gist of his address, adding the local flavor appropriate, but the men expected to hear the commander, if they could. They were bunched in a huge semicircle in front of the redoubt where he stood, units jammed in cheek-to-cheek to get as many as possible within hearing distance

"The Settler is coming north, and he's going to *keep* coming north until somebody stops him—right up to the East Residence, if he can.

"That's what *he* thinks," he continued. "And his army thinks so, too." Raj paused; his foot was on an ammunition crate, and he leaned forward in a confidential gesture. "I've seen his army—"

There was a murmur at that; for a moment his mind blanked, and he realized what the rumor mill had done with the story of the patrol. *Well, well, there's one piece of stupidity that's worked out well.* Unless they thought he was a glory hound who'd get them all killed, of course.

"—and it's a big one, a cursed big one. Pretty, too: a lot prettier than us. Smells better, at that." Digging in dry clay for three days did not improve a soldier's turn-out; there was a sound like a stifled chuckle. "They're so fine they think we're dirt beneath their feet; why, it's presumptuous of us to demand an invitation to the same battlefield as those well-dressed gentlemen!"

Very much the way nobly-born cavalry officers thought about common soldiers: no harm in redirecting some of the enlisted men's anger, particularly the infantry's.

"I'll tell you what they think; they're certain they can walk right over us tomorrow and be in Sandoral drinking and fucking by lunchtime. Are we going to show them different?"

The 5th started the cheers, but they spread rapidly; even the Skinners joined in, although Raj doubted they had understood much. *Although most of them know enough Sponglish for* drink *and* fuck; *they probably think I'm promising them a party.* He let the sound build, then spread his arms for silence before they could begin to taper off.

"This is going to be the biggest battle anyone's seen in our lifetime, or our fathers'. Tonight, there are plenty of people in uniform and out—giving prayers of thanks that they're not here. I tell you, in the years to come, rich Messers who're safe and warm in bed tonight will curse the fact that they weren't here, and each will know that they're not as good a man as you. You'll say: 'I was with the Army of the Upper Drangosh, when we sent Jamal yelping downriver with his tail between his legs,' and they'll hide their faces for shame." *If you don't end up in a mass grave, or legless cripples begging your bread on the streets, no money for pensions,* curse *you, Tzetzas.*

"And I say I'm proud right now, to call you fellow-soldiers, who I trust to do their duty." *And who know I've ordered that any man who withdraws without orders be shot.* "I'm not a politician," he continued, "so I'll end the speech with this: the enemy is coming over that hill tomorrow because they want to. When they leave, it'll be because *we* want them to. Sons of Holy Federation! You are the descendants of the lords of the stars: you fight for your homes, your families, the graves of your ancestors, the temples of the Spirit. To battle! Winner takes all!"

The cheering was more prolonged this time; some of the Descotter units even started to sing, roaring out,

"*Goin' ta Black Mountain, wit' me saber an me gun*
Cut ye if yer stand—shoot ye if yer run—

Raj jumped down from the parapet of the redoubt. The sound died away as the Sysup-Suffragen of Sandoral walked slowly up to the parapet, Star-headed staff in hand, robes shining salt-white under the moons. There was a universal rustle as the soldiers knelt, and a whisper of awe as four priests bore out a litter on which rested a cube of something far clearer than crystal, taller than a man. For a long instant nothing happened; then there was a glimmer of light in the depths of the material, blue white and dazzling. It grew, cool and soundless, until it seemed a star was supported on the priests' arms, and the watchers had to bow their heads to hide their eyes from it; it shone through closed eyelids, even through the hands some threw before their faces.

Then, equally silently, it died away, with a long drawn out breath from the assembled army, a sigh half of wonder and half of regret: this was the most famous relic outside of East Residence, and a lifetime could go by without nonclerics being allowed a sight of it. There was hardly a sound as the priests turned and paced back toward the city, and the men were dismissed to quarters.

"Barton," Raj said. "A question. Where *did* you get those phrasings you passed me? You've got a future in literature, if they're your own."

"Oh, mostly from the *Fragmentary Codex*, sir; very old, written just after the Fall from bits people remembered." Information stored in optical arrays was very little use to people deprived even of electricity. "Mostly in Old Namerique. The references are pretty obscure; who St. Cryssin is and where the Sons of the Griks fought, nobody knows. Pretty words, though."

Well, that seems to be going better than I expected, Raj thought, blinking against the light of dawn. Jorg Menyez had persuaded him to use a regular infantry battalion to hold the skirmish line on the opposite ridge, when the 7th Rangers had been told off for Kaltin Grader's forlorn hope.

Another volley crashed out over the southwestern rise, and the smoke caught the early morning sun, turning orange-white. He scooped a mouthful of the boiled rice from the pot with the flat southern bread. *I didn't think infantry could stand like that*, he mused. It was unusual, a good omen perhaps.

BAM-BAM-BAM, muffled by distance. Almost as crisp as a cavalry outfit would have managed.

Crack-crack-crack-crack-crack, lighter but much more rapid; Colonial repeaters answering. He cocked his head, listening. A *lot* of repeaters. Two battalions at least, advancing by companies and dismounting to volley. The firefight had gone on longer than he expected, and . . . yes.

The first companies of the skirmishing battalion came over the hill, trotting briskly to the rear and holding their rifles at the trail, even as another series of volleys rolled out behind them. He raised his binoculars with his left hand as he ate, resting his elbows on the sandbags of the parapet; the redoubt had two, an upper for the guns and a lower for the riflemen of the 5th whom he had chosen to garrison it. None of the retreating men were running in panic, and none were continuing to the rear except for a few carrying comrades too badly hurt to walk.

Excellent, he thought. Aloud, "Da Cruz, mounted parties to retrieve the wounded, please."

"Ser!"

That would take a minute, the dogs were in covered shelters to the rear, with chain leads to staples in the floors of their bunkers. The infantry had rallied just below the crest; he could see officers walking backward with saber and arm outstretched to either side, setting the lines. Their standard-bearers drove the poles of the staffs into the ground and the men dropped, first rank prone and second kneeling. A perfect leapfrog maneuver, the new base of fire remaining motionless while the men who had been rearguard ran over the top of the hill and down the slope to rally in their turn two hundred meters behind the first. The Colonist cavalry came over the rise at a gallop less than fifty meters behind them, already swinging out of the saddle, expecting to pour fire into the backs of fleeing men. Instead they met three hundred rifles, flashing up in rhythmic unison.

BAM-BAM-BAM-BAM-BAM-BAM. Hideous perfection, point-blank fire, slender-limbed brown dogs and men in spired helms and red jellabas falling in windrows. And the officers and noncoms would be paying the price of the aggressive courage that lead from the front.

"Oh, lovely timing, *lovely*," Raj whispered. *Who did Menyez send?* he wondered. The faces under the helmets looked pale, northwesterners.

BAM-BAM-BAM-BAM-BAM-BAM. The Colonist line was too disorganized to return the volley, but individual fire crackled and spat, at ranges where the light carbines were as effective as the Armory rifles. Men dropped, but the firing lines rose only on order and dashed back in rank; Raj focused his glasses and saw one burly peasant-in-uniform lumbering with an officer thrown over one shoulder and his company standard tucked under the other arm. Another rank of Colonists charged over the hill; these had sabers out and plunged forward, hoping to overrun the retreating line before it could get behind the cover of its comrades.

Raj tensed. The retreating men were masking their comrades' rifles, the waiting companies could not fire without hitting their own men. And they would know it, know they were losing the stand-off power of their weapons; they would be able to see the flashing steel and snarling teeth above the infantry's heads. If they ran . . . There was a movement; the prone rank came to one knee, and the kneeling rear rank stood.

"Prepare for fire support mission, left-flank field guns only," Raj said. A runner sped off.

This time the timing was much closer; the dogs were within five strides when the last of the retreating infantrymen dashed through the ranks of the support companies. The front-rank volley smashed out close enough that the blasts singed the hair on the dogs' muzzles; the line of charging Colonists seemed to stagger in mid-leap. Braced bayonets met them, and the rear rank fired over their comrades' heads. Melee for a moment, pistol and saber against rifle and bayonet, and then the men who had been running a moment before were turning, walking back towards the fight as they loaded. A trumpet called from the ridgeline, high and brassy-sweet, and the Colonists reined in their dogs and retreated. Just in time, as the first field guns fired from the flanks of the V formation, airbursting over the retreating cavalry.

"Well done, well done, oh, *well done*," Raj shouted, hammering his fist into the sandbags beside him, as cheering erupted all down the five-kilometer line of trenches. The Skinners on either side of the redoubt were firing their massive rifles, into the air or at the backs of the retreating Colonists; nearly two kilometers, but they made some hits. Men on dogback were scooping up the wounded, loping to the rear.

"Color-party—" Raj began, then looked down at his right hand, which had squeezed a lump of bread and rice into a ball. "Color party, follow me." He rolled out of the firing slit and trotted to meet the oncoming infantry battalion, with his honor guard and the colors of the 5th Descott behind him.

"Salute!" he barked, drawing his sword with a flourish. The 5th's colors dipped, and the infantry actually formed up to pass in column as they headed back for their section of the line.

Their commander came up; it was Jorg Menyez himself, grinning like an urchin under a covering of powdersmoke. The saber in his right hand had a line of red along the tip.

"Spiritdamned, that was well done, insubordination or no," Raj said, shaking his hand. "You should have delegated that."

"You're one to talk," Jorg replied, and then his smile faded. "It was expensive," he said. "But they needed to see the Messer would stand with them . . . and that they could do it." The 31st Kelden County Foot was mostly recruited from the area around the Menyez estates, Raj knew. "The other line battalions might not have been able to do it . . . but they're closer to being able to, for having seen it."

"MAMMM! MAAAMMM!" the boy screamed, arching his back on the canvas-covered table. "*Mam, help me, mamaaa.*"

"*Hold* him, crash your cores," the Renunciate barked.

The first casualties, after yesterday's construction accidents. The first wave of a rising tide. At the foot of the table Zenafir bore down on the leg with both hands, turning her head aside to vomit into the empty wooden tub.

Fatima felt the bones creak in her hand; she had gripped the young soldier's with hers, relying on the weight of her elbows to pin his arm. He was no older than she, and probably handsome when his face was not turned to a gorgon's mask by an agony greater than flesh was meant to bear. The cords in his neck stood out like cables as the priestess-doctor's scalpel probed and sliced.

"Iodine and clamp," she snapped; her acolyte moved up.

"More opium, reverence?" Fatima asked desperately.

"No, damn you, the first dose hasn't taken effect yet." The Arab girl suspected that it was taking effect, just a little, enough to prevent the boy from passing out with shock, but there was no time to waste. "Spirit *damn* all wars, there's nothing left of this knee but bloody splinters. It'll have to come off at the thigh. Clamp there, idiot. *Hold* him."

Across the great room with its dozens of tables there were other shrieks; one voice was babbling, *we held them, we held them, we held them* over and over, as if it was a talisman.

"Needles ready," the priestess said between clenched teeth; they were hooked things like instruments of torture, threaded with catgut. Fatima looked aside and swallowed as the doctor took up the saw; the boy began screaming once more, pulsing in time to the hideous grinding noise. She closed her eyes. *That is what the tub is for*, she realized. And it was a large one.

"I thought you were going to assign that," Raj said, as they slipped back into the redoubt.

"I did," Menyez said. He grinned, and the long usually-solemn face looked boyish for a moment, streaked with sweat-channeled dirt. "I assigned it to me."

Raj cursed and looked back through the binoculars propped on the sandbagged vision slit. The Colonial advance-guard showed no signs of wanting to do more than wait on the crest of the ridge and lick their wounds; he could imagine the enemy commander up there, writing up his report and handing it to a courier to take back to Jamal. Not that he could tell much; unless *everybody* was disobeying his orders, most of the men were sitting on the firing steps with their heads below the parapet, and the guns were all run back.

"Now," he continued, "how many, Jorg?"

Menyez shrugged. "It's raghead-land out there. Carpets of marching wog as far as the eye could reach, Raj. Foot and cavalry and guns; Tewfik's banner is there, too, now. From what I saw before their advance guard hit us, their support elements are making camp about three, four kilometers back. Tewfik's force looks to be about half the size of Jamal's, but more cavalry and light artillery."

"Mmmmm. At a guess, he came straight up the west bank and then swung west as far as he could to cover Jamal's bridgehead. They'll probably put their gunline on the hillcrest for the direct-fire weapons or just behind it. We can't search the reverse slope, much . . . and they'll parlay first. Better bring up those Ministry of Barbarians delegates; pointless, but delay helps us more than them."

Menyez nodded. "Thank you for saluting my men," he added quietly.

"They earned it," he replied. After the other man had left, "And so will we all, before it's over."

"Sir." Captain Dinnalysn, the artillery chief. A middle-class East Residence vowel-stress: a hint of a breathed "h" in the *seyor*.

Why everyone who'd been in on the fiasco at El Djem wanted another try was beyond him, Raj decided, but useful.

"Yes?"

"Just confirming, sir; the militia gunners"—the part-timers handling the big cast-iron fortress guns—"said they've got those wogboys up on the ridge well within range."

"And you told them, Captain Dinnalsyn?"

"That the first one pulls a lanyard gets tied over the muzzle for the second shot, sir." A thin smile. "Got some of my lads there to do it, too."

"Ser." The nasal rasp of Descott; M'lewis. "Ser, Quartermaster requests confirmation of yer order."

For an instant Raj had to struggle to remember which *one*, there had been so many, and then a hologram showed him a rifleman's hand scrabbling frantically in an empty bandolier. Normal procedure was for troops to be issued a hundred rounds before action, and for further requisitions to be delivered after signed authorization by an officer or noncom; it was the only way to prevent troops in garrison from selling ammunition for booze money.

"M'lewis, my respects to the Quartermaster and I want opened boxes one to a platoon for all units on the firing line, and I want it *now*."

"Mmmm, polite er forceful-loike, ser?" Another gold-toothed grin; give M'lewis a job and he got it done, but over-enthusiasm could be a problem, too.

"Polite, as long as he *does* it."

The thunder of the drums shook the earth. Raj looked up at the sky; not quite noon yet. The drummers must be just behind the crest of the rise, so tempting to order his heavy guns into action on it . . . but knowledge of his artillery's capacities and locations would be a gift like a visitation by Mohammed for Jamal and Tewfik. They were taking full psychological advantage of it, too; not just the drums, but as each unit came up the noise increased, and it marched over the rise and along it in column, down the entire five-kilometer length of open ground. Cavalry and foot and guns, all looking like they had done a hard day's march, but all looking as if they knew their business, too. Gerrin was taking a steady stream of notes as Foley dictated, leaning into the tripod-mounted telescope.

"I make that . . . one-hundred-six guns, so far," he said. "About half pompoms, a quarter 70's—" much like the Civil Government's 75mm rifles "—and the rest a mixture, fair number of howitzers. Anything heavier, they're not showing."

"I wish they'd stop that damned drumming," Gerrin cursed. "Bad for morale . . . that's a *lot* of artillery, Raj."

"Well. The game begins . . . Oh, Spirit, what're *they* doing?"

Raj stepped up onto the parapet again; the redoubt had two, one above for the guns, and this one for the men of the 5th, putting their rifles just at ground level. The Civil Government entrenchments faced up the opposite slope, which meant that any projectile they fired would remain at man-height all the way to the crest, and possibly do damage when it dropped over . . . but it also limited his view somewhat.

"Ser," one of the lookouts on the roof of the redoubt bunker called. "It's the Skinners!"

"What're they doing?"

"Dancin' and singin', ser! In time to them drums." Raj blinked, leaning half-out of the slit to see. The Skinner groups were on both sides of the redoubt; he wouldn't have been surprised to see them out sunning themselves on the sandbagged roofs of their trenches . . . but they *were* dancing, stamping and leaping in lines that wove in and out of each other, linking arms, whooping out a chorus to the simple thudding of the enemy drums:

"*En* roul'en, reyoulouran, *En* roul'en, reeeeboula—"

The song was punctuated by shots fired in the air, or to kick up dirt on the slope near the marching Colonials; every now and then a Skinner would turn his back on the enemy and bend over, flapping up the rear of his breechclout, wiggling and slapping their buttocks at the Muslim host.

Raj put the binoculars down, feeling blank for a second, then coughing to cover the bubble of laughter that forced its way up his throat. The men of the 5th were not trying; one by one they forced their way to a forward position to see, and collapsed hooting to the packed dirt floor of the redoubt. The laughter spread down the line and to the cavalry bunkers just behind it; he could imagine men crowded pleading around their officers for the loan of binoculars. The Colonist high command would be learning just what the Skinners thought of their martial display as well . . .

"It's the first time in my life I've ever wanted to kiss a Skinner," Gerrin wheezed, leaning against the parapet. "So much for morale, for now."

"I'd be jealous if I didn't feel the same way," Foley laughed, wiping his eyes. "You know, that's the most organized thing I've ever seen them do? Oh, shit, wait—isn't that Juluk Peypan, their chief?"

"What?" Raj looked around from the trenches to the ground before them. A lone Skinner was trotting his red-and-white hound out towards the Colonists. "Message to both Skinner groups, no attack!" he barked; the runner hesitated, gripped his amulet and dashed away. Raj raised his binoculars. Yes, no mistaking that zigzag scar on the man's bare chest; he had his feet out of the stirrups, and his monstrous two-meter rifle casually over one shoulder.

Halfway to the enemy, the Skinner broke into a gallop that made the big ears of his mount flop like wings. He rose, stood on one foot, dropped on one side of his dog and bounced to the other, stood on his hands . . . it was a dazzling display of dogsmanship, and it had certainly caught the attention of the marching Colonists, making their neat ranks falter for a second; Raj could imagine their officers' nine-thonged whips flashing. Juluk finished up by standing in the saddle and dropping backwards, then spinning on his back with his legs splayed wide. The long barrel reached out between them and vomited smoke and flame; on the hillcrest, a banner toppled as its bearer's head splashed away from the 15mm sauroid-killing bullet.

That produced a reaction; a pompom swung around and began to spit, shells cracking into the ground around the barbarian chief. He reined in with insolent calm, lighting a pipe and puffing on it, before turning to trot back to the Civil Government lines. Halfway there, he turned in the saddle and extended a clenched fist at the Colonists, shot out the middle finger and pumped the forearm back and forth before clapping heels to his hound.

"The preliminaries are over," Raj said. "Now we'll parlay."

"Salaam aleyikum, amir," Raj said carefully, bowing to Tewfik and touching brow, lips, and chest.

"And upon you, peace, Messer Brigadier Whitehall," the Colonist prince-general replied in accented but fluent Sponglish, extending his hand. Both men ignored the elaborate formalities that were going on where Jamal met the Governor's negotiators; nothing would come of that.

They shook, looking at each other curiously. *Odd*, thought Raj. *Center's shown him to me so many times, yet it's the first glimpse in the flesh.*

"You are young for such a command," Tewfik was saying; his hand was hard and callused in the same manner as his opponent's. There were four men behind him, mostly younger than the Colonist's thirty-five; two who looked like well-born Arabs; one who towered and showed a spiked blond beard beneath cold grey eyes; and a black almost as tall and broader. Tewfik's closest retainers, trusted men with high commands, from the richness of their use-worn weapons and the hard set of their faces. They in turn appraised the men behind him; Jorg Menyez, da Cruz, Gerrin Staenbridge, Foley.

"But you were young in El Djem, as well, and you surprised me there." He hesitated. "It was well of you, not to fire on our wounded from the skirmish this morning."

"We're fighting men, there's no need to act like a jackal," Raj replied. "I was rather surprised myself, back in the Valley of Death. How *did* you get those men there so fast?"

"Is that what you call that battle? Appropriate enough. Well, if the truth be told, I was bringing my riders up for a raid on *you*, using El Djem as a base," he said, with an engaging grin that lit the serious square face for a moment. Tewfik was running an experienced eye over the positions downslope as he spoke. "Not bad," he continued. "But not good enough, of course. It is unfortunate for you that your Governor can never trust an able man with an army large enough to do much good."

"I think you'll find this one amply large," Raj replied.

"There is no God but God; all things are disposed according to the will of God." From Tewfik it did not seem the automatic formula that it might from another man.

"And the Spirit of Man of the Stars shapes our destinies," Raj replied with equal sincerity. "It seems we have something in common."

Their eyes met, turned to the Settler and the envoys of Governor Barholm.

"Indeed," Tewfik said. "Indeed, young kaphar."

"You shouldn't have come," Raj whispered into Suzette's ear. It was an hour past midnight, and they sat on the edge of the redoubt wrapped in a single cloak. She huddled closer, running her hands into the too-large sleeves of her uniform jacket. There was nobody else on the flat stretch of sandbags over timbers, except Gerrin and Foley at the far corner, standing hand in hand. That was far enough for verbal privacy, at least.

"I wanted to," she said. "Spirit knows, there's little enough of doing what we want, in this life." Silence for a long moment. "Raj, I told Falhasker the five fougasses on the left were hooked up—"

"*What*! The *right*, I said tell him the *right*—"

"And I told Wenner Reed that it was the five on the right." A pause. "Trust me."

Raj signed. "I do. And if I didn't, we've not got enough time to waste arguing. Not tonight." Softly: "There won't be much time for anything, tomorrow."

Crack. This time the vicious bark of the pompom's explosion was followed by screams, further down the line. Raj ducked, ears ringing, as dirt blasted through the half-meter space between parapet and roof.

"Shit," he muttered, dusting off his jacket and binoculars. Above him there was a long roar as one of the heavy guns cut loose; they were working a counterbattery shoot at the high-velocity Colonist guns on the ridge, the ones that were pounding his men's firing slits. Diminishing rumble of thunder as the huge weapon ran backward and up the curved wooden ramps behind its wheels; then a gathering return as it rolled back and stopped with a *whack* of anchor ropes. *Ssssshhhhhhhhhhh* as the gunners ran water-soaked sponges down the barrel on rams to quench any sparks.

"Reload, contact fuse, full charge," the crew commander was shouting, voice a little shrill. The militia knew their gun well enough, they had been practicing for many years, but they were holy-day soldiers, members of some trade guild or religious cofraternity or whatever who liked to peacock in fancy uniforms once a week, not combat troops. Being shot back at was a new experience; with any luck they would concentrate on the automatic motions they had practiced, using the familiarity to distance themselves from an environment full of fear and uncertainty.

Raj peered up at the enemy line. Smoke was already dense in the valley bottom, the raw burnt-sulphur stink of it clawing at the lining of the throat and making his eyes water. There was more up there, where the enemy guns flashed through the man-made murk, and more still rising and thinning toward a sky where the stars of dawn were just now fading out. Then there was movement behind the guns;

a waving ripple, as men marched in column through the artillery positions and down the slopes. He focused his glasses. Dismounted cavalry, they had scimitars at their sides rather than the short chopping-blades the Settler's infantry wore. More and more of them, five battalions at least, they would be the first wave. The guns behind fell silent briefly, muzzles shifting, and then the firing recommenced. All at the left flank of his V, and the columns of marching men were slanting in that direction, too.

"Well, now we know who sold out, don't we?" Suzette said, in a voice as flat as the blued metal of her carbine-barrel; she was speaking loudly, to carry over the continuous roar of gunfire.

"You know, I'm glad it wasn't Falhasker," Raj said. *I hate his guts, but he's something of a man, at least.*

"Frankly, I don't give much of a damn," Suzette replied.

Up on the slope two kilometers ahead the attacking columns were spreading out, color-parties marching in place while the men deployed into open line formation. Airbursts slashed the sky above them; tiny stick figures fell or flopped; black pillars sprang out of the earth around them with a brief spark of red fire at their hearts, dirt and metal and pieces of human flying into the air. The lines ignored it all, swinging forward at a uniform jog-trot; even through the bombardment their keening shout was audible. Behind them the upper curves of black hulls showed over the ridgeline, armored cars waiting for the Civil Government artillery to be silenced.

It was going to be a long day.

"Ser," a voice whispered at Kaltin Gruder's ear.

"What is it, Fitzin?" he said normally. Nobody was going to hear them, not with the roar of artillery along the wog gunline up there on the hill half a kilometer north. He scratched at the ferocious itch of snapperworm bites; he'd be painting those with iodine for a month, thank the *Spirit* none of them had gotten under his jockcup. The spoiled-honey smell of native vegetation was a choking reek, but it would cover their scent very effectively, even from the most alert enemy dogs.

"Ser, when are we goin' to move?"

Which could be fear, or just eagerness, or both; Kaltin looked back into brush that swallowed vision within meters, down the gully to the flat where the 7th Descott Rangers waited beside their crouching dogs. Taking an occasional sip from their canteens, gnawing hardtack, slapping at the biting, stinging, burrowing life of the gulch. Listening to the guns, knowing they were half a kilometer behind the enemy's line and three from their own. A bit resentful of being led by a stranger, perhaps, but he was *here*, which would probably count for a good deal.

Raj had mentioned that he had Fitzin Sherrek in mind for a commission; it would be as well to explain, since there was no hurry.

"It's all timing, Fitzin," he said, pointing.

From here they could see the whole rear of the Colonist position, five kilometers or more stretching to the west, bowing south slightly as the ridge over the dry waterbed curved. The field guns and pompoms were on the ridge itself, or just a little back with only their barrels showing; taking protection from the terrain, and low earth berms thrown up in front. Shells were bursting among them, and here and there a tangled mass of burning wood, scattered wrecked metal, stretcher-teams carrying away wounded or dead. Their teams and caissons were well back, men were trotting back and forth humping loads of ammunition. Other guns were behind the slope, stubby-barreled howitzers firing their missiles up at fifty-degree angles.

The enemy infantry were further back yet, kneeling in ranks that stretched down along the road toward the tent-city of their camp. An occasional shell cleared the rise and exploded among the closer of them; men opened out like flowers around the blast-centers, but there was no motion except for the wounded and the stretcher-teams. Every few minutes a trumpet would sound, flags dip, and a new battalion column would surge to its feet and trot toward the hill and over it, more men being fed into the Colonist attack on the left flank of Raj's position. Infantry now, not the dismounted elite whose dogs waited with their reins spiked to the ground.

"We're waiting until the ragheads are bent over

concentrating," Kaltin continued. "All their attention nicely fixed. Raj will tell us when." He grinned, conscious of the slight pain of the scars that made his face ugly when his muscles pulled, but for once he did not mind; his mind was rerunning over and over again the sight of Evrard falling with half his torso gone. "And then we just run right up behind and buttfuck them."

Thud.

Howitzer shell, Raj thought; they had a tendency to bury themselves deep before they exploded. Much louder up here on the roof of the redoubt, surrounded only by the sandbags and boiler-plate of the observation post, but at least you did not have to hug the ground and cough in the dust it shook down from the timbers above you . . . One plunging shell had opened a crater in the trenchline a half-kilometer to his left; through the binoculars he saw panicked infantry pouring out of the shattered fortification, running toward the rear and throwing down their rifles. The next volley from the bunker of the cavalry battalion behind them tore into their ranks; one more, and they turned and ran back to the trench before a fear greater and more certain than the shells or the attack rolling down the long slope towards them.

The cavalry positions were still volleying, crisp and neatly spaced. Far too many of the infantry positions in the front rank were showing a wild crackle of rapid individual fire through the thickening clouds of smoke, and far too many of the guns there had fallen silent under the hammer from the ridge. He hesitated for a long moment, looking to his right; the infantry there were silent, out of range or blocked by the bulk of the redoubt from bearing on the attack hitting the left of the position. The guns were throwing shot and smoke toward the Colonist positions, but only in long-distance counterbattery fire. He swallowed past a raw throat and thrust head and shoulders through the trapdoor, down into the gun-platform of the redoubt.

WHUMMP. WHUUMP. WHUUMP. The massive fortress guns fired; this time the crews threw buckets of water on the barrels before they spunged, and the metallic steam that sizzled off the glowing metal gave a swamp-sauna tang to air already superheated from the muzzle blasts. The crews were stripped to the waist now, their colorful jackets thrown down and trampled underfoot, bodies striped, powder-black, showing the natural brown where sweat had cut through the clinging grim, splotches of red where boiling droplets had rained back from the guns.

"*Dinnalsyn!*" Raj shouted. "*Gerrin!*"

The gunner arrived before the cavalryman; a page full of scribbled calculations was clutched in one hand, and a ranging instrument in the other.

"Sir!"

"We need more fire support on the left flank," Raj yelled. "It's not going to hold. Have the guns switch to cannister at three hundred meters, send a runner—" Dinnalsyn nodded "—and then go yourself, limber up *all* the mobile guns on the *right* flank—" the 75's, the breechloading field guns "—and run them over to the left; prepare to receive armored vehicles."

A hesitation; the communications road behind the flanks of the Civil Government position was protected by heaped spoil from the fieldworks, but it had no overhead protection, and the guns would be hammered mercilessly by the Colonist firing line. The counterbattery exchange had gone against the enemy so far despite their numbers, but that was largely because of the superior protection of his guns. In the open, hitched to dogs driven frantic by the noise and smell of death . . .

"Do it, do it *now*," Raj said. Dinnalsyn nodded and left at a run, calling to his staff.

"Raj?" Gerrin's face.

"Take a look." The other man swarmed up the ladder and looked left.

The Colonist attack was sweeping down the slope toward them. A line would bob erect and dash forward, five seconds, six; then they dove for the earth, their carbines snapping; the men behind leapfrogged them, and the maneuver would be repeated. There was no cover to speak of on the bare scraggly silt of the hill; even the occasional scrub bush had been uprooted while the Army of the Upper Drangosh dug in. Shellfire plowed through the ranks, shrapnel whined and lashed dust from the ground in pocked circles;

wounded men rolled into shell craters and were blasted out again in gobbets as fresh explosive fell from the sky. A kilometer to cover under artillery fire, and then another to advance through the killzone of six thousand rifles, and still they came . . .

Raj focused on the crest. More banners marching over in a continuous stream, deploying and surging forward; infantry now, the second wave. One unit wavered when it saw what waited below, the drifts and tumbled windrows of bodies, still or screaming and moving feebly, half-hidden by the patchy cloud of gunsmoke that covered the whole length of ground from dry stream bed to crest. The officers' whips glittered as they whirled, and a pompom slewed to blast a string of craters at their heels; the men hunched their shoulders as if walking into a storm of sleet, and plodded forward.

"Spirit of Man, but those are good troops," Gerrin said, watching the front rank of Colonists dash forward another ten meters.

"No," Suzette said loudly behind them. "I don't want them to be brave. Kill them all." They gave her a glance; the slanted green eyes were fixed, not seeing da Cruz nod agreement beside her.

"Gerrin, the infantry's wavering. Take da Cruz, get down there, get them volleying again." If they did not, half the rifles would overheat and jam, dippers of water or no. *Perhaps I should shift Jorg from the right*—No, Jamal had enough reserves to launch an attack there, too, he needed someone rock-steady to hold that flank with half their guns pulled out. "Tell them I have absolute confidence in them."

Fifteen minutes, Raj thought as Gerrin and the Master Sergeant dropped through the trapdoors. Kaltin would need that, to get his men into place through that brush.

"*Rockets*," he barked. The trooper on the other side of the pillbox had a cigar clenched between his teeth; he removed it, blew on the end until the ember glowed and thrust it through the firing slit, touching the wicks of the three signal rockets outside. They shot skyward with a *hooosh* that was lost in the cannonade, but the crimson bursts would be visible as far as Sandoral and the Colonist encampment behind the ridge.

"Well, that's it, he muttered to himself. All that could be done, had been done. . . .

The beetling shapes of the Colonist armored cars lurched over the crest of the ridge, grinding and sliding down toward him; their engines threw a haze of black fumes above the riveted iron hulls. They were moving to the left, all the enemy formations had done that. If nothing else, it got them out of the path of fire from the Skinners to the right of the redoubt faster . . .

"*En boon, mes garz!*"

His head turned right, and his helmet clanked on the boiler plate around the slit as he scrambled to see. The right-wing Skinners were on the move, boiling out of their trenches and climbing the roof of the redoubt. Some continued all the way across it, whooping and laughing as they ran to join the band of their fellows to the left of the fort. Others were unwilling to wait that long, or perhaps to fight beside men of hostile clans; they stopped at the edge of the redoubt, standing to brace their long guns on the crossed shooting sticks, or kneeling. One of the armored cars lurched, pinpricks of light flashing from the soft iron armor as the 15mm bullets skidded over its surface or punched through. It stopped, slewing; orange tongues belched out of the firing slits and the pintle mount of the pompom in its bows, and then it blew apart in a globe of orange fire as the fuel from its ruptured tanks sprayed into the flames of the fighting compartment.

Men were falling, too, but the other armored cars continued; a dozen of them rattling down the slope toward him. Wounded Colonists crawled aside, or vanished under the tall metal wheels. The pompoms of the fighting vehicles were beginning to snap out single shots at the Civil Government artillery in the firing line; the guns had shifted to cannister, plowing wedges of lead shot through the Colonist ranks, but no menace to the men behind armor. The front ranks of the enemy advance were more ragged now, remnants of a dozen battalions mixed among those closing to within three hundred meters. Their carbine fire was more effective now, men gaining confidence as they sensed an end to their ordeal. At close range their numbers and magazine rifles would slaughter the Civil Government soldiers, and the trench that protected them now would only serve to hold them in place as targets. Behind them banners slanted as the follow-up waves rose to their feet and ran forward, lines like waves beating toward a storm-locked shore, waves that screamed like files on stone.

The Colonist artillery began to fall silent, as their own men masked the Civil Government line.

"Fire." Kaltin shouted, slashing downward with his sword. Getting the men up here had taken less time than he had expected, but it would not be long before the wogs noticed, even with their attention locked on the other side of the ridge. The Colonist army had a fair assortment of uniforms, but none of their units wore round helmets, blue jackets, maroon pants . . . or carried a banner with a Starburst topping the pole.

BAM-BAM-BAM-BAM-BAM-BAM. The 7th Rangers rose from the edge of the scrub and caught the flank of the column surging up toward the ridge.

BAM-BAM-BAM-BAM-BAM-BAM. Men running cheering to victory shuddered to a halt, even though safety now lay ahead of them. Shouts turned to screams; the impact of unexpected danger is always greater than that of one a man has steeled himself to face. *And they sent in the best troops on this flank first,* Kaltin thought coldly, as the rifles barked again. *These are the ones they kept back to feed in and give weight to a successful push. Got to keep moving, don't let them realize what's happening.*

BAM-BAM-BAM-BAM-BAM-BAM. A gun on the ridge ahead turned and fired toward the Civil Government force which had appeared, impossibly, where no enemy could be.

"Mount!" Kaltin shouted. The 7th scrambled into the saddles of their crouching dogs, slinging the rifles over their shoulders for want of time to scabbard them. Steel hissed free, flashing all along the line.

"Trumpeter, sound *charge.*" Dogs howled, thunder-loud, over the shouts of their riders. "Hell or plunder, dog-brothers—now!"

"UP AND AT 'EM."

"Now! Commander says now!"

Barton Foley started violently at the hand on his shoulder;

he had been standing just behind the forward line as they stepped up onto the parapet and volley-fired to the left. The forward section of the redoubt could rake the whole first rank of the Colonist advance now, they were so close to the Civil Government trenches; shots from the Skinners on the roof were killing three and four men at a time.

He pulled his eyes from the hypnotizing clamor; the other platoon-commanders and noncoms could handle it as well. Barton stepped back with the front rank; the second pushed past him, leveling their rifles as they braced to the firing slits. Foley turned; the two troopers assigned to it were already pumping at the arms of the portable generator with a grinding of iron gears and a rising whine from the clumsy hand-wound armatures. Three scissor-switches were tacked to an improvised board, each of them running back to three copper wires. The wires fanned out, disappearing between sandbags and into the meter depth of dirt that covered each of them.

The young man braced his hand against the wooden handle of the first switch. *I hope nothing cut the lines*, he thought. *I really, really do.*

His palm slapped down, and a fat blue spark snapped.

The explosion from the Colonist gun line was loud enough to carry even over the noise of the battle; a pale sphere of fire rose behind the silent guns and flung things that might have been human into the air. *That's an ammunition dump going off*, Raj thought, with sudden wild relief. *Kaltin.* Running figures appeared among the guns, and others among them, on dogback, swords glittering as they cut.

A pompom round from one of the armored cars slapped into the sandbags of the observation post, with enough force to toll against the iron core below. Raj felt something well up from his chest past his neck, white and cold; it cleared his grit-filled eyes, and made the world go sharply clear. He walked to the barred door at the rear of the pillbox and kicked it open.

"Signaller, standard-bearer, follow me," he said, stepping out over the body of a dead Skinner. Live ones raised a whoop to see him, their fire raking the Colonist line. It had reached the edge of the Civil Government's left flank now, and the foremost men in jellabas were sticking the muzzles of their carbines up into the firing slits from the dead ground immediately below, working the levers and firing blind into the trenches. Bayonets probed back for them, and vanished again as the armored cars came forward to pound point-blank. The Colonial attack might yet succeed, simply because the first wave were too busy to notice what was happening.

"*Look back, you stupid wog bastards,*" Raj roared, as he strode to the edge of the blockhouse. Bullets went by with a continuous *crack-crack*, and the standard bearer fell to his knees with a coughing grunt. Another of the color-party snatched the pole before it could fall and followed. A woman's voice behind him, "Raj, no—"

That didn't matter now. "Behind you, you raghead idiots! Behind you!" His sword chopped toward the Settler's banner on the hill to the south. "Look south, they're behind you."

A few men actually looked up. It was the explosion of the first armored car that really caught their attention, however; it shattered noisily, spattering hot metal and burning fuel along a hundred meters of the trenchline to either side, catching the men it had been supporting. Raj looked north, and saw the second and third of the 75's galloping out from behind the mounds that sheltered the communications road, slowing and wheeling into firing positions level with the cavalry bunkers a few score meters behind the trenchline. One went over from a too-sharp turn, bouncing and flipping end-over-end as the crew flew off in screaming arcs and the dogs twisted in their harness under the inertia of a tonne of moving metal. But the others were firing, belching knives of orange flame over open sights as they came to bear on the Colonial armor. Another armored car blew up, and then another.

A fougasse fired, far to the left. The bursting charge was not large, only ten kilos of powder, but it was enough to spray a huge fan of burning oil and naphtha across the hillside into the faces of the Colonist second wave. The sound was a loud diffuse *fffumph*, as men ran screaming and burning across the barren earth. *Ffumph*, as the next went, then fifteen more, spaced at intervals all across the left flank, two hundred meters out. Not many men were actually caught in the flames, but the sight of human torches running back towards them was the last unbearable thing for the follow-up waves; they turned and ran, screaming, shooting or hacking down the officers who tried to stop them. Even then, the Colonials who had made it beyond the line of flame-weapons hesitated. Another armored car went up in a crash, sending a pillar of smoke like nothing else on the battlefield into the sky; the rest began to pull back as.rapidly as they could, and the soldiers followed, throwing down their rifles and running.

"Sound *Cavalry, general advance*!" Raj shouted. "Get my dog, somebody get my fucking dog! Runner, tell the armored cars to get out of their holes and attack, move it, now."

The carbine bullet cracked past Kaltin Gruder's ear. A second later his saber punched through the Colonial gunner's stomach with the weight of man and dog behind it; he wrenched it free with a twist, reining in suddenly enough to make the dog rear. Others were surrounding the pompom, tossing their lariats over the breech and snubbing them to their pommels to drag the weapon away.

He wiped a forearm across his eyes, the left; his right was sodden to the elbow. Gunners were running west along the line, back to the intact and uncommitted Colonial right where it waited behind the ridge; units were forming up, wheeling to face what had been their own right wing moments before.

"Lieutenant Ynez," he barked. "Wheel some of those cannon around to bear, here. Fire at the wogs who're running, and pepper the guns too far to reach over west there. I want a three-company firing line, ready to back and volley."

He stood in the stirrups and looked back; the last of the Colonial armored cars was burning halfway up the slope towards him; the Civil Government machines were lurching out of the front of the redoubt, and he could see men swarming out of the trenchline, mounting up before the cavalry bunkers behind it. Clots and masses of Colonial soldiers were streaming across the field, retreating in a diagonal towards the part of the ridge still held by their forces; masking their own guns, he saw with a hammering glee, as smoke belched all along the trenchline and raked the fleeing men. More than enough of them to come straight back and swamp the 7th, but the fight was out of them for this day at least.

"I think—" and something sledgehammered him out of the saddle. *But we won*, his mind whispered. The ground struck him.

Barton Foley dashed back to the firing slit as the last of the fougasses fired; one hand went to the back of his neck under the chainmail flap, unconsciously kneading against the tension of suspense. The nearest Colonists were wavering, flinching away from the Skinner's fire as their armored cars reversed and left them.

They're going to run, he decided. *If they're pushed*. It was calm and rather remote, as his right hand lifted the pistol from its holster. He thumbed back the hammer and braced his left on the sandbags ahead of him; remote, like a description of tactics in one of Gerrin's books.

"Follow me," he said, and levered himself up. The troopers did, with a howl that burst out of the bunker like the cries of wolves.

"The Merciful, the Beneficent," Fatima whispered to herself, pausing as she came back down the stairs from the upper gallery of the Temple and paused. A bell was ringing, signal that more carriages and wagons had come through the city gates with wounded.

She had washed her upper body and changed her blouse while she fed her son, but the skirt swung sodden and ill-smelling against her legs. The skin all over felt prickly, as if grains of cold sand had been shaken against it; her stomach heaved again, but she clenched her teeth against the taste. The square outside the windows was carpeted with pallets and stretchers and bodies; men were loading the dead onto wagons, rough in their haste because the still-living needed the room. Doctors ran through the outskirts, among the latest wave, making the quick judgments that sorted the incoming. For those too far gone to save, a massive dose of opium for the conscious, and they were taken to the side street of the hopeless cases; worst was when they knew what had happened, and stretched out imploring hands to the priest-physicians as they were carried away. The lightly wounded were left with their field-dressings in the square, to be dealt with as time allowed.

Fatima swallowed, and walked down the last of the stairs toward the table to which she was assigned. The cleanly order of the dawn had vanished, leaving a fetid chaos that had only the minimum structure necessary to keep from completely seizing up. Men with stretchers shouted and cursed as they elbowed past the men and women dragging out the bodies of those who had died on the tables that crowded the great room, or tubs full of shattered pieces of those who lived. Physicians and volunteers called for medicines, water, bandages; wounded men shouted or moaned or wept. The floor was slippery-sticky on the soles of her feet as she descended the last steps into a blast of stench and noise.

Almost, she did not recognize the man on the table; Damans pushed past her for her rest period, staring with a blank stiff expression Fatima recognized from the feel of her own. The patient was chalk-pale with loss of blood, under a natural light brown; an officer, from the pistol holster and epaulets, and young . . .

"Get away from me, you bitches, not my arm, bitches all of you get away get *away*—" The doctor's aide staggered back, almost dropping the glass full of liquid opium and rum she had been trying to feed to the struggling man.

Fatima moved in and gripped the wounded limb below the elbow joint; the tourniquet was on the upper left forearm, and what had happened to hand and wrist was enough to make her look away even now. Especially as she knew that hand well . . .

"Barton!" she said, leaning over so that he could see her face. The wildness left his eyes, a little. "Barton, you die unless let doctor help. Gerrin left all alone if you die; I left alone. You brave soldier, act like it!"

The straining body slumped back, and the young man closed his eyes with a sigh. Fatima raised his head and gave him the sedative herself.

"Are we retreating?" she asked, distracting him as he drank and the doctor picked up a probe.

"No," he said wearily. "We won. This is victory."

✧ ✧ ✧

"Most Sacred Avatars," Raj whispered hoarsely. "It's only an hour past noon."

The others with him sat equally stunned, watching as the Colonials removed their dead and wounded from the slope; Tewfik's envoy had pleaded for it, and the pause was as much to the Civil Government army's advantage.

"How many, do you think?" Dinnalsyn said, passing a canteen.

"Five thousand dead, maybe six," Gerrin Staenbridge said quietly, taking a swig.

"And ours?" Raj said, beginning a motion to wipe the spout on his sleeve; he stopped it as the wet heaviness of the cloth dragged the arm, and took three quick swallows himself. The water was cut one-third with nun, and the burning put a little strength back into his stomach.

The Colonists lay in a long swath down from their starting point, curving away to the left like a wave that shears away from a subsurface breakwater. They were thicker just in front of the trench line, like a frozen surf of death; the miasma rose into the hot afternoon sun, along with the lingering stink of powder and the continuous low moaning of the injured as they waited to be carried back up the hill they had charged over so confidently.

"Eighteen hundred, two thousand, mostly in the counter-attack," Gerrin said.

"Damn Tewfik," Raj nodded. It had almost been a rout, but the Colonist left had not run; they had wheeled about, presenting a front that the Civil Government troops were too few to break; a single push had shown that. He looked out at the still-burning armored cars, a dozen of the Colony's and four of his. "He knew we *still* couldn't win a battle of maneuver. . . ."

"What do you think he'll do?" Menyez asked. Of all of them he looked the least worn. "His own force wasn't committed for long; they're still fresh."

"So's our right, and they saw Jamal's men run today," Raj said. He looked up; another nine hours of light, but then it would be dark-black for most of the night.

"Dinnalsyn," he continued. "How many enemy guns did we bring back?"

"Twenty, pompoms," the artilleryman said. "Destroyed about the same, but our gun line's going to be weaker tomorrow, too."

"That doesn't matter, if it's strong where it counts," Raj said. "Menyez, pull . . . six . . . no, four battalions out of the right flank, it'd be suspicious if there were more, march them over to the left and have them help with the cleaning up. Then," he continued, "after dark, trickle them back, and every second battalion from the left, too; the least-hurt ones. Dinnalsyn, leave those guns on the left and make like you're digging them in. Then bring them all back to the right, and all the mobile guns originally on the left as well."

They all looked at him; Raj let his hands fall between his knees, watching the smoke of his cigarette trickle up. "We can't be strong everywhere," he said. "They've still got more men, and more weight of metal; and the left was our stronger flank. We'll just have to bet that they won't lead off with the same formations again."

Even for an army as large as the one the Settler had brought up the Drangosh, the losses had been gruesome. Still, those were brave men, well-disciplined; they had proven it today.

"What if Tewfik shifts front, too?" da Cruz asked. Even the veteran noncom was looking a little shaken; nobody in the Civil Government's forces had seen carnage like today's, not in twenty years. The Colonists' had, of course, in the Zanj wars . . .

"*He* might, I don't think Jamal will," Raj said. "And this is two armies we're facing; I'm betting with the confusion back there, it'll be too much trouble to redirect everything. Jamal will do the straightforward thing, hit us with the other hammer on the other side of the head."

"And if you're wrong?" Menyez said, looking at him curiously.

"We all die," Raj said. *The only consolation being I won't see it*, he thought.

" . . . *will fall and wind will blow—*
Lost men die in the mountain snow
Souls break their wings on Heaven's wall
Dark night must come, come to us all—"
Spirit-damned cheerful folksongs the Stalwarts have, Raj

thought, leaning his head back against Suzette's knees. The plangent silver strings of her *gittar* tinkled as she played, singing the ancient songs a nurse from the western tribes had taught her as a child. The troopers seemed to like it; a hundred or so had come from their own fires to listen, here behind the redoubt. Nobody wanted to sleep in the redoubt, if it could be avoided. For that matter, nobody seemed to want to sleep, much.... He had been able to get them a hot meal, sent out from Sandoral on wagons, at least. More than the enemy had, from what the prisoners said; evidently they had come north with nothing but hardtack and jerky, enough to see them through into the fertile lands north of the city, but no more. And it would be a cold camp over there, not enough firewood left around here to roast an avocat.

One more time, he had told the men, doing the rounds of the fires. *One more time, and they'll break. Nobody could take what we dished out today more than once more.* The question was, could *his* men take it once more?

A burst of firing out of the night brought men rolling to their feet.

"Stand easy," Raj called, hearing it being echoed through the long jewel-chain string of campfires behind the trench line. Not enough firing to be an attack, and he had Skinner and Descotter scouts in plenty on the slope. Suzette followed him as he climbed to the roof of the redoubt and watched the spiteful fire-tongues flickering through the dark, frowning.

"Fucking Tewfik!" Raj said with sudden anger. "*Fucking* Tewfik!" Shaking his head in admiration.

"What?" Suzette said.

"The fougasses, he's not leaving anything he can to chance either," Raj said. "They're really not as dangerous as a round of cannister, but they've got lots of mental impact. On our men as well as his, seeing them go off would be a big plus. At a guess ... yes, from where they are ... he's going for the fougasse detonator lines. Messenger!" A trooper ran up. "Off to the scouts, and tell them to concentrate on the fougasses, don't let the enemy damage them."

"Can you replace the lines?" Suzette asked, standing closer and hugging his arm.

"No," he said, returning the embrace. "But I've got a trick or two like that myself." He looked down into her face, and thought of trying to persuade her to leave again. *No*, he thought. *Useless*. Besides, there were limits to a man's unselfishness.

"Meanwhile, I don't much feel like sleeping," he said.

"And we have a whole bunker, all to ourselves. . . ."

"We're not going to stop them," Menyez said flatly.

Raj looked out the slit of the observation pillbox. It was like one of those horrible recurring dreams, where you die over and over again, never able to vary your actions. The same hammering cannonade back and forth, the same stinking clouds of smoke . . .

Of course, there *were* differences. The gun lines on both sides had thickened up from yesterday; dawn had shown him most of the remaining tubes on the ridge above shifted over to positions facing the Civil Government's right. *Fucking Tewfik*, Raj thought with weary irony. *That's becoming my motto. Although I'm the one who's getting screwed*. The attack had been different, too, faster and a little looser. These were Tewfik's own men, the Colonial Army of the South, and they had been with the prince-general during the Zanj wars in the lands beyond the Colonial Gulf. They had come with the same leapfrog tactics, but sprinting rather than trotting, and their rifle-fire was damnably accurate.

"We wouldn't have held them this long if we hadn't stripped the left flank," Raj said.

"Which won't hold either, not if *they* come down," Menyez said. The ridge to the left was quiet, but the reformed battalions of the Settler's Army of the North had marched a little past it, and their ranks had held under the light shelling of the muzzle loaders in the Civil Government gun line opposite. The lanky Kelden County man sighed; the battle on the right wing was turning into a short-range firefight, the front lines of Tewfik's riflemen only two hundred and fifty yards from the trenches.

"You can probably get most of the cavalry back to Sandoral," Menyez said, turning to go. He stopped when Raj touched his shoulder.

"Suzette," Raj said, "what was that toast the Brigade ambassador gave, last year?"

She stood beside him. "He fears his fate too much, and his reward is small—"

He finished the words: "—who will not put it to the touch, to win or lose it all," he continued. "Battles are won or lost in the minds of men . . . signaller, the rocket."

A single trail of smoke rose from the redoubt, above the wreathing smoke of ten thousand rifles and two hundred guns. Behind the trenchline cavalrymen jumped up and ran to the captured pompoms, jerked the lanyards. They did not attempt to aim, nor could they have even if the front was not blanketed with heavy smoke. The Colonist weapons had a single clip each . . . and only one target; each had been boresighted on a fougasse that morning, before Dinnalsyn's gunners were called to serve their own weapons. The pompoms hammered . . .

. . . and the flame-arcs erupted, not in a smooth progression but all within fifteen seconds of one another. Men jumped and ran, screaming, struck by a weapon their leader had told them was disarmed. The snapping of carbines faltered for a moment.

"Signaller," Raj called: "All left-flank units, general advance. All cavalry, prepare for pursuit."

"Tewfik's men won't break, we haven't hurt them enough," Menyez protested. Below them came the pig-snarl of armored car engines, and all along the left flank of the Civil Government line men were clambering out of their trenches, forming line for a sweep into the Colonist flanks. "You can't do that, Jamal's men still outnumber us and they'll take us in the rear!"

"No, they won't," Raj said softly. His binoculars were trained on the motionless units on the heights, battalions cut to the strength of companies. A banner wavered and then dropped; he could see the officer behind it pistol the soldier who had thrown it aside, then fly back as a dozen rifles fired with their muzzles pressed almost to his flesh. "They'll run . . . from their own memories. Why do you think I allowed them a truce, yesterday? They spent four hours in hell, then ten picking up the results and burying them."

He drew his pistol; Horace had been led up to the edge of the redoubt, whining with eagerness after a day spent bridle-chained to the floor of a bunker.

"Fucking Tewfik," Raj said. *I've got to stop that.* "Damned if I don't like the man," he continued.

One of the 75's beside him on the ridge crashed, and a spout of water flashed up white and black beside the giant bridge. It had been an impressive structure under construction; from the hills above its terminus on the western shore it was even more majestic. A blossom of flame came from the entrenchments on the eastern bank, a slow earthquake rumble that ended in a massive gout of dirt on the plain below. The surface of the road across the Drangosh was red with fleeing Colonist soldiers, most in disorder; the shrinking semicircle around the head of the bridge traded slamming volleys with Civil Government cavalry who had pursued them all day.

"Why—" Menyez began, then withdrew a little distance to cough his lungs free. For *this* he had been willing to ride a dog, counting a week's illness a small price to pay. "—do you say so?" he continued, face red and flushed.

"Because he wasn't concerned with anything but getting as many of his men out as he could, once there wasn't a chance of turning things around. Not even his baggage train." The 5th guarded that now, with a picked band of Companions about certain heavy chests. Not M'lewis, who was here; there was no point in pushing a man too far. "Too bad for him he has to work for that butcher Jamal," Raj continued, sighing.

I thought victory was supposed to bring triumph, he thought. *Maybe I'm just too tired; all I want is Suzette and a bath and bed for a week . . . sleeping the first two days.*

"Eh, mun ami!" Juluk Peypan was in high good humor. "*Jey ahz un caddaw per tuh!*"

A gift? Raj thought. The sun was almost down, the banks of the river in enough shade to make the muzzle-flashes brighter than reflected sunlight; the thousand and one details of administration marched through his mind like weary troops. *Oh, well, it's certainly better than defeat*, he mused.

"Yes, I gots this for you!" the Skinner continued, grinning from ear to ear as he reached into a bag tied to his saddle.

Jamal's teeth were showing as well, but Raj would have judged the expression one of surprise. It was difficult to tell, since much of one side of the face was missing.

CHAPTER SIXTEEN

"Well, it's a little different from the last time, isn't it?" Foley said, pausing before one of the wall mirrors in the steamboat's lounge. His Captain's uniform was immaculate, the chain mail of the epaulets matching the mirror polish of the hook where his left hand had been. The stump was actually still a little tender for it, it had only been a month or so, but appearances had to be kept up on a visit to court.

"All relative," Raj replied abstractedly, watching out the window as the multicolored lights of East Residence swam by; the Palace was lit like day, new arc-lights throughout the grounds. The humid air felt soft on his skin, after the dryness of the southern border, but his gut tensed again; fear, different from the scrotum-raising tension of combat, but fear nevertheless. "We got a little more time, but then again, we won."

"This time," Menyez said, laying down his book. "Is he really planning to send us to retake the Southern Territories?" A pause. "You know, my family originally came from there? We had estates around Port Murchison, back when: got out just before the Squadron took the city." Another pause. "They can keep it, frankly, as far as I'm concerned."

"Well, that will be the Governor's decision, won't it?" Suzette said neutrally. She was frowning as she adjusted the court dress; not formal, the official reception would not be until tomorrow, but it was unaccustomed after so many weeks in riding clothes or uniforms.

"Maybe it's Tzetzas who wanted us back," Foley continued. "He's going to have Raj sent to the frying pole for not turning over all Jamal's pay chests. Remember that message he sent when he found out you'd ordered half invested for life pensions to the disabled?"

"'Fiscally irregular,' I believe the phrase was," Muzzaf said; the Komarite was sitting at one of the lounge desks, carefully blotting his pen on a scrap of paper. His new northern-style civilian trousers and jacket were Azanian silk themselves, and a ruby stud glowed in his cravat. "Shall I tell Messer Gruder our journey was uneventful?" he continued, finishing the letter.

"Tell Kaltin to stay flat on his back, for another four months or so," Gerrin Staenbridge said, stretching cat-content. A bullet through the inner thigh and a fractured legbone were no joke, especially after a bad infection. Of course, another inch to the right and Captain Gruder would have been the *last* of the Graders, whether he survived or not. "He's used up about all his luck as it is. . . ." He glanced east, toward Sandoral. "You know, I hate to have loose ends, and I'm a little anxious leaving someone bedridden in charge back there; did they ever find that wog who murdered Reed, for example, what was his name, Abdullah?"

"No," Suzette said, in a tone even more detached; they all looked over at her. The shuttered, unreadable manner seemed to be inversely proportional to the distance from Court.

"Probably intended to disorganize the militia for the assault, had they won," Gerrin observed.

"Probably," Raj agreed. Suzette's eyes flickered to his, and then away.

"Well, I'll be damned!" Menyez exclaimed, from the dockside window. There was a blast from the whistle, and a slight jar as the boat was warped in to the dock. Trumpets sounded. "The 2nd Gendarmerie is providing our escort!"

"'Half-Ass Stanson himself?"

"For the Spirit's sake, watch that," Raj laughed. "I hear he's recruiting a better class of thug, these days." The hundred-or-so survivors of the 2nd's mad-dash retreat from the Valley of Death had learned something, at least. Not least a strong determination never to leave the capital again, from what his correspondents in the Palace said.

"You were planning on seeing the Governor at once?" Stanson said, leaning back against the cushions on the other side of the coach.

Raj blinked, glancing aside at Des Poplanich. It was irregular that his old friend's brother should have come to meet them with the escort, being persona extremely non grata at Court, and the way Stanson had insisted on taking Raj alone in the lead coach was even more suspicious.

"Well, yes, of course," Raj said, suddenly conscious of the pistol at his side and the sword lying across his lap.

Don't be ridiculous, he told himself, glancing out the window. A crowd was leaving a theater, laughing women in gowns and feathered hats and jewels, men in brilliant uniforms handing them up into light town coaches, lacy things of crystal and steel and glass. The bright gaslights glittered on the jewels and metalwork, the marble of the buildings, the embroidered liveries of slaves who held the bridles of coach teams whose coats were brushed to a shine as perfect as the ladies' wigs. Maxiluna was full, hovering over the palace; the streets were loud with the sound of iron wheels on the cobbles, the cries of pushcart-vendors. *Nothing's going to happen; except a lot of tedious parades and speeches, when the troops get here. And* maybe *a war next year, but the Southern Territories are our rightful possession.*

He glanced back; Des seemed embarrassed, but there was a bright tension to Stanson's posture. Raj remembered the way he had handled his pistols in the surprise attack last year, like extensions of his hands; this was Stanson's home territory, and here he was as much at home as Raj was on a battlefield with a clear enemy in front of him.

"It would really be better . . . very much better," Stanson said quietly, "if you would send a message saying you were tired, and that you'd see the Governor at the morning levee." A silence, broken only by the rattle of the wheels that changed to a rumble as they neared the Palace and the surface of the street switched from cobblestones to more recent concrete. The soft thudding of the dogs' paws remained, and their panting.

"Better still," the 2nd's commander continued, "if you'd taken a day or so longer getting back from the frontier; I understand some of your people are still recovering from their injuries."

Unspoken threat; Raj looked out the window again. The 2nd's new uniforms were beautifully tailored, but the jackets were a sand-colored khaki now, and they were riding with the butts of their rifles on their thighs.

"Well," he said after a minute. "I suppose you're to be the new Governor, Des?"

Des Poplanich stuttered; he was plumper than his older brother had been—is, Raj thought *he's not dead, just . . . out of circulation*—but had much of the same well-meaning earnestness. Raj had always rather liked him; Des was very much what his brother might have been, without the force of will and with only nine-tenths of the brains.

"Raj, you know I'm not an ambitious man," he began. Raj nodded; that was the only reason Des was still alive, that and Barholm's thorough-going contempt. Des continued:

"But this . . . it's for the good of the State. Barholm's a madman, and he's . . . Raj, you've been away from Court, but he's getting worse. This religious policy, it's insane! Yes, we can't allow outright heathens like the Christos equal rights, but that's no excuse for confiscating their property or denying them all basic liberties. The taxes are grinding half of what's *left* of the free-farmer class into debt-peonage, and where's it going? Where is every penny going? To line Tzetzas' pockets, and creatures like him, and what's left over is squandered on new temples and crazy schemes like this cross-country railway to Sandoral, and foreign wars that enrich nobody but mercenaries and contractors—Tzetzas again . . .

"He has to go, Raj; him and that *whore* he had the effrontery to make Governor's Lady. Did you know," he continued bitterly, with the offended pride of fifteen generations of patricians, "that he's had her face put on a coin? That respectable Messas have been banished from court—

even imprisoned—because they wouldn't treat a common *prostitute* like one of themselves?"

Raj nodded; because that was all true, yes, and because he needed to know as much as he could. *Although most of those Ladies . . . at least Anne probably always gave value for money.*

"Barholm's a son-of-a-bitch, right enough," he said. Stanson watched him with slitted sauroid eyes. *Careful, he's no fool.* "And Tzetzas is worse; he's not just robbing the treasury, he's tried to rob men under my command." A slight relaxation; his own clashes with the Chancellor were legendary, by now. "But I swore Barholm an oath, and I'll not be party to his murder."

"Raj!" Des said, genuine wonder and offense in his tone. "You know me better than that! Barholm, and even his . . . woman . . . well, they'll be kept under heavy guard, of course, and we couldn't allow them back into Descott County—no offense—"

Raj nodded; the County had gotten used to having one of its own on the Chair, and a good quarter of the Civil Government's native cavalry were recruited there.

"—he'll be taken to Chongwe Island, one of his estates. He can drink himself to death in his own time, or indulge in religious dementia—I think he's already half convinced he's an Avatar—or whatever. That'll be enough vengeance for Thom, and my grandfather."

Stanson had coughed and covered his face with his hand, but the reflection in the window behind Des' head had worn an expression more suitable for a hunting sauroid in the unguarded instant before; one of the smaller, nimbler kinds that killed by biting hunks out of their prey on the run. Raj thought he detected a change in the other man's posture, as well; he had probably been prepared to shoot Raj on the spot if he fell in with the plan suspiciously easily, and damn the complications. Perhaps it would *be* worth the trouble to become a fast-draw artist himself, and Suzette could study poisons—*Des, Des*, Raj thought. *You should have stayed in your townhouse, or better still gone to your estates and written philosophy and plays and spent your time being a good Messer to your tenants.* He felt a deep sadness; covered his own eyes and sighed wearily.

Because when you run with the sicklefeet, you'd better be equipped with claws.

"Who's behind this?" he said aloud. "Because Stanson, I'm not stupid enough to think you could bring it off by yourself. You don't have enough influence in the Army."

The other officer leaned forward and began reeling off names; Raj nodded at the progression. Several million acres of land, including most of the rich Hemmar Valley—Trahn Minh was in on it, no surprise—and another million or so FedCreds worth of East Residence shipping and manufacturing. Men who were not likely to rejoice either at the taxes necessary to pay for reconquests in the western territories, or at the disruption of the export-import trade it implied.

"Well, that's impressive enough," Raj said. "I'm . . . not a suicidal man, whatever the newsmongers say. I've got eight men, myself and Suzette—"

Stanson winced slightly.

"—which is scarcely enough for a firefight; and I don't think you're stupid enough to try it without putting the 2nd in control of the Palace, either, Stanson. It's not as if Barholm were the best Governor we've ever had"—*just essential to the purposes of the Spirit of Man, somehow—*"so as long as I'm not expected to participate in anything against my oath," he shrugged, "what can I do?"

Des leaned over and clasped his hand warmly, beaming. "Everyone knows you're as scrupulous of your honor as any officer in the Army, and the most able field commander in the Civil Government. But not one of these crazy fanatics who think we can restore the Holy Federation overnight, you care for your men too much for that," he said. "When you accept a high command under me, all decent men will rally to my side."

You'd be a puppet, Raj thought coldly, as he smiled and his mouth said words, *and with Stanson in on this, I'd be unsuspiciously dead in about a year.* That could not be allowed to matter, but the consequences to the State which embodied Holy Federation here on Earth—

least unfavorable possibility, probability 15%, 200 years after this date, plusminus 20. observe.

❖   ❖   ❖

—East Residence was burning; it was this street, in the city Raj knew, but worn somehow, buildings aged and not repaired for decades. Grass grew through patchy cobbles, and the harbor was empty. The clothing styles on the men and women who lay in the streets were altogether strange, those who were not naked or in rags. A motley line of infantry stormed a barricade; the people behind it looked to be ordinary East Residence types, but the troops were black Zanj in Civil Government uniforms.

highest probability. 83%, plusminus 4. observe.

—East Residence was burning. A line of troops retreated down the street outside; he recognized the banners of the 7th Descott Rangers and his own 5th. Cannister plowed gruesomely through their ranks, and other men in Civil Government uniforms pursued; Rogor Slashers, Kelden Foot, and the odd short jackets of Brigade soldiers mixed in. Citizens on the roofs above threw tiles and chamberpots, until the Kelden infantry turned and fired a volley upward—

Civil war, Raj thought. At best, centuries in the future when all hope had rotted away. More probably within the year; he knew his Descott gentry, they were not going to stand for a regime dominated by cityman merchants and worse, the Hemmar Valley counties and their lords. The lowlanders had money in plenty, but were unlikely to trust their peons with arms; they would hire outsiders, which meant *both* sides would be forced to seek help abroad. He shivered.

"And?" Stanson prompted. They were through the outer wall of the Palace district. Raj met his eyes, turned up his hands.

"Anything is better than civil war," he said. "Anything at all."

Belief, because Stanson was a good judge of men in his way, and he was hearing absolute truth.

"But it'd be very suspicious indeed, if I don't at least pay a courtesy call on the Governor." Stanson's fingers flexed, moving with an independent life.

"Alone?" he said flatly. The inflection implied a question,

but the face did not; Des Poplanich looked from one man to the other, puzzled.

"No, that'd arouse questions, too," Raj replied. "A man of my rank can't move about without the dignity of an escort, even if he's known not to stand on ceremony. But of course," he continued, "Suzette mustn't be allowed near Lady Anne."

Stanson nodded vigorously. "Of course not," he said.

"Right," Raj said, tapping one thumb against his chin. "You could detach a few of your men, escort her to her quarters—an honor guard, that'll sound right, and I'll take two of my men and just drop in briefly on Barholm. Then I'll rejoin Suzette in our apartments—" *considerably larger ones, the message from Lady Anne had said* "—and we'll lock the doors while you do what you have to."

Stanson thought for long seconds, then nodded. Raj was offering his wife as a hostage. Himself, too, for that matter, taking only two men into the Governor's quarters; if worst came to worst, Des could simply be told that his friend was unfortunately caught in the crossfire.

"Yes, that would be perfect," Stanson said, cutting across Des Poplanich's thanks.

Shows you how much authority he'd *have as Governor,* Raj thought.

"Perfect. We do have to be careful that no harm comes to Lady Suzette—"

That's Lady Whitehall, you son of a bitch—

"—at any cost. I, ah," he hesitated, "I remember very well that she saved my life. Whatever other disagreements we'd had, the wog was coming for me, my guns were empty and there wasn't any *time* and then she shot him—"

"Yes, I remember it, too," Raj said. *A pity, but then Suzette's like that.* "Whatever happened to Merta?" he continued; remembering himself, how the girl had thrown herself between her man and the steel. Better to put things on a man-to-man basis, and keep Stanson's uncomfortably acute treachery-antennae numbed by memories that brought a rim of sweat-beads to his brow.

"Merta?" Stanson said; then his face cleared. "Oh, the redhead. I married her off to one of my farrier-sergeants, and got them a rent-free farm," he said.

Raj blinked slightly in surprise. Rather decent, for—
"It was Lady Suzette who suggested it, in fact."
—Stanson.

"What's going on, Raj?" Suzette whispered furiously.
Raj stepped back; Stanson was watching with the same unblinking reptile stare.
"Warrant M'lewis," he said. "Messer Staenbridge."
They both looked up, alerted by the form of address as much as the tone. The Companions were all out of their carriages now, and the twenty troopers of the 2nd were formed up on foot as Palace servants led their dogs away. This was the Old Harbor courtyard, near the Apartments of Honor; ancient buildings about three stories high, the most prestigious section of the residential wing. Behind them bulked the Governor's Tower, fused stone from before the Fall, as alabaster-perfect as it had been a millennium before.
"You'll be accompanying me while I report to the Governor," he said, drawing off his gloves. "Meanwhile, these fellow-soldiers—" he indicated the men of the 2nd, and saw several of the Companions blink"—will form an escort to accompany Lady Whitehall to our apartments, and will remain until I join you."
Their eyes were on him, a flat alertness that showed nothing in face or body. Foley stroked his hook along the jaw of his young-old face; the outer curve, since the inner was sharp enough to shave with.
"I have *full confidence* in you," he said, in the same loud parade-ground voice. "There have been rumors of disturbances in the city," he continued, "and Messer Captain Stanson has kindly offered these Gendarmerie troopers as additional protection for our apartments and Lady Whitehall."
"Raj, I'm coming with you—" Suzette began.
"—and you will see that she goes there at once and *remains* there, restraining her if necessary. I hold you six responsible for her safety. Is that understood?"
Foley saluted. "*Entirely* understood, my lord," he said. Da Cruz had stepped up to Suzette's side and laid a warning hand on her arm; the other men had quietly moved to see that the rifles and personal weapons in their baggage were

within their perimeter, plucking them out of the hands of the Palace servants with unobtrusive speed.

"And a very pleasant goodnight to you, Messer Captain Stanson," Raj said, squeezing his hand. "I expect we won't see each other until morning?"

"No doubt, Messer Brigadier Whitehall," Stanson replied.

"Your Supremacy, there's a plot against your life, don't look up," Raj whispered, smiling brightly. "Invite me and these two men into the Sanctum, *now* my lord, there's no time."

Barholm stiffened as he pulled him into the embrace of equals. There was not a hint of disbelief. Governors who died of old age were not precisely in the two-headed calf category of probabilities, but not in the majority by any means.

"No formality between me and my best commander!" he said, grinning. Moisture sprang out on his upper lip. "You must join me for a nightcap at least: I wouldn't hear of anything else."

Barholm turned, tucking his hand under Raj's arm; the Gendarmerie detachment at the door to the personal apartments could do nothing. Raj gave their officer a slight helpless shrug; one did *not* refuse such an invitation from the absolute ruler of the State.

"And these two valiant souls with you as well," Barholm continued smoothly. "As the Spirit of Man's Viceregent on Earth, I'd like very much to hear how they've served It against the Spirit-Deniers."

The door of the outer apartments swung closed; it was ebony with a steel core. Barholm swung the handle closed with his own hands, pushing aside a horrified servant; by the time he had turned around M'lewis and Staenbridge were already hauling a great cast-bronze couch across the Al-Kebir carpet to wedge beneath it.

His eyes were glazed as he turned to Raj. "Can these two be trusted?" he said.

"Absolutely, my lord," Raj replied. The Governor's hands were making slight unconscious gestures, the outward expression of a dialogue he conducted with himself.

"Save me and I'll make you both the richest lords in the

Civil Government," he blurted. Staenbridge and M'lewis both gave him a brief bow, hiding disdain under peasant acquisitiveness and aristocratic blandness respectively.

"Come on, come on," Barholm said. "We've . . . the Old Tower, it's impregnable. *Quickly!*"

The servant was still standing there, her mouth making the open-and-close motions of a feeding fish. "Get Lady Anne," Raj told her, simply and forcefully. "Get her *now*."

"My lord," he continued to Barholm, "these are the details I've been able to uncover—"

The innermost apartments of the Old Tower were preFall, oddly shaped and sized by modern standards, despite all that had been done to modernize them since; the fireplaces were of an alabaster as close to the ancient fusemelt as could be found, but somehow they still clashed violently. The ceilings glowed with a cool light that had not varied in all the years since the Fall, and there were no windows below the hundred-meter crown of stone far above. Raj saw the rooms only as a series of tactical obstacles, details discarded by a consciousness focused down to the width of a gunsight. Staenbridge stood beside him, arms crossed and pistol dangling negligently; M'lewis was quivering-alert with the ornamental shotgun he had seized from a blubbering manservant, but not too preoccupied to slip a few articles into his pockets . . .

"They've all turned against me!" Barholm said, sitting slumped in a chair of silver and rock-crystal and silk. "Even Stanson, he was a broken man and I raised him up from *nothing*, do you hear, *nothing*, I paid his debts that would have ruined him and *this* is how he repays me!" There were tears in the Governor's eyes, of terror or real grief, perhaps.

"My lord," Raj said, using patience like a tool that would grind results out of rock, given time enough. His mind showed him Suzette's body torn by a volley from the Gendarmerie troopers, as the conspirators found Barholm's inner apartments barred and locked; he forced it away with a monstrous effort of will. *You've made your decisions*, he told himself. *Now don't waste it.* "My lord, we've very little time. I presume the armored car is still in readiness?"

Barholm drew a deep breath, nodded. "In the level above

the subbasement," he said. "There are, there are jewels and . . . it's fueled for 100 kilometers, the gate there gives directly onto the corniche road." The Old Tower had originally been the heart of East Residence's defenses, and it was still on the seaward edge of the city proper. "We can, we can get away to the Settler, he'd, ah, there's . . . ah, he'd protect us, I've done him favors in the past and—"

"My lord, the Settler is *dead*," Raj said tightly. "You may recall, I sent you his head packed in alcohol about a month ago? But we *can*—"

"Stay exactly where we are!"

Anne, Lady Clerett, knew the value of an entrance. She had taken the time to dress in the full regalia of a Governor's Lady, down to the high tiara and the skirt split at the front and trailing behind half a dozen paces; she blazed with the jewels of her state . . . and Raj could see no fear in her face, no fear at all. An anger as huge as any he had ever seen, yes.

"Barholm Clerett," she continued. "I didn't claw my way out of the gutter—or marry you—to wear a veil and live in a villa on the Colonial Gulf. Or to run away! That's always your answer, isn't it, Barholm; whenever something goes wrong suddenly, you *run*. My protector found us in bed, and you *jumped out the window* and ran naked into the street, for all the city to see and laugh! The *mob* tried to throw you out and put one of those Poplanich worms on the Chair, and you wanted to run then; you'd be running still, if *I* hadn't locked you in your room until you gave the order to send in the troops. And now you want to run again, you *worm*, well I'll show you how a Governor should die, you *coward*, because I'll die here in the Palace, I'll set it on *fire* to be my funeral pyre before I'll lose everything again!"

Bravo, curtain call, Raj thought; but there was a quality in Anne's face that was as daunting as a Colonist charge, in its way. The pistol she waved was a toy, a gold and nielo orchid in steel, but there was almost certainly a round up the spout . . . and she might just decide to kill Barholm *and* herself; this was the sort of trembling intensity of spirit capable of anything.

"And you!" she said, wheeling on Raj. "I—" The frenzy

drained out of her expression, replaced by a smile. "Well, of *course* you don't mean to run away, General Whitehall. You know we can win, the Army can't be all in on it . . . these walls are impregnable, we can hold out for a week or more, they'd have to blast the Old Tower off its foundations to harm it." Which was true enough. "The heliograph on the roof, we can summon loyal battalions from, oh, the coast provinces, from Descott if we have to."

And there will be civil war anyway, Raj thought sickly. If the plotters were given time to consolidate their hold on the Palace. *Wait a minute, though*, he thought suddenly. *They must have thought of that, they know Anne, too—*
observe.

—and Raj recognized the Tower, glowing in solitary perfection. The viewpoint swooped in, down to the basement; all the walls were glowing, now, and a dozen mysterious transparent tubes pierced the floor. Time blurred forward; the light faded from all except the ceiling, and the transparent pipes stood empty and dusty. Men came and sledged them out; they laid brick over the opalescent material of the floor, over the conduits . . . that stretched down into the main sewers. Much later, and other men came, spanning the high chamber with beams to divide it into two stories; they laid stone tile over the beams, and built a trapdoor through it. He was suddenly in the sewer itself; men crouched there, in the uniforms of the 2nd Gendarmerie. There were pry bars and sledges in their hands, carbide lamps to show the circles of brick above their heads. One was setting up a stepladder . . .

"There's a way in from below," Raj said. Anne wheeled to stare at him narrow-eyed. "From the sewers into the level below the main floor, into the storage area." Where the armored car was kept, ready to drive up its ramp and through the gates. "They will . . . that is, they're probably planning to break up through the . . . bricked-in areas, into the chamber with the armored car. There'll be no stopping them after that, the floor over that is rafters and they can break through that, too, and we can't close the staircases in the main section of the Tower."

"Are you a coward, too?" Anne asked, half-raising the gun. "Use the cannon in the car, *shoot* them, *kill* them."

"Lady Anne," Raj said desperately: how to explain to someone with no experience of actual combat? *Although her instincts can't be faulted, certainly.* "My lady, that cannon, it won't depress . . . bend down, enough to hit the floor at all. And once we've blocked the main entrances to the Tower, when they come through the floor they'll do it a hundred strong or more we couldn't . . ." He held up a hand. "Wait. Wait. There is a way." He looked over at the arc lights that could flood the larger rooms with the extra light needed for spectacle.

Hope blossomed on Barholm's face as he explained, and an avidness on Anne's. Raj kept his own as impersonal as a machine; his mind also, focusing on the means and not what they would do.

"Come on, Gerrin," he said after Barholm nodded furiously. "We've got work to do and not much time to do it in. M'lewis, hold the fort."

The end of the pry bar struck through the bricks almost without resistance. *They must have scratched out the mortar days ago, then supported it with a circle of planks*, Raj realized, and drew his pistol.

"Gerrin!" he shouted. "Time, Gerrin, time!"

The bricks fell downward, a circle of darkness lit by the flicker of lamps. He rested his hands on the riveted hull of the armored car and fired, the flash orange in the dim light of the subbasement. A scream from below, and the lights retreated.

"Thirty seconds more, Raj." Gerrin's voice, in the uninflected tone of a man concentrating on a task that requires mind and hands both.

"Whitehall, it's over!" Stanson's voice, and there was a thumping all around the floor, as iron beat on unweakened brick. A crack and clatter, and the bricks over another conduit gave, trembling and then falling back as the mortar went to powder.

"Raj!" Des Poplanich's voice, desperately earnest. "I don't want you hurt; nobody will be hurt, but you *mustn't* be, you *belong* with us, not that murdering usurper Clerett."

"Whitehall, don't worry, we *need* you," Stanson continued. "Everyone's agreed you get the Field Force command on the western border, for as long as you want it." More hammering, and the grinding sound of brick shifting. "Nobody can say you didn't go the second kilometer for your oath, Whitehall, but it's *over*."

Raj thought he heard a reluctant admiration in the other man's voice, impossible to tell whether it was for Raj's courage or the skill he had used to deceive.

"Raj, it's done," Gerrin said.

He fired again, and both men broke for the ladder; the trapdoor tumbled back, and so did a servant who dropped the marble statuette in his hands with a shriek at the sight of Raj's face, streaked with oil and sweat.

"Just what I need, to be brained by a fucking butler," he snarled, as Gerrin rolled out of the entrance. The clatter of bricks below gave way to the stamp of men's feet, the sound of the steel butt-plate of a rifle ringing off the armored car's hull.

Have to get them into position, Raj thought. He fired through the trapdoor, and a huge volley answered it; there must be a hundred men or more below, all the troops Stanson and the other conspirators could trust to actually do the deed and not just accept the results. They would be the core of the plot; he could hear Stanson's voice, Des Poplanich's, others with Messerclass accents. Boots kicked aside brass shell casings.

"Messer," somebody said below. "There's something funny here. . . . I think this is a siphon—"

"Ser?" M'lewis asked from across the room. His hand was on the knife-switch of the arc lights, the one that lit the subbasement below. Supernal light from the glowing ceiling shone on his gold teeth, on the feral tension in his eyes.

Gerrin's gaze met his commander's, holding an identical distaste. Raj straightened. It was his decision, his responsibility.

"Now," he said. M'lewis threw the switch. Current surged, through the power leads and into the great barrel Raj and his Companion had tipped on its side, filled with the coal-oil fuel of the armored car, backed with a powder charge from the ammunition of its cannon. The improvised flame fougasse sprayed across the men packed beneath the trapdoor.

Suzette—

observe.

—and the troopers of the 2nd were sitting outside the door of the apartments, hands sullenly on their necks as the panels swung wide and she flung herself toward him—

—and the first volley from the men he led caught the 2nd's men in the back as they sniped at the barricade of furniture inside the apartments, and Foley was grinning as he rose from behind it, Muzzaf by his side and Suzette was pushing between them, her face lighting as she saw—

probability of harm to lady Whitehall too slight for meaningful calculation. Was there a tinge of mercy in the implacable voice?

Raj opened his eyes again. Barholm Clerett was standing, shaking his fists in the air; the fear was gone from his face, leaving a triumph that was far less pleasant to see. Lady Anne was by his side, reaching out one hand to touch him as if he was a talisman.

"I will rule the world, all of it, *all* of it, the Spirit of Man has decreed it."

Yes, thought Raj sickly. *And I'm sworn to conquer it for him. May my soul find mercy.*

"My lord," he said, "we'd better go upstairs. This floor will probably collapse."

Even with the trapdoor closed, the screams were quite audible.

BATTLE OF SANDORAL

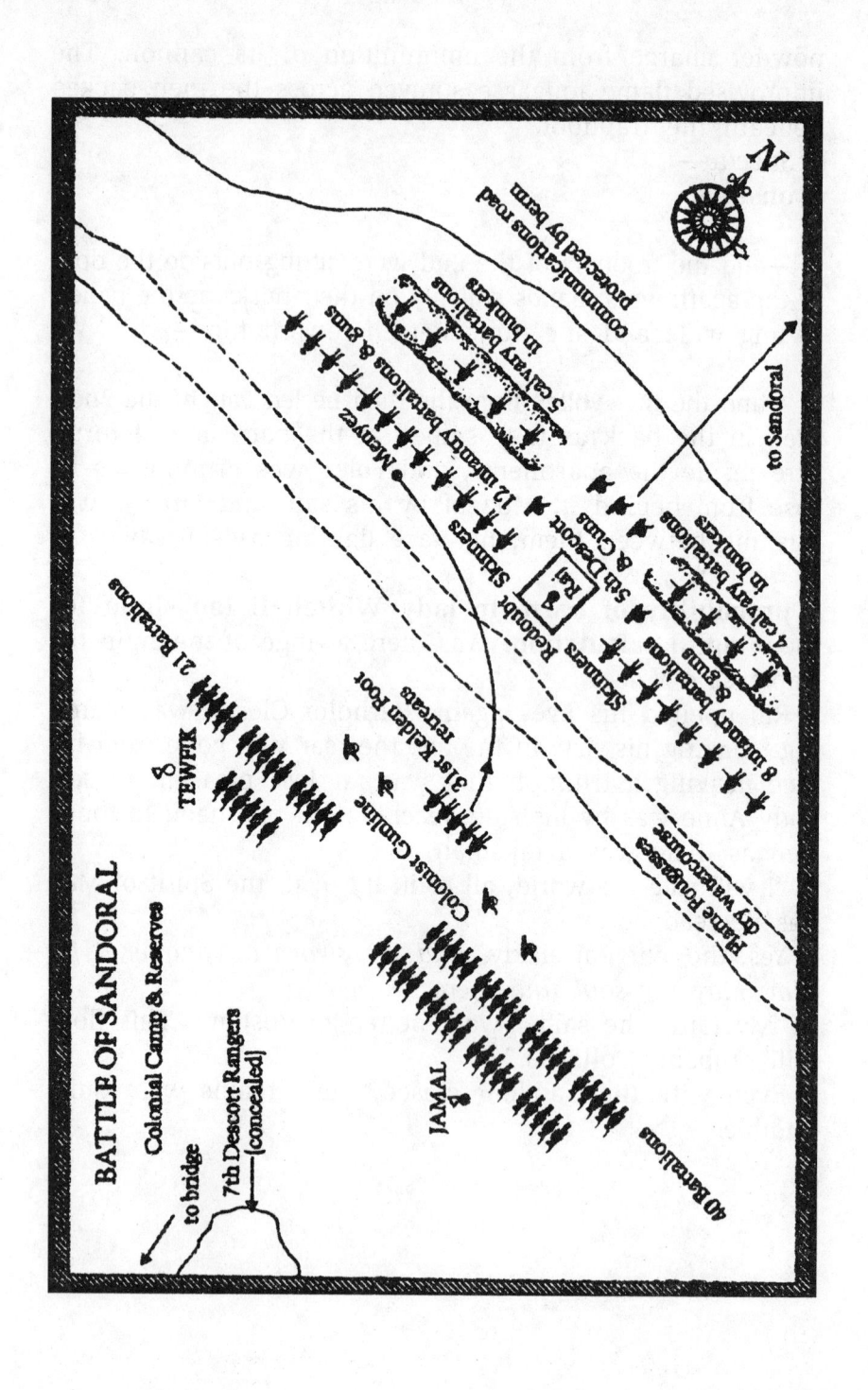

Colonial Camp & Reserves

to bridge

7th Descott Rangers [concealed]

21 Battalions

TEWFIK

Colonist Cuirline

31st Kelden Foot retreats

Skirmishers

Redoubt

Menyez

12 infantry battalions & guns

5 cavalry battalions in bunkers

5th Descott & Guns

Raj

8 infantry battalions & guns

4 cavalry battalions in bunkers

communications road protected by berm

to Sandoral

dry watercourse

Haute Rougesse

JAMAL

40 Battalions

N

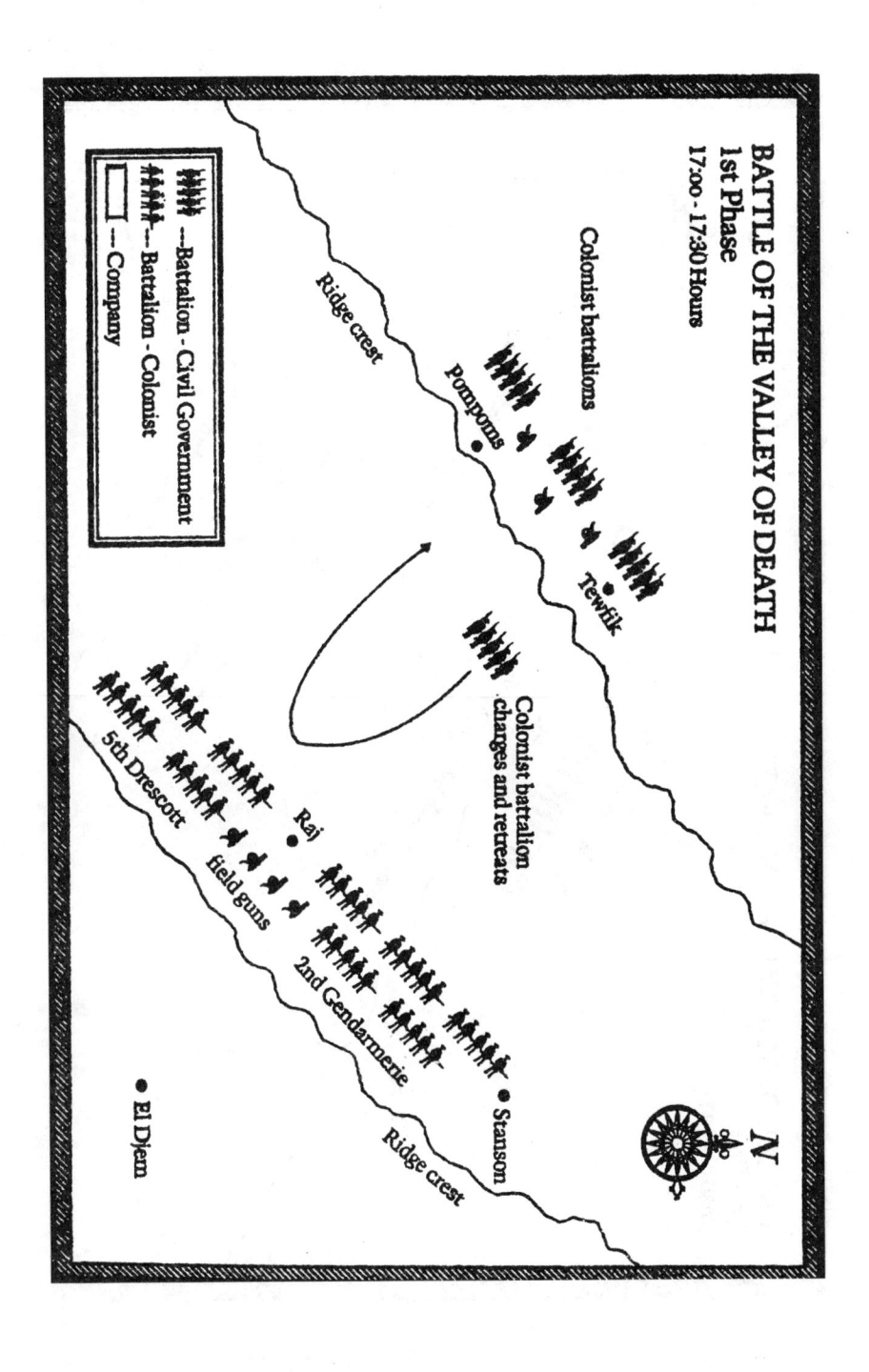

BATTLE OF THE VALLEY OF DEATH
1st Phase
17:00 - 17:30 Hours

Colonist battalions

Ridge crest

• Pompoms

• Tewfik

Colonist battalion charges and retreats

• Raj

field guns

• Stanson

2nd Gendarmerie

5th Drescott

Ridge crest

• El Djem

N

Legend:
- ╫╫╫ — Battalion - Civil Government
- ✝✝✝ — Battalion - Colonist
- ☐ — Company

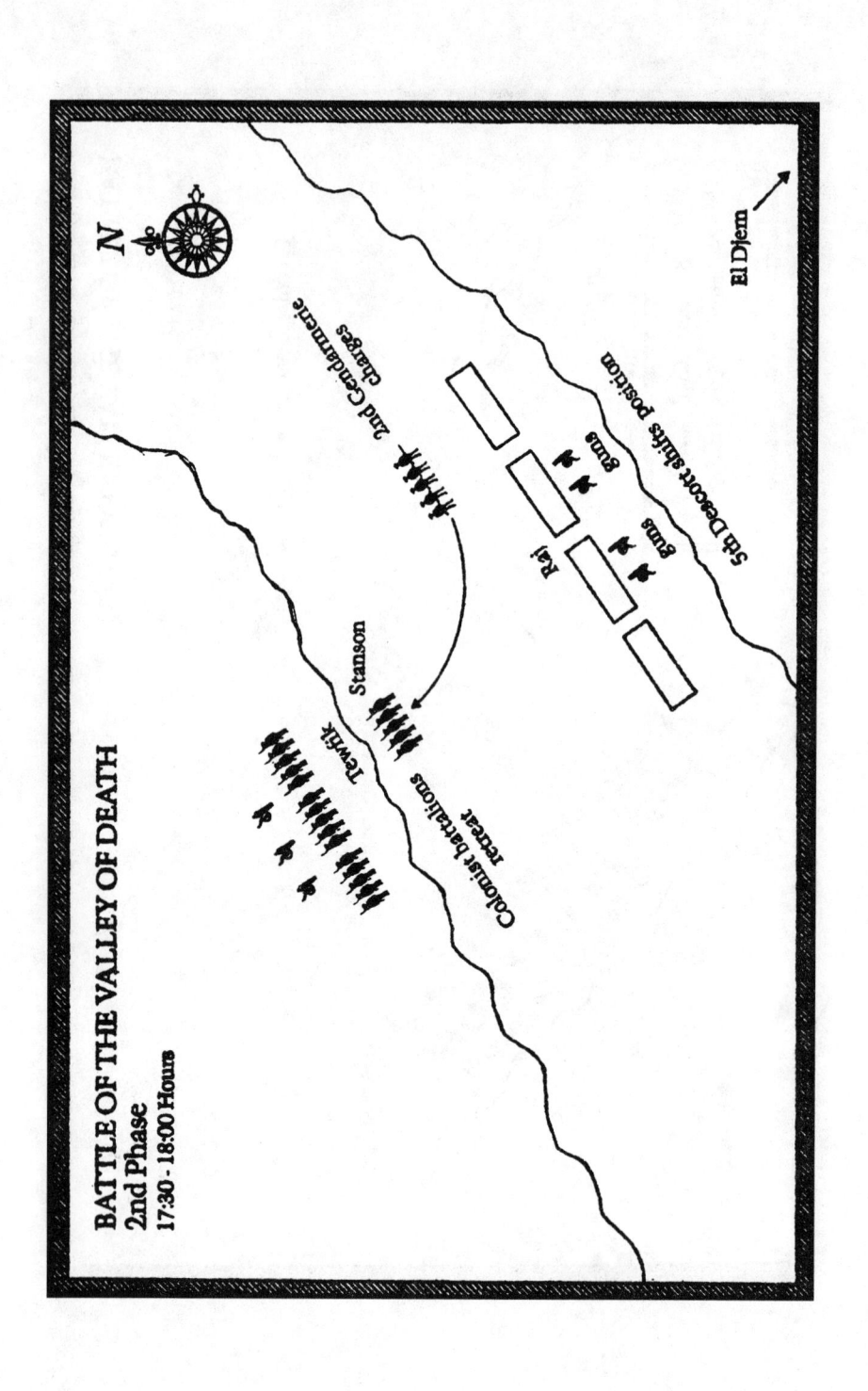

BATTLE OF THE VALLEY OF DEATH
2nd Phase
17:30 - 18:00 Hours

BATTLE OF THE VALLEY OF DEATH
3rd Phase

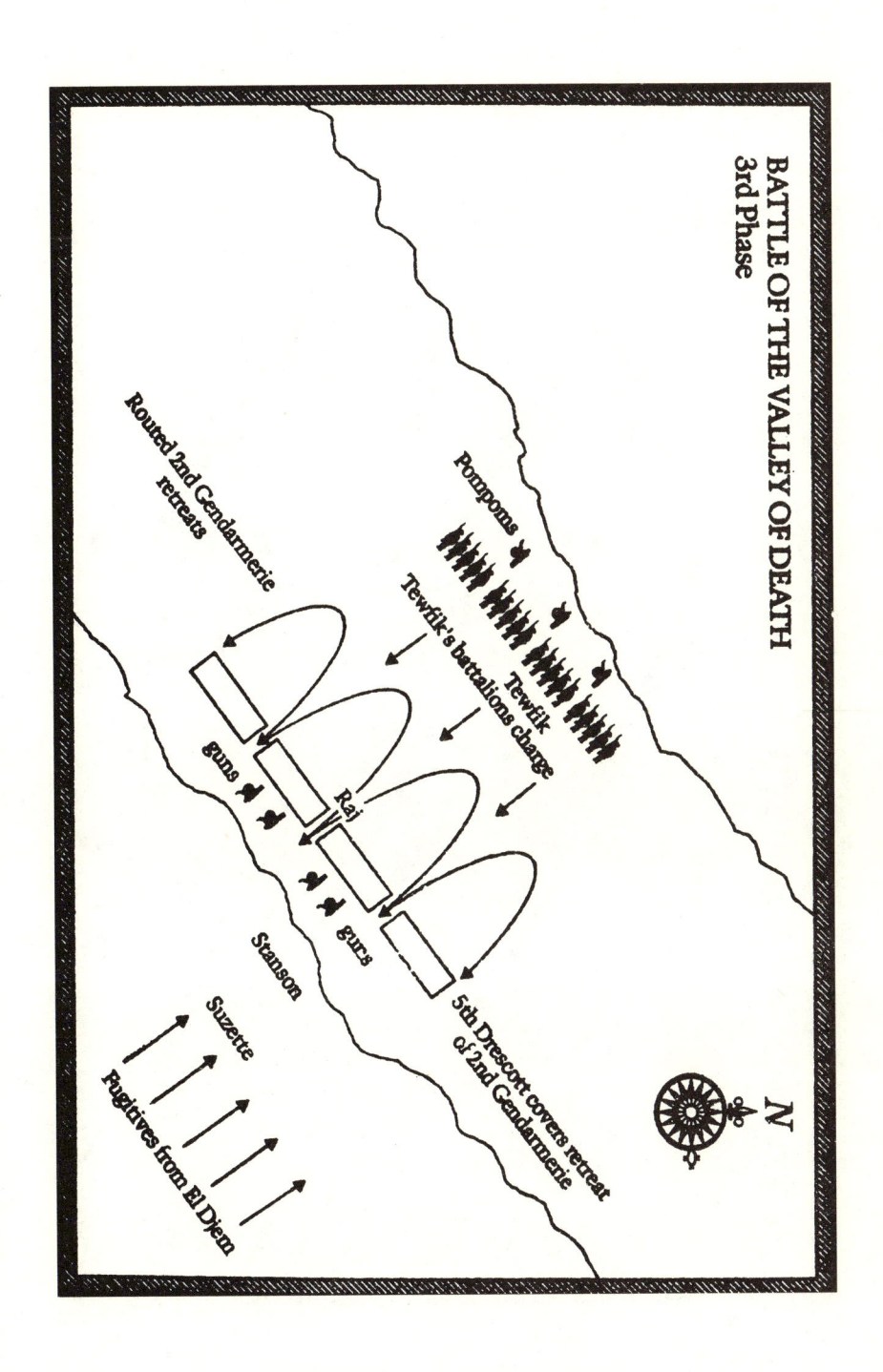

Pompoms

Tewfik's battalions charge

Tewfik

Routed 2nd Gendarmerie retreats

guns

Raj

guns

5th Drescort covers retreat of 2nd Gendarmerie

Stanson

Suzette

Fugitives from El Djem

N

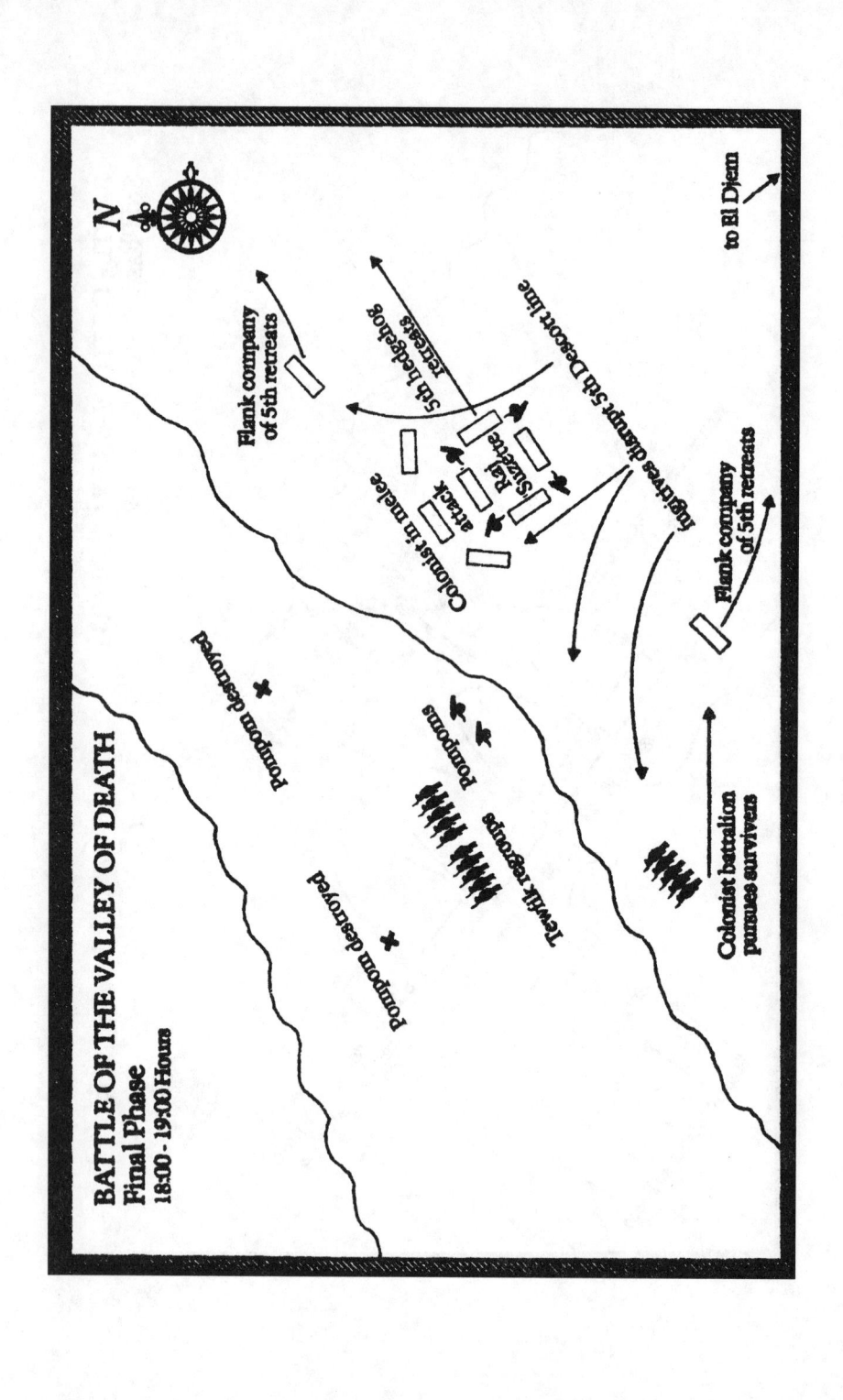

BATTLE OF THE VALLEY OF DEATH
Final Phase
18:00 - 19:00 Hours

N

to El Djem

Flank company of 5th retreats

5th beleaguered retreats

Colonist in melee attack

Rafales Sustained

fugitives disrupt 5th D escort line

Flank company of 5th retreats

pompom destroyed

pompom destroyed

Tenth regroups

pompoms

Colonist battalion pursues survivors

II
The Hammer

To Jan

And to Rudyard Kipling, who said things so well

CHAPTER ONE

"Raj?" Thom muttered. Then, slightly shocked: "Raj!"

The two young men stared at each other for a moment. Raj Whitehall felt his skin ridging in horror; *nothing* had changed here in nearly two years. Nothing at all since that moment when Thom Poplanich had frozen into immobility in the round mirrored room that was the body of the being that called itself Sector Command and Control Unit AZ12-b14-c000 Mk. XIV. Thom still had the unhealed shaving nick on his thin olive cheek, the tear in his floppy tweed trousers made by a ricochet when Raj tried to shoot his way out with his ceremonial revolver. Whereas for Raj . . . a *lifetime*. Thom had remained here; Center had sent Raj Whitehall out to be its agent in the fallen world.

"Raj, you're—"

"Older. Two years older. Everyone's older except you, Thom," Raj said gently, forcing calm into his voice.

He had been forcing calm ever since he made himself go down once more into the catacombs beneath the East Residence. This place was something that did not belong in the prosaic world, in the one thousand one hundred and fifth year of the Fall. Forcing himself not to run at the remembered scent, the absolute neutrality of filtered air, like nothing else in the world . . . The eerie not-floor that somehow supported him without touching his bootsoles, the perfect mirror of the walls that reflected one thing and not another. His hand clutched the grip of his five-shot revolver, not for any good the weapon might do but for the comfort of the honest iron and wood.

This was where his life had changed twenty months ago; the shock in Thom's eyes made him aware of it again, that and the fresh-faced youthfulness of the friend who had been older and wiser and more knowing in the ways of the City. Raj brought up an image of himself as he had been, and as he was: still tall and raw-boned, 190 centimeters, broad-shouldered and long-limbed. The brown, high-cheeked, hook-nosed face was more lined now, and there was something in the eyes . . . .

"What's happened to me?" Thom asked shakily.

"Nothing. Center is—"

thom poplanich has had access to all knowledge in the human universe as of the fall of the Federation, Center said in a slightly waspish mental voice; there was no tone to it, but there was some inner equivalent of inflection, **in addition, he has the services of a Sector Command and Control Unit AZ12-b14-c000 Mk. XIV to guide him through it. surely this is more than nothing.**

"That's right," Thom said, some of the tension easing out of his voice; he licked his lips, and Raj wordlessly handed over his canteen. His friend uncorked it and drank gratefully; it was water cut one-quarter with wine and a slice of lime thrown in. Raj had come properly prepared this time; just a pistol for the rats and native spersauroids, a rope and an old jacket.

"That's right, it's been showing me. . . . Raj, what's happened to Bellevue since we lost FTL travel is like a scale model of what happened to the Federation—"

Thom was never religious before, Raj thought. In fact, Thom had scoffed at his friend's simple belief in the Holy Federation, and the scriptural tales of the days before the Fall from the Stars, when all men were one with the Spirit and there was neither poverty nor age nor death. Now he talked of ancient things as if they were as real and tangible as the prosaic modern world of gaslights and carriages.

"—Center says there's some sort of natural centrifugal effect at work, breaking things down smaller and smaller—"

observe Center said.

✧   ✧   ✧

—and men and women howled, milling across the great square. Some of the buildings around it had the glossy look of UnFallen Man, huge things that looked to be built impossibly of crystal and lacework. Others were more conventional, stone and brick, columns and domes, although not in any style he knew, and ancient-looking beyond words; a great reflecting pool ran down the center, ending in a spikelike monument. A single small moon hung yellow in the night sky, but the lights below bathed the faces of the crowd brighter than daylight, brighter even than the arclights at a Gubernatorial Levee. A man was speaking from a dais on one side of the pool; some UnFallen technological magic threw his head and shoulders hill-huge across one of the great buildings behind him. His voice boomed like a god's, and the crowd shrieked back in an agony of adoration and fear.

Suddenly there was a commotion at one side of the mass of humanity. Troops were pushing into the crowd, heading for the speaker; in dreamlike oddity they were primitively equipped, with helmets and long clubs, and shields that looked like glass but could not be, from the battering they were taking. Locked in a phalanx, they pushed through, a bubble of order in the milling chaos. Then the man on the dais pointed and shouted a command. Bottles and rocks flew toward the soldiers, then a wave of human bodies. What followed was like heavy surf breaking on a reef, but here it was the reef that crumbled. When the mob withdrew, the shield-bearers lay scattered . . . many scattered in separate pieces.

What looked like flying boxes darted out over the crowd. Streaks of fire lanced out from one, trailing smoke toward the man giving the speech. The timber framework of the dais exploded into a ball of orange flame, and more firelances slashed down into the crowd. Suddenly the supernal lights went out, and the buildings were dark except for the light of fires, light enough to see the thousands trampled to death as the crowd fled . . .

—and the viewpoint was in a room. The walls were lined with technology, flat screens and readouts such as you might see on any altar in the Civil Government, but functioning, incomprehensible pictures and columns of figures, the whole giving off a subliminal hum of life. Two men *floated* in the center of the room as if it were underwater; they were dressed in tight blue overalls, the uniform of Holy Federation as preserved in the ancient Canonical Handbook. The younger man was speaking, an urgent whisper. The language was Old Namerique, a tongue that survived only in fragments and in the debased form the western barbarians used, but somehow Raj understood it:

"Admiral Kenner, we've got to cut off the rot in that sector. We *must*, sir. One quick raid, we drop off a Bethe missile on delay, and take out the Tanaki Net. It's like cauterizing a wound, sir."

The older man nodded, his face stony. "Make it so, Commodore," he said, jackknifing to grab a handhold and touch a screen. "I've keyed the release codes in to your access."

"Thank you very much, sir," the younger man said. The Admiral had just enough time to look around and meet the knife . . .

—and Raj was watching East Residence from far above; not the city of his own day, but the ancient town with its broad grassy avenues and dreamlike towers. Then light sparked at its center, sun-bright, and spheres of cloud rippled out across the cityscape in its wake. A cloud rose towering, mushroom-shaped . . .

—and he was in the streets of East Residence, seeing familiar buildings but turned tumbled and weed-grown. Men in the uniform of his own service fought a desultory street-battle, seeming more intent on plundering the few remaining shops and homes. Two tumbled in combat below his motionless eye-point, faces distorted as they struggled hand-to-hand with rifles braced against each other. Then one twisted aside and smashed the butt across the other's face, reversing and driving the long bayonet through his belly. He did not bother to withdraw it before he went through the victim's pockets, ignoring the twitchings and feeble pawings of the dying man . . .

—and the Governor's Palace was a grassy mound grown with oaks; Raj recognized it only because of the shape of the harbor below, a long oval running east-west. You could still see the pattern of the streets through the forest, and here and there a snag of walls, or the humped shapes of the defensive earthworks. The sound of children running and playing echoed through the open parkland. In the foreground two men crouched by a fire; one was skillfully chipping a spearhead from a piece of glass, with the wooden shaft and a bundle of sinew for binding lying near. The other was butchering a carcass for roasting, working with slivers of glass and a stone hammer for breaking the bones. Both men were naked save for hide loincloths and shaggy as bears; it was a moment before Raj realized the body they were butchering was also human. . . .

Raj shuddered; visions of things that had been, that were, that still might be. "That's what men come to without the Spirit," he said.

Thom blinked at him. "Well, that's one way of putting it," he agreed.

Raj nodded, swallowing and looking away. "Yeah. I, ah, well, I asked Center if I could see you, because we're—the Expeditionary Force is leaving for the Southern Territories. The Governor—Barholm; his uncle Vernier died and Barholm's in the Chair—is set on retaking them. I'm certainly going with the army . . . and I'll probably be commanding it."

It was Thom's turn to be shocked. "Congratulations . . . but isn't that a bit of a jump for a Captain, even if he is one of the new Governor's Guards?"

Raj smiled, rueful and bitter. "Things have sort of changed, Thom," he said.

He saw his friend stiffen and a faint almost-glimmer slide across his eyes. Raj Whitehall needed no vision from Center to see what Thom Poplanich was being shown. Raj's memory provided that, and his dreams more often than he liked.

The line breaking at El Djem as the fugitives took them in the back. Suzette wild-eyed, shouting *They're dead, they're all dead* to his question. The milling bulk of red-robed Colonists around the final laager, his own voice shouting *Fall back one step and volley!* over and over again, raw and hoarse, the choking cloud of powder smoke as the cannon cut loose, and the nightmare retreat through the desert.

Governor Vernier dying, and Barholm and Lady Anne Clerett at the foot of the bed amid the ministers and priests and doctors; Anne's face, like something perched in a tree watching a sick sheep. Sandoral, and the Colonist battalions marching over the ridge in perfect order under their green banners, down into the gunsmoke where two hundred cannon dueled. The heaps of dead before his trenches, and that last moment when he knew they weren't going to break and then they did—wondering where the Colonist ruler, the Settler, had escaped to, until the Skinner mercenary brought him Jamal's head grinning at some private joke of death.

"So there are advantages to being a hostage, you see," Raj said with envious sadness.

thom poplanich is not a hostage, Center corrected, with the passionless pedantry that was its most frequent tone, **to release him now would threaten the plan to reunite Bellevue, to rebuild the Tanaki Spatial Displacement System, and if necessary to rebuild the Federation from here.**

Thom smiled, looking up slightly; when he spoke, Raj recognized the tone of a long-standing argument.

"That'll take generations; centuries, even. Provided that it doesn't fail, which you admit is more probable than not."

the shortest journey ends at one false step, Center replied.

Thom laughed, cutting off the chuckle at his friend's bewilderment. "There used to be a saying that the longest journey—oh, never mind, it doesn't translate well into Sponglish anyway." He shrugged, the expressive "unavoidable—circumstance" resignation of an East Residence dweller. "Since Center has elected you its instrument in the crusade, what do you think of the idea, Raj?" he asked.

Raj ran his hand through the short black curls that covered his head.

"I don't know, Thom, I honestly don't. I'm a soldier, not a priest; it's what I was born for."

For five hundred years the Whitehalls had fought the Civil Government's wars, dying in them often enough, and leaving only an urn of ashes or a sword to be brought home to their ancestral lands in Descott County.

"But you know me, too old-fashioned and country-bred to have an original thought. I serve the Spirit of Man of the Stars and the Holy Federation; and since I'm a soldier, I serve them as a soldier must, in the field and under arms. I . . . I don't think I deserve an angel for a counselor, not really. If that's what Center is." It was certainly a computer, and such had been the immaterial servants of Holy Federation, right enough. "I just know I have to do my best.

"I used to think that war was glory. Now . . . the only thing to say for it is that it shows you what men are. I've made some good friends over the past year, damn good. And I think I've got some aptitude for this shit; what that says about me, I don't know. But I have to try."

Thom held out his hand; Raj squeezed it in his. "I know you always will do your best," Thom said. "Spirit, how I envied you that single-mindedness." He laughed shortly. "Starless Dark, this isn't so bad; I was a scholar by temperament anyway; just my bad luck I was the old Governor's nephew. You might say we both had the misfortune to get what we asked for."

Raj made himself meet his friend's eyes. "Thom, there's one last thing. About—"

"Des, yes. Center told me." Thom met the gaze. "He was my brother; he was also an idiot. Letting himself be sucked into that scheme to overthrow Barholm was suicide, Raj. He ran onto your sword."

Actually I burned him alive, Raj thought, swallowing and remembering the sound and the smell from the room below. *Him and about a hundred others.* Most of them had deserved it, although not the hapless troopers who'd gotten caught up in the coup attempt. Des Poplanich had been no more guilty, so naive he didn't even know he was a puppet. And Spirit knew Barholm had done enough to deserve enemies. . . .

"That'll leave Ehwardo as the head of the family—since I'm effectively dead down here," Thom went on; that was his first cousin, and the only adult male Poplanich left. "Raj . . . look out for him if you can?"

"I'll try. He's never shown any interest in politics, or anything but commanding the House battalion, anyway. I've got some capital with the Chair . . . I will try." He drew himself up and saluted, fist to brow. "Goodbye, Thom. I'll be back, if I can."

Even as he turned, Thom Poplanich was freezing into immobility, a statue in the perfect mirrored sphere, nothing alive but his mind.

"Great Spirit, Raj, the War Council meeting is starting in five minutes; where have you—" Suzette halted, forced a smile.

Her eyes flicked over the dirt and ancient dust on her husband's clothes.

In the tunnels, she knew with a chill. Raj had never told her exactly how Thom Poplanich had disappeared down there with his oldest friend . . . which meant he had told nobody.

Barholm thinks Raj shot him in the back and left the body, she knew. *Which shows how much our esteemed Governor knows about my husband.*

Suzette would have done that—Thom had been getting too dangerous to know, with the succession uncertain and so many of the old nobility still loyal to the House of Poplanich—but her family had been City dwellers, court nobles until they lost their lands a generation ago. The Whitehall estates were secure and far enough from East Residence to afford luxuries like honor.

"Well, no matter," she said brightly. "Come on, you useless girls, attend to the master! You don't have time for a real change, darling, but *do* get that rag off!"

"They'll have to wait for me, then—or more likely they won't," Raj said harshly; the new lines graven from either side of his nose to the corners of his mouth deepened. Then he forced relaxation and smiled at her. "I've had other things on my mind," he said more gently.

The maids descended on him in a twittering horde of perfume and rustling linen and soft hands; there were a lot more of them, now that he had bought the rights to the old House Poplanich section of the Palace. Four courtyards, a reception hall, a dining room with enough seating for a forty-guest banquet, servants' quarters . . . and this pleasant terrace with glass-door walls overlooking the gardens. There was a view through tall cypress trees, down across velvety lawns and marble statuary—mostly religious, spaceships and terminals—fountains, topiary and winding paths of colored gravel. The air was cool and fresh from last night's late spring rain, clearer than usual in this smoky city; a tumbled majesty of red-tiled roofs and low square towers spread down to the great warehouses and the docks to the south, a distant surf-roar of noise from the streets.

"Just the jacket," he grunted. Two of the maids knelt and did their best with damp cloths on his boots; others stripped off his coat, brought the walking-out uniform tunic with its epaulets, buckled him into it, fastened the belt and shoulder-strap with the dress saber and ivory-handled revolver, dropped the sash with its orders and decorations over his head, combed his hair, handed him the dress gloves and gilded plumed helmet—both of those were seldom worn but it was de rigueur to carry them at Court functions. . . .

"At least I don't have to wear those damned tights and codpiece," he grumbled. Full-dress uniform was not required for business meetings. *Pity poor Barholm,* he thought ironically. The Governor had to wear twenty pounds of gold embroidery every time he got out of bed. *Of course, he probably enjoys it—he spent enough time scheming to get it.*

"Oh, I think they bring out your . . . assets quite well, my sweet," Suzette said, sinking into her chair and considering him with her chin on one fist.

Raj gave an unwilling snort of laughter, meeting the tilted green mockery of his wife's eyes. His heart gave a little lurch as he watched her, even then; Suzette Emmenalle Forstin Hogor Wenqui Whitehall had that effect on most men. Small, scarcely up to his shoulder, greyhound-slim and graceful, breeding showing like light through fine porcelain. And alive, so alive . . .

"Will you take it?" she asked quietly.

"Probably. Spirit of Man knows nobody else with any experience wants the Expeditionary Force. This is a formality, really . . . unless I screw up."

"Can you do it?"

Raj slapped his gloves into the palm of one hand. "I think so." *One more thing I love about you. You never give me an optimistic lie, and you think, my angel.*

"A lot depends . . . We don't know enough about the

Squadron. The Ministry of Barbarians hasn't been expending enough effort in that direction. Orbit of Righteousness! We've had little enough contact with them for a couple of generations now. At least the Governor has picked the right man for the civil side."

Suzette's brows arched a question.

"Just heard," he said. *Was that Center? Sometimes I can't tell, these days.* "Mihwel Berg; he's from Cyudad Gut, his family trades heavily all through the central Midworld Sea, he's got friends and relatives outside the Civil Government area too. He'll be invaluable . . . *if* he cooperates."

She came over to him, put her hands on his shoulders and stood tiptoe; he bent to take the kiss. Suddenly she gripped him fiercely.

"You *can* do it," she said, whispering in his ear. "You—sometimes I think the rumors are true, you know, and the Spirit *has* touched you."

He straightened, giving her a crooked grin and a salute.

Messa Suzette Whitehall stood as he left, blinking in thought and tapping her thumb against her chin.

"Leave me," she said to the maids. "Not you, Ndella," she added to a tall gawky Zanj woman as the others made their curtsy and rustled out. When they were alone: "Fetch kave, and get me Abdullah and . . . hmmm, Fatima. Bring them yourself. Be discreet."

"Messa."

The black left with silent efficiency. Suzette had been raised in a great household of East Residence, and she had her own ideas on how to manage here in the Palace. Raj would have been glad to find their servants from Hillchapel, the Whitehall family estate, but Descotters were too awkward in the city and free servants too easily corrupted, in her opinion. Like most, she bought her household staff, but unlike most she gave it personal attention. Only those from outside the Civil Government, with neither friends nor family here, only the strong, healthy, and intelligent, and only after careful personal examination. She saw to their training, and education in some cases. Each was paid a small wage, with promise of eventual manumission and enough for a dowry or a shop or a farm. The only punishment was the threat of sale.

Most people underestimated slaves, even more than men underestimated women. And they talked in front of their servants as if they were deaf, too.

Ndella entered bearing a tray. A man in nondescript but respectable clothing followed her, pewter-buckled shoes and dull-gold pants, black coat and plain linen cravat. A plumply pretty young woman carrying a year-old child followed him; she was dressed in the pleated skirt, embroidered jacket and lace mantilla of a respectable city matron, perhaps a bureaucrat or artisan's wife, but her looks were pure Arab. The child was darker, and even barely walking had something of the heavy-boned solidity of a Descotter.

"Peace be with you," Suzette said in fluent Arabic, a tongue they all had in common, and a little safer than Sponglish.

"And upon you, peace," they replied. Ndella served the others and then sank back on her heels. The tantalizing odor of fresh-brewed kave tinged the flower and incense scents of the room; bees murmured in the lilac bushes outside the window.

"Abdullah," she said.

"*Saaidya*," the Druze replied, rising quickly to check outside the window and back through the door before returning to the table. He had been born Abdullah al'-Azziz; technically, he would have been Abdullah cor Wenqui—freedman of the Wenqui family—if the records of that transaction had been in the register. "I have prepared a preliminary report on Messer Berg; his home, connections, wealth, and opinions."

The little Druze pulled a small role of paper from one sleeve of his jacket and handed it to her.

"My summation: Messer Berg is indeed the most promising man for the post. However, he was appointed primarily because he is in disfavor with Chancellor Tzetzas; a little matter of percentages from intervening fees in a tax-farming bid. He is furthermore under suspicion from the Anti-Viral Cleansers"—the investigative arm of the Church—"because relatives of his, living in Brigade territory, have converted to the cult of Spirit of Man of This Earth. All in all, this is a hardship posting for him, a punishment. He may recoup his position either by brilliant success—he probably considers this unlikely, sharing the general opinion of the military probabilities—or by ruining Messer Whitehall, thus gaining the favor of Tzetzas."

She nodded. It was quite possible he *could* somehow contrive the expedition's ruin; and escape blame for it, too.

"Thank you, Abdullah," she said sincerely, tucking the sheaf of notes into her own sleeve. He bowed, smiling. Pleasure at her gratitude, and at the excitement of the task.

"Ndella," she continued.

The Zanj bobbed her head. Her flat black face was exotic to East Residence eyes, and Suzette had added gold snake-coils for her arms and neck to heighten the effect. People in the Civil Government rarely encountered Zanj, and knew them mostly through highly biased accounts from the Colony. The Colonists were commercial rivals of the southern continent's city-states, there were frequent military clashes—full-fledged war quite recently, which was how Ndella had ended up on a Sandoral auction-block—and the orthodox Sunni Muslims of the Colony detested the Reformed Baha'i heresy the Zanj practiced. To hear the Colonists talk, all Zanj were depraved savages who ate their young and mated with anything, carnosauroids included.

So nobody in East Residence would be likely to suspect that Ndella, for example, was literate in four languages. . . .

"Messa Whitehall, I have now access to Messer Berg's Palace household; a few matters of healing, and, ah"—she coughed discreetly—"I have become very good friends with one of the household servants, an undercook." Ndella liked girls, usually a matter of indifference but here rather useful. "Lorhetta has been adding the *capoyam* to Messer Berg's chili, on the understanding it improves his digestion and temper.

"Add the *beyem*," she went on, briefly showing a small glass vial, "to anything he drinks, and . . . heart failure. Perfectly safe for those not sensitized by the *capoyam*. Undetectable."

. . . and nobody would be likely to suspect Ndella was a doctor, either. Women could learn medicine in the Civil Government, although most who did were also Renunciate Sisters, but the Colony was very restrictive. Everyone would assume the Zanj were even more so.

"Excellent," Suzette said. "Thank you, my friends."

Abdullah and the black woman took the hint, leaving quickly. Fatima released her squirming son; the boy ran half a dozen steps and grabbed the cushions of the opposite couch. He turned his head to give the two women a toothless grin of delight, then hauled himself along the settee hand-over-hand, until he came face to face with the house cat sleeping curled up on a cushion at the end. The animal opened yellow eyes and submitted to pats and gurgling cries of pleasure for a moment before fleeing; the baby went on all fours and began a determined pursuit.

Fatima turned back to Suzette with the same bright-eyed interest she had shown for the last half hour; the hint had been delivered, however. She had a child to consider.

Suzette put aside envy; there was no time, not now, later . . . "Young Barton seems to thrive," Suzette said.

Fatima sighed. "Only if his father does," she replied, a little more subdued.

Suzette leaned back, nodding and sipping at her kave. Her own point had been conceded. *Whichever one* is *his father,* she thought. *But both of them are Raj's men.*

The Arab girl had nearly taken out the eye of a 5th Descott trooper while he and his squad tried to rape her, back in El Djem, the Colonial border-hamlet where she had grown up as a very minor daughter of a minor concubine of the town's mayor. Fatima bint Caid, she had been then; Fatima cor Staenbridge, she was now. Two of Raj's officers had rescued her from an unpleasant death by the trooper's bayonet—on a whim more than anything else, being lovers themselves—and she managed to make it back to the Civil Government border with the 5th during the chaotic nightmare of the retreat through the desert. A prudent career move, given the options available to an ex-virgin with no family in the Colony's strict Islamic society.

She had been pregnant as well; by Gerrin or Barton, but it was the heirless Gerrin Staenbridge who had manumitted her and adopted the child. Which made her a free commoner technically, with a nice little annuity and excellent prospects as mother of a nobleman's heir; besides that, she was still the—very occasional—mistress of both men, and well-liked. Gerrin Staenbridge and

Barton Foley were both Companions now, their fortunes as one with Raj's; Gerrin was his right-hand man. "You have been very kind to me, Messa Suzette," Fatima said, in a quiet tone.

That was true enough; Raj and she had stood Star-parent to young Barton Staenbridge, which was a lifetime tie and taken seriously by the Civil Government's nobility. And Suzette had eased her path socially, as well. A mistress could not be received formally, even if she was the mother of an acknowledged son, but informal acceptance was possible—if the consensus of the *Messas*, the gentlewomen, favored it. Suzette had seen that it did, and she had the ear of Lady Anne, the Governor's wife.

"I anxious am—sorry, am anxious to repay your kindness," she said, dropping back into the Sponglish she had made such an effort to learn.

Suzette leaned over and patted her on the shoulder. "Don't worry, my dear—it's just that sometimes we have to . . . look out for the men. Now, what I'd like you to do is drop by on Tanha Heyterez." Berg's mistress, and rather a neglected one, according to rumor. "She's a country girl, just in from Kendrun, and doesn't know anyone here." Hence likely to be desperately lonely and ready to talk. "She needs a friend . . . and *Berg* needs to be brought around to helping—himself, too—rather than hindering.

"So what I need to know," she went on, lowering her voice, "is *everything* about Messer Berg. Particularly the things his woman would know: what he fears, what he likes, what his tastes are."

Fatima nodded slowly. "I understand, Messa Whitehall," she said formally. Then she grinned, an urchin expression that made her face look its eighteen years again. "I have a problem, though. Barton and Gerrin, they don't want me to come on campaign with them this time. Gerrin wants me to go back to his lands, stay with his wife."

"Why not?" Suzette asked. Since a childless wife could be divorced at will, the lady in question ought to be fairly grateful; now that Staenbridge had an heir, she was safe. Nor was there likely to be much jealousy, since, from what Suzette had learned, Gerrin's wife had known his tastes before the wedding.

"Boring!" Fatima said. "Besides, I want be there if they're hurt."

Suzette nodded understanding; she had always followed the drum herself. It was bad enough to send Raj off to battle; to be a thousand kilometers away, not even *knowing* for months—she shuddered slightly. *And he needs me.*

"I can't interfere in Messer Staenbridge's household," she pointed out gently.

"Oh, I take care of that. I got Gerrin to promise I could come as long as I healthy—now he and Barton trying to get me pregnant again so I *have* to stay home."

"You don't like that?" Suzette said, surprised.

"Oh, I like the *trying*, just don't want it to *work*."

They laughed together, Suzette a little harder than she had expected. There had been few enough chances for humor, in the past few months here in the Palace. Maneuvering against Chancellor Tzetzas was not something you could do with less than your whole intent, even if you were a good friend of the Governor's wife.

"That I can help with," Suzette said, wiping her eyes. "Or rather Ndella can, when I tell her to." She quieted. "I'll be glad to get out of East Residence again," she said. "Out where you can see things coming."

Which was odd, she thought, sitting in silence after the young Arab girl had left. Back in her own girlhood—sometimes she had to remind herself she was still four years shy of thirty—Suzette had never looked uphill to the Palace without a stab of envy. That was her birthright, the legacy of the Wenqui *gens*; forty generations of East Residence nobility, ever since the Governors had come, fleeing the military takeovers in the Old Residence. Poverty had kept her out, and the need to care for Father after Mother died coughing her lungs out, leaving Suzette chatelaine of a dying house at fourteen.

Poor Father. Always with his books and a few old cronies, never even noticing. Not noticing when she had to sell off the furniture and the paintings and the rugs to feed them and pay the doddering ancient servants she hadn't the heart to dismiss, when the pitiful rents from their last few farms had to go to keep the townhouse from being sold under their feet. All the years of scrimping and wheedling to get invitations, lessons, research, the coldly calculated dalliances, all aimed at precisely this. A big suite in the Palace apartments, wealth, recognition, to be a known and feared player in the ancient, stylized minuet of intrigue . . .

All wasted, my love, she thought with a warm irony. Whom had she been hoping to meet at Alois Orehuela's garden-party? She couldn't even remember that now. Raj Ammenda Halgern da Luis Whitehall had been just another name on a stolen guest-list, another uncouth Descotter squire down from the northeastern hills, doubtless with a tail of bandits-in-uniform dangling after him and barely able to tell which fork to eat the fish with . . . *and then I saw you, looking like a sword in a silverware set and all that training and effort I went through was for nothing.*

"No, not *quite* for nothing," she mused softly to herself, walking to the windows and out onto the terrace.

Leaning on the railing she could look down toward the graceful but square-built barracks that flanked the main gates. Insect-tiny with distance, the Guard was changing, figures wheeling and halting on the checkered colored brick of the plaza. Faintly the cool brass of trumpets and the rough beat of drums sounded; the blue-and-gold Star banner of Holy Federation was lowered and raised, salutes and ritual words were exchanged.

"Here there are so many enemies you can't fight face to face, with gun and sword and soldier's honor," she whispered. Her face grew bleak as the edge of a knife. "So I'll do it for you, my love. Whether you ever know it or not."

CHAPTER TWO

The four Companions rose from the benches and saluted as the door to the Whitehall apartments opened; a pair of 5th Descott troopers snapped to attention and raised bayoneted rifles to the present. Raj grunted in acknowledgment and returned the gesture; these were old comrades, veterans of the Komar campaign and the Battle of Sandoral out on the eastern frontier. His Companions, to use the archaic phrase they had resurrected in what was only half a joke.

"We'd better hurry, gentlemen," he said shortly.

They fell in behind him, left hands resting on the hilts of their sabers. The whole party fell unconsciously into step, the iron hobnails and heel-plates of their riding boots echoing on the marble flags of the corridor. Like most of the East Residence, this section consisted of two-story blocks set around courtyards; they clattered up a flight of stairs and into an entry hall, where whispering knots of officers and courtiers parted to make room. Brigadier Whitehall was well known, after last year's triumph in the east, and the suppression of the coup attempt that followed. So were his Companions; for that matter, the almost ostentatious plainness of their issue uniforms, maroon pants and blue tail-coats and round helmets, stood out in a Residence crowd.

Kaltin Gruder was the first to speak; he was still limping slightly, from a bullet through the thigh during the battles on the Drangosh. He had been something of a dandy, before he met Raj Whitehall; the Komar raid had left him one brother shorter and covered the right side of his face with lines of scar tissue.

"The 7th's still a bit shaky," he said. The 7th Descott Rangers was his new command. "Lot of replacements, after the casualties."

"I could spare a few NCO's from the 5th," Gerrin said.

Raj's step checked slightly; the 5th Descott Guards was his original command, and it had been expanded recently too. He was still nominal Captain-in-Chief, but Gerrin had taken over the actual running . . . *and you trust him,* Raj reminded himself.

"Thanks, Gerrin; Spirit of Man knows I could use them," Gruder replied. "By the way, did you catch those Brigade ambassadors?"

Antin M'lewis chuckled slightly, showing a few crooked tobacco-stained teeth amid gleaming gold replacements for those knocked out in battle. "Wunnit enough ter fright t'kiddies, though?" he said.

Da Cruz scowled at him slightly, then shrugged in resignation as M'lewis grinned back and jerked one shoulder, marked with an officer's chain-mail epaulet and a Senior Lieutenant's stars. The little ex-trooper from Bufford Parish had been one of the two Companions Raj had taken with him to foil the attempt on the Governor's life last spring, while the rest guarded Lady Suzette. Governor Barholm's gratitude had lasted long enough for M'lewis to get a commission and a moderate-sized estate near the capital; quite a step up for a former rustler and part-time bandit, enlisted one step ahead of the headsman.

At least he didn't have a line command; respectable Descott County yeoman-troopers wouldn't put up with it, even if he was a technical gentleman now. Being from Bufford Parish, the County's disgrace, was enough; never mind his dubious social status. He did well enough with the collection of gallows-bait that Raj had authorized him to recruit, mostly from guardhouses and punishment details. Officially they were the Scout Group of the 5th Descott, more commonly known as the Forty Thieves. Da Cruz had preferred to stay at Master Sergeant rank, even though he had made enough out of the eastern war to buy land of his own back home in Descott County, the farm he had planned to rent on retirement.

"Interestin' weapons them barbs had," the noncom said stolidly. "Not bad shots; surprised they could get that sort of accuracy out of them muzzle-loaders."

The Brigade were fairly civilized for barbarians, having ruled the old Civil Government lands in the far west for centuries now. The emissaries had still been a gaudy sight, fringed buckskins and purple silk, broad-brimmed hats stuck with carnosauroid feathers, gold and jewels and long slashing swords hung over their shoulders. Most of them had had four or five cap-and-ball revolvers slung around them, besides their head-high rifles. They had put on a display of marksmanship in the gardens, smashing bottles at a thousand paces, which was performance as good as you could get from an Armory rifle.

Gerrin tapped a ringed thumb meditatively against the pommel of his saber. "Slow on the loading, though," he said. "Looked as if they were more used to hunting and target-practice."

Kaltin snorted. "Not much real fighting recently, I suppose."

"Not our problem, eh, ser?" da Cruz said dryly. "Anyways, the Squadron won't be as tough as thet-there Brigade, nohow."

The others nodded; the Squadron had come roaring out of the northern wilderness a century and a half ago, to take the Southern Territories from the Civil Government. They had been outright savages then, and the Territories had gone downhill under their management.

"Can't say the men are over-eager to take them on, even so," Gerrin said carefully, glancing aside at Raj. "Not after a year's hard fighting out east. The Squadron's no match for the wogs, true, but you have to sail to get at them. A wet way to fight, and not a Descotter's choice."

Raj grunted again, ducking his head slightly.

observe Center said.

—Raj was standing on the quarterdeck of a three-master, his disembodied viewpoint beside the wheel, looking over his own shoulder. The storm had died down, leaving whitecaps on a ruffled wine-colored sea. The Civil Government sailing-transports were scattered from horizon to horizon, many dismasted or wallowing with their sails blown to flapping rags on bare poles. In among them the Squadron war-galleys plunged, huge plumes of spray flung back from the bronze rams at their bows. Oars worked like centipede legs; they were painted vermilion and white, the long snaky hulls were black. Off in the middle distance more came up, their sails not yet struck for battle; the towering lateen shapes bright crimson with the barbarians' golden Sun-and-Comet. One shocked to a stop, the mast-tops lashing as its ram knifed into the planks of a transport.

The helpless merchantman heeled far over under the impact. Tiny figures flew into the water from the rails, thrashing about briefly until the eager tentacles of scavenging downdraggers hauled them toward gnashing beaks. Others went under the oar-blades as they rose and fell like a mincing machine. Off in the middle distance cannon echoed and smoke rose as a lone Civil Government paddle-steamer loosed a broadside; the solid shot skipped along the waves, and one crashed into the oarbank of a galley, but the other vessels turned nimbly aside to avoid the bigger ship's blundering rush. There was only one in sight. Perhaps, from the smoke, another lay over the horizon; dozens of the galleys, and hundreds of their helpless victims.

The Raj-figure wheeled sharply as a seaman tugged at his sleeve, and the viewpoint turned with him. A Squadron two-banker was boring in on their ship; Raj could see the sea falling off the arrowhead shape of the ram, and the mouths of four brass carronades running forward through the square deckhouse above it. Gunners waited with smoking linstocks; the forward mast bristled with the raven-beak spikes of boarding ramps ready to fall and nail the craft together, and behind them crowded the Squadron marines shrieking and waving their massive flintlocks and axes in the air.

"Yeah, well," he said softly, without looking around, conscious that his step had faltered.

The others had gotten used to these fits of introspection; none of the Companions had known him well before he . . . *became an Avatar of the Spirit of Man of the Stars?* Raj shuddered and worked his shoulders. For the others, it was times like this that he pulled something impossible out of the hat.

As if he was inspired.

"Well," he went on, "I can see how the people who were out east would like a little more rest." That had been the biggest campaign in sixty years, and the first time in forty-odd the Civil Government had defeated the Colony in a major battle. Memory flashed across his mind: Colonist cavalry sweeping toward Raj's shrinking circle in the Valley of Death. Section leaders yipped and waved yataghans, sharpened on the inner curve, but the mass of bright-colored riders were silent because they held their reins in their teeth to work their carbines with both hands. The recollection was so vivid that Raj missed a step.

I could use a break myself, he thought ruefully.

the man you have become in these past two years would not know how to take a break, raj whitehall, Center said. If the mental voice had a tone, it was of regret. **no more than i would.**

Raj shook his head and continued aloud: "The problem is, if I *am* going to be sent to take back the Southern Territories, I'd prefer to have some people with me who've gotten into the habit of pulling their heads out of their arses for a look around now and then."

The Council of State for War was meeting in an old chapel, a semicircle of seats sloping down to the altar; behind it was a smooth wall of the same gray-streaked white marble as the rest of the big room, with a balcony choir-loft above, screened in carved nairstone that glittered silver and rose in the yellow brightness of the gaslights. Lady Anne Clerett was rumored to observe the meetings from behind that screen . . . and the faint elusive scent of jasmine under the wax-and-incense of the room strongly hinted that rumor was correct. The altar was coated in shining electrum, and held a featureless ball about the size of a man's head. The material was part of its mystery; nothing present-day technology produced could even scratch it, should someone be impious enough to try. It was a computer of the Ancients, from before the Fall, timeless and holy.

a 7ec42, Center said in its emotionless monotone, **in**

charge of automated traffic control for a suburb of the Old Residence before the collapse. A pause, **and it had an unacceptable error rate even then.**

The crowd below was all-male, except for one of the Supreme Reverend Syssup-Hierarch's assistants. About fifty present, mostly military, and dressed in a dozen colorful variations on standard uniform. They turned to look at Raj as he and the Companions entered through the big doors at the rear of the arc of seats, relief on their faces. Governor Barholm sat in the Chair before the altar, a shining confection of electrum and brass, pearls and jewels, with a huge golden Star-burst for a back.

"Ah, Brigadier Whitehall," he said.

His voice carried easily in the chapel's superb acoustics, a well-trained instrument. Despite the cloth-of-gold robes, Barholm Clerett looked very much the simple squire from the Descott County hills, a brick-built man with a barrel chest and a nose like a beak in his square dark-brown face. Only a very stupid man would believe that appearance; Clerett had ruled the Civil Government for fifteen years, as Vice-Governor to his ailing uncle and then in his own right, through intrigue and riot and war.

Beside him on a crimson cushion rested a mace, a short weapon forged from a single billet of steel, inlaid with silver and platinum. The emblem of rank only a commander of an independent army corps sent beyond the Civil Government border could carry.

"*Thank* you for joining us," he went on dryly, as Raj and his followers slid into the seats reserved for them in the front row.

A few of the high-born officers in the front ranks smirked; Chancellor Tzetzas leaned back, slimly elegant in his robe of midnight-blue torofib silk from Azania. One eyebrow rose, an expression calculated to the millimeter.

"We were discussing," Barholm went on, "the sacred task of reclaiming the Southern Territories from the barbarian heretics currently occupying them. A task," he added waspishly, "which arouses very little—surprisingly little—enthusiasm!"

"Your Supremacy," an elderly man in uniform protested, "we would serve you ill if we did not counsel you honestly.

My father"—he shuddered slightly—"my father's elder brothers and my grandfather sailed with the last fleet sent to reclaim the Territories."

observe Center said.

—and Raj was on the docks, down where the deep-sea merchantmen came to harbor. It was East Residence, but an earlier one; the East Railway station was not there, and the Messer-class men in view were wearing drooping broad sleeves that covered their hands to the knuckles. A fashion from his great-grandfather's time, like the lace fans of the ladies among the crowd. Miniluna and Maxiluna were both aloft and full, across the horizon from the setting sun, pale translucent crater-marked spheres floating above the darkening sea.

Troops ringed the berths where a dozen transports were docked; gulls chased hissing dactosauroids through the tarry maze of rigging, the sound lost in a surf-roar of voices. The mob was anxious enough to crowd the leveled bayonets. Raj could see the men jab them forward now and then, the long blades coming back red-tipped and the edge of the crowd stumbling away in an eddy; mounted officers with drawn sabers sat their dogs behind the line of guardsmen. Other figures were coming down the gangplanks of the transports, figures in the tattered remains of Civil Government uniforms. They shuffled down the creaking planks in groups, groups of eleven; ten men with their hands each in the belt of the one before them, and pus-wet bandages across the ruins of their eyes. The leading man in each group had one good eye, but no hands. . . .

" . . . and never will I forget my father's words, when he told me how his only living brother came back, a blinded eunuch. Your Supremacy," the old man went on, holding out his hands almost pleadingly; they were calloused from the grip of reins and saber. "Mighty Sovereign Lord, only because my father had not yet entered Holy Church did our line survive at all. I have served the Chair in war all my life, and my sons and my sons' sons. Spare them, Your Supremacy!"

There was a moment of ringing silence. Chancellor Tzetzas coughed discreetly into a handkerchief.

"Most moving, most moving." He was a tall slender man in his mid sixties, with the fine olive skin and delicate features of old City nobility. "Your Supremacy's will is mine, of course; still, this is a rashly adventurous course of action we contemplate. The campaign in the east concluded so successfully last year"—Tzetzas bowed easily in Raj's direction—"did no more than pay its own costs."

Raj felt his lips tighten, then forced an easy smile and a nod of polite acknowledgment. *Because I didn't let you get your hands on all the loot, Tzetzas,* he thought coldly. Some of it had gone on victory-bonuses, a good deal to pensions for troops crippled from their wounds, soldiers the Chancellor had thrown off their land grants as soon as they were registered as unfit for duty.

"Our mighty sovereign lord, Governor Barholm, has embarked on numerous projects to glorify the Spirit of Man of the Stars"—the new Temple, paid for out of an increase in the salt tax—"and to better the lives of the people"—railway extensions, new harbors and dams and steam mills—"and in conclusion, I am forced to confess myself at a loss as to where the funds for this expedition might be found."

"*Take it out of what you steal, Tzetzas.*" The call was a sotto voce whisper from one of the more junior officers up in the higher tiers of seats. Laughter rumbled from all the military men present, although the Chancellor's robed bureaucrats sat in appalled silence. Tzetzas's head turned, and the movement reminded Raj of a carnosauroid he had seen in the Governor's menagerie, one moment death-still, the next snapping an insect out of the air. Then the Chancellor relaxed, smiling thinly as Barholm joined in the bellow of mirth.

I would not like to be the man who said that, Raj thought. There was an old joke about a fangmouth biting Tzetzas; rumor had it that the poison reptile died in convulsions.

observe Center said.

—and a young officer jerked erect in bed; Raj recognized the room, or rather its pattern. Company commander's quarters in an East Residence barracks, although the sleeping woman was decidedly non-regulation. The officer's face was fluid with sleep; he reached out to touch the holstered pistol hanging from the headboard by unconscious reflex.

"Heysos? That you?" he mumbled.

"*Nao*" a voice said, as the door swung open and a masked man in dark clothing stepped through. The naked soldier had just enough time to clear the heavy dragoon pistol from its holster before the shotgun blast caught him in the face, flinging his body back and much of his head across the wall behind him.

The woman screamed twice; the assassin stepped to within a meter of her before he fired the other barrel.

Tzetzas spread his hands. "And in any case . . . military affairs are outside my area of expertise; I would not care to speculate on the chances of success. The dangers to the eastern frontier, however, are, one would think, obvious. We lost several provinces to the Colony when the *last* expedition was destroyed."

Thump. All eyes swung back to Barholm, as he brought the stylized keyboard down on the arm of the Chair. The diamond and padparascha sapphire symbols on its surface glittered, matching the autocrat's robes.

"Thanks to Brigadier Whitehall here," Barholm bit out, "the Colony is without a Settler. Ali and Akbar are still settling who's to be master—"

observe Center said.

—and dark men in doghair robes waited behind an alabaster planter filled with rose bushes, the blossoms plate-sized disks of crimson and yellow. A figure in long robe and cloth-of-gold turban came striding along the pathway beyond, where fountains tinkled among delicate tilework; behind him walked guards, black giants naked to the waist with long curved blades resting unsheathed on their shoulders. The planter overturned and those behind it leapt forward, curved daggers raised, shrieking. Their screams of rage turned to fear as swords hissed and rifles from the snipers on the rooftop opposite spat puffs of white . . .

—and stocky grizzled Tewfik stood in the open flap of a field-commander's tent, dressed as ever in the plain scarlet burnoose and spired helmet of the Colonial Regulars, with the Seal of Solomon on his black leather eyepatch. His left hand was clenched on the hilt of his scimitar until the knuckles showed white, but there was unshakable calm in his voice, and in the face that watched the soldiers drilling. Behind him a man in civilian robe and ha'aik waited by the map table, looking uneasily at the officers who stood around him with their arms crossed. From his expression, he was fully conscious that they would be delighted by an order to take him out—and shoot him as soon as he cleared the rug.

"My regrets to my noble brother the emir Ali," Tewfik ground out, "and my message to him is as my previous message—please, we both know it was read by other than its intended recipient—to my noble brother the emir Akbar; the peace of Allah upon them both. No troops can be spared for . . . missions in the capital. Not now, or until the council of the ulemma has chosen another Settler to lead the faithful."

The civilian hesitated, then bowed. "Peace be upon you, sa'yid," he murmured, and slipped past to his waiting borzhoi.

"And upon you, peace, you viper," Tewfik muttered, when the messenger had gone. Then he wheeled, cutting off the officers with a glare and a chopping motion of his hand. "And there *will* be peace. Either of my brothers will rule well enough—but for me to reach for power would mean civil war; you know the Law." The Commander of the Faithful must be perfect in body. "It will be as God wills; and all things are accomplished according to the will of God."

"Inshallah," the officers murmured.

"—and Tewfik's disqualified, praise the *Spirit* for that." Raj nodded in unconscious agreement; Tewfik was far and away the most able of old Jamal's legitimate sons, but he was missing an eye, lost in the Zanj Wars a decade ago, and by Colonial law that disqualified him.

"Indeed, Your Supremacy," Tzetzas said; his voice had a softly reasonable tone that made you want to agree immediately, for fear of seeming shrill or irrational. "For a year or so the Colony will be weakened. But the conquest of the Southern Territories would take *decades*."

"We certainly can't afford to *strip* the eastern territories," Fiydel Klostermann said; he was Master of Soldiers these days, an administrative command and as close to a Chief of Staff as the Civil Government had. "Which we'd need to do. The Squadron can field a hundred thousand men; granted they're equipped with blunderbusses, and they've no artillery to speak of, that's still two hundred battalions of fighting men." The Civil Government kept a quarter of a million men under arms, but most of those were immobile garrison infantry.

Admiral Tiburcyo Gharderini spoke up; he was a nervous looking little man with gray-shot black hair, in the black-and-gold uniform of the Civil Government's navy. Naval officers often came from the City itself, and from merchant families, unlike the Army, which was dominated by the landed gentry. You could see his consciousness of his own social insignificance as he glanced around at the others.

"Well . . . we *do* have the steam rams and gunboats," he said. "We've managed to keep the Squadron corsairs at a distance, this last generation."

"Mostly," a cavalry commander said dryly. Gharderini flushed darkly.

"But that's a different matter from attacking Port Murchison," the sailor went on doggedly; that was the capital of the Territories. "We don't have enough fleet units to spare to guard a convoy that size, we don't have coaling stations close enough, and we're just too undermanned and underfunded. Begging Your Excellency's pardon," he finished rapidly, with a bob in the direction of the Chancellor.

Barholm was tapping the keyboard-scepter on the arm of the Chair with ominous patience.

A younger officer sprang up. Raj recognized him: Anhelino Dalhouse, commander of the 17th Valley Cuirassiers. Exceedingly wealthy and well-born and without much combat experience, unless you counted putting down the odd peon uprising.

"We sit here quibbling like a lot of old women!" he burst out, the points of his mustache quivering. "What are we, fighting men or duennas at a coming-out ball for our maiden sisters? The Squadron heretics sit on our lands, collecting our revenues and persecuting our people and our church. What more needs to be said?"

The Supreme Reverend Syssup-Hierarch rose, fingering the circuit amulet on his chest. "More than persecuting!" he said angrily. "Your Supremacy, you are guardian of the Church's flock in every land—the Squadron beasts stable their riding dogs in our churches, or worse, convert them to their heretical worship of the Spirit of Man of This Earth"—most of the audience grasped their amulets and murmured a prayer—"and they rob and plunder and enslave our communicants who refuse to follow their beastly superstition. Their Admiral forbids the appointment of Syssups to guide the dioceses of the Territories; Syssups-Missionary I have appointed have been burned alive, priests mutilated, Renunciate Sisters gang-raped. The Spirit of Man of the Stars demands we act! Endfile."

"Endfile," the others murmured piously, touching their amulets. *At least there's one sincere voice,* Raj thought

Barholm nodded, pleased.

Klostermann cleared his throat and spoke: "All respect and reverence to Holy Church and Its Supreme Reverend Syssup-Hierarch, but we've been receiving reports of atrocities for the century or more the Squadron has held the Territories. Why does the Spirit of Man of the Stars demand we act *now*, rather than later when the conditions favor us? Will it serve Holy Church for us to lose another fifty thousand men, and perhaps the borderlands we fought the Colony last year to keep?"

Silence fell again, broken only by the scritch of secretaries writing up the records of the meeting and the slow tick-tock of the brass clock set into one wall of the chapel.

"Brigadier Whitehall," Barholm said at last, softly. "We require your opinion in this matter."

Raj felt cold. *This is the time, Center? The Civil Government really is strong enough now to retake the Southern Territories?*

as i have shown you, raj whitehall, replied the voice in his mind, **i cannot guarantee success, but . . . i did not choose you not to try.**

The young general came slowly to his feet, looking down at the backs of his hands. They were scarred, with faint darker lines on the knuckles, trail-dirt, from long marches, that could never quite be scrubbed away. When he raised his eyes he felt a slight forward sway from the other seats; only desperate fear could have made so many openly disagree with the Governor, who was not a forgiving man. Most desperate of all the fear of being appointed to command the expedition; defeat probably meant proscription as a traitor, death or confiscation of estates for the commander's whole family.

"Your Supremacy," he said, and paused. "On your orders, I've made a study of this problem. I believe the reconquest of the Southern Territories *can* be accomplished." A collective sigh of indrawn breath.

"And it can be accomplished at acceptable cost and risk. No slight to the valiant dead, but the last expeditionary force was neither well organized nor well led. And the Squadron they faced was still the terror of the Midworld Sea, with a first-rate navy.

"They've let their fleet go downhill, and their army too, such as it is. They don't have a standing force, you know. That didn't matter when Admiral Ricks"—the legendary warchief who had led the Squadron down from the north, and then created the fleet that pillaged the Midworld for generations—"called up his warriors for pirate raids every year, 'to make war on those with whom the Spirit of Man is angry' . . . but these days all most of them do is sit on their behinds and watch their peons work.

"Sending fifty thousand men would be an unacceptable risk and far too expensive. With thirty thousand I can be fairly confident of success."

He watched the faces change; Tzetzas relaxing, Barholm tightening into a frown.

you will not be given thirty thousand, Center said. **probability 89% ± 6%.**

Raj sighed inwardly; Center took some of the fun out of bargaining, with its ability to tell you exactly what an opponent would settle for beforehand.

"Fifteen thousand *could* do it: five thousand cavalry as a strike force, ten thousand infantry for garrisons and as a base of maneuver, and thirty guns. I'd estimate no more than a year of real fighting if it's properly handled, and plunder alone will pay the expenses of the campaign, not to mention the revenues afterwards. With less than fifteen thousand, I would regretfully decline to assume any position."

Barholm's face was unreadable as he nodded to Tzetzas. An *I told you so* expression; the Chancellor's face looked as if he was sucking on a lemon for an instant, and his voice actually sounded animated, as good as a shout.

"Even if the expedition *is possible,* that's no reason to *do* it," he said testily.

Raj rubbed a palm along his jaw; the sword-callus that ringed thumb and forefinger rasped on blue-jowled stubble.

"True, Chancellor, if only ordinary matters were at stake. But . . . well, religion may sound odd, in a soldier's mouth, and the Spirit knows a soldier is all I am. Gentlemen—" He glanced around the circle of faces. "Gentlemen, we *are* civilization; we *are* the last representatives of the Holy Federation. The Civil Government is not just another successor-state living in the ruins of sacredness; we have a *duty* to bring all the Earth—"

bellevue, Center interjected, **earth later.**

"—*all* of the Earth and its people back into the Holy Federation and oneness with the Spirit of Man of the Stars. Isn't everyone—everyone, barbarian or Colonist or heretic— made in the Spirit's image? If we deny that, we deny the Spirit in ourselves, and our faith is a sham—"

His voice had risen; he cut himself off abruptly as he saw the others blink at his vehemence, flushing at the murmur of "hear, hear" from many of the other officers, the Supreme Reverend Syssup-Hierarch's gesture of blessing.

"And who should lead this expedition?" Barholm asked neutrally.

"The decision is yours, of course, Your Supremacy," Raj said awkwardly. "But I've thought about this for a long time, and in all honesty I feel that I would be the best choice."

i have thought about it for a thousand years . . . Center whispered at the back of his brain, **at last . . .**

Barholm nodded. "Let it be recorded that Messer Brigadier—no, we'd better make that Brigadier General Raj Ammenda Halgern da Luis Whitehall is appointed Field Commander of the expeditionary force to reclaim the sacred soil of Holy Federation from the Squadron barbarians, with viceregal authority while in the *barbaricum.*

Let all servants of the Civil Government and Holy Church render lawful aid to him in this matter. Brigadier General Whitehall, please submit a list of units and commanders to *me* by . . . hmm, this time tomorrow for my consideration and approval."

He made a sharp gesture, and an aide lifted the cushion with the mace of office on it, going down on one knee before Raj. Raj lifted it in both hands and raised it to his lips; the officers raised a sharp cheer of approval, formal and brief.

The Governor looked around the ranked officers, brows raised. "If there's no further *advice?*" he said with heavy irony. "No?"

The Supreme Reverend Syssup-Hierarch began the elaborate ceremony of dismissal. Holding his amulet and making the keying gesture of prayer with the others, Raj almost smiled at the looks of envy some gave him out of the corners of their eyes.

Envy for a man who's just condemned himself to death, he thought. The mace seemed heavier than worlds.

CHAPTER THREE

East Residence sat on a peninsula that jutted out like a thumb from the foothills of the coast range to the west, enclosing a narrow tongue of water on its south side. Eastward was the estuary of the Hemmar River, flowing from the south out into the Midworld Sea. Both moons were down; the Palace and the inner districts around it were bright with gas streetlights, while the bulk of the capital was a lumpy darkness of buildings and hills, black picked out by the yellow dots of lamps. Off in the west there was a sullen light from the foundries and factories, while to the east on the highest point the gold Starburst on the Temple's dome was underlit by electric arc-lights and touched by the first rays of the sun. There had been no night at the harborside, with thousands of torches to magnify the gaslights.

It was a cool spring morning, the sky cloudy and dark and drizzling down a thin mist of rain; coal smoke drifted down from the city's hills. The bitter smell of it mixed with the silty sewage-tainted tar stink of the harbor, and the smells of thousands of dogs and tens of thousands of men embarking.

The first ships of the Civil Government's fleet were making way out of the inner harbor, but the naval docks were still in a state of barely-organized chaos. Stubby little paddle-tugs and twenty-oar galleys were towing the big three-master cargo ships out east past the breakwaters; as each cast loose the sails went up with a series of rhythmic jerks and the long hulls heeled sharply, catching the northerly wind. Others were still loading, endless files of slave longshoremen trotting up the gangplanks with sacks and crates, the timbers of the cranes groaning as they swung field-guns and wagons aboard. Troopers were leading their riding dogs through side-doors in the hulls of specially fitted transports; most of them had thrown their jackets over the dogs' heads, for the comfort of darkness and familiar smell, but there was a constant whining and occasional outbreaks of thunder-deep barking from the big animals. The infantry stood in ordered clumps further inland by company columns. A hundred or so was the limit for a single ship, and it also served to discourage the press-ganged sailors from deserting.

Raj watched from the shadow of a crane as one unit made ready to embark:

"Company A, 17th Kelden Foot! *Alo sinstra, waymanos!* By the left, forward!" The soldiers marched bowed slightly under pack and rifle, a long centipede of maroon-clad legs and blue-jacketed bodies, faces stolid-set under their bowl-helmets as they followed the furled battalion standard. The hobnails clashed on the granite paving, and the men began a hoarse chanting:

> "*March! The mud is cakin' good about our trousies
> Front! Eyes front, an' watch the color-casin's drip.
> Front! the faces of the women in the houses
> Ain't the kind of thing to take aboard the ship.*"

Star Spirit be with them all, he thought. Raj was standing by a warship; they would cast off last, being all steam-powered. Black smoke poured from the tall twin funnels on each; they were low-slung snaky craft, with big boxlike wooden covers for the paddlewheels on each side of the midships deckhouse, an iron-clad ram at the bows and six light breech-loaders along each side. Those were nearly hidden by the ton-weight wicker baskets of coal standing on the decks, crowding right up to the masts fore and aft.

"There's something wrong with the coal?" Raj asked the man beside him.

"Messer Whitehall, there's not much *right* with it," Muzzaf Kerpatik said. He sneered, the flash of white teeth brilliant against teak-dark skin and his pointed beard and mustache.

"Half of it is shale—and the rest is soft, not hard anthracite. Half the price of good steam coal. Not one half the heating power."

"Tzetzas," Raj said with weary resignation, straightening. The big crane above them chuffed as the handler eased the steam-powered winch into action and swung the heavy net of fuel onto the warship's deck.

Muzzaf was a Komarite, from one of the southern border cities along the Colonial frontier; one of the strange new class of monetary risk-takers, men who invested large sums in manufacture or trade yet were not really merchants or moneylenders or artisans. It still seemed a little unnatural to Raj, gaining wealth without inheriting or plundering it.

"Back in Komar I thought myself wicked because I entered a conspiracy with the Chancellor's men to bilk the Fisc of soldiers' pay," he said. Neither of them needed to add that it was Raj Whitehall who had accepted his repentance, when that conspiracy left Muzzaf's native city defenseless. And Raj who had protected him from the Chancellor since. "Tzetzas . . . since coming to the capital, I have seen his hand in everything," the Komarite confirmed. "He has interests in the Coast Range mines." He straightened, flicking at the black dust on his brown cotton coat and the cloak draped over his arm; normally he was something of a peacock, but today he had limited it to a few pieces of silver jewelry and a spray of colored sauroid feathers clipped to the brim of his fore-and-aft peaked cap. "Messer, I'm surprised anyone ever makes a profit on *anything* in this city. Except the Chancellor and his cronies, of course."

Raj nodded. "I appreciate your work, Mezzaf. You've been invaluable. Try looking into the rest of the supply situation, would you?"

"As you wish, Messer," Mezzaf replied; he bowed and touched brow and lips, already looking abstracted. Behind him the sound of the soldiers' singing faded as they boarded the ship:

> "Cheer! An' we'll never march to victory.
> Cheer! An' we'll never live to hear the cannon roar!
> The Large Birds o' Prey

They will carry us away,
An' you'll never see your soldiers anymore!"

The general gave a hitch at his sword belt as he walked out to meet the commanders one last time. They were standing in anonymous clumps, the heavy military cloaks about their shoulders. His eyes seemed to be ridged with sand, and everything stood out with a slightly feverish clarity. Complete exhaustion: about what you would expect putting this all together on short notice.

Barton Foley stood scratching his chin *carefully* with the point of the hook where his left hand used to be, his right clasped in Gerrin Staenbridge's. Jorg Menyez was talking to Mekkle Thiddo, who was still inclined to look admiringly at his own Battalion Commander's stars now and then; he had been a gentleman-ranker once, and a Lieutenant until the Komar campaign. Kaltin Gruder was saying goodbye to an implausibly large collection of ladies, most of them crying too hard to quarrel with each other as he shooed them firmly away. M'lewis was off to one side, conferring with a few of his Scouts; several of them managed the minor miracle of looking more furtively unsavory than their commander.

. . . and there were the strangers. Ehwardo Poplanich, Thom's cousin, for one. A little older, but with the same thin intellectual's face, a little uncertain in this company. Anhelino Dalhouse for another; and Mihwel Berg, the Administrative Service panjandrum, sulking as usual. He was supposed to set up the civil administration in the Southern Territories, once they took it back; talking to Suzette seemed to be animating him a little. Barholm had said he was a first-rate man who'd be a great deal of help. So far there was fuck-all sign of it, which was odd since the Governor was a judge of men, in his way.

Except he saddled me with Dalhouse, Raj thought sourly. That was fatigue speaking; he hadn't had a decent night's sleep in a week or more . . . about par for the course, out on campaign. Dalhouse probably had too many connections for Barholm to ignore. Besides that, Raj had asked for all the units that campaigned with him in the east—slightly suspicious, from a Governor's point of view.

"Good morning, Messers," he said.

One of the servants handed him his helmet, a plain bowl of black iron with a riveted neckguard of chain mail on leather at the back. The rank-badge over the brows was new, an eighteen-point star of gold and silver on a blue shield, orbited by seven more. He buckled it on, the familiar weight making the war seem real after the paperwork and quartermaster's nightmare of the last month. Dalhouse sneered slightly; *his* helmet was polished bronze with inlay in niello and silver, and the neckguard was torosauroid hide traded down from the northern steppes, the type that grew natural crystals of metal in the skin, brought to a high polish.

"Now, I'm going to give you some final instructions," Raj continued, deliberately dropping his voice slightly. Men leaned forward, straining to hear. "The fleet has been divided into ten sections, plus the naval escorts. While at sea, instructions from *any* naval officer commanding an escort are to be accepted as if they were mine. Is that understood?"

He waited until all the ten section officers nodded. "Admiral Gharderini, your first priority will be to keep the fleet together. If any vessel becomes separated for any reason whatsoever, the fleet will halt until the escorts bring in the strays. If we're scattered by weather, everyone will head for the assigned rendezvous for that section of the journey—check your maps, Messers. Anyone who gets ahead of the fleet may pray to the Spirit of Man of the Stars for help, for he'll get none from me. And anyone"—he paused—"anyone whosoever who turns back without authorization will be shot, and every officer on his ship, and every tenth enlisted man taken at random. Master Sergeant da Cruz, you may inform the men of that."

Slight chance anyone could use a little bad weather as an excuse after that; even if the threat was not altogether credible—many of the officers had family connections powerful enough to rescue them from anything short of heresy—but the men would believe it, and likely shoot anyone risking a decimation. There was a slight stir among the officers, and several of the Companions smiled. Several of the non-Companions looked again at the men who had campaigned with Raj Whitehall, noting the scars and missing limbs and limps; many of them looked a little green. There had been no great rush of commanders volunteering their units for this expedition. Dalhouse waited with elaborate patience, fingers tapping at the glossy leather of his Sam Browne belt.

"Final dispositions will be made at Sadler Island, according to what intelligence information we can pick up there"— *because the Ministry of Barbarians has dick-all here*—"and under *no circumstances* is anyone to attempt to enter Port Murchison without orders. We'll probably land well south of the city and work north by land."

Dalhouse snorted. Raj looked at him mildly, raising his brows. "Yes, Messer?" he said.

"Waste of time, *ferramente*, going all the way past Port Murchison and then walking back," he said, stroking one finger down a waxed black moustache. "We should sail straight into Port Murchison and *kill* the sons of whores, not flounce about in the bloody bundu. They outnumber us, so we should take them by surprise. Sir."

Gerrin Staenbridge laughed. "Advice from the depths of your many years of combat experience?" he said. Dalhouse let his right hand drop to the hilt of his saber and took a half-step forward.

"Messers," Raj said patiently. *Don't provoke him, Gerrin,* he thought. *I know he's a fool and a fop, but the Palace wants him in.* "Messer Major Dalhouse," he continued, "last year we fought the wogs out east. They had an army every bit as good as ours, much bigger, and commanded by Prince Tewfik. So I used the only advantage we had, position, and dug in where they had to come to us.

"Now," he said genially, "we're fighting the Squadron, who are the people the phrase 'dumb barb' was invented to describe. Fighting them, *our* advantages are our weapons, our organization, our discipline. We know what they'll do; they'll rush in like a pack of sicklefeet around a cow. *Their* advantages are their numbers and ferocity." Suddenly he leaned forward, pushing his face into the junior officer's.

His voice went flat. "So I'm not too entranced by the idea of wallowing into a blindsided street fight at close range, Messer Major Dalhouse. I do not intend to imitate a mob of racing enthusiasts in an after-game brawl. I prefer an open-field battle of maneuver to start with, I really do."

Dalhouse looked around. Most of the other officers were staring at him with the shocked almost-consideration they would have given a man who had just been run over by a hansom cab. Young Barton Foley had slipped the leather sheath-cover off his hook and was stropping the razor edge of the interior against a ceramic honing stick. Dalhouse began a sneer. He stopped as he met the young Companion's eyes, flushed darkly under his native olive, and fell silent.

"Now," Raj went on, voice mild and slightly under-pitched once more. "Dinnalsyn?"

Major Dinnalsyn nodded. "*Seyhor*," he said: Sir, with the flat East Residence accent of a City man. The artillery recruited many such, like the engineers and the navy. "Thirty standard fieldpieces, ready to go." Seventy-five-millimeter rifled breechloaders; the Squadron didn't use field guns at all, only fortress guns and muzzle-loaders on warships. It was something of an innovation to appoint an over-all artillery commander, but Grammek Dinnalsyn was a man he trusted. "We stripped out first-rate pieces from other units and dumped anything that looked chancy on them."

"Menyez?"

Jorg's long melancholy face sank deeper into gloom as he ran a hand through his thinning russet hair, damp from the almost-rain. He was from the northwestern provinces, Kelden County, and an infantry specialist by choice. Rare—cavalry was the prestige arm, and the Menyezes were very rich—but he was allergic to dogs.

"The foot regiments are all up to strength. Not too many of them are fresh meat, and they're fully equipped," he said. That was something; away from dangerous frontier posts some infantry commanders equipped their battalions with flintlocks originally made for trade in the trans-border *barbaricum*. His would all be furnished with standard Armory breechloaders. "Apart from that, they're about as usual, except for my 17th and the 24th Valentia."

Tzetzas had been *very* reluctant to let him take even those two infantry battalions from the force he'd had in the Army of the Upper Drangosh, out east. A matter of expense, since Civil Government infantry units were supposed to live off farms granted by the *fisc*, in the neighborhood of their garrisons; the enlisted men were paid only when on the move or in the field, between permanent postings. Cavalry and mercenaries received regular pay in hard cash, but they were the elite troops; infantry were press-ganged from the peons of the central counties, and usually fit only for second-line duties. Barholm had seen little difference between one infantry unit and the next. So would Raj have done, before he saw what Menyez could do with them.

"Making bricks without straw, that's the Army," Raj said resignedly. "Settling in all right with the Slashers, Mekkle?"

The young man grinned shyly. His family were what Descotters called bonnet-squires: possessors of an ancient name and half a dozen small farms, along with several hundred hectares of third-rate grazing; freeholders, but there were yeoman tenants who had more livestock and cash. Not many prospects, living on a Lieutenant's pay, although he had a fair education. *Raj doesn't care about your birth, only what you can do,* he thought. You worked harder under him than a mine-slave, but he'd bought back land his grandfather had lost, and married Maria. . . .

"The 1st Rogor Slashers are ready for action, sir," he said. "Took some getting used to—they're not as, hmmm, unflappable as Descotters"—the Slashers were recruited from the southern border—"and they don't like to sweat much, out of the field, but they'll fight, Spirit knows."

"Good, keep at them. Southerners tend to have more dash than sense. All right, Messers. Dismissed."

He saluted; the Companions leaving for their units stayed a moment longer, and they all slapped fists together in a pyramid of arms.

"Hell or plunder, dog-brothers," da Cruz said, the old Descott County war cry, and the officers dispersed to their commands.

Ehwardo Poplanich lingered for a moment. "Hmmm," he said, clearing his throat. "Sir?"

"Yes, Major?" Raj asked.

"I'd . . . like to thank you, on behalf of the men," he said quickly. At Raj's raised eyebrow: "I heard rumors, convincing rumors, that Poplanich's Own was to be disbanded after the . . . problem last year. I'm happy for the men's sake; they're used to serving together."

Raj nodded. The special uniform, dark-green with gold piping, told that story. Poplanich's Own was recruited from the family's estates, from among the more prosperous tenants-in-chief and bailiffs and such, and the family coffers paid for their initial equipment, against a remittance of land-tax. It was not an uncommon arrangement, particularly a few generations back, and it had the advantage of helping build unit esprit. Of course it also had its political risks, with a family that had fallen from power and favor but not from some political popularity among the older nobility.

Especially after Des Poplanich was fool enough to let himself be put forward as a figurehead for a coup attempt, Raj thought brutally. It was amazing that a man as smart as Thom had had a brother so politically naive. He remembered the screams when the flame-fougasse he improvised went off in the tower basement. The screams, and then the smell. "I did point out it would be a shame to waste a loyal unit," he said mildly. Ehwardo's personal fate had also hung in the balance, but Raj liked the fact that he thought first of his command.

"Yes. And"—in a rush—"I never believed those rumors about you having something to do with Thom's disappearance. He was your friend."

Raj nodded, his face implacable. "He was. However, Des was not. And I *did* kill him. With regret, but I did it."

The man who thought himself the last living Poplanich met his eyes. "I know. Messer Whitehall—" He stopped and looked both ways before lowering his voice. "I'll be honest with you; I don't approve of many of the Governor's policies, and I approve even less of some of his ministers. The Poplanich gens have a better claim to the Chair, too, although I wouldn't take that job if the Spirit of Man came down from the Stars and handed it to me. But Barholm isn't the sort of disaster that has to be deChaired at all costs; and the Civil Government can't afford an internal war. That above all."

He extended his hand, and Raj gripped it for a moment. *That'll look bad if anyone's watching,* he thought. And: *To the Starless Dark with that.*

"Those noncoms you lent me did a world of good," Poplanich added.

Raj smiled grimly. "This isn't a border skirmish we're going off to," he said. Poplanich's Own had been a central-provinces garrison unit until the change of dynasties, and doing routine patrol work up north since then. Ehwardo was conscientious about his profession—not a universal characteristic among well-born officers with a patrimonial unit—but inexperienced, despite being a few years older than Raj.

"It's perked up the men in more ways than one," Poplanich said. "A little regional rivalry; your veterans thought my people raw, and were pretty plain about it. The troopers are eager to show you can be a fighting man without being a Descotter born in a thunderstorm, half-Doberman and half sauroid . . ."

Raj joined in the chuckle, until an infinitely cold voice spoke in the back of his mind:

observe Center said.

—and a solid roaring wall of sound lifted from the crowded docks of East Residence, signal rockets lifting from the shining bulk of the Palace above as the bunting-decked ships edged toward the docks. Sailors and soldiers crowded the rails, waving bits of prize loot—

—and a single warship plodded wearily into the harbor, masts chopped off level with the deck for emergency fuel. A huge wail went up from the city, as the black flag at the masthead came into view—

CHAPTER FOUR

"Ser."

Raj blinked open eyes that felt as if the lids were fastened with birdlime.

"Ser." It was da Cruz, looking worried. "Trouble, ser."

The general sat up on his cot and swung his feet down; he had gone to sleep mostly dressed. Too much work to do, three days out of East Residence. Sailing south along the Coast Range and stopping every night to let the troops sleep under canvas. Easier on the men to start with—mass seasickness on a troopship was no joke, not to mention dogs going berserk with fear—and easier on the supplies: this way they could buy from civilians without dipping into the jerky and hardtack that would have to last them, later. Too much paperwork, and nobody who really knew their administrative jobs. Last year at Sandoral had been easy by comparison; the army had just collected in and around the city and sat there for months before the Colonists moved north.

Spirit damn it to darkness, we should have some sort of permanent contingency command and staff for things like this, he thought, not for the first time. *We're too defense-minded.*

The Master of Soldiers, East Residence, controlled pay and overall logistics, but that was for routine operations in garrison. Field armies' administration had to be improvised out of the handbooks for a particular campaign . . . and he didn't know how anyone before him had coped, without Center to prompt and to remember things.

... *then again, the you can see why the Governor would be antsy about a permanent mobile force.* More than one Governor had been overthrown by a victorious general; a few had even been shot off the Chair by defeated ones.

He stamped his feet into his boots; a valet came in with hot towels and hot water and soap and began to shave him. *Some compensations to general rank, at least,* he thought ironically. Another was laying out his jacket and a clean shirt and bringing in kave.

Damn Berg for keeping him up. No *way* he could afford to snub the man by refusing to eat dinner with him, and every one turned into a bloody banquet with potted delicacies from East Residence. Did he think this was a bloody *picnic*? And a man with a full day's job of work ahead simply couldn't sit up drinking all night.

Suzette had seen him off with a joke about worker bees and an ironic toast from Berg and his cronies and some dashing young rips in uniform like Dalhouse . . . Her cot was still neatly made up. Lamplight made the big tent an oasis of light in the darkness of predawn; only a sliver of Miniluna was up, and a frosty sheeting of stars. It was not quiet, not with nearly twenty thousand human beings about, but the noise was a murmur of voices and deep resentful *wuffs* from cavalry dogs sensing they were about to be led back on board the detested ships.

"Report," Raj growled through the suds. The barber was an artist, and the blade slid through thick blue-black stubble effortlessly. Raj would have preferred a soldier-orderly, but a general had to keep a certain minimum of staff to maintain respect. More of Suzette's work. "What the Starless Realm is going on?"

"Devil's work right enough, ser," da Cruz said; he pulled at the orange-black-red neckerchief all the 5th Descott wore, souvenir of a looted warehouse in El Djem. The lamplight danced across the heavy keloid scars on one cheek, drawing the corner of his mouth up into a parody of a smile. "Killin' over a dice game."

Raj swore; that was *not* his job, and the Top Soldier ought to have known it. "That's their bloody Battalion Commander's—"

"Skinners, ser; 'twas Skinners did it. A civilian. Probably

usin' crooked dice, but they cut 'im cold without warnin'. Local man; then they broke bones when the *guardia* came for 'em. One lad looks like to die."

"*Scramento*," Raj said: shit.

The Skinners. Mercenaries, and barbarous ones even by comparison to the Brigade, or even the *Squadrones* he was sailing out to fight. They lived on dogback, up in the northern steppes, hunting the big grazing sauroids and anything else that moved with their huge two-meter 15mm rifles. Endless trouble in camp: not so much their viciousness—although the Star Spirit knew that was bad enough—as their habit of doing exactly as they pleased whenever they pleased. He sometimes wondered whether the flop-eared hounds they rode had trained their masters in that, or vice versa.

And afraid of nothing, nothing at all. But the ill-temper fell away from him like a cloak; there was work to be done. He took the towel from the servant and wiped his face, ran fingers through the curly black mass of his hair and fastened his helmet. Shrugging into his uniform jacket and buckling his swordbelt made him feel halfway normal despite three hours of sleep; his hands drew the revolver and snapped it open, spinning the cylinder and clicking it home again. Scalding-hot kave heaped with sugar, and a cornmeal bannock gulped while he thought, helped even more.

He ducked out the tent flap, past the sentries who snapped to attention and presented rifles. The sun was coming up behind him, over acres of tents, dog-lines, cookfires just starting into life as they prepared the morning meal and dogmash. Most of the smaller transports were drawn up on the beach, their masts canted over where the tide had left them; the bigger merchantmen and the steam warships lay at anchor farther out, their riding lights yellow-blue stars on the purple-dark water. It was very calm—Admiral Gharderini had kittens every time he thought of what a storm could do to the ships at a time like this—and the water had a surface like a dimpled mirror, throwing back the fading stars. Just chilly enough to be glad of a jacket, and the sparse reddish grass on the sandy soil was damp with the morning dew.

Raj nodded to himself as his mind made lists. "Duty officer," he said.

"Ser!" Antin M'lewis stepped forward and saluted; he had gotten more enthusiastic about that since his promotion.

"M'lewis, turn out the guard."

Company A of the 5th Descott answered his barked orders, coming up at the trot and leading their dogs by the bridle. The bulky rectangle of their formation filled much of the space before the command tent, over a hundred men and dogs. Barton Foley commanded it; he saluted silently and waited beside A Company's standard: a silk serpent covered with red-enameled brass scales. It slithered limp against the pole in the motionless air, a metallic rustling noise.

"Get me Dinnalsyn." A messenger clapped heels to his dog and pounded away, throwing sand over them.

"Written orders to the following battalion commanders: Staenbridge, 5th Descott Guards; Gruder, 7th Descott Rangers; Menyez, 17th Kelden Foot; Thiddo, 1st Rogor Slashers; Poplanich, Poplanich's Own—" He continued down the list; five ought to do it, even with Skinners. "Turn out with battle kit and stand by; prepare for movement to encircle the Skinner camp. When the drum beats to arms"—normally the command to turn out and stand to—"be ready to move quickly. Staenbridge to assume tactical control." The artillery commander came up, fastening his jacket. "Ah, Grammeck."

"Sir?" he said, saluting casually; the other hand was full of kave-cup. "What guns have you ashore or accessible in the next thirty minutes?"

The artilleryman straightened, his light-hazel eyes narrowing, taking in the waiting troopers. "Three," he said. "No, two—one's got a suspicious-looking trunnion."

"Two will have to do; turn them out and get them here and stand by, full load in the caissons, all canister. I'm anticipating some trouble with the Skinners; hopefully not fighting, but goodwill and artillery will get you more than goodwill."

"Yes, *sir*," Dinnalysn said, spinning on his heel. He tossed the cup to one side as he strode. "Captain Har-ritch!" he shouted. "*Hadelande!* Move—"

Raj nodded absently, tapping his hands together to seat the gloves. A groom had brought up his hound, Horace, and was sliding on the bridle, a complex leather-and-iron affair that pressed levers against the cheekbones to turn the animal's muzzle. Horace sat and dropped his barrel-sized head on Raj's shoulder, rolling a huge brown eye toward his master.

"Right, it's up to us, now, old boy," the human murmured, scratching under the dog's chin and pushing it aside as a washcloth-sized tongue lapped at him. He straddled the saddle, and Horace rose underneath him.

"M'lewis," he said. The wiry little man looked up from the papers on his desk, a kitchen table outside the commander's tent. "In exactly one half hour"—officers synchronized their watches daily at the sunset service—"have the drummers beat to arms." That would get everyone standing in place, at least. The Skinners would ignore it the way they did most any Army ritual. "Captain Foley, to me. Da Cruz, lead on."

The night watch had set up their holding cage near the little fishing-hamlet of El Sur, whose strong springs were the main reason for the fleet stopping in this particular spot. This area was south of the point where the Coast Ranges turned east and became the Oxheads; it was dunes on the coast, and rolling dun-colored hills of sparse grass elsewhere, pasture for sheep, with an occasional cash-crop of barley. Further inland several rivers came down from the north, and there were irrigated lands and cities; where there were cities there were sutlers and whores and gamblers, and plenty of all three seemed to have guessed right about the Expeditionary Force's stopping place. Their straggling town of palm-leaf shacks and tents lapped over the date palms of El Sur and out into its stubble-fields; the villagers were huddled behind their mudbrick wall and locked gates.

"Sir!" the officer of the watch said, coming to his feet and saluting as Raj rode up. "Lieutenant Orfirio Dyaz, 23rd Hemmar Valley Foot."

The Lieutenant was a graying man in his forties, with the face of a tired basset hound. Infantry outfits were a dead end, and watch duty was the sort of thing that got handed down the pecking order to the most defenseless. He had a rickety wicker table in front of him, with a jug and some paperwork; overhead was a spindly looking oak tree, the only sizable one in sight.

"Report," Raj said.

Some things were obvious from first glance. Two Skinners in the portable iron cage, both bleeding from half a dozen cuts and sporting spectacular young bruises. They were wrapped in rope like mummies from neck to knees. One was semi-conscious; the other crouched like a carnosauroid in a corner, glaring at them all. Shaven headed except for their scalplocks, horribly scarred, with brown skin and button noses and tilted eyes, they were little men, square-built and solid, wearing beaded dogleather leggings, soft shoes, padded and decorated breechclouts, and little else. They both looked half-naked without the monstrous 15mm rifles, shooting-sticks, cartridge belts and half-dozen or so knives that lay piled on a saddle blanket nearby. They probably felt that way, too.

There were two bodies on the ground, covered in blankets; a woman crouched near one. The feathers in her hennaed hair and the gaudy-gauzy cut of her skirt and blouse proclaimed her occupation; she was weeping steadily, tears running through the thick makeup and turning her clown-faced in the harsh light of morning. Half a dozen other men of the 23rd Foot were being treated for injuries ranging from broken ribs to an ear bitten half off; two dozen hale, armed ones surrounded the cages with leveled bayonets. A further clot of civilians stood under guard some distance off, raggedy-bright women and men with a fair bit of metal flashing from belts and ears and fingers.

"Sir," Dyaz said. "At a dice game run by the deceased"—he glanced down at a pad—"one Halfas Arreyo, freeman of Cyudad Harenaz, the deceased was assaulted and killed by the accused, the two Skinners there—they refuse to give their names, sir. Multiple witnesses. The accused resisted arrest, resulting in many injuries and one fatality, Private Third Class Floreyz Magon."

Raj winced inwardly. A soldier dead, a Regular; that put a different complexion on things, even if he was only an infantryman.

"Let me see the bodies," he said. A soldier pulled back the blankets. The dead infantryman looked to be about seventeen, his head lolling in a manner that left no doubt about the cause of death. A bristle-haired recruit haircut, and a thin pockmarked brown face like a million others, still gaunt with malnutrition; the Army had probably been his first experience of eating his fill.

The other figure had probably been well-dressed. It was difficult to tell that or much else about him. One arm was off at the elbow, and thrown on the bulging intestines that showed through the rents in his belly; half his face was lying down in a flap that exposed a red-and-white grin, and his testicles had been sliced off and stuffed in the gaping mouth. Both eyes lay in smears of jelly across the face, and the flies were already like a black carpet from feet to forehead. The hard stink of blood and shit was underlain by a little of the sweetness of decay. Behind him Raj could hear the A Company standard bearer swear softly, and Foley's quick *"Silence in the ranks!"*

"That's the gambler," the Lieutenant added helpfully.

"Yus!"

Both men looked around; it was the prostitute, standing now and forcing herself to look straight at the officers. Her fists were clenched by her sides. At first glance they looked to be covered in brown gloves; then you could see it was dried blood coating her arms up to the elbows, where she had tried to staunch impossible wounds.

"Yus, Messers, he were a gambler," the woman said, in a thick singsong south-country dialect, spiced with Arabic loanwords. "He were a liar and a thief and a pimp, too, jus' like I's a whore. That weren't no call fur yer tame barbs to cut him! He were shit like me, but he were m'man, what'm we and me *beni*, me kids to do now? I ask yer justice, m'lud; or ain't there no justice fur the likes a' us?"

Raj raised his brows. The infantry officer flipped his notebook:

"Dohloreyz cor Arreyo, freedwoman of—"

"The deceased, I know," Raj said. He shut his eyes, pinching the bridge of his nose between thumb and forefinger, and—

if you do not rule your army, Center said, **then your army will rule itself, observe.**

—and officers and non-coms were trying to push a mob of soldiers back from the edge of the surf. The men's faces were distended with fury; out on the edge of sight a flotilla of ships had hoisted sail, turning tail and running for home, and the men were screaming *come back, come back*—

—troopers looking at him with dull-eyed peasant defiance, refusing to move, standing shuffling in the trench while the broken Squadron troops rallied just out of rifle range, rallied and prepared to come back again across the ground littered with their dead—

—and Raj was standing on a hilltop, watching a whole battalion breaking forward out of the battle line, charging in ragged clumps; over their heads, over the scrub to their right he could see the sun winking on the steel of the dismounted Squadron warriors. Powder smoke filled the air, the rhythmic crashing of volley fire. Frantic orders spilled out of the viewpoint-Raj's mouth, and messengers spurred their dogs down from the hillock, but it was far too late. The Squadron gunmen crashed through the screen of brush and rose to fire their double-barreled muskets, loaded with ball and buckshot. The muzzles of the flintlocks were bell-shaped; that did little to spread the shot-cones, but it made the discharges thunder-loud. Thousands of lead balls made their own sound, like the humming of wasps. The hill was just too far away to hear much of the screaming.

Another wave of flame and noise, and another; the barbarians were carrying two or three muskets each, throwing them aside when fired and unslinging the next. Then they were drawing the great chopping blades slung over their backs and charging forward.

The binoculars came up to viewpoint-Raj's eyes. Tattooed faces with long drooping mustaches sprang out. Many of them were frothing at the mouth as they shambled forward; some were chewing on the thick back edges of their long swords—

—and he was standing on a three-legged stool under a long beam, with a coarse sisal rope around his neck. It was fastened to the beam above, tightly enough that he had to rise on his toes on the wobbling surface. He could tell that, despite being limited to sight and sound in the vision, because of the little desperate catches of breath as he shifted; it is not easy to balance like that, with hands tied tightly behind the back. A crowd of Squadron civilians shifted and seethed behind a barrier of warriors standing with the points of their swords resting on the earth; they screamed curses in guttural Namerique and threw things, lumps of cow dung and tomatoes. A barbarian noble was walking along in the shadow the beam threw, black on the white dust of the square. His floppy-brimmed leather hat was tooled and inlaid with silver, and there were jewels in the hilt of his sword. Raj's viewpoint saw him pause at each stool, each stool supporting a Civil Government officer.

At some he kicked the support out with a booted foot, watching for a moment while the prisoner writhed and kicked. Before the others he put the point of his sword on flesh and pushed with gradually increasing force until the victim's feet slipped. Each time there was a roaring cheer from the bystanders. His grin was broad as he stopped before Raj and rested the point of the blade on his genitals—

—and Raj opened his eyes and looked down at the woman.

"You'll have justice," he said, laying a hand on Horace's neck. "Military justice."

Which was to real justice as military music was to music, but you settled for what was available.

"Captain Foley," he said, swinging down out of the saddle and looping the reins over the pommel. Horace folded to the earth with a grateful *muff and* laid his chin flat on the ground, watching and hiking up his ears. "Attend, if you please. Lieutenant Dyaz, you as well. Have your man bring chairs: do you have a watch-stander here?" Watch-standers received extra pay and reduced duties in return for literacy.

"Ah, yes—Sergeant Hiscobar."

"Have him join us and take notes, if you please, Lieutenant. We'll use this table. And—" He looked behind him; yes, the 5th's chaplain was with the guard platoon. "Under-Hierarch Dohminko, do the honors, please."

Dyaz's dull eyes flickered with belated recognition—three commissioned officers were the standard for a court-martial on a capital case—and began to snap orders. Soldiers of the watch platoon set up the cleared table facing the cages, with three chairs behind it.

"You," Raj went on, "get those witnesses here. You and

you—" He changed his mind and turned to the ranks of the 5th. "Lieutenant Gonhalvez, a squad to bring out the prisoners, please."

Eight of the Descotters dismounted and started toward the cage, winding the lashes of their dogwhips around one hand to use the flexible hafts and iron-bound pommels as clubs. The infantry backed away, keeping their bayoneted rifles leveled. The Descotter noncom in charge of the squad checked for a moment, turning to look at them.

"Ye peon dickheads, put them stickers *up*, an' git yer fingers off the triggers," he snarled. "Now, do it *now*, er we'll ram 'em up yer bums."

The infantrymen backed away and fell into line, nervously clicking on their safeties and sloping arms.

"And hand over t' key." One of them extended it gingerly.

"Right," he said, turning his full attention back to the cages. "Everybody ready." The cavalry troopers withdrew the sabers from the taches at the left sides of their belts and stacked the weapons in tripods, brass basket hilts together; then they rolled up the sleeves of their uniform jackets.

The cells were cubes of welded iron bars, fastened along the edges with thumb-thick nuts and bolts for easy take-down. The door was fastened with an ordinary iron padlock. He turned the lock with a click and threw back the door.

Whump. The dazed-looking Skinner came up off the floor like a hyperactive sack-racer and sprang into the air, kicking out with his bound feet. His judgment was a little off, or he might have missed his footing on the uncertain iron-bar floor, and the sergeant was already blocking; instead of breaking the trooper's neck the feet punched into his stomach and knocked him back a dozen paces, winded. The other Skinner hopped forward, growling.

The Descotters piled into the cage, cursing and swinging the weighted handles of their dogwhips. The sergeant followed, limping.

The chaplain was standing before the officers, holding out the small-print copy of the Canonical Handbook that was part of his kit. All three extended their left hands to touch it, gripping their personal amulets with their right.

Saint Wu, aid me now, Raj prayed fervently. The circuit-board amulet he bore had been blessed by her, over a century ago. Beside him Foley was licking his lips nervously; it was hard to remember the boy—man—was still over a year short of twenty, sometimes. And he had never sat on a court-martial.

"You are met here to decide on a matter of human life," the priest said. He spoke pure Capital-dialect Sponglish, a bit surprising, since his features and the old saber-slash down one cheek made him look like a caricature of a thirty-year man out of the County backwoods. "Do you acknowledge this?"

"We do."

"The Spirit of Man of the Stars is with us always; Its justice is perfect, even as all data is stored in Its cores, ROMed forever. Do you acknowledge this?"

"We do."

"Do you swear to act with impartial justice, excluding all tainted Data Entry, exercising only the Authorized Codes, deviating not from the subroutines of Correct Evaluation?"

"We do."

"Then may your souls receive Input from the Holy Terminal, be lifted into the Orbits of Righteousness, and be as one with the Net; spared from all infection of the Virus of Corruption, in the name of Holy Federation Church. Endfile."

"Endfile," they murmured.

Raj sat, his left foot making the automatic sweep that knocked the scabbard of his saber out of the way; the homey familiarity of the motion bringing home the strangeness of the action. *I've killed and ordered killings before,* he thought. *But these are my men.* Part of the force under his command, at least . . . *So was Private Floreyz Magon,* he reminded himself coldly. *And even Halfas Arreyo was a citizen of the Civil Government of Holy Federation.*

"Bring forth the prisoners," he said.

Battered and bleeding anew, the Skinners were shoved and hauled to within double arm's length of the table. The sergeant was a disciplined man, and did not use the improvised club in his hand on them again, although it was quite obvious how much he would have liked to.

Raj's head turned to the clot of witnesses. Several of them flinched, trying to hide among a miniature crowd of a dozen or so; most of them looked to be the type for whom any sort of court was bad news. He pointed at one in a brown jacket with the remains of a good lace cravat and silver-buckled shoes.

"You. Did you see the deceased killed?"

"Yes, Messer General," the man said.

"By the accused?"

"Yes, Messer General."

"Did he provoke them?" A blank look. "Did he strike first? Insult them?"

"No, Messer General. Halfas was pretty dumb, but not *that* dumb. He just sort of smiled when he raked in the pot."

"Were the accused drunk?"

"Yes, Messer General, at least, they'd been knocking back the arrack pretty fast. Hard to tell with barbs, you know? Staggering drunk, I'd've said, but then they moved *so fast*... Anyways, there was a pipe going around, *mahrawan*, and I think it had some opium in it."

Raj nodded. "Did any of the rest of you see the fight?" he said.

One of the witness half-raised his hand. "Weren't a fight, m'lord," he said. "One held him, other cut him. Cut him slow. When the gunboys got there, the barbs just grabbed the first one and turned his head around till it looked backways, then the others, ones that didn't run, just started hitting the barbs with their rifle butts and stuff. Would have run myself if I hadn't had to go within reach of 'em to get out the door."

Raj turned back to the Skinners. "*Hustai able Sponglishi?*" he said: do you speak Sponglish? Blank looks answered him; he was close enough to smell the mercenaries, a mixture of the fresh sweat and blood that ran down their bare brown chests and a heavy spoiled-butter stink.

"*Say hum,*" he said, scrabbling mentally for fragments of Paytoiz, the Skinner tongue. Suddenly they were there, with the crystalline authority of Center's insertions.

"*Say hum,*" he repeated. "This man, did you kill him?"

The more alert-looking of the Skinners blinked, then grinned broadly at hearing someone speak his language. Even then, Raj wondered suddenly why Center hadn't provided such fluency last year; it would have been useful dealing with the Skinner troops out east.

unlike mine your information storage capacity is limited, Center replied.

"*Napas hum,*" the Skinner said: Not a man. "Just a farmer. I, Luk Belhok, I kill him; he steal our money, the pig." The Skinner lofted a gobbet of spit toward the mutilated corpse. "You got any drink, sojer-man? My friend and I are thirsty."

"Did you kill the soldier?"

"No—too drunk, too much black smoke. My friend, Loway Daygus, he kill the blue-shirt." The other mercenary looked up and nodded, smiling himself. "He look so surprised! We laugh very much."

"Did you know that that was against the law of this army?"

Both the Skinners broke into high-pitched giggling and hoots.

"We *fraihum*, Real Men!" the first said indulgently, as if explaining something to a retarded child. "Kill when we want, take what we want. Maybe we kill you, eh? Where is the drink?"

"Let the record show," Raj said, pitching his voice slightly higher, "that the accused have confessed to the crime." He glanced to either side. Foley was slightly grey under his natural brown, digging at the wicker of the table with the point of his hook.

"Guilty," he said softly, not meeting his superior's eyes.

"Guilty," Dyaz said stolidly, slightly bored.

Raj stood. "By the authority vested in me, and under the judgment of Holy Church, I pronounce these men guilty of the murders of Halfas Arreyo, freeman of Cyudad Harenaz and citizen commoner of the Civil Government, and of Private Third Class Floreyz Magon. The murder of Halfas Arreyo was with insufficient provocation; the murder of their fellow soldier without provocation. Sentence is death on both counts. May the Spirit of Man of the Stars edit their core programs and reunite them with the Net. Endfile."

He dropped his eyes from the eastern horizon, sun-dazzle sparkling across his retinas as he turned to the Descotter sergeant. When he spoke again his voice had the unmusical timber of struck cast iron.

"Hang them."

"Yes, *ser*," the noncom said.

Two troopers trotted their mounts out from the guard

company and tossed the nooses of their lariats over a branch of the oak tree, snubbing the other ends through the rings on the horns of their saddles, vakaro style. The Skinners struggled for a moment as the squad hustled them toward the dangling loops, then began singing in a high-pitch chanting wail, their death-songs.

Muffled by distance, drums began to roll in an endless *ratatatatatat,* beating to arms.

CRACK.

Another of the 15mm Skinner bullets went by overhead, slanting off into the west. None of the fire had been aimed, not yet, but the noise inside the Skinner encampment was growing steadily; screams, shrieks of rage, the throb of tomtoms. He could see clots of them eddying about, some dancing in shuffling circles, barking and wailing, others talking with the wild gesticulations Skinners used when they were upset. A few would run out of the tangle of hide shelters and bedrolls every now and then to shout defiance at the thin scatter of Regulars they could see on the ridges around their bivouac, turning to wiggle and slap their naked buttocks at the Civil Government troops above. A chant was growing throughout the camp, centered on the largest shelter, where a two-meter sauroid skull stood on a long pole. *Mi-*herda *mau*-dit, *Mi*-herda *mau*-dit . . .

Raj raised his binoculars, and the toothy grin of the beast-head standard sprang out, the hollow eyesockets and fangs the length of a bayonet. The chiefs were beneath it, arguing furiously.

That thing would have been fifteen meters tall, when it was alive and walking on its hind legs. Fifteen meters and twenty-five metric tons of muscle coated in hide that secreted metal into its scales.

"Raj Whitehall, this is *stupid,*" Gerrin Staenbridge hissed beside his commander's ear. Quietly enough so that nobody else could hear, of course.

"Quite possibly, but it has to be done," Raj replied distantly. *Does it?* he asked in silence.

this course of action has the best probability of accomplishing the mission, Center said, **probability of your death is 21% ± 7%. within acceptable parameters.**

Acceptable to you, *perhaps,* Raj thought. Aloud to Staenbridge: "Now, soldier, shut up and soldier."

success will increase your charisma factor by a useful degree as well, Center added.

Raj closed his eyes for a moment and prayed, raising one hand and laying the other flat against his ear in the formal gesture. *O, Spirit of Man of the Stars, guide me,* he asked. *I do not fear to die in Your service*—much—*but I ask that You ensure that it furthers the return of Holy Federation and our reunion with the Stars. Download unto me that which I most need, though it be that which I fear most. Endfile.*

He opened his eyes. Suzette was standing beside him, in pleated white-linen riding pants and tunic, but still in her blond court wig and party makeup. There was no mistaking the stubborn set of the cupid's-bow mouth, though, or the white-knuckled grip on the Colonial repeating carbine she carried. Her palfrey Harbie stood behind her, tugging slightly at the reins and wagging its tail with a supplicating look. The bitch knew when its owner was about to ride into danger. . . .

"*Scramento*" he said, letting his shoulders slump. It really was dangerous to pray; you might get what you asked for.

"Get *out* of here. I don't have time to argue," he said in a fierce hiss.

"No, you don't. And you can't afford to in front of the men, not right now," she said, sliding a hand through his elbow. Her smile was a little forced, but only a little.

messa whitehall's presence reduces the possibility of your failure by a factor of 10% ± 3%, Center said unhelpfully, **a public quarrel at this time will substantially increase probability of failure of your mission.**

"*Scramento!*" he said, with more feeling. And there was no time to order a couple of troopers to cart her off bodily. For that matter, only 5th men were in sight, and they might refuse. A lot of the 5th Descott considered their general's Messa to be a lucky charm, or a witch, or both.

"All right," he said bitterly. "If you *must* give me more problems."

Suzette winced at that, but she walked back to mount

Harbie without another word. He regretted the words, but there was no time for others.

Raj straddled Horace's back, the toes of his riding boots finding the stirrups automatically. Iron hobnails clicked on the steel, and Horace whined at the smell of his rider's fear, looking over one shoulder.

"It's all right, boy," Raj said. *I hope.* As an afterthought he took off his helmet and clipped it to the ring on the saddlebag.

The volunteer standardbearer closed up on his right and Suzette on his left. It was his personal banner, awarded with his promotion after Sandoral: the ancient Whitehall blazon, a stripe of white over a stripe of red, with a blue triangle at the staff-end marked with a single star. Legend had it that an ancestral Whitehall had borne it from the planet *Tekhanos*. . . .

He looked behind, nodded once to Staenbridge—*poor bastard, you'll be in charge if I die*—and touched a heel to Horace's flank.

"Nice and slow, boy," he said; the dog twitched ears in recognition and went forward at a walk, up and over the ridge. It was no accident the Skinners were camped in a hollow; nobody in their right minds wanted those sauroid-killer guns with a clear field of fire toward anyone else. The Skinner idea of a practical joke included things like shooting a cigarette out of your mouth at a hundred meters.

If it took your head off instead, that was even funnier.

Silence fell as the three dogs walked over the ridge and down the long slope, rippling out like rings in water from the men who noticed them first. The chant that had been growing—had been whipping the whole six hundred or so of the savages into a blood-frenzy—faltered and died as the mercenaries recognized the general. Many of them had been with the Army of the East in Sandoral last year, and most of the rest had seen him since. Raj kept moving at the same slow swaying walk until they were a hundred meters down the shallow slope, more than halfway to the first of the straggling hide shelters. Close enough to see the faces of individual men, and to see the round muzzle-holes of the big rifles. A hundred or so were pointing his way, enough to tear him and Horace both to butcher's-meat gobbets.

Him and Horace and Suzette too.

Raj let the reins slack on Horace's neck and clicked his tongue softly. The hound stopped and stood stock-still, lowering his head and lolling tongue. Then Raj stood in the stirrups and raised one hand in the air.

A buzz of sound came from the Skinner camp. Behind him came the thud of nearly a thousand feet, and the multiple rattle of equipment. The 5th Descott's color-party stopped on the ridge, the bannerman planting the staff and letting the bullet-marked silk and the campaign ribbons flutter free, trumpeter and drummer to either side. All along the ridge the unit deployed in dismounted close-order, the first rank marching over and going to one knee, the second halting when head and shoulders showed over the ridge. Bayonets flashed as the rifles went to slope, held at a forty-five degree angle across the chest. Not aiming, but ready. Regularly spaced along the line were the company pennants. A few sharp calls came from noncoms and junior officers, correcting dressing, and then the loudest sound was the wind snapping the banners.

Raj waited until the voices died down among the Skinners, then slowly swung his arm and pointed to the right, the east. Barked orders sounded, and the ridge sprouted a crop, glittering bayonet points and the burnished gilt bronze of the Stars on the tops of the flagstaffs, then the rounded helmets of the men. *Tap . . . tap . . . tap* went the drums, over the crunching of boots in the soft soil; Kaltin Gruder called halt beside the banner of the 7th Descott Rangers, and the whole long formation crashed to a stop, then rippled as the front rank knelt and both brought their rifles to port.

He swung his arm over left, and the spectacle was repeated. The Rogor Slashers this time, frontiersmen from the southeastern districts. Then Raj pointed ahead, due south, where there was low ground and a view of sandy flatlands and the curve of the beach. Another battalion double-timed into view to close that gap, trotting in earth-shaking unison in column of fours, a long snake of steel and blue coats and maroon legs; the officers beside their units with their sabers sloped back over their shoulders. Jorg Menyez and the 17th Kelden Foot: big fair men from the northwest, no better than any other despised peons in uniform, until their commander convinced them otherwise. He called, and the color party around him turned smartly left and marked time. Officers fell out and stood beside their pennant-bearers, holding out saber and arm to mark the line. The drum tapped one last time and the trumpet blew; the foot soldiers halted and faced left like one man.

Behind them two eight-hitch teams of dogs appeared, each pulling a 75mm field gun and caisson. The gunners rode the guns, or the lead pair of dogs. Both weapons turned right and halted; the crews were leaping down before they fully stopped, unhitching, riding the teams out of range, the rest opening the caissons and pushing the fieldpieces forward through lanes between companies of the 17th. Ready to spill their canister loads of shot into the Skinner camp. Behind guns and infantry a battalion of cavalry came into view: smart-looking men in green-and-gold uniforms on currycombed Border Collies, sauroid-plume crests nodding from their helmets. Poplanich's Own, recruited from the estates of his old friend,

And the estates of his brother I killed to keep Barholm Clerett on the Chair, but let's hope they overlook that, Raj thought.

The cavalry halted and reined about, the dogs' muzzles dipping and rising as they turned. A shouted command, only a blur at this distance, and six hundred hands slapped down on saber hilts. Another, and the blades came out with a rasping clatter, bright and long, flashing up and then back to rest on the right shoulders of the troopers. The glitter was like sun on rippled water, almost painfully bright, moving as the dogs shifted weight from foot to foot and growled in basso unison. The Skinners were shouting again now, and a few random shots banged into the air. Solid as stone, the soldiers of the Civil Government waited.

Behind him Suzette's voice whispered. "I love you," she said.

"I love you too," Raj said quietly, through a focus that was narrowing his vision like a tunnel, down to the strait confines of the next five minutes.

The standardbearer chuckled softly. "Spirit bugger me blind, 'tis a honeymoon."

That brought Raj back to reality; he turned slightly in the

saddle to bring the man's face into view. He was grinning, as if to ask what punishment Raj had in mind—being sent on a suicide mission, perhaps?

"What's your name, soldier—ah, Hallersen M'kintok, isn't it?"

"Yesser," the trooper said. "Yer won't catch me sleepin' this time, ser."

Ah, that snap inspection last year, Raj thought, facing front once more. *Now, just enough time for the realities to sink in.*

The Skinners were in a box; all the Regulars could deliver plunging fire without hitting each other, the cannon could rake them, and anyone who broke through would be cut down by the mounted men. Not that many would, with nearly three thousand rifles firing volleys at close range, not to mention the canister rounds from the guns. The Skinners' range and accuracy would be irrelevant, and the Armory rifles were faster-loading than the long guns the barbarians used.

The Skinners were savages but not stupid. The problem was that physical hardihood and courage were practically a religion with them. Skinner warriors would not, *could* not admit that fear of death altered their actions, especially not to themselves. No threat alone would be sufficient, no matter how deadly. He touched the heel of his boot to Horace's side again, and the three walked their dogs forward. Dead silence fell as they passed the perimeter of the Skinner camp, if anything so loosely organized could be called by that name. It stank, although not too badly after only one night ashore, just smelled as you'd expect where six hundred men and riding dogs had all been pissing and crapping wherever the impulse took them; he shuddered to think what their transports must be like. More and more of them fell in behind him and followed, a few mounted, most walking afoot with a bowlegged swing. When he drew rein before the skull-standard there were hundreds pressing about him, their breath and body-odor rank.

The chiefs looked up at him silently. That was bad; no ritual insults, no half-serious threats, and no offer of liquor. Raj waited impassively until the senior chieftain spoke; it was the same man who had commanded them last year. The one who had brought him the head of Jamal, the Settler of the Colony, when they drove the wogs back over the border in defeat.

"You kill *mes gars*, my men, sojer-boy," he growled. "I, Juluk Paypan, no like! Hang on rope, not warrior death, no death for *fraihum*, Real Man."

"Yes, I killed them," Raj replied loudly in the man's own language; he saw the Skinner blink at his sudden command of Paitoiz. "They killed a Civil Government tribesman"—as close as you could get to "citizen" in this hog-tongue—"and one of *my* men, without cause."

He stood in the stirrups. "Any warrior who feels a wrong can come to me with it, as a free man to his chief. Anyone who mutinies, anyone who kills his comrade, I will kill like the mad dog he is!"

Another murmur from the Skinners, and the long rifles slanted up and away from him.

Juluk Paypan scratched himself. "You got balls need both hands to carry, sojer-man," he said half-reluctantly; he eyed Suzette sidelong, fingering charms against witchcraft. "Wrongs—we got plenty wrongs!"

"Then come and tell them to me, in one hour at my tent. Tell me to my face, not whining in corners like old women."

He turned Horace sharply, the dog twisting into a U to reverse in its own length, then rode at the same ambling walk directly at the wall of Skinner bodies, free hand on his hip and eyes raised to the middle distance. The barbarians parted from them; he heard whispers. *Baraka*, spirit-power; *wheetigo*, devil-saint-wizard. None of them looked back until they were through the ranks of the 5th and over the slope from the Skinner camp.

Raj hung over the pommel of his saddle for a moment, gasping.

"Darling! Are you all right?" Suzette asked; her face was gray as well, white around the lips.

He took a deep shaky breath, and scrubbed a hand across his face. The palm came away slick.

"I just didn't expect it to work," he said frankly, and then grinned, fighting a surge of light-headed well-being as dangerous as panic. "I *thought* it would work—wouldn't have done it, otherwise—but I didn't *believe* it would work, not really."

my calculations, Center said with a trace of reproach, **are invariably accurate within the limits of available data.**

"Come forward, fellow soldiers," Raj said.

He was seated at his table in the command tent, with the front flap pinned open to leave a three-sided room four meters on a side; over the delegations' head he could look down through the bustle of the camp to the beach and the ships at anchor beyond. The tide was coming in, coming quickly with Miniluna and Maxiluna in harmony, and the first black lines of troops were forming up to board the ships small enough to come aground. Longboats ferried more to the big three-masters farther out, and columns of black smoke reached into a cloudless sky as the warships stoked banked furnaces and made steam. There was a fresh breeze setting in parallel to the coast, smelling of salt and coalsmoke.

"Come forward," he said again. The Companion officers were standing behind him at easy parade rest, with their helmets under their arms, and the open flap of the tent was flanked by troopers standing at ease. "No names, no pack drill; I said I'd hear your complaints, and I will."

The delegation was about a dozen men. Not just Skinners; there were the blue coats of Regular officers, and four or five commanders of tribal levies and mercenaries. Two big blond Halvardii, with butter-slicked braids and long halberds and multiple flintlock pistols stuck through their belts; a few Brigade types in their short-waisted fringed buckskin jackets; and a Stalwart from the far northwest, with the back of his head shaved and dressed in a long horizontally-striped knitted jersey and jerkin. His face, arms and legs were pink and peeling with sunburn; the leather jerkin was sewn with bracelet-sized iron rings, a dozen of them serving as holders for light throwing-axes. For the rest he carried two cut-down double-barreled shotguns in holsters, and a full-length model in his hands.

"You Messers first," Raj said to the Skinner chiefs. At a sign an orderly brought them cups of gin.

"Pig vomit," one said after tasting, and then both gulped the clear liquid down.

Good, Raj thought. *They've calmed down.*

"Look, sojer-man," Juluk said almost genially, speaking Sponglish for the others' benefit: "We Real Men, we want go home, hunt sauroid, fuck our own women, teach our sons. Bargain with Big Stone-House Chief Barholm say we fight one year, then one more year if we say yes. One year finish in three tens of days, and we say no more. Fight enough. We not like your way, all the time, don't do this, don't do that, get on big water and puke our guts."

The Stalwart nodded somberly, and spoke next in a nasal dialect of Namerique; the man beside him translated:

"True, lord. You are a harsh man; one of my warriors was fined because he beshat as a man should, behind a bush. We do not like this digging of holes. Or walking back and forth while blue-coat soldiers with marks on their arms shout at us. We fight as men should, running forward to meet the foe whenever we see him. Another of my men was whipped like a slave because he took the blood of one who called him a heretic! We do not like your harsh, cruel ways. We will follow you and fight because we are true to our salt. All know we will every man of us die in far lands beneath the Squadron guns and lie in nameless graves forgotten of our kindred. So you should be less harsh and unforgiving and ungracious with us. I, Hwilli Morgen, have spoken."

He thumped himself on the chest for emphasis, making several of the axes jingle. Since he had the shotgun in that hand, the men to the side ducked back to avoid the muzzle.

"Your pardon, Messer General," one of the Regulars said, taking a half pace forward and saluting crisply. "The barb's right, more or less. Spirit knows few enough of us are likely to sail back into East Residence. Sir, doesn't it make sense to cut the men a little slack?"

The Halvardii nodded and thumped the butts of their halberds on the ground; Raj waited, but the mountaineers were as notoriously parsimonious of their words as their money.

"That's all any of you have to say?" the commander said. "Very well." He paused, looking down at his fingers on the table, then back up at the men.

"Messers," he began, meeting their eyes. "I'm a soldier, like yourselves. I know we're going into a dangerous campaign, we're outnumbered, all of that." He let the words sink in. "So our hope, our *only* hope of coming through alive, most of us—and of winning—is with the Spirit.

"Yes, the Spirit of Man"—he left out the "of the Stars"; several of those present were Spirit of Man of This Earth cultists—"is our *only* hope. And the Spirit will not be with an army if that army forgets justice—justice within its ranks and justice to the helpless it is our duty to protect."

His hand thumped the table as he stood. "And so in this army there *will* be justice—justice enforced the only way it can be, by *discipline*. For all our sakes, because without that the Spirit will forsake us, and I say to you that I know as if a holy vision had told me that without the Spirit we will wander in little bands across the Southern Territories. And the *Squadrones* will fall on us like an avalanche from orbit and slaughter us piecemeal. So you can obey me or kill me, Messers, because I'll die where I stand rather than fail to do my duty, for the Spirit of Man and for the army the Spirit has called me to lead."

Silence echoed; the delegation stared at him wide-eyed, as did many of the guards outside. A feeling like a warm flush crossed his skin, and suddenly he felt conscious of their stares. *Did I say all that?* he thought.

"Wheetigo," Paypan murmured. The others shuffled their feet, speechless.

"Dismissed," Raj said. "We have an army to embark."

He sat as they walked away, beginning to talk among themselves, feeling as if the strings of his tendons had been cut.

i had not expected the situation to be defined in these terms, Center's mind-voice said, **but it seems to have served the purpose.**

Purpose indeed, Raj thought *But whose?*

CHAPTER FIVE

" . . . and those are the Malfrenek Mines," Muzzaf Kerpatik said.

Raj nodded and gestured for silence; the Komarite was a mine of information himself, but given the least encouragement he would give you much more than you wanted to know, mostly about trade. He could see the small black smudge on the distant land where the smelters' coal-smoke stained the sky; Kobolassian cast-iron and steel were famous throughout the Civil Government. There was no hint of the sulfurous smell, only the huge purity of the waves, white-capped across the darkening sea, breaking in thunder-foam on the breakwater of the harbor of Hayapalco Town, where the fleet waited to enter.

Elsewhere the high spine of the Kobolassian peninsula hung like a dark-blue saw to their south and west, tinged with blood-red where the evening sun touched the glaciers. The upper slopes of the mountains were dark with forest, reddish-brown native whipstick and featherfrond, black-green with beech and silver fir. Lower the steep mountainsides gave way to open hills covered in russet grass and dotted with olives and cork-oak; lower still narrow irrigated valleys drew wandering strips of green through arid scrub occasionally scarred by mine tailings or marble quarries. Whitewashed villages stood amid orchard groves and small checkerboard fields; the narrow coastal plain bore scrub, coconut groves, sisal plantations, and estates on recently drained and irrigated marsh with large square plots of cotton, indigo, sugar, and rice.

"Coal's available?" Raj said.

"In plenty, Messer," Muzzaf said. With a tinge of bitterness: "The best and cheapest in the Civil Government. I have kin here"—he seemed to have relatives in every province south of the Oxhead mountains, come to that—"and much money has been invested in collieries of late, and railways. Yet high-priced trash from the old Coast Range mines has the monopoly in East Residence, even in the Armory foundries."

"Tzetzas," Raj said.

"Tzetzas," Muzzaf confirmed.

"You two using foul language again?" Suzette asked, coming up behind them; she stood a little behind Raj, squeezing his arm.

Her fingers were slim and strong on the muscle of his biceps. The faint jasmine scent she wore carried lightly through the odors of tar and sea. Muzzaf moved down the rail, and they waited in silence while the little galley-tug came out to take them in tow. The strong choppy motion of a ship riding "in irons" changed to a longer plunge as the sailors made the towing-line fast. The transport inched through the narrow channel between the breakwaters; each ended in a massive stone-and-concrete fort, the walls sloping upward to the gun ports. The snouts of huge cast-steel rifles showed through, and after that it was not surprising that there was no seawall.

It's grown, Raj thought.

He had studied perspective and plan-drawings of all the major cities in the Civil Government, mostly with an eye to their fortifications. Hayapalco was medium-sized, forty thousand at the last census, but the old-fashioned curtain wall he remembered had been torn down and a broad avenue laid out in its place. There were suburbs and tenements and factory developments beyond, although most of the town was a tumbled maze of pastel and whitewash cubes climbing up the hills to the district commissioner's palace and the Star temple. A new aqueduct showed raw in cuttings and embankments on the mountain slopes beyond, a big new bullring, and the beginnings of modern earthwork ravelins and forts adequate to stand up to siege guns. The docks were thronged, with everything from little lateen-rigged coasters and fishing smacks to the big three-master beastcatchers, hunting craft for taking the big marine thalassasauroids. Wharfside was black with people, and massed cheering roared out as the first of the fleet steamed in.

The sound of brass bands followed. "I hope they keep singing," Raj said grimly. His hand touched his wife's. "I . . . need to talk to Berg," he said.

"I hope you'll report that Hayapalco shows its loyalty," Sesar Chayvez said.

The District Commissioner of Kobolassa leaned back, making an expansive gesture out the french doors; the brass bands that had followed the command group up to the Palace were still playing. Behind them the city streets were filling with more purposeful sound, marching feet and the heavy padding of riding dogs as the Expeditionary Force disembarked. There would be a week or so to exercise the men and mounts, lay in supplies of fresh fruit and meat . . . and have a last taste of city delights before the campaign, of course.

Which probably accounts for the citizens' good nature, Raj thought cynically. Fifteen thousand well-paid men with hard coin in their pockets could do a great deal of spending in a week. *Although the Arch-Syssup's blessing was probably sincere.* All the southern territories were notoriously pious: inland, because of the Colony and its Muslim hordes just over the border; here on the coast for that and for the ever-present menace of Squadron pirates. The western barbarians were followers of the heretical Spirit of Man of This Earth, which added extra zest to their plundering of churches and burning alive of any clergy they could lay their hands on.

He looked at the Commissioner: a southerner, much like Muzzaf in appearance if you added thirty years and ten kilos, his tunic shining white Azanian torofib, clanking with decorations; the hand that stroked his goatee and double chin shone with rings. It had taken several strong hints to get this meeting before the ceremonial banquets began, and the round of bullfights announced in honor of the visiting troops, and the ball . . . *and their little cats too,* he thought.

Even more hints to strip the meeting down to himself, Gerrin Staenbridge, Suzette, Berg, the Commissioner, and his private secretary.

"I hope so too, Your Honorability," Raj said. "Unfortunately, there's a small problem. Two small related problems."

"Problems?" Chayvez said, frowning slightly.

There was a noise outside the doors, shouting, the heavy *thump* of a steel-shod rifle butt striking a head. Barton Foley stuck his head through the leaves, winked and saluted with his hook before drawing them shut. Outside the glass panes on the other side of the room a line of figures took stance at parade rest. The Commissioner's head swiveled to note them: Regulars in bluejackets and maroon pants holding rifles with fixed bayonets, not his private troops. A closer look showed stocky beak-nosed brown-skinned men. Descotters.

"Don't worry, I've just taken the precaution of replacing the Palace guards with men from the 5th Descott," Raj said soothingly. Chayvez jerked slightly; everyone knew that was the unit that had followed Raj to hard-fought retreat at El Djem and massive victory at Sandoral. "For the duration.

"Now," Raj went on, "first there's the matter of the coal."

"Coal?" Chayvez echoed. His face was fluid with disbelief, anger struggling with the shock of sudden physical fear.

"It seems the wrong variety was loaded in East Residence. An accident, I'm sure. Luckily, you have excellent steam coal here in Hayapalco, I'm told, so we'll just unload what's left of ours and take on all that we need from the government stores. We'll exchange it weight-for-weight, and pay the difference with sight drafts; do be prompt in paying them, won't you?"

Raj drew his pistol and rapped sharply with the butt on the satinwood table, leaving a dent in the soft silky-textured surface. Even then Chayvez winced; he had been Commissioner for over a decade, and must have a highly proprietary attitude to the Palace.

The doors opened again; Antin M'lewis came in, leading two troopers with slung rifles. The *solhados* carried a box between them, one hand gripping the rope handles on either side. They heaved it onto the table with a thump, and M'lewis flipped it open. The interior was filled with dark brown rectangular biscuits. A stale, musty odor filtered out.

"It's the hardtack, you see," Raj said.

"Hardtack?" Chayvez said, with a lift of his brows.

"Hardtack, Messer," Raj said. "Such a humble thing, isn't it? But armies march on hardtack, when they're far from home and markets. As on a long sea voyage away from landfalls, which the Expeditionary Force is about to make." To M'lewis: "Show him."

"Yis, ser," M'lewis said cheerfully, leaning over the table.

He picked up one of the biscuits and held it on his palm in front of the bureaucrat's nose, then slowly closed his wiry brown fingers. The hardtack crumbled at once, falling onto the brilliant white fabric of Chayvez's tunic in streams of dirt-colored powder; when the soldier opened his fist nothing was left but a single weevil, hunching its way over the calloused palm. M'lewis grinned with golden teeth and crushed it between thumb and forefinger, wiping the remains off on the priceless torofib silk. The Commissioner's protest died unspoken.

"Yer knows," the ex-trooper said companionably, "this stuff oughten t' be baked twice. Costs summat, though; gots to use charcoal."

"And," Raj continued in a voice suddenly flat and gray as gunmetal, "this hasn't been twice-baked from whole-wheat and soya meal. Fired only once, using dry dough to hide the fact; so now I have several thousand tones of moldy wheat dust in the holds of my ships. An *unaccountable* accident—since the Chancellor's office listed all of it as first-class ration biscuit from approved contractors, *didn't they, Messer Berg?*"

The Administrative Service representative's face was sheened with sweat, far more than the dry heat could account for. The soldiers' heads turned toward him like gun turrets tracking, and he smiled sickly. It was far too late now to back out; he had said too much.

"*Bruha,*" he mumbled softly. "She's a witch. He's *mad, but she's a witch.*"

"What was that, Messer Berg?" Raj asked implacably.

"Ah, *ferramente,* certainly, the books"—he gestured at a large leather-bound ledger, with the Star symbol of the Civil Government embossed in silver on its cover—"show it quite clearly."

Chayvez hesitated, giving Berg a venomous glare before smoothing his features into a bland smile.

"Well, Messer General, you know these accidents happen," he said, with a broad men-of-the-world gesture. "In any case, it shouldn't be a problem, not at all. You must have specie along to pay your troops"—at six-month intervals, although advances were sometimes given—"so you can just buy ordinary flatbread here, and make up the difference from plunder after your victorious campaign in the Southern Territories is concluded."

"Well, that's one possibility," Raj continued. M'lewis had gone round to stand behind the Commissioner. "I really don't think much of spending the troops' pay on rations for which the Civil Government has already paid—Messer Administrator Berg . . ."

"Eighteen thousand four hundred sixty-four gold FedCreds," the functionary said.

" . . . more than eighteen thousand gold."

"There doesn't seem to be much alternative," Chayvez said, licking his lips.

"Messer Berg?" Raj said.

Berg wiped his face with a linen handkerchief and opened the account book, spreading out several loose sheets of paper stamped with the golden seal of the Central Land Registry Office.

"According to these records," he said, coughing. "Ah, according to these, our Most Excellent Chancellor owns a grand total of twenty-three thousand four hundred and twenty-two hectares in landed estates in the four Counties making up Kobolassa District. Of which five thousand fifty-six are irrigated grainland, not counting smaller amounts on fighting-bull ranches and—" Raj rapped the pistol-butt on the table again.

"Ah, yes. Yielding—according to the taxability receipts of the fisc"—which meant a fifty percent underestimation—"over a quarter of a million bushels of wheat, barley, maize, and rice. The wheat and barley should be just harvested and threshed."

"That much!" Chayvez said, blinking. Then he nodded: "I'm sure the Most Excellent will be glad to sell sufficient for your troops."

"I'm sure he would," Raj replied. "Unfortunately, I haven't the hard currency to pay for it, so he'll have to accept barter. To be precise, thirty-kilogram boxes of double-baked wholewheat and soy meal biscuit."

Raj looked over at Berg. The man swallowed unhappily and began to recite:

"Fifteen thousand troops, three weeks' rations at one and a half kilograms of bread equivalent per day, plus four thousand sailors, equivalent, plus three thousand two hundred civilian auxiliaries, ditto. Carrying the boxed biscuit at book price, East Residence quote—"

"Don't forget a reasonable shipping charge," Raj interjected helpfully.

"With ten *sentahvos* per ton-kilometer, the value of the biscuit should cover all necessary grain purchases," Berg said, his voice speeding up into an almost-babble. "Plus a surplus of two thousand three hundred gold FedCreds. That's after grinding, transport, and baking expenses, of course."

"Of course," Raj said, "we'll take the surplus in cash, or salable assets from the estates." He slid a parchment with multiple seals across the table until it nudged Chayvez's hands. "The requisition and exchange order, signed by Messer Berg, as representative of the Administrative Service and the fisc, by me as Expeditionary Force commander—and by you, Your Honorability, right there at the bottom, as head of the District government."

"I'd as soon sign my own death warrant," Chayvez whispered. "You fool! Do you think—"

Raj nodded. M'lewis moved, his fingers snatching at his belt and tossing backhand; the woven-wire garotte hummed as it cut through the air. The other wooden toggle slapped into his left hand as it completed its circuit around Chayvez's neck and he pulled on his crossed wrists with a knee braced against the soft tooled-leather backing of the chair. The garotte did not cut the bureaucrat's skin yet, although it sank nearly out of sight; it was not piano wire. It did begin to cut off breath and blood, and if M'lewis used all the strength in his arms against the leverage of the loop it would amputate all the way to the neckbone.

Chayvez's eyes bulged, and his hands scrabbled strengthlessly behind him. Raj waited until he smelled the ammonia stink of the other man's bladder releasing, then leaned forward on both hands.

Benefits of having an ex-bandit among your followers, he thought bitterly. Bufford Parish was famous for its rustlers and bushwhackers even in not-very-lawful Descott County . . . and Antin M'lewis had made even Bufford unwelcoming enough that the Army seemed a better proposition. *Loyal man, though.* Service to Raj had brought him from *despoladho* to riches.

The bureaucrat's private secretary had started to reach inside his jacket; he was a boyish nineteen, but his hand moved very quickly. Gerrin Staenbridge seemed almost leisurely by comparison, but before the long *schinnnng* sound of steel on wood was over, the point of his saber was tucked under the young man's chin. A single point of blood showed on the clear olive skin, then trickled slowly over the damascened patterns in the steel. Staenbridge's wrist was thick, and his hand held the sword as motionless as a vise, but the secretary froze.

"There's a good fellow," Staenbridge said, with a charming smile. "Under other circumstances we might be good friends—but right now, would you please bring whatever-it-is out with *two* fingers, and slide it over the table to me?" It was a four-barreled derringer, with a carved grip of sauroid-tooth ivory. "Splendid taste."

Raj waited impassively, until the Commissioner's feet began to scrabble at the El Kebir rug. "Ease off a little," he said. M'lewis obeyed, and Raj pushed his face into Chayvez's, until their eyes were only centimeters apart. The bureaucrat took several cautious, whooping breaths, and the black flush faded from his cheeks.

"Now, Your Honorability," Raj said bleakly, "are you listening to me? *Are you?*"

A nod, quickly checked as it dragged the wire deeper into his flesh.

"You see, Your Honorability, I'm a soldier. I'm used to being screwed over by people like you . . . or our beloved Chancellor. But *nobody*—absolutely *nobody*—fucks over my men's rations or pay while I can do anything about it. I have a job to do, for the Civil Government of Holy Federation and the Spirit of Man of the Stars, and I'll do whatever I have to do to get it done. Anything at all. Understood?"

"*Ci! Ci,* Messer General, yes, yes, I'll sign, get him away from me *pahvor,* please!"

At Raj's nod M'lewis freed the garotte with the same easy motion, flipping the left-hand toggle to the right with a hard snap that swung it around to clack into his right palm. Then he stepped back carefully, swinging the wire back and forth through the air with a whisking sound.

Chayvez coughed raggedly, massaging his throat where a thin red line circled it. Staenbridge withdrew his sword and wiped the tip carefully on one sleeve, sheathing it without looking down. The young secretary's eyes were as steady as the hands that opened a writing-box and handed his employer a freshly dipped pen. Only then did he pull a handkerchief from one sleeve and press the cloth to the underside of his jaw. Staenbridge smiled toothily.

"I'll just keep this, thank you," he said, scooping up the derringer. His right hand rested on the butt of his revolver.

The Commissioner signed the document in the three blanks left for him; his secretary peeled the greased-paper cover off a disk of soft wax and fixed it to the empty circle on the bottom of the page. Chayvez banged his signet-ring down on it with unnecessary force.

"You'll be here more than a week," he said. With triple authorization there was nothing—nothing legal, at least— that Chancellor Tzetzas could do; and the Governor had already made clear that Raj Whitehall was a tool nobody else could break. Sesar Chayvez would simply have to *plead force majeure* with his patron; it was even possible it would work, if he made up enough of the loss from his private funds. There were fifteen thousand troops in the city, after all. That was a major force by anyone's standards.

"Much longer than a week," the Commissioner went on. "The bailiffs on Tzetzas's land aren't government employees. They're going to think a lot more of the Chancellor's anger than any paper you wave at them. If you wave guns, you'd better be prepared to shoot, and explain *that* to His Supremacy."

Raj nodded. The Tzetzas estates would be run the usual way, rented out on five-year leases to men who were themselves gentlemen of some wealth, able to furnish working capital and making their own profit on the difference between the rental and the net sales. It was a variation on the tax-farming system the Civil Government used to collect its own revenues, and like that worked well enough if carefully supervised to prevent the lessee running the estate down for short-term gain. Tzetzas would see to the supervision; nobody had ever accused the Chancellor of being stupid or lazy, and nobody in their right mind would cooperate in stripping a Tzetzas estate. Not if they knew what was good for them. There would be endless delays . . . and it would not look very good to send Civil Government Regulars out on plundering expeditions against the private property of the Chancellor. "I have my methods," Raj said, almost smiling.

"Va, va!" the wagoner cried. The oxen leaned into the traces and the ungreased wooden axles groaned.

Gerrin Staenbridge leaned to one side in the saddle, and his dog skittered sideways, upslope from the road. The long train of wagons wound across the hillside; tall reddish-tawny three-leafed native grass rippled, under the twisted little cork-oaks and silver-leafed olives men had brought here a millennium and a half ago. The road was cut into the low hillside and ditched on both sides, surfaced with a packed layer of gravel. That crunched and popped under the iron wheels of nearly a hundred vehicles, two- and four-wheeled, drawn by anything up to a dozen yoke of oxen. The hot dry air had the hard musty smell of sweating cattle, gritty dust from the road, and the lanolin and dung scent of the big herd of sheep being driven in downslope of the path.

The wagons were heavily loaded with woven sisal sacks of grain, figs, dried tomatoes, and beans, but there was no point in denying the men a little fresh meat, either. The dogs would be glad of the offal and bones.

The estates being put under contribution had furnished the transport, most of it standard gaudily-painted farm carts; they could haul the Expeditionary Force's worthless biscuit back if they pleased. Pigs might eat it, if they were hungry enough.

Staenbridge whistled sharply, and a platoon of troopers

peeled away from the double column at the end of the wagon train. Master Sergeant da Cruz and a special squad of double-pay men were sticking close to one small cart with sealed heavy chests ... and Barton was leading up the duty platoon. He felt the familiar twist of guilt at the sight of the hook flashing in the sun; Foley would not have left to follow the drum so young if Gerrin had not—

Guilt's an emotion for shopkeepers, he told himself.

Foley reined in and saluted, grinning. *He was a pretty boy,* Staenbridge thought, *and now he's an exceedingly handsome young man and even more irresistible.* The dogs paused to sniff noses, panting slightly and waving their whiplike tails; they were farmbreds, mottle-coated, point-nosed animals sixteen hands at the shoulder, weighing in at about a thousand pounds each.

"You think those recalcitrants will be ready to pay up?" Foley said.

"After having a troop of Skinners as house guests for a week?" Gerrin said. "My dear, they'll be *enthusiastic.* And we'd better be prepared."

Foley turned to the soldiers. "Sergeant Saynchez, rifles at the ready, if you please. We're paying a call."

"Ser!" the noncom said, and half-turned in his saddle. "Plat-oon, rifles at the saddle ready—*draw.*"

A multiple rattle sounded as thirty-two hands slapped down on the rifles in their scabbards by the right knee; polished brown wood and blued iron flashed as the long weapons were flipped up. *Slap* as the forestocks came down in the soldiers' rein-hands, then chick-*chack* as the right thumb was thrust into the trigger guard-lever. That brought the bolt down, its grooved top making a ramp for a thumb to push one of the heavy 11mm cartridges into the chamber; then chack-*chuck* as the levers were drawn back to lock position.

Foley looked back and nodded satisfaction; the sergeant straightened, and Gerrin suppressed a slight smile of his own. Barton had had some problems with the men when he was an aide, protege-cum-boyfriend of then-Captain Staenbridge; very little since he had carried Gerrin's unconscious and bleeding body into the laager at El Djem; none at all since he lost a hand and won field promotion and the Gold of Valor at Sandoral.

"Remember, we're visiting our *allies*," the young officer said, turning away. He snapped open his combination watch and pocket compass and chopped one arm forward across the ridge to their left; the farm lane lay in the valley beyond.

Behind them the sergeant whispered hoarsely: "That means *yer arse* if ye pop off without orders, Hermanyez."

The soldiers rested the butts of the rifles on their thighs and settled into a steady trot behind the officers. They crested the ridge in a flutter of tiny dactosauroids startled out of their nests, little jewel-scaled things about the size of a man's hand, with skin wings and long naked tails that ended in diamond-shaped rudders. One flew past Staenbridge's face close enough for him to hear it hiss and see the miniature fangs in its lizard mouth as it banked and glided down the slope ahead. The dactosauroids paused to dart at the insects stirred up by the cavalry's paws. Wings flashed above, and a red-tailed hawk dove in turn, snatching one of the little pseudoreptiles out of the air.

There's a metaphor for you, Staenbridge thought.

"*We're ridin' on relief over burnin' desert sands,*
Six hundred fightin' Descotters, the Major an' the Band
Hail dear away, bullock-man, ye've heard t'bugle
blowed,
The Fightin' Fifth is comin, down the Drangosh road!"

The soldiers were singing for amusement, and to let the Skinners know they were coming and were not afraid; the tune was a folk song from Descott County, roared out by thirty strong young voices. As they rode along the little country lane. Staenbridge cast an eye left at the mountain spine of the Kolobassa peninsula and sighed slightly.

"Homesick?" Barton teased.

"Only when I'm not there," Gerrin replied dryly.

This was actually prettier country than most of Descott— the County's landscape was often grand but seldom pretty— and much richer. The Staenbridge *kasgrane,* manor-house, was a stone barn compared to most of the estates they had visited here. Home was bleak volcanic upland, sparse rocky twistgrass pasture, badlands, canyons, thin mountain forests, here and there a pocket of soil coaxed into production with endless care. Descotters lived more from herding than farming, and nearly as much from hunting—wild cattle, feral dogs, and the fierce, wary native sauroids. There were no towns except for the County capital, and that was a glorified village; no peasant villages, just scattered steadings; no peons and few slaves. The Civil Government had never gotten much in the way of taxes out of Descott; what it *did* produce was men like those riding behind him, sons of the yeoman-tenants and vakaros. Hardy, independent, and bred to saddle and gun. *And I miss the homeplace, now and then.* He even missed his wife occasionally, and he was a man who did without women quite well most of the time.

"Skinner," Barton said quietly. His head inclined slightly, indicating a copse of umbrella pines a thousand meters to their left; extreme range for Armory rifles, but middling for the great sauroid-killing guns the northern barbarians used.

"Ah, for the eyes of youth," Gerrin said.

There were probably others they had not seen, possibly within a few meters. The road was lined with waist-high whitewashed stone walls, and planted with eucalyptus trees, dipping down toward a small lake held back by an earthwork dam. Staenbridge stood in the stirrups and held up a hand for halt as they rounded the last corner and started down the road to the *kasgrane* of the estate.

"Whew," he whistled softly.

The big wooden mill-wheel down by the dam was a twisted, charred wreck; so were the timber and tile buildings that held the gristmill, cane-crusher and cotton gin. Water poured unchecked through the mill-race, already eroding the earth away from the stone channel, probably flooding the irrigated lands that spread away downstream like a wedge where the land opened up toward the coast, too. The fields and orchards there were empty, and so was the peon village of adobe huts along the edge of the main canal. They had been gone before the Skinners arrived, driving the stock up into the hills. . . .

The manor had survived, mostly. The windows were all gone, except for shards that sparkled in the flat afternoon sun; it had been a big square building around a patio, two stories high and built of whitewashed brick overgrown with bougainvillea. Most of that had been stripped away, for some unfathomable barbarian purpose or for its own sake. There were plumes of black soot above several of the windows; a pit had been dug in the garden before the main doors and a whole bull roasted above it on a fire kindled with furniture. Half a dozen Skinners were baiting another in the open space of the drive, stripped to their breechclouts. The bull was a prize fighting animal nearly as tall at the shoulder as a man. As the soldiers entered the driveway, one of the near-naked men leaped forward to meet its charge, whooping, bounding up over the horned head and backflipping over its rump. A long knife flashed in his hand as he landed, and the animal gave a bawling cry of pain as its tendons were slashed. Laughing, the others waded in to butcher it alive as it threshed, crowing mirth at its struggles and at one of their number who took a deep stab in the thigh from the horns.

A few of the Skinners lounging around the open ground looked up from the killing; they were variously occupied, sleeping or working on their weapons, playing odd games with pebbles and boards scratched in the dirt, or fornicating with an assortment of cowed-looking women, girls, and boys from the manor's household staff. Their dogs mostly just slept, huge flop-eared hounds with brindled markings and drooping-sad faces; a few of them raised their muzzles and growled warning at the cavalry mounts.

"Deploy, if you please," Foley said to the platoon sergeant.

"*In* line—walk-march, *halt*," the noncom barked; the platoon peeled off in two columns of twos to either side, halting smoothly in a double rank behind the officers and facing the Skinners. The ones butchering the bull barely even looked up, a knot of glistening-red figures reducing a thousand FedCreds of pedigreed ring-bred animal to ragged gobbets. One of the recumbent Skinners rose, scratching his buttocks vigorously and urinating on a pile of tapestry. Elaborately casual, he rearranged his breechclout and lit his pipe before walking over to an upended barrel of brandy and sticking his head into the broached end. Coming up blowing, he spat out a mouthful, drank hugely and then picked up a battered golden cup from the ground beside it and filled it to the brim.

"Eh, sojer-man," he called, walking over to where Gerrin sat his dog, kicking aside bits of shattered crystal, trampled cloth, human excrement, bones, and dog turds. "Why I no kill you all now, eh?"

He stood grinning at arm's length; a Bekwa Skinner, with four-inch sauroid teeth through the lobes of his ears, face a mass of scars, some ritual, and crossed belts of huge brass shells on his chest. The feral smile on his flat slant-eyed face showed two incisors filed to points; even with the nose-stunning smell of the courtyard, the rancid butter smeared on his skin and shaven scalp was noticeable. A scalplock, woven with diamonds and rubies and bits of crushed gold jewelry, bounced down his back.

At least he speaks some Sponglish, Staenbridge thought as he reached down and took the cup, mouthing a swallow and spitting it out on the Skinner's feet.

"Where did you get this dog-piss?" he said; actually, it was excellent brandy, but you had to observe the amenities. "I spit it on your sow-mother's grave, corpse-fucker." He drank the rest, letting a little trickle out of the corners of his mouth, crushed the goblet in his fist and threw it over his shoulder.

The Skinner's grin grew wider. "You got nuts *cum pomme,* like apple, sojer-man," he said, and slapped his chest. "Moi—me—Pai-har Tradaw, fils d' Duhplesi, shef bukkup—big chief. Who you, what you want?"

"Gerrin Staenbridge, and I bring you word from the *shefdetowt,* the big chief of chiefs, Raj. He says get off your useless arses, come down to the ships—we go to fight"

"Ahh, Raj—he *mal cum mis,* bad like us, that one!" The chief's face almost split with his smile. "Hang, shoot—kill all de time! We go, make big *thibodo,* kill lots."

Still smiling, he turned and let the two-meter rifle drop from his shoulder; his hand released the crossed shooting-stick at the same time, and the heavy weapon fell neatly onto it. He fired without bothering to bring the weapon to his shoulder, and two hundred meters away an iron weathervane pealed like a bell and sprang into blurring motion. The long lance of flame from the rifle's muzzle stabbed into the sky, and before the puff of gray-white smoke had drifted roof-high the Skinners were in motion. Men sprang up, snatched their sacks of loot and jumped onto the backs of their dogs. The bull-killers paused a minute to pile lumps of the raw meat into the animal's hide and roll it up before joining the rest; big Skinner hounds jumped the low garden wall as outlyers and scouts poured in. Four minutes from the shot thirty Skinners boiled out of the estate's gates at a pounding gallop, screeching shrilly and firing their weapons in the air.

"Mamma, yer won't see *that* comin' down t'road from Blayberry Fair," the sergeant said with a slight tone of awe in his voice. "Orders, ser?"

"*Allya waymanos,*" Foley said; all of you get going. "Picket the dogs out in that paddock—not worth our while cleaning up here."

He swung down out of the saddle and walked over toward one of the women, still lying huddled on a blanket; her stringy hair clung to her shoulders in black rattails, and she scuttled backward with a shriek as she saw the hook gesture.

"Shhhh, *danad malino nayw, machacha,*" he said soothingly: nothing's the matter now, girl. "I won't hurt you. The Skinners are gone, understand? Gone."

He flushed with embarrassment when she came forward on her knees and seized his hand, kissing it fervently.

"*Stop* that," he said firmly, rapping her lightly on the top of the head with the back curve of his hook. "Now, go find your master"—it was a safe bet all the house servants knew where the bailiff had taken the estate stores and money—"and tell him they're gone, and won't be back *if he comes down and cooperates. Comprene?* Understand?"

Between hysterical fear and the singsong southern dialect of Sponglish it took a few moments before she did; then she wrapped herself in a blanket and sprinted out the gate and up a path into the higher hills beyond the olive groves.

Foley walked back to his dog shaking his head. "That's disgusting," he said quietly, his face troubled. "I don't like seeing women mistreated like that, even if I don't have much use for them myself."

"Don't let Fatima hear you say that, sweet one," Gerrin grinned. "She's hard enough to handle as it is. Next campaign *I'm definitely* parking her back in Descott with the wife—between the two of you you're going to wear an old man like me out."

"Oh, she's an exception," Foley said, raising a foot to the stirrup.

"Don't let her hear you say *that*, either."

The younger man snorted laughter, then looked around at the wreckage. "I hadn't realized how true the stories about Skinners are," he said.

Seaborne Skinner raiders from north of Pierson's Sea had landed in Descott County a century or so ago, and the tales were still told; presumably in the northern steppes as well, since only half a dozen wounded survivors had escaped, and nobody had tried that again since. Besides which, the Skinners had killed off all the inhabitants of the old northern coastal towns who had once furnished them with ships and seamen.

"This isn't the half of it," Gerrin said, brushing the backs of his fingers over the other's cheek as he swung back into the saddle. "Well done, by the way, my dear. No, this is how Skinners act when they're on good behavior." His eyes scanned the ruined house.

"Back when I was about your age and a new-minted Ensign, I was up in the northwest provinces, around Byrgez, when we had a bad raid. They fight like devils . . . but it's worse than that: they're the death of the land, wherever they go. They burn forests and poison wells and break down irrigation canals because they can live in total wilderness and nobody else can. Compared to them the Brigade are Renunciate Sisters and the Stalwarts a bunch of boon companions."

"Well, what about the Squadron?" Foley said, smiling and leaning into the hand for a second.

"The Squadrones, my heart, are the essence of evil."

"Why?"

"Because they're going to be trying to kill *us*. Compared to that, the Skinners seem as cooing pigeons. Back to the ships; Stern Isle awaits."

CHAPTER SIX

"Piggie! Su-su-su-su! Come t' papa, piggie, pappa loves yer—*git 'im, boys!*" Sergeant Hallersen M'kintock called; emphatic, but not loud. This was the first opportunity for some fresh meat since they landed this morning, and he didn't intend to waste it.

The pig was a rangy young shoat, half-wild and suspicious of the strange-smelling men; it turned and made a dash off through the scrub, leaving a scent like bergamot as it crushed the native succulents. A riding dog with its reins looped up over the saddle horn rose in its path and lunged, snapping shut its half-meter jaws with a sound like a wet door slamming. Squealing panic the shoat turned at a ninety-degree angle and made tracks. Two troopers leapt for it; one landed facedown in a patch of wait-a-while thorn, and the other across the pig's hindquarters. He rose with a grunt of effort and his arms locked around the animal's midsection. Another soldier stepped in and grabbed the pig deftly by the ear, avoiding its frenzied snap, and drove the bayonet in his hand up under its jaw. The beast wheezed, kicked a few times and died.

Two others were grinning as they helped their luckless comrade out of the organic barbed wire. The brush rustled, more so when several chicken-sized sauroids with short horns on their noses and lines of feathers down their forearms scuttled away from under the thrashing body.

"Better 'n the circus, Halfons," one of the troopers said. "Saynchez, ye and Smeeth git 'im bled out an' gutted," the sergeant cut in, cocking one eye up at the sun through the branches of the maquis. About four hours until they were relieved . . . "Carmanaz, bait the dogs with th' offal 'n find us sommat wild garlic 'n greens."

Halfons Carmanaz was a recruit signed up only a few months before the Expeditionary Force left East Residence, fresh down from the County.

"Yer never goin' to waste the blood an' guts, Sergeant?" he said, mopping at his scratched and bloody face and gaping at the noncom. He hung his head when the other soldiers laughed.

"Yer not home on yer daddy's fuckin' farm, butt-fuckin' sheep, Carmanaz," the sergeant said patiently. "And yer momma ain't here t' make us all blood sausage 'n' chitterlin's, neither."

"Tum-te-*tum*," Billi Saynchez hummed, stripping off his bluejacket and the gray cotton shirt underneath. He pulled a short double-bladed knife out of his boot—a bayonet was as long as a forearm, far too much for butchering—and made two diagonal slashes in the pig's throat as his companion threaded a thong through its anklebones and hauled it up on an overhead branch, turning it to one side to avoid the first thick stream of blood.

"Say, Sergeant—what is this place, anyhows?" he said, making the long incision from anus to neck. It was a pleasant, homey task; he stopped to strop the knife on his pocket hone before making the next cut. *Reminds me a' fall*, he thought nostalgically. Pa and his brothers diving into the pen and catching the slaughter pigs on a frosty morning, Ma and his sisters getting the big scalding-pots boiling, the dogs wuffling in the stable as they scented blood. . . .

"Thisshere's Stern Island," the sergeant said.

"Them Squadron barbs run it?"

"Nao. Different bunch a' Spirit-deniers, t' Brigade—friendly heathen, loik, er so the El-Tee says. Er at least theyuns don't like the Squadron much. We'z t' rest up an' refit here, loik. Buy stuff. Mebbe a week. Then we sails on an' gits to the fightin'."

"They say them Squadron barbs is all crazy fer blood, 'n they *eat* their prisoners' *balls*," Carmanaz said.

The others chuckled. "Don't git yers all drawed up, every one a' them barbs dies when yer shoots er sticks 'em," Billi said, hooking his fingers underneath the skin and slitting it away from the layer of fat. "Hey, Sergeant—d'ye think they'll be hoors, here?"

"What's it to ye, Snow-Balls—" the sergeant began; then a call came, like the trilling of a dactosauroid. That was one of the lookouts.

"Scramento," the sergeant said, diving for his rifle and helmet. Half the squad went to ground along the ridge where they had caught the pig; the others followed M'kintock down the slope. Their dogs came to heel at call and trotted sure-footed at their masters' wake, through scrub and then an apricot orchard, until the ground leveled out. There was an old stone-lined irrigation channel there, fairly well-kept and gurgling with cold water from a spring a kilometer to the south; the road ran just west of that through an orange grove, an eight-meter curve of rutted dirt sketchily covered in gravel.

"Sergeant," a soldier in the top of one of the trees said. "Riders comin'. 'Bout fifty er sommat more, ridin' obvious-loik."

The troops fell in on either side of the road, taking firing positions behind the tufa boulders that scattered across the soft volcanic soil, with their dogs crouched behind them. Sergeant M'kintock slung his rifle and drew his saber, waiting in the middle of the road.

"Yer a credit t' the County," he called up to the observer. "Smeeth, ye ride t' get the El-Tee. These is supposed t' be good barbs. So any bastid pops a round before I tells him, gits a new asshole cut with this." The blade went back and forth twice with a *whirt-whirt* sound.

"What if they ain't friendly barbs?" Carmanaz asked, nervously working the lever of his rifle and licking his thumb to wet the foresight.

M'kintock grunted and spat aside. "Then they gits to learn t' price of a Descott boy's balls, eh? Shut yer gob."

"How do you keep the outposts so alert, Major?" said Regional Commander Boyce. "I didn't see the ones under cover until that sergeant stopped us."

"Discipline and constant vigilance," Kaltin Gruder replied. Not least the outposts' vigilance about inspections, when there wasn't any real danger. No need to mention that to the Brigade overlord, of course.

Farther back in the mounted column one of the Brigade nobles muttered something in Namerique, something about *dishonorable hiding like bandits.* Probably he didn't expect the Civil Government officer to understand his language. Few non-Brigade members did, and members generally dealt with their civilized underlings in Spanjol, which was the common tongue of the provinces the Military Governments had overrun, and still officially the second language of the Civil Government. Kaltin Gruder spoke Arabic and Spanjol and Namerique and had a fair smattering of Old Namerique and Neosawhil and Afraantu as well; it was a minor gift, like the ability to learn juggling quickly.

He turned slightly in the saddle. The fifty or so brightly-clothed figures behind him bore no more than ceremonial arms, and many had brought their wives; the thirty battalions of Civil Government troops in the Expeditionary Force vastly outgunned anything the Brigade had on Stern Island. They were assuming—rightly—that the Civil Government did *not* want a war with the masters of the Old Residence, yet. Either that assumption was correct, and they were safe, or it was wrong—and then nothing short of a relief force from Carson Barracks would be any use. And Carson Barracks was over a month's sail away.

Gruder's face swept the line of guests, flanked between two double columns of 7th troopers. There were other ways of communicating than with languages. . . . He knew they were looking at his face: not that the scars were anything very drastic, just a series of white lines reaching up from the high cloth collar of his uniform tunic and over the cheek and into the hair. One cut a little V into the lower lip. Nothing very bad, although he had been a handsome man in a square-jawed Descotter fashion. He still was, they told him; at least, women still seemed to like it, although usually women of a rather different type than before. It always made him flush, though, when people looked at the scars, and that made them stand out more despite his oiled-wood natural color. It made him remember his brother looking around, and then his chest splashing open under the pompom round—

Which had an effect on his expression he knew quite well by now. His eyes met one of the Brigade officers, and the man looked aside. Suddenly realizing that the geopolitical considerations did not necessarily apply to *him,* personally.

Well, he had to be an idiot or totally inexperienced to say something like that, Gruder thought, turning back. The Brigade had not seen much serious fighting around here for a generation or more. Though come to that, he could think of Civil Government aristocrats just as brainless. Some of them with the Force.

Commander Boyce had noticed the brief byplay, and his lips compressed into a line for a moment. Boyce was a diplomat.

I don't envy that loudmouth, Gruder thought ironically.

"We should be coming up on our perimeter soon," he said aloud.

The escort party was riding down out of the hills that made up the spine of Stern Island's western peninsula. They were closer to the coast here on the northern shore; Wager Bay was ten kilometers away on the south side, a fine natural harbor and the island's largest city amid broad coastal plains. On the north the forested hills gave way to a steplike series of tablelands, some in mixed scrub of illex and thornbush, some cultivated in orchard crops.

The noonday sun was hot, and sweat soaked his armpits and trickled down his back. The Expeditionary Force had traveled south into summer as they sailed. It baked out smells of resin from the umbrella pines along the road, lavender and the cooking-spice smells of native Bellevue scrub. Life-forms not intimidated by riding dogs or humans whirred or fluted or hissed. . . .

And the delegation stirred, murmuring, as they rode a switchback down the last escarpment and got their first clear view of the encampment.

"How long did you say you'd been here?" Boyce said, then answered himself with a wave of his hand to show the question had been rhetorical: less than twenty hours. "You've been busy."

Gruder nodded. Impressing the locals was not the object,

but it was a useful by-product. Almost all of the force was ashore, the smaller transports drawn up on the broad, gently curving beach, the others anchored out in the bay, and the dozen steam warships in a rank beyond that. On shore the tents were going up in severely regular rows along the camp-city's streets, grouped by company and battalion, each one holding an eight-man section. The dog-lines stretched endlessly, equally neat, with a thunderous barking as the evening tubs of mash were carried out. The artillery park stood at the eastern end of the camp, thirty guns standing nose-to-tail with the harness laid out ready for the teams. A ditch, earth berm, and firing-trench ran all around the perimeter, and groups of men could be seen marching or riding in formation along the streets or in the broad trampled space outside the main gate.

The marketplace was to the west, behind rope barriers, and even that was fairly organized under the vigilant eye of troops with *guardia* armbands. Muzzaf's work, Kaltin knew; the Komarite could tell you exactly how to get merchants to do what you wanted with the minimum of fuss. Wagonloads of fresh produce were already streaming in, herds of slaughter stock milled, and a coastal schooner was unloading sacks of flour and vegetables.

Most of the Brigade people looked *extremely* impressed.

Thank the Avatars of the Spirit they weren't there to see the first couple of camps, he thought, leaning back in the saddle as the dogs took the last of the slope. *Shambolic chaos.*

"Advance and be recognized!"

"Major Gruder and escort, with the Honorable Messer Commander Boyce and party," Kaltin replied. The officer of the watch saluted with his saber and the men lowered their weapons.

"Pass, friend."

"What are those men doing?" Boyce's wife said, pointing across the broad stubble field.

"Drill, ma'am," Gruder said, with a broad smile. The woman was built like a wine tub and dressed in implausible gauzy fabrics, now rather dusty, and mounted on a slim little Afghan that was wheezing with the heat and the load. "That's the Colonial Countermarch, I think." Menyez was supervising, on his long-legged riding steer.

Several of the more militant Brigade members were watching with more than idle curiosity. Two infantry battalions were marching at the quickstep to the tap of the drums across the drill field, trotting with their rifles held across their chests; moving rectangles parallel to the road, four men broad and a hundred and fifty long. Twelve hundred feet struck the earth in unison, a sound that thudded through the dirt as much as the air. The colors at the head of each unit were cased in their cylindrical leather covers, but Gruder recognized the 17th Kelden Foot and the 55th Santanerr Rifles. He grinned to himself. Jorg Menyez had been working the foot soldiers unmercifully—a real shock after years in sleepy garrisons where little was expected of them. A tenth of their officers had been broken out of the service, and as many again had resigned their commissions. Raj had remarked what a pity it was that he couldn't do the same with some of the cavalry units—although their commanders had too much pull for that.

Bugles sounded and the drums beat. The columns had been following each other, well-spaced. Now the head of each turned sharply toward the road, making an L that shrank along one arm and grew on the other until the whole battalion was moving at right angles to its original course. Gruder's eyes narrowed; the 17th was doing it with machine precision, the inner man stamping in place while the outer lengthened his stride, but the 55th were having problems, bunching and sagging and losing their dressing. More showed when the bugles sounded again and the columns split into a T, double files peeling off at right-angles from the marker of the color party. That was supposed to leave the whole battalion deployed in double line with the colors in the center . . . but not if men forgot which way they were supposed to turn, which several of the 55th's embarrassingly did.

"*Halt!*" The drums crashed into silence.

"*To the right—face!*"

Now the two battalions were facing the road.

Menyez rode slowly down the line, from the ruler-straight 17th to the clumped and ragged 55th. At last he spoke.

"Soldiers . . . men of the 55th Santanerr Rifles. I am disappointed in you." He pointed to his left, at the 17th. "*That* is the way to do it properly." His arm swung back. "This is *not* the way to do it."

There was a ripple down the ranks which grew to an almost moan as Menyez signaled, and the color party of the 55th marched out and turned over the pole with the furled banner to the detachment with the commander. Menyez reached out and touched the flagstaff gently.

"You will get it back when you've *earned* it. 17th may return to quarters."

The 17th's banner-party advanced to the front five paces, turned smartly right and marched down the line. When they came to the end of it they reversed, and the double file of men there followed, bending the formation in a U; when they reached the other end the battalion was back in a formation of fours, and it made two sharp turns onto the road and marched back into camp. Jorg Menyez spurred his beast over to the Brigade party, grinning under a covering of dust.

Behind him a stentorian bellow rang out in a drawling Kelden County accent. *"BLOODY MARTYRED AVATARS' BLEEDING WOUNDS, DOES YO MOMMAS STILL HAVE TO HOLD YUH COCKS WHILE YO PEE? NOW WE DO IT AGAIN, GIRLS, AND THIS TIME—"*

"Kaltin," Menyez said, smiling. He inclined his head back to where the luckless 55th was trying the formation again, and going without dinner to do it. "I've lent them Master Sergeant Tobol. They're not happy, but he has a magic charm for making riflemen out of mud."

Kaltin made the introductions; Menyez nodded amiably enough, slapping at the dust on his tunic.

"I'm for a bath," he said finally. "See you at Messer Raj's for the reception."

Gruder was conscious of Boyce's slight surprise; interesting that he caught the linguistic subtlety. That was the form of address an old family retainer might use for the young master, not what another member of the upper classes would employ. The whole army had taken it up, now: *Messer Raj will do you right,* or *Try and old-soldier Messer Raj and you'll be sorry and sore.*

He grinned. Raj hated it, of course.

✧   ✧   ✧

Mill and swill, Raj thought disgustedly. *What a waste of time.*

He composed his face hastily; Boyce was *very* sharp for a barbarian. Hardly a barb at all, despite the orthodox fringed leather jacket, beard, and huge sword. Of course, the Brigade presence had always been thin on Stern Island. Better than half the bigwigs Boyce had brought along were of the old nobility, the families who had ruled before the Brigade took the Western Territories from the Civil Government. Nor were many of the Brigade the hulking blonds of legend; then again, that would be true even in Carson Barracks, these days. Most of the Spanjol-speaking inhabitants of the Western Provinces were lighter-skinned than those of the Sponglish-speaking areas around East Residence; the Brigade members here seemed to be only a little taller and fairer, on average. Raj suspected many of them spoke Spanjol at home and Namerique only at formal gatherings.

The Squadron would be closer to the raw Northern beginnings.

"I was impressed with your camp, General," Boyce said. "And almost as much at the way you could entertain us so lavishly, at such short notice."

He made a gesture with the wineglass in one hand and the canape in the other.

"Largely Messa Whitehall's work," Raj said, sipping at his own glass.

It was Hillchapel *slyowtz,* plum brandy from the Whitehall estates in Descott County; meant to be sipped, but the locals were knocking it back fairly fast. Tearing into the buffet, too, one or two Brigade types reverting and picking up joints in their hands, and the civilian nobles shying aside with mortified expressions. There had been only one suitable building on the bay, a small manor-house owned by a civilian, non-Brigade landowner. Suzette's charm and East Residence polish and a substantial golden handshake had persuaded him to rent it and visit relatives elsewhere. Her traveling household and the manor servants had laid out this spread on the patio, decked it out with hangings and tapestries and Al Kebir rugs. The wrought-iron grilles of the gate framed a broad circle of beach and gave a view out to sea, where the moons cast two glittering paths over the water as the sun inclined to afternoon.

A squad of cavalry went by on the beach, heading out west to patrol, their rifle butts resting on their thighs. Raj smiled as he saw Boyce's eyes follow his.

"Yes," the chieftain said, turning back. "She's certainly put our local ladies in the shade."

Suzette was holding court, half a dozen local nobles vying for her attention and Administrator Berg looking smug. She was in full Court regalia, white-on-white patterned skirt of torofib, slit down the front and pinned back to show the glittering metallic embroidery of her tights and the platinum-and-diamond nets over her sandals; her belt was fretted silver, the bolero jacket above it cloth of gold with ruby dragons, and an ancient Star symbol crafted around a display crystal hung between her breasts. The long blond court wig hung shimmering down her back, covered with a fall of Novy Haifa lace and bound at the brow with padparascha sapphire. Every gesture and intonation was a work of art, and it was not the least of that art that she never seemed stiff or artificial.

It was more than that, or the clothes or the prestige of a great lady of East Residence, that gathered the crowd, though. Even from here, even after all these years Raj could feel the magnetism; the dour middle-aged politician beside him did too.

Raj took another sip of the plum brandy, somewhat larger this time. Boyce smiled and shook his head and looked away.

"There are times I'm glad to be fifty," he murmured to himself in Namerique. Then in his smooth capital-dialect Sponglish: "I'm happy to see that the diplomatic envoys of the Civil Government have been well-treated here . . . even if there are so many of them."

"Yes," Raj said, equally bland. "It's important that we reach the Lion City area with no unfortunate incidents. The Stalwarts are so difficult to deal with, little sense of civilized restraint."

That was the *official* reason the Expeditionary Force was here, that they were going to "discuss" the status of some port cities in the Western Territories held by the Stalwarts after several decades of war with the Brigade. Claimed by the Civil Government, of course, but not held by it for better than six hundred years. *If I can make him believe that, I can sell pork to the Colonists,* Raj thought.

Boyce smiled whitely in the vast pepper-and-salt bush of his beard. "Indeed. It's unfortunate that my government has had so little success in its diplomatic dealings with the Stalwarts."

Almost as little as in its military dealings, Raj noted. The Brigade had a more advanced military structure than the Stalwarts, but there was something to be said for several score thousand shrieking berserkers, too.

"Yes, conditions are unsettled. I understand there's trouble down in the Southern Territories, too."

Boyce raised a shaggy eyebrow. "Well, there's been rumors of trouble on Sadler's Island," he said; that was just off the west coast of the main peninsula that made up most of the Squadron lands. "But no, I wouldn't say there's been much trouble. Apart from that I couldn't say at all; my government has excellent relations with the Squadron—we are relatives and fellow-believers, after all—and I wouldn't dream of interfering in their affairs in any way."

In other words, letting us land here is as far as they'll go.

"A pleasure to meet you, young man," Boyce said, shaking Raj's hand; the grip was unexpectedly firm. "I'm sure you'll go far."

"And you likewise, Messer Boyce," Raj replied.

"Oh, I've gone just as far as I want," Boyce said. "Staying there is the problem." He bowed slightly to Raj and left, heading for the buffet and several cronies.

"Ah, Raj darling," Suzette said. It was her Court voice, smooth as buttered rum. "*Look* who Messer Berg has caught for me."

"Messer Hadolfo Reggiri, at your service," the man said. He was ordinary enough, well-dressed in a conservative southern provinces style, plain silk cravat and dark jacket with only a little jewelry. Slimmer than Berg, a little gray in the black of his hair and mustache, with the weathered look of a man who spent much time at sea.

"Hadolfo and I were at the Cyudad Gut town Academy together," Berg said expansively; his face was flushed a little with the wine. "He was always more adventurous than I, alas—he's been here on Stern Isle these twenty years, trading and doing very well."

"Trading in . . . ? "Suzette asked.

Reggiri looked at her, blinking. Normally a shrewd face, Raj thought, probably closed and secretive; you would have to be, trading in these waters, where there was little law. Now he looked as if he had been hit between the eyes with a rifle butt, quite hard.

"Ah, Messa—ah, saltpeter and rosauroid hides, mostly; wine, grain, dried fruit, wool, ironware, slaves—but mostly nitre and hides."

Aha. Raj felt his ears prickle. There were only two really good sources of saltpeter west of the Colony. One was in crusts in some soils of Diva County, part of the Civil Government . . . and the other was in caves on the desert fringe of the Southern Territories. Back before the Squadron took them, that had been one of the district's main sources of tax revenue, a government monopoly. Doubtless something of that sort now, too; Southern Territories saltpeter was exported to powder mills all over the Midworld Sea, even to East Residence, since it was cheaper than the domestic product. And rosauroids came from the central rocky hills just south of Port Murchison; their hides had high concentrations of silica, and were much in demand for factories, as power belting for transmission from steam engine drive shafts.

Anyone who dealt widely in those products would know a *lot* about the Squadron. He could tell the Squadron a great deal, too; and would, if he was thinking straight. A Civil Government administration in the Southern Territories would make the saltpeter a monopoly again, as sure as Tzetzas stole.

"Hadolfo . . . Messer Reggiri has been kind enough to invite me and Messer Berg to dinner at his country place," Suzette said. Her slim fingers rested on Raj's forearm. "Do say yes, my dear. We'll need an escort of course, but it's *quite* safe and only a few kilometers away."

"By all means," Raj grated. "I'm afraid I can't come, far too busy, but by all means . . ." Berg glowed, preening before his old friend. "Kaltin!" the General called.

"Messer Raj?" the younger officer said.

I wish they wouldn't keep calling *me that,* Raj thought, gritting his teeth against the need to lash out "Do me a favor, would you, and take . . . oh, a company, and M'lewis, and escort Messa Whitehall and Administrator Berg to this gentleman's manor? They'll be staying for dinner—and I'm sure you'll be welcome as well?"

Reggiri nodded without even taking his eyes off Suzette. "I'd be glad to," Gruder lied coldly.

"And now if you'll excuse me:—my dear, make my apologies to our guests—I have a great deal to do." *At least I inflicted M'lewis on him,* Raj thought vindictively. He tossed back the slyowtz. M'lewis had the morals of a dactosauroid and the effrontery of a dockside rat . . .

The camp had settled into late-night routine by the time Raj was finished with the last of the personnel reports. *Damn, this is like being a mayor of a city,* he thought. Worse; most County capitals in the Civil Government had fewer people than the twenty-thousand-odd concentrated here. He was working in his tent; if the men slept under canvas so would he. *And I used to be able to know the names of every man I commanded,* he continued, pouring himself another glass of slyowtz and lighting a cigarette. *Now I'm damned lucky if I can remember the officers and a few hundred more.*

He took the glass and leaned on the tentpole, looking down the main avenue of the camp. There was little traffic, it was quiet enough to hear the *laplaplap* of waves down by the beach. Most of the troops were sleeping as men did after a hard day's work, glad enough of a hot meal and solid dry ground with room to stretch out. The camp had already taken on the universal smell of an army on the move: sweat and dogshit and greased iron and woodsmoke. Both moons were out and full, low on the horizon, silvering the sea and giving enough light to read by even without the coal-oil lantern hanging from the roof behind him. He took a long drag on the tobacco, holding it until it bit the lungs in a peculiar pleasure-pain, then blew it out at the moons.

The Canonical Handbook said that the True Earth had only one moon, smaller than either Miniluna or Maxiluna . . . there were whole schools of theology which debated whether that was literal, revealed Truth or mere allegory, like the Personal Computer that was supposed to watch over every soul, or the wars in heaven between the angels of the Apple of Knowledge and the Ibemmeraphim. Or whether this had once been the True Earth and so had only one moon, later split into two at the Fall, although that was dangerously close to the Spirit of This Earth heresy.

"I know," he murmured, taking another mouthful of the plum brandy. It burned, like white fire along his gullet, and he exhaled with a hard *sshhha*. "I've seen the True Earth and the Single Moon. I *have* a personal angel, access to all the wisdom of the Spirit's Mind."

"Sir?" The guard officer was a figure in shadow.

"Nothing, son. As you were."

exercise more care, Center said coldly in the back of his mind.

Quiet, he replied. "We all have our Operating Code, try and edit it as we will." *You too, I suppose.*

Faintly he heard the sound of a challenge and response from the main gate, and the squeal as the spike-studded logs were pulled aside. The muffled thumping of paws sounded down the deserted alleyways; another challenge came from a roving internal patrol, close enough to be separated into words.

"*Who goes?*"

"*Escort party a' th' 7th Descott, returnin',*" he heard.

"*Advance and be recognized . . . Pass, friend.*"

But there were too few, far less than the company that had gone out. Eight men, a squad, and a ninth on a big shambling Chow. Administrator Mihwel Berg, sliding off with a sulky look on his face as he stalked into the puddle of yellow lamplight outside Raj's tent. His own was nearby, here in officer country.

"Messer Berg," Raj said. "Where are the others?"

Berg's thin face looked as if he had bitten into a lemon, and bloodshot eyes blinked behind his glasses. "Back there. With *my friend* Messer Reggiri. Your *wife* decided it was too late for anyone to come back, but *I* made it well enough." The bureaucrat glared at him like a rabbit turning on a hunting sauroid. "What do you propose to do about it?"

"Do?" Raj said. "Finish this bottle. Come on in, half drunk is only half done."

The remaining hundred and fifteen men of the escort company came into camp an hour after the dawn service. Most of the troops were at drill or fatigues, but there were enough left in the 7th's billet area to groan and whistle their envy at the escorts. The men were riding their usual dogs, mostly Descotter farmbreds, but each was leading two or three others on checkreins. The led dogs were Ridgebacks, a short-muzzled, long-legged breed easily distinguished by the odd upright curl of hair along the spine that gave the breed its name. These were pedigree animals, clean-limbed, bitches and geldings of two or three years and broken to the saddle; the breed was famous for its endurance in hot weather, and each animal was worth a year's pay for a cavalry trooper, possibly more. Their pack-saddles held coils of sausage, flagons of wine and boxes of cigarettes, sacks of Zanjian kave beans and cured hams from the Stalwart territories.

Gruder, M'lewis, and the company commander, Tejan M'brust, had extra dogs as well. They were also each accompanied by a woman on a palfrey-dog. The girls—none of them looked over seventeen—wore the collars that Brigade law required of slaves, but theirs were of thin chased silver. They carried light parasols to shade their complexions, necessary since two were blondes and one a redhead, and any of them would have fetched five hundred gold FedCreds in East Residence; not to mention their clothes and jewelry, and the twin suitcases each had on a packdog.

The officers reined in in front of the command tent and saluted; all of them were stone-faced, and Gruder did not meet Raj's eyes.

"Sir!" he barked. "Returning as ordered. Permission to report to my command, sir?"

"Nothing to report, Major?" Raj asked.

"No, sir."

"Dismissed."

He heeled his dog around with unnecessary violence; the slave-girl squeaked and clutched at the pommel of her saddle as her mount followed his. Suzette dismounted and handed Harbie's reins to a groom.

"What, no presents for me?" Raj said softly, with a stark grin.

There were spots of red on her cheeks, but her eyes met his steadily as she offered a sheaf of paper. Raj took it and looked down at the first page. Then he grunted as if belly-punched.

"Fellow soldiers," Raj began.

A long slow roar built up through the crowd, a huge semicircle of blue jackets and brown faces, spotted with the green-and-gold of Poplanich's Own, the gorgets of the 17th Hemmar Valley Cuirassiers, and the multicolored blaze of the barbarian mercenaries. A corner of the berm and the gentle slope leading up to it gave seating sufficient that most of the army could see him and the Companions seated on the improvised dais. The officers of the force were down in front where they could hear him; many of the men could too, and there was a rippling murmur as his words were relayed back to the rear ranks. Only the officers could see the map on the easel behind him, but that was not much of a drawback.

The cheer had started with the men who'd served under him in the east, then spread to the others. Da Cruz had told him—with an innocent expression—that the story of the hardtack had gotten out.

Spirit damn it, shut up, he thought. *I may be leading you all to death, for Spirit's sake.*

"Fellow soldiers," he continued, when the noise had died down. "You all know that we're embarked on a dangerous mission. Well, I'm glad to say I have some good news for you; it's still dangerous, but it's not suicide. The Squadrones—I have this on the best of authorities—the Squadron still has its head tucked up its behind—they don't know we're coming!"

This time the cheer was a roar.

"The Squadron's Admiral thinks everything he's heard about us is just smoke and mirrors, rumors like the ones that come up every couple of years since the last expedition failed." Raj leaned forward, grinning like a sauroid and tapping one fist into a palm. "Isn't he going to be surprised?"

The soldiers howled laughter. "In fact, the pick of the Squadron levy, ten thousand men, sailed three weeks ago for Sadler Island, to put down a revolt." His swagger-stick traced the course, from Port Murchison away around the western coast of the north-pointing peninsula. "Under Commodore Curds Auburn, the Admiral's brother and his best general. With all their fleet, every war-galley they have in commission. The biggest threat to this force was being intercepted at sea—and now it's gone. The Spirit has put its protecting hands over us."

He spread his hands for silence. "Wait! Cheer when we've won, not before!" More grimly. "This means we've got a better chance, not a walkover. There'll be hard fighting yet.

"Now, here are the general orders. We'll take the shortest sea route from here"—he tapped their position on Stern Island—"to here." The stick traced a line directly south, landing on the indented coast south and east of Port Murchison. "We'll land and concentrate in this bay and establish a base.

"Nobody," he went on, tapping the stick into his palm, "is to leave the landing site without orders; nobody under *any circumstances whatsoever* is to enter the Port Murchison harbor. We're going to land close enough to panic them, then grind up what they send out."

He paused. "Any questions?"

Gharderini shot to his feet. "You say there won't be any interception at sea," he said furiously. "How can you be so sure? Did the Admiral send word, or the Spirit of Man of the Stars inform you personally?"

Raj stood and let his hand fall on Suzette's shoulder. "The information," he said slowly, "is from a source I trust absolutely."

as you should, raj whitehall, Center said, **as you must.**

"Hear us, O Spirit of Man of the Stars," the priest intoned.

"*Hear us,*" the massed troops answered. Everything was aboard except the men; the tide was making, and a breeze blowing down from the hills and out to sea.

The priest lifted his hands to the last of the stars, vanishing as night faded under the spear-rays of the sun.

"Code not our sins; let them be erased and not ROMed in Thy disks."

"*Forgive us, O Star Spirit!*"

As Raj led the response, another voice spoke in the back of his mind:

observe Center said.

—and a high surf beat on a rocky beach under a gray sky. Dinghy-loads of troops and the light transports drove in regardless, men leaping into head-deep water and wading ashore with their rifles over their heads or clinging to the saddles of swimming dogs. The first of them were just forming up when the Squadron troops rose from behind the dunes, their double-barreled muskets blasting at point-blank range—

—and viewpoint-Raj was clinging to a rope-line, on the deck of a ship lost in sea and spray. The sound of the storm was beyond belief, a solid roar in all the frequencies a human ear could perceive. Walls of water rose higher than the masts, but the wind tore off their tops and flung them as a horizontal sheet of spray like low cloud, until there was no telling where air began and sea stopped. The ship rose as a wave belled out beneath it, and for a moment they could see the rocks ahead. Then they struck, and the hull exploded into fragments beneath their feet—

—and the fleet was crowding into the bay, the beach black with men and the sea with dinghies and swimming dogs. Everyone's head came up at the first cannon shot. The Squadron warships came around the headland in a surge of gilded beaks and vermilion oars, the first flying the sword-and-comet banner of Commodore Curtis. Its bow-guns cut loose, the roundshot skipping over the low waves and into the side of the first Civil Government warship. Timbers smashed over the paddle wheel, and then the deck came apart in a shower of splinters and white smoke as the boiler ruptured. Behind the galleys came the transports, their rigging thick with the elite troops of the Squadron roaring out their war cries. . . .

"The Spirit of Man is of the Stars and all the Universe; this we believe."

"Witness our belief, O Star Spirit!"

"As we believe and act in righteousness, so shall we be boosted into the Orbit of Fulfillment."

"Raise us up, O Star Spirit!"

"Deliver us from the Crash; from the Meltdown; from the Hard Rads; spare us."

"Spare us, O Star Spirit!"

"We receive diligently the Input from Thy Holy Terminal, now and forever."

"Forever, O Star Spirit."

"As we believe, so let Thy Holy Federation be restored in our time, O Spirit of Man of the Stars; and if the burden of a faithless generation's sin be too great, may our souls be received into the Net. Endfile."

"Endfile!"

Raj looked out over the sea of bared heads. "Right, lads. Enter your sins at the Terminal, and fight with the Spirit at your side."

The priest lowered his hands. "The Spirit be with you."

"And in thy soul."

CHAPTER SEVEN

The longboat cut through the darkening purple of the waves toward the shore of the bay. Senior Lieutenant Antin M'lewis crouched in the bows, his eyes flickering restlessly as the muffled oars beat behind him. No way of telling if the barbs were waiting for them . . . probably not. He looked up for a second; low scudding clouds, and a wet breeze from the east, overland. Rustler's weather, they called it at home in Bufford Parish. Home to the only men in Descott County, or so his Pa had told him the first time he took him out to try for some of Squire Rahmirez's sheep. It had been Squire Rahmirez got him into the Army, too, after the little matter of those two riding dogs he'd sold him. Well, good Spirit bless, did the man think he'd *bought* them, to be selling them at that price? Good-hearted of him to sponsor M'lewis's enlistment, though. "The Army will be the making of you, me lad," he'd said.

Truer words never passed yer teeth, Squire, M'lewis thought, and spoke under his breath:

> "An' if you treat a barb to a dose a' cleanin'-rod
> He's like to show ye everthin' he owns
> When he won't produce no more, summat water on
>   the floor
> Where yer hear it answer hollow to yer boot
> When the ground begins to sink, shove yer
>   baynet down the chink—"

"El-Tee?"

"Jist some ol' Army musik," M'lewis said.

The keel grated on sand, very quiet. He turned to look at the other boats, half a dozen, with the tethered dogs swimming alongside. None of them made any sound as the men leaped overboard with their rifles over their heads and led the animals up beyond the high-water mark before crouching down beside them. M'lewis slapped palms with the petty officer in charge of the detail—to whom he had been careful to lose money as yet unpaid—and vaulted over the bow, running quickly through the shallow water before too much could soak into his boots. His dog followed with the reins in its mouth, silent-trained, and they all ran crouching up to the lee of the ridge six hundred meters inland. It was good to feel solid land again; the last night had not exactly been a storm, but the wind had been up high enough.

"All right," he whispered, as the others crowded round; there were twenty-two, not forty as battalion legend had it. *I has me standards,* he thought ironically. "Ye bastids all know yer assignments," he said. "One last word. Yer here t' scout, not finger. Any one a yer stops to lift a shiny pretty or a skirt, better run fuckin' fast an' far."

His hand blurred, and suddenly the man across from him was gasping, hands clawing up to his neck at the coil of wire that had whipped around it. Then he froze, his eyes rolling down in a frantic effort to see the knife-point pricking just above his belt-buckle.

"Fast an' far, because I'll be behind him wit' me little friend here t' take yer breath away. That means ye partic'lar, Dommor Alleyman. *Comprene?*"

"Grrk! ci!"

M'lewis flipped the toggle and unwound the wire, patting the man on the cheek. "Good. When th' fightin's done, ye'll all have more gold 'n yer can carry, more likker n' ye can hold, 'n big-titted barb princesses spreadin' wide and askin' fer it. Until then, do yer fuckin' jobs!"

Silent nods, and then they dispersed; two began to put up the big tripod-lantern that would flash directions to the fleet and guide them in safe to the center of the bay. M'lewis smiled to himself; he had chosen them all well. Most were old neighbors—some even from Hole Canyon, his family's subdistrict—and they all had a professional's deep respect for a really successful operator. He pulled the pocket compass out of its case at his belt and took a reading. Surprising how few men realized the value of tricks like that. Gentrydoings, they'd say. How did they think the gentry got on top in the first place?

"Thissaway," he said to the six with him, straddling his dog. "Go."

The felt-muffled surfaces of the stirrups made no sound as he slipped the toes of his boots into them. *Well, I'm gentry now. Of sorts; his sons would be Messer-class . . . Keep yer mind on business, ye butthead,* he told himself. The dogs moved off, paws almost silent in the deep soft dust of the road, spaced out to ten-meter intervals. *Messer Raj's business. A shooting Star of a man, and if you hitched your cart to his harness he'd draw you along. Or you'd go over with him in a crash.*

M'lewis smiled into the warm summer night. They were coming up on a hut, and lantern-light leaked through the warped shutters.

"Dicinsyn, Felodez," he whispered. "Around the rear. No killin'." Time to find out some local news, then on to that well the map marked.

"Yer map's not bad, but sommat incomplete, ser," Antin M'lewis said. "Anyways, no concentration of barb sojers anywhere within three hours' ride. Hardly spotted a man under arms; no Squadrones t' speak of."

"Bring that lantern over here!" Raj called over his shoulder. The landing was going surprisingly well, considering that it was night and there was a moderately stiff onshore breeze. At least the transports had not had to tack their way in.

The coal-oil lamp was the bull's-eye type; Raj took it and clicked open the shutter to illuminate the map. M'lewis crouched. He had burnt cork on his face and hands, and a black bandanna around his head. The map was copied from originals more than a century and a half old. The gross terrain features would be there, but the most valuable parts of the Ordinance Survey, the houses and field-boundaries and woods, would have changed drastically.

"Thisshere ridge"—his finger pointed inland, to their west—

"don't have the houses over the edge what's marked, ser. Jist a couple'a huts. I got two, three men in each. Land over t'ridge is all split up inta little fields croppers work fer th' barbs. I got a couple, they talkin' pretty free. Don't love them barbs, nohow. Then here"—he touched a spot marked with the symbol for an inn—"'tis a village now. Mondain by name. 'Bout two hundred houses, rubble wall shoulder high. Not hardly no problem. Some militia; we kin take it an' use it fer a base right off, yer gives the word, Messer Raj."

Raj thought, turning again to look at the bay. With both moons down, the night was pitch-black, and the beach was milling chaos. Lights darted back and forth on the water, and he could see a dull red glow from the funnel of a steamer, but the running lights of the vessels were out by his order. This was far too close to Port Murchison for safety; only twenty-five kilometers, one day's forced march and less than that for a ship. As he watched another transport ghosted in, the long rumbling crunch of its keel bedding in the sand ending in a louder crackle as its prow struck a ship already ashore. There were yells of fury ending in the *thwack* of a rope's end on a bare back, and the moaning whimper of a frightened dog.

"No," he said. "First things first; we'll get this sorted out." He leaned forward and slapped the little ferret-faced man on the shoulder. "Good man. Excellent work." He looked up. "Captain! How many of your company ashore?"

Foley stopped in mid-stride. "All of them, sir," he said. "Gerrin's in the next boat; we've got about half the dogs in. Bloody hell getting them over the rail in the dark."

"Good; get two platoons up on the ridge. There are some of the Scouts in those two hovels on the ridge. Relieve them, get up there, and lay me out a perimeter defense. I'll feed men up as they arrive. Now, M'lewis. What I want you and your scouts to do is get me some farmers. And their wagons; collect them, tell them they'll be paid—*no, pay* them, for whatever spare supplies they'll bring in."

"Already done, Messer Raj; figgered we couldn't nohow leave 'em t' run off to the barbs after they'd seen us."

"Good. Put a dozen wagons aside—"

Menyez came by, with a pair of infantry battalion-commanders in tow. "Sir," he said. "It's going according to plan, but Dinnalsyn says we can forget about the guns until tomorrow or until we can get the floating pier up, whichever comes first."

"Fine. That transport?"

"Rock under the sand; broke her spine. Hopeless."

"There's some good in everything; get some fatigue-parties breaking her up for fuel. Warm or not, I want the men dry; dig fire-pits, no big blazes."

"Sir!"

Raj turned back to M'lewis "—and leave them half-full. Fodder, for choice, hay, anything like that." He gave the map a last glance and stood, considering. Men with banners were forming up on the beach, a few hundred meters between each, calling—

"3rd Chongwe! 3rd Chongwe!"

"88th Seyval! 88th Seyval!"

Out of sight of his men for a moment, Raj rubbed his temples, his knuckles rapping against the rim of his helmet. The landing was a complete ratfuck. A thousand Squadron cavalry—the personal retainers of a single major landowner—could slash the force into bloody windrows at the edge of the surf.

How are we doing, Center? Raj thought bitterly.

better than expected, Center replied.

Raj stiffened in surprise; the machine voice sounded almost jovial.

if the enemy reacts perfectly, both in making a plan on the basis of statistically-insignificant intelligence and in execution of that plan, then they could successfully attack us tonight. in that case, i will begin to believe in a god myself. A pause, perhaps a heartbeat long. **theirs.**

More than half the 5th had already gathered around their standard; he came up to it himself just in time to see Gerrin Staenbridge wading up from the surf, sopping water from head to foot and sneezing.

"Evening, Raj," he said cheerfully. "Stepped out of the boat into a bloody sinkhole."

They slapped palms. "Glad to see you. As soon as the next wave of men and dogs are ashore, take the 5th inland to the ridge; Foley's setting up there. Dig in, and push out some patrols, men who won't fall over their feet in the dark.

M'lewis has supplies and wagons coming in; I want everyone who can to have a hot meal and at least a couple of hours' sleep. I'll send some infantry up, relieve you eventually. Staff meeting one hour before dawn."

"Got it," Staenbridge said. Then he looked beyond Raj's shoulder. "Ah, Messa Suzette. More radiant than ever," he said.

Raj turned; Suzette was in her riding clothes, linen and leather looking stained with salt

"You flatter, Gerrin."

"Not in the least," Staenbridge said; he smiled warmly and raised the extended hand to his lips for a brief moment. "Not being as blinded as most men by the exterior, I can see better within."

Some of the rest of the household came up behind her. Fatima first; the nurse and her son were back on the ship, until the beachhead was secure. She had a cork-insulated flask in her hands, and began pouring cups for Suzette and the Companions.

"Ahh, nectar," Raj said; it was hot black kave, sweet and with a dash of brandy. The Southern Territories were dry enough that even an early-summer night could be chilly, and there was a sea breeze.

Fatima handed cups to the others; Mekkle Thiddo came up, his boots sloshing, and passed his clipboard to Raj.

"Gerrin," she said, with a mock pout. "How come you kiss her hand and not mine?"

"Because, mother of my son, you are an imp and she is a very great lady. *Sahud!*" he finished, raising his cup.

"*Health*," they replied.

"Where's our good Administrator?" Raj went on, looking over the papers Thiddo had handed him. "Outstanding, Thiddo. All right, bivouac them. One company up to the ridge; Gerrin will assign the sectors."

A fleeting hardness went across Suzette's face as she shrugged and answered her husband. "Still puking his guts out on the flagship, while Admiral Ghardineri runs around looking at the sky and tearing out his hair," she said. Then she smiled and took a deep breath of the damp, chilly air. "It's much nicer here."

Raj threw back his head and laughed. The stars were very

clear through the gaps in the clouds. Suddenly he felt bright, almost transparent, at the cusp of a moment more rare than diamonds.

"A night landing in a high wind, on hostile soil, with a battle to fight tomorrow. Not enough sleep, or intelligence . . . maybe all the Squadron's hosts roaring down on us."

"Marriage to you is an education, darling."

"Perfect, sir."

"Couldn't ask for better."

"Hareem was so *boring* compare to this."

"You *can* throw a party, Whitehall, I'll say that for you."

They looked at one another, grinning, and touched fists in a pyramid.

"Well," Suzette went on, "Fatima and I will scare up those priests and Renunciates and get the infirmary open. There'll be enough broken legs and smashed hands from *that*," she said, nodding out to where yard-arms were being used to lower nets of supplies to men standing waist-deep in the surf.

"Men, ammunition, dogs, food, and medical supplies *in that order*, Captain," Raj said patiently. *You ruddy imbecile*, he thought. Patience was like a millstone that could crush out results if you gave it time. The young man looked harassed and bewildered and out of his depth, here under the curving stempost of the ship.

"Yessir. I see, sir."

I hope you do, Raj thought. "So that's why we have to push this ship off even though it's still partly loaded. The wheeled transport and tents can come ashore when we're more secure. See to it—"

A voice spoke at his elbow, more insistently when he made shooing motions. He turned; the torchlight was dim, but—

"Admiral Gharderini," he said resignedly.

"General, we must stop this—stop this unloading immediately!"

For a moment Raj stared at him, then looked up and down the crescent beach. Firelight provided more visibility now, but the operation was just getting into high gear. Soldiers with *guardia* armbands were getting most of the ordinary soldiers off the beach and to their unit bivouacs quickly enough, though that often meant pushing a way through the working parties carrying supplies up to the piles just above the highwater mark; stiff, grumpy dogs were led up out of the surf, their heads held high. A torch hissed as one stopped and shook himself in a spray like a salt thunderstorm. The dogs would have to be watered, and soon, or they would be very unhappy indeed. Unhappy five-hundred-kilo carnivores were bad news anywhere, and worse than that on a crowded sandspit in the dark with fifteen-thousand-odd men trying to find their unit assembly areas. There was a freshwater spring just under the ridge inland. . . .

"There is an onshore storm coming, I am *sure* of it," Gharderini said, making a hand-washing gesture. "I can *smell* it. We cannot let the fleet be caught on a lee shore! Embark the men—we can beat off the coast and sail right into the harbor at Port Murchison, they'll never suspect on a night like this, and the fleet will be safe behind the breakwaters."

For a moment Raj simply stared at the naval officer. When he took the smaller man by the elbow and steered him several steps into the darkness, it was more gently than he had first intended. Gharderini was afraid for his ships, not himself, and he was a competent seaman; he'd done a pretty good job of getting everything here. The problem was that he was focused on his own aspect of the task, not taking in the big picture—which was Raj's responsibility, sure enough. His responsibility to make it clear to Gharderini, without an open quarrel, which would be bad for the men, bad for morale.

"*Listen* to me, Messer Admiral," Raj said, facing the man. His hand was on the other's shoulder, his saber-hand, and he used willpower to prevent it dosing like a mechanical clamp through the Admiral's deltoid muscle. "That doesn't matter." Gharderini bleated. "The fleet is expendable; the troops are not. If worse comes to worst, beach your ships and get the crews ashore. We can fight as long as we have the soldiers and their dogs and rifles." *Although the Spirit knows I'd appreciate having my artillery ashore.* Dinnalsyn was moving mountains getting a temporary pier rigged, but it was man-killing work.

"Lose the *fleet?*" Gharderini said, with a tone much like that of a man just asked whether he would like to eat his children. "*Ground* the warships?" The steamers were much more heavily built than the transports, but grounding their rams in a surf would mean having them pounded to bits in short order.

"If necessary," Raj said. Then he thrust his face into the naval commander's. "Do—you—understand—me?"

Gharderini pulled himself free and stumbled clear.

It would have to do. *Damn, I wish I had time to get him on-side,* Raj thought. *Now, what was I doing before that damned interruption—*It was going to be a long night and a longer day.

"Who goes!"

Several of the men at the fire had started up. Two more walked out of the shadow, rifles leveled at the cloaked figure. Raj let the hood slip back, and the men halted, gaping.

"Suh!" the corporal said, springing erect.

"No need, not tonight, men," Raj said, walking forward into the light of the fire. The soldiers were infantry, he could tell from the blanket-roll packs some of them still had slung. He returned the noncom's salute. "Mind if I warm myself at your fire a little?" he said.

There were awkward murmurs; he sank into a crouch and warmed his hands at the coals glowing in the pit they had dug in the sand while they shuffled and sank back to the ground. He looked around the little encampment. Two sections, sixteen men; they'd laid out their shelter-halves as groundsheets, and stacked their rifles regulation-wise, in tripods with the helmets hanging off them like grotesque fruit. Down by the beach unloading went on, but more slowly; most of the men were ashore, and only some of the dogs and the heavier supplies waited for dawn. A pier of longboats covered with planking had been rigged, braced with cable, and a jib-boom crane was lowering a field piece onto the seaward edge of it. It swayed and dipped under the weight, but the waiting crews were running it forward as soon as the wheels touched wood, a sound like thunder over the loosely fastened planks.

There was a pot of bean soup bubbling on the fire, and a stack of flatbread laid out on somebody's blanket-roll next to a helmet full of small ripe apricots.

"Just stopped by to see you lads had what you needed," he said. "Water all right?"

From the lack of conversation before he walked in, they'd been sitting and worrying.

"Yes, suh," the corporal said. "Got a length o' sausage 'n summa ham fuh d'pot. 'N other stuff."

Raj took out a packet of cigarettes and handed them around. One of the soldiers broke his in half and tucked the other part behind his ear before lighting it.

"I really hope you paid for it all, too," Raj said. The troops nodded, although the older man who had broken his cigarette frowned slightly.

"Yas, Messer General, suh. Seems a might waste a' money, it do. Weuns doan' see much cash-money."

"Well, lads, think of it this way. The most of you were croppers, before you went to follow the drum, right?" They nodded, a circle of ox-eyed faces still struck with awe to see the general within arm's reach. "These farmers here, they're not our enemies. They're croppers too, only for heretics who don't worship the Spirit of Man of the Stars, as we do—and as the peasants here do, too. No, they have to pay tithe to the heretic church at peril of their souls, and hide their priests like rabbits. On top of all that, they don't need us to come and steal their pigs and chickens, do they? We're here to set them free, not afflict them."

The others nodded, although the old sweat looked a little skeptical. "We'll be fightin' tomorrah, then, suh?"

"Probably, fellow soldier. And the day after: but not tonight; you'll have time for a meal and some sleep. It was only the thought of the barbs attacking us when we came ashore that had me worried; but the Spirit was with us. That's why we have to act with justice, lads; the Spirit won't fight for an army that doesn't." More nods, round-eyed and solemn with agreement.

"Messer Raj, suh," one of the young soldiers said. "Kin Ah ask a question, suh?" At Raj's smile and nod, he plunged on. "It's muh ma, suh. Mah pa's dead, 'n if Ah was to die . . . she'd be hard put to it without mah guvmint-farm. She worries 'bout me sumthin' awful, she do."

Raj slipped his notebook out and jotted briefly. "Don't worry, lad . . . Private Dannal Huiterrez, isn't it? Spirit preserve you, but if you fall we'll see the campaign bonus and your share of any plunder gets sent to your family. I'll have a note sent her, by the way; it's a good son thinks of his mother, and she should know."

And I should know why the officers of the 88th Seyval Infantry haven't attended to that, he thought to himself. He sighed and stood, butting out the cigarette.

"Spirit of Man of the Stars with you, boys. Get your rest."

"Spirit bless ye, Messer Raj!" they chorused; there was a buzz of excited talk as he left. *Much better than brooding silence,* he thought.

The next campfire he stopped at was some distance away; a group of the 5th Descott. Some of them were cleaning rifles or putting a last edge on a saber or bayonet, or just leaning back against their saddles watching the chickens they had turning on an improvised spit over their fire. One man was strumming at a guitar:

> *"Listen to 'em callin'—callin' with all their might*
> *All a summer's evenin', and halfway through the*
>   *night—*
> *Donna—"*

The music broke off as he strode up; you needed a different approach with County men.

"Hello, dog-brothers," he hailed them. "Wouldn't happen to be wine in that water, would there?"

Mondain woke early, like any farm town; it had perhaps two thousand souls, almost all of them land workers. A gong was ringing from the little church of the Spirit of Man of This Earth; by far the minority congregation in the village, but by law the only one allowed to have bell or signal. Woodsmoke rose from chimneys, or through the smokeholes of houses too humble for that. Most of Mondain was narrow lanes partly cobbled and partly packed dirt, between houses of peeling whitewashed adobe. A few houses near the central well were more substantial, multiple rooms around small patios, although the exterior of the Star Spirit church was deliberately humble. Men rose yawning, to eat the morning gruel prepared by women who had been up for an hour or better. The smell of kave came from a few of the better-off households: the priest, a notary, the headman, and the single half-breed Able Hand who was the Squadron's only representative in town. Riper smells came from middens, compost heaps, and the honeybuckets of the night-soil collectors, taking their contents toward the gate and the farmers' fields that would receive it.

At the gate, grumbling fieldworkers waited for the militia guards to open the woven-lath doors, leaning on spade and hook and bill; the militiamen were freeholders or artisans, but the laborers had walking to do before their day's work on nearby estates. Beyond, the narrow dirt road wound away into the fields, dusty olives and figs near the village, with reaped wheat and barley beyond. A dozen or so carts were waiting to enter the village, high-wheeled and vividly painted, mostly loaded with alfalfa fodder for the town's few oxen. It was a brilliant early-summer morning, last night's unseasonable wind and cloud gone, still crisp but with a hint of the heat that would turn afternoon into a white blaze.

"'lo, Danyel," Aynton Mugirez said to the first farmer outside as he leaned against the midpoint of the gates to swing them open. "Spirit bless." He was corporal of town militia; no great honor, but it brought a little extra blacksmith's work his way, paid in hard coin.

The farmer mumbled nervously; from the loose hay behind him a rifle was poked firmly against the base of his spine. He chucked to the oxen and they walked forward with the stolid, swaying pace of their breed, the ungreased wooden axles protesting. Farmworkers crowded past, and the wheeled traffic within waited impatiently in side lanes. The militia leaned their backs against pounded rubble of the town wall, waiting for the second gong that would send them to home and bed, free for another month of the irksome duty barely worth the tax remission. Wagon followed wagon, until half were through the gate and curving down the lane. It was then that the militia corporal grew suspicious. The farmers driving the carts were *very* quiet; Mugirez's eyes widened, as he thought of the tricks bandits sometimes played.

The Squadron lords were supposed to scour bandits out of the hills and wild woods. Some attended to it, others ignored anything that did not threaten their rents. Some actively connived at outlaw gangs, as long as they raided a neighbor's estates: Most outlaws were of Squadron blood at that, broken men or ones who'd lost their lands. *Bandits*, Mugirez thought. Rape, fire, the best young people dragged off for foreign slave markets, the survivors starving without the seed corn and plow-beasts, and the rents for the masters would be abated not one *sentahvo*. He stepped toward the nearest wagon, raising his musket.

"Hoy!" he shouted. "Stop them—"

A figure catapulted from the hay. The militia corporal leveled his musket and pulled the trigger. *Whang*, and the other's rifle swept it aside; the ball thumped into hard-packed dirt. The blacksmith roared and tried to club his weapon, but the follow-through stroke drove the steel-shod butt into the side of his head with force enough to send him reeling back. It was only as he slid down the wall clutching his bleeding head that he noticed the men exploding out from the wagon-loads of fodder were dressed in uniforms—blue jackets and dark-red pants.

M'lewis held his aiming-point on the militia, grouped in a frozen tableau, half-rising from their resting positions. *Rick me fer an ijit volunteer*, he thought bitterly. *I had t'go 'n have ideas. Mother M'lewis didn't raise no volunteers.* . . .

"Drop it, drop it, *drop* it," he shouted. The words were comprehensible enough; Sponglish and Spanjol were closely related tongues, and many simple words were very similar. The leveled rifles spoke volumes more, and the taut grins of the dark hard-faced men behind them. "Nobody gets hurt if yer drop 'em!"

The muskets clattered to the ground; the soldier winced at the weapons' rough treatment, and one hammer did click home. The flint sparked against the frizzen, but the musket misfired. Shouting grew and died in the immediate area as the ones under the menace of the guns backed up against the nearest wall and froze. A murmur ran among them: *Gubernio Civil.* Civil Government, the fabled overlords their great-grandparents had known. Awe touched their faces, growing when the man beside M'lewis unfurled the blue-and-silver Star banner of Holy Federation. A few raised their hands in prayer or touched amulets.

Other Scout parties were on the wall elsewhere around

the town. M'lewis nodded at one of his men, who raised a small rocket on a stick and struck a match.

" . . . come to set you free," Raj concluded, hooking his thumbs through his belt. He was standing on the steps of the headman's house, the only stone structure in the village, and it gave him a good vantage.

The people of Mondain stood silently in the little plaza of their town; all of them, save for the sick and two-score This Earth heretics, under guard in their chapel. They were not that different from a crowd of central-province peons back home; dressed in unbleached cotton pants and shirts, holding their floppy straw hats respectfully at their chests. Women in blouses and skirts of the same fabrics; both sexes mainly barefoot, and smelling fairly strong. Taller and lighter-skinned than most in the east, although lives spent working under the sun could hide that. Very old legend spoke of migrations from different worlds—or countries, it was unclear which. *Tekhanos, Sonoras,* and *Pairhagway* back home; *Hargentin, Hespanya,* and *Hile* out here.

"No soldier will steal or kill," Raj went on, keeping it simple. His Spanjol was book-learned, and probably hard for these peasants to understand. "They will pay for everything they need, in good silver." That brought a stir, and an incredulous murmur. The concept of armed men paying for their food was strange. "If any causes harm, tell an officer, and the criminal will be punished. Let us pray to the Spirit of Man of the Stars."

He made a gesture with one hand, and the local Star priest came forward with the 5th Descott's chaplain beside him. They raised their staffs of office and began to chant a hymn, one of the most ancient of the Star faith; the peasants joined in, showing more enthusiasm than they had for the speech. Religion was something they understood very concretely, and they knew no public service had been held in their faith since the Squadron came. A few of the older villagers were in tears, weeping with joy as the soldiers joined in the song.

I hope tears of joy are the only ones I bring you, Raj thought. *But I sincerely doubt it.*

CHAPTER EIGHT

The army of the Civil Government was a moving city as it marched north along the coast road; a rippling pattern of human organization, transforming the landscape as it passed, like a weather-front. There was a shudder ahead of it, a froth of Squadron refugees lucky or canny enough to abandon everything but ready cash and spur their dogs toward Port Murchison. Many even of those met roving bands of Skinners and died, on the inland western flank. Next came the scouts, mounted and moving by half-squads at a steady wolf-trot, probing at gullies and woods, sniffing around the outskirts of Squadron manors and farms. Information flowed back to the main body, and the first most of the enemy knew of the army was the arrival of a raiding-column of cavalry. Dun clubs of smoke marked the spots of resistance, towering up into the hot cloudless sky; that and livestock, wagonloads of household goods, and the dwellers roped neck-and-neck as they moved back to the main column. Those willing to submit and swear allegiance to the Civil Government were left their lives and property, except for arms, riding dogs, and wagons. A third of their lands would be forfeit later, but that was for peacetime.

The main body moved like a hub at the center of those spokes, spokes carrying inward plunder and produce brought for sale by native peasants, outward scouts and well-paid emissaries promising good treatment for those who surrendered. The coast road ran north through rolling plain scarred by the odd gully, mostly wheat and barley stubble with the odd patch of woodland, orchard, or vineyard; most farmers lived behind walls in tight-packed villages. An observer waiting in the road would have seen lines through the heat-shimmer of late afternoon, first marked by pillars of dust.

Those became company columns of cavalry, spaced out at regular intervals a half-kilometer or so across the line of march; blue of uniforms, dun-brown of dogs, the long formations wiggling a little as the animals instinctively kept to the level. An occasional glitter marked them—the star at the point of a pennant, the brass guard of a saber—but mostly they were faded to the color of the earth they crossed. At a walking pace the feet of the dogs were only a muffled thudding scuff. Louder was a clatter of metal buckles on harness, the steady bang of scabbards on stirrup-irons, an occasional hoarse command. The men rode with an easy swaying slouch, but they were alert enough; the cavalry would deploy to screen the rest of the column if an attack came. More mounted units flanked the road on the vulnerable western side; everyone knew the Skinners were *supposed* to be out there somewhere, but nobody was going to stake their lives on it. Galloper-guns with eight-dog hitches followed, a three-gun battery to every five companies, ready to wheel about and form a firing line.

Behind the mounted men came the foot-soldiers, marching by battalions, eating the outriders' dust. They were grouped three battalions abreast, one on either side of the ditch and one on the road; ten thousand men would have stretched forever, lined up like beads on a string. Rifles on one shoulder, blanket-roll over the other, they moved with a swing born of short marches and good rations. Six hours into the day the drummer-boys had fallen into a common beat, and the ten battalions at the head of the column were singing:

> "*Sojer boy be full a' fight—sojer boy be randy:*
> *Mind the drumbeat—mind the step*
> *And with the girls be handy—*"

The command group followed them, in a dust-cloud still more dense; behind shambled the mass of the wheeled transport and camp followers. More guns, dogs panting wearily; the heavy mortars on their ox-drawn carriages; wagons with tools and tents and ammunition and provender; herds of cattle and sheep and bleating goats; several small, heavily guarded carts carrying iron-strapped chests of coin and high-value plunder . . . And the army's civilians: Priest-doctors and Renunciate nun medicos in their ambulance-clinics, cavalry troopers' servants afoot, officers' valets, sutlers, the loot-fences and slave-traders who followed war the way the vultures did, girls picked up in the days since the landing, enlisted men's wives smuggled aboard the transports against all regulations, the odd officer's lady on her palfrey. The mounted guards who chivvied them on had standing orders that anyone who couldn't keep up was to be kicked out of the line and left. That was no problem with most who had followed the drum before, but all too many straggled and sprawled and chattered, as chaotic as the livestock and harder to manage. Then the remainder of the infantry—four thousand men—and behind them the cavalry screen.

"They're shaping well," Raj said critically, lowering his binoculars.

Then he looked around; he and his trumpeters and bannermen and messengers were on a slight rise half a kilometer to the east of the road. Men in the red-striped blue trousers of the artillery were laying out a camp with pegs and rope; five hundred meters to a side, with diamond-shaped bastions at each corner, and a regular gridiron of streets within centered on an open square. Spots were allocated for each unit, for the dog-lines, for the infirmary and the knockdown shrines that housed the battalion standards, for the camp-followers and the wagon park and the latrines. There was a little stream nearby, still flowing, that would do for water; woodlots stood conveniently near, but not close enough to give an enemy shelter.

"This is a nice little piece of work, too," Raj went on. He mopped his face with the orange, red, and black checkered bandanna of the 5th and opened his canteen. Any Civil Government officer was supposed to be able to do basic surveying and lay out fieldworks, but the artillery did it better, no doubt of that. "Water?"

"Thanks, sir," the artillery major said, lighting a cigarette. "We've all had four days' practice. Not that it's a forced march, either."

Raj grinned at the hint and looked at his watch: 1600 hours. "I have my reasons," he said. Center painted a map across his sight, distances and times. Six kilometers a day since they landed. They were only a day and a half from Port Murchison.... "It's an excellent regulation that the army has to entrench every night on hostile ground; they used to say barbarians were more easily defeated by seeing us go into camp than by fighting us. I intend to see it's strictly enforced.

"Trumpeter," he went on. "Sound *attention.*"

Everyone was expecting it; the column fell silent except for the jackdaw-chatter of the civilians and one tapping drum per battalion. The avalanche sound of thousands of bootheels slamming down echoed across deserted countryside.

"Sound *general halt.*"

A more complex rhythm: ta-*ra*-ta-*ra*-ta-rarara-*ta-ra*, twice repeated. Unit trumpets sounded to relay it, and shouted commands for smaller groups. The halt began at the rear of the column, the only way to prevent people running into the heels of the men ahead; it rippled down the long line of humans, dogs, and vehicles like a wave through a pond. A second ripple as the infantry units called *slope arms* and *stand at the easy;* multiple rattle of hands on iron and wood, then the thudding of butt-plates on dirt or gravel. There was a slow-motion traffic pileup among the transport and camp-followers, but that was to be expected.

"And *fall out to quarters,* if you please."

What followed was almost as complex as a dance, along a front of nearly two thousand meters. The cavalry screens closed in to group by battalions and then stood to in three directions around the campsite, acting as an outer guard. The infantry battalions marched off the road at a trot with their rifles at the trail, and swung into the campsite by the notional gates in each string-marked wall. Standardbearers and officers trotted down the streets to their assigned sectors. The men halted, dispersed to drop most of their gear on their squad plots, then three-quarters of them formed up stripped to the waist, with only rifle, bayonet, and bandolier. Each company hurried at the same jog-trot to its assigned sector of wall; by the time it arrived, wagons had dropped offloads of shovels, picks, and baskets.

Raj looked at his watch: 1620, and the first spadefuls of earth were flying. In another ten minutes nine thousand men would be working; hours before sunset there would be a ditch two meters deep and precisely two meters wide around the entire camp. Inside that would be a steep-sided embankment the height of a tall man: working parties of camp followers were being shepherded to the nearest patches of wood—for fuel, and for the stakes that would be rammed into the top of the mound and woven together with brush. Guns went by below, headed out to the bastions; emplaced there, they could shoot outward, or rake any side of the square with enfilading fire. Hammers sounded on tent-pegs all across the camp; a more musical sound cut in, cavalrymen driving in the metal rods that anchored the picket-lines of dogs for the night. A file of them went by, trotting behind a single handler and standing in a well-trained row while he snapped their bridle-chains to the wire cable stretched between the steel posts.

Latrines, fire-pits, field kitchens, water-barrels at set intervals . . .

"That reminds me," Raj said. "Da Cruz, no drinking the water from the stream, or barrels until they've been blessed." The priests used a ritual with a short prayer and a sprinkling of chlorine powder.

The senior noncom nodded. "If ye order, ser," he said.

Raj half-turned in the saddle. "Meaning I wasn't always so superstitious, Top?" He shrugged. "Let's say a little voice told me it'd be a good idea. Haven't had many down with the squirts, have we?"

Diarrhea was no joke in an army: it killed. More men than bullets, when you took them into an area with strange food and uncertain water, even if it didn't bother the locals.

"No, ser." He saluted and wheeled off. Dinnalsyn flicked away the butt of his cigarette and chuckled.

"They didn't call you the King of Spades, either, a while ago—but I'm not objecting," he said. "I remember Sandoral—if there's one thing worse than sitting in a hole while someone shells you, it's not *having* a hole when someone shells you. Ah, our brothers in arms."

The battalion commanders were riding up, some of them with a few of their subordinates. Dalhouse looked to have brought all his company commanders and most of the Lieutenants. The Cuirassiers had a little polished ceremonial breastplate on their tunics, a reminder of the time when they had worn back-and-breast armor. To Raj it had always seemed a curious habit in a combat zone—rather like hanging a *shoot me here* sign on your chest—but Dalhouse swore by the tradition. His crony Hingenio Buthelezi of the 1st Gaur Rangers was with him.

The officers reined in and saluted; Raj answered it and leaned forward with both hands on his pommel.

"Excellent work, Messers," he said. "We'll have sunset service at 1900, reveille at 0600, then, if I give the order—there may be a change of plans depending on fresh intelligence—we'll demolish the camp"—there was no point in leaving a usable fortress right behind them—"and make another day's march."

"Sir." Dalhouse made the word a half-insult; but then, his voice usually seemed to have that tone of throttled impatience, a *you fool* to all the world. The tips of his mustache were still waxed, and they quivered as he flung an arm northward. "Do you intend to stop and camp with four hours of daylight remaining?"

Raj let his eyes rest on the thousands of men entrenching the army, then looked back to Dalhouse.

"Yes, Messer Major, that's more or less my intention." Somebody coughed to hide a chuckle.

"Sir, we're moving like a collection of old women on washday! Every barbarian in two hundred kilometers will know we're here; they're already stripping their estates of stock and goods before we get there."

"Well, Major Dalhouse . . ." Raj went on, with a slight smile, pausing to light a cigarette. *Who I would strip of his command and bust back to East Residence if I could,* he thought wistfully. Far too influential for that, worse luck.

The match went *scritch* between thumb and forefinger. " . . . this isn't a razziah or a slave-raid, you know. It's a campaign of conquest."

"How are we supposed to bloody conquer them if we *don't fight* the sons of whores? We spend all our time digging dirt like peons. You—" He reconsidered. "We're giving them time to concentrate."

Raj looked behind Dalhouse at his junior officers.

tell them, Center said, **as i told you. some of them will listen and learn.**

As I listened and finally learned, Raj thought dryly. *After arguing for a swift thrust at Port Murchison, because I'm so afraid of crawling along, waiting to be hit with everything the Squadron has....*

"Exactly, Major," Raj went on aloud. "Exactly. My actions are quite precisely calculated to *make* them fight; at a time and place and in a manner of *my* choosing, not theirs. I'm giving them enough time to mobilize some of their strength, and not enough to gather all of it. Making them come to us in bite-sized chunks, as it were.

"You see," he went on, making a spare gesture with the hand that held the cigarette; it trailed a curve of blue smoke. "We of the Civil Government have the most disciplined army in the world; apart from the Colony, the only disciplined army on earth."

bellevue, said Center.

"The strength of that discipline is that it provides for a series of set contingencies of battle, but no drill can cover *all* the possibilities. So it behooves us to avoid the ones that aren't provided for, does it not? Our army is a battlefield army; all its weapons and its training are for set-piece battles in open country, where volley-fire and formation count. Its great weaknesses are close-quarter ambush and night attack; you may note, Major, that I'm carefully avoiding the possibility of either."

He indicated the pillar of smoke that marked a Squadron farm in the middle distance.

"By advancing slowly on their capital and scorching the earth, we accomplish three things. Some of their chiefs will surrender, to spare their estates. Others will try to pressure their Admiral into a premature attack on us, also to spare their estates—and he can't afford to alienate too many of them. This is the richest land in the Southern Territories; the most influential nobles own it. And thirdly, we make the *Admiral* fear native uprising and a siege of Port Murchison—not that I intend to besiege it. The fortifications aren't modern, but we don't have a siege train—and sure as a tax-farmer grafts, if we sat down to siege we'd get a visit from Corporal Forbus."

Cholera morbus; a few of the men winced. A close-packed camp in hot weather was an invitation to it.

observe said Center:

—and rows of men lay on pallets soaked in feces. They shook, and their faces had the fallen-in look of famine victims. Flies crawled over them in sheets; Raj saw one man too weak to blink as they walked over his eyeballs, although his chest still rose and fell. Renunciates in soiled white jumpsuits and overrobes went down the rows, trying to make the victims drink; water mixed with sugar and salt was the only thing that did cholera victims any good, that and the careful nursing that they could not give so many—

—and Raj watched from a mound as the armies closed in on both sides of a fortified siege-camp; the Squadron host from landward, a huge mass of men and metal that surged in disorderly dots from horizon to horizon, the whole land-levy of the enemy. On the other side stood the walls of Port Murchison, old-fashioned curtain and tower built but cored in concrete and faced with huge granite blocks, immune to the pecking of his fieldpieces. The gates opened, and out poured another army itself larger than his, the garrison of the town and Commodore Curtis Auburn back from Stern Island with the elite of the barbarian armies, moving to some sort of coordinated command. Viewpoint-Raj looked down. The parapets were thinly manned, units at half-strength or less. As he watched one man collapsed, knees too weak to hold up his weight even leaning against the firing ledge, and nobody moved to aid him . . . .

probability of serious epidemic 80% ±, 6%, Center said, **probability of city surrendering to siege before return of Stern Island force 6% ± 2%. probability of decisive results from siege operations, too low to calculate meaningfully.**

Raj blinked back to awareness, shocked as always at how little time had passed. Dalhouse was talking:

"—so how do we know the garrison *will* come out? Or that the Admiral will attack before he's reunited his forces?"

"Two reasons, besides the ones I've listed," Raj said, holding up his fist. He raised a finger. "First, because the Squadron are barbarians, who think like children—like thirteen-year-old boys, really. Honor demands they attack at once; glory and fame to those in the forefront, eternal shame to the laggard; they'll overthrow the Admiral if he doesn't lead them to battle, and he knows it. They haven't had any real wars to temper it with common sense lately, either. Second." He raised another finger. "What time of year is it, Major?"

Dalhouse blinked bewilderment. Raj swung an arm to indicate the harvested fields.

"Wheat and barley and beans, Major, a holy trinity like the Christo's. All cut, and carted to the villages, and stacked—hence easy to burn—but not threshed or bagged, and certainly not carried into Port Murchison. I doubt they have a year's reserve on hand, either."

The officers nodded unconsciously; even absentee landlords who visited their estates only to hunt, collect rents, and lay the odd peon girl knew that threshing grain was the longest task in the farm calendar; not time-pressured like harvesting, either. A well-thatched stack would keep the grain safe for half a year, rain or no, so you threshed it a bit at a time, as the other demands of the land allowed. A few of the best-managed estates near East Residence had simple ox-powered threshing machines—more of an affectation than anything, with labor so cheap—but such would be unknown here. They had all seen signs of neglect on the march, old irrigation channels allowed to silt, fields left to grow back in ruddy native scrub. Yet the Southern Territories still exported grain in most years, apart from the odd dearth or famine such as any area suffered, so reserves must be low.

"So," Raj finished gently, "it's easy to support a *moving* army—there *was* a reason for attacking this time of year, Major—but even the Squadron leaders aren't going to cram fifty or sixty thousand people and thirty thousand dogs into a city living on what's left of last year's yield. Not when they think their mighty warriors can crush our little band; after all, they won last time, didn't they?"

Dalhouse was silent for a moment. "Sir—what if you're wrong?"

"This isn't a safe profession, you know. If I'm wrong, we all die. And now, Messers, I think we should attend to the men."

❖ ❖ ❖

"Spirit, Raj, you could have fired a locomotive by sticking Messer Bloody Dalhouse in the boiler and letting the steam coming out of his ears do the work," Kaltin Gruder said.

A guffaw ran around the table in the command tent. All the Companions were there, and Ehwardo Poplanich—it suddenly occurred to Raj that he might be sliding into that category too. *Poor bastard.* They were sitting Colonist-style on cushions around a wicker table; a sauroid somebody's men had shot was the centerpiece, a local biped grazer about man-size, with a head like a sheep and a feathered ruff around its neck. It had been baked in a temporary earth-oven with strips of bacon over the back, and the crackling skin had covered succulent flaky white meat, ranging to brown on the haunches. Bowls of new potatoes swimming in butter flanked it, with fresh piles of fresh flatbread and olives and a salad of greens; the main course had been reduced to hacked remnants, and they were all leaning back with fruit and cheese and another glass of the local wine. The whole army was living well, from plundered storehouses, or what they bought from the peasants with plundered goods. The main supply problem was keeping the men from getting their hands on too much booze, which they *would* drink if they could.

It's a bloody military picnic, so far, Raj thought. None of the Companions expected it to last, of course . . . but there was no use borrowing grief beforehand when you knew it was coming down the pike. M'lewis seemed mostly concerned about his table manners at a Messer-class gathering, fairly futile since most of the others were resting their boots on the table or spearing bits out of bowls with their daggers.

Gruder, M'lewis, and Tejan M'brust had brought along the girls Reggiri had given them. Joni, Mitchi, and Karli, of Stalwart stock captured young; they all spoke Sponglish and had been given a social education. Fatima was there as well. She and Barton were throwing clandestine peach-pits at each other across a recumbent and indulgent-looking Staenbridge. It reminded Raj that young Foley was still a little shy of eighteen. It also reminded him that Suzette was not there; she was dining with Berg and his cronies. Berg's feathers had come unruffled since Stern Isle; Berg was seeing less of Dalhouse, and Dalhouse and Berg together had far too much pull at Court . . .

To the Starless Dark with it.

"Come on, Mekkle," he said to the young Descotter; Mekkle Thiddo was silent, looking at an opened locket. His wife of one year was back in the County, pregnant according to the latest letter, that having been suspected but uncertain when he left. "You're the honeymooner—give us *Road to Santanerr.*" Ehwardo looked a little alarmed; that was a very old tune in the Civil Government's army, and officially strictly forbidden. Then he shrugged.

"*Hole*, Mekkle—start us off!" he yelled, leaning back and loosening his collar.

Well, at least here Ehwardo gets to relax without looking under the rug for Barholm's spies, Raj acknowledged. Even if the life-expectancy of Companions was not very good.

"*Hadelande, dhude!*" Gerrin called. *Go for it, youngster!* He reclined sultanic on a pile of the cushions, with a head on each shoulder.

Thiddo grinned and ducked a half-eaten apricot. "On your own heads—and eardrums," he said, and threw back his head to sing in a strong young baritone:

"*When I left home for Lola's sake—*
By the Army road to Santanerr
She vowed her heart was mine to take
With me and my sword to Santanerr
Till our banners flew from Santanerr—
And I've tramped the desert—and Sandoral
And the Diva's banks where the snow-flakes fall
As white as the smile of Lola—
As cold as the heart of Lola!
And I've lost the desert, and Sandoral,
And I've lost home and worst of all,
I've lost Lola!"

From his place at the head of the table Raj could see down to the west gate of the camp, and north along the coast road. From the edge of sight northward a shuttered lantern blinked. That was where the main cavalry picket guarded the approach from the north; from Port Murchison, among other places. *Party—escort—embassy—truce flag,* he read. The gate acknowledged: *Proceed.* Two lights glowed, bobbing as the embassy rode southward with a squad of the cavalry to guard them. It was probably some Squadron noble looking to save his skin. Amazing how these pirates turned meek when the devastation showed up on their own doorsteps. Old Admiral Geyser Ricks, the conqueror of the Southern Territories, must be spinning in his marble-and-gold mausoleum.

They all joined in:

> "*When you go by the Cantina Bellica*
> *As thousands have travelled before,*
> *Remember the Luck of the Soldier*
> *Who never saw home any more!*
> *Oh, dear was the lover who kissed him*
> *And dear was the mother that bore;*
> *But then they found his sword in the heather,*
> *And he never saw home any more!*"

The torches reached the gate, and paused for challenge and response. They spurred up the long shallow incline, up the main cross-avenue of the camp to the open space before the commander's tent. Raj raised an eyebrow; they were cantering at least. Something must have impressed them, and Civil Government regular cavalry were generally not easily impressed by barbs. The troopers pacing guard outside the open tent door were fighting back grins; the song everyone inside was roaring out was a flogging offense, officially—and the next verse was the reason. No Governor liked it, especially the ones who shot their way onto the Chair:

> "*When you go by the Cantina Bellica*
> *from the City to Sandoral,*
> *Remember the Luck of the Soldier*
> *Who rose to be master of all!*
> *He carried the rifle and saber,*
> *He stood his watch and rode tall,*
> *Till the Army hailed him Governor*
> *And he rose to be master of all!*"

A jingling and flash of bright metal in the square; he could see the dark forms of the Regulars around the jewel and gold brightwork of the barbarians. The officer of the guard ducked into the tent and bent to talk to Muzzaf Kerpatik. Raj raised his glass in an ironic toast; he had given the Komarite the job of compiling a list of Squadron notables. He had done it with smooth efficiency, drawing on his commercial contacts; right now he looked more interested in staring sideways at Joni, M'lewis's new concubine. She was leaning back on one elbow in a way that did interesting things with the front of her sheer linen blouse. . . . *Duty calls,* he thought

The voices rose to a bellow:

> *"It's twenty-five marches to Payso*
> *It's forty-five more to Ayaire*
> *And the end may be death in the heather*
> *Or life on the Governor's Chair*
> *But whether the Army obeys us,*
> *Or we serve as some sauroid's fare*
> *I'd rather be Lola's lover*
> *Than sit on the Governor's Chair!"*

Muzzaf came back in; his face was like a bucket of cold water amid the shouts of laughter. He bent down to whisper into the commander's ear, and Raj came erect like an uncoiling spring. Silence spread outward. "Messers, I think we'd better bid the ladies goodnight," he said.

"You're Ludwig Bellamy?" Raj said in Spanjol.

The barbarian noble stepped forward: He was young, no more than twenty, taller by a hand than the general's 190 centimeters, broad-shouldered and handsome in a thin-nosed blond way: His hair was in braids tied at the right, and the back of his head shaved in the old Squadron style, but he had only the beginnings of a beard. The retainers behind him were scarred men in their thirties, looking naked without the flintlocks and long swords. The younger man's empty scabbards and belts looked to be worth the price of a thousand Merino sheep, and the fringed leather jacket was sewn with platinum sequins.

"*Ci, heneral-hefe Whitehall,*" he said in excellent court Sponglish: *Yes, Supreme General Whitehall.* "*Ludwig Bellamy este, mi, elto spreyt d'Karl Bellamy, ho esten gran Capetain do sojadas marihenos en afilo d' Ahmiral Rick, Ispirito Persona dondi fahor on el*": I am Ludwig Bellamy, oldest son of Karl Bellamy, who is Senior Captain of Marines, descended of Admiral Rick, upon whom be the blessings of the Spirit of Man.

Ludwig licked his lips; his eyes did not dart to the shadowed figures of the Civil Government soldiers around them. "Perhaps, Messer General, this is not the place?"

Raj smiled grimly, left hand resting on the hilt of his saber. This place would do quite well, with the light from the tent behind him casting his shadow over young Bellamy's face. Raj would be a featureless silhouette, with all the ordered sleeping power of the encampment behind him. *Karl Bellamy*, he thought. About fifth from the top in the Squadron hierarchy, fantastically rich, personal lord of thousands of armed Squadron vassals and tens of thousands of native peons, warships, merchantmen, mines, slaves, herds . . . and father of only two legitimate sons, by Muzzaf's account. This one matched the description in the files, down to the crooked left finger that had healed wrong after being broken in a hunting accident.

"This will do quite well," he said. He carefully refrained from offering refreshment, which would make the noble feel he had the quasi-sacred status of a guest. "I take it your father—if you are who you say—wishes to make obeisance to the Civil Government of Holy Federation?"

Ludwig paled. "That is, Messer General—Your Excellency—we were given to understand—"

"—that those who surrender unconditionally will have their lives and most of their estates spared," Raj completed. "In a word, yes. But loyalty must be *proved*, and proved in person. I won't treat with an emissary. Let him come himself."

The Squadron noble closed his eyes for a second, gathering strength. "Messer General, you must understand . . . these things take time—"

"If he hasn't surrendered by the time we reach him, his life and lands are forfeit," Raj interrupted brutally. "We have a saying in the Civil Government: *time to crap or get off the pot.*"

A sigh and a nod. "Yes, of course. Messer Whitehall, my father—you see, if there is any suspicion by the usurper Admiral . . . Well, my father waits at a manor not three kilometers from here. He has with him only a dozen of his most faithful guards; come with as many men as you like, Messer Whitehall. We have more than submission to offer. We have vital information, most vital to the progress of your campaign."

Raj stood for a moment, his eyes probing the other man while his mind raced. *This is Bellamy's land we're on . . .* and Bellamy would know a great deal of his monarch's plans; the Squadron mobilized for war by sending a summons to the chief nobles, who called out their followers in turn.

"Get our guest a cup of wine!" he called. Bellamy's shoulders slumped a little in unconscious relief; the veterans behind him kept the same silent cornered-carnosauroid tenseness. "I'm afraid we can't offer more, since we'll be returning immediately."

He turned on his heel and walked back to the open flap of the tent.

"M'lewis," he rapped out. "Turn out your dog-thieves; I have some scouting for you. Gerrin, I want the 5th by the west gate in battle order in fifteen minutes, if you please. The rest of you—Companions, I suggest you get some sleep; I'll be back in a couple of hours—battalion commanders' meeting at 0300. Then there are likely to be happenings tomorrow."

A wolfish growl swirled past him, to where the barbarians waited under the Descotter guns.

"Ser."

Raj looked down, slightly startled. M'lewis had appeared out of nowhere, at the entrance to the Bellamy *kasgrane*'s gardens; his face was blackened, but the gold teeth shone. It was dark under the high stone arch, but . . .

"All safe, ser, me men's in place. Nobbut a dozen a' th' barbs, loik they said, even th' slaves've run er been sent off. Coulda took them's dogs 'n siller too, easy-loik."

"Good man. Come along."

M'lewis whistled softly, a hissing note like a night-flying dactosauroid; his dog walked out of the underbrush with its reins in its teeth and dropped them at his feet. He vaulted easily into the saddle and fell in as they spurred back into a lope. Glancing back brought only a gleam of eyes under the faint light of half-full Miniluna, a dark mass rising and falling as the battalion swept down the long curving drive. Gravel crunched under paws; the soft warm night was full of the smells of eucalyptus from the bluegums along the road, of warm dog and powdered rock and fading spring flowers.

Karl Bellamy was waiting on the portico of his manor, under a lantern that showed him and his retainers standing with no arms but their swords. It was an old building, far older than the Squadron conquest, mellow marble and tile. A tall fountain stood before the steps, a marble maiden reaching for a globe that danced on her fingertips. One foot was missing, and a well had been sunk through the stone pavement beside the basin. Hitching posts showed that it was a watering trough for visitors' dogs, now. Raj beat down a rush of irrational anger and flung up one hand. *Van-dals*, he thought.

The command party reined their dogs and the animals sank back on their haunches, breaking in a spurt of gravel and dust that billowed to the front steps of the portico. Behind them the 5th split both ways and peeled into a single two-deep line of men and guns, wet dog-fangs catching the lantern as the animals panted.

"Captain Staenbridge, secure the area," Raj said, swinging down. Behind him boots clattered on stone as the flanking companies deployed on foot; the banner-men and trumpeter stayed mounted, the long poles and silk-fringed cloth swaying overhead.

The Squadron men saluted in their manner, right fist to breast and then straight out; Raj tucked his helmet under one arm and inclined his head very slightly.

"Captain Karl Bellamy?" he said.

"I am the Bellamy," the Squadron leader said, in a slow deep voice that seemed to rumble from his chest; the Sponglish was much more accented than his son's, but understandable. His gray-shot beard reached nearly to his waist; the kettle belly beneath it only added to the aura of gross strength about the man.

"Brigadier General Raj Ammenda Halgern da Luis Whitehall," Raj said.

"This is my son Benter." A younger version of his brother Ludwig, staring at the dark foreign faces with a boy's delight in wonders. "Be welcome on my land; drink the guest-draught with me and be peace-holy."

Bellamy took up an heirloom drinking cup, priceless ancient plastic cradled in modern silver filigree; his sons drank first, a solid mouthful each, before their father. Some of the wine spilled into his beard; he wiped his mouth on one paw and offered the guest-draught. Raj drank in his turn, moderately—there was still a quarter of a liter, excellent red wine—and handed the rest to Gerrin. *Let all my officers be peace-holy and none of us drunk,* he thought ironically. Still, by all accounts most Squadron members actually put some store in this sort of thing. With a Stalwart, say, you knew an oath was the time to look out for the hidden knife; *their* favorite sport was fratricide.

Bellamy blinked solemn pouched eyes, sad as a hound's in their nests of cheek-beard and bushy eyebrow.

"We must speak," he said. None of the retainers objected aloud when a squad and Gerrin Staenbridge accompanied the two leaders, or when another squad sealed off the door behind them. Bellamy led the way through shadowed corridors of faded magnificence and gaudy splendor to a small room. He glanced at Staenbridge.

"This man is my kinsman and right arm," Raj said. True enough: They *were* fourth cousins or something of that sort. Every gentry family in the County was related somehow, just as every one had a vendetta or two if you went back far enough.

Bellamy nodded slowly. "I will not snipe with words," he said. "Admiral Auburn is no friend of mine. The Bellamys were kin to old Admiral Tonbridge. *He* would not have sent our best men away when war threatened!"

Actually, he was an even bigger idiot than the present one, Raj thought. Also the old Admiral's mother had been a very minor relation of the previous Gubernatorial family in East Residence, sent to the *barbaricum* as a maiden sacrifice to the gods of diplomacy. Many Squadron nobles had thought him too influenced by his mother, and suspected—quite rightly—that he leaned to the Spirit of Man of the Stars. The change of dynasties was one of the official *causi belli*, not that it mattered. A bit ironic coming from the equally usurping Cleretts . . . .

"The Auburns are usurpers," Raj nodded. "The Spirit will not favor a usurper in war."

"You promise—" Bellamy began, stroking his beard. "You promise those who swear to you keep their lands?"

"Yes," Raj said firmly. "Minus one-third for the Civil Government." Bellamy winced, but it was better than losing everything and being sold to the mines. "Just as I promise oblivion for those who resist. The Civil Government would rather have you as loyal subjects—we can use your fighting men, for one thing—but if I have to grind you into dog meat to pacify these Territories, I will do it."

Bellamy's thick-fingered hands twisted at each other, and sweat broke out on his ridged forehead.

"So you say, Messer General. Yet you will not be king here—will the next Vice Governor abide by your word?"

A good question. Once the Civil Government was firmly in charge, a reversal of policy would be nearly impossible to resist.

"Probably. I'm privy to Governor Barholm's War Council, and the policy is to conciliate where possible. We want to rule stable and productive lands, not put down rebellions every other year. And the Southern Territories are a long way from East Residence . . . I'll not mince words; you'll find our taxes hard—Spirit knows, most of *us* do—and we'll probably see that a lot of your young men see military service elsewhere, on the Colonial frontier, for example; but that's not altogether bad. We don't hold a gentleman's origins against him in the Army"—much—"and your sons, for example, could go far as officers. Perhaps on my staff . . . .

"The rest of you will be disarmed, at least at first. In return you'll get stable government, peace, and prosperity."

Bellamy leaned forward. "These are good words. But what of your Church? What of the Viral Cleansers?"

Raj winced slightly. "Well, that *is* something of a problem—especially given the way you've treated members of *our* faith.

Certainly the church properties will have to be restored. I can only say that my policy will be tolerance, and the civil administrator appointed to follow me thinks likewise. As long as you don't try to proselytize or worship in public . . . Not one in a hundred of the people here is a This Earth follower, anyway. Those who want to rise in the Army or at Court will have to embrace orthodoxy, of course."

Bellamy hunched back in his chair, covering his eyes with one hand; after a moment Raj was startled to see silent tears trickling down into the bushy beard.

"*I must preserve my sons' heritage,*" he whispered hoarsely in his own language. "*I cannot destroy the Bellamy line for Auburn's folly. . . .*"

Suddenly his face froze in Raj's sight; lines and patterns moved across it. The mottled image hung imposed over the living man, then jumped toward the general in silent leaps. Arrows sprang out around it, indicating the pupils and the pattern of coloration.

stress analysis indicates subject bellamy is sincere, Center said, **probability 96% ± 2%.**

"You speak honestly, like an honorable man. I will swear," Bellamy said. "Fetch my sons! They too will swear to you!" He rose and then fell to his knees.

Raj stood and awkwardly took the noble's hands between his, stumbling through the ritual of allegiance; this was *not* the time to explain the difference between swearing loyalty to an individual and to the State. *All the same, it's lucky nobody but Gerrin is here. Put the wrong way, this could be sticky back in East Residence.* Ceremony complete, Bellamy went over to a desk whose grace and sauroid-ivory inlays were incongruous beside his bulk. When he turned there was a sheaf of papers in his hands.

"Admiral Auburn has summoned the war host," the Squadron commander said, all business and flat impersonal tones now. "He attacks tomorrow, thus—"

"So the city garrison, under Commodore Conner Auburn, the Admiral's youngest brother, will sortie south down the coast road. Twelve thousand men, give or take a thousand."

Raj looked up, across the circle of officers grouped around the map table, under the swaying lantern. It was 0330; some of them were bleary-eyed, others gulping kave or gnawing on bannocks. There was sand under his eyelids as well, and sleep was a distant memory of childhood. Seventy thousand men were in motion, barbarian and Civil Government, like huge ponderous pieces of machinery in a big steam engine. His mind felt like that too, like machined shapes of iron and brass whirring and camming in oiled precision; everything was bright-edged and clear.

"They're expecting to hit us around noon—which means they're probably leaving Port Murchison around now. Conner Auburn's a hothead even by Squadron standards, so I expect the ones on the best dogs to arrive first and the rest to straggle. Major Staenbridge, I'm sending you with the 5th and the 7th"—the 5th was overstrength, so that meant fourteen hundred men, and very good ones—"and two batteries, six guns, to meet him around—" His finger stabbed down on the coast road about halfway to Port Murchison. "—here. Get there early; otherwise I leave the details to your discretion, but don't get out of reach or let them flank you. Bloody their noses and fall back on the base here if they press you—fire and movement."

"Understood, sir." Gerrin rotated his shoulders, frowning at the map and unconsciously flexing the heavy muscles like a plowman looking at the field and preparing for a day's job of work.

"The next element of the enemy's plan," Raj went on, "is a diversionary attack by two thousand picked cavalry—some of Admiral Auburn's household troops—coming in from our west and planning to hit us around 1000 hours and make us face front west while the other forces approach from north and south. I've sent the Scout Group of the 5th to get their exact position, and Master Sergeant da Cruz to get the Skinners moving to block them."

Raj's finger moved south until it was below the Expeditionary Force's original landing site, then moved north parallel to the line of march but farther from the coast.

"Admiral Auburn has been sweeping up from Sefex"—the southernmost city on the Territories' east coast—"calling out the home-levy of the Squadron, plus anyone who's managed to get out of our way and run southwest. He has the remainder of his household guards, fifteen hundred men, and whatever he's been able to rally: at least thirty thousand, perhaps forty." *Or possibly more; they're likely to answer the call whole-hearted, with us here burning and killing.*

There were grunts around the table; Raj's expression might have been called a smile, by someone who did not look too closely.

"They'll have all the unit coordination of a street brawl after a racetrack meet—but don't forget. They're fighting on the doorsteps of their homes, for their families and Church and the graves of their fathers.

"There are only two real routes of approach from the south for a force that size"—which could not get far from potable water, for one thing—"here and here. Major Zahpata, you'll take your battalion, the 1st Gaur Rangers, and the 3rd Chongwe Dragoons with one battery, and push down this route."

Haldolfo Zahpata of the 18th Komar Borderers nodded, stroking his pointed black beard. He was a leathery middle-aged professional, experienced but not ambitious, and middling gentry at home. Buthelezi of the 1st Gaur was a crony of Dalhouse's, but he wouldn't give Zahpata trouble.

"Major Thiddo, you'll take your Slashers, the 21st Novy Haifa Dragoons, the 17th Hemmar Valley Cuirassiers, and likewise one battery." Putting Dalhouse under Thiddo was a calculated risk; the man was insanely birth-proud, and senior to boot. On the other hand, putting Poplanich in charge of that column was out of the question; nobody with any ambition, of which Dalhouse had more than his share, was going to associate with a Poplanich. *I can accompany that column in person,* Raj thought

"Both of you: Your mission is to fix the front of Admiral Auburn's column and force it to deploy—which, knowing the Squadron, will take quite some time. Move forward fast, but do *not* allow yourselves to be drawn into a melee. Remember, you have four times the range of their weapons and five times the rate of fire; put one battalion up on point, and keep the other two and the guns on overwatch from defensible terrain every time you move forward. When you make contact, have your lead battalion gall them with long-range fire. When they charge, fall back on your base-of-fire and give them volley fire and shrapnel until they start to envelop you. Then fall back and repeat the process. The column which hears the other engage first will ride to the sound of the guns and repeat the process; draw them back on the camp, but as slowly as possible.

"Colonel Menyez, you will be in charge of the camp and the infantry," Raj went on. Menyez nodded, wiping his nose on a handkerchief in his perpetual allergy problem. "Keep them standing to arms; light combat load, hardtack, water, and double ammunition, but man the walls and stand ready to support either cavalry force if it's driven in, or to move forward." Only a couple of the infantry units were really steady enough to face cavalry in the open. "Major Poplanich, you will act as central cavalry reserve at my or Colonel Menyez's discretion." At that, Ehwardo could be relied on to work with an infantry officer without complaint; not something to be assumed with many of the others.

"Major Staenbridge will move immediately; the cavalry columns at dawn, when the camp beats to arms. And if that's all, Messers, I suggest those of us who can get some rest and the remainder attend to business. It's going to be a long day."

The meeting broke up quickly; nobody was in a mood for chitchat. Raj stood by the outer post of the tent; the two Descotter battalions were outside, filling the square as the men sat beside their crouching dogs.

"Keep them in play while you can," Raj said to Gruder and Staenbridge. "I'm giving you all I can spare because I'd really rather fight one battle at a time, if I could."

Gerrin nodded, slapping his fist into his palm to tighten the gloves. "City militia and sailors on dogback," he said, "apart from Conner and his house-men."

Kaltin grinned. "Mebbe we'uns kin do summat fer ye, loik, ser," he drawled in broad County dialect

They all slapped fists together, and Raj watched them walk out to their commands with envy. *Damn, but I'd like to have just one job of manageable size,* he thought as he watched.

"Mount!"

The troops swung into the saddle; forward file-closers in

each company carried lighted torches of bundled oilwood sticks, so that the formations could keep position in a fast night march.

Gerrin Staenbridge stood in the stirrups and pitched his voice to carry:

"Right, lads, it's time to earn our pay and show the enemy what County men are made of. These barbs make a lot of noise and look a sight, but they'll go back faster than they come forward after they meet us. Just remember to mind the orders and aim low." His right fist shot skyward and then chopped down to the front. "To Hell or plunder, dog-brothers—walk-march, *trot.*"

Suzette came up behind Raj, sliding her hand through the crook of his elbow as they watched the streaming fires pour down to the gate and turn north on the coast road; the moons were both down, and there was only the rippling frosted light of the stars to show them against the white dirt of the track. Her voice was a murmur at his shoulder.

"You should sleep, my darling," she said. "A little while, at least."

He put an arm around her waist. "Can't," he sighed. "Too wired—hell, too much kave."

"Come." She pulled him gently toward the rear of the tent. "I can make you sleep. Come with me, my love."

"Raj. Raj, wake up."

"*Huh.*" Raj sat upright with a jolt, out of dreams of fear and flight. It was still hard dark; Suzette was there in her wrap, touching his shoulder. He slid the pistol back under the pillow and swung his feet to the floor, scrubbing his face with his hands, then splashing water over it from the basin and running fingers through his hair. Right now his brain felt muzzy, worse than if he had not slept at all, but he would be better for the rest in a little while.

"It's da Cruz," Suzette said quietly.

Swift and skillful, one of the servants was laying out fresh kit: trousers, boots, underclothes, belt, ammunition pouches, slide rule, mapcase, binoculars. And another mug of kave with a cup of goat's milk. *Spirit,* he thought, swigging them down in alternate gulps. *If the Azanians ever cut off our supply of kave beans, the Army high command is doomed.*

"He's wounded," she went on. "Not seriously. It was the Skinners, not the enemy."

Scramento, he thought, grunting. "There goes the western flank." And a three-battalion force of the Admiral's death-sworn household guards getting ready to fall on him out of nowhere, too.

"Don't worry," he said, laying a hand on her cheek for an instant. "Just the usual desperate emergency."

Da Cruz was swearing as Raj dipped a shoulder through the doorflap into the outer room of the tent, fastening the collar of his tunic and knotting the red-and-black checked bandanna. The noncom was on a stool, bare to the waist while a Renunciate medico in jumpsuit and robe worked on a long superficial cut on his forearm. The coal-oil lamp showed the stocky torso and knotted arms laced with scar tissue; knife, sword, bullet, and shrapnel had all left their marks, and it looked as if someone had once tried to write their name on the Master Sergeant's stomach with a hot iron, getting as far as the second letter before trailing off.

Now he had a new wound, a long shallow slash along the outside of the arm from wrist to elbow. The nun swabbed it out with iodine, washed the arm with blessed water, and began building a substantial bandage with linen and gauze.

"Spirit's holy static, careful with that, Sister!" he said.

"Watch your language," she snapped back. "No hope of getting you to rest it?" She clicked her tongue. "Boys. Well, try and keep it clean."

"What happened, Top?" Raj said.

Some of it was obvious from da Cruz's uniform tunic, thrown on the floor. The left arm was blood-soaked and slit— it had taken a *very* sharp blade to do that—and one of the tails had been cut off as an improvised bandage. A Skinner *patcha* knife, Raj judged, the arm-long type they kept as general-purpose chopping tool. It had been originally designed to cut firewood and hack through the massive bones of grazing sauroids; but the Skinners were nothing if not versatile.

"It's them Skinners, Messer Raj," da Cruz said. He took the water-jug a servant offered and drank, Adam's apple bobbing. Wounds made a man thirsty, and he looked to have lost some blood. "Theyun er five klicks outa position, an' boozin' summat fierce in a Squadron *kasgrane*. Tole 'em to git movin'—git this fer my pains, ser. Lucky to 'scape wit' me life."

"Joy," Raj said.

Think. This is your job, think. The Squadron battle plan was a monstrosity, even before it was compromised; it depended on things going right and precise coordination between what were little better than armed mobs. The two thousand out west were the only enemy force that was really mobile, and the only one that was all full-time professional fighters—not really soldiers, but they would have *some* idea of what they were doing.

"The Skinners won't listen to anyone else, and they're the only force in reach," he said, mostly to himself. "The Forty Thieves have the line of march pegged"—that bunch of guardhouse rejects and throat-cutters really *could* do reconnaissance now that M'lewis had put the fear of the Spirit into them—"but only the Skinners can intercept them."

Unless he committed his only reserve battalion of regular cavalry . . . but the roll call of battles won by the last man to commit his reserves stretched back beyond recorded history. *Here's where I start cursing sending Kaltin and Gerrin both,* he thought. Then: *It was the right decision. We can't have them catching us like a* pinyata *between two sticks.*

"Suzette?" he called. She came through the curtain in her riding costume, holding the Colonial repeater carbine and thumbing a last round into the tube magazine through the gate above the lever. "Sorry, darling—you're staying behind this time. Officer of the guard!"

"Get me Colonel Menyez." Cavalry snobbery be damned; Menyez would have to hold the fort, and send the two columns south. Poplanich would be his second . . . *and if I'm ever in a position to do it, we're going to have a regular table of ranks and establish permanent brigades,* he decided. Damn the political risks. *We need formations that are used to working together.*

CHAPTER NINE

Four men are just right for this, Raj thought.
Not a squadron of Poplanich's to clank and clatter in the night, though they were shaping to be good battlefield soldiers. Just himself and da Cruz and two of the Scouts, for quiet work in the dark. One was a cousin of M'lewis's, a little rat-faced man everyone called Cut-Nose, because most of his had been removed with something sharp; the other was a silent hulking brute called Talker from the northeast border of Descott, on the mountainous fringe of Asuaria County. The battalion rolls listed their former occupations as vakaro and sauroid hunter; offhand, he judged Cut-Nose for a sheep-stealer. Talker had the eyes of someone who just liked to kill—people by preference, though sauroids would do at a pinch. If either had come calling back home he'd have had the vakaros whip them off, or hang them for the County's peace. Both rode with an easy slouching seat, reins knotted on their pommels and eyes never still; their rifles they cradled in their arms, and both weapons had rawhide sleeves shrunk onto the forestocks.

And Spirit, but it's good to be doing something myself *for a change,* he thought.
It was very quiet in the hour before dawn, somehow blacker than deep night. Dew beaded the dogs' coats to the breast as they pushed through a rustling cornfield, chill on the soaked cloth of trouser-legs. Their way led through the last of the coastal plain, foothills heavy with fruit-orchards

where springs welled up at the foot of the escarpment. Water rippled in stone-lined ditches beside the road.

Da Cruz reined in beside the general. "'Tis thissaway, ser," he said quietly, nodding at a rutted cart-track that led up the face of the limestone ridge that loomed at a sixty-degree angle on their west.

"This way's quicker."

The holographic map hovered over his vision at every turning, and beneath it he picked out the trail better than his eyesight could have done; somehow Center looked through the darkness even though It had only his vision to use. He remembered the visions It had shown him, of the floating *satellites* that had been Its eyes before the Fall. *They* could have looked through absolute darkness or deepest cloud. . . . Not for the first time, he wondered how an angel came to be condemned to the cislunar sphere of Fallen corruption.

The hillsides ran upward in steep scree-clad illex and whipthorn, then leveled off into a plateau; once a herd of wild grazing sauroids fled in honking, hissing confusion and a little later a wild boar held the way against them for an instant.

One of the troopers hissed a little through his teeth at the commander's certainty, and Raj smiled silently to himself. "That way," he said, cutting his palm over the fields.

There are advantages to having a legend, he thought.

"Cowards!"

Raj let his voice roar out over the patio, as the dogs picked their way in among the broken glass and rubble of the Squadron manor's courtyard. Horace stepped delicately over a Skinner facedown in a pool of vomit, and up the steps, not even looking aside when two Skinner hounds growled and raised their hackles at him. A human leg was hanging by a cord around its ankle from the wrought-iron balcony above the main entrance; judging from the bits and pieces scattered around, they'd hung whoever it was off alive and then used him for target practice until the body fell apart.

"You cowards hide like old women!" Raj shouted again. "Your ancestors die again with shame to see you run from battle!"

Roars and grunts answered him as troll-figures stirred amid the doors and shrubberies. A squat shape appeared on the balcony and jumped down, long gun over one shoulder.

"Eh, sojer-man! Neck-stretcher!" The banter was less friendly than usual. "What you want, eh? *Tu peti lahpan hilai kouri ahvent nus coup,* you little rabbit, run away before we get skin—mebbe we skin you now, eh?"

"I want you to *fight,* Juluk," Raj said, leaning over. "Or is killing farmers and drinking all Skinners can do?"

The chief grunted. "No Squadron men here—all run away," he said a little defensively.

Raj lifted one hand from the pommel of the saddle to point behind and to the left, southwest. "There are two thousand Squadron troops there, moving fast to the east—no more than three kilometers away. I ask you again, Shef Juluk Peypan—will you fight, or just sit here drinking while better men do battle?"

The Skinner chief grunted again and leaned on his long rifle, making a motion with one hand. Three of his men leaped to dogback and pounded out of the courtyard; others were moving about, readying gear and kicking their dogs to wakefulness. Then they gathered around the little group of Descotters, staring with the steady hungry gaze feral dogs gave guard-hounds. Barely half an hour passed before the scouts returned, shouting in Paytoiz. An exultant yell went up from the assembled warriors, and a deafening chorus of howls from their hounds. Juluk had been standing with a hunter's patience, both hands on the rifle and one foot crooked behind the opposite knee; now he straightened and unhooked a flask from his belt.

"Today we doan' skin you, sojer-man," he said, holding it up.

Raj took the ceremonial drink, fighting not to cough.

Gah. Juluk had really done him honor; not looted wine or brandy but *arak,* the date gin spiked with red pepper and gunpowder that was the Skinners' own favorite drink.

"I'll piss out this sauroid-gall on your grave," he replied politely. "Now, can you keep the Squadron troops off my men's flank, while we fight our battle?"

"*Hoya-hey!*" The chieftain laughed, and the others joined him in a barking chorus. "Six hundred Real Men against only two tens of hundreds of long-hairs?" he chortled, using the Skinner's slang term for any of the western barbarians of the Military Governments. "We chew their bones! We kill them all, take their dogs and cattle and guns, fuck their women, burn their houses! *Hoya-hey,* it is a good day to die!"

He pulled at one long drooping mustache, leering up at the Civil Government commander. "You come with us, kill long-hairs?" he said. "You got balls enough to fight like Real Man, sojer-boy?"

Raj looked up at the eastern horizon; the sky was paling slightly behind the distant mountains. *On the other hand, I can kiss goodbye to any chance of controlling these wild men if I don't,* he thought.

"Can you girls fight like me?" he said.

Juluk swung onto his hound. *"Fray hums!"* he shouted, shaking his rifle in the air. *"Hoya-hey,* it is a good day to die! Let's go fight!"

Yipping and howling, they poured out of the gate at his heels. Raj and his men heeled their dogs into the same loping stride.

"When we make contact, I'll send you back with the news," Raj said to the senior noncom. They swerved apart a little to avoid a cork-oak tree in the middle of a pasture, then set their mounts at a thorn-hedge beyond, leaning forward into the saddle. Their dogs soared, *wurfing* slightly and lashing their tails to match the pack-excitement of the Skinners' dogs.

"No ser," da Cruz said in the same stolid tone, as they landed and continued stirrup to stirrup.

Raj looked around at him in surprise. Da Cruz was a long-service man, only two years short of the thirty-five maximum, steady to a fault. He'd bought Casanegri Farm from Squire Dorton back in the County on his last leave, the property he'd thought to retire to as yeoman-tenant. Bought it free and clear and stocked it well, with the prize-money and plunder from the campaign against the Colony, and married a sensible woman of middling years who was managing it until he returned. That had been his private dream, to be a well-respected yeoman freeholder with a good farm.

"Didn't figure you for a fire-eater, Top," he said with deceptive mildness.

"Ser," da Cruz replied; the slick surface of the massive scars on his face caught at the starlight. "Them barbs run me off. Not goin' ter let them see me turn tail again, beggin' yer pardon. Nor leave yer wit' nothin' but those two at yer back."

He jerked a thumb over one shoulder at the two Scout troopers. Raj looked behind him; the two soldiers were a half-dozen meters back. Cut-Nose looked nervously alert as they rode to battle, but Talker . . . his face was still basalt-still, but there was the edge of a smile in his eyes.

"I take your point," he said.

"Gittem, Gittem!"

The Squadron battle cry sounded over the dry valley. It would have been difficult for Raj to estimate their numbers, if he had not known; they came in clots and bunches, each under the flag of some chief of note and his principal henchmen. They paused as they topped the low ridge and saw the Skinners ambling toward them on the opposite slope, grouping together into larger clumps. Then the clumps slid down into the valley, gathering speed. They howled, shaking their swords or muskets in the air, and they glittered in the dawn sun with metal and jewelry. Raj drew his pistol and pulled back the hammer; from the looks of it they would keep corning right to close quarters.

It was three thousand meters from one side of the valley to the other; reaped wheatfields flanked it, but the slopes were too rocky to be tilled. Even the dusty-gray olive trees that spotted it were few and straggly, although the remnants of tumbled stone terraces hinted that cultivation had been more intensive once. The morning sun cast broad shadows from every tree, every low native brush, throwing a blushing pink shade that seemed to foreshadow the blood to come. It was almost a relief to have only himself to fear for, at the beginning of an action; the dry tightness of his stomach and the brittle clarity of sight were less terrible than the knowledge of thousands of other lives dependent on him making the right decisions.

Juluk Peypan knocked the dottle out of his pipe and

shouted. Men began sliding out of the saddle in the long loose line of the Skinner warband, scores of them. Their dogs dropped flat, and the warriors stuck the iron butt-spikes of their shooting sticks into the ground. The rest continued on their way at a brisk walk, holding their weapons across their laps with an ease that belied the ponderous weight of iron and brass and wood.

CRACK. The first 15mm rifle spoke, in a long gout of flame and puff of off-white smoke. A Squadron officer dropped fifteen hundred meters away, next to the main banner. Raj leveled his binoculars in time to see the round take off the skull at eye height and the man's head splash away from the lead.

"*GITTEM, GITTEM!*"

This time a full two thousand throats roared it out, and the whole Squadron host rocked into a gallop, big men on long-limbed dogs pounding through a fresh-raised cloud of dust. More of the huge sauroid-killer guns spoke, and when the dismounted Skinners fired, a man died at every shot. More than died—the thumb-sized bullets ripped off limbs, drove fist-width holes through men's bodies, and splashed their comrades with blood and bone-chips and pulverized flesh. Dead men were torn out of the saddle, and when the bullets struck dogs the big Ridgebacks and Banzenjis went spinning head over heels as if struck by invisible sledgehammers in the hands of giants. The Skinners around Raj hooted and giggled at the sight, grinning and jostling each other like little boys on an outing.

When the Squadron charge reached six hundred meters every Skinner opened fire from the saddle. The noise was stunning, loud as artillery, and a dense bank of smoke hid the front for a moment.

Spirit of Man, Raj swore to himself as the brisk wind tore it away.

The whole great block of Squadron warriors seemed to shudder in mid-step; it was like watching a sandbank eroding under a high-pressure hose. Where two or three in the front rank went down together, the men behind had to leap their dogs over the head-high obstacle or collide and join the writhing tons of man and dogflesh. War cries and the bellowing of dogs on the attack were suddenly swamped by screams of human and canine agony. The Skinners were not quite so accurate firing from the back of a moving dog, but with a massed target, even rounds that missed their first mark often went home. Yet the Squadron men kept the charge coming for a full hundred meters more.

One dismounted giant came forward at a lumbering run, whirling his long sword over his head. A Skinner thumped heels to his dog and rode out to meet him. The first shot smashed the steel out of his hands, sending it pinwheeling end-over-end into the sky in a blurring circle. The Squadron fighter stood stock-still for an instant, looking incredulously at his numb and ringing hands, then leveled the big blunderbuss slung over his back, fumbling with the hammers. Laughing, the Skinner went down on the opposite side of his dog, holding the pommel of the saddle with one foot. Lead balls hummed through the space where he had been, and he bounced back to his seat as if pulled by rubber bands. Then he was at arm's length; something bright flashed as he rode by, and the Squadrone toppled like a felled tree, a sheet of blood running from his throat beneath hairy clutching hands. The Skinner swooped far over and came erect waving a string of silver medallions the dead Squadron warrior had been wearing around his neck, whooping as he rode back.

Spirit, withdraw for the Spirit's sake, Raj thought; but the Squadron men had more courage than sense, it seemed— or perhaps just no command structure to tell them to get out. Instead they were dismounting and going to cover behind dead dogs or rocks or olive trees and bushes, trying to return fire. Skinners darted forward in twos and threes, sometimes firing point-blank; he saw many lope up and spring out of the saddle with knives in both hands, screeching like a powered saw going through rock. But at close range the shotgun blasts of lead balls from the Squadron smoothbores were taking effect. A Skinner ahead of Raj took one such in the face and slumped backward off his dog, his head a mass of red meat and shattered yellow bone. The others ambled on, the good cheer in their voices undiminished, their long guns bellowing with the regularity of triphammers.

Those Squadron barbarians could be good soldiers if they

had training and decent weapons, he thought. This was a victory, of sorts, but it offended his sense of workmanship to see first-rate material wasted.

The advance continued at a brisk walk; Skinners were dismounting to loot the hundreds of Squadron corpses and to slit throats. A few were taking heads or scalps, ignoring the men firing at them from less than a hundred meters away. At this range the 15mm bullets blasted right through tree trunks to kill the men behind them. . . . Raj heard the sharper crack of Armory rifles from his rear and glanced over a shoulder; Cut-Nose and Talker were firing from the saddle. Ahead a Squadronite slumped down and lay draped across the low branch of the olive tree. Another leaped up from behind a low stone terrace-wall and turned to run. Talker fired again and the barbarian seemed to leap forward with a red splotch on the leather between his shoulderblades.

Smoke hung over the battlefield like a drifting pall, heavy with the scent of burnt sulfur. A third warrior rose from behind the rocks, leveling his musket. They were close now, close enough to see the pockmarks on the man's face, the polished bronze scales sewn to his leather jacket . . . and for both barrels to be circles, tunnels to hell. The battle had been curiously detached until then, but now Raj felt a raw stab of scrotum-tightening personal fear. He leveled the revolver and fired. The big weapon kicked in his grip, and he let the weight bring the muzzle back down onto the target. Da Cruz was firing beside him; bullets pocked the stone around the kneeling man. The hammers of his flintlock snapped forward. There was a dreamlike slowness to it, a flash of sparks as the flints struck the steel, a puff of smoke from the firing pan, then a world-waiting pause until the gun fired, a jet of sullen red flame and smoke.

TUUNNNgggggg. A slapping blow snapped Raj's head around, throwing him back against the cantle of his saddle, and the chinstrap of his helmet broke. Savage pain lanced down his neck as the vertebrae grated together. Blood spurted from his nose. *Whack,* and something icy-hot coursed the length of his forearm. A second later two Armory rifles barked behind him and the Squadrone flipped backward, the blunderbuss arching from his outflung hands. Raj reeled in the saddle and forced himself erect; his helmet fell off and he grabbed it by reflex with his free hand, almost dropping it again as the metal bit at his palm. A gouge of bright steel and smeared lead showed across one side of the black enamel, where the bullet had struck glancingly. His arm was untouched, but the sleeve of his uniform tunic floated open almost to the elbow, cut as neatly as though with shears.

"Hunnh."

It was da Cruz. He was slumped over the pommel of his saddle, clutching at his belly; then his eyes rolled back in his head and blood came out of his mouth and nose. Raj reached for his shoulder, but he fell with a boneless finality that told its own story. His dog bent itself in a circle, trying to support the body with its muzzle, then sniffing frantically at the dead man. It flattened to the ground an arm's length away, whimpering.

"Oh, bloody hell," Raj whispered. Da Cruz had been a County man of the old school, and a first-rate professional . . . *and he should have died at home on his own land, among his sons.* "The bullet doesn't care if you're ready," he repeated to himself, the ancient Army motto.

It had taken only a few seconds for da Cruz to die, but when Raj looked up the battle was over. *Such as it was,* he thought. The only living Squadron men visible were lashing their dogs into a gallop, or stirring weakly on the ground.

Juluk reined in beside the Civil Government commander; he laughed uproariously at the sight of the bullet-grooved helmet in Raj's hand.

"Mebbe you wheetigo, maybe you one big devil!" he said. "Eh, you want prisoner, man to sell, man to ransom?"

"No," Raj said softly. "Kill them all. No prisoners. And when you're finished, head east—that's where the fighting will be."

He leaned down and closed the dead man's eyes. "You!" he barked. Cut-Nose was rifling the Squadron dead, but Talker showed more interest in those still alive. A neck parted with a wet crunch as the big mountaineer wrenched a head around to look back between its shoulder-blades.

"Ser!" Cut-Nose said, saluting with one hand and stuffing a pouch under the tail of his tunic.

"Trooper, bury this man—a cairn. Then rejoin Lieutenant M'lewis; he's to rendezvous with me at the camp or on the trail there." He caught the hideous little man's eye. "*Understood?*"

Cut-Nose went slightly gray under his natural brown. "Yisser!"

"Ah, suh, tank Spirit yuh here!" the sergeant cried. The infantry picket of the 17th brought their rifles up to salute with a snap.

Raj swung up a hand; the Forty Thieves reined in behind him. He stood in the stirrups and closed his eyes for an instant; yes, firing to the north. Heavy firing, volley fire by Armory rifles. Staenbridge and Gruder were engaged, something more than two or three kilometers up the road toward Port Murchison. The sun was over the eastern horizon now, 0930 hours; but the cavalry were still standing beside their resting dogs, command banners beside the main west gate, nearest the road. A murmur ran through the blocks of men as he and the Scouts plunged past them toward the gate, gravel spurting from beneath their dogs' paws.

"What the Starless Hells of Darkness is going on here!" Raj roared, pulling Horace up on his haunches before Menyez's banner. "I ordered the columns out!"

Most of the battalion commanders were grouped around a map table; he could tell from the set of their shoulders that they had been arguing. Now they were bracing to. Most of them had the grace to look a little shamefaced, or carefully blank. Dalhouse's face was still dark with rage, and Suzette—*what in hell is she doing here?*—Suzette's hands were clenched on the stock of her Colonist carbine until white moons showed beneath the nails. Her eyes closed and her lips moved in prayer as she saw him; thanks, he supposed. Even young Ludwig Bellamy was there, skulking around the edges of the gathering.

"Colonel Menyez!" he snapped, swinging down to the ground. He checked a half-pace as he saw the others' eyes on him, on the blood and dust smeared across his face and the bullet-rip in his sleeve, the lead-splashed helmet.

"Sir," Menyez said. "Sir, the flanking force?"

Raj made a chopping gesture of dismissal. "Dead. Slaughtered to a man." Somebody offered him a canteen, and he rinsed his mouth and spat. The news was spreading in whispers out from the circle of officers, and cheering broke out from the infantry units for a moment.

"I'm waiting, Messer," Raj went on, dangerously quiet.

Menyez met his eyes squarely, hands folded behind his back. "Disputes arose, sir, over the best course to take, with you out of communication. Major Dalhouse felt that as senior officer he should lead the column assigned to Major Thiddo; Major Buthelezi concurred. Several officers were of the opinion that the force should be kept intact to go to your rescue; Messa Whitehall also forcefully expressed that view. Sir."

Raj stood silent for a moment. Suzette went white around the mouth under his stare.

"My lady Whitehall," he said softly. "Please stand aside for the moment; this is not your place." He made a signal behind him with one hand; the twenty Scout troopers dismounted and formed up behind him. Two swift steps brought him in front of Dalhouse, and he took the waxed mustaches in thumb and forefinger of each hand. The move was swift and utterly unexpected; Dalhouse rose on tiptoe as Raj jerked his hands up toward his face. That left their noses almost touching.

"You refused an order to advance in the face of the enemy, Dalhouse," Raj said. His voice was metallic. "For which the penalty is *death.*"

He released the smaller man. "And I'll have you shot here and now if you question an order again."

Dalhouse took a step back, his hand not quite touching his saber. He cast a quick glance from side to side. Mekkle Thiddo was smiling with relief, no surprise in Raj Whitehall's crony . . . but so was Hadolfo Zahpata of the 18th Komar, who was a professional's professional. And Hingenio Buthelezi was keeping his face to the front and carefully neutral. Dalhouse looked beyond Raj for a moment, and met the eyes of a hulking Scout trooper. The trooper started to smile.

He swallowed and made a stiff salute. "As you command, General."

"Exactly," Raj said. He turned ninety degrees on one heel. "Colonel Menyez, all of you, I am not pleased. This is supposed to be a civilized army, under discipline, not a barbarian warband."

He gave a brief nod, dismissing the matter for the moment. "Now. Major Poplanich, you'll accompany me with Poplanich's Own. Colonel Menyez, I want the highest possible state of alert on the part of the infantry. Majors Thiddo and Zahpata, you have your instructions; move your columns out. In the event of your being driven in on the base, you'll be under Colonel Menyez's orders until I return. And, gentlemen, I expect effective coordination." He looked around, found the white robes of a priest. "Reverend Father, the three-minute battle prayer, if you please."

"*Spirit of Man, Spirit of the Stars, make us strong for battle in Thy name—*"

PAMM. PAMM. PAMM.

The sound was muffled in the distance as the battalion column of Poplanich's Own jogged forward. A rattle of shots echoed it, like very loud and slightly blurred rifle shots stuttering one after the other. A faint tinge of sulfur drifted down the wind; so did flocks of winged creatures, skipping from tree to tree and falling again to disappear in the wheat stubble on the rolling fields—skin-winged dactosauroids mostly, and the toothy-mouthed feathered types that were almost birds but could only glide, and behind them true birds of Earth descent.

"What's that, my lord?" Ludwig Bellamy asked nervously, nodding forward at the noise. He was riding to Raj's left, near where Suzette sat her palfrey with the butt of her carbine on one hip. The Squadron turncoat had his sword, but no firearm.

"Cannon," Raj said absently, frowning over the map in his hand. They were nearly to where Staenbridge had planned to set up. Whatever had happened, it was not the slow retreat they anticipated. "Field guns and volley fire." There was a burbling chorus of dull pops behind the crisp sound of the Armory rifles; *that* was Squadron smoothbores, but there was no need to point it out.

Ehwardo Poplanich lowered his binoculars. "I'd say rifle

fire from about four, five companies," he said. "Not in any great hurry, either."

A whistle sounded from ahead, and a Scout came pounding back along the rutted, potholed gravel road. Sunlight flicked across him in bars between the roadside trees as he pulled up.

"Barbs, dead, ser," he said, raising a gloved hand to his helmet-brim. "Looks like some action."

The road rose slightly to an almost imperceptible ridge, marked in the fields to either side by a low fieldstone wall. Metal glinted amid the stubble along the near side of it, thin brass cartridge cases for the Civil Government breechloaders. The column topped the rise, and Raj flung up his hand. Behind him the trumpet sang, *walk-march—walk,* and then *halt.* Ahead lay a windrow of bodies, men and dogs lying in layers on the road and spilling off to either side. He counted about a score of men and as many dogs; it always looked like more, when they lay like this. Every man and beast bore multiple wounds, with exit-holes the size of fists where the hollow-point 11mm rounds had punched out. Enough blood had followed to make mud of the dusty surface of the road; the musky stink of it was already growing under the warm sun, and flies swarmed. Dozens more corpses scattered the fields to either side, and the road for a half-thousand meters back.

"Walked right into it," Poplanich said absently.

"That they—" Raj began; he was interrupted by Bellamy, who had spurred closer to the main clump of bodies with a handkerchief held to his face.

"*Gawdammit!*" the young noble swore in Namerique. "*Eh bi gawdammit!*" He wheeled his mount, pointing at a richly-dressed corpse. The dead man's face was undamaged, a jowly pug countenance with brown muttonchop whiskers. Ludwig stuttered, then forced himself back into Sponglish:

"That's Conner—Conner Auburn, the Admiral's brother, the Grand Captain of Port Murchison. He's *dead.*"

Ehwardo's mouth shaped a silent whistle. "Very," he said.

Raj rapped his knuckles on the pommel of the saddle; Suzette met his eyes with a quirk of raised eyebrow.

"We may find that convenient," he said, and turned to the Scout trooper. "Arnez—take the head and bag it."

✧   ✧   ✧

"They ran," Ludwig Bellamy said, with something halfway between anger and shame in his voice. "They all ran."

He looked depressed. The Squadron bodies littering the road merely looked dead, as if they had been caught and time-frozen in a dozen different postures. Most were lying facedown here, where the pursuit had caught them as they galloped their dogs back down toward Port Murchison much faster than they had marched south. Few of the bodies were of dogs; it had been saber-work here, and the barbarian bodies lay tumbled with great black sprays of blood where the blades had left them. Cuts across the neck were most common; half-severed limbs, and multiple slash-wounds to the shoulders and arms where they had tried to turn in the saddle and defend themselves.

"Not all of them," Raj said, rising in his stirrups.

They passed through a stretch of fig trees, and on the other side there was a windrow of bodies a hundred meters or so out into the open ground—several hundred of them, some deployed out into the fields. Dactosauroids and gulls were busy crawling over the bodies and squabbling for dainties, and packs of little knee-high carnosauroids burrowing their fanged heads into the soft parts of the bodies. There were plenty of dogs here, caught by case-shot and shrapnel by the tattered look of them.

"Well, Spirit eat their eyes," Ehwardo said. "You thinking what I am?" The road stretched twisting ahead of them, sparsely lined with trees and rising and falling over hills and small valleys. The noise and smoke were closer, now.

"I can hardly believe it," Raj murmured. "They came down the road straggling any old way—hardly two or three hundred of them together in a single bunch. Conner right out ahead like a point-man. Gerrin just deployed, shot them to ribbons, stayed in line abreast across the axis of the road as he advanced. Chased the survivors into the next lot, then repeated the process. Is repeating it."

"Ser!"

Two of the Scouts were waving from fifty meters farther down the road. The officers spurred over, to find a wounded Descotter propped up against a roadside gumtree with his dog standing at stiff-hackled guard. The man had the shoulder-flashes of the 5th, his rifle by his side and a wadded red-soaked bandage around one thigh; a stocky young man of medium height, face gray-brown and sweating, but grinning at the Scouts.

"*Bwenya dai* to ye, dog-brothers," he said. "Got sum-mat ter drink? Mine's empty." He swigged at the offered canteen. "Ahh, good." One of them jostled his leg slightly as he reached for it again. "*Son of a bitch!*" The dog barred its teeth and growled. "Down, Jaimy, down."

"Trooper Hesus M'Kallum, isn't it?" Raj said, drawing up.

"*Ci*, seyor," the soldier said, sketching a salute.

"Report, soldier."

The man seemed a little light-headed with pain, and he laughed until the jiggling moved his leg.

"*Scramento!* Sorry, Messa. Ser, it warn't nobbut a sauroid-shoot. Them barbs, they come alang loik 't was they were ridin' groomsmen ter a weddin', right at dawn, loik. T'Major, he jist sings out *volley fire,* an' then we starts gobblin' em loik a dog eatin' a snake headfirst, all alang t'road. Chase 'em till they clumps up, then out a' the saddle and shootin' by platoons an' up comes t'field guns. Not hardly no casualties fer us, 'cept I didn't check an' one were shammin'. Major Staenbridge, he says ter tell ye he 'spects they kin keep goin' right ter the gates a' Port Murchison, ser. Ser, happen ye have some brandy, loik?"

Suzette touched her toe to Harbie's foreleg and the dog crouched; she walked over to the wounded man carrying a pouch from the saddle and knelt at his side.

"Brandy isn't what you need, soldier," she said. The man stiffened and closed his eyes as she slit the field-dressing with a small razor-edged knife and examined the torn flesh carefully, maintaining pressure with a pad of gauze. "Did you use the blessed powder?"

"Yis, m'lady," he gritted. "Hurt summat." Iodine did that.

"It will probably save your leg," she said; the man slumped slightly in relief. "The bone's broken, but it's a clean fracture and the hamstring's not cut. I can feel the ball—close to the surface, right here." She taped a new cover over a fresh bandage. "There'll be an ambulance cart along to take you to the Sisters soon enough, and you'll be fit for duty in six months. Take some of this. Not too much; we don't want you passing out."

"Ye're an angel, m'lady," the man said fervently. "Spirit bless ye an' Messer Raj too!"

The officers looked at each other. "Doesn't really seem to be much for us to do here," Poplanich said mildly, then broke into a broad grin. His hand shooed away some of the swarming flies; the cries of the scavengers, hissing and shrieking, were raucous in the background.

Raj smiled back, for the first time since he returned to camp. "And we're likely to be needed back south," he said. *Gerrin's finished off twelve thousand of the enemy. Now we've fifty thousand more coming at us.*

CHAPTER TEN

"Sixty thousand if it's one, Major, Spirit be with us," the Slasher captain said in his singsong borderland accent. "*Malash.* The Spirit appoints our rising and our going down."

An' ye'll nivver see that *comin' down t'road from Blayberry Fair,* Mekkle Thiddo quoted to himself in County dialect. Instinctively he crouched a little lower on the ridge, pressing his body against the rough-barked trunk of the olive tree.

"Well, that solves the problem of which route they're taking. They're using all of them. Runner to Major Zahpata with the other column, Captain Belagez: our location, and that we're engaging."

The sight of the Squadron host was stunning enough, spreading from the sea on the east to the edge of sight on the west. A huge clot of them were shambling down the road, ox-drawn wagons and a rabble on foot that must be the servants and unarmed followers. The mounted Squadron lords and their retinues sprawled over the open country by twos and threes, by scores and hundreds; enough of them that they flowed over the stubble and through the orchards like dark water on the sere yellow and green. A huge mist of dust smoked up over them, hiding the endless waves that followed, and the packs of spare dogs. The sound was like a long slow roar of surf.

Thiddo raised his binoculars. Faces jumped out at him across the kilometers; there were groups ranging from a lone freeholder with a rusty musket, ambling along on a gray-muzzled dog, to the households of magnates glittering with metal-studded saddles and jewelry.

"Nothing to worry about, Peydro," he said. *Although it's more than enough to piss your britches for.* He touched the amulet at his throat, and the locket with the picture of his wife. "Not a cannon among them, and most of these barbs have never heard a shot fired in anger."

There might be a few ox-drawn brass guns among the host, but if so they were back among the transport and useless. The border barons who fought the desert and mountain tribes were too far away to have answered the summons so soon, and the best of the Squadron levy were away with Curtis Ashburn. And sixty thousand more were barreling down on his three battalions. *My three battalions.* A third of the Expeditionary Force's striking power, fifteen hundred lives, and they all depended on *him.*

Spirit.

He turned and slid back downslope to where the others waited. "Right," he said, in the cool tones he'd heard Messer Raj use. "Majors Dalhouse and Istban, keep your force well-concealed on this ridge. When we come back"—because he was damned if he was going to put the tricky part in Dalhouse's hands, not when everyone's arse depended on it being done right—"give them rapid volley fire by companies as soon as we're clear. Lieutenant Muhadez, open fire with airburst shrapnel at three thousand meters."

The gunner nodded, looking up from his rangefinder. "Seyor," he said, nodding. The commander of the Novy Haifa Dragoons added the same; Dalhouse grunted wordlessly.

Thiddo gave a final look both ways. The two supporting units were spread along the ridge just below the crest in double file, with their dogs crouched only a few meters behind them. The guns likewise, with the teams crouching in their harness and still hitched to the caissons; all they'd have to do was let the last round roll the weapons back from the crest, slap the trails onto the caissons and gallop away.

Nothing to do but stand ready and then shoot, he thought, turning to his own command.

The company officers crowded around him: dark as Descotters but more slightly built, mostly bearded, with the ends trimmed to points. They had khaki-colored cloths wound around their helmets and crimson sashes under their sword-belts; merrier than County men, swifter-witted on average although less steady, and fine foray-and-ambush fighters from generations of fighting Bedouin raiders on the Drangosh frontier with the Colony . . . and from raiding over it themselves, of course. Like weasels in a henhouse with civilians, unless you watched them. They grinned at him now, unconcerned at having an outsider appointed over them as long as it was by Messer Raj, the Spirit-blessed general who'd sent the head of the Colony's Settler back to East Residence in a keg of arrack.

"Right, men," he went on. "We'll do some Slashing now, eh?" More grins, punctuated with spitting on the ground and holy oaths; every man of them was jingling with Star amulets, circuit chips and display modules in a display of the violent piety of the southern border.

"Open-order column until we're within a thousand meters. Then we'll deploy into line by companies; company advances, fire and retreat by alternates on the trumpet. Spirit of Man be with us."

"Holy Federation Church with us, brothers," they answered. "*Hingada thes Ihorantes!* Kill the Infidels!"

He swung into the saddle as the rest of the battalion raised their amulets and fell into line behind the color-party and the banner; then he raised his hand and chopped it forward. The trumpet sounded and the mass of men and dogs rocked into a lope, opening up to two-meter spacing between each man in the column of fours as they crossed the ridge. The banner flapped behind him, the silk making a ripping noise as they picked up speed; he knotted the reins and let them lie on the horn of the saddle as the column rose over the ridge. There were parties of Squadrones all over the plain, mostly surging forward, but a few moving south on errands of their own. None of them had the geometric order of Civil Government troops, but it would be a moment before they were noticed. He waved his arm twice and pointed toward the largest clump of enemy troops; his body adjusted to the long swooping movements of the dog with a lifetime's ease.

Two or three thousand of them just in that one bunch. Merciful avatars.

Dohloreyz had told him to be careful, before he'd left from his last leave. The house had still been in chaos with the additions going on, the barns and cottages first for the help and the new stock for the land he'd bought. Pa and his younger brothers still looking at him as if the sun rose behind his head, Ma wringing her hands—she always distrusted good fortune, little though the family had had of it in her lifetime . . . Dohloreyz wasn't sure if she was pregnant yet, hard though they'd tried since the wedding. Everyone had wanted to know them all of a sudden, relatives who hadn't called in years; they'd even had that greasy Christo moneylender sniffing around again, and the satisfaction of flogging him off their now-unmortgaged estate.

"*Scramento,*" he muttered; the Squadron unit ahead had definitely seen something.

Better than a kilometer to go. The Slashers' formation slid down into a hollow like a ground-hugging snake, and when they came up the opposite lip the enemy unit was milling like a kicked anthill. Messengers splattered out from it toward the others around, and the remainder clumped about the tall cloth-of-gold standard in its midst. Thiddo signaled to the trumpeter and he raised the curled brass to his lips. *Ta-ra-ra-ta.* The color party slowed, and the column of fours behind them opened out on both sides like a fen. Three minutes, and the whole Battalion was trotting in a double line abreast, with each trooper two meters from his neighbor and double intervals between companies.

Damn, but these are good troops, Thiddo thought with a glow of pride. Just over two thousand meters to the target. He lifted a clenched fist and pumped it twice into the air. The trumpet sounded again over the thunder of massed paws and the growing buzz from the enemy. Three companies launched themselves forward, out of the line like teeth on a saw. The slender desert-bred dogs rocketed forward in a stretched-out gallop, hindpaws coming up between forelegs and bounding off again.

"*Despert Staahl!*" the men screamed. *Awake the Iron!,* the war-cry of the southern borders. Then: "*Aur! Aur!*" in an endless yelping falsetto chorus. They stood in the stirrups as the lines pounded forward, rifles leveled over their left forearms; the enemy ahead of them was still milling. A few rode forward to meet the attack; some others were already firing at the Civil Government soldiers.

Might as well try to hit the moons, Thiddo thought contemptuously. That was beyond range for Armory rifles, much less smoothbores. *A thousand meters. Eight hundred. Six hundred.* Anything beyond two hundred was safe from Squadron weapons, more or less. *Four hundred meters. Now, now!*

As if in answer to his thought the first rank of charging Slashers fired. Not quite a volley, more like a rippling crack down the line: *BAMbambambambam.* The dogs dropped their haunches and reared, turning; the second line galloped through the first and fired ten meters farther toward the Squadron troops, then turned as well; less than a minute and the three companies were galloping back along their own path, reloading as they guided their mounts with knees and voice. The trumpet sounded, and the two companies with Thiddo rocked into a gallop in their turn.

Nobody could achieve any useful degree of accuracy against individual targets from a moving dog, not at these ranges. With enough practice, you could learn to hit *large* targets—several thousand men bunched shoulder to shoulder would do nicely—and the Slashers, like most units recruited on the Colonial frontier, made a specialty of this maneuver—the *fantasia,* it was called. The mass of Squadrones ahead of him was littered with dead men, and with dogs dead or thrashing around wounded, which was much worse. He could hear their howling, and a flurry of blurred *whumps* from Squadron smoothbores as the animals were put down before they turned on the nearest human.

Closer; six hundred meters. More groups pouring across the plain, angling out toward his men or in toward the golden spaceship-and-planet banner . . . *Spirit save me, that must be the Admiral we're attacking, no* wonder *they're upset.* Five hundred. Four hundred, and he drew his saber; a pistol was about as much use as a holy-water sprinkler at that range. It flashed up and then down in a shimmering arc. *BAMbambambambam,* another stuttering crash, louder this time as the tongues of flame shot forward from either side of them. He wheeled his dog, the big animal scrambling sideways as it killed velocity and threw clods of dust and wheat-straw, then riding back and *BAMbambambambam* behind him as the second file fired. Ahead the first three companies had reined in and turned, galloping back toward him.

Aur! Aur! They passed in a flash of combined speed; the trumpet sounded *rally* as Thiddo reined in and turned.

"Well, that's got them worked up and no mistake," he said to himself.

The whole mass of odds-and-sods around the Admiral's banner was rocking forward into a wild charge, waving swords and blunderbusses, banners flapping. The sound of their bellowing was almost as deep as the massed baying snarl of their dogs; more and more groups merged into the galloping mass, as individual noblemen and their retainers rallied to the Admiral. The last *fantasia* was from barely a hundred meters, and whole sections of the Squadrons went down before it. A few Slashers were hit by the return fire; a few more were dismounted, and swung up pillion by their comrades. The loose dogs mostly followed the retreating companies; two remained with bared teeth to fight and die over the bodies of dead masters.

"Sound *retreat*," Thiddo said.

The Slashers heeled their dogs and headed back for the ridge; the companies closed up and fell in one behind the other as they rode. The ridge grew ahead: The gap with their pursuers was growing; the Civil Government cavalry were on faster dogs and knew where they were going. A mob as big as that following them would include a lot of slow riders, and not many wanted to be right out in front. Especially when the rear ranks of the pursued were turning in the saddle to shoot backward occasionally....

POUMM. A pulse through the air as much as a noise, and a long tongue of flame from a field gun among the olive trees on the low ridge. *POUMM. POUMM.* The shells went whistling overhead with a sound like ripping canvas. Thiddo looked back. Two of the shells airburst over the advancing host with vicious *crack* sounds. Dirty blackish smoke-puffs at ten meters height, and oblongs opening below in the dark densely packed mass of galloping men and dogs. Thiddo winced slightly: the casings of the shells were loaded with hundreds of lead balls packed around a bursting charge. A third shell's time-fuse was off and it exploded on contact in a dark poplar shape of pulverized soil. That one was less deadly than the airbursts, but there were bits and pieces of men and dogs among the debris cast skyward.

POUMM. POUMM. POUMM. Three more shots, ten seconds later. There were ten thousand of them at least following him now, a huge moving carpet that heaved and sparkled in the sun, sparkled with steel and brass and polished iron musket-barrels. More riding in from all over the rolling plain. But the Squadrones were not used to artillery; the front rank faltered, and hundreds of dogs went wild with panic, throwing their riders or attacking those next to them—always a risk with animals who had not trained together—or riding off across the battlefield in uncontrollable funk with the men sawing at their reins. "Shooting stars," they were called. . . . The huge roaring noise of the charge changed timbre, mixed with the frenzied screaming of wounded dogs.

Major Anhelino Dalhouse cursed as the 75s let out another salvo and his wolfhound attempted to curvet.

The third gun of the battery had fired with a CRACK! an instant after the BOOM/BOOM of its sister tubes. Recoil from previous shots had driven the gun far enough back that this round was from the top of the ridge itself. The other two guns were still down the forward slope where the mass of earth and rock deadened their muzzle blasts. The shift in timbre made Dalhouse's knees clamp, multiplying the dog's own nervous reaction. The men behind him were murmuring to their crouching mounts spaced out through the sparse olive grove; a chorus of whines and growls sounded.

"Redlegged muckeating wogs!" Dalhouse snarled as he fought his mount back under control. No way *he* was going to dismount, of course.

The artillerymen ran their gun forward, heaving at the tall iron rims of the wheels to get it started as it disappeared down the forward slope again. Rifles volleyed at a greater distance, cutting through a sound like heavy surf that he couldn't identify. *I can't see a damned thing from here,* Dalhouse thought, his mouth working. He had a gleeful momentary vision of heavy bullets scything down the gunners, ringing on the gun tubes . . . the caissons exploding, blowing to hell the whole *damnable* mess of stinks and noises and men with as little social position as the mongrel mule-dogs that drew their guns.

"How close are they, sir?" asked Ensign Meribor, Dalhouse's aide—a cousin from the wealthy side of his wife's family. His restive mount tried to lick the muzzle of Dalhouse's wolfhound, causing the latter to first snap, then growl in embarrassment at being startled.

Dalhouse fought his reins. "How in the bloody Starless Dark would *I* know?" he snarled. "And keep your dog back! What do you think you are, you shopkeeper on dogback, a *bleeding gunner?*"

"Sorry, sir."

Boom. Boom. Boom.

A bullet whickered high overhead. Probably a ricochet, certainly no threat to anyone . . . but an evil sound, and a reminder of the things that *might* be taking place unseen on the other side of the ridgeline.

The thought decided Dalhouse in the instant it flashed across the surface of his mind. If that incompetent heathen-loving Descotter savage Thiddo thought he was going to leave Dalhouse to be shot down when a wave of Squadrones appeared on the ridgeline, he had another think coining . . .

Dalhouse spurred his mount toward the ridgeline from which he could view the battlefield for himself. "Come along!" he ordered Meribor.

Dalhouse wore rowels with long spikes for the look and jingle rather than need, but tension dug his heels deeper than he'd intended this time. The wolfhound yelped and brought its long jaws around by reflex, before it realized that the target was its master's booted leg—and therefore sacrosanct. The beast lurched forward, whining deep in its throat.

Boom.

"Sir, should we be—"

Boom.

"—leaving our position?" Meribor called desperately from behind Dalhouse. The boy wasn't a natural rider. He was a city lad, raised in the East Residence in a house which would have stunk of trade were the smell not smothered by so *much* money.

Boom.

One has to be practical, even in matters of honor.

Dalhouse glanced over his shoulder. Meribor's mount had followed Dalhouse's own, unbidden, catching the boy unprepared. His left hand was tangled in the wolfhound's curly neck fur, a white-knuckled grip that instinct said was safer than the reins.

"We're not leaving our position!" Dalhouse snapped.

Beyond Meribor, the helmets and polished brassards of the 17th Hemmar Valley Cuirassiers blazed with reflected sunlight, framing and concealing the faces of the troopers watching their commanding officer. They were glorious next to the rather drab issue uniforms of the Novy Haifa Dragoons.

"Do you think I'm going to trust a Rogor County half-wog to decide when *my* troops—"

CRACK! and the rest of the sentence—"advance"—was shocked out of Dalhouse's mind by the muzzle blasts; a field gun and volleying Armory rifles no longer blocked by the ridge that his wolfhound had just surmounted. His head whipped around just as the other two guns let loose together. They bounded backward uphill behind a red flash an instant before their paired *CRACKCRACK* slammed Dalhouse's ears.

The view across the ridge was as sudden a shock as that of the unmuffled gunfire. Dalhouse had never been good with numbers. "Fifty thousand Squadrones," Whitehall had said, but that meant nothing, it was not *real*. It was like listening to a bailiff talking about tithes and harvests, when all that mattered to Dalhouse was that there be a sufficiency of money to buy whatever his whim required.

The mass of men and weapons and brightly caparisoned dogs now visible in the valley before Dalhouse was *real*. It was enough to sweep the whole world before it and grind anything that tried to stop it into dust The sound he had wondered at was their voices and the paws of their dogs, beating like the roar of surf, like a natural force, an earthquake or forest fire. Three guns and a handful of the Rogor Slashers—irregulars, near as no matter, half-breed wogs—

would be swallowed up unnoticed by the Squadrones' advance. Even as Dalhouse stared, half of Thiddo's force turned their dogs and galloped toward the doubtful safety of the ridge.

A round musket-ball, flattened into a miniature frisbee when it ricocheted from a stone, moaned *burrburrburr* past Dalhouse's ear.

Powder smoke, white and sulfurous, lay like a gauze shroud over the valley. A breeze curled hazy whiffs up the slope. Dalhouse, breathing through flared nostrils as he considered the situation, the *impossible* situation, gagged as something like the blade of a buzzsaw scoured the back of his throat. His dog whined and pawed its nose.

Dalhouse wheeled his wolfhound. "Ensign Meribor!" he ordered. "Ride back to the camp! Tell whoever's in charge there to advance at once and support us. At once! Or it'll be too late!"

It was no doubt too late already. Well, a gentleman of the Civil Government was willing to die when honor demanded. . . .

Without waiting for Meribor to respond, Dalhouse spurred his mount into a deliberate trot toward the standard-bearer of the 17th. He had been betrayed. Thiddo and Whitehall had put him out here to die. Everyone knew what Descott County was like. Whitehall's blood father was undoubtedly some groom his mother had taken a fancy to, as sure as Whitehall's wife was a whore!

Meribor's mount passed Dalhouse at a dead gallop. The ensign clung to the big wolfhound's neck with both arms. He'd managed to lose the stirrups, and his brassard turned on its chains to jingle against his back. The stirrup-irons beat a tattoo in time with it on the mount's ribs.

Meribor was shouting—perhaps to the dog, perhaps to his mother. The dog, at least, took no notice.

"Pull him up!" Dalhouse bellowed. He spurred his own mount in pursuit. Dalhouse's wolfhound, nervy already from the noise and smoke, put its long head down and bolted after its companion.

Dalhouse realized his mistake at almost the instant he made it. He sawed his reins, but the half-ton carnivore had taken control of its immediate future and ignored the levers pressing on its muzzle. Neck and neck, the two dogs and the officers astride them swept around the southern flank of the 17th Hemmar Valley Cuirassiers, heading for the far hills. The color party and trumpeter dashed out to keep their station by the commander.

Like a sweater unraveling, the twin glittering ranks of the battalion began to trail off behind Dalhouse and his aide.

POUMM. POUMM. POUMM.

Mekkle Thiddo stood in the stirrups and stared ahead at the ridgeline: Where was the glitter of ranked riflemen moving forward? He heard a bugle blowing, sounding *stand, stand to,* and *halt.* The bottom seemed to drop out of his stomach as he swept over the ridge. The artillery was there, gunners slamming fresh shells into the breech and rolling the pieces forward by the wheels to their firing positions. And about a company of the Novy Haifa . . . and the backs of everyone else, spread out in wild disorder and racing full-tilt back north toward the camp.

There were shouts behind him, rage and fear as the men of the Slashers realized what had happened. The halt was ragged when the trumpet blew, but they halted . . . Mekkle Thiddo felt the collar of his uniform tunic cutting into his flesh, tasted a sudden rush of acid bile at the back of his throat. *Defeat. We're all fucking dead. Disgrace . . . Dohloreyz—*

"Turn!" he screamed. "Battalion firing line along the ridge—keep your dogs with you—move, move, *now now now!*

The trumpeter sounded it, again and again; the men moved, a little slowly at first and then with desperate speed. The five companies wheeled out into line just behind the crest of the ridge, the dogs crouching flat and the men staying seated in the saddle. The Squadron was spread out over three, four times their frontage and beginning to come forward again, although there were milling clumps where the dogs were still panicked by the shellfire, and swirling confusion where the rear ranks pressing forward had run into them. *No more than a minute's leeway,* he knew. Suddenly everything was diamond-clear; his own lips seemed too slow, too numb for the words he must pour out of them.

Major Istban of the Novy Haifa came up, weeping tears of rage and shame. "The Cuirassiers bugged out. It was like a dam breaking—Dalhouse couldn't hold them and when they didn't rally he took off after them"—There was red dripping from the edge of the other officer's sword, a sign of how he had turned back some at least of his own men.

"Shut up," Thiddo said calmly. "Take those you've got, rally what you can on the way, set up there—" He pointed to a clump of eucalyptus four thousand meters to the north. "Lieutenant Muhadez!" The gunnery officer had come running. "Limber up after your next shoot, then get the hell back there and support us as we withdraw. We'll slow them down, you shoot hell out of them as they come over the ridge—leapfrog. Understand?"

He nodded. "Go!" The guns fired once more, but this time the crews caught them as they finished their recoil and used the momentum to run them to the caissons. An iron clang sounded as the trails were dropped onto the loops and holding-bars slammed home, then they leaped to saddle and handhold, and the men mounted on the lead pairs of the dog-teams shouted their mounts into a gallop. The remnants of the Novy Haifa Dragoons followed the bounding, jolting passage of the guns.

Then there was nothing but his own command and the pounding thunder of the Squadron host starting their climb up the long shallow slope to the ridge. Light flashed across the raised sword-blades: The front of the charge was a thousand meters, and the ranks were packed up to fourteen deep.

"Wait for it!" Thiddo shouted, keeping his voice flat and his mount well back so that only his head and shoulders were above the crestline. The last thing the men needed was to hear him screeching. "We'll be giving them five rounds and then pulling back to the next position."

Gray sweating faces under the helmets on either side. A thousand meters to the spray of brave men on fast dogs the Squadrones were casting ahead. Nine hundred. They would be firing down a long slope into the mass of the enemy. Beyond the Admiral's standard the whole plain was alive with growing clumps of them, gathering and heading toward the sound of combat. Down along the line he could hear officers and NCOs giving last-minute instructions:

"Steady, brothers, and aim for their feet, aim low."

"Malash, Malash, the Spirit is with us—and I'm behind you, Assed."

"Volley fire by platoons and rank. Prepare for rapid fire."

Eight hundred meters. He heeled his dog forward to the crest, the standardbearer and trumpeter following, and raised his saber. The men stood; they were in double file, with the ranks staggered so that the rear men had a clear field of fire through the gaps in the front rank. There was a yell and surge through the Squadron formation as the figures rose as if by magic among the edge of the olives. The enemy vanguard recoiled on those behind. . . .

"Aim." The front rank brought their long Armory rifles to their shoulders with a single smooth jerk; there was a barely perceptible ripple as each picked his target.

"Fire!" His saber slashed down.

BAM-BAM-BAM-BAM-BAM. Like five blurred shots, very loud walking down the line from the left; three hundred fifteen rifles firing, the sixty-man half-companies ripple volleying. Very crisp, the sound of long practice. All along the Squadron front men and dogs went down in threshing tangles. A cloud of smoke rose from the line, drifting up into the flickering velvet-silver leaves of the olive trees. A few last dactosauroids fluttered up with it.

"Aim!" The rear rank's rifles came up in unison; the front were working the levers of their weapons and reaching back to the bandolier for a fresh round to push into the breech. Clatter and snap amid the shouting and echoes. Six hundred yards.

"Fire!"

BAM-BAM-BAM-BAM-BAM. A horizontal comb of red tongues reaching out for the enemy. The whole formation staggered; it was turning into a C with the open end pointed at the ridge, as the solid bar of volley fire punched into the middle of it like a fist. Dead men and dogs were piling up all across the frontage covered by the Slashers' line, but there were too many Squadrones, too many swinging wide around the barrier of flesh.

"Fire!"

BAM-BAM-BAM-BAM-BAM. You couldn't fault their courage, at least; there must be hundreds dead and more wounded, but the dismounted were coming on at a run, leveling their flintlocks, more pushing up on either side, and new bands galloping full-tilt to join them.

"Fire!"

BAM-BAM-BAM-BAM-BAM. A bit of a stutter in the line now; if the Squadrones got to handstrokes his command would be chopped into dogmeat in less than a minute. Four hundred yards . . .

"Fire!"

BAM-BAM-BAM-BAM-BAM.

"Withdraw!"

The trumpet sounded, and the dogs knew the call as well as the men. They surged erect under their riders and wheeled; the whole formation was moving back at a trot in a few seconds. A huge bellow of triumph came from behind them, as the Squadron force poured forward. Thiddo glanced to either side; the formation was tight and the men were keeping their dogs well in hand, as some of the shock of betrayal faded. Most of the men were riding with their rifles in their right hands, the lever down to let air cool the barrel and chamber. Extraction-jams were the great weakness of the Armory rifle, the fragile brass cartridges ripping when softened by heat or coming loose from the iron base. A few men were hammering at the levers with knife-hilts or trying to pick the cooling metal scraps out of the breech with the points as they rode.

Ahead of them the cannon had drawn up; they flashed as the Slashers reached the flat ground below the ridge. Men ducked as the shells went by overhead. This was extreme range, and if someone had turned a time-fuse improperly— or if the trail of powder in it burned a little too fast . . .

Thiddo looked behind. The ridgeline was a mass of men, many halting with screams as they heard the shells again; the three airbursts speckled the front behind them. Six hundred meters gap, and they would push it to three times that by the time they got to the guns and wheeled to sting their enemies again. Ahead, Istban had managed to draw up nearly two companies of his Dragoons off to one side from the Slashers' line of retreat, so he could take the

Squadrones in enfilade and open fire while the battalion covered the last thousand meters.

"Peydro!" he shouted. Senior Lieutenant Peydro Belagez angled his galloping dog over beside the battalion commander. "Messengers to Zahpata and Messer Raj, verbal reports."

Another flight of shells went overhead and cracked open their loads of hissing metal. The Squadron might be chasing him and the Slashers, but they would pay for the privilege.

The Squadrones would *pay first*.

CHAPTER ELEVEN

"And who ordered this withdrawal?" Raj said coldly.

The Cuirassier captain flushed and braced to attention, staring to the front. "Sir. The withdrawal was spontaneous. I attempted to rally the men—"

"Which was why you ended up in front of most of them?" Raj asked, dangerously mild. "Shut up."

He looked to the front; there were several hundred men immediately ahead of him—

two hundred seventy-four, Center said.

—and more straggling in across the fields. The base was half a kilometer behind him; he could hear the steady throb of drums as it beat to arms. Menyez's own Kelden Foot were moving out from the gate, forming in square and marching smartly to the tap of the drum, out to cover the entrance in case the retreating columns of cavalry came in fast with the Squadron on their heels. The mid-morning sun was bright, bleaching the fields to a yellowish-white and making the clumps of trees almost black by contrast A pillar of dust over most of the southern horizon was growing steadily closer; the air was already dry with it, even though the wind was from the north.

"Captain . . . Hermano Suharto, isn't it? Captain Suharto, right now I'm about convinced that I should have every officer in the 17th Cuirassiers shot, and the unit's enlisted men decimated, for cowardice-in-the-face. So you'd *better* rally them, right now, and bring them along smartly. Convince me to change my mind, Captain. Work hard at it."

Suharto gave an unanswered salute and rode off to the men; they responded quickly, losing a little of the lost expression as they heard orders. Sergeants began to push them into line, and troopers accreted in their platoons and companies.

"Ehwardo," Raj said, "this looks like a complete balls-up, and we're going to have to pull it out of the pot. Form up for a company advance in line"—that meant a column a hundred and twenty men wide and six deep—"ready for extension, rifles out and a round up the spout.

"Jorg," he went on to Menyez, "I'm not going to let them besiege us if I can help it." Everyone nodded; the position was impregnable, but badly supplied. Once closely invested, the Civil Government army would be swamped if it tried to come out and starved if it did not. "We'll draw up a battle line here." There were two kilometers or more of clear ground to their front, only a few shaws and the odd dip in the ground to provide cover. "Spread the infantry across in a shallow crescent. When the cavalry comes in we'll dismount two battalions on each flank and keep one in reserve."

He pointed. "Anchor your right flank on that," he said, pointing to a deep ravine to their west. "But be careful, use your best—I don't like the look of the ground beyond it"—broken, and largely covered with olives and cork oak. "Left flank over on the ravine opposite." That one was open to the east, but the western bank was higher, a sheer clay wall. "Grammeck, guns in three bastions—left, right, and center. Quickly, Messers, if you please."

"Ser," the bannerman said, leaning forward behind him and pointing. Three riders were coming across the open ground, slanting in from the west.

They pulled up and saluted: A sergeant and two troopers, with the sand-dune and palm-tree shoulder blazon of the 18th Komar overlain with its motto: *Dehfenzo Lighon*, Defend the Faith.

"Zur," the sergeant said. "Message frum Major Zahpata." He handed it over.

Raj unfolded the paper. *Am heavily engaged and my flank is exposed by withdrawal of first column*, it said. *Request permission to withdraw more quickly as my left is in danger of encirclement.*

"Sergeant, verbal reply: inform Major Zahpata that the western and northern Squadron forces have been completely routed. I'm bringing up Poplanich's Own to rally the first column. He's to fall back as slowly as possible and bloody their noses. Understood?"

"Zur!" They swung off, leaning over the necks of their galloping dogs.

"On our way, Ehwardo," Raj said.

"Walk-march . . . *trot*"

Suzette fell in beside him as they broke into a lope toward the highest and nearest of the dust clouds. "Is it going very badly?" she said. Harbie whined, catching his mistress's anxiety.

"No," he replied, slightly surprised and blinking away one of Center's maps. "It just isn't going according to plan."

" . . . and I take full responsibility, Sir," Mekkle Thiddo finished.

Raj looked at him, and then at the action ahead. The Slashers and Poplanich's Own were in line on either side of the guns; the steady crashing of their volleys complemented the louder bark of the field pieces. The vast mass of the Squadrones had stopped cold and was withdrawing from the suddenly extended front. Parties of the enemy edged forward on either flank; officers ran down behind the firing line, indicating new aim-points with their drawn sabers.

Raj looked over to his right: the remaining four hundred or so of the Cuirassiers were standing in solid ranks, and Suharto seemed to have them well enough in hand. Dalhouse and the others probably wouldn't stop until their dogs died.

"Runner. C Company is to face right and fire in support," he said. The man dashed off and the outermost of Poplanich's companies came to and stood, shuffling backward and pivoting on the left like a door swinging back to face the Squadron units lapping around them. "Runner, to Senior Captain Suharto. Prepare to see that party of barbs off."

BAM. BAM. BAM. C Company had opened fire, rifles coming up and dropping like the motion of a loom's shuttle.

There were four noblemen's banners among the Squadron flanking party, and about eight hundred men; two of the glittering flags went down under the hail of 11mm rounds. Through the growing haze of smoke and dust, he could see men pitching out of the saddle, and the whole body bent and curved a little away from the fire. The Cuirassiers' banner dipped toward him in acknowledgment and readiness; he waved his arm around his head twice and chopped it forward to the right. A trumpet sounded and the Cuirassiers moved from stand to walk, from walk to trot. The sabers came out with a uniform snap and rested on their shoulders, then forward as they rocked into a gallop and swung wide right to charge; the volley fire continued in their support almost to the moment of impact. The disordered ranks of the Squadrones shattered under the impact of the boot-to-boot charge, only a few of them managing to fire their flintlocks; then the Civil Government soldiers wheeled and galloped back, emptying more saddles.

They cantered back into place, bloodied sabers in their hands, and dressed ranks again. Raj nodded; Senior Captain Suharto was taking his words to heart.

"Runner to Major Zahpata," he said, pulling out his notepad: *Major, I expect the Squadron to fall into disorder for a short period. If you can break contact easily, pull back to the left flank of the main position.*

"No, Mekkle," he went on, "I'm not relieving you. Quite the contrary—you kept your head when all about were losing theirs, and turned what could have been an unmitigated disaster into a mitigated one." *Although when I find Major Dalhouse* ... Thiddo looked stunned; until then he had been a mixture of relief at having someone to take the responsibility off his shoulders, and dread of what his leader would say.

Raj leaned forward and slapped him on the shoulder. "If you'd lost those guns and come barreling into camp with the barbs on your heels ... well, you didn't. My friend, this is not a business in which elegant plans buy you any yams. The ability to retrieve matters when someone screws up is much more important.

"Now," he said, viewing the field.

They would have to pull back soon; someone on the other side was finally realizing they were in a meeting engagement. The Squadron host was clumping into four main groups—what he could see of it—with the transport train far behind pulling into a classic Military Government-style circular wagon-fort. And dismounted Squadrones were working their way to the east through the patch of broken country that was protecting his left. Fairly soon they'd be through it—and he couldn't afford to be pinned. Raj massaged the back of his neck under the leather and chainmail guard; the day—he glanced up; about 1100 hours, morning rather—had been a real surf-ride. *In garrison, we complain about the boredom. But when you consider the alternative . . .*

"Sir?" Thiddo asked. "Ah, I expected—"

"You can't," Raj went on, "let yourself get too focused on a plan, Mekkle. Actually things are going rather well. We've lost, oh, two hundred men"—da Cruz's face came before him for a moment, and he pushed it away—"including those who just buggered off, and how many do you think the Squadron's lost? Two thousand? Four? Six?"

They both glanced to the front. It was difficult to tell through the drifting mass of powder smoke, but there was a positive carpet of unmoving figures on the ground out beyond the Civil Government line. Another series of volleys slapped out, hiding the Squadron front for a moment; smoke billowed from the enemy, too far away to do any real damage.

"And more important, they're still coming on the way we want them to. Notice anything about them, Mekkle?"

"Ummm—they do tend to react like a bull stung by a *pihkador*, sir. Confirms what we were told."

"Hit them in the nose and you can lead them by it," Raj nodded. A trooper came up with a flagstaff; the banner on it was pure white. "I've got something for you to take to the Admiral," he went on, reaching for a bag tied to his saddle "that will concentrate his mind even more. Yes, things are not going badly at all. Trumpeter, call *cease fire*."

"Hnnnng."

The soldier arched his back as the Renunciate cut away the remains of his boot. Sticky blood had pooled inside the leather, and it slid out in a gelatinous mass. One of the assistants wilted and began to sag; Fatima cor Staenbridge reached out and shook her sharply.

"Scrub," the nun said; the pants-leg had been slit far back. "*Come* on, I've got to see what I'm doing here."

The soldier—the boy—was glassy-eyed from opium, but it was dangerous to give too much when shock was involved. Fatima gripped his wrist and hand more firmly and leaned over him, smiling; it seemed to make it easier for them to bear, if someone was looking at them. *At least there aren't many.* A Descotter trooper with a shot-broken thigh right at the beginning, and a few more ever since; they had even had time to treat some enemy wounded. Not like Sandoral; she remembered the tubfuls of amputated legs and arms at the bottoms of the operating tables . . . just a trickle so far. The word was that the north force was almost to the city. Soon they would be there, under the walls and the cannon. Gerrin and Barton would be there.

The boy with the mangled foot had a shield-shaped shoulder—flash with crossed sabers over a black numeral "5," and the motto *Hell o Zpalata* above—"Hell or Plunder." The 5th Descott Guards.

"What's your name, soldier?" she asked.

His eyes darted to her, and his teeth showed in something like a smile; they were yellow-white in the muddy shock-molded brown of his face.

"Hylio Carasyn," he gasped.

"You're in the 5th, aren't you?" she said.

"Yis, ma'am," he said. A probe clicked down by the foot of the table, and his hand gripped hers until the bones creaked; it was his saber hand, and he was a strong young man. "Yer t'Major's lady, eh?"

She nodded. "What happened up there?" she said. *Allah—Spirit of Man*—she prayed silently, remembering Foley on the table, his ruined hand . . . *Please, let anyone die but them.*

The soldier was panting, and his eyes slid out of focus. "Barbs," he muttered. "Gunmen, swordsmen. Barbs, thousands, I shot 'im and he—*nnnnnnn!*"

"Ah, *got* it," the stern-faced Renunciate said, her arms glistening red to the elbows. The probe held a misshapen piece of lead a little larger than a pea. "Clamp there, move sharp!"

There was a clatter at the door of the tent "Mediko, mediko! More of 'em!"

Young Hylio Carasyn had fainted. Fatima put her hand on the sweat-cold forehead. *You don't know any more of what's going on than I do, poor baby,* she thought

The doctor looked up. "Get me that damned catgut," she said, frowning. The assistant handed her a curved needle. "Time to close this one up."

"Took them long enough," Raj grunted, raising his binoculars. He had drawn a little ahead of the group around his banner, messengers, and aides.

The firing had finally stopped, along the front at least. Wind drifted the smoke away; unfortunately, it also showed the true size of the Squadron war-host again, looking all the more terrifying because it had hauled itself together. It would show them how few their enemies in this particular skirmish had been, as well—which might be either good or bad, depending on how bright they were. Raj turned and looked down the ranks. The men were resting stolidly, faces and hands black with burnt powder; a few were taking sips from their canteens and carefully spraying a fine mist into the open breeches of their rifles, then wiping them with the tails of their coats. Hell on maintenance, but you did what you had to when it came down to cases.

"Did we really have to send Mekkle?" Suzette asked.

"It's a favor," Raj said absently. "I'm demonstrating that he's still trusted. Which," he added quietly, lowering the binoculars for a moment, "might not have been necessary if somebody hadn't interfered in the chain of command this morning."

Suzette looked away. "That was a mistake," she said.

"It was. My heart," he went on more softly, "we're partners, I know that. You were concerned . . . but I don't take unnecessary risks. Don't second-guess me on my specialty, or you *will* get me killed."

She nodded stiffly, and he raised the glasses again. "And it would be an insult to send a man of no rank to treat with the Admiral," he went on.

The group around the Admiral had advanced a little to meet the party of Civil Government troops under the white flag. Admiral Auburn was a tall portly man, with a spray of gray-brown beard covering half his chest, and small sapphires and diamonds on the ends of the leather thongs that fringed his jacket. He glittered as he moved, leaning forward with a hand cupped to his ear. It was like watching a puppet show; the big barbarian reared back in the stirrups, shaking his head. *Probably refusing to believe his brother Conner's been defeated and killed,* Raj estimated.

Mekkle was handing over the canvas bag. Auburn ripped it open and sat gasping for a moment, while men recoiled all around it and his dead brother stared at him in eternal surprise. Then he dropped the head, fumbled for it as it bounced off his saddle and fell to the ground, rolling. Buried his hands in his beard and began to scream, half-falling as he slid from his dog's back to the object it was sniffing curiously. Screaming and moaning, he rocked back and forth over the head, and one of his hands came free with a handful of hair in it. There was chaos around his banner, as men turned to each other, shouting into faces, waving their weapons. Sections of the Squadron line surged forward; the news spread outward as ripples did from a stone dropped in a pond.

Good man, Raj thought, as Mekkle and the trooper carrying the flag of truce turned and began to canter back to the Civil Government line. Then he stiffened as dozens of weapons leveled behind the envoy.

"Son of a bitch—son of a *bitch!*" he shouted, as they fired in a flicker of smoke-puffs with red spearhead cores of fire.

The flag of truce went over as the trooper and his dog collapsed. Mekkle slumped forward over the neck of his dog; the animal laid back its ears and ran, howling, one paw flinching every time it struck the ground. Raj and his color-party were galloping forward too; they met the wounded man a hundred meters in front of the Civil Government line. The wounded dog crouched, and Horace sank to the ground beside it, snuffling and licking at the injury. Raj took Thiddo's shoulders, easing him to the earth; Suzette ran up with her medical box, then halted, eyes wide. The shotgun blasts of the Squadron had pulped the muscle off the young officer's back, and the yellow bone of spine and ribs snowed through it, along with loops of gut. The flow of blood was slowing even as they watched.

Raj leaned over the dying man. Thiddo's mouth moved, but nothing came out of it but a spatter of blood that flecked across the general's face. Dust from near-misses spurted around them both as Raj set the dead man's head back on the ground and rose; several of the others flinched slightly as he turned back toward the enemy.

"Get a record of those banners," he said, pointing to the standards of the noblemen grouped around the Admiral. The whole Squadron force seemed to be paralyzed for the moment. "Get a record of every one of them, because afterward I want to identify them."

The Admiral was still kneeling by his brother's head, wailing and beating the ground with his fists; many of the men around him were doing likewise, or gashing their faces with their knives as a sign of mourning. Their howls were nearly as loud as those of their dogs, and as inhuman.

Children, Raj thought. *Vicious grown-up children, and nothing but the Army to keep them from wiping out all the adults in the world.*

in the universe, Center said. **a universe of vicious children for us to school, as we will do in time.**

"And now," Raj went on, "Major Thiddo bought us some valuable time. I suggest we use it."

CHAPTER TWELVE

The sun was nearly overhead and a little to their west; Raj squinted into it as he and his command group rode down the front of the Expeditionary Force's position. His personal banner dipped each time he passed a battalion standard, and he saluted; the men raised a rolling cheer that swelled and pulsed in his wake. At each he stopped for a moment.

"It's all very simple now, lads," he said for the tenth time. "They run up to us, we shoot them down. Mind the orders, keep the muzzles down, and everything will go fine. Spirit of Man with you!"

The cheer swelled and then died down again as he galloped back to his post on the west corner of the formation, next to Poplanich's Own. The palisade of the overnight camp was just visible behind, and closer were the light two-wheeled ambulance carts. It was intensely hot in the early afternoon. Insects whirred, and a bellows sound came from the rear, where the dogs lay and panted. The men were down on one knee in orderly rows with their rifles held in the right hand; sweat darkened the blue tunics. The air smelled of it, and dust; on the border of sight to the east, the sea added its tang of salt.

"Here they come," Ehwardo Poplanich said.

"Took their time," Raj replied, looking at his watch: 1300. "Better than an hour."

He looked left and east, along the Civil Government position. It stretched between the two ravines like a huge shallow C; the infantry in the center had had time to dig sketchy fieldworks, throwing up a meter-high ridge of dirt. With the front rank prone and the second rank kneeling that would give them excellent cover if the enemy came close enough to hit anything. The guns were more elaborately protected; each had a man-high bulwark in front of it with a V-shaped cutout for the muzzle, and a sloped earth bank behind it so that it would rise with the recoil and run back into the battery. Three battalions of dismounted cavalry under Hadolfo Zahpata held the seaward flank; the other four were anchoring the right wing, under Raj's personal eye, although that included the still-shaky Cuirassiers and Novy Haifa. There had been time to bring water carts up, as well; water the dogs and men, issue bread, stack spare ammunition close at hand but protected by sandbags. Time to have the priests parade down the front, sprinkling each banner with holy water and censing it with fragrant smoke.

The horizon to the south turned black as the Squadron came on—black edged with winking brightness from their weapons and flags. There was a rumble that seemed to shake the earth, the paws of more than forty thousand dogs pounding the dirt; dust towered into the sky over the barbarian host. They slowed as they approached, less from caution than from the way the terrain was squeezing them down like a wedge. Those in the front were nobles with a reputation for valor, or the desire for it. They were there of their own free will; the Admiral could direct their advance, but not stop it. The Civil Government line looked frail and still by comparison, delicate and structured as a snowflake.

Raj leveled his binoculars. The area in front of his position was bare, except for the poles marked with colored rag that gave the distances.

"Major Dinnalsyn," he said. "Commence firing for effect at four thousand meters on my signal. Don't get fancy; rapid fire at the foremost edge of their formation." The artillery chief nodded.

"Colonel Menyez?" Raj asked.

"Everything in order, General," the infantry commander said. "All sights have been checked, and set initially at nine hundred meters; the men've been drilled in readjusting, and aim-points established. I'd like to have had more firing-range work—the fisc has been shorting ammunition training allowances for years—but they'll do."

"Go to it, then," Raj said.

The three of them slapped fists, with Ehwardo Poplanich joining in a little awkwardly; then the others dispersed to their commands. An aide handed Raj a sandwich of roast beef and mustard; Horace looked over his shoulder at his master and whined plaintively.

"Shut up, you son of a bitch, you were fed this morning," Raj said, then relented and tossed him a scrap. It was only a token to the huge jaws that slammed down on it, but dogs liked to share and have eye contact while they ate. The cavalry mounts were all pretty frisky these days, what with plenty of bones and offal to go with their mash of boiled grain and beans.

Young Ludwig Bellamy spoke; he was watching the Squadron host advance with his hands white-knuckled on the reins, but his voice was calm.

"Your warriors must be men of iron, to watch that and not fear," he said, glancing sidelong at the silent ranks of the Civil Government battalions. Nothing moved except the bright silk flags crackling in the breeze from the sea, and dogs shifting restlessly from foot to foot under mounted officers.

Raj grunted bitter laughter through a mouthful, and swallowed.

"The only warriors here," he said, waving backward with the sandwich, "are *there*"—he indicated the battalion equivalent of Stalwarts and Halvaardi held in reserve for the unlikely event of a hand-to-hand melee—"and *there*" sweeping across the southern horizon.

The Squadrones had begun to chant, paced by drums and oxhorn trumpets: "*Ha*-ba-da, *ha*-ba-da, *ha*-ba-da."

"My men are not warriors, they're soldiers, Messer Bellamy—and they're about to demonstrate the difference." He finished the sandwich and wiped his mouth. "While the Squadron is doing exactly what I've been trying to get them to do in the week since we landed."

"What else *could* they do?" the young man asked.

Center offered map displays of alternatives, but Raj knew them well already. Center had always given its human tool the whole truth, the ways that a plan could fail—inevitably more numerous than the ways it could succeed.

"Leave enough men here to pin me and go around," Raj said. "I don't have enough troops to divide my forces; I'd have to backpedal, and then they could do it again and again until I was trapped against the walls of Port Murchison. The Expeditionary Force is big enough to fight a battle with the Squadron—it *isn't* big enough to occupy any significant area of land. As long as the Admiral keeps a large force in being and hovers around, I'm stuck—we certainly can't charge them at bayonet-point. I desperately *need* a battle; the Admiral might well defeat me and force me to withdraw by skillfully refusing one. That he isn't even trying shows that Auburn and his principal advisors are all incompetent."

"But . . ." the Squadron noble tugged at his braids. "You killed Conner Auburn—honor demands that the Admiral attack you! The levy won't follow a commander without honor. And the nobles can't run from a smaller force; their men would laugh at them."

"Exactly," Raj replied, with a grin like a carnosauroid.

I hope. The sandwich lay like a lump of molten lead in his stomach; his mind knew what he said was true, but his gut heard fifty thousand voices howling for his blood. The chanting dropped off a little, and the horns sounded in unison. The Squadron array was divided—somewhat—into three successive groups, "Battles" as they called them. The first seemed to gather itself a kilometer or more away. There was a huge metallic ringing as they pounded musket-barrels and swords on each other, and a shout fit to stun the ear of heaven. They charged, the mass of the first Battle stretching like warm toffee over the ground.

"*GITTEM, GITTEM!*"

Center reeled off ranging figures before his eyes as he watched; he raised one hand. The Squadrones had rocked into a full gallop, a mass of fangs and faces and long flashing swords looming up out of white dust, bellowing deeper than thunder. The glowing-green numbers scrolling over his vision came up to 4100, and his hand slashed down. An aide touched his cigarette to the match-paper of a signal rocket, and it arched over the empty space to the center of the C. There it burst in a green *pop*. And twenty-seven field guns fired within half a second of each other; a great *POUUMMMMPH* of noise that hit the lungs from the inside, echoing slightly with the distance between the three artillery redoubts.

With hideous perfection the shells airburst directly over the Squadron line. A thousand men and dogs died fractions of a second later as shrapnel sleeted through the close-packed ranks. The men behind had no chance of avoiding the sudden bloody shambles ahead of them; massive six-deep pile-ups of dogs and men blossomed, the collisions killing nearly as many as the explosions. The whole galloping mass of Squadrones checked, as if a single beast had stumbled hard.

Raj looked to his right, into the artillery position. The guns had run up the earth ramps the gunners had shoveled behind them; now they hung suspended for a second and rolled forward again to jerk to a halt against wooden chock-blocks. As they did, the gunnery teams jumped in, moving with metronomic precision: breechman to jerk open the lever that swung the block aside, spongeman to swab out the chamber, loader to slam home the next round; even as the breechman swung the crank back up to close the eccentric-screw breechblock, the gun captain was squatting over the trail, sighting. His hands moved and the others spun the elevating screw under the barrel; the muzzle depressed, and the gun captain sprang aside and jerked the lanyard.

This time the sound was much longer, as slight differences in the loading speed of the crews told: A stuttering POUM-POUM-POUM that lasted six seconds or so. Half the shells were airburst and half contact-fused explosive, hammering up tall candles of dirt and flesh from the front of the Squadron line. Clouds of smoke were rising from the artillery emplacements as well, bending over to the right as the breeze from the sea blew them away. The crews had settled into a steady implacable rhythm of three rounds per minute, the pace that preserved barrels and broke armies. Raj raised his binoculars again.

"Yesss . . ."

Those overgrown adolescents in floppy hats were as brave as anyone who ever forked a dog, and it was impossible to actually *kill* fifty-thousand-odd men, even with massed artillery. The dogs were a different matter; they were already nervous and overstressed from being forced into close contact with strangers, and it took long and careful training to accustom the big animals to the sound of artillery. He saw one turning in circles as the pressure of the cheek-levers in its bridle fought against its determination to turn and run. Then it caught the rider's thigh in its half-meter mouth and ripped him screaming out of the saddle, shook him until he struck the ground in two places. The man behind pressed his blunderbuss to its chest and pulled both triggers, but his own frantic mount dropped and rolled over him before rising to dash off with flapping reins and wet-red saddle.

The Squadron formation shredded away from the rear as men still out of range of the guns let their dogs turn; they had little alternative, with thousands of snarling uncontrolled animals fighting their way back to safety against anything that tried to stop them. Oxhorns blew and flags waved from the group to the rear around the Admiral, as the guns hammered retreat into rout. Only the motionless bulk of the second Battle kept the first formation from charging off the field altogether. Down the line of Civil Government troops there were cheers and ripples as men shook their rifles in the air.

But the sound was quickly quelled. "Damn your eagerness!" Ehwardo Poplanich shouted as the noise reached his battalion. "Silence in the ranks!" Then he took another glance to the front. "Sweet merciful Avatars and the Constellation of Saints," he said, when he lowered his glasses. From the point where the Squadron charge had begun, a thousand meters of ground was carpeted with bodies. Many of them were still moving; a heap of them slid aside as a dog burrowed its way from underneath and hopped three-legged back toward the south. The whimpers and moans were strong enough to reach the Civil Government line, and so was the copper-salt stink of blood and feces.

Raj glanced around. *Ah. He's never seen a large-scale pitched battle before,* he thought. "Sandoral was worse," he said. "More guns, on both sides."

He studied the enemy. It was difficult to make out details through the smoke and dust, but the wind was freshening. Shouting, waving swords, more horn-calls; he saw one man dismount and shoot his own dog as it cowered and whimpered and tried to lick his face. Others were grouping again on foot around the banners of their chieftains, flags with the skulls of dogs or carnosauroids or men, lofting up through the dust. Warrior after warrior snapped the sheath of his sword across his knee, and more were dismounting as they reached the second Battle, servants leading strings of dogs off to the flanks and rear.

"They won't turn as easily next time," he said quietly. "They've been shamed."

Ehwardo lit two cigars; Raj took the other gratefully and dragged the smoke down into his lungs. It took a good half-hour for the enemy to prepare; just getting the riderless dogs out of the way was difficult enough.

"Runner, message to Colonel Dinnalsyn," Raj said thoughtfully. "Have case-shot on hand."

"Here they come," somebody murmured.

"*GITTEM, GITTEM.*"

This time the enemy came in some sort of formation, an irregular blunt wedge. Raj focused and saw them tramping stolidly with their heads held rigidly up and hands clutched on swords and muskets. *Must be uncomfortable marching in those boots,* he thought; the Squadron model was thigh-high and had a pointed heel, designed strictly for the saddle. They roared as they came, chanting and gradually picking up the pace, trying to work themselves into the famous barbarian frenzy of the Military Governments. A few in the front ranks were already glaze-eyed and frothing, gnawing on their weapons and throwing aside their clothes to run forward naked.

There must be at least thirty thousand in this wave, Raj thought.

thirty-eight thousand four hundred ± three hundred, Center said.

"*GITTEMGITTEMGITTEMGITTEMGITTEMGITTEMGITTEM GITTEM—*"

4100 meters.

The general's hand chopped down and the rocket rose. The guns spoke and the Squadrones broke into a run, crouching over in useless but human reflex. Air-bursts blasted circles in the edges of the formation, and explosive rounds hammered into the center of it. Banners fell, and other men caught them up and ran forward; the whole mass of humanity was running forward, more people than the average city in a single block, a thousand men across and thirty deep.

3000 meters.

"Run away, you poor brave silly buggers, run away!" Raj whispered, slowly drawing his saber. "Go home!"

There was a long wave through the enemy as they clambered over the last of the bodies from the first attack and came pounding on across the open ground. The guns were firing faster, as if the teams had caught the contagion of madness. He dropped his binoculars into their case on his belt and fumbled it closed one-handed; there were some things it was better to see no more clearly than you must.

2000 meters.

The giant wedge was more ragged; another two or three thousand down in the last few minutes. Close enough now to see the figures grow from ants to dolls by naked eye, close enough to see contorted mouths and for their roaring almost to drown the shellfire. A quiver ran down the long thin blue line of Civil Government soldiers. Only the guns spoke. The Squadron ranks were packing tighter and tighter as the men on the outside edged in away from the artillery redoubts on either wing.

1500 meters.

"Ready," Raj said, raising his blade. The aide puffed his cheroot and went down on one knee.

1000 meters.

"May the Spirit forgive us," Raj whispered.

900 meters.

"*Now,*" he said in a clear loud voice.

The sword came down in a glittering arc, and Horace danced a half-step sideways. The rocket arched skyward and exploded in a silver dazzle.

Seven thousand men came to one knee and fired. The sound was loud enough to drive needles of pain into the ears.

What happened to the enemy was hidden for an instant by the cloud of flame-shot smoke that erupted from his line. When that parted, he saw that the whole front of the enemy host had vanished; the heavy hollow-point 11mm bullets drove right through bodies and into the men behind. Time seemed suspended, moving in amber honey so slowly he could see the faces of the charging barbarians turn from fury or fear to uncomprehending shock.

Then the second rank of his men stood and fired over

the heads of the first. Ahead there were muzzle-flashes and reports along the Squadron front line—what had suddenly become their front line—as men reflexively tried to strike back. Some of the ones in the middle of the formation fired too, into the air or into the backs of the men ahead, as the unreachable death combed them. All of which meant that even if they did get to within a hundred meters of the Civil Government line they would be helpless, since nobody was going to stop for the tedious business of reloading a flintlock in the middle of *this*.

"They're still coming on," Ehwardo said in disbelief. "All guts, no brains."

Raj stood in the saddle. Directly ahead of him an officer of Poplanich's Own shouted *"By half-companies, volley fire!"* Others were repeating it all along the line, and a steady column of smoke rose from the riflemen, like a long thin chimney across the face of the battlefield, and a stuttering rattle of BAMBAMBAMBAMBAM underneath it, continuous. Noncoms ran down the lines of the infantry units, pushing rifles down and checking that men were adjusting their sights; most of them were firing blind to verbal direction, into the pall of smoke ahead.

"Oh, the evil, evil bastard," Raj breathed. Behind the engaged Squadron units still more men were dismounting and running forward into the smoke, into the artillery and massed rifle fire. Admiral Auburn was sending in the last Battle. The bulk of the Squadron troops were slowing; exactly the wrong thing to do, but inevitable as terror balanced and fought against courage. The rifle-fire beat on, under the steady roaring of the guns; more and more of the enemy were falling flat and trying to crawl forward, or taking shelter behind bodies.

400 meters.

A new sound from the artillery, long *PAAAMMM* reports as they switched to case-shot. No bursting charge, just a giant shotgun shell with hundreds of half-ounce lead balls ahead of the powder . . . they whistled through the air with a malignant hum, like giant wasps, and where they struck they carved pathways through the packed Squadron fighters, as clean as wedges cut by a giant invisible knife. Raj walked Horace forward between two companies of Poplanich's Own, coughing with the powder-smoke and peering out. The Squadron attack had stalled . . . or rather, it was acting like a stick of butter thrust slowly onto a hot frying pan, melting away at the front despite the pressure thrusting it forward from behind.

A last knot of men ran out of the smoke, grouped around a banner. The Captain to Raj's left barked a command—probably unheard in this racket—and swung his sword. Muzzles turned; the next volley ripped half the men around the flag off their feet. They came on, feet pumping; more fell, until there was only one to scoop the banner out of the dirt and continue with bullets kicking clods out of the dirt all around him. He staggered, red spots blossoming on his chest, came on again, sank to his knees and thrust the iron spike of the flag into the ground and slid down it, arterial blood pouring out of his mouth. Raj sat watching as bullets snapped the flagstaff and the folds dropped over the last man to hold it.

The steel of his saber tapped against Horace's stirrup-iron. *Three hundred meters*, he thought. *I doubt any of them got closer than that.*

Behind, through the gaps in the smoke, he could see the Squadron forces disintegrating. They had been locked for a moment as the last ranks trapped those in front when they turned to flee, but shell fire had knocked holes in that wall. Now the last Battle were fleeing as well, some still mounted, individuals and blocks scattering away. Panic spread faster than ripples in water, and in moments scarcely a hundred Squadrones were facing the Civil Government line. Hundreds more died as bullets and shrapnel took them in the back, as they ran sobbing with exhaustion and fear over the bodies of the dead.

"Sound *rifles cease fire*," Raj called.

It spread down the line, faster than the sea breeze pulled away the dirty cotton blanket of smoke. The guns cracked on, hammering the fleeing enemy.

"Sound *prepare for general pursuit*," he said; that rolled out too, a complex of drums and bugles.

Down the line of infantry orders barked. Men stood, and there was a ten-thousand-fold glitter as the long bayonets snapped onto the bars and cleaning-rod fasteners beneath the barrels. Banners swayed to the front and drums beat; in a long waving front like sea-surf the infantry advanced at the walk. A staccato rattle of aimed individual fire swept out ahead of it, marksmen and NCOs shooting and reloading as they advanced. Around Raj the cavalry line dissolved as men raced back for their dogs and slid their rifles into the scabbards before the right stirrup: There was a scent of scorched hide over the sulfur stink, as the glowing metal burned the liners; then a massive jingling as twenty-five hundred riders formed by battalions behind him: He heeled Horace forward as the banner of Poplanich's Own moved up to one side.

"Sound the charge!"

At both ends of the Civil Government line sabers slithered free by the thousand, a blinding mirror-brightness.

His sword swept up and then down, pointing to the dispersing mass of the enemy.

"*Charge!*"

"Coward! Whelp! You fled, you fled!" the women screamed at the defeated Squadron warriors.

Many of the Squadron levy had brought their households along with them to share the victory, leaving them in the wagon-fort a few kilometers behind the line. Now the women stood on the wagon-beds with their black shawls fluttering, striking clumsily at the fugitives who had made it this far, at their husbands and brothers and sons; they had swords and clubbed muskets in their hands, or stock-whips.

"Coward, coward!"

Some of the wagons were burning, and women threw themselves into the flames. Others cut their children's throats before stabbing themselves, or hanged themselves from the tall wagon-poles with their children at their heels. Raj passed a family strung up thus like obscene fruit; beyond them, inside the great circle of wagons, men who had thrown away their weapons were rolling under the feet of the milling frantic oxen to die. Their bawling covered the screams, an undertone to the roar of flames and the occasional crackle of shots. A field-gun went bouncing by, on its way to some pocket of holdouts.

WHUMP. A powder-wagon blew up a thousand meters

across the fort, and a globe of orange fire strobed for seconds across retinas in counterpoint to the ringing in ears stunned by the blast.

"Let's get some order here, Spirit-dammit!" he shouted hoarsely, waving the revolver at a clump of cavalry. "Get these people under control!"

They cantered over and began prying two wagons apart, slashing at the hide bindings with their sabers; one trooper looked up as dead feet brushed his head, swore and cut twice to sever the rope. His comrades shouted curses as they heaved and bodies rained down on their heads. Infantry were already at work inside, rounding up the survivors, stunning and binding; when the wagons were heaved apart a column of prisoners came through at a stumbling run, kicked, prodded with bayonets, and whacked along with rifle butts. A blond girl fell almost at Raj's feet; she would have been very pretty, except for the swelling purple bruise across one side of her face. She spat at his feet and stumbled off with the rest, holding a torn blouse across her breasts as a shoulder pushed her.

"You, Captain," Raj said. The officer saluted. "Get more of these wagons dragged apart or we'll lose them all to the fire. Move the oxen out but keep them bunched. And for the merciful Saints' sake, keep the men in hand!"

Ludwig Bellamy was looking white, even in the ruddy light of the fires and the dust-shrouded afternoon sun.

"Your father made the right decision," Raj said, sweeping his pistol in a circle over the scene. His voice was a little louder than need be, even with the level of background noise. "He knew the Squadron was going to lose. This is what defeat is, Messer Bellamy. Avoid it."

Raj heeled Horace into a canter, and the command-group and the Scouts followed, past growing roped-off squares where Squadron prisoners sat under guard with their hands behind their heads. The fires were dying as the soldiers pulled the wagons away; other men were spreading the tilts as groundsheets and piling loot in a rough-sort, separate heaps for fabrics and weapons and whatnot. Many of M'lewis's men were casting longing glances at the wagons—a sack was one of the rare pleasures of a soldier's life—but their Lieutenant was there . . . and Messer Raj had a name for seeing his men right.

He halted as Muzzaf Kerpatik rode up with a platoon of the Slashers: The men dropped back as they halted their mounts nose-to-tail, and Raj leaned forward to listen. The little southerner was not formally a fighting man, but his face was black with powder smoke under his cap and puggaree, and the Komar-made pepperpot pistol stuck through his sash had seen use this day.

"I have the Admiral's wagons under close guard," he said. Leaning closer and speaking in a whisper: "I estimate the value of what we found at two hundred twenty thousand gold FedCreds, Messer Raj—and he escaped with the best of it. Many of his private papers were left, as well."

Even then Raj shaped a silent whistle. Enough to equip and mount the entire Expeditionary Force, and pay it for a year; that was making war support war with a vengeance! So *much for Tzetzas*, he thought; the Governor would be very well pleased indeed.

"Also, I have these men," he said. Raj looked at the column of prisoners behind the Slashers, roped neck and neck. Ordinary-enough Squadron warriors, from their looks; a few had the rich equipage of high nobles. Then the Slasher Captain rode up; it was Pehdro Belagez, the new commander. He carried a Squadron banner over his shoulder, and swung it down for Raj to see.

"These *Ihorantes* dogs are the ones who killed our commander under a flag of truce, *mi Heneral*," he said in a gentle voice, with an almost kittenish tone. "Messer Kerpatik brought us to them as they tried to escape with their sows and spawn, for which the Spirit of Man of the Stars will shine upon him. What is your will concerning them, my General?"

"The families? Slave market."

"And the men?" Belagez asked. The troopers leaned forward in their saddles: Mekkle Thiddo had been a popular commander.

Raj looked at the big burly figures who stood with downcast eyes in their bonds.

"Crucify them," he said.

CHAPTER THIRTEEN

"Thank you, no," Raj said firmly.

The delegation under the high arched gate looked downcast and astonished. It was fairly impressive for something cobbled together on short notice: the heads of the merchant guilds in long robes of a cut that had been fashionable in East Residence fifty years ago; a scattering of old aristocracy families who had hung on under Squadron rule; the underground Arch-Syssup of Port Murchison, understandably overjoyed to be representative of the State church once more; with a chorus of hymn-singing girls in garlands and white dresses and a flock of priests. . . .

"Messers, Messas," he went on, in careful Spanjol, "my troops have just won a major battle and their blood is up. The war isn't over, and it wouldn't do discipline any good to let them scatter in a rich city at night—nor, to be blunt, would it do your city much good, at all. We'll enter the city tomorrow, and I'll call you together then to settle billeting and other arrangements."

"But . . . but, there are still Squadrones inside the walls, thousands of them!" the head of the delegation said. Even now he was visibly afraid of the overlords. All to the good, or else the mobs would have torn them all limb from limb.

Former overlords, Raj thought. "Are they under arms?"

"No—no, most of the fighting men marched out with Conner Auburn." And died, many under the walls when the gates were shut against them. "They crowd into the Earth

Spirit temples, and into our Star churches, even, seeking sanctuary."

"Then give it to them. Post guards. Tomorrow, Messers, if you please."

Raj stretched and sighed, looking upward. The stars were very bright, with only a three-quarter Miniluna to dispute the heavens; it was mildly warm as they rode away from the torchlit bulk of Port Murchison's walls. Those were the old-fashioned curtain type, twenty meters high and ten thick with a rubble core in none too good condition, but they bulked huge in the darkness. The cookfires of the Expeditionary Force were a glowing constellation of their own, through the groves and gardens outside the city; it was rich land, well tended with noblemen's country-seats. Wagons and handcarts were creaking out of the city with food and cooked delicacies, although the guards were supposed to be turning back anything too blatant in the way of liquor or whores. Mostly the men seemed too tired to be restless and too excited to sleep.

"You sure about the war not being over?" Gerrin Staenbridge said, as he and Foley fell in beside their commander. "What happened today . . . that was about as decisive as anything I've seen or heard of."

Foley nodded. "We must have killed, oh, eight or ten thousand," he said with a slight shiver. "Toward the end they couldn't fight and wouldn't give up . . ." Gerrin reached over and squeezed his shoulder.

Raj nodded absently. "It was no more trouble than slaughtering pigs in a pen, Spirit strike me blind for a Christo if I lie," he said. *Except to poor Thiddo and a hundred or so others, every one of them as dead as they'd be if the barbs had won.* "I doubt if five thousand of their main force got away: we took twenty thousand fighting men prisoners, and twice that number of civilians. They must have lost nearly thirty thousand dead—over forty thousand counting the ones here and the two thousand the Skinners slaughtered. We'll have plague unless we get them underground fast, in this weather."

That meant half of all the Squadron males of fighting age were dead or captured, if the Ministry of Barbarians' figures were anything like accurate. Of course, the Squadron could mobilize every non-cripple; they didn't have the vast peon mass the Civil Government did.

"But the Admiral got away, worse luck, and the evil, senile old bastard will probably do his best to get *all* his people killed. He can still raise another forty or fifty thousand men from the western counties, if they answer the call, and the ten thousand Curtis Auburn has out on Sadler's Island are their best anyway."

"Gah," Gerrin said. "I didn't join the Army to work in an abattoir."

"Well, we can't *count* on their being as obliging next time," Raj pointed out. "See you in the morning," he said, as they came up to the villa that was his billet.

He walked Horace into the courtyard, then halted him with a silent touch of the rein. Suzette was sitting on the veranda in a pool of lantern-light, playing her long-necked *gittar*, and two-score men were crouched motionless on the flagstones at the base of the stairs; roughneck Scouts as quiet as the officers and Ludwig Bellamy, who was looking at her with the expression of a man who has just been struck hard on the head.

> *"For we are all one way riders—*
> *Riders on that one way street,*
> *That runs across a golden valley*
> *Where the rivers of joy and hope run deep."*

It was her favorite song, one a Stalwart nurse had taught her as a child.

> *"Rain must fall and winds will blow—*
> *Lost men die in the mountain snow*
> *Souls break their wings on heaven's wall*
> *Night must come, come to us all—"*

She rose and set the instrument aside as he walked toward her, lamplight sheening on the raven's-wing hair and gilding her eyes. He knelt and kissed her hand, then swept her up effortlessly in his arms as he rose and carried her indoors. Good-natured cheers followed them as he kicked the door shut behind him.

CHAPTER FOURTEEN

A roaring chorus of soldiers' voices echoed back from the houses of Port Murchison, louder than the frenzied cheering of the crowds:

> "The heathen in his blindness bows down to dirt an' stone;
> He won't obey no orders, 'nless they is 'is own;
> He keeps 'is side-arms awful: he leaves 'em all about—
> Then up comes us Regulars and we poke the heathen out!"

The Expeditionary Force was marching into the city down the Sacred Way in a mass two battalions wide, each in column of fours. Raj and his household first, and then the 5th Descott and Poplanich's Own, in the position of honor at the front; then the Arch-Syssup of the diocese with a chorus of priests and nuns, then cavalry, guns, infantry, long columns of stumbling prisoners roped neck-and-neck, wagons filled with captured banners and weapons . . . The citizens were massed on the sidewalks behind barriers of infantry holding their rifles across their chests, on balconies and rooftops; they threw streams of flowers at the soldiers, muck and rotten vegetables and dogshit at their former overlords. Star Spirit priests stood on every corner to bless the return of the True Faith.

"Spirit-damned waste of time," Raj muttered to himself, keeping his gaze fixed straight ahead.

"We all have our burdens to bear," Staenbridge said beside him. Ehwardo snorted laughter on the other side, brushing flower-petals off his tunic. Suzette smiled regally, nodding and waving to the crowd.

Well, they certainly can't afford to have the Admiral back after this, Raj mused. Which was also the reason Ludwig Bellamy and his father were in the parade a little farther back, conspicuously well-treated and armed.

Gerrin muffled a shout of laughter, looking over his shoulder. Raj snuck a look back himself, pretending a genuflection to a Syssup spraying holy water from a platform. Kaltin Gruder had fallen out by the outer line of the 7th Descott Rangers, sweeping off his helmet and bowing in the saddle as his dog caracoled and pranced. A striking young woman in the mantilla and shawl of a matron was waving from the wrought-iron balcony of an affluent-looking townhouse; she covered her face with her fan and flung a rose. Gruder snatched it out of the air and bowed again with the stem between his teeth before galloping back to his position at the head of the battalion.

"Damned fast work, even for Kaltin." Staenbridge laughed.

"Damned bad example," Raj said grumpily. Although Gruder's reputation didn't do him any harm with the troopers, to be sure.

Port Murchison was much like a Civil Government town, of a rather old-fashioned type; the streets were lined with three-story buildings of whitewashed brick and stone, arched arcades on the ground floors and screened balconies above. No gaslights, and not much of a factory district; the fountains were not working, and though the houses and shops were fairly well kept, the surface of the road was not, cracked and uneven and actually muddy in places.

"I just hope they love the Civil Government as much once Tzetzas's tax-farmers get here," Raj said ironically.

Ehwardo snorted. "Even Tzetzas only loves Tzetzas because he's paid to," he said.

They wound into the plaza, a big U-shaped pavement surrounded by public buildings and the townhouses of wealthy nobles. There was a dry fountain in the center, the marble pile of the Palace of the Vice Governors—the Admirals, for the last three generations—at the head. The ancient Star Temple, with a high golden dome and pillared portico, stood to its right; there was no many-rayed Star at its peak, though. Raj's lips tightened in genuine anger. He had been in to survey the route, earlier, and he had seen enough of the damage the Squadron had wrought in the churches, even in the ones they had converted to their own cult. Holy statues splashed with bullet-lead—the Squadrones seemed to have a particular liking for shooting off the noses—mosaics ripped up, icons burned . . .

"Vandals," he muttered. "Nothing but a bunch of fucking *vandals.*"

a universe of vicious children, raj whitehall, said Center, **and us.**

Grooms ran to take their horses as they stopped before the steps of the Palace; he laid the ceremonial mace in the crook of his arm and turned to hand Suzette down from Harbie. She stepped regally by his side, her fingertips resting on his arm and the plumes of her headdress nodding. The officers and civil dignitaries followed him as he walked up, seating themselves as he turned at the marble plinth that divided the stairs and served as a raised podium; that put him nearly a story above the level of the pavement, with a fine view out over the plaza and down to the wall. He rested easily with his left hand on his saber hilt, letting the breeze ruffle fingers through his dark curls and watching the remainder of the Expeditionary force march in and drop to parade-rest. All except the units already busy, of course.

And the Skinners. Not even the Spirit of Man with a thunderbolt in hand could control Skinners in a town; he'd camped them a kilometer from the walls, with a continuous stream of high-proof liquor and highly paid entertainment, and a cavalry battalion to watch them. Muzzaf's work; invaluable man . . .

At last the final unit came to a halt and crashed into parade rest; the prisoners were elsewhere, filing off to the bullrings he was using to pen the Squadron captives and their families for now. The other half of the square was black with civilians, including a clump of important personages directly below the stairs.

"Citizens of Port Murchison," he began in Spanjol. The

acoustics were superb, as they had been when the long-ago engineers laid the buildings out. "You are once more united with the Civil Government of Holy Federation—and with Holy Federation Church." Deafening cheers from the crowd, while the soldiers stood patiently at the easy.

"Soon we will begin the work of rebuilding this province and making it secure for all time. Rest assured that the Army of the Civil Government is here as a liberator, not a conqueror. All citizens will be protected in their persons and property"—*as long as they don't go near the Skinners*—"and any offense by military personnel should be reported immediately. By the same token, any disloyalty, any treason, any failure of cooperation with the new and lawful authorities, will be crushed without mercy."

Everyone had seen the bodies from Gerrin's pursuit piled in windrows under the gates, and selected individuals were being marched out to see the battlefield and help with the mass burials. Most of the inhabitants would probably get the point.

"Please disperse, and remember that this city and district remain under martial law for the present. Go about your usual business, and further instructions will be issued as needed. The remainder of this day is a public holiday, and the warehouses are to be opened for an issue of free wine to the citizenry."

That brought hearty cheers, and the crowd began to flow out rapidly enough, helped by soldiers with *guardia* armbands. When Raj resumed, it was in the Army's own Sponglish:

"Fellow-soldiers," he began, then had to halt while a roaring cheer battered at him. He blinked in slight surprise, then held up his hands for silence.

"Fellow-soldiers, I'm not a politician, so I'll keep this short. We've come a long way together, and done great things. By our count, every one of you has done in at least three barbs"—massed laughter—"which is a good start. Remember, the job's not over yet! The barb Admiral is still loose, raising more troops, and Curtis Auburn isn't back yet either. There's more fighting to come, so don't let your guard down.

"Also remember this is a city of our own people, not a conquered enemy. You're guests where you're billeted—act like it. There's enough honest liquor and willing women in this town without acting like bandits. Everyone will get leave over the next week, in rotation; and just so you can drink the Governor's health, I'm authorizing a donative of six months' pay for everyone—"

This time the cheers were enough to make the stone vibrate slightly under his feet, and lasted for minutes.

"—as an advance. You've all done well and I'm proud to lead you. Dismiss to quarters!"

Trumpets blew, but instead of scattering the men began to chant:

"*RAJ! RAJ!*"

He waved good-humoredly, but the chanting did not stop; the men surged forward around the stairs, their helmets thrusting upward on the muzzles of their rifles.

Spirit, some idiot will start hailing me for the Chair next, he thought with genuine alarm; no Governor forgave demonstrations like *that*, spontaneous or no. He smiled and saluted and turned, leaving the officers and dignitaries to follow in his wake.

The huge audience hall was almost full as well, with a crowd whose gowns and jewelry shone under the skylights high above; soldiers with polished bayonets stood at rigid attention, clearing an aisle down which ran a red-velvet carpet. The Arch-Syssup of the Diocese of Port Murchison greeted him, and Raj knelt to receive the anointment of power, a dab on both temples and a touch of the the wired headset that symbolized contact with the Spirit's Net. There was a certain irony in it, for him. . . . Then he was striding toward the Chair, high on its dais at the end of the room, blinding-bright in a peacock glory of sapphire and emerald and silver. Blazing mosaics covered every wall; even the Squadrones had not touched the huge abstract Star that covered the solid portions of the ceiling, glittering with burnished platinum.

The only drab things in the chamber were the uniforms of his troops, grim and worn. There was a certain symbolism in that, too. His boots sounded, harsh metal on the stone of the dais; there was an iron clatter from the chape of his saber scabbard as he turned, holding aloft the mace of office. Heads bowed like flowers rippling before a breeze, and stayed bent in a low bow until he seated himself and laid the mace on the broad arm of the Vice Governor's Chair. Suzette took the consort's chair, lower down the stairs.

"Gentlemen," he said, "we have a program of work before us. I suggest that we begin."

Faintly through the doors and the thick stone, he could hear the soldiers chanting his name.

"Spirit damn you, get those drumsticks back! Don't drip grease on this!" Raj said again, resting his palms on the map.

The big room was buzzing with officers, administrators from Berg's contingent, and members of the Port Murchison city administration; few of those last had been Squadrones, anyway, and most seemed enthusiastic about the new order. Cork-boards were ranged around the walls, covering the murals, and maps and lists were pinned to them; more were scattered down the long glossy table. Suzette had gotten the household organized in record time, and Admiral Auburn's own servants were wheeling around trays and dispensing a working lunch. Some of the officers showed a tendency to gnaw on the honey-garlic sauroid sticks while leaning over important documents. . . .

"We've got to patrol vigorously," Raj went on, his finger tracing a circle around Port Murchison, "but not in penny-packets; Auburn's men will be trying to snap up foraging parties. Gerrin, see to it. Which reminds me—Muzzaf, what's the news on grain supply?"

"No more than two weeks currently, counting the extra mouths," the Komarite said, looking up from a huddle of clerks at the foot of the table.

"Right. Put out an offer for, hmmm, ten percent above current market for clean threshed grain, beans, meat, fruit, alfalfa fodder—payable in hard cash. The enemy will try to stop us, of course; coordinate with Gerrin. We can name collection points and use the captured wagons."

"Messer."

"Grammeck?"

The artilleryman flourished a pad. "Messer Raj, the walls are in a mess—crumbling on the outside, down to the rubble core in places. The city services—it's a pigsty, looks like nothing has been kept up in a century. You *saw* what the main avenue was like—the delivery pipes from the aqueduct blocked years ago, and the ham-handed pigs have never gotten them properly fixed. The sewer system—" He shuddered. "Don't ask."

"Do what you can; organize night-soil carts if you have to. I'm worried about the bull-rings"—where fifty thousand Squadron men, women, and children were crammed; plague was no respecter of nationalities.

He looked over at the *halcalde,* the mayor, a sleek-looking civilian named Carlo Arrias. "Messer Arrias, do you have anyone who knows the systems?"

"Certainly, Messer General," the man said, rubbing his hands together and grinning. *Well, somebody's happy, at least.* "The Squadrones would never authorize the funds—as long as the whorehouses and bars were open the city was working fine to their tastes; *real* warriors live out in the country." A trace of bitterness there. "There's emergency repairs we can do. A relief to finally get something *done* in this job."

"Grammeck, see to it; you can use on-duty units for labor, and prisoners when we've gotten them organized. Maximum priority on the defenses." His first impulse was bunkers and earthworks, but against the barbarians a nice high masonry wall would do, if it stood. "Then roads, here and around the city."

Thank the Spirit *we didn't have to fight in the rainy season,* he thought, sipping at a cup of soup. Even the main arteries near the city were in shocking condition.

"Will do, sir."

"Now, about billeting," Raj said. Arrias frowned.

"Messer general, couldn't more of the troops be accommodated in Squadron properties?"

Raj grinned. "Not until they've been properly inventoried and stripped," he said. "I can keep them from stealing too much from living, breathing fellow-citizens, but not from absent barb heretics. Speaking of which, Jorg; I want three full battalions of infantry on continuous patrol as *guardia;* I'm authorizing you to take over whatever police arrangements this city had—"

He looked at Arrias. The man spread his palms: "The Admiral didn't like civilians having any sort of armed organization," he said apologetically. "We had a volunteer watch, but it was mostly poorer Squadron members."

"Well, we'll work out something permanent later," Raj went on. "Jorg, I want strict control. Come down like a ton of cement on anyone who so much as stiffs a barkeep or a hooker."

Menyez dragged off three of his infantry Majors and they went into a huddle at a side table over a street map of the city.

"Kaltin," Raj went on.

Gruder looked up, alert and smiling; he was nattily turned out, freshly shaved, and had a ruby stud in one ear; rumor had it that a prominent young widow had already invited him to use her townhouse as billet for his headquarters.

"Kaltin," Raj went on, "I'm still concerned about Curtis Auburn and those damned ten thousand men of his; it's only a week's sail from here to Sadler Island, he's going to have to hear about what's going on *sometime*. If he lands outside and joins his brother the Admiral, well and good—but he *might* just try attacking us here. Go over the harbor defenses—personally, and whatever records you can scrape up: get Grammeck to give you some of his people. I want a fallback plan for defense against simultaneous assaults on the walls and the outer harbor."

Port Murchison had two linked lagoons; the outer was the merchant docking area, and the smaller circular one farther inland was the military. They were joined by a canal, but only the merchant harbor was directly accessible from the sea.

"Which reminds me," he continued: "Security. We want no tales getting out to the hot-blooded Curtis."

"Ahem," Arrias said. Raj raised an eyebrow. "Messer General Whitehall, I have here"—he pulled out a slip of paper—"a small list, compiled with the help of the Reverend Arch-Syssup, of—hmmmm—questionable non-Squadron persons. You will understand, since the barbarians ruled here so long . . . and to tell the truth, there are those not anxious to see our city back under East Residence rule."

For which there are good reasons, Raj admitted. The Admirals had been sloppy, inefficient, lazy, corrupt, and occasionally oppressive rulers. The Civil Government was nearly as corrupt, but vastly more sophisticated and energetic. The Southern Territories would be better-organized and more productive now, but the local ruling class would not necessarily reap the benefits. He made an inquiring noise.

"Guildmaster Ferteryo Saylazar, to begin with," the mayor said. "He was instrumental in having the Civil Government's resident merchants interned when the news of the invas— of the liberation first arrived. And—"

Iron-heeled boots slammed to attention outside the door, and hands slapped on iron as rifles were brought to salute.

"The honorable Messer Senior Administrator Berg," a voice said briskly, as the doors opened.

"Ah, Messer Administrator Berg," Raj went on; the man came through the door and handed his riding cloak to a servant, accepting a glass of lemonade and dusting himself down.

Raj raised an eyebrow. "You didn't come in with the fleet?" he said. Orders to bring the fleet and enter the harbor sometime today had gone out to Admiral Gharderini right after the battle, while the fleet worked north in concert with the Army. There had been little contact, but according to the last report—his eyes flicked down to the map—the fleet had been resting in a cove about three kilometers south.

"No," Berg said, puzzled. "Admiral Gharderini sailed immediately on receiving news of the victory, right after Major Dalhouse arrived with his detachment. But I had some matters to get in order first . . ."

"Wait a minute—*quiet, please!*" The buzz of conversation died. "*When* did Gharderini sail? With *who?*"

"Yesterday: Your courier arrived, then Major Dalhouse with about a hundred men. They embarked, and steamed off right then, well, actually around midnight . . . Why?"

Raj held up a hand to stay him and turned to the halcalde. "Messer Arrias?"

"Ah—then the four warships weren't supposed to be in dock?" the mayor said nervously. He looked around, touching a finger to his cravat. *How can I avoid getting sucked into Army politics I know nothing about?* was written plainly enough on his face. "They've been, ah, loading supplies since last night."

"Supplies?" Raj said flatly.

"From the Admiral's warehouses. A number of export trades were the Admiral's property . . ." His voice trailed off. Raj spun on one heel like a gun-breech closing.

"Who's got the harbor sector?" he snapped.

"17th Cuirassiers," Jorg Menyez said. Everyone was suddenly conscious of the absence of Captain Hermano Suharto.

"Major Gruder," Raj said. "Turn out the 7th Descott and get them down there. Find out what the *hell* is going on. See that all naval personnel return to their ships; and if you find Dalhouse, put him under close arrest and bring him here, immediately."

"Sir!" Gruder said; suddenly the carefully brushed tunic looked like the glittering skin of a hunting carnosauroid. "If he resists, sir?"

"Kill him."

Captain Hermano Suharto needed the two troopers on either side to hold him up; the bandages on his face and side were still leaking red. He tried to salute as Raj stood.

"Get this man a chair, for the Spirit's sake," he snapped. "Kaltin?"

"Gharderini right enough," the scarred young Descotter said. "And Dalhouse with some of his cutthroats, and Hingenio Buthelezi and about half a dozen others—officers from the 17th and the 1st Gaur, mostly. That seagoing counter-jumper and his Blackjackets"—marines—"had a cool half-million worth loaded by the time we got there. Captain Suharto had some of his own men there; he was arguing with Dalhouse, then the *hijdaput* drew down on Suharto and cut him. There would have been a firefight right there and then if we hadn't ridden up; the warships fired blanks over our heads while the bastards got back on board, then they made steam. The last anyone saw of them, they were heading right out to sea."

Raj sank back in the chair, his hands clenched white on the arms.

observe said Center:

—and Dalhouse bowed before the Chair. It was a private audience in the Palace, in the Negrin Rooms; the Governor, Lady Anne, and Tzetzas seated, Dalhouse, Buthelezi and Gharderini standing as petitioners. Cool evening light came through the tall windows, picking out the ancient murals of waterfowl and reeds.

"Sovereign Mighty Lord," Dalhouse said, rising from the prostration. "With a heavy heart I bring Your Supremacy news of your servant's treason."

"Explain," Barholm said dryly. Lady Anne frowned, and the Chancellor steepled his slim fingers and raised a brow.

"Whitehall's arrogance is beyond belief, Your Supremacy!" Dalhouse's face contorted with anger. "He appoints known traitors like Poplanich and baseborn nobodies, peasants and infantrymen, to command over loyal men of good birth. Why? Because they owe everything to him, of course! Instead of sending back his loot to Your fisc as is his plain duty— as we loyal men have done—"

Tzetzas leaned forward and handed the Governor a slip of paper; this time Barholm's brows rose at the amount.

"—he spends it on donatives to buy the loyalty of his troops. I fear, I greatly fear, Your Supremacy, that Whitehall intends to make himself an independent ruler in the Southern Territories, using the Expeditionary Force and Squadron lords he's won over by bribes and by favors to their heretical cult. Already he's forbidden plundering of the abominable Earth Cult shrines, while they drip with a century's stolen wealth from Star Spirit churches."

Barholm nodded. "You may go," he said, and the three officers withdrew.

"Well?" he said.

"General Whitehall is a very able man," Tzetzas murmured, riffling a file of papers. "Even Gharderini's report concedes a smashing victory over the Squadron army. Very able . . ." He spread his hands; the dangers of extremely able commanders were never far from a Governor's mind.

"Well, we certainly can't panic on the report of a spiteful little backstabber like Dalhouse," Lady Anne said.

She glared at Tzetzas; the feud between them was old and bitter, running back to her childhood as a dancer down in the stews. Tzetzas had been her client then, in the years before she met and captivated the rising star of Barholm Clerett. Most men would have flinched before that gaze; the Chancellor merely smiled thinly and inclined his head in a show of deference as she went on:

"Either Raj Whitehall is loyal or he isn't—Lady Whitehall certainly is, and she's proved it. We can't do anything until we receive unbiased reports."

"The matter needs more thought," Barholm said, biting his lip. "We'll—"

"Good riddance," Raj said, shaking away the vision. "Major Gruder, I approve of your actions; the last thing we need right now is a major battle among ourselves. In the unlikely event that we see those swine again . . . Captain Foley"—Gerrin's friend was the most scholarly of them—"draw up formal charges of mutiny, theft, and attempted murder against them all; we'll forward it to headquarters."

"And now," he went on, "back to work."

CHAPTER FIFTEEN

"No, I'm *not* going to the pen-pushing bastard's party," Kaltin Gruder said, rising on one elbow. The servants had cleared the remains of the picnic lunch away, all except for the stone jugs of lemonade and thrice-watered wine. He sipped moodily at his. "Neither is Raj, you'll see."

"I really don't see what you've got against Berg," Gerrin Staenbridge said, leaning back against the oak tree and linking his fingers behind his head.

It was a comfortably warm summer's day, with the breeze off the sea; the headland park they had chosen was the highest land inside the walls, once a nobleman's pleasance, now the 5th's headquarters bivouac. Two weeks in Port Murchison had seen them well settled in, enough that the officers could take an hour or two for lunch. The air smelled of sea and warm grass, and he felt pleasantly drowsy, amused at the bitter passion in the other man's voice.

The rest of the picnic party were farther down the hill. Raj Whitehall was on all fours, with toddler Barton Staenbridge riding on his back and crowing delightedly; Hadolfo Zahpata crouched and gibbered in front of him, giving a remarkably accurate imitation of an arborosauroid. Barton Foley and Ehwardo Poplanich were lying on the rugs scattered under the jacaranda tree, singing to Suzette's *gittar* while Muzzaf kept time with a spoon on his knee. Pehdro Belagez and Hermano Suharto were doing slow-time fencing with wooden sabers in front of a wildly enthusiastic audience composed of Fatima and her new friends, Joni, Mitchi, and Karli. The three girls from Stern Island had turned out to be sisters, and they had all adopted Fatima as mentor.

"Berg should keep his hands off other men's wives," Kaltin spat.

Gerrin abandoned his abstract enjoyment of the four young women jumping up and down as they squealed and clapped—it reminded him of flowers swaying, especially given the varying hair colors—and turned wide eyes on the younger cavalry officer.

"Please," he said in a choked voice. "Tell me I didn't just hear the Rooster of East Residence, the Stud of Descott County, the man who's fought three duels over married women in the past year, say—" His coughing turned into helpless whoops of laughter.

Kaltin struggled and gave in to a sour grin, shrugging. "Well, that's different," he said, turning his own gaze on the fencers. Redheaded Karli blew him a kiss. He smiled briefly, then continued with a frown: "There's Raj's honor to consider."

Gerrin shook his head, pulling a handkerchief out of the sleeve of the uniform jacket next to him and mopping at his streaming eyes.

"You *mehmacho* types," he said, "just don't appreciate women."

It was Kaltin's turn to stare round-eyed. "Apart from the part between navel and knees," Staenbridge amplified. "And you might remember that Berg's testimony may very well be all that stands between us and the frying post when we get back." He sighed. "Not to mention putting Dalhouse there, where he belongs."

"Endfile to that," Gruder said; his hand stroked the hilt of his sword. "Although I'd prefer to see him get what that traitor Saylazar got."

Staenbridge grimaced; the evidence had been fairly damning, but he was still surprised that Raj had ordered the merchant impaled. He looked over; the General was bucking, with Barton Staenbridge's hands wound in his hair and heels drumming on his ribs. There were a few threads of silver in the thick black curls ... and Ferteryo Saylazar was still alive that morning on the steps of the Palace, standing straddled over the sharpened stake rammed up through his anus. A strong man could survive three, perhaps four days on a short stake.

"I'd rather shoot Dalhouse in the back and be done with it," Gerrin said. "And speaking of sneak assassins, have you heard what M'lewis found?"

"Ah-*ha*." Kaltin shook off lesser matters. "The Admiral?"

"Might be. In which case . . ."

"Battalion sweeps," Gruder said happily. "Hi! O Great Leader!"

Raj stood, holding the squirming child under one arm while he dusted himself off with the other. Fatima reclaimed her son amid a cooing crowd of her three protegees; the fencers came drifting over too, arms over each other's shoulders. Belagez had been very fond of Mekkle Thiddo, and anyone who tried to arrest the man who betrayed him was a blood-brother, even if he did now command the 17th Cuirassiers.

"Who gets the first rip-and-run at the Admiral's beard?" Gruder asked.

"Well—" Raj began, and froze. The others turned at his expression, to see the heliograph on the topmost tower of the Vice Governor's palace clicking out its sun-bright flickers.

"*Confirm please,*" Gerrin read. As one, they all pivoted to watch the eastern horizon; the hill was nearly as high as the tower, and they could all see the reply from the warship stationed at the edge of visibility.

"*Multiple—sails—*stop*—estimate +40—*stop*—approaching—northwest—*stop*—Squadron—galleys—and—transports—*stop*—am—heading—in—*stop*—estimate enemy will arrive two hours minimum four maximum.* End."

Four voices whispered it aloud. Seconds later the women and child were alone on the hill, staring after the soldiers.

Barton Staenbridge began to cry.

"Bloody hell, bloody *hell*," Raj said, squinting up the dockside street.

Port Murchison rose on low rolling ground from the water it enclosed on three sides. Like most cities originally laid out in the Civil Government, it was built on a partial grid plan; most of the waterfront was cut off by three- and four-story warehouses, there were tangles of alleys in parts, but the major streets ran more-or-less straight up from the water.

And on one of them, a barricade of wagons was visible. "Runner!" Raj said. "Message to whoever's in command up there, *get those wagons into a side street and keep them there until the word's given.*

"You," he went on, jabbing a finger at the harbormaster as the messenger clapped heels to his dog. "You've got the tugs ready?"

"*Say, Messenor,*" he replied in nervous Spanjol: Yes, my lord.

They were tubby little vessels, with ten two-man oars to a side and a raised catwalk; a tiny lazaretto stood under the wheel at the stern. Two more just like them were towing the final Civil Government steam ram into the inner military harbor; the bosuns danced down the catwalk swinging their ropes' ends, and the oars splashed with haste. Low smoke showed over the stone forts, as the remaining six warships made steam in there; no help for that ... He turned to the Captain of the 5th standing at his elbow.

"The men have been thoroughly briefed?" he said.

Tejan M'brust stroked his long black hair. "Yes, sir," he said cheerfully. "No sound unless the barbs catch on. Then they toss a grenade into the rower's pit and swim for it."

Risky duty ... but the best way to keep the oarsmen honest, and *they'd* been told the orders too. M'brust would be going on one of them himself.

"Go to it, son," he said.

"Move, move, *move*," Menyez shouted.

The drum beat in a long continuous roll: *to arms, to arms.* Men poured out of the houses down the long narrow street, some hopping as they jammed their feet into boots, others buttoning tunics loosened for the *siesta.* Hobnails clattered as they fell in by platoons, then dashed off with rifles at the trail; at the intersection outside, traffic directors in *guardia* armbands were grabbing file-closers and pushing them in the direction they should go, then halting everyone in a chorus of bone whistles as a battery of guns went by, the iron wheels rumbling on the cobblestones.

"Look," Menyez went on, turning to the assembled company commanders. Not his own 17th Foot—they didn't need a pep talk, although he'd be with them when it started—this was the 10th Melaga, an ordinary line outfit.

"You showed the dogboys what you could do at the Slaughterhouse"—that was the nickname for the first engagement with the Admiral—"and now you're going to do it again. It's all quite simple; you stand in reserve at the assigned locations, *keeping out of sight from the harbor.* No noise, no movement—the longer it takes until they realize we're here, the better. Then when the signal comes, get the stuff across the street, lie down behind it and shoot. In the unlikely event they get as far as your positions, give them the bayonet. Understood, gentlemen?"

"Sir yes sir!"

"I make it thirty-zero-and-one meters," the sentinel sang out from the rooftop above.

"Keep it peeled and be ready to call it," the commander of the mortar battery said, before he turned back to Grammeck Dinnalsyn.

"Should be ready to go in less than twenty minutes, sir," he said.

The mortars were massive weapons; most of the weight was in the big circular baseplate of welded wrought iron and cast steel. Those had clanged to the pavement minutes ago, and the wheels on their cranked axles had been dragged away. Now the crews were pounding long iron spikes through its slots into the ground and shoveling dirt from the little plaza's garden into the trough that ran around the edge. The barrel was a stubby tube of cast steel with a 100mm bore, mounted on a ball joint in the center. As he watched, the men finished rigging a knock-down lifting tripod over it and ran a cable through an eyebolt at the muzzle. The aiming frame waited to take the barrel, a thing of rods and screw-wheels. Others were unloading crates of shells from a wagon.

"Good," Dinnalsyn said. "Remember, I want those things dropped right on the decks if I call for them."

"You'll get it, Major," the lieutenant said. "Glad to have someone in charge who knows a gun isn't fought from the same end as a dog," he went on.

"You'll find Messer Raj fully aware of that," the artillery specialist replied.

"Well, of course, *him*, sir!" The tone strongly implied Messer Raj used ships only because walking on water was tiring.

"Carry on." He mounted and heeled his dog, cantering until he came to the Captain at the head of a two-battery train of field guns.

"Got your position?" he said. The man looked up from a map he was holding across his pommel against the wind of passage.

"Checked it yesterday, sir," he replied. "The road goes over a lip there, no sight-line to the harbor. We can set up and then just manhandle the guns forward, and we'll cover the outer harbor mouth nicely. *And* the road down to the docks."

The forts at the outer entrance were useless for this work; they had been intended to keep ships *out* of the port, and were ruinous anyway.

"I'll go along to see you get that infantry support company," Dinnalsyn said.

The iron racket of the gunwheels echoed back from shuttered houses amid the whining panting of the dog-teams. No civilians were in sight: War had come to Port Murchison with a vengeance . . . and most of them would be indoors, imagining a vengeful Squadron force turned loose on the city that had betrayed their Admiral and their families.

"Do *not* break the windows out, you fools!" Barton Foley snapped. The trooper froze with his rifle butt poised. "*Open* them."

"Yisser," the soldier said, flushing.

Like children, Foley thought. *They just love to break things.* It seemed to be an ineradicable enlisted-man trait, like pyromania . . . *Good men, though. Steady.* None of them showing any nerves at being rousted out of a comfortable billet for a surprise battle.

There were a dozen men of A Company, 1st Platoon of the 5th Descott setting up in here; a fire team and a set of 500-round ammunition boxes back by the door. The room had been some merchant's salon until a few moments ago, when the Descotters broke in and threw the protesting family out to find their way uptown against the massive flow of military traffic. He stepped to the tall narrow windows and looked out over the balcony; the slanting road below made a dogleg here, giving a clear field of fire right down to the main docks. Across the way more troopers were settling in along the roofline with only their eyes showing, and he saw movement at the windows; at ground level there was a pounding of feet and tap of drums as company columns pounded past doing the double quickstep.

"Where's Lieutenant Ahlvayrez?"

"Up t' roof, Cap'n."

"All right, men," Foley said; acutely conscious of his own youth for a moment. He made a sweeping gesture with his hook. "Remember, don't let them *see* you—just like a sauroid hunt. This is a blind over a game-trail . . . memorize your firing positions and the terrain, then get well back and wait for your corporal to give you the word. Understood?"

Nods and grins, even on this unfamiliar urban terrain. None of them were townsmen by birth, and none of them had fought in a built-up area before either. That was rare enough that even the handbooks didn't deal with it, much.

"Carry on."

Gerrin was coming upstairs outside the room, slightly out of breath; they had time for a quick hug.

"Everything in place?" the older man said.

"More or less. They'll be settled in in about fifteen, twenty minutes." They both looked at their watches; an hour and a half since the heliograph message. "It's those cow-handed peon infantry I'm worried about—they take a week to chew the cud of an unfamiliar idea."

"Raj thought of that," Gerrin said, taking a deep breath. He squeezed the younger man's shoulder. "I'm off to the command post. Be careful, my dear."

Foley grinned and flourished the hook where his left hand had been. "Always," he said.

"Bloody odd way to run a battle," Raj said, leaning back in the deck chair and raising the binoculars.

The overall command post had been set up on a rooftop patio with a good view down to the harbor and a crenellated wall; that was meant to be ornamental, but the stone was thick and the gaps for riflemen quite functional. There was a map table set up, and a rank of messengers waiting; a portable heliograph stood with the operator's hands on the levers. The soldiers seemed incongruous among the potted rosebushes and bougainvillea.... The city had fallen very quiet; perhaps quiet enough to be suspicious, but there was not much he could do about that.

Not much I can do about anything, he thought, swallowing acid.

does it distress you to have to give orders and trust others to carry them out? Center commented drily.

Raj laughed, drawing awed looks from some of the troopers. *It's easy for you,* he thought.

is it?

Raj blinked in surprise, then turned to Suzette. "How's our mutual friend Berg?" he said, raising the glasses again.

The first transport was being towed between the ends of the breakwater; he could see the long blue swells creaming into surf on the rough line of interlocked stone that guarded the harbor. A substantial ship, bluff-bowed and three-masted; sailors were standing on the bare spars, at their ease—and away from the rowdy mass of Squadron warriors crowding the rails. *Getting ready for the knocking-shops if they're from the country, and home to the wife and kiddies if they're not,* he thought

"Nervous," Suzette said quietly. "He's . . . not a fighting man, after all."

"Well, I hope he doesn't bugger off for the bundu—the Admiral's out there somewhere," Raj said.

Two more ships were coming into the harbor mouth; there was a crowd of them dotted across kilometers of calm ocean, rising and falling with the long swells, bows to the wind under jibsails as they waited for their tows. Forty or more sail, and beyond them the long snaky shapes of war-galleys, their beaks flashing as the crews dipped the oars just enough to keep them head to the waves and holding station. They made a brave sight, familiar from the visions Center had sent him; from what he'd been told, they could be smelled a kilometer or better downwind. The Squadron navy used chained slaves and convicts as rowers, ten men to an oar and single-banked. The slave-barracks over on the military harbor had provided thousands of extremely enthusiastic volunteer laborers for the Civil Government forces, even though they were three-quarters empty with the decline of the Squadron's naval power.

"Feel that trembling in the ground?" Raj asked.

"What?" Suzette replied.

Raj gave a harsh laugh. "That's old 'Geyser' Ricks trying to burrow back from Starless Hell and strangle his descendants for ineptitude," he said.

Suzette sat beside him and took his hand; he squeezed back gratefully, feeling a little of the tension go out of his back. "What's going to happen?" she said softly.

"I don't know," he replied honestly. "As far as I can tell, I've got everything covered . . . but this isn't like a normal battle where you can sit on a hill and *see* everything." Most battlefields were less than a kilometer on a side, and in open country. "Even the reserve is decentralized—and I've got to keep enough men on the walls, just in case. I've told the front-line people to use their initiative."

The first transport was nearly to the docks, and a dozen more were inching in as the tug crews bent to their oars. It would be the men first, the dogs second, and then the warships following through to the inner harbor; tradition, for the Squadron. Convenient for him . . .

"Spirit knows what'll happen when they do *that*."

Hereditary Sector Commander Henrik Martyn leaped down the gangplank and fell full-length to kiss the grimy concrete of the dock.

"Home!" he howled, between smacks. "Eats! Booze! Pussy! No more hardtack, no more hairy hardcases!"

The men behind him on the ship yelled good-naturedly and poured down after him, slinging their weapons; servants and slaves would follow with their baggage.

"Fuckin' waste of a campaign," one of them said.

Martyn nodded, rising and dusting himself off; he was a tall young man, full-bearded and with shoulders like a bear. "Damn straight, Willi," he said. "Go to Sadler Island, sit in front of the city walls, scratch our butts, come back because somebody's seen a Civvie boogieman behind a peach tree."

"Too much peach brandy, maybe," one of his friends laughed. "Hey, come back to my place for dinner? Try out your lies on Marylou."

"Sure, can't head home until tomorrow anyway—then I'll kick some peon butt. Lazy bastards probably let my wheat rot in the fields."

They shrugged their slung flintlocks to their backs and strolled off away from the docks, peering around for the friends and family who should have been there to greet them. The broad paved area along the piers was deserted, except for the thousand or so men from the ships fresh in dock. No stevedores but the few handling the ground-lines, and those went about their work with heads down and mouths shut; no bustle around the anchored merchantmen, no trains of carts and slaves at the warehouses. It even *smelled* quiet, like a hot dusty day out in the country or in some little *puheblo,* not like Port Murchison. Granted it was siesta time, but this was ridiculous.

"Where the fuck is everyone?" he asked, as he and a half-dozen others ambled up one of the cobbled roads toward the central plaza. "There a bullfight or a baseball game on today?" He hitched uneasily at his swordbelt

"Naw—nothin' scheduled; it's Holy Week, remember? There aren't even any *natives* around. Earth Spirit—you don't think there's something to those latrine rumors about the Civvies invading, do you?"

"Those rabbit-hearted bastards? You've got to be—*hel*lo, *that's* better."

One of the dockside taverns seemed to be open, from the tinkling of a piano coming through the rippling glass-bead curtain that closed the entrance. A girl was standing in the doorway; Martyn angled over for a better look. *Rowf!* he thought: a high-breasted young one, with long shining blond hair and a complexion to match. She pouted at him as he approached, raising a wineglass to bee-stung lips and shooting out a hip. That made her slit skirt fall open, showing one long smooth leg right up to the hip; she turned and vanished into the door with a bump and grind as he came near.

"Hooo, darlin', wait for *me,*" he called. "C'mon, boys, a drink before dinner!" he added, over his shoulder.

He ducked through the bead curtain of the door, blinking in the dim light. Then his eyes focused on the girl; she was leaning her buttocks back against the rail of the bar and raising her skirt in both hands. A *natural* blonde. Martyn roared happily and reached for his belt-buckle as he stepped forward.

Darkness, and the floor rushing up to meet him.

"Is he dead, Antin?" Joni asked anxiously, dropping her skirt and hurrying forward.

Antin M'lewis chuckled as he slapped the chamois leather bag of lead shot into his palm, then bent to expertly slit the Squadron warrior's wallet loose from his belt. It was gratifyingly heavy; he tossed it to the girl.

"Joni," he said; then paused for a moment. Outside a single shout sounded, a few meaty smacks as of steel buttplates chunking into flesh, and the distinctive butcher's-cleaver sound of a bayonet driven into a belly. Scouts dragged bound or dead or feebly twitching bodies in through the door.

"Not th' first man led ter ruin by 'is prick—er the fifty-first, Joni," he went on. "Ye jist git yer pretty ass back t' th' door; keep on earnin' that there manumission an' dowry, flies to the honeypot. Hell, er a 'baccy shop fer yer very own!"

A calloused hand smacked down on her backside. She pouted uncertainly and resumed her pose in the door as a voice sounded softly from the second story.

"More comin!"

"Mounted party, Cap'n," said the man with the mirror on a stick poked up above the window. "'bout twenty a' em. Real important lookin' barbs, fer sure. Nice dogflesh."

"Wait for it, everyone," Barton Foley said. "Not until they get past the dogleg." His stump was itching; it always did, just before. It itched, and he saw the hand—what was left of the hand—just after something snatched at it, and he looked around from urging his men on toward the Colonists and it was *gone*.... He checked his weapons one more time; the cut-down double barreled shotgun in the holster across his back, the pistol, the saber—*and my hook*. Better than a hand in some ways.

Dog paws thudded in the street outside, and suddenly he felt fine. Fine and clear and light; that always happened too.

Almost as good as reading the old poetry or making love, except that this was a feeling of being *more* in control, not out....

"Now."

He turned and rose, as the men knelt up and leveled their rifles out the ground-floor window, and more from above and across the street. The pistol was in his hand as he stepped out into the sunlight. Twenty mounted Squadrones, right enough; one with a banner covered in stitching and brightwork: the comet-and-planet of the Admiral's family. Gaudy richness on the sleek, beautifully groomed dogs— and *that* must have taken some doing on shipboard; jewels on clothes and belts and weapons. The men were roaring in surprise, clawing for their weapons; mostly in their thirties, hard-looking even by Squadron standards.

One lifted his flintlock. *Crack*, and the top of his head spattered away from a bullet. A twin file of men double-timed out behind Foley and formed up with bayoneted rifles leveled; the Squadrones' heads swiveled, their faces liquid with shock. More rifles bore on them from rooftop and window. Nor could experienced men doubt the trembling intensity of spirit in the eyes of the young one-handed officer standing with his revolver making small prodding motions. The dogs wuffled uneasily, snuffling their masters' fear. Two extended curious noses toward the blood and brains leaking out on the worn paving stones, and the dead man's animal whined in distress.

"Drop the weapons and out of the saddle by three or you're all *dead*," Foley shouted. "One! Two!" The hook rose.

The Squadron noble next to the banner swung down to the ground and unbuckled his swordbelt; the others followed suit, moving like men drugged or newly wakened. Troopers in bluejackets and round helmets with chainmail neckguards darted forward to lead off the dogs and drag away the corpse.

A gaping Squadron warrior blinked in disbelief. "Earth Spirit! It's the *cunnarte gisuh sharums*," he blurted in Namerique: the phrase translated into Sponglish as *chicken-hearted little darkies*.

The man screamed and fell to his knees as a Descotter

rammed his rifle butt home over the kidneys. Foley took him under the chin with his hook, very gently.

"Times," he said to the wide-eyed face, "have *changed.*"

The senior Squadron warrior shook off his bewilderment as troopers grabbed his elbows and began to lash them together behind his back.

"Take your hands off me, you peasant dogs!" he roared. "*I am Curtis Auburn!*"

"Oh-*ho!*" Foley said. Auburn stared at his smile and fell silent. After a few seconds he began to shake.

"They captured *who?*" Raj asked incredulously; the runner grinned back at him and saluted with a snap. The General shook his head. "Get him back here by all means—immediately. And my congratulations to Captain Foley. By all means, congratulations." He was still shaking his head as he turned back to the harbor, standing close to the parapet and using a tripod-mounted telescope. The wharves were black with men, now; all the transports had docked. The war galleys were spider-walking in toward the inner harbor, a dozen or so still outside waiting. More shots crackling across the city; a half-dozen here or there, then the unmistakable slamming of a platoon volley. He focused on the docks; men were milling around in circles, twisting their heads to look up into the city, shouting questions at each other. Weapons were flourished overhead; a banner went up, and an ox-horn gave its dunting snarl. Warriors formed behind that, shouldering their way through the press toward the main road up from the harbor.

"It's time," he said, looking up to the man at the heliograph. "*Now.*"

"Now!" the commander of the mortar battery said, swinging his saber down.

Two men dropped the heavy cylindrical shell into the muzzle of the mortar. *SCHUUMP,* and a tongue of flame and heavy smoke shot into the air; the bomb was almost visible, a blur arching up over the rooftop and down toward the harbor.

"Overshot seventy-five," the observer lying on the tiles of the roof shouted.

"Up three," the officer snapped. Men spun the main screw-wheel beneath the muzzle, and the fat barrel swung a fraction higher. "Fire!"

SCHUUMP.

Smoke was beginning to haze the street, drifting away slowly west. The loading crew had stripped to the waist, only their Star amulets swinging against their hairless brown chests as they waited with hands poised over the next shell.

"On target, right in the middle of 'em!" the spotter shouted exultantly.

"Fire for effect—all tubes—five rounds!"

"Now!" the infantry officer barked.

His men put their shoulders to the sides of the wagons and pushed; the ironshod wheels rumbled as they ran the vehicles out of the laneway and across the broader avenue. Boots thundered behind them, and they heaved in unison to tip the four-wheeled farm carts over. Scores of strong hands dragged them together, and the footsoldiers crowded up behind them as their sergeants cursed and pushed them into order.

"Aim!"

The bayonets winked as the long rifles leveled, a line three deep. Four hundred yards down the road, a black mass of Squadron warriors halted their tentative advance. There was just time for them to let out a scream of rage and begin to dash forward.

"By platoons—volley fire—*fwego!*"

"Now, lads!" Gerrin Staenbridge said.

Four hundred rifles spoke in a stuttering crash; from behind the barricade of furniture and boxes across the road, and from rooftops and windows along it. The head of the charging column disappeared; a two-wheeled cart they had been pushing ahead of them shattered in a shower of splinters and fell sideways. A wheel broke free and rolled away backward toward the harbor, overtaking some of the fleeing men who ran or limped or tried to drag wounded comrades back with them.

"Ser!" a man called from the back of the room.

Staenbridge turned just in time to hear the shot and see him stagger back with his face pulped by a shotgun blast.

"Face about!" he called crisply, bringing the blade of his pistol's foresight down on the window.

The rear of the room was a row of windows, giving out on the courtyard of the house. A Squadron warrior blocked one for a moment, and then the revolver kicked in his fist, the recoil a surprise as it always was when the aim was right. The body slumped and lay across the sill. Men turned from the street windows and fired from the hip, the ricochets as dangerous as enemy fire; one plucked at the sleeve of his coat as it wasp-whined by. Then the enemy were pouring through. He picked his targets and shot four times, dropped the empty weapon and drew his saber. Steel clashed about him, sword on bayonet; a charging barbarian came at him with long blade upraised above his head and practically ran up the outstretched point of Staenbridge's weapon.

"Feh," he said, kicking the man free of the saber and blocking another cut, locking wrists. The Squadron warrior fell away as a trooper drove his bayonet into his back, blade carefully horizontal to the ground to avoid catching on the ribs. The room fell silent.

"Lieutenant," Gerrin said, in a clear flat voice. "Take your platoon and check the courtyard and roofs, if you please."

"Messer Raj!" the company commander said in surprise.

"Damned if I'm going to sit on a couch *all* the way through a battle, Captain," Raj said, sliding out of the saddle.

The reserve company of the 5th was standing to arms in front of the pillared forecourt of a Star church, short a platoon already called away. The men were quiet, straining attention toward the firing nearer the docks; they gave a cheer as Raj's banner rode up, though. A panting runner skidded around a corner and jogged up to the steps.

"Ser," he said, facing Raj. "Major Staenbridge reports infiltrators tryin' to use the courtyards an' alleyways to git around his block-force. Thinks it's some Squadron chief got hisself a bright idear. Asks fer reinforcement to block it, got enough on 'is plate where we are."

"Sir, that must be—" the Captain began.

"I know, Captain Saynchez," Raj said. Center was painting a map on his eye, the most efficient route strobing across it in a red line. "Fall in and follow me."

There was a murmur of awe as they did, and a quick three-minute run to the mouth of an alleyway that gave into a gated internal patio shared by four houses. Downhill toward the harbor it was divided from a service lane by a low wall.

"Take up positions under that wall," he said. "Strict silence."

They crouched, the only sound their panting; these back alleys were heavy with the scent of stale garbage, and less pleasant things. Raj could hear nothing, see little, but Center shone a red light in front of his eyes. Then voices muttered on the other side of the wall; more and more of them, trying to be quiet. The narrow-heeled boots of Squadron warriors grated on the flagstones out there, and a sword clanged as it was brushed against a wall. The light before Raj's eyes turned green. He shot out a fist, conscious of the eyes on him, and extended one finger. Two. Three.

"Aim!" the Captain screamed, as the men leaped erect and leveled their rifles over the wall.

The Squadrones were massed not ten meters away, at least two hundred of them in the irregular opening beyond the wall and more down the five-meter alleyway between the houses. All their attention had been on the rooftops and to the west, where they hoped to filter through the buildings and move to take the 5th Descott's roadblock in the rear. Most of them had just enough time to look around when the rifles came level.

BAM. Smoke hid the enemy for a second; then it showed what happened when seventy-five rifles were fired into a confined space. Most of the bullets had found two or three targets, and the misses were bouncing down between the stone walls that lined the narrow lane.

BAM. The Squadrones were screaming in sheer horror as the rifles spoke again. A few managed to fire back; the young Captain beside Raj dropped, pawing feebly at the wound on his back. The legs did not move, except for a few pithed-frog twitchings as the severed spinal nerves sent their last impulses.

BAM. An attempt at a charge broke up in bloody chaos; Raj aimed his revolver carefully and gave mercy to a man crawling toward the Descotter guns with a mask of blood across his face.

"*Marcy, migo!*" A few voices called it out first: Mercy, friend. Then more, many more: "*Marcy, varsh!*" Mercy, brother. Some down at the end of the alley tried to run out, and more gunfire greeted them. All the Squadrones were throwing down their weapons now, those who could, and falling to their knees, crying out for quarter.

"Cease fire!" Raj shouted. A few more aimed rounds pecked out, and a man in front of him flopped backward, still kneeling, his long brown hair dropping into a pool of blood from the massive exit-wound in his back. "Cease fire, I said!"

The rifles fell silent, and men vaulted the wall to round up the stunned survivors. Raj suddenly felt a stab of pain and put a hand to the seat of his trousers; it came away red.

"Yer wounded, ser!" one of the troopers said, leaning his rifle against the wall and fumbling out the package of blessed powder and boiled gauze on his belt

"Only a graze," Raj said. There was a flat sadness in his tone as he watched the Squadron prisoners stumble by, disbelief on their blood-flecked faces. *And only in the arse. The poor bastards couldn't find their own.*

"Cease fire," Dinnalsyn said, raising his head from the telescope. "Signal the mortars to cease fire too."

All around him in the little park men slumped to the earth; air quivered over the scalding-hot barrels of the field guns, and the brass shell casings that littered the earth behind them.

Ships were burning and sinking all over the outer harbor; over the inner, too, from the smoke. One was on fire right in the mouth of the breakwaters, aground on the moles. Tiny figures dropped over the rails, wading on the half-submerged rocks; eager tentacled forms cruised just below the waves, moving forward to the scent of blood. Beyond them in the ocean the last half-dozen galleys were well out of range, helpless spectators to slaughter. A long black shape churned out of the inner harbor and turned for the outer, its low-slung ram casting back twin waves and its stacks fuming. Five more followed it in line, paddles beating the harbor water to froth, moving with a butting purpose utterly unlike the organic grace of sailing craft.

"Sweet merciful Avatars and Holy Saints," he murmured. The water was actually tinged with blood—pink more than red, but . . .

He turned the binoculars on the nearest street. Three field-guns fired as he watched, and the Squadron rush dissolved as the canister shot filled the roadway and bounced between the walls. Freakishly, the man who had led it remained standing for a second; he had dropped his banner because both arms were off at the shoulder, and he stood screaming amid the fragments of his men. The dismounted cavalry below the guns gave him a volley in mercy. Further down the street the last Squadron holdouts were trying to return fire from prone position behind bodies, but each time one raised himself on his elbow to reload his muzzle-loader, a Descotter marksman fired. From the roofs of some of the larger buildings heavier weapons were firing, huge rifles in the hands of squat figures in leggings and breechclouts who danced derision between shots.

"Not much longer," Dinnalsyn whispered.

"You made the right decision, calling for surrender," Raj said.

"I, ah, I—" Curtis Auburn stuttered.

The dogs whined as they picked their way among the hot shell-casings. The gunners were dropping them back into the round holding slots in the caissons, using tongs. Beyond the gun positions the sloping surface of the road was black with powder residues; beyond that, littered almost to covering with spent rifle cartridges. Auburn's eyes were farther down the street, though, on the windrows of bodies: the dogs whined more loudly as their riders pressed their knees tighter and forced them onto the slick-slippery surface. Prisoners were busy, working under guard to throw bodies and body-parts onto handcarts. Load after load was lumbering away, down toward the harbor.

There was a cleared lane down the center, more or less, but that was reddish-brown with a scum that pooled and clung. More flies than Raj had ever seen in one spot swarmed about, making the mounts toss their heads: The late afternoon sun was hot, and a miasma was already rising from the street.

"I've heard the expression," Raj murmured to himself as they proceeded at a slow walk. There seemed no end to the carpet of bodies, no impression the carts could make on their number. "But this is the first time I've actually seen a street run with blood."

Administrator Berg had been riding behind them, with a handkerchief pressed to his face. Now he stumbled out of the saddle and to the side of the road, bending over and heaving with his eyes squeezed tightly shut to avoid seeing what he was spattering with vomit Raj turned his toes inward to touch Horace's ribs; the dog stopped and began to sit, then straightened at his jerk on the reins. He looked around, feeling as if there was a thin pane of glass between him and the world. *Only two hours,* he thought. *Only two hours.* The blood had splashed and stuck far up the sides of the whitewashed buildings; blood and bits of flesh.

"We'll have to flood the streets and scrub everything down," he mused.

They were coming into the wider open areas around the warehouses; the bodies were scattered here, with room between them, although the blood from higher up had pooled and clotted around the dams of flesh. Many of them had been bayoneted or sabered in the back; others had the mutilated look produced by the 15mm Skinner rounds. On the dockside itself thousands were squatting with their hands on their heads, or helping to put out the fires that smoldered on the wrecked ships. The sea breeze was a touch of cleanliness—if you ignored the glistening shapes that cruised just below the surface of the harbor, broad smooth humps as they nearly surfaced, a fluke or a beak or a writhing arm protruding when they turned to dive. Shots had taught them to keep back from the dock—you could see intelligence in the huge unwinking eyes that showed now and then—but the water writhed when a corpse-cart was backed to the edge.

"And I hope you can persuade your brother to do likewise," Raj went on, in the same emotionless voice.

Curtis Auburn shook himself; on the third try his voice functioned roughly.

"Ah, I'm sure, recognition of the Civil Government's suzerainty—" he began.

Suddenly Raj reached out and grabbed the Squadron leader by the knotted braids on the side of his head.

"*Look*, Auburn!" he shouted, his voice a shocking roar. He forced the other man's head around effortlessly, despite the bull neck's resistance. A cart piled high with bodies tipped and slid two-score more into the waiting serrated beaks. "Look at that!"

The Grand Captain of the Squadron wrenched his head away and buried his head in his hands. Raj waited, lighting a cigarette and turning his eyes away.

"Don't try to bargain with me, Auburn," he went on, when the other man was calmer; his own voice had the metallic flatness back. "I beat Conner, I beat your Admiral Charles, and now I've beaten *you*. We've lost less than a battalion, and killed half the fighting men in your entire nation. Once might have been luck, twice a mistake—three times is the Voice of Heaven, man!"

He offered a cigarette, and a light when Auburn's hands shook. *Not fear, not really,* he decided. *Shock.* Curtis Auburn's entire world had vanished in an afternoon; this morning he'd been a ruler of a century-old kingdom, leading home a powerful army. Three hours later, the army was downdragger food—and he was a rightless prisoner.

"What do you intend for my men—for your prisoners?" he said quietly.

"Well, under the laws and customs of war, they're mine to do with as I please," Raj said grimly. Quite true; he could execute, enslave, or ransom them—and their families—as he pleased or his ruler instructed. Auburn would be remembering what his ancestors did to the Civil Government prisoners from the last expedition, blinded and castrated en masse. Raj let the silence stretch for a moment

"But Governor Barholm has decreed as much mercy as possible," he went on.

"Only those who refused to surrender when summoned on the march north will be enslaved." Several thousand, and a profitable object-lesson. "And any among the prisoners who refuse to swear allegiance, of course. Those who do swear will be formed into military units under Civil Government officers, and sent back to East Residence for retraining and deployment to the eastern frontier. All their property here is forfeit, of course—only those who came in voluntarily will keep their lands—but they'll have their families, and if they give good and loyal service, they can expect to rise in the hierarchy of Earth's proper government."

He leaned forward and caught Curtis's eyes. "If your brother comes in and makes unconditional submission, you and he can take your households with you; you'll be granted estates near East Residence"—carefully watched, of course—"and Charles's followers will get terms at least as good as those yours do. Failing immediate surrender, tell him he can run but he can't hide; I will send every living Squadron man, woman, and child to hell or the auction block and *I will send Charles Auburn's head to the Governor packed in salt.* By the living Spirit of Man, I swear it."

"Are you a man or a demon?" Curtis asked hoarsely.

"*I am the Sword of the Spirit of Man,*" he said, with the conviction of absolute belief. "Now get out—and tell your Admiral what you've seen. Tell him everything."

"Well, a great victory, yes," Administrator Berg said. His eyes were carefully unfocused as they rode back toward the Palace; he seemed to be trying to avoid seeing either the man beside him or the world around. Raj handed him a clean handkerchief, and he accepted it gratefully. "We've been . . . very fortunate, yes, the Spirit has favored us."

"Oh yes, not with luck," Raj said calmly. Berg jumped a little at the normality of the tone. "The enemy made every mistake they could . . ." He paused to return the salute of a detail marching back to quarters. "And with men like these behind me, if they *hadn't* screwed up we'd have won anyway."

CHAPTER SIXTEEN

"It's him," Muzzaf said, bowing beside the Vice Governor's chair. "All the most important lords are with him, Messer Raj; but . . ."

Raj sat calmly, his hand on the Mace. The audience hall of the Palace was not nearly as crowded as it had been for the assumption of power, leaving plenty of room for the Squadron nobles—soon to be ex-nobles—who would be brought in to swear submission with their leader. Much of the rest of the room was piled with captured Squadron battle-flags, and not even the thick incense from the priest's censors could entirely hide the smell of the rotting blood many of them were soaked with. The Admiral and his retinue had also been routed past the mass graves . . . and the soldiers and their weapons lining the whole route in from the gates and up to the Chair were also an exercise in education.

There was no point in being subtle with barbarians, not if you wanted to be clearly understood. Sometimes he thought that applied to most civilized men as well.

"Yes?" he murmured to the Komarite.

"Ah . . . the Admiral is, shall we say, not entirely well. Functional, but not well."

Raj nodded; there were rumors about hereditary instability in the Auburn family—and Spirit knew the man had had enough shocks of late. The Companions glanced at each other a little uneasily, and there was a ripple of comment through the civil dignitaries below the dais at the exchange they could see but not hear.

"Don't worry, my friends," he said quietly, smiling. It had been three days since the battle, and they were all thoroughly relieved that there wasn't going to be another. "Charles Auburn can be a raving lunatic for the rest of his life, as long as he sings out loud and clear today. How's the loading going, Gerrin?"

"Right on schedule," the older man said, in the same low murmur. "We should be able to get ten thousand Squadrones to East Residence in the first wave, without overcrowding. With the cadre of Regulars they'll need; they can start their training as soon as they're sworn in, and continue it as they march east."

There were rumors that Ali had consolidated his position and was looking for revenge for the death and defeat of his father Jamal. Not to mention a victory that would rally his *emirs*.

"Ali may get a surprise," Raj nodded.

The noise through the great open bronze doors became a swelling roar. The troopers at the door snapped from at ease to attention, and the motion rippled down the silent ranks lining the red-carpeted corridor with the smooth regularity of falling dominoes. Halfway down the corridor was a structure of spears lashed together, forming an arch about chest-high. Charles Auburn checked slightly as he saw it, checked again with a grimace of hatred as he saw Karl and Ludwig Bellamy standing in places of honor at the foot of the dais. Then he came on, with the defeated lords behind him; they all bowed their sackcloth-covered shoulders to pass under the spears.

Then Auburn was grinning as he reached the first of the stairs. Raj's foot was resting on the staff of the last Squadron banner, the ancient flag of Admiral Ricks, taken from the great Temple now restored to the Holy Federation Church after one hundred and twenty years. The faded gold silk spilled down almost to the last Admiral's feet, and he bent to finger it.

"Vanity!" he cackled, looking up. Raj felt a slight chill; there was something inhuman there. "It's all vanity . . . I was vain with flags, now you are—vanity, vanity, all vanity!"

Curtis Auburn nudged his brother sharply, and the glaze left his eyes. He dropped clumsily to his knees, and the others behind him; Charles drew his sword and unloaded pistol, laying them down. Officers bore them up to the Chair and laid them at Raj's feet, and the trumpeters behind blew a fanfare. All the spectators cheered, as the Auburns and their followers were led away.

"Messer general," a voice said at Raj's ear. He looked around, and felt a small cold shock at the expression on Barton Foley's face.

"Yes?"

"There's a courier from East Residence, sir. From the Palace; it's Colonel Osterville."

One of Barholm's Guards; as Raj was himself, technically. A jack-of-all-trades, specializing in discreet strongarm work.

"Sir, he demands immediate audience . . . and his dispatches carry the Seal."

The voices of an infantry regiment marching down to the docks to embark came clear through the windows. That was the only sound to break the nervous silence, as Raj and his officers waited in the upper audience room:

> "Where have you been this while away,
> Peydro, Peydro?
> Out with the rest on a picnic lay.
> Peydro, my Peydro, ah!
> They catted us out of the barrack-yard
> To Spirit knows where from Residence-ward
> And you can't refuse when you get the card
> And the Guv'nor gives the party!"

Osterville was in an immaculate uniform of white and gold; he checked a little as he entered, under the glares of the Companions. His hard smooth face showed nothing, though. Barholm Clerett was a judge of men, in his way. He made his way briskly to the head of the table, saluted and presented a thick parchment envelope stamped with a gold-and-purple seal.

"Sir," he said, "I present the order of the Governor."

Raj took the envelope and turned it in his hands. "Upon whom may the Spirit shower blessings. I acknowledge receipt, Colonel. Do you have a verbal digest?"

Osterville looked around at the hard glares.

"I have no secrets from my officers . . . unless the orders are confidential?"

"No." The Guard cleared his throat. "You are directed to turn over your command to me and to return immediately to East Residence, there to render accounting to the Chair for your actions."

There was a chorus of oaths from lower down the table; Kaltin Gruder leaped to his feet and slammed his fist down on the teak.

"Actions! 'Account for his actions,' like a criminal? He's bloody well destroyed the Squadron in three weeks' campaign—after everyone else failed miserably for a century—and left the Civil Government richer by a province, by twenty-five thousand soldiers and a million gold FedCreds! *Those* are his fucking actions, you Palace popinjay, you lapcat for—"

"*Major Gruder!*" Raj barked. Kaltin sank back into his seat, but his left hand stayed clenched on the hilt of his saber. "If you can't restrain yourself, you are excused!"

Raj's fingers broke the seal; he touched his amulet to his lips and then read the vermilion ink.

"Accurate, Colonel. The written version's a little more formal, but accurate."

He closed his eyes, his fingers playing with the thick paper. Barholm was suspicious to a fault, and Dalhouse *had* been back quite a while. Successful generals were always under a cloud; it went with the territory, and he was the most successful for a long, long time.

observe said Center:

—and Raj was seated once again on the Vice Governor's chair. This time the viewpoint was well back; he could see his own face, stiff as if carven in stone, as the Arch-Syssup lowered the regalia on him—the sacred keyboard and headset that only Governors could wear. Below, an audience of Expeditionary Force soldiers and Squadron nobles cheered in a frenzy of adoration: *Conquer! You conquer!*, the traditional call for an Enchairment—and a city was burning. Sandoral, he thought; the great eastern bastion he had held against the Settlers' armies. Now it burned like a pyre, a throbbing red pyramid reflected crimson in the waters of the great Drangosh River. Behind it innumerable lesser fires marked farms and villages in all the stretch of fertile irrigated land that ran to the foothills of the Oxheads. Troops marched by on the road, men in the spired helmets and scarlet jellabas of the Colonial regulars. Flags waved above them, the green and crescent of Islam, the peacock of the Settlers, Tewfik's Seal of Solomon—

—and a Raj aged beyond belief lay in a bed he recognized, the Admiral's quarters in this very palace. Each halting breath was a struggle; the flesh had fallen away from the strong Descotter bones of his flesh. Priests prayed, and a few elderly officers wept. Outside came the sounds of gunfire and the clash of steel, as men fought for the old king's legacy—

Better for the Civil Government that I had never lived at all, if I make myself ruler here, he thought. *Of course. These men are the best troops we have.*

accurate, Center said implacably, **although oversimplified.**

And nothing I built here could last.

97% ± 6% indicates immediate civil war and continued fission upon your death, Center said, **the centrifugal process will continue unabated on bellevue until maximum entropy is attained, the next upswing of the cycle will, with a high probability, take at least eight millennia.**

Raj remembered the vision of flint-knapping cannibals crouched on the ruins of East Residence and shuddered. The soldiers' song came louder through the windows, as the battalion passed along beneath the Palace windows:

> *"What did you get to eat and drink,*
> *Peydro, Peydro?*
> *Standing water as thick as ink,*
> *Peydro, my Peydro, ah!*
> *A bit o' beef that were three year stored,*
> *A bit o' mutton as tough as a board,*
> *A sauroid we killed with the sergeant's sword,*
> *When the Guv'nor gave the party."*

He opened his eyes and smiled wryly. "Vanity, vanity," he murmured. Then aloud: "We'll need a few formalities, but for the present—" He lifted the Mace of office and stood, offering it to Osterville. There was a gasp and long sigh of exhaled breath from the others as the Guard took it in his hands. "If you'll excuse me and these officers, Colonel," Raj went on softly, "we have a few administrative matters to prepare for you."

Osterville looked around; by the strict letter of the instructions all Brigadier General Raj Whitehall should do now was walk down to the docks, but there were times when initiative was necessary.

"By all means, sir," he said.

The babble broke out the minute the door closed; Raj looked at the faces, tense with anger and concern, and smiled gently.

He waited until the noise died away.

"Thank you," he said sincerely. "My friends, I thank you more than words can say. But before anyone says a word that might be considered treasonous—*no*. Not for any reason."

"But, Raj—he'll *kill* you," Barton Foley said. A tear trembled at the edge of one eye. "Spirit damn it, it isn't *fair*."

"Well, it's possible that will happen," Raj said, taking a cigarette out of a box on the table. He contemplated his hands for a second.

"Understandable, perhaps. Generals have shot their way into the Chair before"—*including Barholm's uncle Vernier Clerett*—"always with disastrous results. But hell," he grinned, "it's not an arrest order, after all. As Kaltin pointed out, I *have* accomplished the mission assigned—and going back peacefully as ordered will be the best testimony possible. Plus I'll have yours, of course."

A chorus of agreement; Administrator Berg rapped his water glass down.

"By the Spirit, mine too!" he blurted; the soldiers' eyes turned toward him. "It's well, only just," he said. "Besides," he added shrewdly, "when the Governor sees the figures on what we're bringing him, even Chancellor Tzetzas will have to sing Messer Raj's praises. Three years' total revenue! Not *counting* the value of three-quarters of the lands in the Territories, now forfeit to the fisc."

There was a thoughtful silence inside the room, and a ruffle of drums from outside the window:

> "What did you do for knives and forks,
> Peydro, Peydro?
> We carries 'em with us wherever we walks,
> Peydro, my Peydro, ah!
> And some was sliced and some was halved,
> And some was crimped and some was carved,
> And some was gutted and some was starved,
> When the Guv'nor gave the party."

"And even if the worst happened, rebellion cannot be justified," Raj said. "Say what you like about Barholm Clerett, he's a strong Governor—the strongest we've had in generations. Gentlemen"—he leaned forward in an unconscious attempt to drive home the lesson—"these barbarians we just fought, *they* started off as soldiers of Holy Federation as well; look what rebellion's brought *them*, over the years. Beyond that, Barholm has my oath, which is all the honor a soldier has; and beyond *that*, he's the Vice Regent of the Spirit of Man of the Stars upon Earth."

He rose and offered his arm; Suzette took it. "Gerrin, if you'd draw up movement orders for the Skinners? I promised them they'd be sent home, and Osterville might not consider himself bound." A wry smile. "See you on shipboard, gentlemen."

"There goes," Gerrin Staenbridge whispered, as the door closed behind them, "a true hero. The poor luckless bastard." The Companions sat in silence, listening to the receding footsteps and the fading song:

> "What was the end of all the show,
> Peydro, Peydro?
> Ask Messer Raj, for I don't know,
> Peydro, my Peydro, ah!
> We broke a King and we built a road—
> And a Star church stands where our boot-heels goed.
> And the harbor's clean where the raw blood flowed
> When the Guv'nor gave the party."

CHAPTER SEVENTEEN

"Raj," Suzette went on, looking up from the table, "at least don't rush straight back to East Residence!"

Her delicate tilt-eyed features were furrowed with anxiety. The brass cabin lantern cast moving shadows over the captain's cabin of the transport, commandeered for the General and his lady. The sterncastle windows still shed more light, from the westering sun behind them. The manifold creak and groan of timbers and planks surrounded them, the almost-living noise of a wooden ship under full sail. The huge salt smell of the sea filled the cabin, with the warm brass scent of the lantern and clean wool from the bed. Raj turned from watching the long white wake of the ship and the long-winged dactosauroids hovering over it as his wife went on:

"Darling, stop over in Hayapalco. You can say you need to rest the men, it's a long voyage . . . and then *I* can go back to East Residence and talk to Lady Anne. You can be sure *she* isn't listening to that tattletale Dalhouse, who's been sniffing around Tzetzas for years now."

Negotiate, Raj knew she meant. With Lady Anne pleading his loyalty, and thousands of troops at his back; negotiate terms with the threat of insurrection unspoken in the background.

observe Center said.

—and Barholm sat on the Chair, the arc-lights blazing on the gold-tissue robes and peacock jewelry of the Chair as it rose on its soundless hydraulic cylinder. He stared down impassively at the kneeling figure of Raj Whitehall; only someone who knew him well could see the cold anger in the expressionless black eyes.

"Our well-beloved servant General Whitehall is returned victorious," he said. "Let all honor—"

"Yes, that would work," Raj said quietly. "For a while. Maybe for a year; maybe even for four or five, Barholm's a cautious man. Then he'd kill me . . . or I'd have to kill him to stop him." He paused for a moment, and his voice grew sharper: *"Wouldn't I?"*

Suzette nodded unwillingly, nervously lighting a cigarette and jamming it into the ivory holder with unnecessary force.

probability of disgrace/execution at a later date 60% ± 25%, given hayapalco scenario as outlined by lady Whitehall; large variant factor due to subsequent dependent variables, Center said.

"So I wouldn't be much improving my chances. If I have to die, I want it to have some point—and trying to make Barholm bargain under my guns would make it meaningless."

"Sailing right into East Residence and being sent to the Pole has *meaning*?" Suzette asked.

"Yes." Raj's eyes were focused on something beyond the rafters. "Why am I in this fix in the first place? Because Barholm Clerrett is a paranoid ingrate?" He shrugged. "He's a politician, that's much the same thing. But Governors have a *reason* for being afraid of successful generals, and *that* is the reason we've never been able to subdue the barbarians. The Civil Government has more than enough power to reunite the planet; it just doesn't have the will, not as long as whoever occupies the Chair is more afraid of his own Army than of foreigners."

Suzette blinked, her eyes wide with incredulity. "You're going to sacrifice your life—our lives—to reassure Barholm? Or some future Governor?"

Raj smiled, running fingers through his curls. "No. To reassure future rulers *and* to teach future soldiers that there's no honor in rebellion. I'm not going to contribute to the climate of fear that's rotting us out from within." His smile turned to a grin. "And Starless Dark, I don't expect Barholm to give me the chop, anyway. It'd be crazy, and he's not that crazy. Yet."

probability of eventual clinical paranoia in barholm clerrett is near certainty if subject's lifespan extended past 60 standard years, Center noted.

"To make a point? You're risking everything just to make a *point?*"

"There *has* to be a point," he said, driving one fist into a palm. "Or what's it all for? I—we—killed *sixty thousand men* out here, Suzette." He wiped one hand across the back of his mouth. "I can still see it . . . That wasn't a battle, a whole nation died there. What for? To make a reputation for me? Or to give Tzetzas a new province to loot—for a while, for a few generations, until some new bunch of barbs takes it away again? No."

He shook his head, turning to look at her with his hands clasping behind his back. "I don't fight wars because it's the most efficient way of piling up corpses. I'm not spending my men's lives for that. It has to have some point, or I might as well do the world a favor and blow my own brains out." More gently: "Don't you see?"

Suzette's shell of control cracked, and she flung herself against Raj. He held her, stroking the sleek black hair; it caught occasionally in the cracked calluses of his saber hand.

"Spirit, I'm afraid, Raj!" she said. "He's mad with jealousy . . . I'm so afraid."

"I'm afraid too, darling," he said gently. "It's for the best, though. Believe me, it's for the best."

It was evening, cool and gentle in the bows where Raj sat alone. His feet dangled over the netting that linked bowsprit to deck, almost within reach of the spray as the ship took the swell with all sail set in the mild breeze. The water was dark-purple beneath, fading to almost black at the edge of sight, rippled with white foam. Six-winged flying things skipped in shoals over the waves and then dove; stars were coming out, a frosty bridge from north to south across the sky. Miniluna and Maxiluna were both full on the eastern horizon, throwing brilliant paths of silver ahead of him, on the road to home.

—and the image of red-hot irons glowing toward his eyes faded.

probability of blinding, 22%, Center concluded, **±4%.**

Well, at least it's less likely than outright execution; I'd prefer that, he thought.

Stretching, he rose and took a last puff on the cigarette, letting the breeze ruffle through his hair like a woman's slender fingers. Off to the left the smoke of the escort-warship had a ruddy tinge from the fires of her furnace, only visible in the hours of darkness. He flicked the butt away, and it was a tiny meteor toward the water that slapped with thousandfold hands at the hull.

And whatever comes, it doesn't really matter. I'm obeying the Spirit that made all—his gesture took in the night and the horizon.

i am not god, Center said; there seemed to be a troubled overtone to its monotonous internal voice, **i cannot guarantee a desirable result, i can only indicate actions whose results are most probably beneficial to human society, optimization for you as an individual would be a completely different calculation.**

"I am the Sword of the Spirit," Raj whispered, raising his arms to the arch of stars. Once men had traveled there. "And I will obey that Spirit—whatever the cost."

APPENDIX

Southern Territories Expeditionary Force
Order of Battle
Mai 1, 1106 After the Fall

REGULAR CAVALRY

5th Descott Guards —800
Major Gerrin Staenbridge (Companion)
Captain Barton Foley (Companion)
Captain Tejan M'brust (becomes Companion during *The Hammer*)
Senior Lieutenant Antin M'lewis (Companion)

Recruitment area: Descott County.

Insignia: a black "5" over crossed sabers.
Motto: "Hell o Zpalata" ("Hell or Plunder") across top of shield.

* * *

7th Descott Rangers —600
Major Kaltin Gruder (Companion)

Recruitment area: Descott County.

Insignia: a black "7" over a running dog.
Motto: "Fwego Erst" ("Shoot First") across top of shield.

* * *

1st Rogor Slashers —590
Major Mekkle Thiddo (Companion)
Senior Lieutenant Peydro Belagez (becomes Companion during *The Hammer*)

Recruitment area: Upper Drangosh Valley, north and east of Sandoral and in the southeastern foothills of the Oxhead Mountains.

Insignia: a black "1" on a rayed star. Motto: "Hingada thes Ihorantes" ("Death to the Infidels")

* * *

Poplanich's Own —620
Major Ehwardo Poplanich (becomes Companion during *The Hammer*)

A House regiment, recruited mostly from the estates of the Poplanich family (in the provinces along the Coast Range seaboard, south and west of East Residence). Officers from gentry families related to or clients of the Poplanich.

Insignia: Chrysanthemum (Poplanich sigil) on a blue background.
Motto: "Eweyz Widya" ("Always Faithful")

* * *

21st Navy Haifa Dragoons —610
Major Hemilo Istban

Recruitment area: Northeastern frontier, near the Singre mountains.

Insignia: a black "21" on a silver background, flanked by rifles.
Motto: "Singre Guzzlah" ("Blood Drinkers")

* * *

17th Hemmar Valley Cuirassiers   —608
Major Anhelino Dalhouse
Captain Hermano Suharto

Recruitment area: Central Provinces, mostly the Hem-mar Valley near East Residence.

Insignia: black "17" on a light-green background. Motto: "Waymanos" ("Forward!")
(N.B. After the Southern Territories campaign, tavern brawls frequently start when members of other units say "Backwards!" in the hearing of a member of the 17th Cuirassiers.)

* * *

3rd Chongwe Dragoons   —610
Major Hesus Anderson

Recruitment area: Chongwe Island, a large island in the middle Midworld Sea, and the westernmost Civil Government province.

Insignia: black "3" on blue background, over a stylized wave. Motto: "Rahpeedo" ("Swiftly")

* * *

1st Gaur Rangers   —628
Major Hingenio Buthelezi

Recruitment area: Central Provinces; upper Hemmar Valley, near the north flank of the Oxhead Mountains,

Insignia: black "1" on purple background, crossed bayoneted rifles.
Motto: "Sehuro Comphadres" ("Faithful Comrades")

* * *

18th Komar Borderers —559
Major Hadolfo Zahpata (becomes Companion during *The Hammer*)

Recruitment area: Central southern border country, on the frontier of the Colony and on the south flank of the Oxhead Mountains.

Insignia: black "18" on stylized sand-dune with palm tree. Motto: "Dehfenzo Lighon" ("Defend the Faith") on the top of the shield.

Total Regular Cavalry = 5625 (9 battalions)

IRREGULAR CAVALRY

Skinners —600
Chief Juluk Paypan
Chief Pai-har Tradaw

Halvaardi —500
Chief Francor Genhuvaa

Stalwarts —581
Leader Hwilli Morgan

Total Irregular Cavalry = 1,681

INFANTRY

17th Kelden County Foot
Colonel Jorg Menyez

24th Valentia Foot
Major Ferdihando Felasquez

55th Santanderr Rifles
Major Fitoriano Huarez

1st Kendrun Foot
Major Pernardho Reyez
88th Seyval Infantry
Major Franhesco Alleyman

10th Melaga Foot
Major Alfaro Orzoco

23rd Hemmar Valley Foot
Major Lazaro Trahn

71st Upper Hemmar Foot
Major Sule Mihn

1st Asaurian Mountaineers
Major Andreu Three Bears

3rd Upper Drangosh Light Infantry
Major Algrood Naxim

42ndjernelle Marines
Major Dohminko Falcones

9th Irtish Skirmishers
Major Tentito Cortinez

21st Ceres Guards
Major Omar Sherf

101st Forest Hangers
Major Nortesinho Negrotete

2nd Gurnyca Mountaineers
Senior Captain Luis Ordhaz

1st Malga Foot
Major Heanar Fillipsyn

3rd Denson Foot
Major Jenkynz Ordonto

32nd Straits Rifles
Senior Captain Daniel Villegaz

9th Hayapalco Volunteers
Major Nikros Arayfet

Total Regular Infantry = 10,721

ARTILLERY
Colonel Grammeck Dinnalsyn, commanding.

No siege guns were taken on this expedition. Thirty standard field pieces were embarked. These were 75mm (3-inch) rifled cast-steel breechloaders, with iron-bound wooden wheels and iron carriages, drawn by four pairs of dogs—usually Alsatian-Newfoundland crosses. The muzzle velocity is 650 mps, with a range of approximately 4,500 meters with shell and 4000 with shrapnel. Canister (lead balls with no bursting charge) is effective to 500 meters.

Rate of fire is 3 rounds per minute. (Note: since the gun has no recoil system, it runs backward after every shot and must be manually returned to battery.)

Five mortars were also taken. These were 100mm smoothbore weapons, firing from 45 to 95 degrees. They were mounted on a modified gun-carriage with the cast-steel firing base slung under the tube.

Guns required a crew of eight, and were organized in three-gun batteries. Four of each crew had their own riding dogs, and the remainder rode on the gun, caisson, or the two lead dogs of the team.

Each battery was commanded by a Lieutenant, and included a squad of eight supplementary personnel to perform auxiliary tasks and replace casualties.

Gunners carry rifles and sabers as their personal arms; officers and noncoms also carry 5-shot revolvers.

ORGANIZATION

All regular Civil Government forces were organized in *battalions* (Sponglish: *bandata)*, of 500-800 men (average around 600).

A battalion was made up of *companies* (Sponglish: *tabora)* and *platoons* (Sponglish: *campadra)* of roughly 120 and 32 men each, respectively.

A battalion would normally be commanded by a Senior Captain or Major; companies by Captains or Senior Lieutenants, and platoons by Lieutenants.

Platoons were comprised of eight-man *squads*, commanded by a Corporal or Sergeant. Enlisted men were *privates* (infantry) or *troopers* (cavalry); there were several grades within these ranks, based on skill (e.g., "marksman"), seniority or other skills (e.g., "watch-stander," open to literate soldiers).

Each squad generally bunked and messed together, shared a tent, and in the cavalry each squad was allowed one general servant to help with fatigues. (This provision was often exceeded.)

Units larger than a battalion were organized *ad hoc* as situations demanded. While there was a schedule of ranks above Major—Colonel, Brigadier, Brigadier General and General, with administrative titles (e.g., "Commander of Eastern Forces")—there was no permanent unit organization above the battalion.

Companies and battalions would also have their senior NCOs—Master Sergeants—and a larger formation might have one appointed by the overall commander.

RECRUITMENT, PAY, AND RATIONS

The Civil Government's army still bore some traces of a period when units had been raised by provincial noblemen on their own initiative. Battalions generally had a number (denoting when they had been first mustered) and a county or district designation, showing where they had been raised. (Proprietary battalions were named for the individual who first raised them.) Recruitment was largely, although not exclusively (particularly for infantry), from the same area. Enlisted men and officers below the rank of Major almost always stayed with the same battalion throughout their careers.

In theory, all male subjects of the Civil Government were subject to military service. In practice, this had long ago been commuted to a compensatory land-tax (levied on farm units, not on the owners from whom they were generally rented), for most of the central provinces. In many frontier or upland areas the tradition of direct service continued; families were required to send one son per generation, and pay for his equipment as a cavalry trooper; service was for ten-year enlistments. In return, the family holding was exempt from tax. Those without suitable recruits could find a substitute, and volunteer enlistments from the same areas—with a substantial enlistment bonus—were also common.

Cavalry districts tended to lie on the frontiers, or in remote wilderness; Descott County alone, with about 6 percent of the Civil Government's population, furnished over 20 percent of its mounted troops. Cavalry soldiers came from the Civil Government's closest equivalent to a rural middle class: freeholders, or what in Descott were called yeoman-tenants, men renting substantial areas and able to afford riding-dogs. In other counties tenants-in-chief, overseers, and bailiffs might furnish such recruits.

Cavalry officers generally came from middling or wealthy landowning (Messer-class) families with a tradition of service to the Chair.

Infantry were effectively conscripts for the most part, or "volunteers" one step ahead of the courts, or sons of soldiers with no other trade; generally they were men their landlords were eager to see the last of. Most of them (with the exception of Asaurian units from the semi-civilized mountaineers of that County) came from the arable heartlands of the Civil Government, in the Peninsula, the Central Territories and the Hem-mar River Valley and were peons—debt-bonded peasant sharecroppers—in social status. Their main role was as garrison and internal-security troops.

Infantry troops were issued their equipment, but did not

receive payment in cash unless mobilized for field service. In time of peace they were supported by moderate-sized (30 hectares, or more if the region was infertile) farms on state-owned land; this land was worked by State peons, but managed by the soldier (who often spent as much or more time helping on the farm as drilling, in consequence). When an infantry unit's base was moved, new farms were assigned.

A battalion's commander was paid a lump sum, dependent on the number of men fit for duty; an infantry commander in garrison received cash pay for his officers and senior NCOs, as well as substantially larger land-grants. Periodic musters (inspections by muster-masters sent by the Master of Soldiers) were held to check on readiness.

Cavalry and artillery troopers were paid in cash, twice yearly. Stoppages were made for replacement of equipment and for rations, where issued.

Infantry soldiers generally drew their food from their land grants, and sold the surplus for cash to pay for their uniforms and equipment. Most cavalry troopers bought their rations (and their dogs) out of their pay; many units arranged to do this by clubbing together and buying in bulk. Where sutlers—merchants specializing in the military trade—were not available, food would be issued, and the soldiers' pay debited. Many cavalry battalions had unit savings funds, mutual-benefit clubs which stored their members' money and paid funeral expenses and small pensions out of the interest. Particular commanders might also buy annuities for the disabled and the dependents of casualties.

Pay for cavalry troopers amounted to 55 FedCreds per year; this was roughly equivalent to the annual earnings of a skilled artisan such as a blacksmith. Various stoppages would generally take about 10 FedCreds off the total, but there were bonuses for seniority or for foreign service. A Master Sergeant would make twice that; Lieutenants 150 FedCreds, Captains 250, and a battalion commander 500 (plus, in some cases, the pay of men carried on the rolls after their discharge or death—a common abuse).

Many officers had at least some independent income as well, usually from landed property.

Infantry pay schedules were half those of cavalry, when in the field; an infantry private made roughly the same wages as a dockworker or bricklayer.

Plunder and bonuses. In legal theory, the persons and property of areas outside the Civil Government which refused obedience, or ones within it in case of rebellion, were forfeit. This was rarely enforced with full rigor, for political reasons. On campaign, plunder was (theoretically) collected from assigned areas by battalions after an action was complete, then shared out according to rank, length of service and accomplishments (conspicuous gallantry, etc.). Troops might be allowed to "glean" through an area already picked over. Under certain conditions—e.g., refusal to surrender when summoned—towns might be turned over to the troops for a sack. Successful generals often used the proceeds of large-scale looting (e.g., sale of confiscated lands, or prisoners to the slave markets) to give cash or property donatives to the troops under their command. This was immensely popular with the troops, but frowned on by the authorities—especially by Governors nervous about too-popular Generals.

UNIFORM

Most cavalry and all infantry in the Civil Government's regular forces wore a uniform of calf-high boots, buckled at the sides with two straps, rather baggy maroon-colored trousers, a blue swallow-tail jacket with a high collar, (the tails ending just above the knees) and a bowl-shaped iron helmet. Enlisted men wore a canvas belt with shoulder-strap carrying a bandolier with 125 rounds of ammunition, bayonet, canteen, and messkit. (Bayonets were worn on the left hip by infantry; cavalry wore their sabers on the left hip, and the bayonet beneath the bandolier.) Other equipment was carried on the dog, or in a blanket roll worn over the right shoulder by foot-soldiers. Cavalry helmets usually had a neck-guard of leather covered in chain-mail; line infantry went without. Officers and many cavalry troopers wore a leather belt of similar pattern with a shoulder strap. Officers wore their sabers on the left hip, pistols on the right, and carried no bandolier. Their standard equipment included binoculars, map case, and slide rule. Cloth for uniforms was generally bought either by the soldier, or by unit commanders in bulk, and made up by local tailors to central-government patterns. Cavalry uniforms were usually of much better material.

Battalions that had originally been proprietary might wear distinctive uniforms; usually these would be of different colors and better cloth than standard, and might have "extras"—e.g., plumes on the helmet.

Noncommissioned rank is indicated by chevrons on the arm, of red or silver cloth. Commissioned rank is indicated by Star insignia on the epaulets and on the front of the helmet, as follows:

Lieutenant: one small seven-pointed silver star on each shoulder; one likewise on the helmet.

Senior Lieutenant: one small seven-pointed silver star on each shoulder, points enclosed in a thin gold circle. Likewise on the helmet.

Captain: As per Lieutenant, but with two stars on each shoulder and on the helmet.

Senior Captain: As per Senior Lieutenant, with two stars on each shoulder and on the helmet.

Major: Three golden stars encircled with a silver band; one of these on each shoulder and one on the helmet

Brigadier: One large eighteen-rayed silver and gold star on a blue shield, on each shoulder and on the helmet.

Brigadier General: A large eighteen-rayed silver and gold star on a blue shield, "orbited" by small silver stars; on each shoulder and on the helmet.

General: A large eighteen-rayed silver and gold star on a blue shield, "orbited" by small silver stars and enclosed by a gold band with overlaid stars at 10mm intervals; on each shoulder and on the helmet.

Dress uniform has more elaborate rank insignia, with the Star emblems on the collar, braid epaulets, cuff-braid, etc. Soldiers customarily wear the insignia of their battalions on shoulder-flashes, shield-shaped cloth badges sewn to the upper shoulder on the right arm.

WEAPONS

All Regulars in the Expeditionary Force were equipped with the *armory rifle*.

This is a breech-loading, single-shot, lever-operated rifle of 11mm (approximately .45) calibre.

To operate, engage the end-loop on the trigger guard (directly to the rear of the trigger) with the thumb and press downward until the lever is at 90 degrees to the stock. The bolt will retract, ejecting the spent cartridge directly backward, and slide down. A grooved ramp on the top of the bolt surface will then act as a guide to the next round, which is pushed home with the thumb. Pull the lever back into the original position, and the bolt will come up and forward, engaging two locking lugs at the bolt-face, and the firing pin will be cocked. The weapon is now ready to fire.

Sights are a forward blade and adjustable rear notch; the weapon is sighted, rather optimistically, to 1000 meters.

There is an iron cleaning rod carried under the barrel in the forestock of the weapon.

Range is approximately 1000 meters against massed targets and 600 against individuals.

Ammunition is a wrapped-brass cartridge on an iron base, with a center-fire percussion primer; the bullet is cradled in a papier-mache wad at the upper end of the cartridge case. The cartridge is rather fragile, and care must be exerted—particularly when the weapon is hot from rapid fire—not to jerk the lever too hard, as this may tear the base off the cartridge and jam the action. Drawn-brass cartridges were available but very expensive.

The bullet is unjacketed lead (lead-antimony) alloy, with a hollow-point nose driven by a 50-grain cake of compressed black powder. At battle ranges it has excellent stopping power.

The 220 mm (10-inch blade) *bayonet* is attached by a ring and bar system under the barrel. The bayonet is a straight single-edged sword-knife model, with the reverse edge sharpened for 50mm back from the point; the hilt is wood, with a brass strip guard.

Cavalry also carried single edged *sabers* as sidearms; officers of all branches of service, and artillerymen, also carried sabers. These were usually of about a meter in length, very slightly curved and suitable for thrusting as well as slashing; the blade was sharpened along the back for about 75mm back from the point. Scabbards were of wood, covered in leather and with metal chapes and mouths, worn slung from a saber-tache attached to the left side of the belt.

Officers and NCOs of cavalry and artillery, and infantry officers, also carried *revolvers*. These are 11mm weapons with swing-out 5 shot cylinders and fairly long barrels, firing a shorter, lighter version of the rifle bullet; they have a quite heavy kick.

Almost all troops carried privately purchased general utility knives.

NAVAL FORCES
Admiral Tiburcyo Gharderini, commanding:

10 steam warships. These vessels are between 1000 and 2000 tons displacement, with wooden or wood-and-wrought-iron frames and wooden hulls. They are flush-decked and 65 meters long by 11 meters maximum beam, with a single-story deckhouse and bridge amidships, pierced by the twin funnels.

Each is propelled by two 275 hp two-cylinder double-expansion steam engines; each engine drives one paddle-wheel at the midships position. The engines are coal-fired, with cylindrical three-flue riveted iron boilers, producing steam at 50 psi pressure. Salt water can be used, but requires frequent down-time to clear the pipes and boilers.

Maximum speed under steam, 11 knots.

The warships each carry two masts, schooner-rigged, and can cruise under sail at up to 8 knots with favorable winds.

Armament is six 75mm breechloading rifles per side on the upper deck or as bow and stern chasers; these are modified versions of the standard cast-steel field gun, on heavy metal pedestal mountings. Swivel-guns (25mm break-open rifles on pintles) were carried on the rails and deckhouse for use against boarders. The ships also carry a reinforced, steel-shod ram just below waterlevel on the bows. This is a very effective weapon, but its use requires great skill and if mishandled may damage the ship.

Standard crews per ship were 150, including 25 marines and 60 in the "black gang," the engine-room crew. Officers include Captain, First Mate, Second and Third Mates, Chief Engineer and Lieutenant of Marines.

Ordinary crew were recruited by conscription—press-gang—from merchant sailors, as necessary; Marines were transfers from infantry units. Officers were usually townsmen of mercantile background, more literate and technically-minded than Army officers but looked down upon socially.

The several hundred transports used to carry the troops and supplies of the Expeditionary Force were wooden-built merchantmen under contract to the Civil Government, with their usual crews. Size ranges from 40 to 1500 tons, with 200-400 being average; most of the ships were three-masters, with a mixture of square and fore-and-aft sails. A half-dozen of the largest had auxiliary steam-powered paddle wheels, usually used only in calms or when entering and leaving harbors.

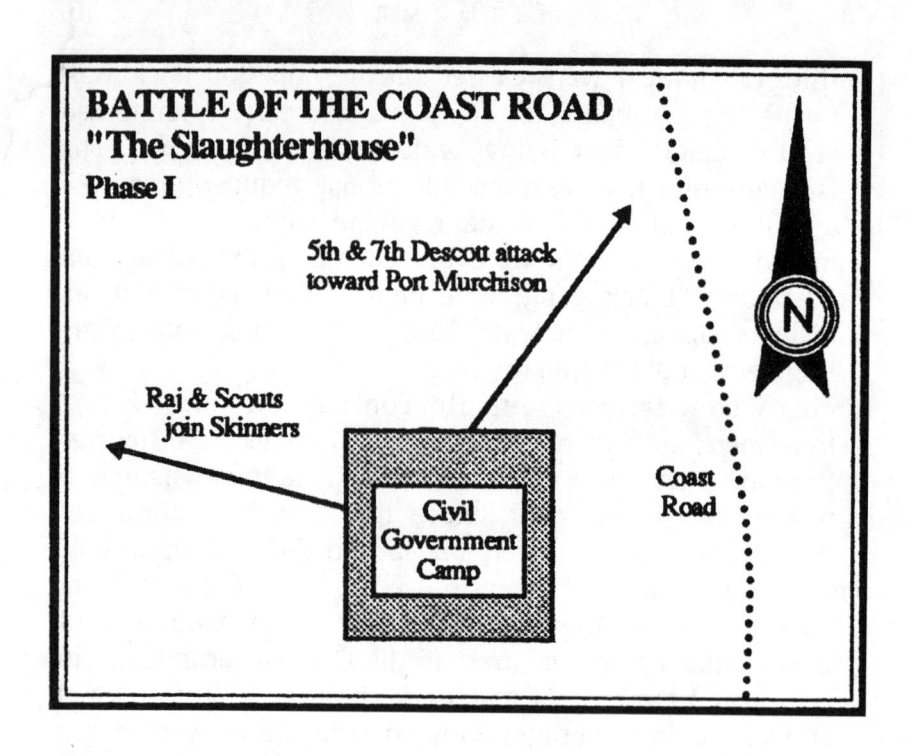

BATTLE OF THE COAST ROAD
"The Slaughterhouse"
Phase I

5th & 7th Descott attack toward Port Murchison

Raj & Scouts join Skinners

Civil Government Camp

Coast Road

N

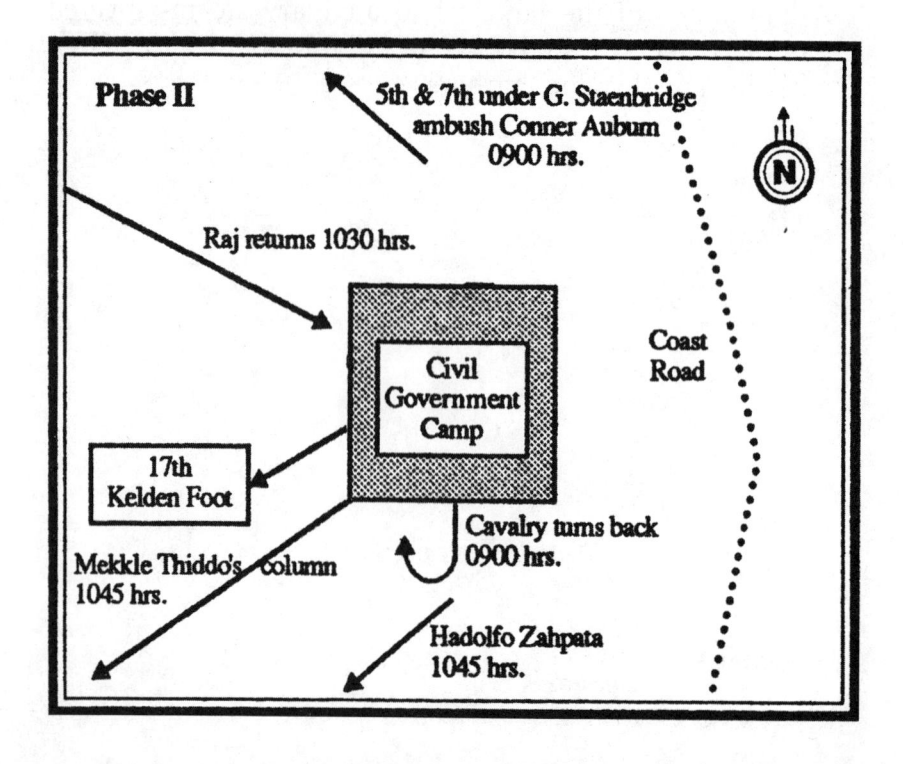

Phase II

5th & 7th under G. Staenbridge ambush Conner Auburn 0900 hrs.

Raj returns 1030 hrs.

Civil Government Camp

17th Kelden Foot

Mekkle Thiddo's column 1045 hrs.

Cavalry turns back 0900 hrs.

Hadolfo Zahpata 1045 hrs.

Coast Road

N

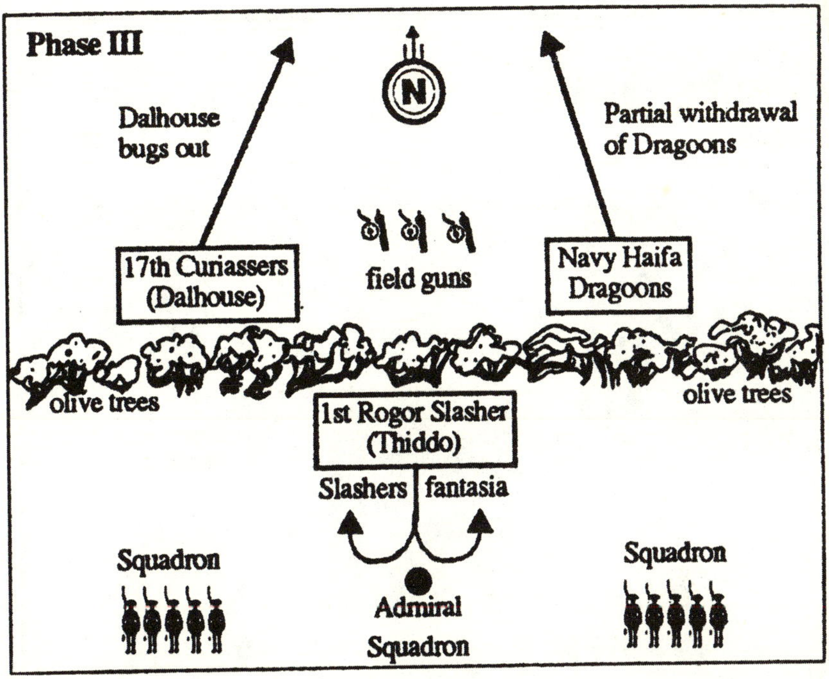
Phase III
N
Dalhouse
bugs out
Partial withdrawal
of Dragoons
17th Curiassers
(Dalhouse)
field guns
Navy Haifa
Dragoons
olive trees
olive trees
1st Rogor Slasher
(Thiddo)
Slashers fantasia
Squadron
Squadron
Admiral
Squadron

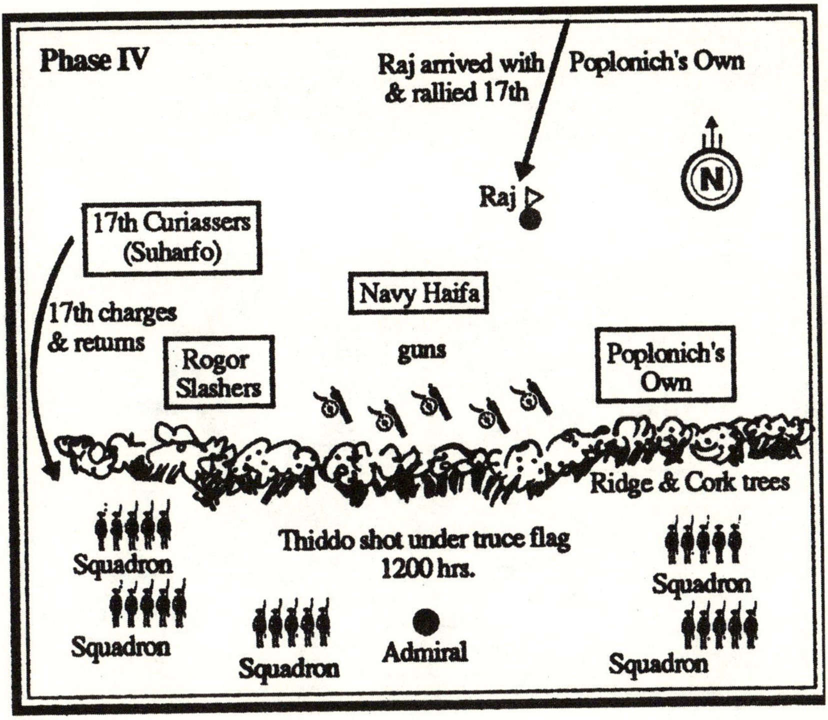
Phase IV
Raj arrived with
& rallied 17th
Poplonich's Own
N
Raj
17th Curiassers
(Suharfo)
Navy Haifa
17th charges
& returns
Rogor
Slashers
guns
Poplonich's
Own
Ridge & Cork trees
Thiddo shot under truce flag
1200 hrs.
Squadron
Squadron
Squadron
Squadron
Admiral
Squadron

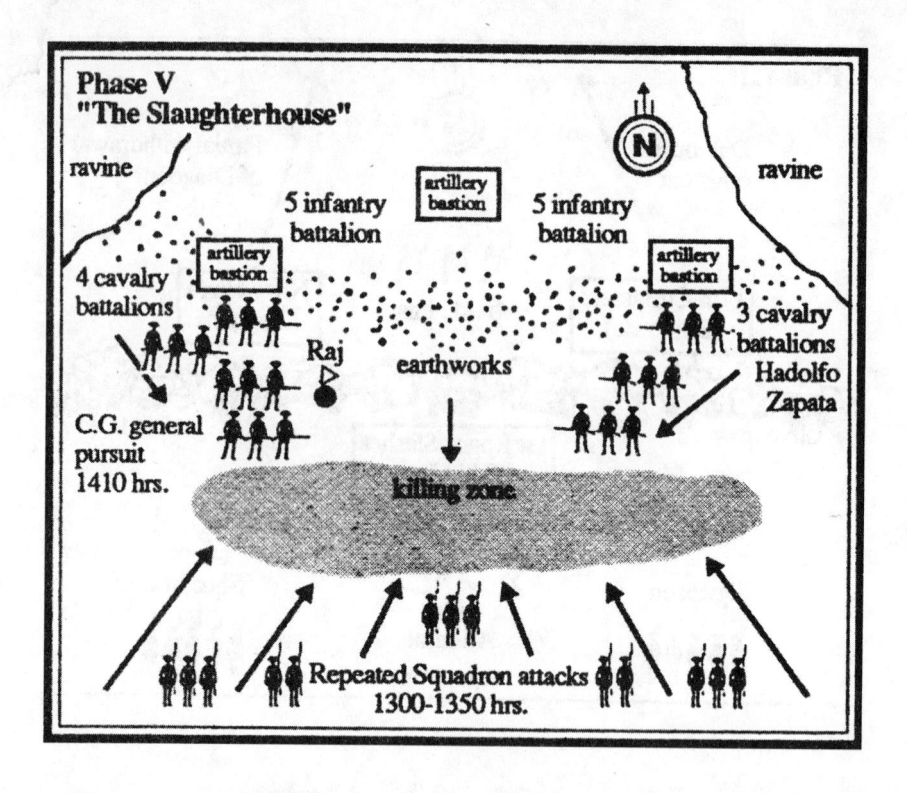

Phase V "The Slaughterhouse"

- ravine
- 4 cavalry battalions
- artillery bastion
- 5 infantry battalion
- artillery bastion
- 5 infantry battalion
- artillery bastion
- 3 cavalry battalions
- Hadolfo Zapata
- ravine
- Raj
- earthworks
- C.G. general pursuit 1410 hrs.
- killing zone
- Repeated Squadron attacks 1300-1350 hrs.

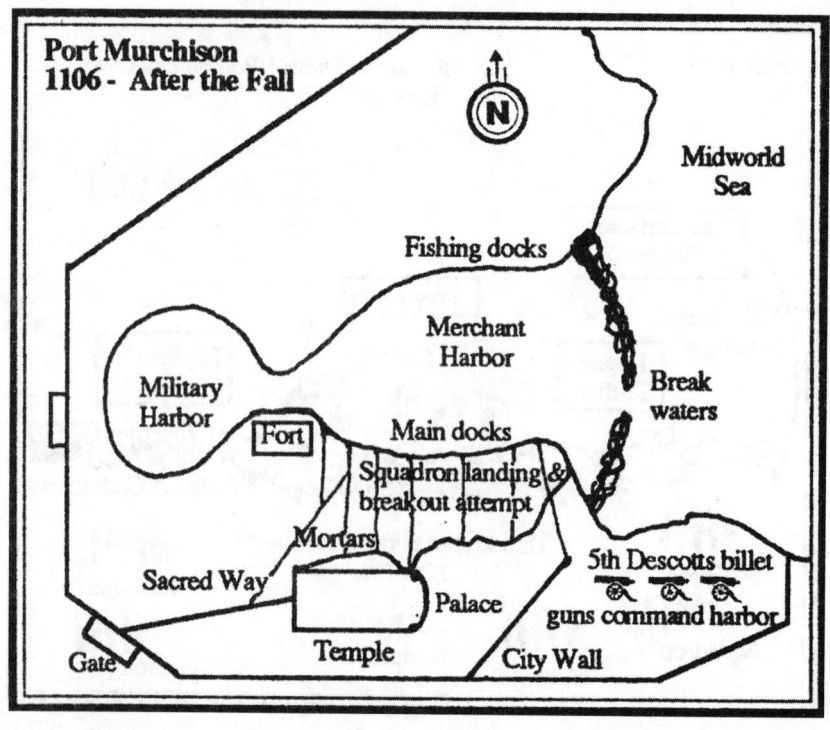

Port Murchison 1106 - After the Fall

- Midworld Sea
- Fishing docks
- Merchant Harbor
- Break waters
- Military Harbor
- Fort
- Main docks
- Squadron landing & breakout attempt
- Mortars
- Sacred Way
- Palace
- 5th Descotts billet
- guns command harbor
- Gate
- Temple
- City Wall